NAUGHTY BRITS

AN ANTHOLOGY

SARAH MACLEAN   SOPHIE JORDAN

LOUISA EDWARDS   TESSA GRATTON

SIERRA SIMONE

A Duke Worth Falling For, Copyright © 2020 by Sarah Trabucchi

Better With You, Copyright © 2020 by Sharie Kohler

Not a Bad Boy, Copyright © 2020 by Louisa Edwards

Songbird, Copyright © 2020 by Tessa Gratton

Supplicant, Copyright © 2020 by Sierra Simone

Cover Design: Hang Le

Cover Illustration: Angela Day

Editing:

A Duke Worth Falling For, Julia Ganis of JuliaEdits

Not a Bad Boy, Songbird, and *Supplicant*, Erica Russikoff of Erica Edits.

Proofing: Nancy Smay of Evident Ink

Print Edition ISBN: 978-1-949364-07-1

Digital Edition ISBN: 978-1-949364-06-4

CONTENTS

A DUKE WORTH FALLING FOR
SARAH MACLEAN

BETTER WITH YOU
SOPHIE JORDAN

NOT A BAD BOY
LOUISA EDWARDS

SONGBIRD
TESSA GRATTON

SUPPLICANT
SIERRA SIMONE

A DUKE WORTH FALLING FOR

SARAH MACLEAN

CHAPTER ONE

THESE SHEEP WERE NOT STORYBOOK sheep.

Sure, they came with rolling English hills and a gentle mist, but these sheep were not soft and fluffy and they did not gently bleat. These sheep were muddy and pungent and noisy.

And they were advancing.

Lilah Rose planted her rain boots into the slick mud of the Devon countryside, lifted her Nikon and stared down the lens as the herd approached, an enormous black-eyed, gray beast leading the charge.

There it was, that familiar thrill, the one that came every time she knew the perfect shot was in reach—the thrill that came with the edge of threat, because she had one chance to get it.

"That's it," she said softly, the words barely a breath. Lilah might not have shot fashion for eighteen months, but twelve years as a style and portrait photographer were instantly there, hardwired as she cooed to the massive ewe. "Just like that."

Click.

The whisper of the shutter summoned the beast, which increased its speed. Lilah backed away, her steps sure. How many times had she photographed this exact personality—foreboding, absolutely certain of its power, and completely unaware of its vulnerabilities? Wasn't that what had made her the most coveted celebrity photographer out there?

It didn't matter how impossible the subject, how impenetrable the personality. Lilah Rose could capture truth on film. She'd photographed playboys and presidents, longtime A-listers and hot new stars, athletes and socialites, billionaires and royalty. And she was great at it.

At least she had been.

Lilah swallowed around her frustration, hot and thick in her throat, willing away thoughts of Met Galas and Oscar after-parties and the three-thousand-square-foot Tribeca loft she'd once called home base.

It didn't matter that at this exact moment, two years earlier, she'd been in that very loft, shooting the cover of the *Bonfire* Silver Screen issue—a famously impossible task. It didn't matter that she'd been the first photographer in thirty years to get every one of the actors on the cover to agree to a single shoot, in the same room, at the same time.

It didn't matter that working with Lilah Rose had been enough for them to agree. Not even thirty, and it had been *her* name that had brought ten sets of famously longtime Hollywood rivals together—in New York City no less!—and without a single superstar screeching for an agent.

It didn't matter that she'd had to sell the studio when magazines had blacklisted her and her own agent and manager had stopped answering her calls, and the celebrities and power brokers who routinely invited her to parties and dinners in the hopes she'd decide to take their picture had seemingly lost her number.

Stars . . . they're just like sheep!

None of it mattered anymore.

What mattered was getting a picture of this damn sheep.

"At me, beautiful. Right for me."

The ewe didn't hesitate to follow directions. She was ten yards away.

Click.

"That's right."

Eight yards. Coming fast.

Click, click. Lilah was fast too. Too much closer and she'd lose the shot.

Her heart started to pound. She loved this moment on the knife's point, the moment before she either got the picture or lost it, and would never get it back. She crouched, changing the angle, making the beast larger than life.

Five yards.

Not low enough.

She sat, leaning forward, ignoring the cold wet that immediately soaked the seat of her jeans. She'd done worse to get a shot.

She waited, checking the frame, the way the late-summer grass swayed in the viewfinder. The sheep advanced, herd behind.

Enough time for a final shot.

Don't blink.

"Come and get me, you gorgeous girl," she crooned.

"I wouldn't pass up that offer, Mabel."

The shutter fired even as Lilah gave a little squeak and snapped her head around to find the source of the cool words—a pair of grimy Chameau boots about six feet away. She'd just begun to raise her attention higher than the laces to the man who'd spoken, when the sheep—apparently named Mabel—reached her. Along with Mabel's friends.

And then Lilah couldn't worry so much about the man, because she was headbutted by the enormous ewe, who was, as indicated previously, decidedly *not* a storybook sheep.

Mabel was *strong*.

And Lilah was down for the count.

"Argh!" she shouted, half indignation and half terror, and did the only thing that came to mind—rolled to her side, tucked her knees, protected her camera with one hand and her head with the other. Bleating and baas surrounded her, along with the pounding of hooves and the distinct funk of wet livestock. She took a hoof to the kidney. "Gah!"

"Christ!" the boots said, loud enough to be heard despite their distance. The word was punctuated with a high-pitched whistle and the deep, heavy woof of a dog that Lilah hoped was big enough to run off—a hundred sheep? A thousand? Infinity. Infinity sheep.

Another collection of urgent woofs, and the sheep parted.

Good dog.

Lilah lifted her head just enough to take stock of her surroundings. The herd passed on either side of where she was curled in a muddy ball, apparently having decided that trampling her was not worth the hassle of—

"Are you all right?"

The words were grumbled from above, equal parts concerned and irritated.

"I'm fine!" she reported, checking on all her important bits before returning her attention to the boots and beyond . . . up, up over a pair of dark jeans, worn in the knees and thighs, past the warm, wheat-colored sweater to the man staring down at her.

Lilah's mouth went instantly dry.

Good lord. And she'd thought the sheep was big.

Anyone else wouldn't be in the best position to judge his size, but Lilah Rose had spent a decade photographing small men from low angles. This man didn't need the angle. He was *tall*. Over six feet. She quickly catalogued the rest of him, broad in the chest and shoulders with a long, straight nose and a jaw that was comic book levels of square, dimpled chin and all.

Take his picture.

The thought was wild and absolutely terrible judgment. After all, she was a half-hour's walk from anything approximating civilization and very likely without cell service, and this enormous man was not for picture taking. Definitely not while he glowered down at her.

Wait.

He wasn't glowering down at *her*.

He was glowering down at her camera.

And then the glower became something worse. Those lips she'd catalogued flattened into something like disdain, colder than the muck seeping through her jeans. She knew that look. She'd had her fill of it as her life imploded and everything she'd worked for fell to pieces.

She'd run all the way to the English countryside to escape it.

But there was no outrunning it, only fighting it.

Lilah scrambled to sit up even as his hands—very big and warm, not that she noticed—wrapped around her elbows and hauled her upward.

In another situation, she would have been grateful for the help, considering there was no graceful way to rise from the slippery mud of a sheep pasture, but she was *definitely* not going to thank this disdainful jerk for laying hands—no matter how big and warm, not that she noticed —on her.

Before she could pull herself from his grasp and tell him exactly what he could do with those hands she did not notice, he released her, putting immediate distance between them, his jaw setting into stone.

"I've seen you people go to some lengths, but nearly getting trampled by a herd of sheep is new."

Lilah blinked. "We people?"

His gaze narrowed. "There's no need to play coy. I'm immune to it—cow eyes or no."

What the hell? "*Cow* eyes?"

"Big. Empty."

Who did this guy think he was? "Wow. You know what? You're an asshole." She probably shouldn't have engaged with him at all, but she'd had enough of men who used intimidation as a weapon.

"To your kind? Absolutely."

Ugh, she took back all the complimentary thoughts she'd *almost* had for this guy. He was clearly the *worst*.

"My *kind*? You mean civilized humans who were having a perfectly nice time before being manhandled by jerks?" She paused. "I don't know what your problem is; *you* approached *me*."

Lilah turned on her heel and walked away, as gracefully as she could, considering she was covered in mud. The white and gray sheepdog danced around her, enormous tongue lolling out of its mouth.

"Atlas," the jerk said, and the dog immediately returned to his side. He called after her. "Of course I approached you! You were about to get trampled!"

"I would have happily taken my chances, considering what the alternative turned out to be," she tossed over her shoulder before looking to the dog, happily watching her, tail waving wildly. "You did great though, Atlas. You should find yourself a better owner."

"I'm a fine owner. The kind who came to help when you were *lying on the ground*."

"*I was trying to get a shot!*"

And dammit, she hadn't even gotten it. Or, if she had, it would be pure luck. Which meant she hadn't gotten the shot.

Instead, she'd gotten kicked in the ribs by attack sheep and yelled at by the handsomest man she'd seen in a long time.

Not that she'd noticed.

"So you admit it," he shouted back.

She turned to face him as he strode toward her, his steps sure and firm, as though he'd never dream of slipping in the mud. As though the mud would never dream of misbehaving for him.

In a decade as a style photographer, she'd come up against egos of epic proportions, but nothing like this. This man—he wasn't ego. He was certainty.

There'd been a time when Lilah had been certainty too.

Never let them see you sweat.

She squared her shoulders, and looked him dead in the eye. "Admit what?"

"You're a photographer."

"Why wouldn't I admit it?" She lifted her chin. "I'm the best photographer you'll ever meet."

If she believed this was a man who had ever in his life been surprised, she might have imagined she saw surprise in his whiskey-colored eyes before he caught himself and said, coolly, "If I'm lucky, you'll also be the last one I ever meet. You're trespassing."

Lilah didn't hesitate. "No, I'm not."

"You're on Weston lands. Uninvited."

"How do you know I'm uninvited?"

He raised a brow at her. "Because I'd know if you'd been invited."

Lilah had seen the mammoth estate house on the drive into the property owned by the Duke of Weston—it was hard not to see it. Maybe big old estates came with handsome security details.

Not handsome.

"Castle guard, are you?"

"Something like that."

"You're missing your armor."

"It's being repaired."

"Broadsword?"

"Shall I fetch it?"

She resisted the urge to smile. This was not a man for smiling at.

Back to the task at hand—putting him in his place. "Well, apparently you're not the king's favorite anymore, Lancelot. Because I've got keys to the castle."

The cottage on the eastern edge of the estate wasn't exactly the castle, but it didn't matter.

"Impossible," he said.

"Why don't you call his lordship and check?" she said, reaching into the back pocket of her jeans. "I'll lend you my phone."

"It's His Grace, actually."

Lilah, who had photographed six royal families and knew proper forms of address in every one of their countries, smiled. "I don't care."

Something flashed in his eyes, recognition. "Lottie."

Lady Charlotte Arden was a friend of an old art school friend of Lilah's—and had kindly offered up the cottage on her family's estate for two weeks.

Lilah nodded. "Lottie."

"You're at the cottage?"

She nodded, though the descriptor amused her. This "cottage" wasn't a one-room affair. It came with a sun room, a formal dining room, gorgeous woodwork, creaking floors, a big, four-poster bed, a bathtub bigger than her kitchen in New York City, and an ancient, beautiful Aga stove that made a girl wish she had a reason to roast something. "It's very nice."

He grunted. It should have been off-putting. "She should have told me."

"Oh yes, you seem like the exact right person to bring guests a welcome basket."

"I saved you from Mabel, didn't I?"

"Practically rolled out the red carpet."

"I might not have if Lottie had told me you were a photographer." He said the word like someone would say plague. Or cockroach.

"Gosh, it's almost hard to imagine why she didn't."

Truthfully, Lilah would have liked to have had a little warning about this . . . farmer? Watchman? Whatever he was, he was comfortable enough with the owners to call the daughter of a duke by her nickname.

No one had warned Lilah though. She'd received directions to the cottage, instructions to find a key under a rock near the door, and an assurance that she was more than welcome.

Lottie is over the moon to have you at Salterton Abbey! She's a HUGE fan!! Sophie had emailed a month ago, her excessive use of caps and exclamation points throwing the truth of the words into question. *Don't think too hard about it!! It's solitary and YOU'LL LOVE IT, and it comes with sheep, which I assume you ADORE now!!*

Lilah had picked up the email from a cliffside hotspot in Sicily, where she'd been photographing goats. After the hard sell, Sophie had added what she'd really been thinking.

Take two weeks to steel yourself for your return.

Return. Period.

Sophie had left out all the bits that came after return.

Return, after eighteen months out of the public eye.

Return, after her career had been destroyed.

Return, but not to the world she'd lived in for a decade. To a different world. One that might not accept her.

She pushed the thoughts aside and eyed the man in front of her, who, when he wasn't looking so irritated, was probably the poster boy for the Devonshire Farming Society with his broad shoulders and long legs and sure steps and his sweater that matched the barley in the fields beyond and also his eyes—not that she noticed.

She smiled her photographer smile. The one she used to settle starlets and Sicilian goats, princes and Peruvian llamas. The one that had not worked on grumpy sheep, but would hopefully disarm this incredibly grumpy man. "I'm Lilah."

Another grunt.

Her brows shot up. "Your turn, Lancelot."

She expected the irritation that flashed across his handsome face, but she didn't expect the rest of the emotions—there and gone so fast that if she wasn't used to watching the world at shutter speed, she wouldn't have noticed. Suspicion. Surprise. And something she might have discovered was longing if she'd been able to study the film.

He ran a hand through his hair and a lesser woman would have called it endearing. "I'm . . . " A pause, like he'd forgotten. Like he'd never known.

Lilah waited. A trick of the trade.

Don't blink.

"I'm Max."

And like that, Lilah knew there was a story in this man. This wasn't a family-friendly story though. It didn't come with once upon a time and happily ever after. Because just as his sheep were not storybook sheep, this man was not a storybook man.

Lilah knew that without question. She recognized it, because her life was not a storybook either.

Not anymore.

CHAPTER TWO

Rupert Maximillian Arden, Fourteenth Duke of Weston and Earl Salterton, was waylaid from entering the Fox and Falcon, one mile from his estate house, by the sound of his mobile.

Pulling the phone from his pocket, Max cast an irritated look at the screen, where his sister's face smiled up at him. He turned away from the pub and lifted the rectangle to his ear, crossing the street into the manicured greensward that marked the center of the town named eons earlier for his family. "I've been trying to reach you for two days."

"Roo!" His sister shouted over the riot of noise wherever she was—no doubt one of London's poshest clubs or some party thrown by some toff looking for a few pictures in *Tatler*.

Max gritted his teeth at the diminutive he'd only ever heard from two women in his life—Lottie, who'd given it to him when she was a baby, and his ex-wife, who'd thought it charming and claimed it as hers when they were at St. Andrews and he'd been too young to stop it.

"Dearest darling Roo!"

His sister always spoke in superlatives and exclamations when she knew she was in trouble. Which was often. The tabloids adored Lady Lottie, activist and street artist by day and delightful scandal by night, and Lady Lottie loved being adored. She was the opposite of Max, who would happily walk into the sea to avoid questions about his status as Britain's Most Eligible Bachelor.

Of course, the tabloids had not chronicled the downfall of his sister's marriage minute by minute.

"I've been *so* busy! I installed a half dozen pieces around Shoreditch a few nights ago, and between avoiding HMP and the rest of it, time has been absolutely impossible."

"It's almost as though vandalism doesn't pay." The words were dry as sand, and held no ring of truth. Max was as wild about Lottie's art as the rest of the known universe.

"I'm ignoring that!" his sister singsonged. "The very moment I was able, I called! Tell me everything! Leave nothing out!" The sound muffled for a moment as Lottie spoke to someone else, then cleared when she returned, deep bass throbbing on her end of the line. "I am fully and completely yours."

Max ignored the obvious untruth, looking round to be sure he was alone. "Your friend is here."

"Right! Lilah!"

Lilah. It was a pretty name—he'd liked it the moment she'd said it in the field. Old-fashioned and perfectly suited for someone with a riot of curls and a riot of freckles.

"You should have told me."

"That she was using the cottage? Why would you care? Is the drafty manor house too much for you? Finally unnerved by the ancestors in the paintings?"

"I care very much that she is a photographer."

"Did she try to take your picture?" His sister was suddenly very focused, ice sliding into her tone. She might be an absolute loss when it came to remembering—or caring—that her decisions impacted others, but she was fiercely loyal when it came to protecting her family.

"No."

The chill was instantly gone from his sister's voice. "Of course she didn't! Everyone knows she doesn't do celebrities anymore."

The words turned his stomach. "I didn't know she *did* celebrities in the first place."

"Ugh. Roo. It would do you well to read the news now and then."

"Celebrity photographers are not *the news*."

The line muffled again—he'd lost her to another conversation. He sighed and looked up at the sky, clear and sparkling with stars. It was later than he'd thought.

"Sorry! Sorry! I'm back!"

"I'm not a celebrity, Lottie. That's the point."

"We know," Lottie replied, disdain and boredom in her tone. "You're a perfectly ordinary duke in hiding, as though that's a thing. Look. It doesn't matter. She doesn't do portraits any longer. She's photographing wheat or fish or cocoa farms or something for some sustainability thing now. She's far more likely to be interested in the sheep than in you."

I was trying to get a shot!

Lilah had been telling him the truth. A hint of guilt flared, and Max pushed it away. He'd been right to be cautious, dammit.

" . . . all I know is that she needed some time alone, away from the world."

The tail end of Lottie's words collected his attention again. "Why?" The question was out before he could stop it, and he closed his eyes, instantly full of regret.

Lottie was silent, the heavy throb of music the only indication that she was still on the line.

"Never mind," he said.

"Rupert Maximillian Arden," his sister said at the exact same moment, "are you asking me . . . about a woman?"

"No." His denial was instant. "I'm asking you about the photographer you allowed onto my estate."

"First, it's the *family's* estate. And second, I promise you that Lilah Rose is far, *far* too skilled an artist to care one bit about you."

Lilah Rose. Max resisted the instinct to repeat the full name—softer and prettier as a matched set.

Not that Lottie would have heard, as she was still talking. "—she's certainly not there to take the first picture of the Dusty Duke in a century or however long it's been."

Nine years. It had been nine years.

Max grimaced at the odious nickname that the tabloids had bestowed upon him when he'd turned his back on London and the aristocracy and returned to Devon to take up the work of land steward on the Weston estate. He was about to take Lottie to task for using it with him when she added, "In fact, I'd bet now that she knows you're a duke, she's going to steer well clear of you—with what they say happened . . . "

His admonition evaporated. "What do they say?"

"Sounds like you're asking me about a woman, Roo."

"I'm not. But if she's going to guillotine me—"

Lottie's laugh tinkled through the phone. "Dukes really have it rough these days, don't they?"

He gave a little huff of laughter at the words. "Terrible. Can't even get our sisters to return our calls."

"She's not going to guillotine you, Roo. And she's not going to take your picture either." Lottie's exasperation was palpable. "She's not after the title."

She doesn't know I have a title.

That thread of guilt again—but different now. Lingering, as though he should have told her who he was when they were in the pasture, covered in mud and grouching at each other. At first he'd thought she was playing coy and already knew, but then . . . then there'd been something freeing about her *not* knowing. And now—

"What happened to her?" He hated that he asked. It wasn't his business.

And it didn't matter anyway, because his sister answered in her smuggest tone, "She's really adorable, isn't she?"

A memory flashed, Lilah curled on her side in a muddy field, his heart pounding—terrified she'd be trampled. "I wouldn't say that."

"Are you sure?"

Lilah, toe to toe with him in that same pasture, covered in muck, and still ready for battle. Enormous brown eyes framed by thick lashes. Freckled face flushed with frustration and indignation, a smear of mud on her pink cheek.

Wide, full lips that made a man think wicked thoughts.

There was nothing adorable about that woman. She was stunning.

"I'm sure."

"Then you won't mind steering clear of her for two weeks."

"Two weeks!"

"Sorry! Can't hear you!" his sister shouted. "Mobile service is pants here!"

"You're in London."

"Headed into a tunnel! Ring you later!"

"Dammit, Lottie!"

"Bye-ee!"

The line went quiet, the sudden absence of Lottie's cacophonous world making the silence of the greensward unsettling. Max pulled the mobile away from his ear with a choice word. Sisters.

He didn't know how he'd expected the conversation to go—it wasn't as though Lottie ever admitted wrongdoing. She had spent most of her adult life as a tabloid darling because of it. And even if she had offered up an apology for installing a complete stranger at Salterton Abbey without telling him, it wouldn't have changed anything.

Lilah would still be there. For two weeks.

Pocketing the phone, Max crossed the street back to the pub—one of the few places in the world where he was not Weston, Britain's Most Eligible Bachelor, the Dusty Duke, or Roo.

He'd spend the evening the way he spent any ordinary Thursday evening—he'd have a pint, throw some darts, let the ancient old men inside take the piss for a bit. And then he'd go back to the real world, filled with scandalous sisters and an estate in constant need of attention, and a title that came first. Always.

Tonight, he would put all that out of his mind, along with Lilah Rose, whom he only had to avoid for two weeks. Not so hard, that. It was an enormous estate, and the odds of coming into contact with one freckled photographer were slim to none.

He pulled open the door, an unexpected chorus of masculine cheering within. Max's brow furrowed as he scanned the interior of the pub, all leather and mahogany, shadowy corners and—usually—quiet.

John, Richard and Paul—the three older men who were as much fixtures in the space as the ancient casks in the corner—were turned from their usual spots, rheumy-eyed attention riveted to the dartboard at the far end of the room.

Not the dartboard.

The woman walking toward it, where three red darts were sunk into its bright red center.

Lilah Rose.

He had no reason to recognize her. Her back was to him, and her muddy jeans had been traded for black leggings and a long, white cable-knit sweater that fell to mid-thigh, hiding the curve he'd pointedly *not* noticed when he'd helped her out of the mud. Her hair was no longer piled high atop her head in a messy knot—it was long and wild, the color of roasted chestnuts, gleaming in the gold light of the stained glass wall sconces.

Of course he recognized her.

Even if he hadn't, his body—instantly tight and aware—would have.

"A tenner says ye can't do it again!"

"I'll take your money all night," came her laughing reply as she yanked the darts from the board and turned back to the room.

She stilled, seeing him immediately. He read the surprise in her eyes as her pink lips parted, just barely, on an inhale. She wasn't expecting him either.

She regained her composure quickly, spreading her hands wide, the darts held tight against the palm of her right hand. "No camera."

He should have been gentleman enough not to look her up and down as she stood for inspection. But he wasn't. He looked, cataloguing the line of her long neck, the swell of her full breasts, the flare of her generous hips beneath the sweater, down over the leggings to the red canvas trainers she wore.

When his gaze returned to hers, her head was cocked to one side as if to say, *Finished?*

He didn't want to be.

He cleared his throat. "I was a prat."

She smiled, and he enjoyed the way it filled him up and made him want to earn it. "That's one of my favorite British insults."

His brows rose. "There are others you'd have liked to have used?"

She tilted her head, nearing, and Max went hot, though whether it was from embarrassment—the boys were watching the scene roll out before them—or from her own frank appraisal, he didn't know.

"Numpty?"

He nodded. "That's a good one."

"Wally?"

Simon—the owner of the pub, who'd been Max's friend since birth—snorted from his place.

Max winced. "Also appropriate."

"Can I say knob in polite company?"

"No one ever called us polite!" chortled John, the rest of the assembled men adding their laughter as Max slid the ruddy-cheeked farmer a look.

"No one's ever called 'im a knob around here either," Richard pointed out.

Lilah looked to Max again. "You're usually better behaved?"

He dipped his head in sheepish reply and said, "I am, actually."

She nodded, her gaze on his, as though she was searching for the truth in the words. As though she expected them to be a lie. She must have seen something she liked, because she finally smiled, wide and winning, stealing some of the air in the room before she said, "So, Max, do you play darts?"

And like that, Max remembered that Lilah didn't know the truth—that he was Duke of Weston. That the castle on the hill belonged to him, and the ten thousand acres of farmlands that surrounded it. That the town, complete with the land the pub stood on, bore his name.

Even here, at the Fox and Falcon, Max hadn't been free of that name. The locals within might have known him since he was in nappies, and they might not treat him with ducal reverence, but they'd never quite treated him as an equal either. He'd been baptized Earl Salterton and spent his years at school with people who befriended him to be close to the title, one of the oldest in Britain. But it wasn't the earldom anyone wanted. It was the other title—the one he'd inherited before he'd had a chance to discover who he was without it.

And along with it, the responsibility for this land and this community and his family—wild Lottie, and Jeremy, his younger brother who had left the UK the moment he'd been able to, bound for particle physics at MIT, where he'd received his PhD and control over a research lab before marrying an equally brilliant virologist and raising two terrifyingly intelligent nephews.

The last time Max had FaceTimed with the family, his brother had leaned into the frame to say one thing—*Met any nice girls?*

It was as tactful as Jez got. He wanted nothing to do with the family business and certainly didn't want it for his boys, who would inherit it if Max didn't meet a nice girl and do his duty. Wife. Heirs. Legacy.

But Lilah didn't know any of that.

She didn't know that he was rich, or powerful, or that half the tabloids in the country would allow her to name her price for a photograph of him. Lottie's words echoed.

She doesn't care one bit about the Dusty Duke.

She didn't know who he was, and it was glorious, because when she smiled, she smiled at *him*, and not at the duke.

And he didn't want that to change.

Not tonight, at least. Not when he could take this rare chance to live out a fantasy he barely allowed himself to contemplate.

Not when tonight he could just be Max.

"I do play darts, in fact."

"Well enough to lay money on it?" Her smile went crooked and he was struck by the fact that his sister was right—Lilah was adorable.

He was right too; she was stunning. And he didn't care that she looked perfectly happy to fleece him out of whatever he had in his pocket.

Max was happy to be fleeced, and Simon and the boys—not one of them younger than seventy—were thrilled to watch it happen. A chorus of chortles rose as he reached for the darts in her hand, his fingertips grazing her soft skin.

Did he imagine that small surprised breath?

He didn't imagine the reaction he had to touching her. Tight, wanting. Just as he'd been in the field. Wanting to do more than compete with her.

Wanting to pull her close and kiss her, steal that breath for himself. Own the pleasure in it.

"Go ahead," she said, softly, and for a moment he thought he'd spoken his desire aloud and she was on board with it.

But no. She meant the darts.

"As I am feeling magnanimous . . . *and flush*," she added over her shoulder at the men watching, who groaned and jeered in unison, "you can go first."

He raised a brow. "No concern about local advantage?"

"Not in the slightest."

He let his first dart fly and landed it in the outer bullseye. "Oh-ho!" Paul said, brandishing his half-empty pint glass. "Well done!"

Lilah cast a critical eye at the dart before turning back. "Would you like a drink?"

Max raised a brow. "Are you trying to get me drunk?"

"Not at all," she said with a grin. "Unless you think it will help me win."

He laughed, the sensation foreign. When was the last time he'd been free enough to laugh? The last time he hadn't worried about his siblings, the estate, the name, the world beyond Salterton Abbey?

What was the harm in giving himself up to it?

What was the harm in pretending to be Max, the land steward, for a little longer?

His gaze dropped to her lips for a heartbeat, soft and perfect, curved in an open, teasing smile. For him.

One night.

No harm in one night.

Tomorrow, he'd be duke again.

CHAPTER THREE

Two HOURS and five rounds of darts later, giddy with triumph, Lilah toasted Max with her second pint. "I'll say this for you, Lancelot, you gave it your very best."

He offered her a very good-natured grin—more good-natured than anything Lilah would have been able to drum up—and said, "A man knows when the battle is lost."

She smiled. "Wherever he falls, there shall he be buried?"

He approached, sandy brown hair falling over his brow as he waved his hand toward the scarred oak floor between them and said in perfect seriousness, "Might as well measure out my grave."

Lilah couldn't help her laugh. He was really very cute. Dangerously cute, if she was being honest, with his laughing eyes and his winning smile and the dimple in his left cheek that matched the dimple on his chin . . . and all that before the rest of his assets—tall and broad with beautiful forearms that she'd had no choice but to notice while they were playing darts.

But she'd made a career out of being unaffected around handsome men. Good genes weren't what made this one handsome. He was just so effortlessly charming. Self-deprecating and funny, no trace of the gruff, unsettling farmer who'd grouched at her camera the other day. In his place, this man who was one of the handsomest she'd ever seen—Sexiest Men Alive had very little on him—and somehow, impossibly . . . easy.

The kind of easy that made a girl wonder what it would be like to wake up on Sunday mornings with him. To make Sunday dinner with him. To take after-dinner walks with him. To tumble into bed with him and do it all over again on Monday.

Lilah's life had never made easy possible, but two hours of darts and drinks with this man and his motley collection of friends could tempt her into just that.

He was in front of her then, staring down at her, one dark brow cocked in sheepish curiosity, as though he knew what she was thinking.

As though he was daring her to reach out and try easy on for size.

Dangerously cute.

She tilted her chin up. "You're lucky I am feeling benevolent tonight."

He reached into his back pocket and extracted his wallet. "By my count, it's fifty quid for the losses?"

She shook her head. She didn't know the going rate for an English estate farmer, but fifty pounds was a lot for anyone. "The reward is the win itself, don't you think?"

"Not if you lord it over me for the rest of your stay."

"Aren't we on the ancestral lands of a duke?" she asked, all tease. "Do you think he'd mind if I took on the lording for a bit?"

The words were barely out of her mouth when the pub went silent, the only sound the thud of one of the elderly men's pint glasses on the bar.

Max's gaze slid to the sound, and something flashed across his face. Frustration? Irritation? With her? She followed his attention to the men who had been watching their darts, rosy cheeks gone ruddy against pale skin, their eyes now trained on Max.

He didn't look so easy now.

Lilah couldn't tell if she'd said something wrong or if something had happened that she simply hadn't noticed, but the air had definitely shifted. Grown cooler.

So much for flirting with the hot farmer.

Hiding her confusion and her disappointment, Lilah grabbed her messenger bag from the sturdy stool where she'd left it. "It's late," she said. "I should go."

Before she could sling the bag over her shoulder, the oldest of their audience—a tall, white man, all long limbs and sharp joints, who had reminded her of the farmer from any number of British children's films when he'd introduced himself as John—said, "Do *you* think *he'd* mind?"

The words drew her attention, but John wasn't looking at her. He was looking at Max. As were the other men.

Lilah looked too, though she didn't know why. Her brow furrowed as Max cleared his throat and said to John, "I don't think he'd mind, as a matter of fact."

Confused, Lilah tracked the conversation back to the bar, where Paul, portly and quick with a smile, raised a brow in Max's direction. "*You* don't. Think *the duke* would mind."

Those strange emphases again, and Max, that strong, sturdy, unflappable farmer who took her teasing in stride was gone.

Strong became stoic.

Sturdy became stiff.

Unflappable became unbending.

The stark change could mean only one thing: there was something Lilah didn't know about Max and the Duke of Weston. Bad blood of some kind, maybe? Which didn't really explain how protective he'd been of the duke when he'd thought she was paparazzi.

Maybe the duke was a terrible boss. Lilah had certainly met her fair share of rich and powerful men who were terrible bosses.

Who were terrible, period.

And Max, out in the muddy fields with his good dog, likely with no choice but to take whatever garbage the lord of the manor doled out. She knew what that was like.

She knew the danger of not taking it too.

He looked away from their audience, and she wanted to do something. To say something. To touch him. Anything that would show him he wasn't alone. But he wasn't looking at her either.

"Have you met the duke, Lilah?" The bartender, this time, who'd introduced himself as Simon. He was in his thirties and handsome, and big as a house, with a broad chest and muscled forearms covered in tattoos.

She shook her head and approached the bar, opening her wallet to pay her tab. "No," she said.

"Imagine that," John said.

"Is that so strange?" she asked.

"Strange?" Simon said, looking to Max, who was watching him intently. "A bit, I'll be honest."

She set her near-empty pint glass down on the bar and plucked a leftover dart from where it had been forgotten. "Don't dukes have things to do besides rolling out the red carpet for guests? Balls to dance at? Rolls Royces to drive? Cravats to tie?"

The men assembled laughed. All except Max.

"He doesn't wear a cravat," Max grumbled.

She smiled. "It was a joke."

He didn't seem to think it was funny. "She's Lottie's friend."

Simon said, dry as sand, "And she hasn't met the duke."

"I'm not really her friend," Lilah was quick to correct. "I've never even met *her*. Lady Charlotte and I have a mutual friend."

"All the more reason for her to meet the duke, Max," John said. "Not every day a girl gets a chance to meet a real live title."

Lilah laughed and shook her head. "It's not necessary. I've met plenty of real live other things, and learned not to believe the hype."

"Right. Lottie says you're a posh photographer," Simon said.

Max shot him a look. "What are you doing talking to Lottie?"

The bartender shrugged one shoulder. "I like to keep up with goings-on." He looked to Lilah. "Who's the poshest person you've photographed?"

"Oh, for—" Max said, looking at Lilah. "You don't have to answer that."

"It's okay," she said with a laugh. "I've taken a lot of pictures. Actors, authors, world leaders, athletes."

Simon whistled, impressed. "All right then, who's the biggest tosser you've ever photographed?"

The one who got me blacklisted because I wouldn't sleep with him.

"Simon! Christ!" Max turned to her. "You *really* don't have to answer that."

"I only ask because she's not impressed by the duke," Simon interjected.

Lilah let the dart fly, watching it land in the dead center of the board. The men assembled shared a collection of impressed looks before she turned back toward them. "In my experience, men who are born with money and power are more trouble than they're worth. And considering the castle on the hill, the duke is a great deal of trouble."

"Oh-ho!" John chortled from his seat.

"Brazen, sayin' such a thing on the man's land," Paul chimed in, though it was less criticism and more delight.

"I don't mean to sound ungrateful. He's got a very cool sister and a beautiful estate that I'm more than enjoying—especially the company," she added with a smile. "Let's just say it's not him . . . it's me."

"He's not a bad geezer," John said.

Max looked to him. "He's not, as a matter of fact."

"I believe you," Lilah said.

"Ugly bastard," Simon chimed in from behind the bar with a wicked smile that, combined with the wicked gleam in his blue eyes, probably made knees weak across the county. "Babes scream just to look at him."

"That much is true," Paul confirmed.

"That is patently false," Max said. "He does all right."

"Good thing he's a duke, is all I'm saying," Paul replied.

"It's not the face I'm worried about," John said, tapping the side of his head and looking straight at Max, "it's the faculties." The men assembled—minus Max—nodded their agreement as he added, "Makes brainless decisions."

"That much is true," Paul repeated.

"Not as a matter of course," Max said, defensively. Maybe she'd misread the dynamic between them. Someone who didn't like his boss wouldn't be so affronted by criticism of him.

"Nah, but when he does, they're big 'uns," Richard said. "Great fun watchin' the fallout!"

Max let out a low grumble at the words, as though he didn't know whether to defend the duke or agree with the men assembled. Lilah chalked it up to some kind of long-standing cultural view of the aristocracy and tried to change the subject.

"Truthfully, I'm not really a meet-the-duke kind of girl." She looked to Max, surprised to find him staring directly at her. She tried for humor. "I'm more of a meet-the-shepherd-in-a-muddy-field kind of girl."

Paul blinked. "The shepherd . . . "

"Max!" John said, as though he'd just learned the fact.

Simon chimed in. "Course it's Max! What else would he be?"

Someone was drunk. And Lilah was certain it wasn't her.

"Lilah was taking photographs of the herd the other day," Max said, approaching, his wallet still in hand. "We met and I was a . . . "

"Prat."

"Numpty."

"Wally."

"Knob."

The descriptors were offered in unison, in myriad tones of sheer delight.

Suddenly, Max wasn't so stiff anymore. His lips quirked in a small, sheepish smile that made her insides do strange things, especially when paired with the gleam in his brown eyes. "Right."

Lilah couldn't help her own smile. "You really take a beating, don't you?"

"Deserved, innit?" He lifted a noncommittal shoulder, one lock of shaggy hair artfully draped over his brow, like he'd just stepped out of a rom-com. *Easy.*

Would he kiss like that? Easy?

She imagined he would, slow and smooth, lingering like he had a lifetime to explore. And when he did explore? His hands on her? His body against her?

Lilah's heart skipped a beat thinking about how easy it would be to slide a hand up his chest and into that soft hair. How easy it would be to fit herself to him and forget that the rest of the world could be so difficult.

She should leave now. Before she tumbled into something that could only end up a bad idea.

She set her empty glass on the bar with a smile for Simon before looking to the rest of the men who had kept her company for the evening. "As much as I adored this evening, gentlemen, I am out far past my bedtime."

She'd reached into the side pocket of her bag to find a few pounds when Max set a hand on her arm, electric heat shooting through her at the touch.

"At least let me pay for the pint." The words were low and soft, like a promise, and it occurred to Lilah that she might have agreed to anything he'd offered in that particular voice, close enough for the words to vibrate around her.

"That, I'll allow," she said, wondering how her own voice had gone so breathy. "Thank you."

He opened his wallet and tossed several twenty-pound notes onto the scarred bar. Simon straightened lazily to collect the money and the glass. "Lilah, you shouldn't walk back alone."

A chorus of elderly masculine agreement followed, including Richard's excited addition, "Absolutely not. Too dangerous."

"Dangerous?" Lilah laughed. "What, precisely, is dangerous out here in the middle of nowhere?"

"Can't be too careful. There's tales of marauders."

Her brows shot up. "Marauders."

"Tales of 'em, yes."

"Tales from when, 1700?"

"And more recently," Paul said, all expertise. "We had a high-wayman in the 1820s. He took one look at the young duchess and thieved her right out from under the duke."

"Max, tell her," Richard said, hefting a pint in their direction.

She looked to Max, who'd shoved his hands in his pockets and grinned. "It's true. She was never seen again. Legend had it she became a highwaywoman and they terrorized the countryside for years."

"Are we afraid that this nineteenth century Bonnie and Clyde might rob me on the walk home?"

He tilted his head, rubbing a hand up around the back of his neck and over his hair, ruffling it in a way that made her insides do those strange things again. "You never know."

Lilah laughed. "I think I'll take my chances."

He leaned down, his lips close to her ear, and the temperature in the pub was instantly warmer. "There are no marauders."

The words were a rumble of pleasure, and Lilah shivered at his nearness, her heart pounding. If she turned her head, he'd be *right there*. His lips would be *right there*. That easy kiss would be *right there*.

"But it is dangerous."

She sucked in a breath and pulled away, using all her willpower to do so. "What's so dangerous?" she asked, softly, even as his lips curved in that slow smile that made her want to do very bad things.

She didn't think anything was more dangerous than what she suddenly wanted very much to do to this man.

"The sheep are still out there, Lilah."

The laugh came, full of surprise and delight. *Easy.*

What if she took easy?

There was no harm in one night.

"All right, Lancelot. Walk me home."

CHAPTER FOUR

MAX CLOSED the door on the Fox and Falcon and the censure of the men inside. Exhaling, he looked to Lilah, turned to him in the warm golden glow of the pub's windows, a curious half-smile on her lips.

"They can be a lot."

Her smile widened. "They're perfect. If someone asked me to close my eyes and describe the contents of a pub in the Devon countryside, those men would be it."

He gave a little laugh. "Three men who've been in those exact chairs for as long as I can remember?"

She nodded. "Fixtures."

"They are that," he said, waving a hand in the direction of the dark road that would lead them back to the estate.

She fell into step beside him. "You've really known them your whole life?"

"Feels like more than that," he said.

"So you grew up here."

The question was so casual. Just conversation. One thousands of other people answered without hesitation on any given day. One he could answer without hesitation. And still, he hesitated.

She looked at him, enormous brown eyes clear and patient, like she'd wait forever for him to tell her the truth.

I'm the duke.

She was going to find out eventually. He should say it. Get it out of the way, before he decided he liked more than the curve of this woman's smart mouth.

But he didn't want to. He didn't want to feel the air shift between them. Didn't want to hear her voice slide into a higher octave when she said one of the things people always said when he referenced his title for the first time.

Oh!

A duke!

You are?!

What is that *like?!*

Have you met the Queen?!

And he didn't want the rest either. The sudden sizing up, the reassessment. The knowledge that every opinion she formed of him after the revelation of his title would be clouded by the title itself.

The unavoidable, malicious whisper: *She doesn't see you. She only sees the duke.*

Worse: *She doesn't want you. She only wants the duke.*

And then: *She doesn't love you. She only loves the duke.*

Her brows rose as the silence stretched between them. "Max?"

No harm in one night.

"I was born here."

She nodded and returned her attention to the road, visible in the bright light of the moon. "And you still live here, with people who care about you."

"For people who care about me, they certainly enjoy taking the piss."

She laughed at that, the sound lovely and rich. "I think that's how you *know* they care about you."

"It is, honestly."

Lilah watched him for a moment and then said, "That sounds like you have proof."

In his darkest moments, as his marriage disintegrated before God and tabloids, it had been those men who'd smacked him surely on the back and bought him pints and let him privately grouse to them. And during those moments, Max had been certain they'd remain private. After all, he wasn't ever going to talk about them.

So he would never know what made him respond, "Let's just say that when your marriage falls apart, you could do much worse than those four."

She didn't hesitate, her footsteps sure as they turned off the road and onto the long drive to the main house. If only Max could take the moment in such stride. In the nine years since its demise, he'd never once spoken of his marriage. To anyone. Not even the men down the pub.

Until this freckle-faced, doe-eyed, red-shoed darts shark had appeared.

Silence stretched between them, and it should have been uncomfortable, but it wasn't. She nodded. "I'm happy you had them, then."

No questions. Just honesty.

She sighed and looked up at the stars, clear and bright against the night sky. "You could do worse than them, and you could do worse than here."

The words were kind and light, but there, in the tail end of them, Max heard it. Wistfulness. Sadness. Nostalgia. Something else. Something he couldn't name but somehow understood, because it was familiar.

Someone had disappointed her too.

She's going to steer well clear of you—with what they say happened. Lottie's words.

He should leave well enough alone. He shouldn't push. Everyone had secrets. God knew he did. And yet, "What about you, Lilah Rose?"

She slid a surprised look at his use of her last name. "Checking up on me?"

"Wanted to make sure you weren't planning to rob the place."

"The oil paintings are safe." She laughed. "I won't have the wall space when I get back to New York." A pause, and then she added, "Come to think of it, I won't have walls when I get back to New York."

Knowing he shouldn't—knowing it wasn't fair play to ask her for secrets when he wasn't sharing his own—he grasped the string and pulled. "Why not?"

She lifted a shoulder in a little shrug that revealed more than she realized. "I sold my studio space eighteen months ago."

"For what, backpacking across Europe?"

"Around the world, actually. This is my last stop. Ten more days."

"What's in ten days?"

For a moment, there was nothing but the sound of her footsteps as they walked, the steady crunch of her worn red Converse trainers on the graveled path. "I return to the real world."

"What does that look like?"

She shook her head and looked at him, and there it was again, the sadness. The uncertainty. Max clenched his fists in his pockets, resisting the impulse to pull her close and wrap his arms around her. To keep whatever demons haunted her at bay. If he wasn't careful, he'd turn into Lancelot. Pledge her his sword.

And everyone knew what happened to Lancelot. He didn't get the girl. In fact, he was her downfall.

She looked to the main house, windows lit in the darkness. "Does it have a folly?"

The question was so unexpected it took him a moment to follow it. "It does."

Lilah smiled. "Two years ago, I shot Henrietta Wolfe, Vivienne Darby and Margot McKennett at a folly at Highley Manor."

Lottie had said Lilah was an artist, but photographing a trio of Shakespearean actors, each well into their eighties, each made a Dame by the Queen, who were collectively considered Britain's greatest treasure . . . Max couldn't help being impressed. "What was that like?"

Her voice filled with wonder. "Unbelievable. I've taken pictures of some amazing things, but those three? They've lived hundreds of lives in their work, and you can see it in every line of their faces . . . " She trailed off for a moment before she said, "The camera—it loved them."

Max could see her pleasure. Hear her breathless excitement. And he knew, without question, that she had loved that day.

She doesn't do celebrities anymore. His sister's words from earlier in the evening.

Why not? "What happened to the pictures?"

Like that, Lilah closed up. He'd said something wrong. "They were never run."

Sadness again. Loss?

Why?

He didn't ask. Maybe because he knew she wouldn't answer. Maybe because he knew that if she did, he wouldn't like what it revealed.

She filled the silence. "Anyway—before that shoot, I didn't know follies were a thing. I mean, who could imagine that people would build entire buildings for no purpose whatsoever?"

"Not for no purpose . . . they served a very clear purpose of showcasing the aristocratic love of excess."

"I never think of the English as being overtly excessive." She paused. "Estate houses aside."

He gave her a little smile. "Oh, never overt. That's the point. The folly here, which right now serves absolutely no purpose whatsoever, *looks* exceedingly useful."

"Useful in the sense of . . . "

He put on his best ducal accent, the one perfected during years of schooling. "How else are we to guard the northern border?"

She laughed and turned toward him, walking backward up the drive, the moonlight gleaming on her mahogany curls. "Back to marauders, are we?"

He watched her, riveted to her pretty, open face. Wanting to do more than watch it. "I thought we agreed that it was sheep."

She slowed, the laugh trailing off as his words echoed the moment in the pub, when he'd leaned in close and whispered in her ear, the scent of her wrapping around him like sun-drenched linen. It had taken every ounce of his self-control to resist pressing his lips to the soft, warm skin of her neck.

Soft, warm skin that tempted him even now, from beneath the collar of her sweater.

"Right," she said, softly, stopping altogether, turning her body toward him, and he would have given his whole fortune to know what she was thinking.

Enormous brown eyes, hooded. Full lips, parted.

He didn't need the fortune to know what she was thinking.

Lilah Rose wanted him.

And she wanted *him*. Not the Duke of Weston. Not Rupert Arden. Not St. Andrews or the Mayfair townhouse or the massive estate.

She wanted Max.

Christ, she was perfect here in the darkness, the crisp autumn air whispering through the trees, the night sky like a blanket, the universe closing around them.

He pulled his hands from his pockets, slowly, not wanting to ruin it. Not wanting her to think he'd only walked her home for this. To touch her. To kiss her.

It was true, that. He liked her. He hadn't wanted to say goodnight. Not yet.

And he wanted to kiss her.

But a gentleman wouldn't—

And then her fingers were on the bare skin of his forearm, stroking over the hair there, leaving a trail of fire in their wake, down his arm, over the back of his hand, until they laced into his for a heartbeat, just enough to make him wonder what she would do if he tightened his grip on hers and pulled her close.

Just enough to make him wonder how well she'd fit against his chest.

What she would taste like.

How quickly he could make her sigh with pleasure.

"Will you take me there?"

He'd take her wherever she wished.

No. That wasn't what she was asking.

The folly.

"Now?"

She smiled, and her touch slid away. "No. In daylight. But I imagine it's beautiful at night under the stars."

You're beautiful at night under the stars. "I'll take you there."

"Thank you." The words were soft and perfect, and they made Max want to give her everything she could ever want, just so he could hear her say them again. He wanted to lay her down in his bed and pleasure her until she was sighing them into his ear.

He cleared his throat at the thought and waved a hand in the direction of a turnoff from the main drive. "You're up here."

She looked off to where the light from the cottage shone through the trees, then back to him. "Where are you?"

He waved a hand in the direction of the estate house. "Other direction."

Not a lie.

Not the truth, neither.

Lilah looked back up the path toward the cottage, and he heard the breath hitch in her throat, as though she wanted to say something but wasn't quite sure what it was.

He would have waited there all night to hear it.

Finally, she looked back at him, her brown eyes gone black in the darkness. "Tell me something, Max . . . "

Anything she wanted.

" . . . are there sheep between here and there?"

"Could be," he said, his heart pounding, awareness thrumming through him. He wasn't young and he wasn't a fool. He knew what she was asking. "Shall I walk you the rest of the way?"

She led the way, through the darkness, beneath the ancient trees that had witnessed any number of lovers headed for that particular cottage in the dead of night over the last three hundred years.

When they reached the cottage, Lilah turned to watch him for a moment, and Max couldn't shake the idea that she was searching for something. Truth? Trust?

Whatever it was, she found it, and her fingers were back, sliding over his, threading through them. Her face tilted up to the moonlight. To him.

"Come inside." Not a request. Command. Pure temptation. Easy to follow.

It was his turn to touch her, to reach for her, his fingers stroking down the side of her face, along her jaw and down the column of her neck. She shivered, leaning into the heat of his hand, bringing one of hers up to hold him close.

His grip tightened, and she pressed herself to him—tight enough that he could close the distance between them without trying. Settle his lips on hers and steal her kiss.

He growled deep in his throat, frustration humming through him. "I can't."

"You can, though."

"The pub," he whispered, setting his forehead to hers, closing his eyes. "The drinks."

"Two pints. Three hours. I'm not drunk, Max."

She stepped closer to him, her free hand coming to his chest, warm and firm like a promise. His fingers flexed. He'd never wanted anything the way he wanted her. But he was trying to do the right thing.

"It's sweet you think you'd be taking advantage of me," she said, softly.

"I would," he said, matching her tone, leaning down and inhaling at the place where her neck met her shoulder, breathing her in as her fingers slid into his hair and tightened, holding him there. "I'm *already* taking advantage of you."

I'm taking advantage of the fact that you don't know who I am. That you don't treat me the way every other woman I've ever known has.

His lips brushed the soft skin of her shoulder, warm beneath the collar of her sweater, and she caught her breath.

"Don't stop," she commanded, pressing him closer, and he responded, his tongue circling against that magnificent, smooth skin, just once.

They both groaned at the sensation.

"Or maybe it's you, taking advantage of me," he spoke to her neck, his lips sliding along the column, over her jaw, to her ear.

Lilah's fingers tightened in his hair, tugging, and he lifted his head at the delicious sting, looking to her. She smiled, and it took all of his willpower *not* to give in. Not to take what he wanted. "I would really enjoy taking advantage of you."

And then she leaned up and kissed him, and he knew he shouldn't, but he let her, groaning into the caress, his fingers tightening on her waist, pulling her closer—was he pulling her? Not really. She was coming for him, fingers sliding in his hair, body pressed against his, all soft curves and perfection, and her mouth—pure, lush, beautiful sin.

She sighed into his mouth, and they took advantage of each other, just for a moment.

Just long enough for Max to slide his tongue against hers, just for a taste. Just long enough for him to know what he would miss when he remembered that he shouldn't be kissing her right now. Just to know her sweetness, so later he'd know what he missed when he lay in his own bed in his own house and stroked his cock and imagined her with him.

She tasted like spring.

But he wasn't the only one tasting—Lilah was stretching up to him, her arms wrapping around his neck, her own tongue meeting his. Exploring him as she pressed against him, her warm body fitting against him as she ended the kiss and whispered, "You taste like autumn."

He went instantly hard and pulled her tight to him with a growl, his hands falling to her ass and lifting her against him, her legs wrapping around his hips as he set her back to the closed door of the cottage with a thud that somehow set them both free.

She exhaled on a low, delighted laugh and looked up at him through her lashes—a lethal combination that sent a straight shot of pleasure through him. "So strong," she whispered, her hands stroking over his shoulders and down his arms, testing the muscles that strained there.

"I could hold you here forever," he said, setting his lips to her neck, her jaw, her cheek, and then kissing her again, meeting her tongue as it darted into his mouth and giving it a long suck, until a little cry sounded in her throat, and she rocked her hips against his, her core hot and perfect and too fucking far away, separated from him by layers of clothing.

He groaned as she increased the pressure there, where he wanted her beyond reason, and they kissed again, heavy and intense. She was like flame in his arms, hot and perfect, and sexy as hell, and the kiss went on and on, rioting through him until time disappeared, and place, and him—leaving nothing but Lilah.

"I could be held here, forever," she whispered, breaking the kiss, looking him straight in the eye. "Max . . . " His name came like a siren's call, punctuated by another slow rock against him.

Christ, she felt good. *This* felt good. Better than anything he'd ever experienced, and he gripped her tighter, pressing into her more firmly, one hand sliding into her thick curls, holding her still as he rocked against her, once. Twice.

She sighed. "Please, Max. One night."

One night.

Temptation incarnate. And what if he gave himself up to it? He'd thought it himself, earlier. One night. One night with her, and without the rest of the world. Max met her eyes, dark pools, heavy-lidded with want. He understood that too. He wanted her just as much. More. When was the last time he'd wanted something so much?

No harm in one night.

Except he knew now, even before he'd had her, that he wouldn't be able to stop at one night. He'd need more for what he wanted to do to her. For how he wanted to consume her.

For the look in her eyes, like she had delicious plans herself.

One night would never be enough.

Max lowered her to the ground in a slow slide that had him gritting his teeth from the pleasure of her body against his, of her indulgent, wicked smile, of her decadent sigh, of the throbbing ache of his cock.

And he lied.

"One night."

CHAPTER FIVE

IT WAS A MISTAKE, of course. Lilah knew it even as she pulled Max through the ancient oak door into the entryway of the cottage. She was going to London and then to New York and she absolutely did not need the complication of a hot British farmer, who was way too perfect for a one-night stand.

Or a one-week stand, for that matter.

This was the kind of man who made you want to stay.

But that was a problem for *future* Lilah. Present Lilah didn't have any problems at all.

She toed off her shoes as Max kicked the door closed behind them and reached for her with a growl, one arm sliding around her waist and pulling her to him.

She wrapped her own arms around his neck as he lifted her again, and she let out a little squeal. There was no three-hundred-year-old wall behind her this time, and Lilah wasn't exactly pixie-sized, but he carried her like she weighed nothing, and he wasn't even winded.

She threaded her fingers into his hair and wrapped her legs around his waist. "So much for the gentleman, huh?"

"Turns out I'm the marauder."

Pleasure coursed through her, pooling deep. "What will you do with me?"

One hand slid up her back, large and warm and firm, and he said, low and dark, "I have some ideas."

"Me too," she whispered, leaning down, her lips a hairsbreadth from his. "Should we see if they match?"

He groaned, his fingers sliding into her hair, pulling her down as he took her kiss, hot and lush, licking over her lips in a rough stroke that set her on fire. How was it that this man kissed like this? How was it that he tasted like wheat and smoke and sun and rain? How was it that he made her feel like she might spend the rest of her life searching for another kiss like this one—addictive and perfect?

They lingered there, in the foyer of the cottage, kissing for what felt like minutes or might have been days, and when he broke the caress it was only because they were both gasping for breath.

Lilah opened her eyes, finding his whiskey-colored gaze on her. "Okay?" he asked.

"Perfect."

He grunted his approval and took her lips again, the world tilting beneath them. No, not tilting. He was walking, headed for the stairs behind her.

She broke the delicious kiss and said, "Wait."

He stopped short, like he'd hit a brick wall, and pleasure shot through Lilah.

"I just want you to know," she leaned back and put her hands to his cheeks, staring down at this big, beautiful man who was carrying her through the house like they were in a romance novel, "I don't have someone in every harbor. I haven't had someone in *any* harbor in . . . a while." She closed her eyes. "I'm making a hash of it, but . . . it's important I say it . . . so, yeah. I choose you."

Something relaxed in her when she said it. Something that hadn't been fully relaxed in eighteen months.

He nodded. "Kiss me again, Lilah Rose." And she did, long enough to soften into his arms again. And when she did, he broke the caress to whisper, "I choose you too. And I haven't had anyone in any harbor in a while either."

"Okay." She smiled and kissed him again. "Do you want . . . " She trailed off . . . not quite knowing how to finish the question, but feeling like she should be polite. " . . . a tour?"

His laugh was a low rumble as he stepped onto the bottom stair. "No."

She clung to him as he carried her to the first floor of the house. "Something to eat?"

He stilled on the landing and met her eyes. "Mmm."

The sound curled through her, sending heat pooling to the place where he was hard against her. "Mmm," she repeated, soft and almost breathless. Lilah pointed toward the bedroom she'd chosen. "There."

He was already moving.

Inside, he flicked on the lights and set her down beside the big bed, his warm, strong hands coming to cradle her face, his thumbs stroking over her cheekbones until her lips parted from the soft pleasure of the caress and he leaned down to give her what she wanted, a long kiss that made her squirm. When he lifted his lips, he slid them across her cheek and to her ear. "You like that?"

She sighed her answer. "Yes."

"Mmm." That low growl. God, how was it that a mere sound made her wet? And then his hands were stroking over her hips and waist, up to where she was heavy and aching for his touch. "You like this?"

"Yes," she said, frustrated, wanting him to touch her breasts.

"But you want more."

"Yes, fuck. Yes," she said, the fingers of one hand clutching his strong forearm, the others tangled in his hair.

He gave a low laugh.

She turned to him. "Touch me."

"Tell me where."

She did one better, grabbing his hand, moving it. He exhaled, his fingers flexing over the flesh of her full breast, and she gritted her teeth, wanting her clothes gone. Wanting *their* clothes gone.

"It's not enough," he growled.

She shook her head. "I want more."

"I want it all," he said, and the words came like a confession, as though he shouldn't.

She met his eyes, recognizing the understanding flashing in them.

Understanding and something else. Something like hunger. One that matched her own. "Take it." After a long moment studying her, Max released her, and Lilah swayed with the loss of his touch.

And then his hands were on the hem of her sweater, clutching the fabric and pulling it over her head, and Lilah had never been more grateful for putting on a decent bra. He exhaled, reaching for her, one fingertip tracing the scalloped edge of the delicate red lace. "Red." He smiled. "Like your shoes."

"I like red," she said, her breath hitching as that wicked finger found the peak of one hard nipple, swirling over the lace, making her want to scream.

"Take it off," he said, the command like a shot in the room.

She didn't hesitate, reaching behind her to unclasp the bra before she looked up at him and said, "You take it off."

His gaze flew to hers and his hand fisted around the fabric, pulling it down, baring her to him. He stilled for a moment, watching. Riveted, and her nipples went impossibly hard under his scrutiny. "Look at you." He lifted a hand to his lips, rubbing his gorgeous mouth as though he was starving and she was a meal. And then his gaze came to hers. "You're beautiful."

She blushed.

"Shall I tell you more?"

Yes. Yes yes.

"You are." He was reaching for her again, that finger returning, circling until she thought she might lose her mind if he didn't— "Does it ache here?"

She looked to him, full of need, and told him the truth. "So much."

"Mmm." That sound again. Pleasure. Hunger. And then he took the tip of her breast into his mouth, working her gently until she sighed and her fingers came to his head, holding him there even as she wanted to beg him to move, to do more.

"God, Max, yes."

Another low growl and he released her. "Do you like that?"

"I can't remember," she replied. "Do it again."

He laughed against her skin as he moved to the other breast, giving it the same attention, long, slick, rhythmic sucks that opened a line of pleasure straight to her core, as though he was already inside her.

And then, like he knew what she wanted, he lifted his head and stole her lips in an equally delicious kiss, walking her back until her knees hit the bed and she sat, Max lowering himself with her, but not to the bed.

To the floor.

To his knees.

Between hers.

Anticipation flooded her as his hands found the waistband of her leggings and pulled, taking her underwear with them over her hips and thighs, down her legs, until she was completely bare.

Lilah was suddenly very aware of being naked in that room, in the glow of the porcelain bedside lamp, while this man—big and strong and beautiful in his own right—studied her.

And he did study her—his whiskey gaze tracking over her skin, devouring her, making her ache.

Instinctively she moved to cover herself, but Max was having none of that. "No," he rumbled. "I want to look."

Before she could reply, he touched her again, his strong hands stroking up her legs, searching for and finding all the places that made her shiver. Her ankles. The backs of her knees. The soft swell of her belly, the undersides of her breasts.

He kissed her at the base of her neck, his tongue making a little circle until she sucked in a breath and he laughed again, low and sexy as hell.

Those hands disappeared, back to her knees, easing her thighs open. "I want to look," he whispered, the heat of his breath against her skin like a promise. "Will you let me?"

She bit her lip. "Yes."

"Mmm." He sat back on his heels, his hands sliding along the soft skin of her thighs, pressing her open, wide.

And then his eyes were on her, and she couldn't stop herself from watching him. God, he looked like he was about to devour her. And she wanted it. Badly.

She moved, flexing her hips beneath his gaze, setting off a low rumble in his chest. His hands stroked again, down to her knees and back up over soft skin, until they found the tight curls at her core, brushing over them once, twice, until she rocked against him again. "Max."

"You like that?"

"No," she said. "Stop teasing me."

He parted her folds, gently. "Christ, you're wet. That's for me, isn't it?"

She lifted her hips toward him, the movement rewarded by one of his long fingers stroking, just barely—just enough to make her hiss her frustration at the barely there pleasure. "*Max*," she said again.

The bastard laughed. "That?"

"More."

The word came out harsh and directive, and Max's gaze shot up to hers. "Now *that* . . . that *I* like."

And he gave her what she wanted, that finger stroking over her slit, up and down over her straining, aching flesh, back and forth, never quite getting to where she wanted him most.

She grabbed his wrist. "Now."

The word was barely out of her mouth and he was there, his finger on her tight, aching clit, circling, pressing, stroking, until he found the rhythm that threatened to break her apart.

She rocked against him, and her eyes found his as he worked her, over and over. "Fuck, you're beautiful," he whispered. "I'm going to watch you come again and again, all night long."

Whatever he wanted. She'd give it to him. "Yes."

"But first . . . "

His touch was gone in an instant and Lilah cried out, the sound garbled and frustrated, even as he was pressing her thighs wide and lowering himself between them.

"Shh, love," he whispered. "I know."

"Max . . . " His name came out on a cry.

"I know, love. But you see, I changed my mind," he said to her core, the words soft temptation against her as he tucked his shoulders, wide and perfect, between her thighs, holding her open for him. "It turns out I do want something to eat."

Her laugh immediately became a groan as he set his mouth to her, his tongue tracing the path his finger had blazed earlier along her soft heat, savoring the taste of her as he licked and kissed in long, lingering strokes, as though they did not have one night . . . as though they had forever.

And Lilah, unable to do anything else, gave herself up to the twin pleasures of feeling . . . and watching. Because Max watched her the whole time, his eyes on hers, hot and dark and full of need, reading her pleasure as he manipulated it. As he controlled it.

Her fingers found his hair again, clenching there, holding him to her. "Yes," she whispered as she rolled her hips against his magnificent mouth, in time with his steady, languid licks. "God, *please.*"

She watched his eyes light with a wicked gleam as he growled against her and gave her what she wanted, finding her clit, swirling his tongue around it and flicking over it, slow and delicious, until she couldn't watch anymore, her eyes sliding closed as she lay back on the bed and gave herself up to this magnificent man.

One of his hands came to the swell of her stomach, warm and enormous over her, pinning her to the bed as he continued to fuck her with his mouth, flattening his tongue against her and working it against her, again and again.

She fisted his hair and rocked against him. "God, yes, don't stop," she whispered, and he didn't, this gorgeous man, instead pushing one thick finger of his free hand into her, pressing deep, searching, fucking her, and he didn't stop.

He didn't.

He worked her and he played with her and he fucked her with his hands and his mouth and his *eyes*, still watching when she flew apart, coming up off the bed, her own eyes opening, instantly finding him as she came, and came, and came, his name on her lips, laying waste to her thoughts.

And he stayed there as she came down from her pleasure, his fingers stilling, his tongue gentling, stroking in long, slow licks that sent delicious tremors of pleasure through her until she found the strength to release the hold she had on his hair and fall back against the bed, sated and thoroughly pleasured.

No. Not thoroughly. There was another thread of need there.

Need to be closer to him.

Need to be with him.

She sat up and he was there, meeting her kiss as she came for him, consuming her with lips and teeth and tongue so she could taste herself on him. In him. With him. And that taste, that moment, that kiss—

"You are wearing too many clothes," she whispered, reaching for the hem of his sweater, yanking it up over his head and sending it flying across the room, instantly forgotten.

Her eyes went wide as she took him in, broad and muscled with years of working in the fields, the opposite of every man she'd ever been with before. Those men had all been lean and lanky. But Max . . . well.

Name was destiny.

Her hands stroked over his wide shoulders, his broad chest, down the ridged muscles of his abdomen to the waistband of his jeans. She stilled, her eyes on his. "Do you mind if—"

One side of his mouth kicked up in the sexiest smile she'd ever seen. "I do not."

Her fingers were on the fastenings of his jeans then, tearing open the button and lowering the zipper, her curiosity taking over as she reached inside the shadowy opening and found him, hot and heavy and *huge*.

Her eyes went wide. "Max," she said softly, nibbling at his earlobe when he grunted his reply. "Turns out you *do* have a broadsword."

He stilled, a little exhale the only indication that he'd registered the words before he ran his hand through his hair, over the back of his head, and looked away, sheepish. "Sorry."

She couldn't help her laugh. "That's the most English thing I've ever heard."

His gaze shot back to hers. "What?"

"Apologizing for your penis size." She stroked it, measuring its length and girth beneath soft fabric. "Listen to me, Max. You have *nothing* to apologize for."

He growled, low and dark, in reply, and that hand that had been the hallmark of his chagrin reached for her, cupping her chin. When he kissed her, it wasn't apology. It was claiming.

And she *loved* it.

Without breaking the kiss, he removed his clothes. She scooted back onto the bed as he joined her, eager to feel him bare in her hand. She pushed him to his back and came up to straddle his thighs. "Let me see."

The gorgeous man did, putting his hands behind his head and watching her as she explored him, straight and thick and beautiful. She couldn't stop herself from stroking him in a long, slow slide, crown to base. Again. And again, this time marveling as a drop of liquid revealed itself as his foreskin slid back. She rubbed it into his skin with her thumb, and he swore softly.

Her gaze flew to his at the sound. "You are so beautiful," she whispered, leaning down to press a kiss to the sensitive head, to taste him, earthy and salty and perfect, and he cursed, one hand coming to her hair, stroking her curls.

"Lilah," he growled. "Not like this."

She lingered there. "Just a taste, Max. Just one . . . please."

"Christ." His hips rocked into her grip.

"Just once," she promised to the velvet tip of him. "Just once, and then I want you to fuck me." She sucked him down as he groaned her name, loving the feel of his cock, thick and heavy on her tongue, and the sound of his filthy mouth thick and heavy in the room around them. And then he was pulling her up off him and rolling her to the bed, and she was squealing her displeasure. "Not fair!"

"What's not fair is that you are a witch."

She smiled, feeling powerful enough for it to be true, and spread her thighs, cradling him between them, his heavy, hot shaft against her. "Shall we try for real magic?"

"Mmm," he said, stealing another kiss, quick and dirty, before saying, "Don't go anywhere."

He was gone to his wallet just long enough to fetch a foil packet and return, climbing up her body again, placing long, lingering kisses along the way, until she was writhing beneath him, wet and ready.

The broad head of his cock was at her entrance, and Max pressed into her, slowly, aware of his size and clearly wanting to give her time to adjust. Lilah strained for more and he held back, sinking into her by impossible measures, each time pulling out slowly, until only the head of him stayed with her. Until they were both breathing ragged, devastated breaths.

And only when she was wild with need for him did he give her what she begged for. He began to thrust, slow and—yes, so easy—so smooth and even and perfect, like they'd been doing it for a lifetime and not just one night. "Oh, God," she said, her arms around him as she tilted her hips up to his. "Yes."

"There."

"More."

"Please."

"*Max.*"

And then he was fucking her, hard and smooth and unleashed, and he was whispering the filthiest things in her ear, rough and beautiful, and she was doing as he asked, sliding her hand between them to rub her hard, straining clit again, and he was lifting himself up, giving her more room, and thrusting deep and fast and she'd been right.

It was so easy. Like home.

It would have scared her if she'd let it, but she didn't have time to think about it, because electric pleasure was coursing through her and she was coming hard around him, harder than she could ever remember coming, milking his own release from him and reveling in the harsh shout of her name on his lips as he came in long, heavy thrusts that sent ripples of pleasure through her.

He was glorious.

It was glorious.

When they'd recovered, Max collapsed onto his back, pulling her over him, pressing a kiss to her temple and tucking her into one of his big, warm arms, as though she belonged there.

And the strangest thing was that she *felt* like she belonged there.

He rumbled again, that rolling "Mmm" pure satisfaction beneath her ear, and the sound sent a little thrill through her even as it settled her, heart pounding, into something else entirely.

Something like happiness.

She'd think about that in the morning.

But first . . . sleep.

CHAPTER SIX

LILAH WOKE to sunshine and the smell of coffee, neither of which were things she usually experienced, because she was usually up before the sun, and it had been a long time since she'd had someone to make coffee for her. But she didn't usually wake in sheets that smelled like autumn leaves and sex.

Max.

He'd stayed.

She'd woken twice the night before, the first time to his lips on her skin, pressing warm and soft kisses over her shoulder and neck until she'd rolled to her back and directed his touch to where she wanted him. He'd made her come twice before she slipped back to sleep.

The second time, it had been nearly dawn, the sky outside that perfect charcoal that came right before light. He'd been asleep, and it had been Lilah's turn to wake him with lips and hands, to follow his wicked, wonderful instructions until they were both sated.

This time, it was morning, and he could have left.

But he'd stayed.

She should have been unnerved by the realization, but she wasn't. In fact, as she stretched in the beam of warm sunlight and catalogued the lingering effects of the night before—a tight muscle here, a delicious twinge there—she was filled with an undeniable thrill.

Minutes later, having pulled on a pair of soft yoga pants, a tank top and a cardigan, brushed her teeth, and ensured she looked properly, artfully mussed, she made her way down the ancient creaky staircase to the kitchen of the cottage. Hesitating in the doorway, she watched him, tall and broad and . . . freshly washed. Wearing different clothes than the night before.

He stood at the scarred wooden counter next to the stove, chopping something that he had to have found wherever he'd found his new clothes, because last she'd checked, the cottage refrigerator contained a bottle of rosé, a carton of milk, half a wedge of Stilton, three Cornish pasties and an apple—none of which was producing that delicious smell.

"I've heard about these English fairies," she said, moving into the room. "Bringing clean clothes and eggs"—she peeked around him—"and thyme?"

"I had to feed Atlas," he said, setting the knife down and looking to her. "I thought you might be hungry. I kept you up late."

And like that, the air in the room shifted, the memories of the night before between them, full of pleasure. "I am hungry," she said, not meaning for it to come out quite so soft. Quite so wanting.

But it did, and his gaze heated, and she wondered what he'd do if she suggested they table breakfast and head back up for round four.

"Lilah Rose," he said, the words a delicious rumble. "I have plans for this morning and if you keep looking at me like that, you're going to ruin them."

She inhaled at the words—direct and perfect, like this was normal, every-day-after-ordinary-sex breakfast and not extremely not normal, morning-after-excellent-first-time-sex breakfast—and smiled, coming closer. "Would we say *ruin*?"

He reached for her then, one big hand grabbing the waistband of her tank top, fisting the fabric and pulling her close for a kiss that should have been a normal daytime kiss and was instead extremely not normal and incredibly sexy, his tongue stroking deep, sliding against hers until she sighed and went loose in his arms. Only once she was clinging to him did he release her. "Pour yourself a coffee and wait for breakfast like a good girl."

Unf.

She did as she was told, telling herself that responding so thoroughly to being called *good girl* was offset by the fact that she was absolutely going to sexually objectify this wildly handsome man while he cooked her breakfast.

She tucked one leg beneath her and sat down on the wide bench on the far side of the large oak table where she'd set up shop earlier in the week, her laptop and equipment on one end, and watched him work, moving two saucepans around the ancient Aga and navigating the kitchen, finding everything he needed without pause.

"You know this house well," she observed. He did pause then, his shoulders stiffening just barely, just for a moment—so quick that you'd have to be incredibly skilled at reading people to notice.

She waited through the hesitation—a lesson learned in years of training. Hesitations revealed truth. *Don't blink, or you'll miss the shot.*

"I lived here for a bit." Her brows shot up, but she bit her tongue, staring at his broad, hunched shoulders. She was rewarded for her patience when he added, "When my marriage was falling apart. I didn't want to be in London, and I didn't want to be at the main house. So I stayed here."

Lilah looked down at the table then, at the map of the grain, crossed with scars and dings and divots, and her thumb traced the edge of a knot in the oak, imagining him here, nursing a broken heart.

They'd both come here to mend wounds.

They'd both come here to start fresh.

"Well," she said, finally, returning her attention to his back, "I think you should have stayed for the stove, honestly. I'm in love with that stove. If I *were* a thief, that's what I'd take."

"This cooker weighs at least a tonne and was installed before you were born, Ms. Rose; you'd need a team to nick it." He laughed, grabbing two plates from a shelf nearby and turning one perfect omelet and then another onto them before he collected napkins and forks and approached the table.

She took a moment to admire his lean hips where his dark Henley met the waistband of his worn chinos. "Why do you think I'm making friends with a very strong farmhand?"

He set the plate in front of her. "Mushrooms, herbs and goat's cheese. Eggs fresh today from the girls. How's that for farmhand?"

She blinked. "You collected *eggs* this morning?"

He shrugged, taking the chair across the table. "It was on the way."

She wasn't sure it was, but she wasn't about to turn down a home-cooked meal. She lifted a fork and took a bite. "Max, this is *delicious*."

"It's nothing." He dipped his head, that blush spreading across his cheeks again. If Lilah had more than this vacation from reality with him, she'd make it her personal goal to summon that blush once a day.

"It's *not* nothing. I should know. I've been living in Airbnbs for eighteen months." She waited for him to look at her. "Thank you."

He didn't look away then. Instead, he replied with absolute honesty, "Thank *you*, Lilah Rose."

And it was Lilah's turn to blush.

He watched her for a long moment, and she could see the pleasure in his gaze. She wanted to preen beneath it until he cleared his throat. "So, you've seen the world."

"Not nearly the whole of it, but a lot more than most."

"And what was that like?"

She looked to her gear at the end of the table. "At first? Terrifying."

He waited patiently.

She took another bite of the omelet, using the time to find her answer. "When I left New York—" She paused, not quite knowing how to tell him the truth without telling him the truth. "Well, I didn't know if I'd ever be able to take pictures again. I sold my studio and packed my gear and left with my passport and a list of old friends from art school who I thought I might be able to beg a couch from here and there."

"And?"

"And about four months in, I was in India and a friend told me a story about a woman who lived nearby, who was changing the world."

"How?"

"Organic fertilizer. Devi drove me to a farm in Andhra Pradesh and introduced me to Aarti Rao, one of the preeminent minds in sustainable farming. She's developed a natural treatment to protect seeds and young plants from fungus that can devastate crops and livelihoods on small farms across India."

His brows rose. "This sounds a long way from the red carpet."

She grinned. "I know a lot about cow urine now."

"Fascinating stuff. Would you like a job here?"

She shook her head. "Too late. Dr. Rao is on the board of Common Harvest, an NGO in support of sustainable farming—"

He nodded. "I know it. Salterton Farms is a member."

"Well then you know that Common Harvest is always looking for ways to elevate sustainable farming. To make it . . . "

"Cool?" he supplied, his tone indicating that he found it anything but.

Lilah laughed. "Don't be so quick to doubt. People love the idea of sustainability. Farm-to-table is everywhere, farmers markets are having an absolute renaissance, there are Instagram accounts devoted to celebrity farmers all over the world."

Max couldn't hide his surprise. *"Why?"*

She pointed a fork at him. "Do not underestimate the appeal of a beautiful person holding a piglet!"

His brows shot together. "A piglet!"

"Maybe you and Mabel should team up," she suggested, trying to keep a straight face.

He grimaced at the suggestion. "I'm not sure either of our dispositions would suit."

"Fair." She laughed. "But the truth is, the world is getting bigger and bigger, and people are feeling more and more disconnected, and so we are all thinking more about what it means to be closer to the things that keep us . . . " She searched for the word. Found it. "Happy."

"And farms make you happy?"

This one could.

She bit back the reply and pointed to the omelet on her plate. "How much of this came from here?"

"All of it."

"And you too, so farms make me very happy today."

He smiled, small and satisfied, and she resisted the urge to swipe the plates to the floor, crawl across the table and kiss that satisfaction from his lips. He was proud of his work, and that was something she understood.

"So. You're to make farming cool."

He didn't know that not long ago Lilah Rose could have made anything cool—even cow urine.

"That's the job," she said. "Aarti lobbied hard for Common Harvest to hire me, and when I told them what I wanted to do, they agreed. I drove back out to her lab and took pictures of her. And then I traveled the world, taking pictures of a dozen other people in their labs and on their boats and farms and with their beehives."

"And was that terrifying?" he asked.

She shook her head. "No. That was incredible. Exhausting and challenging and weird at times . . . but really incredible."

And it had been. She'd found her feet again, camera in hand, taking portraits of interesting people. Which was what she'd loved doing in the first place.

"Where are the photos now?"

"They'll be shown at the Common Harvest gala in London. Next week."

A pause, and then, "The end of the journey."

All those months traveling, taking pictures, trying so hard to rebuild herself and forge a new path back . . . She nodded. "Nine days. And then back to the world."

And maybe, just maybe, back to her life.

"And will they do it? Make farming cool?"

If he'd asked her that question two years ago, she would have answered, categorically, *yes*. Two years ago, Lilah had been on top of the world, the most in-demand photographer around. She'd been able to choose her clients, name her price, and set her standards. She'd been in the perfect place—old enough to no longer be a wunderkind, young enough to have a lifetime of opportunity ahead of her.

And then, in an instant, the walls of her carefully constructed palace came tumbling down.

Frustration flared, along with self-doubt and disappointment, all emotions that she'd learned never to show. But she wanted to show it. Here, in this place, with this man who had no tie to the world of wealth, privilege, glamour and high society that had made her famous. He didn't care that she was famous. And there was freedom in that.

Space for honesty.

"I don't know," she said. "But if anyone can make it cool, it's me."

"A lifetime of practice."

"I've made a lot of people cool."

"Would I have seen your pictures?"

She was good at her job, and wasn't ashamed of it. "Probably."

Max watched her for a long moment, long enough that she wondered if she'd said something wrong. "Show me."

Her stomach flipped. "Show you what?"

"Show me what Lilah Rose can do."

She almost didn't. But it had been so long since someone had seen her work and judged her on its merit, and not on the stories they'd heard —the lies they'd been told.

That, and she wanted him to see them.

She reached for her laptop, opening and unlocking it, pulling up a search window and turning it to him. "There's excellent Wi-Fi out here."

"The sheep riot if they don't have it," he deadpanned, setting his fingers to the keyboard and typing her name.

She tried to stay still. Tried to pretend she didn't have to see the results of his search. But she was only human, after all, and he was about to stare into her soul, so what was a girl to do?

She got up and went around the table, doing her best not to grab the computer and curate the images he saw. Show him the ones she knew were best. Instead, she pressed herself back to the heavy wooden chopping block at the center of the kitchen, and watched over his shoulder as he scrolled.

Scroll scroll *pause*.

Scroll scroll *pause* . . . on an image that had been cropped by some website and now looked absolutely awful.

Lilah bit her tongue, willing him to keep going, and when he did, she watched his strong fingers work the trackpad on the laptop, and her attention fell to the Breguet chronograph on his wrist, recognition coming with no small amount of surprise. She'd photographed enough celebrities styled to the teeth to know that the watch easily ran twenty thousand dollars. Apparently there were some perks to working for a duke.

"I've seen some of these before," he said.

She didn't know what to say to that, and she didn't want small talk about the work. She wanted to know what he thought of it. So Lilah held her tongue and watched his face.

"I know this woman," he said, pointing to a stark black-and-white portrait—a woman standing alone outside the marriage bureau at City Hall in Little Rock, Arkansas, a proud glint in her dark eyes.

"VM Mathers," she clarified. The author of *Self Love*, a book that had spoken to every woman who had ever been with the wrong person and vowed to seize her own happiness. "I took that one a few months after the book came out."

He nodded, recognizing the name. "What's she like?"

Lilah smiled. "Not what you'd expect from a self-help juggernaut. Badass. She took me to the best barbecue of my life immediately after I got that shot."

It was the last shoot Lilah had done before the one that had ruined her.

"And this one . . . Ian Hale—why do I know this one?"

"I don't know," she said. "You don't seem like the kind of person who subscribes to lifestyle magazines." She took a step forward, not trusting herself to get close enough to take over his browsing. "That was my first *Bonfire* cover. I was sick to my stomach showing up for it—I wanted to do something different than shirtless-action-hero-leaning-on-a-rusted-out-car." She paused, then added, "Celebrities often have their own ideas of how they want to be photographed, and they're usually pretty banal and terrible. I knew there was a better-than-even chance he would hear my ideas and storm out."

"And did he?" The words were low and gruff, like he might hunt Ian Hale down if he had been rude to Lilah. She shouldn't like that, but she did. "No. He was great."

Max had enlarged the photo—the cover. A flawless shot. One that revealed more of Ian Hale than any of the dozens of covers he'd been on before or since. She was proud of that one.

Max grunted his reply and for a heartbeat Lilah wondered at the sound—was it possible he was *jealous*?

"And this one—I remember this picture of the American president."

Half the newspapers in the world had run it on Inauguration Day— the president of the United States, head bowed, framed against nothing but blue sky. "I remember every second of that day. The first woman president, and she wanted me to take the portrait." She shook her head, still in awe. "A thousand other photographers to choose from, and there I was."

"Not a thousand. None like you," he said, softly, drawing her attention.

She met his eyes. "No," she said, the word as much an agreement as it was a reminder to herself. Of who she'd been then. Of who she might still be. "None like me."

"You love it."

I do. She loved the excitement and the people and the knowledge that she could capture a moment that would show *everything* and only because she was astute enough to see everything first.

She loved it, and she wanted it back.

Looking at the screen—her entire past laid out in a mosaic of thumbnails—she was consumed with emotion. She'd worked so hard. She'd done everything right. She'd done magnificent work.

And now . . .

"Nine days," she said, softly.

"Not long," he replied.

Nine days, and she was on a train to London. Away from this place that had somehow already begun to feel like more than a holiday.

Away from this man—his whiskey-colored eyes and his rugged face and his beautiful mouth, set in a firm line that might have been disappointment if she let herself think about it. But she didn't want to think about disappointing him—this man who had impossibly begun to feel like more than a holiday himself.

He closed the laptop and stood, turning to face her. "More than one night though."

Her heart began to pound. "We passed the one-night mark when you went and collected fresh eggs, I think."

He didn't laugh at the joke, instead closing the distance between them. "How many more will you give me?"

She swallowed at the direct question, her lips falling open in surprise. "You don't mess around."

"You leave in nine days, Lilah. I don't have time to mess around." His hands came to cup her face, tilting her up to him. "Nine days, and you go back to your world. To the glitz and the glamour and the parties and the pictures."

She was losing herself in him. In the deep brown of his eyes. In the rumble of his voice that made her forget what it was she was so desperate to get back to. "Yes."

"Nine days," he repeated, stealing her lips in a soft, lush kiss. "I want them."

Yes.

He was kissing her again, hot and lingering. "Give them to me." She opened her eyes to find him watching her. "Let me spend the days making you laugh and the nights making you come."

This man was absolutely a marauder. "Yes."

With a growl, he walked her back to a clean section of the counter and lifted her up to sit on it, his hands already divesting her of her clothes. Not that she was complaining.

"I thought you had plans for the day?"

"Mmm," he rumbled at her ear, the sound like sin. "They've changed."

CHAPTER SEVEN

THEY SPENT the next two days living on sex and sleep and whatever they could throw together to eat before they started all over again, and Max did his best to discover every bit of Lilah's glorious body, memorizing the places that made her sigh and the ones that made her laugh and the ones that made her moan.

He liked those the most.

On the third morning, as the early afternoon sun turned the grass in the north pasture the perfect autumn gold, he made good on his original plans, and took Lilah to the folly, Atlas leading the way. At some point after the morning she'd agreed to give him her time at Salterton Abbey, he'd gone to fetch the sheepdog, who seemed as happy to linger with Lilah as Max was.

And he was happy to linger with her, he thought as they crossed the estate in the direction of the tower at the northern edge of the land.

Happy to pull her close and pretend she needed help navigating the collection of stones that would become a brook in the spring.

Happy to thread his fingers through hers as they climbed the small hill just to the north.

Happy to stand back and watch her turn in a circle there, taking in the estate, reaching into the bag she'd slung over her shoulder before they'd left the house to retrieve her camera.

He could have watched her for hours, taking pictures of the land, of the mottled sunlight across the patchwork fields, of the storm clouds on the horizon, of the sheep in the pastures beyond.

And as he watched, it occurred to him that it was he who should have taken photos. Lilah who should have been the subject.

Because in six days she would be gone, and he would have nothing but the memory of her here, with him. And it didn't matter how happy he was here and now—it didn't matter how happy they both were, even as he watched the gleam of pure joy and contentment in her rich brown eyes.

This happiness, like all happiness in Max's experience, was temporary.

At least this time, he'd known it from the start. He'd never expected Lilah to stay, and he could not afford to let himself believe she might. That way lay bitter disappointment and despair. He'd learned that years ago. It was a lesson he'd do well to remember now as the sight of Lilah looking so peaceful and at home on the land that was his birthright and his legacy tempted and threatened.

Six more days, he promised himself. And he'd be damned if he gave up a single moment of them.

Lilah raised her camera, looking through the viewfinder at the estate house rising up on a hill in the distance, far enough away to settle it into the landscape and still imposing enough to give pause.

"You know, I think you can get that exact shot in the gift shop."

She looked up instantly. "Excuse me, you can absolutely *not* get my exact shot in the gift shop."

He laughed at her affront. "I beg your pardon."

"You'd better," she said, feigning seriousness before looking back at the house. "How many rooms are there?"

"One hundred and forty."

"Good lord."

It was ridiculous. "The family lives in about twenty of them. The rest is open to the public."

She nodded, returning to their walk. "I took the tour."

His brows shot up. "You did?"

"I did! The morning after we met."

"I could have given you a tour," he said, suddenly embarrassed and frustrated that she'd been in his home and he hadn't known.

Neither had she.

Embarrassed and frustrated and *guilty.*

"You didn't exactly bring me a basket of baked goods when I arrived, Max."

"I saved you from Mabel."

"Okay, first, I think Mabel and I would have worked it out," she said with a laugh. "And second, I'm guessing that the lovely elderly woman who gave the tour probably knew more about the portrait gallery than you did."

The portrait gallery filled with portraits of his ancestors.

"Although she *really* wanted to talk about the duke."

He snapped his head around to look at her. "She did?"

"Oh yes. According to Judy, not only is he a billionaire, he's *quite dishy and unmarried.*"

She said the last in a perfectly theatrical British accent. Max's cheeks warmed. "Mmm."

Lilah waved a hand in the air. "Unfortunately for all of us sad single-tons, however, he's also *very secretive* and nursing a *legendary broken heart.*"

"What rubbish," he scoffed. Who was this Judy woman?

She shrugged. "I don't know, I thought it was a pretty nice way of getting around the fact that he probably loathes having to mix with the masses. She really sold it. I confess, I was about ready to go Lizzie Benneting around to see if I could find him in the lake."

Right. He wouldn't sack Judy.

"Careful," he said. "If you found me in the lake, I'd do more than Mr. Darcy you."

She turned a delicious smile on him. "Promises, promises."

He kissed her, lingering at that smile. "Unfortunately, we don't have a lake handy."

She shook a head. "What even is the point of having an English country house if you don't have a lake?"

"I don't know. You should ask Judy the next time you take the tour."

"Okay, I give," she said, threading her arm through his. "Regale me with tales of Salterton Abbey."

"What do you want to know?"

"You have an apartment in the main house?"

"I do." *Tell her.*

Tell her, and lose every moment of those six days of happiness.

"You see? And Judy said *nothing* about the hot farmhand."

"Land steward, actually," he corrected. It was the truth. Just not all of it. "But let's get back to me being hot."

"No. If we do that, I'll never see the folly."

That much was true.

"What's it like living in something . . . Versailles-sized?"

He turned wide, affronted eyes on her "Versailles! Please. Balmoral. Windsor. But not *French*."

He loved making her laugh. "I'm so sorry to offend. Please don't tell your boss. I wouldn't want him to kick me out."

He resisted the urge to flinch. "He wouldn't, you know."

"I'm happy to hear it," she retorted. "Do you know how hard it is to find a good hotel room on such short notice? I'd have to convince Simon to let me stay at the Fox and Falcon."

"First, you are *not* staying anywhere near Simon."

Her brows rose. "What's wrong with Simon?"

"He's a bounder and a cad," he said without hesitation. "And besides, you're allowed to stay as long as you wish."

"Even if the duke knew I compared his castle to Versailles?"

"Even then."

"Ah. He's the good kind of duke, then?"

He looked away. "He tries to be."

Except for now. He can't seem to be the good kind of man right now. Not when it means losing the pleasure you've promised him.

They walked in silence for a while, waving to a young family who had come to the estate for a wander. An older girl was attempting to teach a little one how to do a cartwheel, and Lilah slowed to look, giving Max time to watch her.

To wonder what it would be like if she were his to watch, always.

When the little one toppled over almost instantly, Lilah chuckled, and the woman with them looked over with a smile and a shrug.

"I like that the estate is public," Lilah said as they resumed their journey.

"I do too." Max waved to the family from a distance. "I like that it belongs to residents of and visitors to Salterton as much as to the title," he said, repeating his father's words, repeated from his grandfather.

"But not to photographers," she said, teasing.

One side of his mouth lifted. "We make an exception for hot ones."

She grinned. "So I'm hot now, too?"

"Shall I show you how much?"

He reached for her, but she slipped from his fingers with a laugh. "No deal, Lancelot. I was promised a folly. Tell me more. You've lived here your whole life, you said."

"Yes." *The truth.*

"Family business?"

"Mmm," he said, hating the non-answer.

She shook her head. "Wild. And you never thought about leaving?"

"I did leave, for a while."

She understood instantly. "The fallen-apart marriage."

"The very same."

They walked for a bit longer, and Max was grateful that Lilah didn't pull away from him. He wanted to tell her this truth—even if he didn't want to tell her all of it.

And she waited for him.

"We were young and in love," he started, surprising himself with the words. "But I'd lived here my whole life and she'd spent her life in London. She didn't want sheep and hay and lazy evenings down the pub. And I didn't want the city, the parties, the people." He'd never told anyone the rest. "I thought I could love her enough to get her to stay. And Georgiana thought she could love me enough to get me to leave."

She nodded. "You were on different paths."

Just as we are.

He'd seen the longing on her face when she'd talked about her work in that world—Christ, she'd taken photos of presidents and princes and superstars—and he could see how much she wanted to get back to it every time she lifted her camera to her eye.

Could see, too, that someone had taken it from her. He'd seen that look before on a woman he loved. Disappointment and sadness and something worse. *Regret.*

He'd never be someone's regret again.

Lilah would never have cause to regret Max. She would leave in less than a week, none the wiser as to his title, and he would remain a lovely, satisfying interlude in her long and interesting life—a happy memory. He could hope for that. He could be that.

Because she *would* leave. And he would stay. And that was where this story ended.

"How long were you married?"

He looked out toward the tower, just visible at the center of a copse of trees on the next rise. "We met at eighteen. Married at twenty-three. Divorced at twenty-six."

"Wow," she said, softly.

"My greatest failure," he said.

"Please. You were young and in love and believed it was enough. We all do stupid things for love at twenty-three."

He looked at her, loving the matter-of-fact way she said it. Like it was true. "What did you do?"

She shook her head. "I went to *art school*, Max. About the only thing I didn't do is get married to the wrong person, and honestly only because I was falling for a different wrong person every week."

The confession freed Max. "And do you still do that?"

"What, fall for the wrong person?"

"Mmm."

"Ask me in six days," she teased, not looking at him. Instead, she took in the wide expanse of Weston lands, but Max missed the vista with its enormous rolls of baled hay dotting the fields, lush wood in a riot of color, and the house itself in the distance.

He was too busy watching Lilah, more breathtaking than the land beyond.

"Growing up here must have been amazing," she said, pulling him from his thoughts.

"It was," he agreed. "Summers, when we were home from school— Simon and I . . . we'd spend every minute of daylight exploring."

She smiled. "Bounders and cads in training?"

"He was the bounder and cad."

"And you? Scoundrel and rogue?"

"In training. How did I do?"

She tilted her head. "Terrible."

He raised a brow. "I shall endeavor to try harder."

"See that you do," she said before adding, "And what about other kinds of friends?"

He slid her a look, feigning ignorance. "What other kinds of friends?"

"Girls, Max," she said, as though speaking to a small child. "What about girls?"

They were nearing the top of the rise, closing in on a cluster of trees that had been there for two hundred years. "I'm familiar with the concept."

She laughed. "I bet you were a heartbreaker."

"I did all right."

"Tell me about your first kiss."

He stopped in his tracks. "I most certainly will not."

She burst out laughing. "That was the most British you've ever sounded! Are you afraid you'll ruin her reputation?"

"A gentleman would never."

Lilah grinned. "Surely there's a statute of limitations on kissing and telling."

"How long would you say that is?"

"Twenty years," she said, all certainty.

"Fair enough. Her name was Claire, we were ten, and it was very fast because we were absolutely certain we were about to be discovered by the vicar."

"The vicar!"

"The vicar. We only ever saw each other after services on Sunday mornings."

She made a show of looking shocked. "Kissing behind the church hedgerow is scandalous, Max."

"It wasn't behind the hedgerow; it was in the graveyard."

Lilah's pretend shock disappeared. "Wow. I'm honestly impressed.

And a little jealous. My first kiss was in the back row of my high school auditorium with Brock D'Avino during rehearsal for the school musical."

"Young Brock deserves a talking to, no doubt."

"Well, I can't remember anything about him but his name, so I don't think it was very memorable. The point is, it wasn't anywhere near as interesting as a *graveyard*."

He winced. "Don't say it like that. Makes it seem really grim."

"Sunday morning cemetery snogging is better?"

"I wouldn't exactly call it a snog."

"Chaste smooching."

He chuckled. "Better."

They walked for a bit longer, and Lilah asked, "So, what happened to Claire?"

"Living quite happily with her partner and their twin girls in London, last I heard."

"Too bad."

He cut her a look. "Not so bad." Suddenly, nothing in his past felt bad. None of it could, if it had led him here, to her. To this. To her, beautiful and fresh-faced and him, here, now. If just for a moment. And if six days of her was all he ever got, it would be enough.

Lie.

She stilled, pulling him around to face her, and he read the understanding in her eyes. The desire in them—a desire he recognized because it was his as well. "No," she agreed, softly. "Not bad at all."

She came up on her toes to meet him as he dipped his head and they kissed, and he didn't want it to stop, soft and sweet and full of pleasure.

When they broke apart, Lilah's eyes remained closed for a heartbeat, and Max took the moment to drink her in, warm and sun-kissed, a dusting of freckles across her cheeks, where her dark lashes lay. And then she whispered, "If I'm not careful, I'm going to like you more than six days' worth."

He already liked her. Too much.

He swallowed the realization, grateful that they'd arrived at their destination. The little tower stood a few yards away now that they were at the top of the ridge. Clearing his throat, he waved a hand in its direction. "The folly. As requested."

CHAPTER EIGHT

IT WAS PERFECT. A little stone tower, complete with arched windows and a rooftop parapet, made to look like a tiny medieval castle out here in the middle of nowhere.

Lilah let out a little gasp of excitement. "Can we go in?"

"Of course. What good would it be otherwise?"

She didn't need to be told twice. There was nothing inside—the small door led to a staircase, winding around a great central column to the roof. In the doorway, she turned back to Max, still outside, still watching her. "Are you coming?"

He followed as she made her way up the winding stairs, catching up to her when she stilled on the small platform halfway up the tower to look out the tall, narrow opening there, the breeze whispering through the arch, cool and crisp. Atlas was already bounding off into the distance, released from herding humans for a while.

She lifted her camera and took a picture a thousand other people must have taken. She didn't care. It wasn't for the world. It was for her.

To bring her back, when it was over.

"The view is better from the top," Max said, the low rumble curling through her.

He was right.

They climbed through the small doorway at the top of the turret and Lilah walked to the edge, nothing in the world going to stop her. Camera in hand, she set her bag down at the base of the tower wall, peeking over, surveying the land. "This is like the greatest tree house ever. Did you play here as a kid?"

"It's an excellent hiding place, if you are ever looking for one. Visitors never come this far north, and everyone on the estate forgets it exists."

She shook her head. "England is real wild."

He laughed. "Americans love a castle."

"And what's wrong with that?" she tossed over her shoulder. "I, for one, feel like the heroine in a romance novel," she said. "Out on the ramparts, watching for soldiers coming home from battle."

"Mmm," he said, wrapping an arm around her waist and pressing a kiss at the place where her neck met her shoulder. "I like the idea of coming home from battle to you."

She turned in his arms as his touch and words warmed her. "Mmm," she repeated, teasing. "Maybe I'd like to come home from battle to *you* on the ramparts."

"Waiting to warm you by the fire?" His tongue swirled against her pulse. "No. We go to war together."

"Sword in your sheath, blade in my kirtle?" She sighed.

"Sounds proper filthy. Let's do it."

She laughed and pulled away from him, finding the sunlight on his face, his eyes bright and warm with pleasure and teasing, and the sound trailed off. "My God, Max. You're so pretty."

He dipped his chin at the words, and she loved that she'd embarrassed him.

"Let me take your picture."

His attention immediately returned to her, his brow furrowed, like he didn't know what to say.

"I'll be gentle," she said with a smile. "You won't feel a thing."

He laughed and rubbed a hand back and forth at the back of his neck. "I don't know anything about being a model."

She shook her head. "No modeling necessary. I just want—"

I want to remember you.

Lilah swallowed around the thought, hating the tightness in her chest. "I just want to take a picture of you, here. With the land you work behind you. With the sun that loves you on your skin."

"Only if I am able to take a picture of you at the end."

"You drive a hard bargain, but I accept. And you will be very, very disappointed to know that I do *not* photograph well."

"I don't believe it."

"It's true," she said, lifting the Nikon, watching him in the viewfinder as she joked, "Mine's the kind of beauty that moves."

He laughed.

Click.

"I wasn't ready."

"You were perfect," she said, immediately reframing.

He hesitated.

Don't blink.

There.

Click.

"*You're* perfect," he said.

The words sent a shot of pure pleasure through her. She lowered the camera, wanting to remember this moment, his eyes on her, seeing her in a way no one had ever seen her. She swallowed, her heart pounding. She was excited. Nervous.

Photographing Max, here, felt like she was taking pictures for the first time.

"Are you sure you don't model on the side, farmhand?"

"I've been practicing for my new Instagram account."

Click. That sly smile.

She laughed. "Too few piglets."

Click. And the easy one, like home.

Click. Watching her. Not posing.

"You love this."

On autopilot, Lilah readjusted her grip, moving with the light, backing away. Considering the angle of the shadows behind him as they lengthened in the afternoon sun. "It's all I've ever wanted to do. Since I was a kid and my dad dug an old Polaroid camera out of a box in the attic and let me have it." She paused. "Remember those?"

Click. Memory.

"I don't think we ever had one."

"I loved them, because you could see the shot in minutes. My dad bought up as much instant film as he could find at yard sales and thrift shops. And I took about twelve thousand pictures of the cat."

Click. The handsomest of grins.

"How old were you?"

"Seven or eight," she said, lowering the camera. "After the cat, I turned to portraits. My parents, my friends, my teachers, strangers. We took a summer vacation to the Outer Banks and I convinced a dozen people in line for ice cream to let me photograph them." She shook her head, stuck in the memory. "My poor mother. She didn't know what to do with me. But I still remember that when we developed that roll of film—she turned to me and said, in her thickest Georgia drawl, 'Well, Lilah Rose, I suppose you're going to be an *artist.*'"

"They were good?"

"They would have been better if I'd been able to develop them myself, but my mom vetoed turning the downstairs bathroom into a darkroom for some reason." She lifted the Nikon. "They bought me my first digital camera for my next birthday, and no one in my life was safe."

"Not even me," he said.

"Especially not you. Too many good angles."

"You like my angles, do you?"

The words coiled through her as her focus narrowed on him, tall and broad in the golden light. "I might need a better look."

That smile. So easy. Max spread his arms wide. "I present myself to the artist for inspection."

Yum.

She turned away for a heartbeat, just enough time to set her camera back in her bag. Max had relaxed against the parapet wall again, a modern-day knight. His arms were stretched across the edge, the collar of his navy blue sweater unzipped to reveal a hint of sun-kissed skin. He wore the same Chameaus from their first meeting—crossed one over the other like he had all the time in the world for her blatant appraisal.

"Applying for position of muse?" She approached, slow and deliberate. When she was close enough to touch him, she stopped, drinking him in. Shadows and light, hard lines and smooth edges.

"If you'll have me," he said, the words rough like stone.

She went heavy with want and stepped closer, setting her hands to his chest, tracing the lines of him, out over the wall, the weight and sinew of his strong arms, the ridges of muscles down over his chest and abdomen, beneath his sweater. She slid her fingers beneath the hem, finding the warm skin of his waist, and he sucked in a breath at the touch of her cold hands.

"It's difficult to decide," she said, unable to keep the need from her words. "With all these clothes."

"Mmm."

She loved that sound. When this was over, that low rumble would follow her forever. She'd summon it on late nights, in the dark, when she let herself remember this week, slipped out of time.

Pushing the thought of *over* out of the way, Lilah stroked one hand down the outside of his trousers, finding his cock hard beneath the fabric.

"Visitors never get this far north?"

His eyes went liquid with heat and understanding. "Everyone forgets it exists."

Lilah rewarded the words by tracing the ridge of him, heavy and thick, and delighting in his low groan, in the way her touch undid him. She leaned in and pressed a lingering, soft kiss to the skin at the open collar of his shirt. "May I?"

He swore, and she took it as a yes.

"Hands on the wall, please," she whispered in his ear before she traced her lips across his jaw, down the column of his neck, the slide mimicked by another, lower, his trousers opening, releasing the swell of his cock into her waiting hands.

"Lilah," he whispered. "You're going to kill me."

"Mmm," she said, still playing her part, pulling the fabric down and revealing the stunning, straining length of him. Her mouth watered as she stroked over him, reveling in the feel of him, hot and hard. She couldn't help her whisper, "Look at this gorgeous cock."

"Fuck, yes," he said, harsh. "Look at it."

Her gaze flickered up to his, finding him staring at her. She fisted him, stroking from base to tip, loving the way the movement wrecked him, his eyes going hooded, his chest rumbling with a low growl of pleasure. "I don't just want to look at it, Max."

His eyes narrowed and he leaned down, not taking his hands from the wall even as he claimed her mouth—ever the marauder—tongue delving deep, stroking over hers until she gasped with pleasure.

"Whatever you want, love."

Love.

She ignored the way the word rioted through her, filling her with a wave of pleasure, leaving her hot and heavy with need, instead returning her attention to him, tracing ridges and veins, "I want it all."

"Christ," he said, "I can see how much you want it. Fuck, you're beautiful—" She stroked him again, and his words were lost in a groan as his hips rocked against her touch.

"You like that," she whispered.

"I like that very much," he said with a laugh. "I like *you.* Kiss me again."

She did, heat pooling at her core, making her ache in the best possible way. As she continued to work him over, fucking him with her hands, memorizing the length and feel of him, his thick shaft and the beautiful pink head of him, moist with the evidence of his need for her.

"Fuck, Lilah, you look . . ."

She could see it. She could see how she looked in his eyes. On his face. "Hungry," she whispered. "I'm hungry, Max."

She slid to her knees in front of him, and he gritted his teeth, the muscles of his jaw working as she knew he did all he could not to touch her, this gorgeous man, giving himself up to her whims. God, he was perfect.

This is perfect, she thought as she stroked him, loving the way his strong, lean hips met her movements, and she watched, feeling the straining steel of him, reveling in his size as she looked up at him, in the cords of his neck and the clench of his jaw and the white-knuckled grip he kept on the parapet wall because she'd told him to.

She rewarded them both, licking over the tip of him, salty sweetness exploding on her tongue as his curse exploded in her ears, one hand coming off the wall, uncontrollable, threading into her hair, tightening in her curls until she groaned too, at the delicious sting of his touch.

And somehow this glorious man didn't move, even as she teased him, keeping his pleasure from him. From her, even as his cock throbbed in her hand and his breath hung between them, ragged and uneven.

"You want to fuck me, don't you?" she said to the straining length of him, knowing she tempted fate.

"No," he bit out, summoning her surprise. She looked up at him, meeting his eyes, his pupils blown with need. "I want you to fuck me."

The words were her pleasure and her power and fucking perfect.

And then he added, "But I want you to fuck yourself too."

She stilled.

His pleasure. His power.

"I want you to spread your legs and slide your fingers beneath your clothes, and tell me how wet you are." He slid one booted foot between her knees, helping her widen them. "Go on, beautiful."

She did as she was told, her fingers sliding over her pussy, her breath catching with the pleasure of her own touch.

"That's it," he said, encouraging her even as she could hear the way everything about this moment was wrecking him. Wrecking them both. "Find the place where it aches, love."

She did, her eyelids flickering when she stroked over her clit.

"There it is," he whispered. "Are you wet for me?"

She nodded.

"Mmm."

Wetter for him now.

He used his fist in her hair to tilt her up to him. "Are you sure you don't want me to do it? Sure you don't want me to lay you down here in the sunlight on this tower and eat you until you scream? I want that," he said. "I want the taste of you on me all day, like sex and sin."

He was destroying her. She did want that.

But she wanted him more. "No," she said, loving the surprise in his eyes when she leaned forward and licked the underside of him, long and lingering and wet, until she reached the tip of him. "I want this."

And she parted her lips and took him in, loving the heavy slide of him over her tongue, the salty fire that came with it, the hard heat of him. The way he let out a long, slow breath as she drew him deep, one hand stroking over his shaft, reveling in his ragged breath and his filthy words as he reached for control.

As she unraveled him. The pace, the pressure, the places that made him wild, summoning more of those deep-throated rumbles.

"Don't stop," he whispered, looking down at her, drawing her attention to his face.

She wasn't going to stop; she wanted everything from him.

She took him deep, and his fist tightened again, stopping her movements. "*Don't stop,*" he bit out. "Make yourself come."

The words set her on fire, and she fucked them both, taking him in long, lush strokes, again and again, over and over, and stroking herself, wet and wanting, until she had to focus on one of them, and of course it would be him—because his pleasure was hers, the sounds he made, the filthy words he whispered as she found the rhythm that was his undoing, until finally, the hand he'd kept on the wall came to her hair, stroking soft and reverent and he groaned, "Lilah, love, if you—I'm going to—"

Yes. She willed him. *Give it to me.*

He grew, impossibly harder, impossibly thicker against her tongue, pulsing against her.

She took him deep and he came, shouting her name, loud and rough and devastating, to the land and the sky and this tower that she would never forget, salt and musk and Max, her hands stroking up his thighs, over the trembling muscles of his stomach as his touch gentled and he caught his breath.

She stayed with him until he returned to himself, easing himself from her lips, and Lilah sat back on her heels, looking up at him as the expression on his face moved from pure pleasure to something that looked more than a little dangerous.

Her eyes widened as he yanked up his trousers, ignoring the fastenings on them, and came to his own knees before her, reaching for her, pulling her in for a deep, intense kiss. When it was over, he growled against her lips. "I said *don't stop.*"

"I was busy," she replied.

"Mmm. Well, it looks like I'm going to have to take matters into my own hands."

She squealed as he flipped her back, reaching beneath her sweater to pull her jeans down past her knees, locking her ankles together as he spread her thighs and wedged his broad shoulders between them. "Max —" she started, but there was nothing more to say, the rest of the words forgotten with the pleasure of his mouth, hard and urgent against her.

"You taste like the fucking sun," he said, lifting his head for a heartbeat, just long enough to slide his hands beneath her ass and tilt her up to him, like a banquet.

Like she was a feast.

And God, it felt like he feasted, his tongue thick and perfect, licking over her, rubbing back and forth over her clit, where she ached for release, again and again, faster and faster until *her* fingers were tight in his hair and she was rocking against him, crying out, "Please, Max."

"Mmm."

That growl, that deep rumble, combined with a thick finger, stroking deep, just there . . . just enough . . . She came hard, shouting his name to the sky. And this time Max held her while she returned to thought, restoring her clothing and rolling to his back and pulling her into his arms, holding her tight against him as her breath returned and her heartbeat resumed a normal rhythm.

They lay there in easy silence, at the top of the folly, for what seemed like hours, the sunlight spilling through the ancient trees, and Lilah traced the shadows of the leaves on his chest, willing time to stop, just for a bit. Just for a few more days.

Just until he wasn't so perfect.

"I didn't get my pictures," he said after a while.

She smiled. "You got something better though, no?"

Silence. And then, "I still want the picture."

Warmth threaded through her, and she shifted, reaching into the back pocket of her jeans to extract her phone.

"Don't trust me with the real thing?" Max said, teasing.

"This one is better for Instagram," she quipped, flipping the camera and handing it to him. "You've got a longer arm," she said, tucking herself against him, adjusting the angle of his reach to avoid shadows, framing the shot with precision.

"You can take the photography away from the girl . . . " Max intoned, his lips curved as he watched her on the screen.

"Hush," she said. "Take the picture."

He turned and kissed her temple.

Don't blink, Lilah. You might miss it.

CHAPTER NINE

MAX AND LILAH lingered on the estate, exploring until the sun had almost set and Atlas had to lead them home through the fast-darkening fields, as he lit the last bit of the journey with the flashlight on his phone.

They tumbled into the cottage like young lovers sneaking home after curfew, cheeks red from the evening chill, and Lilah scraped together pickle and ham and cheese and a packet of Ryvita while he built a fire in the study. After supper, he poured them both a Scotch and they curled together beneath a cashmere blanket he'd unearthed, Atlas by the fire.

Max watched as Lilah pulled up the shots from the folly and proved to him that she was one of the greatest portrait photographers the world had ever seen.

"Here," she'd said, finally finished editing the picture she'd deemed the best of the bunch, one where he looked happy and relaxed on the land. "Let me send you this one. They should put it on the Salterton Abbey website."

He pressed a kiss to her temple and said, "I don't care about the one of me. Where's the one of us?"

With a little laugh, she snatched up her phone from the low table nearby and pulled up the picture. "You know, there was a time when many, many people in the world would have done crime for a portrait session with me. And you want the selfie."

"I want the one with you."

She fiddled with it, opening the edit menu to play with lighting and crop it just so, and he watched, marveling at the idea that anyone could take so long perfecting a photo they'd snapped with a phone.

When she was done, she sent it to him, and they returned to what she called *farmhouse idyll.*

And it felt like idyll, like time had stopped, the world no longer beyond the windows now that her ear was pressed to his chest, the warm weight of her like a gift as he told her about the estate—about goats on the rough land to the west, the sheep in the east pasture, the beehives that would have to be wintered soon.

As she told him stories of the farmers she'd met on her travels—the apiarist in Crete, the cattle crowdfarming initiative in Ghana, the women dry-growing grapes on California's Central Coast.

And it was not lost on either of them that it was perfect.

Or that it was fleeting.

When the fire waned, left to nothing but embers, Max took the empty glass from Lilah's hand and guided her off the couch and up the stairs to bed, where he stripped her bare and lay her down and reset the clock once more, worshipping her long and slow, like they had all the time in the world.

Of course, they didn't have all the time in the world, but neither of them wanted to think about that.

Not that night, with six days ahead of them like a promise. And not the next.

But it became more and more difficult for Max to think about giving her up at the end of their time together. And more and more difficult to hold his tongue when all he wanted to do was beg her to stay.

He'd fallen for her.

It wasn't supposed to have happened. It was supposed to have been nine days—nine days of easy companionship and intense pleasure. Nine days in isolation, without either of them knowing enough about the other to complicate things.

Nine days with Max and Lilah, and no one else.

She didn't know the truth of who he was, and he didn't know the truth of what she'd run from, and every time he thought to tell her or ask her, he resisted, because it was only supposed to be nine days, long and lush and free.

But they weren't free anymore. Because Max didn't want to be free of her.

Wild as it seemed after not even a week, he'd fallen for this woman, and he wanted a shot at forever with her. But forever meant more than Max and Lilah, in the cottage tucked away deep in the Devon countryside.

Forever meant real life. It meant the Duke of Weston hermited away at his estate, and Lilah Rose, celebrity photographer and friend of the glitterati in New York and Paris and Hollywood or wherever.

Except she had stopped. She'd left that world for some length of time. Something had happened, and he'd never pressed her on it. *I didn't know if I'd ever be able to take pictures again.* She'd sold her studio.

Why?

And so, as they lay in bed, tired and sated from another round of the best sex he'd ever had, and likely would ever have, her fingers trailing through the hair on his chest, his tracing patterns over her soft skin, the scent of her filling him like sunshine, he asked her.

"Why did you stop?"

"Stop what?" The reply was full of sleepy satisfaction, and Max nearly didn't clarify. He didn't want to burst the bubble.

But he had to know whether the future was an option.

"Your work. Posh photography."

She stilled against him. "You don't think sheep are posh?"

"Hey," he said, softly, and she lifted her head to look at him. "You don't ever have to use your armor with me."

She watched him for a long moment, and then put her head back to his chest. "I want to believe that."

He waited, willing her to speak. Knowing he couldn't ask her to tell him anything. Knowing she didn't owe him truth. Knowing he didn't deserve it.

And then, "I turned down the wrong man."

Every muscle in his body tensed, and he went hot with immediate anger. "What does that mean?"

She didn't look at him. "I was asked to shoot a cover for *Culture Magazine*. They were doing a huge piece on a very powerful man." No name. Max gritted his teeth, going through the dozens of possibilities. "It was massive—ten thousand words, the first of its kind about someone the whole world knew and, it seemed, no one knew."

More likely, someone everyone knew, and no one was willing to discuss. Max was a member of the British aristocracy—they'd practically invented sweeping scandal under the rug.

Lilah took a deep breath, her body pressing closer to his, as though she needed strength to go on. "To get the story, the editor-in-chief of *Culture* had made a number of promises. The subject got to choose his interviewer, location, approve a list of staff and peers who would be the only people *Culture* could contact."

Fury flared. "And you."

She nodded. "I wanted the gig. I'd worked with the magazine before. I liked the team there. They respected me . . . or so I thought. So I didn't really think twice. He chose the photographer for the piece . . . and the location, date and time for the shoot."

Max cursed, low and dark, his hand going wide over her shoulder, tight, as though he could protect her in hindsight.

"It's funny, how you see it. I didn't. I should have known when they said they were willing to triple my fee. I'm not exactly cheap to begin with. But I was at the top of my game, and hubris is real."

No. Whatever this story—however it played out, it wasn't her fault. "Lilah—"

She cut him off before he could argue. "I'd shot the *Bonfire* Hollywood issue earlier in the year and I had the Finezzi Calendar scheduled. This cover—it would be a hat trick." She paused and looked up at him. "A hat trick is when—"

"I know. It comes from cricket."

"It does? Cool." She smiled and he would have matched it if he wasn't resisting the urge to book a flight immediately to wherever this man was and do damage.

"Lilah . . ."

"He chose his house in the Hamptons. His wife would be there, his staff, his kids, probably. But if I came in the evening, things would be quieter. Would that be fine?"

"Fucking hell." Not damage. He'd do murder.

"I drove out from the city," she said. "I borrowed a friend's car—this nonsense convertible that half the time wouldn't even start—but it was a beautiful spring day and I spent the drive out going over the ideas that I'd had for the shoot. His staff had sent me photos of this mansion—it was bananas. All white walls and chrome and steel and built right on the edge of the Atlantic. I'd been in houses like it before—it was my job not to be impressed. But this house—" She quieted. "Well. It was bananas."

"He was alone."

She nodded. "He was used to photographers, but not artists, he told me, and he thought it would be easier if it was just the two of us. Gross, right?" She paused. "I really thought it would be fine. I'd dealt with slimeballs before." Max growled, and she looked at him with amused surprise. "What was that?"

"Me, resisting the urge to ask you to make me a list."

She let out a little laugh, like he had made a joke. It wasn't a joke. It was truth. This story was turning him into pure vengeance, and he probably shouldn't like it but he was too busy imagining how much he'd enjoy putting his fist into this man's face.

"I handled them just fine," she said, stacking her hands on his chest and setting her chin to them. "Athletes, actors, talk show hosts, princes, every kind of egomaniac you could come up with . . . billionaires are the worst. Here's the thing—they're all the same. They want the power play, but they want the great picture more. So I get in, get the shot, find a way to turn them down, and get out. No problem."

She stopped, the air between them heavy with the story, Max's jaw aching from the clench of his teeth. If this man had hurt her, he would move every mountain he could to punish him. He'd use every inch of the dukedom to ruin him.

"Lilah," he said, her name coming out like gravel. Sounding like he was in pain.

"He didn't touch me," she said quickly, as though to soothe him, and a twist of relief curled through Max, though not enough. He might not have touched her, but she'd been harmed. She'd stopped working, for Christ's sake, and she loved working.

"He went to get something; he said he had a folio of Helen Levitt shots he'd bought at auction—his staff must have done some research, because Helen Levitt is one of the few people who could have made me stick around. Anyway, when he came back, he was naked." She scoffed. "I should've taken a picture of *that*. But I didn't. I took off."

"The car started." There. More relief. More fury.

She gave a little laugh. "Thank God. And I thought it was over. I called my best friend and told her the whole story on the drive back and I still remember coming over the bridge into the city and saying, clear as day, 'But I got the fucking shot.'" She looked at him. "And I did. I had this vision of that shot on the cover of the most respected magazine in the world—revealing what a creep that guy was."

He didn't doubt she'd gotten the shot. Of course she had.

That was her job, and she was remarkable at it.

He stroked his hand down the soft skin of her back, pride warring with a dozen other emotions, not the least of which was fear. The photograph hadn't been enough. Something else had happened. "Then what?"

Sadness clouded her beautiful eyes, and Max's chest tightened. He already hated what was to come. "Three days later I got a call from *Culture*. They were going in a different direction with the story. I'd be paid, but the images wouldn't run. 'Please deliver the files to the magazine and delete any copies.'" She spoke to his chin as he continued to stroke down her spine. Back up. "A few days after that, we got word that *Bonfire* had decided to reshoot the Hollywood issue with a new photographer. A different direction. Literally weeks before the issue shipped. It was unheard of."

Fury threaded through him. Hot and angry and foreign. "And Finezzi?" He didn't know much about the calendar, but he knew it was an enormous win for art photographers.

She shook her head. "Different direction."

"Christ."

"It was going to be great," she said, her eyes meeting his. Max heard the urgency in her voice, as though it was important she say it out loud.

And it was the truth. He knew it. It would have been magnificent. He knew, without question, that Lilah Rose would have made sure the whole world knew about that calendar. "I had this plan to play with hard and soft—I wanted to go back to the original erotic pinup style, but really change the gaze. Shoot the whole thing centering women and pleasure and power. Twelve women who were unashamed of passion. Upend the whole thing."

"That sounds perfect," he said. It sounded like exactly the kind of thing this glorious woman would do.

"It would have been. It was the dream, and I could reach out and touch it. And he robbed me of it." There was anger in the words, along with frustration and sadness and fury. She gave a little wave of her hand. "Like that. He robbed me of my career. And the rest of the world helped. My agent—who'd signed me when I was twenty years old and not even out of art school—she stopped calling me. My mentors, who I thought would stand by me. All those people I thought were my friends . . . " She laughed, the sound without humor. "A few months ago, I was in Ghana?"

Max nodded, hating this story and wanting to hear all of it. Every word.

"I pulled out my phone and scrolled through it, and deleted two hundred and seventy-three contacts. Dozens of people who would make you starry-eyed."

"I promise you they wouldn't make me starry-eyed."

She shot him a look. "They make everyone starry-eyed."

He shook his head. "Not me."

She watched him for a while and then said, "Weirdly, I believe that."

But it didn't help, he could see. It didn't soothe the furrow at her brow that had come with the memory. He touched that furrow. Smoothed it.

"They were supposed to be my friends," she said, softly, and his heart broke a little bit at the words. "But they didn't care about me. They cared about what I could do for them. Ironically, *Bonfire* ran a piece about me once." She smiled as she remembered the headline. "*Kiss from a Rose*. Lilah Rose, whose photos could turn a star into a supernova."

She shook her head, seeming not to be able to find the right words, and he wanted so much to give them to her. "You weren't just good at it," he said. "You cared about it. You loved it. Your work meant something."

"Yes," she said, softly. "I know what it looks like from the outside. I know it seems frivolous and silly. Who cares about the photograph? We all have cameras in our pockets and we've all taken a decent picture now and then. But I really thought . . . " She trailed off, and Max couldn't bear it. The loss. "I built it. It was mine. I was good at it and I gave up everything for it. No real friends, no real love life, no real life in general. Nothing outside of this one thing that I did well and that I loved. And then . . . it was gone." Her eyes met his. "One minute *I* was there and then . . . I was gone too."

He ached for her. He ached for what she'd suffered and what she'd lost and for how hard she'd worked and for how hard she fought, still, for this world that should have lowered itself to its knees and thanked the heavens that it had her.

Just as he would lower himself to his knees if he might have her even a fraction as much.

And he ached for himself, for the keen, clear understanding that the only thing she desired was the thing he would never be able to give her.

His silence had stretched too long, until Lilah pulled back from it. "I'm sorry," she said, pushing up off his chest to move away, her eyes gone liquid. "That was a lot."

"No." He rolled with her, cradling her face, running his thumbs over her cheeks, refusing to let her go until he told her exactly what he thought of her. "Thank you," he said. "Thank you for telling me."

She took a deep, shuddering breath. "No problem."

He couldn't help his small smile. She was so strong. "Now I have to tell *you* something."

For an instant, he considered doing it. Telling her his truth, a secret for a secret, and finally having it all out in the open between them. He wanted it so badly, the words burned in his throat—but this moment was not for him. This moment was for Lilah, and what she'd been through, and the fact that she'd shared it with him, and no one else.

He waited for her to look at him. "You are the finest person I know."

Her eyes went liquid with tears.

"No, Lilah." He brushed the hair from her face, searching it, memorizing it. "You are strong and clever and you play darts like a professional, and you are a brilliant artist with—somehow, though I cannot understand how—a spine of pure steel."

"Thank you."

The tears spilled, and he leaned down to kiss her, sipping the words from her lips, before he pulled back and said, "Now. Who was it?"

She exhaled on a laugh. "Why, are you going to go punch his lights out?"

"It's a damn good start."

She reached up and pulled him down for another kiss. "You're really very sweet, you know."

"I'm not feeling very sweet right now." He was feeling murderous right now.

"I can take care of myself. Remember? Blade in my kirtle?"

He didn't rise to the bait. "Save it. Let me bloody my sword instead."

She tilted her head, her gaze narrowing on his. "Why is that so hot?"

"It's not meant to be."

She ran her fingers through his hair and traced the high arc of his cheek and the straight edge of his jaw, still twitching with anger. "I'm already fighting."

He understood, instantly. "Four days."

She nodded. "Four days. I return. And the pictures—they're a good opening salvo."

God, he was so proud of her. "They'll get you what you want."

"The return of Lilah Rose."

Four days. Four days, and she would be gone.

Four days, and Lilah would head back to her glittering life and her glamorous parties, and she would leave Max here and the farmer she'd once known would fade away as she returned to London, or New York, or Los Angeles or whatever place she needed to be.

He'd tried that life before. And he'd ruined a marriage with his inability to love it. He'd disappointed Georgiana, but somehow the idea of disappointing Lilah was even worse.

"Max?"

He looked down at her, this woman he loved, strong and clever and so beautiful she made him ache. "Yes?"

"Do you own a suit?"

He froze, knowing what was to come next. Knowing it would be the most difficult thing he'd ever done to reply.

She smiled. God, he loved her smile. "Come to London with me."

He hesitated, and she waited, ever patient.

Yes.

Christ, he wanted to say yes.

But he hadn't fallen for her. He'd fallen in love with her.

And the only thing that mattered was her happiness. And he knew, without question, that he could not make her happy. Not forever.

And he couldn't bear the thought of anything less.

"I can't."

CHAPTER TEN

"I BOLLOCKSED IT."

Simon considered Max through the small crack in the door of the Fox and Falcon the next morning, before letting him in, wet and bedraggled, Atlas on his heels. Peering out into the torrential rain in the street beyond, the owner of the pub said, "Must have done if you're out in this."

Closing the door, the pub owner turned to his new guests, wincing when Atlas shook the rain from his coat and went to lie down by the fireplace. "My pub is going to smell like wet dog."

"Think of it as an improvement," Max said before getting to the important bit. "Simon . . . she left."

Simon nodded to a stool at the bar and Max moved to sit. "We knew she was leaving, didn't we? Back to America, no?"

"I had three more days." Max rubbed a hand across his chest, hating the ache there—one he hadn't felt in a lifetime. "We were supposed to have three more days, and she left."

"Because you're naff at women."

"I'm not naff at women."

"All right, I'll play." Simon checked his watch. "Why are you here at twenty past eight in the morning? Instead of abed with your pretty dartsmistress?"

"Because my pretty dartsmistress is gone."

"Because you're naff at women." Simon slipped behind the bar and said, "Pint?"

"It's twenty past eight in the morning, Simon."

"Coffee it is, then." Simon turned away. "So, what, you told her you were duke and she took to the hills, afraid of a long line of aristocratic inbreeding?"

"No."

Simon stilled and turned back. "Shit, Max. You told her you were Duke eventually, didn't you?"

"No," he said. "I didn't think it would matter in the long run. Not if she was leaving. Not if we were just . . ."

Simon stilled. "You didn't think it mattered that you owned the house she was staying in."

The house they were both staying in.

"And half of Devon," his friend added.

Max rubbed his face with both hands, shoving his fingers through his wet hair.

"And a large swath of London."

Christ, he was an ass.

"You didn't think she might like to know that you're one of the richest men in Britain?"

That got Max's attention. Simon and he never talked about the dukedom. They talked about the pub and the sheep and the land, about Lottie's art and Simon's mother's ailments. But they never talked about Max's money.

Simon gave him a half-smile. "You think I grew up in the back room of this pub, in the shadow of Salterton Abbey, and didn't know that my best friend was rich as royalty? *Richer* than royalty?"

"Christ, Si." Max dipped his head, loathing the conversation. "Come on."

"I didn't invent Google. Take it up with your fellow billionaires. Look. You are a good friend, and a great partner in a brawl, and I'm fairly certain you bailed out this place when my father ran it into the ground." It was true, but Max had promised Simon's father that he'd never admit it, and he wouldn't. "The rest doesn't matter. Just as I'm guessing it wouldn't have mattered to her."

"It wouldn't have changed anything," he said. "She'd still be gone. She would always have left. Nothing I could say would change that—telling her the truth would only have hastened the inevitable."

There was a long pause, like an eternity.

"It wouldn't have changed anything," Max said, filling it. "She'd still be gone."

Simon watched him for a stretch, and then said, "You look like you've been rolled down the hill and into my pub. How long has she been gone?"

Max shook his head. "I don't know." He'd left her after she'd fallen asleep on the other side of the bed, out of his arms for the first time since the first night. Gone back to his apartments. Woken at dawn without her and returned to the cottage, ready to explain everything, even if it meant losing out on those last few precious days—and nights—at her side. But it had been too late. She'd left.

As he'd always known she would.

"A few hours."

He filled Simon in, telling him the story of their arrangement, designed only to last until Lilah went back to London and returned to her life, filled with celebrities and superstars and leaving no room for Max, who—even if she knew the truth—would never be able to give her what she wanted.

But that wasn't all Max told his friend. He told him about *Lilah*—about her brilliant photographs, and her easy laugh, and the way she'd won him again and again, and made him believe, more and more, that it was possible for him to be Max forever. And her to be Lilah forever. And for them to live in farmhouse idyll forever.

"When she asked me to go with her, I told her I couldn't," he said. He'd watched as disappointment and resignation had clouded her gaze, even as she'd promised him she understood, hating it even as he told himself it was for the best. That it was the best way to keep her from a larger, more devastating disappointment.

To keep from disappointing her.

"Wait. What?" Simon didn't seem to agree. "Why couldn't you go?"

"Because I'm not what she wants. Not really."

"Sorry," said his friend, leaning down on the bar. "I don't follow. Did she or did she not invite you to London to go to this posh party?"

"She did. But she doesn't know that I've been a part of that world, and I can't make her happy in it."

Silence fell, the sound of the rain on the ancient stained glass windows all there was as Simon turned away to fetch the coffee. Only once he'd poured the cup and slid it across the bar to Max, he said, "Would you like to know, Max, what I thought the first time you brought Georgiana to Salterton?" He paused. "What we all thought?"

Max looked to Simon—his oldest friend, who'd always known about his family and his fortune and never once seemed to care. "I don't suppose I have a choice."

"Ha, no. We all thought you were doomed to unhappiness."

The words were a blow. Max's brow furrowed. "What does that mean?"

"Oh, we threw you a stag and dressed up for church and toasted you heartily and hoped we were wrong, but we could see the truth." Simon backed up to his favorite place for pontificating, against the far wall of the bar, arms crossed over his massive chest. "You and Georgiana what-everhernamewas—"

"Chesterton," Max said. "She's Countess of Hyde, now."

"Good for her," Simon retorted. "Point is, the two of you twenty-three and had the brains to prove it. She was put together as they come—more money than any person needs and reading posh accents at school, or whatever."

"History of Art, actually. And she's not exactly faffing about in Ibiza, Simon. She's head of the British Museum."

"Oh, well, what in hell was she doing with you to begin with, then?"

"That's my point," Max said, lifting the cup. "She shouldn't have been with me. I made her miserable."

"No, you didn't," Simon said. "You made *each other* miserable. She was born for a world with plummy titles and posh friends and her picture in *Tatler* every month, and good for her for realizing that and telling you that she wanted that life and not this one when you were sulking around here, dreaming of a girl who could rate in Wellington boots and didn't mind the stink of your dog."

Atlas sighed in the corner, used to being maligned by Simon, who was still going.

"The point is, you were both wrong. And Lady Hyde is sorted. Turns out she wasn't doomed to unhappiness after all."

She wasn't. Last he'd heard from her, Georgiana was happy and successful and wildly in love with her husband and children.

It had been a long time since Max had thought about happiness.

No. It wasn't true.

Lilah made him happy.

He looked up, meeting Simon's knowing eyes. "I love her."

"Of course you do," his friend said. "You were half in love with her the other night when you were in here playing darts and flirting up a storm."

It had been the best night of his life. Except for all the others with her.

And still, "I don't want to disappoint her."

"How do you know you will?"

"I know, because she's spent the last eighteen months trying to get back to that world. She's been at the center of it for years—she's met more aristocrats than I have! And when she talks about losing it . . . " Max met his friend's gaze, and was surprised to find sympathy there. "When she talks about losing it, I can tell she'd do anything to get it back. She wants someone who will love it like she does. And I can't be that. I've tried, but I can't."

More than that, he couldn't bear to live through the moment when Lilah realized he wasn't what she thought, wasn't what she wanted, wasn't . . . enough.

"Did you ask her what she wants?"

Max stilled. "No. That wasn't part of the deal. The deal was nine days, until she left."

"Oh, well then, if the deal was nine days, then—" Simon's words were dry as sand. "Max. Are you saying, this girl asked you—idiot farmer —to stand next to her during one of the most important nights of her life, and you think that wasn't a blatant invitation to a future?"

Max swallowed back frustration at the question. "I've said yes to that invitation before. And I've made a hash of it."

"Well, seems like you're damned if you do and damned if you don't, mate. But one way, you've got the girl." Simon shook his head. "You know what? You're right. You do not deserve that woman. From what I can see, she is brilliant, beautiful, a ringer at darts, and legions too good for you."

It was all true.

"All right," Simon drawled, as though he was speaking to a small child. "How about this? Has it occurred to you that you have enough money to travel the world and take the woman you love to a gala at the British Museum, or a party in New York, or a week in the Maldives because that's what she wants—oh and because she's a fucking superstar you don't deserve—you can do that, and be back here with your sheep and your hay and your dog within hours? Has it occurred to you that what felt like all or nothing at twenty-two might be more nuanced at thirty-five?"

Hope flared.

"Has it occurred to you that you could try again?"

He didn't have to wait here, on the ramparts, terrified she might never return.

They could fight together.

And come home together.

"This isn't the same, bruv," Simon said, not a hint of sarcasm in his tone. "You're not twenty anymore, trying to work out how to become a man and a duke all in one breath. And she's not twenty, trying to make a go of it in the world and also not disappoint her husband. Lilah Rose is a grown woman who knows what she wants, Max. And—though it flummoxes me more than I can say—I think she's made it clear that she wants you."

"You're an ass," Max said.

"But a brilliant one," Simon retorted. "Why don't you believe her?"

Because no one had ever wanted him for more than that world. From the moment he was born, that had been his value. Access to that world.

Simon seemed to hear the thoughts. He came off the back wall and leaned down, his elbows on the slick mahogany bar. "It might not work out, mate. For any number of reasons, which doesn't make you a special case, by the way. But doesn't Lilah at least deserve the chance to throw you over for the right reason, knowing all the facts? Or to choose to try, eyes wide-open?"

And like that, Max saw it.

He'd been so caught up in thinking about what he could bear and what he couldn't, he'd discounted *Lilah*. Why the hell had he tried to fight this battle alone, when he'd had the strongest, cleverest, most creative and perceptive woman in the world ready and able to help win this war?

Their future was not written.

They could write it. Different. Perfect.

Together.

"And if it doesn't work out," Simon concluded, "you'll come here and drink yourself into a stupor and I'll charge you double for whinging into your pint about how hard it is to be a duke, poor fucking baby."

"I have to tell her who I am."

An idea came, half-formed. Coalescing.

Max felt like one of his marauding ancestors, girding his loins for the battle of his life. "I have to get to her."

"Right then." Simon nodded with satisfaction. "Tell her the dart board is always open for her."

CHAPTER ELEVEN

THE SHOW WAS A TRIUMPH.

The Great Court of the British Museum was awash in warm light, giving the whole space an autumnal feel that Lilah would never have expected from somewhere known for soaring white walls and a roof designed to reveal firmament and nothing else.

And her photos were perfect.

The decorators had followed her careful instructions, hanging the ten enormous prints around the central staircase of the Court, the curves of the room obscuring them until attendees made a full turn of the space. Each one highlighted the work of one of the sustainable farms she'd visited, capturing the people who had devoted themselves to ensuring their land would survive for generations while prioritizing delicate ecosystems.

Seeing them together, Lilah realized why she loved this project—not only because she'd hoped it would return her to the world from which she'd been summarily booted, but because she recognized herself in these people. Passionate. Proud. Purposeful.

And now, she recognized Max in them.

No.

No thinking about Max. He'd made it clear that he had no interest in extending their arrangement beyond the Weston estate. Beyond the nine days they'd promised each other.

Of course, Lilah hadn't given him nine days.

She hadn't been able to, not once she'd realized how much she'd fallen for him in such a short time. Not once she'd realized that he hadn't fallen for her.

We go to war together, he'd promised her that day on the tower.

And yet here she was, in full armor, ready for battle. *Alone.*

Her chest tightened at the thought, enough for her to grab a glass of Prosecco from a passing tray and square her shoulders, willing her heartbeat steady as she entered the room.

She wore a sleek black Paul Smith tux with a cigarette pant that she'd had for years—a nod to sustainability, with the added bonus of it being a comfortable old friend—the deep plunge of the satin lapels revealing a long, narrow wedge of skin. Her hair was wild and loose, a dark, smoky eye finishing the look.

The armor looked good. It had to.

It was her against the world.

She instantly recognized a handful of people. Some, she'd met and photographed during her travels: a Peruvian economist who had perfected small-batch cacao farming that honored a protected biosphere; a Danish chef who'd made a name bringing foraged food into haute cuisine; the grape growers from California.

Some, she'd encountered before she'd been ruined: an Academy Award winner with a passion for environmental causes; several CEOs committed to sustainability; a world-renowned Emirati architect specializing in revolutionary green skyscrapers.

The place was a who's who of activist glitterati.

And Lilah, without her Nikon for protection.

Without anyone for protection.

When was the last time she'd walked into a showing of her work without a battalion of people—people who disappeared the moment she'd been blacklisted? People who lacked loyalty and only attached themselves to her when there was something valuable for her to give them.

She didn't need them.

And if she kept her head high, perhaps she'd forget that the only person she wanted wasn't there.

"Lilah!"

She turned to see Aarti Rao coming toward her with a bright smile before pulling her in close for a warm embrace.

"Friend!" Lilah said, unable to contain her relief. "I cannot tell you how happy I am to see your face!" She lowered her voice. "Do people like them?"

Aarti pulled back sharply. "You are kidding. They are *magnificent*. Look at them all, craning their necks to get a better view. No one cares about the rest of this old stuff tonight, darling." Lilah laughed as her friend waved a hand in the direction of the galleries beyond. "I've told everyone who will listen that they absolutely must come and tell you just how perfect they are." She added, softly, "We are very proud to benefit from the return of Lilah Rose."

For the first time that evening, Lilah's smile was authentic. "I'm so happy you're happy with them."

"We're thrilled. And personally, I am planning on using mine as my business card!"

Lilah looked up to the picture of Aarti in the lab on her family's farm in Andhra Pradesh, at the center of nearly a thousand saplings at different stages of growth. The biochemist's arms were crossed, her pride in her achievements clear as day on her lovely, laughing face. "The best day," Lilah recalled. "I want to come back."

"Anytime," her friend said as they began to circle the room. "But I think that after tonight, you're going to be a bit busy."

Lilah's heart pounded at the prediction—everything she'd wanted. *Not everything.*

She pushed the thought away. It was not for tonight.

She and Aarti were immediately swallowed by the crowd. Each of the subjects of Lilah's portraits were in attendance, deep in conversation with stars and businesspeople alike, finding common ground—which was precisely the point of the evening.

Lilah was thrilled.

Aarti's prediction came true as they circled the space; every few feet, they were waylaid by someone coming to meet Lilah—celebrities, fellow artists, the editors-in-chief of two magazines, wealthy attendees looking to discuss commissioned work. She took every introduction in stride, slowly falling back into the habit of having these conversations about her art—about what might come next.

For eighteen months she had planned for this night—knowing it would be important, because it would mark her return to the world from which she'd been exiled. And she could not have asked for a better reception. Suddenly, everything felt possible.

Everything but one thing, which she refused to think on.

One thing that she knew, later that night, back at the hotel, would make her ache.

"You've caught all of us in these beautiful moments," Aarti said as another enormous portrait came into view. Gianna Simeti—an elderly Sicilian woman seated high on an enormous pile of aging cheese wheels on the farm her family had owned since she was a young girl—stared down the lens of Lilah's camera, a lifetime of work in the lines of her face, and a familiar pride in her eyes.

"It's honesty," Lilah said. "You're all in love."

"That's true," Aarti replied, a gleam of something Lilah didn't quite understand in her eyes. "I particularly like the next one."

Lilah followed her gaze to the next photo, the outer edge just in view.

Her brows knit together and a wash of uncertainty flooded her. It wasn't her photo. She shook her head, moving more quickly. "I didn't—"

She stopped short as the image appeared.

It was her shot.

It was the picture of Max she'd taken at the top of the folly at Salterton Abbey, the estate laid out behind him, white pops of sheep and bales of hay and the fields of barley in the distance, turned gold in the late afternoon sun—the same as the gold in his eyes.

She caught her breath, her chest tightening as she drank in the image of him, a whirlwind of emotions coming with the memory of what he'd said immediately after she'd taken it.

You're perfect.

She could hear the words in his low, delicious voice, carrying on the wind, whipping around them on the parapet, just before she'd put her camera away and they'd made love.

It was a gorgeous shot, one that seamlessly integrated with all the others and still felt like it was ripping Lilah's chest open with its honesty. Max had that same look in his eye as all the other farmers.

Pride. Passion. Purpose.

Except he wasn't thinking about the farm in that moment; he was thinking about her.

He was proud of her.

She shook her head again, unable to look away. "How did you get it?"

"The Duke of Weston sent it over himself," Aarti said. "Direct from Salterton Abbey. He said you'd taken a final picture, and he thought we might like it for the event. As he put up the seed money for Common Harvest, we were happy to . . . "

Her friend's words faded away as Lilah craned to see through the throngs of people. "Is he here?"

"The duke? I think so, as a matter of fact. Another late addition," Aarti said. "It's a coup for the organization, as he's notoriously private, so people will be thrilled with the photo."

"No, not the duke," Lilah replied, the words barely there, caught in her throat as she saw him. *"Max."*

He was beneath his photo, looking nothing like the man above, dressed in a navy peak lapel three-piece suit, the watch chain on the waistcoat thick and modern—reminding her that underneath all that perfect tailoring he knew how to get dirty.

This was a man who was asking to be mussed, and she was absolutely up for the challenge.

Lilah was already moving toward him. "Sorry, Aarti. I see—"

The man I love.

She pushed through the crowd, desperate to get to him.

And then he was there, catching her up in his embrace, and her arms were wrapping around his neck and he was lifting her against him, and she let him, not caring who saw. Caring only that he was here. "You came," she said, like a prayer.

"I should have been here from the start," he rumbled, low and secret.

She reveled in the feel of him against her when he set her on her feet, and leaned down to say at her ear, "I want very much to kiss you, but I'm on my best behavior."

She snapped her head around to meet his gaze. "That is a shame, as I would very much like to be kissed by someone not on his best behavior."

"Mmm," he growled, the breath of air at her neck sending a shiver of pleasure only enhanced by the large, warm hand sliding to the small of her back. "You really ought to provide a warning when turning out looking like you do, Lilah Rose." He slid the tip of one finger just beneath the edge of her lapel, setting the skin beneath aflame as he teased, "I am glad I am here, as this kirtle does not look like it has room for a blade."

She grinned. "No battle necessary."

He shook his head. "Instant victory."

She took a deep breath, the words thrumming through her. "It feels like victory now that you're here."

He lifted his hand to her cheek, rubbing his thumb across her skin, like he'd missed her. She closed her eyes at the touch. She had missed him. When she opened her eyes, he was there, watching her, and he said, low and purposeful, "I'll always be here, Lilah. As long as you'll have me."

And she believed him.

"Do you forgive me for sending the photo? I know it wasn't part of the set, but Salterton is sustainable, and I thought—"

"Shh." She looked up at it—one of the best she'd ever taken. "As grand gestures go, it's perfect."

"You're perfect," he said, an echo of the words he'd spoken the moment after she'd taken that picture.

"I'm so happy you came," she said, the pleasure of the success of the evening now sharper with him here.

He pressed a kiss to the corner of her mouth, then another high on one cheek. "Your photographs—they're incredible. Show them to me?"

Speeches had begun, so they toured the massive prints in relative privacy, hand-in-hand, Lilah quietly telling him about each of the farms she'd visited. He listened like the perfect date, riveted to the images and her stories.

Lilah, too, was riveted—to the way he looked at her work, admiration and pleasure in his gaze. Pride. In her.

And there, in that room that had returned her to the world, Lilah realized that the time with Max had done something more. It had returned her to herself.

When they were once again at his portrait, Max took his cue, and Lilah laughed as he tugged her across the room, barely avoiding a collision with a pretty blond server, stopped in her tracks and glued to the speeches, seeming not to notice as bystanders relieved her tray of champagne flutes.

Tucking into a little alcove off the Court, he wrapped his arms around Lilah's waist, stealing kisses down the column of her neck. She sighed in his embrace, wrapping her own arms around his neck. "I missed you."

"Not like I've missed you," he whispered at the place where her pulse pounded. "I can't sleep. Mabel won't even look at me. Simon says I'm naff at women."

She giggled. "You're not naff at me."

He lifted his head. "I was, though. I thought I would disappoint you."

Her brow furrowed. "How?"

He hesitated, and for a split second—barely an instant—something flashed in his eyes. Lilah saw it, wishing she had her camera. Wishing she could study it. Identify it. But in that moment, she couldn't name it beyond a keen sense that Max had more to say.

"Max?"

He shook his head. "This night, here, it's yours. Everything else will keep." He looked past her to the enormous room, a thousand people in revelry. "They love you."

"No. They love what I do. They love what I can make people feel. What I can make them see. But they don't love me. They don't know me. I'm just the girl behind the camera."

"I know you," he said. Her heart began to pound as he tilted her chin up, meeting her gaze. "I love you."

She closed her eyes, her breath tight in her chest. "Max—"

"Let me finish. Whatever tonight brings. Wherever it takes you. I want to be by your side." He paused and then he said, "Not that you need me."

Tears sprang at the words. *I do need you.*

He was still talking. "I know it's fast. I know we've only known each other for a heartbeat. But I want to be with you. I want to love you. And I'll wait for you as long as I need to."

"Max," she said. "I think you might, in fact, be naff at women."

He smiled. "What does that mean?"

"It means I love you too, you numpty."

He pulled her tight to him with a low, delicious laugh. "It's not quite the delivery I was hoping for, but I probably deserve it."

She grinned. "Definitely. You *definitely* deserve it."

He slipped a finger into the opening of her jacket again. Slightly farther this time. Enough to send shivers of pleasure through her. "I am very open to doing penance," he said, low and dark.

"I can think of a thing or two," she said, low and dark.

"Quickly," he growled, pulling her deeper into the alcove, out of the view of anyone who wasn't expressly looking, and tipped her chin up to press a lingering kiss on her neck. "I promise I won't muss you, belle of the ball."

She threaded her fingers into his hair. "I can't make the same promises."

His laugh was swallowed by a low curse when he opened the single button of her jacket and spread the fabric, revealing her bare breasts. "So beautiful. You are going to kill me, Lilah Rose."

He dipped his head and took the tip of one of them into his mouth, suckling in long, deep pulls that had her writhing against him. "Max."

"Mmm. I'll stop," he said. "But it wouldn't be fair if—"

"No," she gasped, the words hushed and fervent. "It really wouldn't."

She gave a tiny cry when he took her other nipple into his mouth, his knee coming between her thighs, pressing against the place she desperately wanted him. And for a moment Lilah writhed there, rocking herself against him, slow and firm, just enough to set herself on fire. Mistake.

She cursed her frustration when Max pulled away, buttoning her jacket as he rained kisses on her cheeks and temple, whispering a wicked curse there before saying, "That is going to ruin me for the rest of the evening."

"Let's go," she said. "My hotel is a five-minute walk."

He shook his head. "No. This is your night."

"You're right," she said, no longer caring about anything but this moment, this man. The photos would be here tomorrow. Tomorrow, she'd hit the pavement. Find a new agent. Start fresh and aim for everything she wanted.

And she'd get it.

But tonight, she wanted Max. "This is my night, and I want to go." She stroked over the front placket of his trousers, finding his cock firm within. "I'm happy to leave them wanting."

"Poor bastards, I know how they'll feel," he quipped, letting her pull him out of the alcove, back toward the entrance to the hall.

They'd gotten no more than a few feet when a man stepped into their path.

"Hello, Miss Rose."

At the words, delivered in a nasal, American drawl, Lilah skidded to a stop. Her spine straightened as her skin crawled, but she was already turning—there was no other option on the table. And there, tall and reed-thin in an ill-fitting suit that did nothing for his pasty skin, was Jeffrey Greenwood, multi-mllionaire, media mogul, creep, and the man who had destroyed her career.

CHAPTER TWELVE

LILAH HESITATED, not knowing how to respond. Wanting to ignore him. Wanting to tell him off. Wanting to run.

But she wasn't alone anymore.

Max was immediately by her side. "What's wrong?"

"My studio is making a movie with Marcus Anderssen," Greenwood said, pointing to the handsome young actor in the distance, known for his passion for environmental causes. The producer's ice-blue eyes were calculating as he smiled without warmth. "Had I known you were taking these photos, I would have made a much larger contribution." He chuckled, the sound humorless, and pulled a glass of wine off a passing tray. "Next time, I suppose."

The threat was clear as day. Not really a threat. More of a promise. He had enough money to ruin Lilah again and again. For kicks.

Frustration flared, then unbridled anger when Greenwood turned to Max. Easy Max. Wonderful Max, who she didn't want anywhere near this. He extended his hand and said, "Jeffrey Greenwood. Miss Rose took some pictures of me once."

Max couldn't have looked calmer as he clasped the offered hand. "I hear they never made the light of day."

Greenwood's gaze narrowed with understanding, and he tried to pull away. Max wasn't having it.

"Lilah," Max said. "Look at me."

She did, and he read it all. Every truth. Every desire.

He threw the punch before she could stop him.

"Max! Shit!" Lilah said as Greenwood went down with a screech, blood exploding from his nose. "You can't punch him!"

"Too fucking late," he said, shaking out his fist. "We go to war together, remember?"

He was magnificent.

"Oh my God," she repeated, delight and surprise and horror flooding her before concern for Max won out. She grabbed his hand and checked his knuckles. "You've hurt yourself!"

"Worth it."

She couldn't help the little hysterical laugh that came at the words. "Oh my God." A bright light registered in her peripheral vision. An iPhone. "Too bad you didn't start that Instagram account," she said. "You're about to go viral."

"I don't care," he said, staring down at the media mogul who'd ruined her career. "I hope they got every second of it."

And then, from below, "You broke my nose, you asshole! I don't know who you are, but I'm going to fucking sue you into the ground. And your *girlfriend* will go back to not being able to get a job anywhere. The local shelter won't let her take pictures of *strays*. You don't know who you fucked with."

Max stiffened beneath her touch, going hard as steel everywhere.

Panic flared. "Max. Don't. It's not worth it."

"No," he replied, his voice cold and unyielding as he lowered himself to a crouch, sending Greenwood scrambling back. Not fast enough. Max's hand shot out and he grabbed a fistful of the disgusting man's jacket, holding him still. "You don't know who *you've* fucked with. How dare you think yourself worthy of her. How dare you think yourself worthy of looking at her. At her art." The words were no longer cold; they dripped with disdain. "How dare you think yourself worthy of speaking her name." He tightened his fist and pulled the other man closer. "If you come for her again, I will destroy you. Don't doubt it."

God, she loved this man. She loved how willing he was to protect her. How proud he was of her. How proud he was to stand with her.

"Max." He released Greenwood the second she spoke his name, rising without difficulty. He took a handkerchief from his pocket and wiped his hands, and in that moment, in that beautiful pause, he looked nothing like her Max. He looked like pure, leashed power. Expensive and undeniable.

Don't blink.

Several well-dressed security guards arrived as Greenwood scrambled to his feet. One reached to help him. "Get your hands off me. Worry about him." He waved a hand in Max's direction. "That . . . *animal* . . . assaulted me."

Time to go. Lilah didn't want to have to bail Max out of jail tonight. Was it even called jail here? "That's our cue."

But Max simply returned his handkerchief to his pocket and straightened the cuff of his jacket. "We're not going anywhere."

What the hell was wrong with him? "We're not?"

A crowd had collected, phones out, and Lilah could already hear the whispers. Her name. Greenwood's.

Who's the other one?

He's mine, Lilah thought.

"Sir," one of the security guards said to him, "I'm sorry, but you'll have to come with me."

"No, I don't think I will."

"Max," she said quietly. "What are you doing?"

She could see the murderous look in his eyes. "What I am doing and what I want to do are very different things."

Before she could reply, a shocked voice called out, "Weston! What on earth is going on here?" Lilah recognized the tall, stunningly beautiful Black woman moving toward them at a clip in a claret vintage silk Cushnie sheath—Dr. Georgiana Chesterton, the director of the museum.

It wasn't exactly the way Lilah had envisioned meeting one of the greatest minds in art, but life came at you fast.

Dr. Chesterton's attention was moving back and forth between Max and the security guard who had frozen in the act of forcibly removing him. "I don't know what you think you are doing, but this is the Duke of Weston. Unhand him, please."

What?

Lilah turned in shocked surprise to Max, expecting him to wink at her with one of those slow, easy smiles, a laughing denial.

But there was no smile.

In the hesitation, she saw the truth. "Max?"

More hesitation. More truth.

Only this time, Lilah didn't want to see it.

"Once more, this is the Duke of Weston," Dr. Chesterton said, more firmly this time, as though no one had heard her at first. "Weston of the *Weston Galleries,*" she underscored, pointing to the bronzed words installed above a nearby doorway.

The security guard immediately released Max, who rolled his shoulders back. "Cheers."

The woman gave Max a look that indicated more than passing acquaintance. "I confess I, too, am surprised, as in my experience, causing scenes is not the duke's favorite pastime."

He shrugged. "Times change."

Dr. Chesterton sighed. "Do they have to change in my museum?" She waved to a security guard standing nearby, who looked absolutely flummoxed as to how to handle whatever was going on.

Lilah understood exactly how he felt.

"Jonathan, do you mind escorting Mr. Greenwood to my office?"

"I don't need escorting anywhere, I need the police. I'm calling my lawyer." He pointed at Max and repeated his threat—one that continued to have no impact. "I'm going to sue you into the ground."

Dr. Chesterton smiled, the portrait of expensive composure. "I simply thought you'd like an opportunity to collect yourself. And perhaps do a bit of research about who, exactly, the Duke of Weston is. Of course, you are welcome to suit yourself." Finished, she turned her back on Greenwood, as though he was no one.

Lilah's brows shot up in admiration. This woman was incredible.

"You'd better have had a good reason for causing a scene, Rupert."

Rupert. Rupert Maximillian Arden.

"I swear I do," he replied, his searching gaze not leaving Lilah's face.

Dr. Chesterton followed his attention. "I see," she said, a bright smile blooming, as though everything about the evening was perfectly ordinary. "Ms. Rose, if I may? I am a great admirer of your work. I particularly like tonight's photograph from Salterton Abbey."

Lilah must have thanked her. But she couldn't remember doing it. The next thing she knew, she was watching Dr. Georgiana Chesterton disappear into the crowd, all elegance and grace.

Georgiana. Rupert. "You were married to her."

"Yes." No hesitation.

"And you are . . . Weston."

The pieces fell into place. The disdain for paparazzi. The men in the pub. The apartments in the estate house. Lottie. All his strange little hesitations whenever she invoked the duke's name. Whenever she talked about the estate.

Max was the fucking duke.

The crowd around them was already dispersing, headed for drinks and dancing now that Greenwood had skulked off and there was nothing left to watch.

Apparently, Lilah's breaking heart was not worthy of a vid.

"I was going to tell you," he said, softly.

She met his eyes. "When?"

"A thousand times."

"Well gosh, Max, I can see how you didn't get around to it. What with all those days we had together." He winced at the words. "I don't understand. Was it a joke?"

"No. Christ. *No.*" His fingers grazed her arm, leaving fire in their wake, her body instantly remembering that he'd just stretched it tight like a string and it would like its promised orgasm, thank you very much.

Her body had not received the message that he was a lying bastard.

Nope. Not a bastard. A *duke.*

She pulled away from his touch. "Don't." She was hot with embarrassment. "You lied to me."

"It wasn't a lie . . . "

"I thought you were a *farmer.*"

"I am a farmer."

She exhaled, angry. "That's your play? *I'm a farmer?* I asked you if you owned a *suit!*" God, it was mortifying. Of course he owned a suit.

He'd turned up in *Gucci*, for fuck's sake, and not off the rack—bespoke as hell and looking like he'd stepped off the pages of *Vogue*.

She'd invited him to this gala, filled with her work, where she'd laid herself bare for him, desperate for his approval, thinking he'd be *impressed* with her. And he was a *duke*. She laughed. "And then, when I saw you here, I thought you were—"

She stopped, not wanting to reveal more of herself to him.

He pounced. "What? What did you think I was?"

I thought you were mine. I thought you were my partner. Us against the world.

I thought you were my future.

And it turned out, he was a duke. The most glamorous guest at this party filled with glamorous people. And Lilah? She was back to where she always was.

Alone.

I thought you were home.

"Lilah," he said softly, stepping closer. "Please. I wanted to tell you."

Don't touch me. Don't make it harder.

"And how did that end? You reveal you're secretly a duke and I throw myself into your arms and we live happily ever after . . . cosplaying in your collection of medieval suits of armor?"

He blinked. "Is that what you think we would do?"

"I don't know what *your kind* do."

"Lilah," he started, cautiously, but she could tell he was holding back a smile, and she considered giving the British Museum a second punch in the face that evening. "I don't own suits of armor, but I will get some if that's what you'd like."

"Don't," she said. "Don't make this a joke. You lied to me." She turned on her heel and made for the door. Max was at her elbow instantly. "I should have known. Look at you. Of course you're a duke. With your perfect face and your perfect voice and your . . . *watch*."

"What? What about my watch?"

She cut him a look. "I thought it was a gift! But it wasn't, was it? It's just a normal twenty-thousand-dollar watch that you wear on regular days in a sheep pasture *because you're a duke*." She stopped at the coat check, empty now that everyone was inside, enjoying themselves. She spun to face him. "Is this some kind of bullshit game you play with all the girls who wander onto your estate? See if you can get them to bang the hot farmer?"

"What? No!"

She turned her back on him, digging a small white rectangle from her pocket, and passed it to the young woman behind the counter who stared at them, wide-eyed. "Thank you," she said, but what she meant was *Please, God, hurry.*

"Lilah—listen to me."

"No. You listen to me," she said, anger coming hot and furious. "I've spent the last eighteen months of my life trying to put myself back together, trying to work up the courage to trust this world again—this world that turned its back on me. And you—" Tears came, hot and unbidden, and she willed them back. "No. Not you. *Max* made me believe that it was possible. That I could trust again. That I could believe in the value of my work and in my own value. And that I could open myself up again, and triumph, and maybe . . . just maybe . . . also get the guy."

"You got the guy," he said. "I'm here."

"I didn't even know your *name.*"

"Who cares about my fucking name?"

Weston.

Rupert Maximillian Arden. Fourteenth Duke of Weston, Earl Salterton.

That strange, foreign, mystery of a name—the name used with reverence by the staff in the estate house, the one they'd casually tossed around while they'd joked with the boys in the pub, while they'd walked to the folly tower on the edge of the estate, where she'd realized how fast she was falling in love.

And all the while *he'd* been the duke.

He wasn't *Max.*

God, she hadn't even asked him his last name.

Her face went hot with refreshed embarrassment. The laughter in the pub with the boys—the way they'd all guffawed and winked along with her when she'd talked about how she didn't trust rich and powerful men. And all that time, the joke hadn't been on the duke in the castle on the hill.

It had been on her.

Because Max *was* the duke in the castle on the hill.

"Obviously you care about your name a whole lot, Max, or you would have introduced yourself."

He rocked back on his heels, and she turned back to the woman in the coat check. "Thank you," she said, collecting her coat, clutching it to her chest. Armor.

She met his eyes then, those beautiful, whiskey-colored eyes she'd imagined looking into for the rest of her life. Now, somehow, in the face of another man.

Max was gone.

And of all the things she'd lost, this one might be the one that broke her.

Her chest tightened, tears threatening.

She would not cry. Not tonight. Not here.

Which meant she had to leave.

"Goodbye, Max."

CHAPTER THIRTEEN

He'd been so close to telling her.

He'd had a plan. Back to her hotel room, and there he'd confess all of it. He'd tell her he was a duke, and why he'd kept it from her.

He'd tell her that he loved her, and that he didn't want a life in half measures. That he wanted all of it. That he wanted her in his world—no more farmhouse idyll, but real life. That he wanted to be in her world, however it came. Real life. Not just the gala. London, New York, Los Angeles—whatever she wanted.

He'd tell her the truth. That he couldn't imagine the future without her, wherever and whenever and however it came.

And then he would make love to her as Weston and as Max, and give her everything he had.

He'd been so close.

But Max should have known better. Because nothing with Lilah had ever gone to plan, since he found her on the ground, taking pictures of his sheep.

Christ, he'd fucked up. Again.

He watched her leave, pushing through a crowd of people that had congregated by the entrance to the museum, wanting more than anything to follow her. Maybe if he followed her, she would—

"I almost couldn't believe it was you, you know."

Max turned toward the words, finding his ex-wife watching him in that way she always had, calm and understanding, like she was perpetually one step ahead of him. And maybe she always had been.

She smiled, warm and full of fondness. "Surely not, I said to myself. Rupert? In London? By *choice*?"

"I come to London," he grumbled.

"Under duress," she said with a little laugh. "But you're not here under duress, are you?"

"No." He'd go anywhere if it meant being with Lilah.

"You're here for Lilah Rose." Her gaze tracked over his shoulder, to the place behind him where Lilah had disappeared. "Have you taken up an interest in photography?"

"Hers," he said.

Georgiana nodded. "I can understand why. She's set the standard for a generation of portrait photographers."

A pause as they stood in silence, as they had a thousand times before, at school, beyond. Finally, Max exhaled. "I really bollocksed it, Georgie."

"Why, because you thrashed Jeffrey Greenwood? I've no idea what he did, but anyone with sense can see he deserved it."

"And more," Max replied. "But it has nothing to do with Greenwood. It has to do with the fact that she didn't know I was Weston."

"Wait. What?" When he didn't look at her, Georgiana said in her firmest voice, "Rupert."

He did look then. "You needn't talk to me as though I'm a child. How are your children by the way? And Hyde?"

"They are all fine, thank you, but I've no interest whatsoever in discussing them right now," she said, the words coming in a perfect aristocratic clip. "How long have you known her?"

"Two weeks."

"And you didn't tell her."

"No."

"That you're the duke."

"Christ, Georgiana. No. I didn't."

"Right," she said, turning and pointing back at the Great Court, to the massive pictures. "Look."

Max did as he was told. There he was, on the folly tower at Salterton, acres of land spread out behind him. Hay he'd baled. Sheep he'd lambed.

All of it captured by Lilah. And now, none of it important without her.

"In all the years we were together—" Georgiana said, "You never looked at me like that."

No one cares who is behind the camera.

He cared. Christ, he'd never cared so much.

"You're in love with her."

He looked to his ex-wife. "Yes."

She sighed, the sound full of pity. "Roo."

"I didn't want her to . . . " He trailed off, the explanation getting lost in—was that opera playing in the room beyond?

Georgiana finished for him. "You didn't want her to love you for the title, and you not be able to deliver."

He didn't reply. He didn't have to.

"Congratulations. She doesn't love you for your title." Her gaze softened. "And I know you never believed it . . . but I didn't love you for it either. It wasn't the title that ended us. It wasn't the sheep, and it wasn't parties in London."

Max looked to the woman he'd married an age ago, believing that they could love each other enough to give up the lives they'd always wanted. "We never wanted the same things."

She smiled, sad and kind. "No, Roo. We were young and silly and we didn't know what we wanted."

He knew what he wanted now though.

"I want her," he said, to himself as much as to Georgiana.

"I'm very happy to hear it. It's rather wonderful when it all falls into place." She smiled the smile of a woman who'd learned that lesson well. "And does she want you?"

"She wants Max."

"Lucky thing, that," Georgiana said. "As you've always been more Max than Weston."

He looked to her. "I love her."

She smiled. "Then I suggest you go tell her. And please thank her for her gorgeous photographs. From me. And when it's sorted, come round to dinner sometime."

He was already gone, headed to the door at a clip no gentleman would ever use in public, but Max had already broken several of the cardinal rules of gentlemen that evening, so there was no reason for him to stop now.

He pushed through the crowd at the door, a plan already forming. She was at a hotel five minutes' walk from the museum. He'd go to every one of them he could find in that radius, all night long until he found her.

He didn't have to go far.

Max burst onto the red carpet, ready to sprint to the street, to discover that something had happened outside—a commotion of some sort, if the police and photographers were any indication. Whatever had occurred was over now, but the gates leading onto Great Russell Street were closed, penning in anyone who wanted to leave.

Which worked out very well for Max, because there, standing at the center of the red carpet, somehow all alone in a pool of light, waiting for the gates to open, was Lilah.

Relief thrummed through him on a wave of adrenaline as he bounded down the steps, calling her name, loving the way she turned, instantly, as though she couldn't help herself.

Good. He couldn't help himself either.

He wanted to turn whenever she called his name. Always.

He came to a stop in front of her, hating the way she'd crossed her arms over her chest, closing herself to him. Protecting herself from him. God. He'd done this to her—all the times he'd wanted to protect her, and now he'd hurt her.

"I love you," he began. "Whatever else there is, whatever else you believe, whatever else you think of what I've done, know that. I love you. This was not a joke. And it was not a game. And it was not a lie. I might have ruined it, but that is the truth. And that will be true forever. I love you."

She met his eyes then, and he sucked in a breath.

It wasn't enough.

"How can I believe that? I unraveled for you. I told you everything. I held nothing back. I gave you . . . " She paused, and the ache in Max's chest became pain. "I gave you every bit of me. All of it. And you lied to me. From the start."

"I never lied to you," Max insisted, fear and panic thrumming through him as she cut him a look of utter disbelief. She was slipping through his grasp. "I didn't. Christ, Lilah . . . I told you more of my truth than I've ever told anyone. You . . . *you* unraveled *me*. The moment you looked up at me in that pasture . . . I was blown open. I didn't tell you my name. But I told you so much more."

The disbelief was gone now, replaced by something else. Something like doubt. He could work with doubt. It wasn't ideal, but he could work with it. He stepped closer to her. She didn't back away. He could work with that too. "Lilah, if you give me the chance, I'll tell you everything. Whatever you want to know. Every dark secret, every embarrassing moment, every emotion." He paused. "Right now, I'm fucking terrified, love. I'm terrified I've lost you."

"God, Max. You make it sound so easy."

"It's always felt easy with us."

Her lips curved in a little smile, and a sliver of hope flared.

"Lilah, love." He was desperate to touch her. He took a lock of her gorgeous hair in hand, the only touch he'd let himself have. "Let me prove it."

There was a low rumble of murmurs somewhere off to the left, but Max didn't look. He was too busy looking at her.

Lilah did look.

"Max," she said, quietly, shooting a nervous glance at the lines of cameras set up on either side of the red carpet. "We're in full view of every tabloid photographer in London. This isn't exactly the place for—"

"I don't care," he said. "I've spent the last decade avoiding them. But I don't care about any of that now. Let them take their pictures. None of it matters. Not if I don't have you. And I can't have you if I don't tell you the truth, which I should have told you from the start."

She nodded. "Okay."

"My father died when I was sixteen."

Her gaze softened. "I'm sorry."

Of course she would say that. Of course that would be her first thought. God, if he lost this woman, he didn't know what he'd do.

"Before that, I was a lot of things. I was born Earl Salterton. I was Arden to schoolmates and Rupert to my family. Lottie called me Roo. Georgiana as well."

Her lips curved in a ghost of a smile. There and gone, so fast that he almost missed it. But he didn't miss it. He loved it. "I know. *Awful*. I hated it, truly. But you know what I hated most? I hated that when my father died, *every* friend I had . . . *every one* . . . immediately started calling me Weston. Without hesitation. One moment I was Rupert or Arden, and then the phone rang at Eton and the news traveled from one room to the next, and instantly I was Weston. My father, not even cold in his grave. As though they'd all been calling me that in their head for years, anyway, just biding their time until they could tell the world that they were friends with a duke."

Her brows knit together as he continued.

"And it happened like *that*." He snapped his fingers. "Without anyone even thinking to check on me, or to tell me they were sorry that my father had died, I was just someone else. The door closed on the past. Opened on some new future. Time to learn how to live in it." He stilled, thinking on it. Hating that he still remembered the ache of it. Dwelled on it. He scoffed. "But what a whinge, right? I was a duke, and it came with money and power and privilege beyond reason, and everything I could ever ask for. And here I am, complaining that people noticed."

"You were sixteen. And even if you weren't . . . it was your life." She reached up to touch him, her fingers sliding over his cheek, and he closed his eyes, the pleasure of her touch nearly unbearable.

She wouldn't touch him if he'd lost her, would she?

"One minute you were there, and the next you were gone." At her words, his gaze flew to hers, finding tears in her beautiful eyes.

Christ, he loved her.

"Max," she whispered, searching his face.

"No." He took her hand in his and kissed her fingertips. "Let me finish. I was born into this world. Power and privilege and money, with duty to the title absolutely drilled into me from birth. And I was terrible at this part of it." He waved a hand at the museum, large and looming behind her. "I hated being here, in London. I hated parties and people and . . . "

"Paparazzi?"

He nodded. "Them too. And I thought that if you wanted all this, I was doomed to disappoint you." He hesitated, searching for the explanation. "So I stayed Max, telling myself I'd let you go at the end of our time together. Telling myself I'd be able to watch you return to your world and not wildly, desperately, want to be a part of it so I could be near you. Telling myself I could be in love with you and still let you go."

"You should have asked me," she said, her brow furrowing.

"I know."

"You almost broke both our hearts."

"I know. I'm sorry."

She nodded, her eyes searching his. Laying him bare. "No more of that."

"None. I swear it."

She smiled then, small and sweet. "Let's go back to you wanting to be near me."

The tightness in his chest loosened. "Every minute of every day. Wherever you want to be."

"That doesn't sound like it could possibly disappoint me," she said, a gleam of something like happiness in her beautiful eyes. "But it's not all or nothing. This world . . . it's not my world anymore. It's not all I have. It's my work, and I love it, and I don't want to leave it. But there are other things I love. Other things I don't want to leave. Like you. Like Salterton."

Yes.

"Then don't," he said. "You never have to."

She looked him up and down, and he took the way her appraising gaze turned hungry as an extremely positive sign. "Though, truthfully, any time you want to put on this suit and tag along for work, I'm not going to say no."

He laughed. "I think I can manage that."

She stepped toward him, close enough that he could feel her heat. "A duke, huh?"

"I should have told you," he repeated. "I'm sorry. But the idea that a woman like you—brilliant, talented, sexy as hell—would love me . . . *Max* . . . me . . . without any of the rest of it . . . I was terrified of ruining it." He exhaled and looked up at the sky, then looked back at her. "It was like a gift. In all my life before you, I've never been enough. Just me, on my own."

"Max," she said, lifting her hand, pushing a lock of hair off his brow. "I love *you*. I love you, and the men in the Fox and Falcon, and your enormous dog, and your terrifying sheep, and your cottage, and your *Aga* . . . " He laughed again. "And if they come with a title, well, I suppose I'm going to have to try falling in love with the duke too."

"I'm afraid he's the only way you get the bespoke suits."

She laughed. "Well then, I will persevere. I'll get used to the whole world calling you Weston, as long as I can save Weston for special occasions, and call you Max all the rest of the time."

He set his forehead to hers. "Yes, please. Now kiss me."

"If we do that, the Duke of Weston will return with a bang, whether you like it or not."

"If it means you kiss me, I promise I'll like it."

Dozens of camera flashes were already firing as he lowered his lips to hers, a slow, sinful temptation.

"Max?" she whispered, just before he kissed her.

"Mmm?"

"Don't blink."

EPILOGUE

FIVE MONTHS LATER, Lilah opened the door to the cottage, weary from her overnight flight from Los Angeles and the drive from Heathrow. Dropping her bag in the foyer, she called out for Max.

No answer.

Taking off her shoes, she made her way to the kitchen, stopping only to wash her hands and face. She reveled in the quiet peace of the creaky old house—so different from where she'd been two nights earlier, in the delicious mayhem of the Oscars.

Aarti had been right—after the Common Harvest gala, Lilah was welcomed back into the world she'd once given everything to. Greenwood had tried to bury her again—as powerful men so often did—but this time, Lilah stood alongside a dozen other women he'd threatened and harmed, and they'd told their stories together. And it had been Greenwood who was buried.

She'd be lying if she said her time in Los Angeles hadn't been sweeter for that triumph.

Lilah had spent the day of the awards shadowing a young nominee during her first red carpet prep, and the evening taking a collection of group portraits at the *Bonfire* After Party.

Years earlier, she might have spent the rest of the week in a haze of lunches and drinks and dinners and networking—or she would have taken one of the half dozen interviews she'd been offered to discuss the downfall of Greenwood. But Lilah had something far more tempting waiting for her at home.

Max.

The kitchen was empty, late afternoon sunlight pouring through the windows overlooking the wide expanse of green spring pastures beyond. She paused for a heartbeat to take in the view—one of the many reasons they'd decided to live here, in the cottage, and save the estate house for special occasions.

There, on the scarred kitchen table, was a note in Max's bold scrawl.

Checking on Mabel.
I love you.

She smiled. Even as he'd dashed off the note, he'd added his love. As though she might not know. As though he hadn't told her he loved her several times a day since the night he'd told her the first time.

Slipping the paper into her back pocket, she went to the rear door of the cottage, pulled on her wellies, and set off to find him, the thought of him chasing away jet lag and exhaustion. She crested the hill a few hundred yards from the cottage, looking down on the field below, dotted with sheep, Atlas in the distance.

And there, in the center of all of it, was Max. Holding a lamb.

Lilah's chest tightened at the image—her big, broad farmer cradling the little creature—and her stomach flipped with pleasure, hormones standing up and taking notice. It was ridiculous how easy it was to love him.

He looked up as she made her way toward him, his eyes lighting with pleasure before he crouched to set the little creature on the ground and came for her, long strides eating up the green earth. Lilah laughed, distracted by the lamb stumbling and swaying toward Mabel—who immediately provided shelter.

And then Max was there, catching her to him, lifting her high in his arms and kissing her, deep and thorough and desperate enough that anyone watching would think they'd been apart for months instead of a few short days. Lilah met the kiss, just as thorough, just as desperate.

Wildly in love with this man, farmer, duke, marauder, *hers*.

When they finally came up for air, he set her back on her feet, Atlas dancing around them for a hello. "I love it when you come home."

She smiled and said, "I love coming home." She leaned over to give the dog some attention, then peeked past Max to see the lamb. "And you, just hanging out in a field, holding a new lamb. Could you be more picturesque?"

"Mabel and I have always liked making the place nice for you."

She laughed, tucking herself into the crook of his arm as they made their way over to the ewe. "Well done, Mabes," she said, and Mabel seemed to preen under the compliment. Lilah crouched and called to the lamb, who came immediately to her, curious and sweet.

Lilah went to her knees, the two-day-old lamb coming to stand on her thighs, accepting her touch instantly. She lifted it into her arms, cuddling it close. "What a love."

"He likes your touch. I can relate."

She flashed him a grin over the lamb's fluffy white head. "Passionate shepherd flirting is the best kind of flirting." Lifting the little creature into the air, she studied its sweet face and said "I think we should name you Marlowe."

The lamb gave a tiny, high-pitched bleat and squirmed to be free, and Lilah released it to the field and its mother with a laugh. Brushing mud and grass from her thighs, she stood, Max reaching down to help her up.

Once she was on her feet, her laugh caught in her throat as she met his gaze, hot and delicious on her. "Marry me."

She stilled, surprise and a deep, delicious pleasure coursing through her. Had she heard it correctly? "What did you say?"

He came for her, cradling her face in his warm, rough hands, tilting her up to him, until she was lost in his whiskey eyes. "I've resisted asking you that for months. I've wanted to ask you every day since the day you left for London. I wanted to ask you at the British Museum under your gorgeous photographs, and in the kitchen at the cottage, and in the gift shop of the main house that day when you made me go in and introduce myself to the guests."

She laughed, delighted by him and the memory. He'd hated it. And then he'd loved it. "Really?"

"Yes, really. I wanted to ask you when we were in the States for Thanksgiving with your friends. And when we spent Christmas here at the Abbey with Lottie and Jez and Simon. And I wanted to ask you every night we've spent at the pub, and again, as we've walked home under the stars."

She wrapped her arms around his waist, wanting to scream her answer and also to savor this moment—one she wanted to remember for the rest of her days. "So why haven't you?"

"Because I wanted to give you time," he said, softly. "I wanted to give you time to settle back into your brilliant life, and give you a chance to decide that this is enough." He paused. "That I am enough."

She kissed him then, soft and sweet, breaking it to whisper at his lips, "This is perfect. *You* are perfect."

He pulled her tight to him. "Is that what you've decided?"

"I've known it from the start." She paused, then added, "Ask me again."

He smiled, that handsome, crooked smile that stole her breath. "Lilah Rose, will you marry me?"

Max.

"Yes."

He kissed her again, until they were both gasping for breath, and he lifted her high off the ground, her arms wrapping around his neck. She sighed in his arms and said, "Ask me again."

He pressed a kiss to her cheek. "Will you marry me?"

The Duke.

"Yes," she said, turning to catch his lips once more, kissing him until he rumbled his pleasure and lifted her high in his arms, until her legs were wrapped around his waist and he was already headed across the pasture.

"Time to go home," he said. "Now that you've said it twice, I intend to spend the night making you scream it."

The Marauder.

She laughed, full of hope and love and the future . . . and let him lead the way home.

ALSO BY SARAH MACLEAN

The Bareknuckle Bastards

Wicked and the Wallflower

Brazen and the Beast

Daring and the Duke

Scandal & Scoundrel

The Rogue Not Taken

A Scot in the Dark

The Day of the Duchess

The Rules of Scoundrels

A Rogue by Any Other Name

One Good Earl Deserves a Lover

No Good Duke Goes Unpunished

Never Judge a Lady By Her Cover

Love By Numbers

Nine Rules to Break When Romancing a Rake

Ten Ways to be Adored When Landing a Lord

Eleven Scandals to Start to Win a Duke's Heart

Anthologies

How The Dukes Stole Christmas

Dark Duets

ABOUT THE AUTHOR

A life-long romance reader, Sarah MacLean wrote her first romance novel on a dare and never looked back. She is a *New York Times, Washington Post*, and *USA Today* bestselling author, the co-host of the weekly romance novel podcast, *Fated Mates*, and a columnist for The Washington Post.

Her work in support of romance and the women who read it earned her a place on Jezebel.com's Sheroes list and led *Entertainment Weekly* to call her "the elegantly fuming, utterly intoxicating queen of historical romance." Sarah lives in New York City.

Find her at sarahmaclean.net or fatedmates.net, or sign up for her newsletter at sarahmaclean.net/contact.

BETTER WITH YOU

SOPHIE JORDAN

For every woman who dreams of a fresh start.

CHAPTER ONE

"VEE, this is Mr. Moretti from Corps Security. He will be your security detail while you're here."

Security detail. I turned those words over as though struggling to translate them in my mind.

"Bodyguard," I breathed like it was dirty thing.

I couldn't bring myself to look at the man coming up behind me in my UK editor's office. I knew it wasn't mannerly. I should greet him. Shake hands. But I couldn't look at him. I could only gawk at my editor, hoping this was some kind of joke.

"That's right." Melani nodded, her gaze darting just beyond my shoulder. I felt his presence there like a heat-radiating furnace, but I couldn't tear my gaze from my editor. She settled her gaze back on me. "Corps Security prides itself on its discretion. I'm certain you will hardly even notice Mr. Moretti. He'll be a shadow. Entirely unobtrusive." She smiled encouragingly.

I shook my head. "You never mentioned any of this before."

"After your signing last week . . . Anna and I spoke and thought it would be the wisest course of action while you're here."

I tried not to wince at the reference to my event in Washington, D.C. four days ago. It had been . . . *unfortunate*. Anna was my US editor and she was even more rattled by the incident than I was. "Pfft." I fluttered a hand. "That was nothing. It won't happen again."

"I don't think we can make light of this. Employees at the bookstore had to hustle you into a back room and end your event early. The police were called."

"It was an isolated incident. I toured nine other cities and nothing like that happened. I am sure nothing is going to happen while I'm here."

"No one ever expects anything to happen to them," a deep voice contributed behind me. "It's always wise to be prepared."

Galled at this man, this stranger, who dared to insinuate himself into the conversation, into *my* life, I twisted around in my chair, hot words burning on my tongue.

The air left me in a whoosh and I sank back down in my chair, speechless.

He was as unobtrusive as slap to my vulva.

Oh, hell no. I did not need good-looking guys around me.

How was *he* supposed to be unnoticeable? This man did not go *anywhere* without being noticed. He was big. Muscly even in his nice jacket and slacks. No tie. Just a crisp white button-down under his jacket. No amount of clothing could hide the fact that this guy was built. It was partly the way he held himself. I could easily see him in military fatigues, loping through the jungle with a panther-like gait.

I studied him from the cocoon of my wingback chair, digesting that *this man* would be shadowing my every move. I blinked and looked to Melani incredulously.

She gave a pathetic little shrug that told me she had a sense of my thoughts. "Sorry. You're much too important to us, Vee."

I barely held back a snort. I was not *much too important* to anyone. My book was important. The book. Not *me* specifically. It was a crucial distinction.

Self Love meant money to these people. It meant money to me too. As someone who never had a lot growing up, I wasn't indifferent to that.

I never had a mom that packed me lunches. She gave me money for school lunches when she remembered or when she had the cash, which wasn't very often. I qualified for free meal benefits. That meant I received two pieces of white bread with a slice of cheese in the middle and an apple every day. It was a flag to everyone that I was poor. Well, that and the fact that I wore my grandma's hand-me-downs. Mom was too short for me to borrow her clothes. I was the only fourth-grader dressed like a Golden Girl with shoulder pads.

I'd come a long way from that. Now I could afford my own clothes and pretty much anything else I wanted. I'd flown business class to London, where I was served champagne and five courses. A long way, indeed.

My editor was a perfectly lovely person, but this was business, plain and simple. I wouldn't be important—or here at all—if not for three months of a rage-filled writing purge.

It had begun as a form of catharsis after my last divorce. My last and *final* divorce. There would not be another. By the age of thirty-four I had three failed marriages behind me. Yeah. I was done being stupid . . . done falling for guys that looked good on paper, but turned out to be someone else. Someone that didn't really exist. A fourth failed marriage would not be my fate.

I had channeled all my disappointment and frustrations into a book —a book that now, four years later, happened to be in its second year on multiple bestseller lists. The success of *Self Love* had turned me into a household name. I now had a sizable bank account and the pleasure of an international book tour.

Who could have guessed that something good could come from my life's biggest failures?

Melani continued, "Vee, your amazing book has created some waves, which, of course, is part of its appeal and popularity. You had something important to say and you said it. Women don't need men to be happy. In fact, sometimes women are happier without them." She nodded approvingly. "You'd think the concept wouldn't be that shocking, but apparently, men are unused to hearing they're unnecessary."

I arched an eyebrow, knowing there was more coming. "*But?*"

"The truth can offend . . . and not everyone loves what you have to say."

I knew that. My own family didn't love it. According to rumors, my exes *hated* it.

"I'm not going to live under a rock because a handful of Nean-derthals don't like what I have to say . . . or rather, what I wrote."

The mental image of the man at my Washington, D.C. event rose in my mind. His face had been mottled red in rage. I didn't know I could make any individual so angry. Not even my ex, Brent, and he had a temper.

The guy in D.C. had looked ready to hurt me—not that I would admit such a thing to Melani. It would only affirm her certainty that I needed a man to protect me, and that went against everything I had come to believe of myself.

"You don't need to live under a rock, but these individuals cannot be underestimated. We don't want you taking any risks. This security company has a stellar reputation. We've used them before for a few of our controversial authors."

Is that what I am now? A controversial author?

"I really think this is an over-reaction, Melani. And how does it look? I'm all about self-reliance but I need some beefcake for protection?" I shot Moretti a quick glance. "No offense."

"None taken."

I looked back to Melani. "That kind of undermines my platform."

"Better alive and a hypocrite than a dead author . . . at least according to legal."

I winced.

Melani gestured to the over-sized monitor on her desk. "It's not just the incident in D.C. either. I can show you the emails. We need to take this seriously."

"A few angry emails—"

"A few?" Melani moved to her desk and bent over to tap at the keyboard. "I can read you one hundred and seven emails. And these are just the people who felt motivated to email us. *This week.* Anna has received her share. There have been bloggers, podcasts, jokes on chat shows, angry men on the news. And who knows how many wankers out there posting God knows what on social media . . ." She sighed as though her diatribe fatigued her. "I'm sorry, Vee, but it's already decided." The apology wasn't real. She wasn't sorry at all. They were simply words to soften the blow. "Your tour here will be done this way. Anything else is . . . a liability."

A liability?

With a disgusted huff, I rose and crossed her office, staring out the seventh-story window overlooking the city streets, admiring the descending dusk.

"We're so pleased that you were available on short notice," Melani said to Mr. Moretti behind me. "You come highly recommended. Your employer tells me you are one of the best, and that's what we need for our Vee."

I continued to stare out the window. Melani had a perfect view of the iconic BT Tower from her window. All steel and glass, it was like a great spindle reaching for the sky.

As a little girl growing up in an ant-size town, I dreamt of seeing the world. I'd never left the country. I only left Arkansas once when we visited my mom's aunt in Missouri, and I was excited to finally put a stamp in a passport. I was eager to do a little exploring—to walk the streets of a city that I had crossed an ocean to reach and had only ever seen in the movies. The sooner I left, the sooner I could start doing that. So far, I'd only seen Heathrow and the inside of my hotel.

I wanted to visit Buckingham Palace and Hyde Park and walk Baker Street. As a kid, I was a big fan of all things Sherlock Holmes. Reading helped get me through my childhood with Mom and her various boyfriends. Maybe I didn't have time to visit all those sights in the short time I was here, but I wanted to squeeze in as many as I could. Except a bodyguard did not exactly fit into these plans I had envisioned for myself.

Melani continued to chat at my back with Moretti. "You have the itinerary I sent over?"

"Yes, ma'am. I've studied it and will deliver her to all scheduled events."

Deliver me? Like I was some package? God. This was the worst. Here I was, the author of *Self Love*, a book touting female self-reliance, and I needed a bodyguard. I felt like a fraud. After all I'd been through, all I'd learned, it made me sick to be dependent on any man for any reason.

I turned back around.

"Excellent." Melani smiled brightly. "Then you should have everything you need." Melani smiled brightly. "I feel so relieved our Vee is safely in your hands." My editor turned her attention on me. "Now I'll see you at the Common Harvest Gala when you return from Edinburgh. There are several people I want you to meet there. Oh! And Lilah Rose is going to be there. Remember her?"

I nodded. "Of course. She was the photographer for the piece in *Bonfire*." The first magazine feature that took *Self Love* seriously, with the portraits to prove it. Not a dildo in sight.

Melani clapped her hands together. "Yes! Gorgeous photos."

I had to agree. I never looked as good in any of my wedding photos as I did in the four portraits that ran alongside the article.

Melani continued, "Well, apparently her hiatus is over. She's back and revealing her new collection at the gala—something about global sustainable farming?" She waved a hand. "Trying something new, I gather! Anyway, It's going to be a wonderful affair."

I picked up my handbag, moving stiffly. Melani gave me a quick hug. "Text or call me if you need anything." She cut Mr. Moretti a look. "And you have my contact information, as well."

He nodded once, curt and perfunctory. "Of course, ma'am."

Melani moved to the door and held it open for us. There were more words of farewell as she accompanied us out into the corridor, words that were all a blur of sound as I tried to ignore the behemoth close behind us. *Impossible.*

"Enjoy yourself. Have fun," Melani called after us as we stepped on the elevator.

Have fun? As though I was jetting off on a vacation—or heading out the door for a date with some dreamy boyfriend. *Not even close.*

Fine. Maybe he was dreamy. Some women liked the hard-body-square-jawline-smoldering-eyes type. The type of women who were into men. Which I was not. I wasn't into men. I wasn't into *anyone*. Not men. Not women. I was into me. Myself. That was enough. It was the theme of my book, for goodness sake. I didn't need anyone else.

The elevator doors closed on Melani's face and it was just the two of us in the elevator. He didn't stand beside me. He stood just behind me to my right. I felt his presence, energy and heat vibrating so closely. I resisted the urge to look over my shoulder at him.

What was I supposed to do? How did one treat a bodyguard? Did you acknowledge them or behave as though they weren't there at all?

Bodyguard. Ugh. After all the bumps and hurdles in my life I thought I didn't have to deal with things like fear, but I was being told I should be afraid—that I needed to be cautious and that I needed this man to keep me safe.

It was like I was caught up in a movie. My mother would start screeching if she knew and demand I come home. Not that I did the things my mother told me to do—if that were the case I'd still be trapped in an unhappy marriage. In any event, this would definitely be something I left out during our texts and phone calls.

The elevator doors opened and we stepped out into the lobby.

I marched a hard line for the front double doors, feeling his presence close, like hot breath on my neck. He wasn't *that* close, of course. Imagination was a powerful thing. I rubbed at the back of my neck anyway.

I stepped from the building and glanced left and right. We weren't far from London's West End where my hotel was located. I had walked here. It was just a few blocks. I'm sure my publisher had deliberately booked my lodgings close to their offices. I'd already done my research and planned on a nearby pub for dinner. The place had wonderful reviews.

Pasting on a smile, I faced Mr. Moretti. "We can part ways here. I'll just get a car."

His stone expression flickered with the barest reaction. "I beg your pardon?"

I shivered at the sound of his deep voice. Perhaps that was why he went into the bodyguard business. Because his voice alone could strike dread into hearts.

I fluttered a hand down the street as though he could take himself in that direction. "You don't need to babysit me."

"That is precisely what I've been hired to do, ma'am."

"I'm fine. You don't have to stay with me. I won't tell."

"And what happens when someone comes after you?"

"*When?*" I shook my head. "You speak as though it's inevitable."

"My job is to plan and prepare as though it is."

I snorted. "That's silly."

There it was. Something definitely flickered across his face. I'd hit a nerve. "It's called being ready."

I settled my hands on my hips. "I'm not going to be attacked."

"You don't know that."

"No one is going to attack me," I insisted.

His lips flattened into an obstinate line. "I've entered into a contract with—"

"Not with me. *I* haven't hired you."

"This seems like something you should have sorted out in there." He motioned to the building from which we had just emerged.

He was correct, of course. My courage had failed while I was in my editor's office. I had somehow decided it would be easier to persuade him to walk away from me than to convince Melani that I didn't need protection.

Staring at him now with his unflinching gaze, I was not certain why I thought that.

It was rather insulting, I supposed, to assume he lacked integrity, that he was little more than a cheat.

Feeling uncomfortable, I readjusted my handbag on my shoulder and gestured to the street. "I had planned on visiting Buckingham Palace—"

"They're closed for admission by now."

I frowned.

"You can check if you don't—"

"I believe you."

"At any rate, it's too crowded."

Staring at him, I realized it was going to be like this. Moretti calling the shots. Telling me what I could do . . . where I could go. It was a blow to my pride. What kind of expert on autonomy was I?

"Well, then. I'm going to get something to eat—"

"Your hotel has a restaurant."

I exhaled a hot breath. "I've already planned where I'm dining this evening." Plans that I did not intend to change just because he had been thrown into the mix. I was done changing or altering aspects of my life for a man. Granted, there was no confusing him with any of my exes. None of them had ever worn a sidearm under their jacket, but he was clearly packing heat under his.

"I've already assessed your hotel. I'm familiar with all points of entry. I'd be more comfortable with you dining in the hotel restaurant—"

"Wait a minute, wait a minute." I waved both hands in front of me as though chasing away a pesky mosquito. "I can't go to dinner where I want?" I shook my head. This was unacceptable. I was independent and single and did not defer to anyone. Not anymore. *Never* again. I pointed down the street. "I'm going to dinner that way."

Without waiting for his response, I spun around and started walking toward The Figgy Spoon, not caring if he followed me or not.

CHAPTER TWO

OF COURSE HE FOLLOWED ME.

"Ms. Mathers," he called, but I did not stop or look back. I kept a steady pace down the sidewalk. The restaurant was five blocks away and was reputed to serve the best shepherd's pie in London. If he wanted to follow me, that was his right. Eating dinner where I wanted was my right.

I had to stop and wait for the pedestrian light at an intersection.

He arrived at my side. My hand flexed around my purse strap. I tried to pretend he was just a random person standing beside me, waiting for the light to change, too. Just someone leaving work and headed home or to the bar for drinks. It was futile, of course. He wasn't going to let me pretend he wasn't there.

"Where is this restaurant?" he asked, not looking at me. He seemed to avoid looking at me directly. He should work on that. Maybe no one ever told him eye contact was important when speaking to someone.

"One block on the left," I replied.

The light changed and I stepped forward, crossing the street.

I assumed Moretti was behind me as I kept going, walking the length of the block. I didn't bother to verify his presence as I entered the restaurant.

It was crowded. Most of the customers congregated at the bar. Lots of men, I noted. The place had plenty of flat screens playing different games throughout the room.

Crowded or not, I didn't have to wait for a table. A hostess greeted me with a smile and menus in her hand, leading me to a small table for two away from the bar. *A table for two.* Would I have to eat with him? *Great.*

How was I going to make idle chitchat with a man that was hired to babysit me? It was worse than a first date. Not that I did those anymore, but at least on a first date the two individuals wanted to be together and were invested in the conversation. I doubted we would even have a conversation.

I didn't look over my shoulder, but I felt him there just behind me. At the table, the hostess's eyes drifted beyond my shoulder and widened ever so slightly. Yep. He was there. No mistaking that reaction. She probably didn't get too many Henry Cavill dopplegangers in here.

Deciding to make the best of it, I exhaled heavily, fixing what I hoped was not a too strained smile to my face, and lifted my chin . . . to find him nowhere.

He was not seated across from me.

I jerked my head around, searching for him. Was it possible he had left? Given up just as I had requested? It seemed rather rude that he would leave without letting me know, but if he was gone that was all that really mattered.

A genuine smile started at my lips and then died swiftly when my gaze landed on him.

He was still here, seated at a high table between the bar and me, looking fine and at ease in his jacket and crisp white shirt. Again, he did not look at me. He looked around. Everywhere. Anywhere. Just not at me.

His tapered fingers lightly drummed the surface of his table and I couldn't help staring at those broad, olive-skinned hands, the backs lightly sprinkled with hair. Even the glimpse of his wrists was intriguing. Thick and wiry. Strong. Masculine. Maybe it was because I knew that those hands of his were so capable. They existed to protect and go to battle if needed.

I swallowed thickly as my mind took a trip to the gutter, envisioning those hands on my skin, several shades darker, gliding up my thigh . . .

My stomach squeezed a little. Okay, he definitely needed to go.

"I need a drink," I muttered under my breath. As though to mock my wishes, a waitress approached for *his* drink order. Of course. Still no sight of my waitress.

She stood close to Moretti and reached for the cocktail menu at the center of the table, the front of her generously endowed chest brushing his arm. I wiggled my shoulders slightly, suddenly self-conscious of my *not* large breasts.

Women must do that all the time to him—look for the happy accident of brushing against him. His body begged for touch, exploration.

He was like a giant lollipop begging to be sucked.

God. I gave my head a swift shake. What was *wrong* with me? This man was not candy to eat. He was attractive, but I'd seen other attractive men since my divorce. None of them made me think such dirty thoughts . . . or feel quivery inside.

Obviously it was because he was *assigned* to me and would be around me a lot. It had me looking at him. Thinking about him.

Looking at and thinking about him—more than I should.

We were going to Edinburgh. We would be trapped together for hours. He would be with me every day while I was here. I was stuck with him until I left for Paris. I doubted my publisher in France would insist on a bodyguard. At least my French editor had made no mention of that in our emails . . . unless she wanted to drop that little surprise on me like Melani did.

I winced and took a ragged breath.

Clearly I needed to get my head straight.

An evening with my trusty vibrator would help. If I got off, I would probably be a little less tense around him—and less afflicted with these wayward thoughts.

I'd bought myself a vibrator the day after I left Charlie. It had satisfied me ever since, convincing me there was nothing I couldn't handle myself . . . nothing I couldn't *do* for myself.

A waitress arrived for my drink order.

"I'll have a gin and tonic, and can I go ahead and order the shepherd's pie? I've heard wonderful things about it."

"Excellent choice. You won't be disappointed." She nodded with a friendly smile and accepted my proffered menu. "It will be out soon."

Just then Moretti's waitress sidled close to my waitress. "Did you see the bloke at table ten? He's well fit," she murmured in a low voice. Not low enough for me *not* to hear her, but I don't think she really cared. Her face was slightly flushed and she looked like she needed a vibrator of her own—or *not*. What she really wanted was the man at table ten. "I could spend all night climbing him."

"Annie," my waitress chided with a nervous laugh, sending me an apologetic look.

I waved a hand that it was all right. It didn't have anything to do with me, after all, and I was all for females expressing their desires free of judgment.

"I'll be back soon with your drink." My waitress gave me another contrite smile and walked off with Annie—but not without looking back at Moretti herself, no doubt verifying just how well *fit* he was.

"God," I murmured, relaxing back in my chair and starting in on my drink like it could bring salvation. Realizing I would quickly reach the bottom of the glass, I went ahead and signaled for another one, deliberately avoiding looking at my bodyguard where he sat.

Something happened on one of the games on TV because the bar erupted in shouts and cheers. Of course I looked in that direction. Beer was flying as men were hugging and high-fiving each other like they'd just won the World Cup. My gaze caught on one guy as he whooped loudly and embraced a friend. His eyes locked with mine over his friend's shoulder. It was just one of those accidental things that happen when your eyes collide with someone else's gaze.

It was an accident, but it happened.

I quickly looked away, hoping he didn't get the wrong idea, hoping there were no adverse consequences to that brief eye contact. I was not looking to get picked up. Even without the awkwardness of a bodyguard nearby watching me, I wasn't up for that.

My second drink arrived. The waitress took my first glass. "Your dinner will be out in a moment."

"Thank you." I lifted the glass to my lips and drank deeply. I was halfway through my gin and tonic when I felt a presence beside me.

There was exaggerated throat clearing and then, "Looks like you're going to need another drink there."

I glanced up to find the guy from the bar staring down at me. His face was flushed pink—either from revelry or alcohol. Maybe both. I glanced down at my drink, which was mostly ice now. I was going to need another drink, but I didn't need him to buy it for me. Contrary to what my mother had always taught me. I didn't need anything from a man ever again.

"I'm fine, thank you."

"Oh, a Yank!" I wasn't sure what that signified to him, but he looked back at his boys as though he'd just made a great discovery. Facing me again, he asked, "What's your name? I'm Joss."

"Vee," I replied somewhat reluctantly. Uneasiness settled in the pit of my stomach.

"And what brings you here, Vee?"

I hesitated. I didn't want to share the reason for my visit to his country with him. The last thing I needed was some stranger pulling out his phone to look me up. Plus, I didn't feel like wasting my time with this. Or him.

He looked at me with keen interest and settled a hand on my shoulder as if we were intimates and not perfect strangers. I eyed his hand and tensed.

I breathed in deeply, telling myself I could get rid of some rando guy. And we were in a public place. "If you don't mind. I'm just here to eat my dinner."

"Oh." He donned a deliberately crushed expression that I didn't buy for a moment. He was not disappointed. This guy was used to hitting on women in bars and getting his fair share of rejections. "No one likes to eat alone."

"I do." I had been for the last four years and I loved it. Better than any dinner I sat through with my exes. Oh, there were some occasional good meals we'd had together. Date nights. Mostly before we married. Everything before marriage was better. It was a hard lesson, but one I had learned.

"Oh, I don't believe that for a moment." Joss leaned down, propping one hand on the back of my chair and his other hand on the table in front of me. A lump clogged in my throat. I felt surrounded at every direction. Leaning back put me in contact with his arm. Leaning forward—he was there, too. "This place serves the best shepherd's pie in London."

Before I could respond he started wagging a finger in my face. "Hey, don't I know you?"

My stomach tightened. "I don't think so."

"Nah, I've seen you on telly." He snapped his fingers in triumph. "You wrote that book! You're *that* woman!"

Great. Couldn't I get a meal in peace?

Joss turned and called over to his friends. "Hey, mates! You're never going to believe—"

"You can leave. The lady is *not* dining alone." A chair scraped across the floor as it was pulled back from the table. Moretti sank down across from me, all smooth, liquid movements and stoic expression.

Joss straightened, his jovial air slipping as he eyed Moretti. "Right then. I thought she was alone."

"As you can see, she is not." Moretti's dark eyes didn't stray from Joss. Threat emanated from him in palpable waves. "Get lost."

With a departing nod for me, Joss turned and headed back to the bar and his rowdy friends.

I lifted my glass, took a sip, and set it back down. "I could have handled that, you know."

"It's my job though. Isn't it?"

His job. No. That should be *my* job. I took care of myself. "To run off harmless guys in pubs?" I scoffed.

"Allow me to decide who is harmless." He still didn't look at me for a prolonged period of time, and I wondered if an inability to hold eye contact was typical for him. Or was it just me?

The waitress arrived with my food. "There you are, dear. Can I get another refill for you?"

"Yes, please. Thank you." There was a slight tightening of his lips, the barest hint of disapproval. He was probably counting my drinks and worried he was going to have to carry me back to the hotel.

The waitress looked at Moretti. "And what about you, love?"

"Water is fine. Thank you."

"Water?" I asked as the waitress left us. "What? No drinking on the clock?"

"Something like that."

I lifted my fork and dug into my dinner. "Aren't you eating?"

"I'm fine."

"No eating on the clock either?"

He didn't respond to my question this time, but I didn't let that stop me. I was hungry, and I hadn't invited him here. He'd been foisted on me. I was going to go where I wanted. And drink. And eat. And do anything else I felt like doing.

I ate, moaning at my first bite.

A muscle feathered along his jaw as he stared suddenly at my face. His gaze fastened on my mouth, his eyes strangely . . . intent. I swallowed my bite and moistened my lips. His gaze tracked the glide of my tongue and my sex clenched. It wasn't every day I had a man like him really look at me.

And he was *really* looking at me now.

I shifted in my seat, trying to ease the unwanted pulsing between my legs.

"This is delicious," I said, my voice excessively loud. I winced and lowered my tone. "You should try some."

"I'm fine."

"You've got to eat. How else can you keep up your strength and protect me from all the bad guys?" Yeah. I was being a little sarcastic, but he gave no reaction. Either he didn't register or didn't care about my pithiness.

I stretched my fork across the table at him. "C'mon. Have a taste."

"That's not—"

I pushed the food-laden fork up against his mouth. "C'mon."

Maybe I was feeling the alcohol. I didn't remember ever trying to feed anyone before.

Accepting that he had little choice, he opened his lips and took the bite.

"Good?" I asked.

He gave a single terse nod of agreement.

I nodded back, satisfied.

The waitress breezed past, depositing a fresh drink before me and snatching up my empty glass. I took a deep drink and continued eating. "So. Have you been a bodyguard very long?"

"I've been in protection for five years."

"Protection. Ah." I nodded. So that was the professional word for it. "So you're a badass."

He hesitated. I chewed, studying him.

"It's okay. You can say it," I encouraged.

"I can send you my resume if you'd like to go over my qualifications yourself—"

"Pfft." I waved my fork dismissively. "You've already been hired . . . and not by me. You don't need to prove yourself to me. My opinion doesn't matter." Yeah. That stung even as I said it. "So. Have you been a bodyguard for anyone interesting?"

"Specialist."

"I beg your pardon?"

"We're called specialists."

I stretched another bite toward him in offering. He shook his head.

"Huh. Really?" I took another drink. "Have you been a specialist for anyone interesting? Elton John? Adele?"

"I can't disclose the names of any principals."

"Principals," I tested the word. "I'm learning so much. Is that what I am then?" I squared my shoulders as I said it again in a slightly deeper voice. "I am the principal."

He wasn't even looking at me. I watched him as he scanned the busy pub. "What are you looking for?" I asked mildly after another sip of my drink.

"Anything or anyone that is out of place," he answered as he continued to survey the busy restaurant, his profile stern but no less hot. No less exciting.

I shoved that distracting observation aside and took a slow, savoring bite, considering his words. The place was swarming with people of all variety. How could he determine if one of them shouldn't be here or was up to something nefarious? "And how can you tell that?"

"Experience, Ms. Mathers."

I considered him for a moment, waiting, hoping he might elaborate. Guess I wasn't going to get specifics then. Fine. I leaned back, dropping my napkin on the table. "I'm stuffed."

He scanned the room without looking at me and I felt a fresh stab of annoyance at finding myself in this situation—stuck with a man I didn't even know. My first-ever trip abroad wasn't supposed to be like this. I felt . . . constrained. Instead of seeing the world and having exciting new experiences, I was sitting across a table from a man who was better at ignoring me than any of my exes had been.

"I should warn you, you know."

The bar erupted into loud cheers again and his head turned in that direction, his eyes narrowing. "Warn me?" he asked vaguely as though he was not totally listening to me.

I reached for my handbag and dug out my wallet. "Yes." I dropped several bills on the table, more than enough to cover my meal, drinks and tip. "Don't fall in love with me."

His head whipped around to face me, and I found myself the subject of those blistering dark eyes. Yeah. He was listening to me, and it was immensely satisfying to see him so discomposed—and to have his full attention on me. "I beg your pardon?"

"Don't fall in love with me," I repeated. "I won't love you back."

He blinked. "Are you . . . joking?"

My expression threatened to slip. He didn't need to act so very appalled at the idea, even if I was making a joke. "I've seen *The Bodyguard*. Isn't that what always happens in the movies? The bodyguard falls in love with the woman he's protecting, and blah, blah, blah." I shook my head. "It's all so very predictable and cliché." Even if I did believe that kind of fairy tale existed, I was so *not* looking for it.

"I'm sure I wouldn't know."

I stared at his unflinching expression. This guy had absolutely *no* sense of humor. "You've never seen *The Bodyguard*? Whitney Houston? Kevin Costner?" At his lack of recognition, I tsked and shook my head. "You should rectify that."

He looked bewildered . . . and a little horrified. Clearly I wasn't being serious about the whole love thing, but he acted as though I was . . . he acted as though the prospect of loving me was so unpleasant.

Had he been talking to my ex-husbands?

I stood up from the table, my hands a little shaky as I reached for my bag. So far, he was epitomizing the stereotype of a stuffy Englishman. I strode from the pub, not caring if he followed but knowing he would. That was his job and he was unfortunately quite earnest about it. He was solemn like a soldier. And I was stuck with him.

Unless I managed to run him off.

I smiled slowly. Yeah. I could do that. I could make him miserable enough to quit. I knew all about that. I'd been married three times. I knew how to run men off. At least that's what my mother said. My mother, who was husbandless herself, claimed that I ran men off (or forced them to leave me) with my unreasonable expectations.

I left the pub and marched in the direction of my hotel. I felt his gaze burning hotly on the back of my neck as I passed my publisher's office. A quick glance over my shoulder confirmed he was still behind me, trailing me, dogging my heels like a bad cold I couldn't shake.

CHAPTER THREE

THE DOORMAN politely held the door open and I stepped into the blast of cool, gardenia-scented air from the lobby. My wedge heels thumped lightly over the tile floor.

Moretti moved ahead of me to catch the elevator before it closed, his big hand grabbing onto the edge of one of the sliding doors. With a nod at him, I stepped inside the space. He joined me.

I went to my corner and he occupied the opposite one—like two boxers in a ring, ready to engage at the sound of the bell. My lips twitched. Until I thought about how vastly outmatched I would be against him. I frowned then.

Even beneath his well-cut clothing, his muscles were a clear threat, hard and honed. There was also the fact that he had a good seven inches on me, and his shoulders looked like they could be used to effectively ram through a barrier. Maybe bulldozing capabilities were a requirement in his work.

It took everything in me not to look at him. From my peripheral view, I could tell he wasn't looking at me either. He was looking straight ahead.

The elevator opened to the fifth floor and I dove out, walking ahead of him, my footsteps biting into the carpet. This was a waste of my publisher's money. That conviction burned through me. This man could be out there protecting someone who needed protection. Not me.

I knew I probably looked ridiculous, my hips rolling as I race-walked. Believe it or not, I took a race-walking class at a local rec center years ago. I thought it might be a light and easy way to shed some weight. That was when Greg was on my case to lose weight—back in the days when I thought I needed to be a certain weight for a man to love me. Now I knew better. Now I didn't care about a number on a scale. I only cared about myself and what felt good to me.

I couldn't wait to get in my room and have some blessed privacy. A hot shower and some mindless television. Maybe I would order a bottle of wine from room service. Or champagne. I should be celebrating my first time out of the country. I should be doing something to mark the occasion other than feeling this . . . *annoyance.*

I had my key card ready in my hand. Fortunately it worked on the first try and I wasn't left fruitlessly swatting my card against the door. The light beeped green and I pushed the door open. Fixing a brave smile to my lips, I turned to face him. "Well. Goodnight."

He gave a brief nod, his gaze drifting somewhere over my shoulder. Then the unbelievable happened. He pushed past me into my room.

I gawked, struggling to find my voice, the will to do something, anything. Certainly this broke some kind of protocol. *Certainly* I did *not* have to tolerate this man in my hotel room.

I watched as he moved deeper into the room, inspecting the space with a sweep of his gaze. It was an elegantly appointed room. Nothing like the motel rooms where I had stayed at as a kid. The few times we ever went anywhere we stayed at motels with rooms that were accessed from the outside, à la the Bates Motel.

I could still only watch, my body rooted in place, keeping the door from closing. A closed door would be bad. It would seal us in together in a way that felt much too intimate for two people who had only just met. God. I didn't even know his first name. He was merely Moretti to me. Mr. Moretti.

He crossed the small living area, bypassing the sofa and leather armchair, striding to the window. He peered outside before pulling the drapes shut, making certain the edges met—as though even a sliver of space was an unacceptable amount of exposure.

Seemingly satisfied, he again passed through the living area and rounded the small couch, venturing into the single bedroom. *My* room where I'd tossed all my clothes from earlier—including the silk nightie.

After my last divorce, I started treating myself to nice things. Things that made *me* feel good. If that meant a vacation to the beach (Greg hated the sand), Pad Thai (Brent didn't like Thai food) or buying clothes for myself that weren't from a discount store (each one of my exes believed clothes should never cost more than their lunch), so be it.

Silk, I had discovered, felt like heaven against my skin. Better than any man had ever felt against me and that was the unfortunate truth. Or not so unfortunate because that realization had led me to this life of self-imposed singlehood and sudden notoriety combined with a level of financial security I had never known.

I didn't need the notoriety. I didn't desire celebrity status, but as it carried the benefit of fiscal independence, I would not turn my back on it.

As someone who grew up wearing hand-me-downs, I would never take financial security for granted.

I now had a life in which I was entirely at peace with myself. No. Not merely at peace. I was happy. Happy. God's-honest-truth-happy and I wasn't going to let some bogus threat diminish that.

I finally found my voice. A soft, strangled thing in my throat and mouth. "What are you doing?"

He didn't answer me. Just disappeared inside the bedroom.

I stepped forward, letting the door close behind me with a very final sounding snick.

I followed him, stopping on the threshold of the bedroom and observing him as he went to the window, moving with a predator-like gait. He looked out as he had before, and then pulled the drapes closed.

He flicked me a glance. "Keep the drapes closed."

I shook my head, marveling. What? Did he think there was a sniper out there waiting for me? Absurd.

He moved on into the bathroom. The obscured glass shower door clicked open and he investigated the shower's interior.

"What are you looking for?"

He stopped before me, reluctantly, it seemed, giving me his attention. "Standard protocol, ma'am."

"To inspect my room?"

He nodded once.

"You actually think someone could be hiding in here waiting for me?" I motioned behind me. "The door was locked."

"It would not take much to infiltrate a hotel room, or any residence, for that matter. If someone wants in badly enough, they can find a way."

I shook my head. "I appreciate that you're doing your job, but this level of . . . " I paused, searching for the right word. "Caution is not necessary."

He didn't argue, but I knew he disagreed. His actions conveyed that. He went back out into the main room and bolted the door I had failed to bolt behind us. He stopped for a moment and surveyed the room again—looking at what, I had no clue.

I inhaled through my nose, grasping for patience. "Isn't it time you go now?" I waved in the direction of the door. I didn't know where he was staying and I didn't care. I was ready for my privacy. Apparently I would only have that at night when I could get rid of him . . . at least until I managed to run him off. There was still that hope, that goal, nibbling at the fringes.

"Yes. Your room appears secure. Good night." He then strolled across the living area—not in the direction of the door. No, he kept walking a straight line until he arrived at the adjoining door. He unlocked it and swung it open to reveal that the door on the other side was already open.

I stared. Speechless.

I pointed accusingly at the neighboring room and marched closer, peering inside. It was a single room with no living area. A lone bag sat on the king bed. "Who . . . what . . . how?" I shook my head. "You've *got* to be kidding!"

"I checked in earlier today," he explained with a slight shrug. "Your publisher arranged for me to have the room next to you."

This is real? This is happening?

I have to share a space with a man? I never thought I would have to do that again. Never wanted to.

I suddenly felt claustrophobic.

"Wh—I . . . " Words eluded me. I could not believe such lengths had been taken for my safety. Presumably my publicist knew about this. Melani knew about this too.

Moretti waved at the adjoining room's doors. "I would prefer these doors remain open. I can get to you should you need me."

Indignation bristled from my every pore. I didn't need him. I wouldn't need him. "Oh? Would you prefer that?"

"If there is a situation—"

"A situation?" I sputtered. "Like what? "A tricky bottle of lotion I need help uncapping?"

"A threat," he amended.

A threat? I sighed. This was ridiculous. "You're fired."

He blinked at that. His only reaction. And then: "You can't fire me. I don't work for you."

I opened and closed my mouth several times, feeling helpless in the face of this truth. Helpless in a way I hadn't felt in a long time. Vulnerability was something I had banned from my life.

"Do you want to call your editor?" he inquired in an even voice, but it felt as though he was humoring me with the question. I already knew what Melani was going to say. He knew, too. No bodyguard = no tour.

"Fine," I snapped.

I could close the door to my bedroom and pretend he wasn't there on the other side. Just to show him how it was done I marched from the adjoining door and into my bedroom. Whirling around, I faced him, all of me vibrating in outrage. Staring across the distance at him, his stoic expression galled me. The guy was an emotionless robot.

My excitement at being here, at being on an international book tour and living my dream, took its last breath. Irrational or not, I blamed him. I knew it wasn't fair. I should blame the culprits who were sending me stupid hate mail and wrecking my signings.

Grasping the edge of the door, I swung it shut in his face with a resounding bang.

Childish. But it felt good. I felt in control.

I fell back against my door, releasing a huff of indignation.

So much for provoking him to quit. Ha. The only one who felt provoked right now was me.

A slow smile lifted my lips. With a devious little laugh, I made my way to the phone by my bed and dialed room service.

Someone answered promptly. "Good evening, Ms. Mathers. How may I assist you?"

"Um. Yes. Hello. I would like to order your menu."

"I beg your pardon? Do you mean you would like to order *from* the menu?"

"No, no. I would like to order one of *everything* on the menu and could you please send it to room 520. For Mr. Moretti. He has the room adjoining mine."

There was a pause and then: "That will take an hour."

"That's okay. My boo is starving."

"Very good, ma'am. We'll have that sent up as quickly as possible. Good evening."

"Good evening to you," I returned, feeling very pleased with myself. Humming lightly, I hung up the phone.

CHAPTER FOUR

I SHOWERED, availing myself of the luxury shampoo, conditioner, and body wash provided by the hotel.

Wrapped in a towel, I dried my dark hair with the blow dryer, letting the mid-length strands whip all around me while wondering if room service had arrived yet. Moretti was going to owe quite the tip. Grinning, I lathered moisture generously on my face. One thing Mama that taught me that I actually believed in was to moisturize.

I applied lotion to my face and neck, then up my arms, making sure to rub into my elbows. Once that was done, I propped a foot on the edge of the garden tub and applied to both my feet and legs.

Standing, I tightened the belt of my robe that had loosened around my waist and emerged into the bedroom. A quick glance confirmed my bedroom door was still closed. Not that I expected it to be open. I didn't peg him as the kind of guy to enter my room uninvited—at least not unless he heard gunfire.

Shaking my head, I snatched up the remote and turned on the television. I was browsing channels when I heard a distant knock. My pulse jumped as I jumped from the bed and crept to my door. Pressing an ear to it, I listened closely.

Another knock sounded and Moretti called out. "Coming."

My stomach heaved and I had a moment's doubt. Maybe I went too far? My first husband had a temper. This kind of thing would have sent Brent into fits. I was a naïve twenty-year-old when I married him. I didn't know any better. Now I knew to avoid men with short fuses.

Now I knew to avoid men.

Voices carried through the door. Muffled words I couldn't decipher. I heard the squeaking wheels of a cart and I assumed it was the food being rolled into his room.

A few minutes passed and then silence. Had the server left?

I pressed the side of my face deeper into the door as though that might somehow clue me in to what was happening on the other side.

"Oh!" I jumped as a knock resounded directly against my ear.

I pressed a hand against my racing heart and took a steadying breath, convinced I had just suffered a minor cardiac episode.

Shaking my hair back off my shoulders I opened the door wearing the most innocent expression I could manage. "Yes?"

Moretti stood there minus his jacket. He'd undone the top two buttons of his crisp white shirt, exposing the tanned column of his throat and an enticing patch of bare chest. My gaze lingered at the base of his throat and the pulse that seemed to be thrumming quickly against his skin there.

His gaze swept over me. "Your room service arrived."

"Room service?" I blinked innocently and peered around his shoulder. The door to his room yawned open and I could see across the sitting area inside his room to multiple trays of food. There had to be more beyond my vantage that I couldn't see. "Oh. I already ate dinner."

His dark eyes narrowed slightly. "You ordered the entire menu."

I fought back a grin. "I thought you might be hungry since you skipped dinner at the pub. A strapping bloke like you must keep up his strength. Especially in your line of work, I imagine."

His gaze held mine for a long moment and I waited for his anger, fully expecting it. "Thank you, Ms. Mathers. That was very thoughtful of you."

My smile slipped. *Thank you?* He wasn't annoyed with me?

"Ah. Yes, enjoy your dinner. Good night." Determined to not let him see I was annoyed at *his* lack of annoyance, I pasted a fresh smile on my face and closed the door on him.

As soon as the door shut, I got rid of my stupid smile and replaced it with a scowl. What didn't he understand? I was a pain in the ass and I planned on being *his* pain in the ass. He should be looking for a way out of this assignment.

Sighing, I brushed my teeth and got ready for bed. I left the bathroom light on and cracked the door. In lieu of a nightlight, it would have to do. Whenever I was in a hotel or a strange place, I always left the bathroom light on so that I wouldn't be totally submerged in darkness . . . it especially helped if I woke disoriented in the night.

Dropping my robe, I changed into my silk nightie, enjoying the way the fabric swished around my hips and thighs.

Turning off the TV, I moved to my shut door and pressed my ear against it one more time. Not a peep from him on the other side. He was probably in there enjoying his buffet. I'd have to come up with something better if I was going to get rid of him.

Pulling back the covers, I climbed into bed, sighing as my bare legs slid against the crisp sheets. It had been a long day. The nap I'd taken earlier to help recover from jet lag felt like a long time ago. I was exhausted.

In the near darkness, my mind slid into the fact that I was essentially sharing a hotel room with a man. It was something I had vowed would never happen again. *Men and me. Me and men.* Those two things weren't supposed to converge ever again.

After three divorces, I had learned my lesson. Only someone clinically insane would go there again. But here I was stuck with this guy, and all because my signing in D.C. had gotten out of hand.

Before I had been hustled into a back room, the man had knocked over a chair and become belligerent, calling me several colorful obscenities. It had been a little jarring, but I didn't need protection because of one freak incident.

My head was starting to ache, and I closed my eyes, rubbing lightly at the backs of my eyelids.

I was overtired. Sleep now. Later I could think.

I STOOD at the front of a crowd. Faces swam before my eyes. Blurred features zoomed in and out of focus. Mom was there. And Grandma. Both shaking their heads as I talked about things like sex and a woman's right to orgasms and independence—things no female in her right mind should ever discuss publicly, at least as far as they were concerned.

Then my exes were there, all three of them glaring at me in censure.

I faltered in my speech, but continued, asking the audience if they had any questions for me.

Suddenly the man from the Washington, D.C. tour stop stood up from the crowd and tossed a chair at me. My exes cheered and clapped. Even Mom and Grandma looked on in smiling approval—like I was getting what I deserved.

Another chair flew through the air, this one catching me and bringing me down. I scrambled out from under it and ran. He gave chase and then we weren't in the bookstore anymore. We were in a deep wood and he was thrashing through trees and bushes behind me. He was so close. Terror clogged my throat. And then he caught me. His hands were on me, and I was trapped in a real-life horror movie.

A scream burst from my lips. I fought. Punched, slapped, clawed, kicked with all I had.

Hard hands closed around my flailing wrists, restraining them, and I fought against the confinement. One of my hands broke free and I brought my palm cracking against my attacker's face.

Everything stilled in the echo of that slap. The current of it rippled up my arm and through me like electricity.

Then my hand was reclaimed and suddenly both my arms were pinned against the mattress on either side of my head. The long length of him splayed over me, strong thighs straddling me, holding me in place.

I twisted and tried to buck his weight off me, but he was heavy. A solid immovable mass.

"Easy, there." A deep voice spoke above me. "You're all right. You're safe."

I blinked. That voice did not sound like it belonged in a horror movie. It sounded . . . British and soothing.

"Ms. Mathers!"

I blinked several more times. Suddenly I wasn't in the woods anymore.

No. It was worse than that.

I was on a bed, on my back, shrouded in gloom with a man over me.

I whimpered, bewildered, disoriented.

And then I remembered where I was and who was restraining me on the bed.

It all clicked together in my mind like a key and lock coming together. I had a nightmare and I was in bed with my bodyguard. Or rather he was in my bed.

So much for not being affected by what happened in D.C. I swallowed back a sob.

"Sssh. It's all right. You're safe. Everything is going to be okay." One of his hands released my wrist and smoothed over my forehead and into my hair. It felt good. I didn't want it to, but that nightmare was still plaguing me, and his touch felt so damn good.

I buried my face in his neck, forgetting myself and accepting the comfort he was providing. It had been a long time since another human held me—and never had anyone promised me that everything was going to be okay. Not my mother or grandmother. Not any of my exes. And maybe it was something no person could guarantee, but it was nice to hear someone say it. It was nice that someone thought I was important enough to deserve comfort and protection.

I wrapped my free arm around his shoulder, absorbing that he was not wearing a shirt. His skin felt warm and firm and smooth under my touch. I splayed my fingers wide, reveling in the way his back muscles flexed under my palm and the press of each finger, like steel under satin.

His heavy body pushing me down into the mattress felt amazing. I liked the weight of him. My legs widened instinctively, welcoming him deeper into the cradle of my body. And that's when I felt it. He was hard. Full-on erection hard and it felt . . . impressive. Massive. I whimpered and wiggled against it, trying to get it in the right spot against my aching clit.

I opened my lips against him, breathing in his skin—man and soap and pheromones. It was a stimulating mix that I couldn't remember inhaling before. You would think I knew such a smell. I'd been with three men, after all, but never had I inhaled such a heady combination.

I moved my lips, brushing them over the mouthwatering skin of his neck and a tremor rocked him, vibrating through me. I couldn't help myself. My tongue darted out for a taste.

He groaned and I opened my mouth wider, sucking on his neck.

He responded, driving his erection against my sex. I cried out. It was both stimulating and frustrating because of the barrier of my underwear and his briefs.

I dragged my lips down to where his neck met his shoulder and sank my teeth into his skin.

He gasped, thrusting against me again.

His fingers speared through the thick mass of my hair, the pads of his fingers pressing into my scalp and melting my bones. The action stirred up the scent of my shampoo. Pears wafted around us. A soundless sigh coursed through me.

"Christ," he muttered, his accent thicker, deeper, a little less cultivated. He pumped his hips once more, grinding his cock into my soaking-wet panties. "You smell so good . . . feel good."

I shuddered at his words. They were the first from him that sounded personal. Intimate. Not robotic. They were coming from the man, not the specialist.

I was so close. I pushed up against him, seeking that pressure. Needing it like I needed air.

"God," he choked. "You're so wet."

I arched my neck, purring like a cat and settling my scalp deeper into the cradle of his hand. "I'm sorry I hit you."

I flattened my fingers over the planes of his cheek tenderly. His skin felt warm under my fingers and I hoped it wasn't from the burn of my slap. I'd never slapped another living soul, but I'd struck him. I stroked his cheek as though in apology.

He stilled for a long moment, and then he was suddenly peeling my hand off him as though it were something diseased. He leapt off me, landing lightly on the carpet beside my bed. "No worries, Ms. Mathers."

I flinched and expelled a shuddery breath. And just like that, we had returned to formality. Sitting up on the bed, I smoothed my nightie back down over my hips with shaking hands.

He continued, "I'm glad I was here to . . . "

"To save me from a nightmare?" I finished, nodding jerkily.

"Yes. I heard you scream."

I winced. Had the entire hotel heard me? He probably thought I was being murdered. "Sorry about that." Clearly the thing that happened in D.C. bothered me more than I wanted to admit to myself. Or to anyone. But now he knew. Now he knew I wasn't as tough and invulnerable as I pretended.

I winced again. Now *I* knew I was pretending.

I tugged down on my nightie again, trying to make the fabric cover more of my thighs than possible.

"As I said, it's not a problem. Ms. Mathers." Ugh with the Ms. Mathers again. "It's okay. You were scared."

Scared? No. I did not do "scared". Not around anyone else anyway. His words left me feeling . . . *seen* in a way I did not like.

I tucked my hair behind my ear. This was *all* very much a problem. This guy had just nearly made me combust. I was still trying to climb back into my skin. And he was *still* here. Standing beside my bed half naked in his skivvies. Yes, this was a problem. *My* problem.

I tried not to gawk, but he was hard *not* to take in. The bathroom light illuminated his silhouette. A boulder-size lump lodged itself in my throat as I scanned him up and down. His body was clearly built for utility. He was indeed a protector. A weapon to be wielded. The broad shoulders and bulging biceps and defined pecs and ridged abdomen veeing down to a narrow waist were primed for defense . . . among other things.

My mouth dried as my gaze dropped to rest on the not so insignificant bulge in his briefs. God. I could still feel it pushing insistently against my sex. *No no no no no.* I didn't require protection or any of those *other* things from a man. Even one that looked like him.

I could handle everything just fine by myself.

"I'm fine now. You can go back to bed. Thank you."

A long pause. He still stood there in his skivvies. With that bulge I couldn't stop staring at. I did the only thing I could in that face of it. I rolled over and presented him with my back. "Good night."

"Good night, Ms. Mathers," he said softly, and now I was grateful for that formality—for the reminder that what we had was professional and not personal. Not intimate.

I listened as his muffled steps faded away.

———

I WOKE before my alarm went off. I didn't have any more nightmares, fortunately. I'd slept like the dead, dreamlessly and deep.

I turned my phone alarm to silent so it did not have a chance to go off, and then just remained sprawled in the bed for a few moments, rubbing my eyes awake with the heels of my palms. Murky light crept in around the edges of the drapes and the bathroom light still offered its sliver of illumination, but otherwise my room was still comfortingly shrouded in gloom.

I didn't have anything to do until later in the afternoon, but it didn't appear as though I was going to fall back asleep. Once that was determined, I flung back the covers and padded to the bathroom. I brushed my teeth and swept my hair up into a ponytail. I didn't bother with makeup. Right now the thought of coffee, orange juice and some manner of lavish breakfast beckoned.

I exited the bathroom as stealthily as possible. Not too difficult on carpet and with bare feet. I dressed quickly, tossing my nightie to the bed. I slipped on loose drawstring pants and my favorite comfy sweatshirt with the words Schrute Farms scrawled across my chest. It was definitely my stay-at-home-and-lounge-all-day-wear.

I could call room service for breakfast, but that would take forever. It would be quicker to go downstairs myself. Shoes on and handbag slung over my shoulder, I eased open my bedroom door and peered out, holding my breath as though he might hear even that. He was a bodyguard, after all.

The small living area was dark for whatever reason—maybe the drapes were thicker and less light crept into the room from the window. His door was still open. Of course. He hadn't closed it last night after rescuing me from my nightmare. My face burned hot at the memory of that. The light of day did not spare me from or lessen that embarrassment. I was not eager to face Moretti after he had very nearly launched me into orgasm. The entire incident was mortifying. Especially considering *he* had been the one to end it. *He* had been the one to come to his senses. Not me. I would have merrily gone ahead and fucked him.

The sound of a shower running alerted me to the fact that I wasn't the only one awake early. He was in the shower, which meant this was the perfect time to take off. Less worried about the noise I made, I propelled myself through the door and out into the hall.

The dining room was fairly empty this early, and I soon had my food.

I ended up ordering a traditional English breakfast replete with fried eggs, back bacon, sausages, mushrooms, beans, grilled tomatoes, and buttered toast. It was lavish and decadent and probably a million calories, but I did not care. I stopped counting calories right about the time I left Charlie.

I took a hearty bite and chased it with a sip of orange juice. I was halfway through my plate when I spotted Moretti in the threshold of the restaurant. He did a quick scan and then his eyes landed on me, narrowing faintly.

I lifted my coffee cup in salute to him and called cheerfully, "Mr. Moretti! Join me. Would you like some coffee?" I motioned for the waitress to bring another cup. There was plenty of steaming coffee left in the carafe.

He sank down in the chair across from me. For a big man, he moved with grace and ease. He set his hand on the table, his long fingers splayed on the surface in idle repose, and yet he emanated an air that was the exact opposite of calm and relaxed. For all his silence and stillness, he brought to mind an animal ready to spring at provocation. Last night I had felt his strength and power as he had pinned me down. I reached for my juice, suddenly desiring a sip of something cool and sweet.

A waitress deposited a coffee cup in front of him. "Can I get you something to eat, love?"

His gaze flicked to the food spread before me and I tensed, ready for some judgy remark about the bounteous amount of food. Instead, he said, "I'll have what she's having."

Thank goodness he wasn't one of those boiled eggs with a side of fruit kind of men. I thought he might be, given the lack of body fat on his person. He could probably do with two English breakfast platters.

"Very good." The waitress nodded distractedly and looked to the doors. A large family with rowdy children had just entered.

"Thank you," he murmured as she departed.

I watched his hands lift the carafe and pour himself coffee. He dropped in several cubes of sugar into his cup. An odd thing. I couldn't help think a no-nonsense man like him wouldn't need to sweeten his coffee. With a quick stir, he settled back in his chair, bringing the cup to his lips for a slow sip.

He settled his dark eyes on me. "You left without alerting me."

I arched an eyebrow. Suddenly, I realized he was mad. This was him mad . . . which wasn't that different from him *not* mad. It was very nearly imperceptible. A subtle tension on the air. His voice remained even and composed. He was a little more broody, but that was it.

I stabbed at a sausage. I'd stayed in the hotel. It wasn't as though I took off to a restaurant across town. "I'm not required to report my comings and goings to anyone." It had been a long time since I lived under my mother's roof—and four years since I had last been married. I was my own person now and that wasn't going to change.

He traced the edge of his cup and I followed the slow movement of that finger, imagining it trailing over my skin. "You need to let me know when you're going somewhere."

I snapped my gaze back to his face. We stared at each other for a long spell in silent battle. Several colorful replies danced at the tip of my tongue, but I miraculously refrained. Readjusting my grip on the fork and knife in my hands, I vigorously sawed into the sausage I had pinned with my fork. "I was hungry. I did not think I needed permission to eat breakfast."

"You don't. Of course."

I ate a bit of grilled tomato, chewing thoughtfully.

He leaned forward slightly in his seat, his fingers setting a soundless

staccato rhythm on the table's surface. The motion seemed somehow . . . agitated. *I* was agitating *him*. The realization made me smile.

"Do I . . . annoy you, Mr. Moretti?"

His nostrils flared a fraction. "Of course not."

"Hm." I picked up my toast, letting the corner of bread drag along
my bottom lip.

His gaze dropped to my mouth.

"I'm here to accompany you," he said tightly, the sound of his voice
oddly strained. "Where you go, I go. I can be useful. Let me be. Last
night—"

"Last night won't happen again." Heat flushed through me. I did not
think he would be so bold as to mention last night. I wanted to believe it
had been an aberration instead of proof of my vulnerability. He probably
thought I was randy and his for the taking. "I don't usually have nightmares," I rushed to add. And I didn't usually react like an oversexed
divorcee immediately following them when I did.

"But you did have a nightmare." His gaze roamed my face. "What
was it about?"

I wasn't about to tell him.

I looked down at my food, arranging and rearranging it until I had
the perfect forkful—a combination of fried egg, sausage, and tomato. I
chewed and then took a bite of buttered toast. "This is really good."

Something flickered in his eyes as I savored my food. Just a ripple of
something and then it was gone. His dark eyes returned to their normal
obscurity.

The waitress returned and placed his food before him. He wasted
no time tucking in. He didn't savor it with same enthusiasm I did, but he
ate with such whole-hearted focus that I knew he approved of his food.
Even though he started after me, we finished at the same time.

I leaned back in my chair, finishing my coffee.

He wiped his lips with his napkin and looked back up at me. "Do
you have plans today beyond the agenda I received from your publicist?"

"I thought I would pack and get ready for the event this afternoon
before catching the train this evening." I didn't feel up to visiting all the
sights on my wish list with him beside me. That would feel too intimate.
Like we were friends. Like he wasn't someone hired to be with me.

"We're not taking the train."

"I beg your pardon?"

"The train is too crowded. Too many unknown variables. It's safer to drive."

Unknown variables?

I set my coffee cup down. "I have a reservation—"

"I've already cleared this with your publisher. I will be driving you to Edinburgh. It's only a few more hours by car."

I was seething. Now we were doing a road trip together? He was fully entrenched in my life. "Any other surprises you want to spring on me?"

He continued, "Does it really matter how you get where you need to be as long as you get there?"

Did he have to sound so very reasonable?

I breathed in and out of my nose. What mattered was that a man was calling the shots in my life. Again. That was intolerable. You would think Melani would know that. She had edited my book, after all.

I dropped my napkin on the table and pushed back my chair, ready to stand, ready to escape. Even if I couldn't.

Even if I was stuck with him and the completely confusing way he made me feel. I alternately wanted to run from him and climb him. Yeah. Totally confusing.

"I'm sure you can handle the bill. You seem to be handling everything else." Except my orgasm. He'd failed on that score last night, ending about ten seconds too soon when he suddenly remembered that we weren't supposed to boink. "I'm going to get ready and pack."

He nodded as though he had come up with that idea himself. "Yes, I'll take care of that, I'd like for us to get on the road as soon as your event ends."

I stood without giving him the courtesy of acknowledgement. I wasn't in the mood for courtesy right now. Not when things felt so very out of my control.

CHAPTER FIVE

THE LIBRARY WAS PACKED. Over a hundred people were arranged before me in chairs. It was a relief, of course, and I could breathe a little easier. An empty house was always a niggling worry for an author, especially when it was your first book stop on a publisher-sponsored book tour. You wanted a full house.

The library's event coordinator had requested that I perform a short reading. Perform wasn't really the right word, although I did feel as though I was putting on a show. Reading words I wrote four years ago as I was reeling from divorce number three and flitting through varying states of numbness, shock, and rage always felt a little strange now that I was content with myself and my life. I suppose I asked for this though, when I sat down and starting writing.

It definitely felt as though I was on exhibit, broken open and exposed, as I stood before the crowd reading a passage.

" . . . in the aftermath of my marriage, I did not feel alone. Someone else was there beside me. It was me. Just a memory at first. Then a shadow that grew and took form into the girl who used to dance alone in her room, who read Sherlock Holmes late into the night without a care that the light from her bedside lamp might wake her husband at any moment . . . who ordered cheese pizza *with* mushrooms because that was the way *she* liked it. It was me again and I had missed this girl. A lot. I was glad to have her back."

I closed the copy of my book with a muffled thud and faced my audience. For a long moment no one said anything. No one moved, and then a woman clutching my book to her chest timidly lifted her hand slowly in the air.

I nodded at her. "Yes?"

One of the library's staff rushed over to her with a microphone. She cleared her throat. "I just wanted to say I really enjoyed your book and I was hoping I could ask you a question."

I nodded. "Of course."

For some reason a movement in the back caught my attention. Moretti stood there, easing against a column. He scanned the room almost casually, appearing unaware of my words or me.

It was deceptive, of course, because he was not casual at all and he was aware of *everything*. He was on the job. He was wholly aware of our surroundings, and that included me. I could only hope, however futile, that he hadn't been listening closely as I read out loud. I felt rather insecure knowing he had been listening. Absurd, of course. They were words I had put out there for all the world to feast upon. Anyone could read them. Perfect strangers *did* read them. Sure. When I started writing the book it had just been something for me alone, an exercise in self-indulgence, but once it became published it no longer belonged to me. It belonged to the world. It belonged to every reader.

I fixed my attention on the nervous woman before me.

"What do the initials V.M. stand for?" she asked.

Of course it was a question I was not inclined to answer.

I smiled to soften my rejection. "V.M. Mathers is my name."

"But they are initials."

"Yes," I acknowledged, determined to leave it at that. My name wasn't up for public consumption. There was a reason I went by Vee. I wasn't about to put the name my mother gave me on the cover of a book. I'd been harassed enough over it as a child. I did not need to endure it as an adult, too.

The woman took a breath and moved on to another question. "Are you really happy being single forever? I mean . . . do you *never* want to meet someone and fall in love?"

All eyes fastened on me, waiting for my answer.

"But I have fallen in love. With myself. I like myself in a way I never did when I was married. It wasn't until I was single and on my own that I finally flourished."

Several women in the audience nodded as though they commiserated.

The woman asking the question persisted. "But what if the perfect man, your soul mate exists, and he's out there waiting for you?"

I scoffed. "Fairytales. The kind we've been fed all our lives." More nods in the audience. "If we're good enough, sweet enough, patient and obedient little girls, our Prince Charming will arrive and save us. Well, I say wait no more. I say save yourselves." I shrugged. "I don't need a man to be whole. I don't need a man to be happy. I don't need a man to—"

"Orgasm!" a woman cried out.

The audience cheered and clapped and hooted at the interruption. It was probably the most commotion to ever occur inside this library.

I chuckled. "I believed we've now moved on to chapter eight." Smiling, I gave a slight shake of my head. It was the chapter everyone wanted to talk about at these things. "But this is true. Three marriages and I never had satisfaction. No orgasms. Not like what I have now at my own hand. A woman does not need a man for sexual fulfillment."

Applause.

My face heated even though I had spoken on this topic at several gatherings. You could take the girl out of the small town, but you couldn't take the small town out of the girl. It always felt strange to admit such a thing in front of strangers—in front of an audience no less than a hundred deep. But again, I had asked for this when I wrote about such private matters. That anyone cared about my thoughts and opinions still left me in awe. For so much of my life my voice had not been heard or appreciated when I asserted it. Now I was heard, and unbelievable as it seemed, I was helping other women take control of their own lives and bodies and pleasure. Any small amount of embarrassment was worth that.

My face was still uncomfortably warm as my gaze moved over the audience, seeking him again. This time Moretti wasn't scanning the room. He was looking directly at me with his alert eyes, his frame rigid as stone.

There was no mistaking that he had been listening to me. He had heard every one of my words.

A woman does not need a man for sexual fulfillment.

His dark eyes drilled into me as though challenging me . . . challenging my words. As impassive as his expression remained, I felt his incredulity, his disbelief.

Several hands flew up in the air during my pause. I looked away from him and called on a young woman sitting in the front row.

She straightened in her chair and pushed her glasses up her nose. "Uh, Yes. First thank you for your book. It was revelatory to me." I smiled at her. "I want to know though . . . how hard was it to leave your husband? To leave everything you had?"

I nodded slowly. Each time a marriage ended it had been hard, but the last time was the one in which I had unequivocally walked away. I'd left him. My first two marriages, I'd been the dumpee, because I still hadn't figured out how to put myself first—I still didn't love myself. Charlie had been different though.

My third marriage was the one *I* left. I'd decided I'd had enough and that I deserved more. Better. Charlie had a hard time accepting we were over. He'd wanted to cling to our union, glaring defects and all.

"It was hard. But no harder than staying. It's better to be happy alone than miserable with someone." For some reason my gaze drifted to Moretti again. He stared back at me, his gaze inscrutable.

"Blasphemer!"

The audience turned and twisted, searching for the source of the outraged voice. He wasn't hard to locate. I might have noticed him sooner if I hadn't been so attuned to where Moretti was in the audience.

He stood at the back, near the doors to the library's entrance. He was an older man, holding several books in his hands as though he had just checked them out from the library. That happened sometimes. Occasionally, when the venue was at a library, people checking out books stopped out of curiosity to listen to me speak. The library was still open to patrons even as they hosted my event.

This guy wasn't going to buy my book. He had not come to hear me speak, but he had heard me talking. He had heard and he was not impressed. That was his right. But it was not his right to hurl insults at me.

"Jezebel! Harlot! You speak filth." And then he quoted Exodus, "' . . . your desire shall be for your husband, and he shall rule over you!'" He gestured to the crowd. "Do not taint these souls with your wickedness. They may yet be saved."

He advanced, swiping a hand through the air as though he would slice me in half. There was a mad light in his eyes. A zealousness I had seen before. My second father-in-law was particularly avid in his political views. There was no middle of the road for him, and if anyone said anything contrary to his beliefs he would go off like a bomb. His eyes would get all glassy and bright and I would find an excuse to leave the room whenever he erupted like that.

Suddenly Moretti was there. He moved quickly, blocking the angry man from my view and murmuring something that silenced him. With a minimum of fuss, Moretti escorted the gentleman away, looking so damn hot in the process that I felt a little out of breath. As though *I* had been the one dispensing the man. Moretti was good. He'd diffused the situation before it could even become a . . . *situation*.

I exhaled, my pulse steadying at my neck. I was grateful I didn't have to hear him spouting his poison anymore.

A few people sent lingering looks back to the rabble-rouser. Most returned their attention to me, however. I tucked shaking hands into the pockets of my dress and refocused my attention on the crowd with a smile fixed to my face.

It irked me to realize that Melani had been right. I had been wrong.

Moretti was useful, even necessary. I actually *needed* this man's presence in my life, and he knew that. I had determined to never need another a man in my life, but in this instance, I did. I could be in danger. That incident in D.C. was not an isolated event.

Moretti returned, standing at the back of the crowd. My gaze locked with his, and warmth suffused my chest, spreading outward beneath his steady and intense regard. I felt a connection to him in that moment. And maybe . . . trust. I didn't hate that he was here. I was actually kind of glad. He would keep me safe.

CHAPTER SIX

As soon as I finished autographing books, we thanked the library staff and left the building. I shouldn't say *we*. Moretti merely stood at my side like the hulking bodyguard he was. He didn't speak. I did all the talking and when we left the building, he took my elbow and guided me to his vehicle in silence.

We left the city limits of London behind as dusk settled. He drove us north, one hand in a relaxed grip on the steering wheel. For the first hour I avoided looking at him. I just stared at that hand and out the window at the passing scenery.

"Are you hungry?"

"Not yet." My enormous breakfast was still holding me over.

"Maybe when I stop for petrol, we can get a bite to eat then."

"That sounds fine."

My phone started ringing from my handbag at my feet. I retrieved it, noting the caller. Mom. "Excuse me. I need to take this."

He gave a brief nod of acknowledgement as I answered the call. "Hey, Mom. It's like . . . midnight there. Everything okay?"

"Verna Mae," Mom greeted me, ignoring my question and getting directly to her own. "Why haven't you called me?"

I winced at the sound of the ridiculous name she had given me. It was a family name she had wanted to carry on, but there were some names that shouldn't be recycled. Names that got your kid relentlessly bullied should be put to rest.

"I texted when I landed, Mom."

"How do I know that was you? You could have been picked up by some sex trafficker at the airport like in that movie *Taken*. We should have a code word for when you text me so that I know it's really you."

"Mom, you're being paranoid."

She ignored my comment. "When are you coming home?"

"I emailed you my itinerary so you would have it."

"I never check my email. Just tell me."

"In two weeks. Please check your email."

"Brent called me."

I stilled at her blunt announcement. I hadn't heard directly from my first ex-husband in ages, but I knew through the grapevine that he was not a fan of *Self Love*. "Well, I hope you didn't speak with him." Brent might be the worst that humanity had to offer. After I worked two jobs to put him through college, he dumped me for the physician assistant who treated him in the emergency room at the local hospital for alcohol poisoning the morning after the Super Bowl.

"Of course I did. I couldn't be rude. He's furious about the book, Verna Mae. His wife is threatening to leave him."

Did Mom really expect me to care that the woman Brent left me for was upset with him? I imagined she spent a lot of her time being upset with him and it had nothing to do with my book or me. I should know.

Brent loved boozing it up with his buddies and playing softball with his buddies and watching sports with his buddies. Everything he did involved his buddies. The guy was stuck in high school and I actually felt sorry for the physician assistant because I knew the life she was living.

Mom continued, "He said his friends are laughing at him. I told you the book was a terrible idea."

"A terrible idea that paid off your house."

"He said he's consulting a lawyer."

I sighed. "He was never specifically named." My publisher's legal team and I discussed at length how to protect me from liability. I never said anything untrue. Nor did I ever cite anyone by name. Still, I would rather not be dragged into court to defend myself.

"You should still apologize to him and help smooth things over."

"Are you serious? Apologize to him? After everything he put me through?" I shook my head. It amazed me how many times my mom sided with my exes. As far as she was concerned, I was to blame for the collapse of every one of my marriages.

"Verna Mae, this book is causing quite the stir and embarrassing our family and friends—"

"Brent is not my family or friend." That ship pretty much sailed when I caught him in the backseat of his truck with the PA.

The car in front of us suddenly hit their brakes. Moretti's arm shot across my body as though my seat belt wasn't enough protection. "Hold on," his deep voice rumbled.

We slowed down as the traffic reduced to a crawl.

"Who is that? Verna Mae? Is that a man? Do you have a man with you?" Outrage mingled with glee in my mother's voice, and I know the outrage was at being kept in the dark over a potential man in my life. My mother wanted nothing more than for me to find another man. That was the glee I heard. It didn't matter that I had three failed marriages. As far as Mom was concerned, I would never be a success unless I had a man front and center in my life.

I closed my eyes in a tight blink. "Yes. It's a man."

"Who?" At my silence, she demanded louder, "WHO?"

I shook my head. "No one, Mom."

"Did you meet someone?"

"No, Mom." I slid a mortified look at the man driving beside me. He stared straight ahead, his expression unflinching. "I have to go now."

"Don't you dare hang up without telling me who you've got with you."

"He's my . . . handler."

"Handler?" Mom echoed. I could hear the bewilderment in her voice. "Is that some kind of sex thing?"

"Mom," I sputtered. "No. He's in charge of escorting me places on my tour over here."

"Oh." Mom sounded clearly disappointed. Clearly she wished it had been some kind of sex thing.

"I really do need to go now." I sent another quick glance to the silent man beside me. He was a block of stone, but there was no way he had not heard the exchange. This close to me, he probably heard everything my mother had said too. God. That was a mortifying thought.

"Fine," Mom grumbled. "You should take a minute to apologize to Brent though."

Uh. Yeah. Not happening.

I shook my head but didn't bother to disagree. It would only lengthen the conversation. An apology was an acknowledgment of wrongdoing, and I had certainly never done anything wrong to Brent. I wasn't saying I was perfect, but I had spent enough of my life apologizing for one thing or another. I wasn't apologizing for telling the truth and trying to help other women avoid my mistakes.

Hanging up, I let my head fall back on the headrest and looked back out the window. The fading sunlight cast the rolling hills in soft gold.

After a few minutes of driving, he spoke up beside me, his deep voice filling the vacuum. "I couldn't help but overhear."

Of course he couldn't help overhearing. The vehicle three cars up from us probably heard my mother.

Fighting a sigh, I rolled my head and turned to look at him. "Yes?"

"You have an angry ex, I take it?"

I considered that for a moment. "Apparently, yes."

He continued to stare straight ahead. "He doesn't care for your book?"

"Apparently he's embarrassed over a few things I wrote."

"What's his name?"

I hesitated. I'd trained myself to be cautious. I had been careful ever since the beginning of my publication journey to never mention my exes directly by name—partly to protect myself from liability but also because my new life had nothing to do with them.

"Why do you want to know that?"

"To run a check on him, of course. See if he's in the country or—"

"You think he would come here?" I interrupted.

"You've received threats—"

"Not from him."

"Do you know that for a fact?"

I looked out the window again with a huff, not answering. I *knew*, but, of course, I did not *know*. I did not have any proof except my knowledge of Brent. I knew there was no way he would hop on a plane to confront me on my book tour in England. He didn't care *that* much, and he would never leave the country. He thought every place outside the US was too dangerous.

When we'd been together, and I had talked about going to Europe or other dream locations like New Zealand or Iceland or Bora Bora, he shook his head at me as though I were suggesting a trip to the moon.

"It's fairly standard," he continued.

Standard? Nothing about any of this was standard for me.

"His name is Brent Segal and you can go ahead and run your check. You'll see. There's no way he would get on a plane and come here. Honestly, he's too lazy."

"I see." Without another word, he reached inside his jacket and pulled out his phone.

I watched curiously as he punched a key and held the phone up to his ear. He didn't greet the person who answered, merely dove directly into his crisp dialogue. "I need you to look up a Brent Segal, American. Yes. His location and recent travel. All the usual data." He murmured something of assent. "Yes. Thanks, Tandy."

He ended the call with Tandy (I had a vision of Moneypenny somewhere clicking at a keyboard making magic happen) and tucked his phone back away.

I stared at him for several moments, grappling with my bewilderment—and thinking he would turn to me with some explanation. After a few more moments of nothing happening, I asked, "What was that?"

He shot me a bland glance. "What was . . . what?"

"You can pick up the phone and get information on anyone you want?" I snapped my fingers for illustration. "Just like that?"

He lifted a single shoulder. "My agency has resources."

"Corps Security," I said, recalling the name of his agency from Melani.

"Yes."

"What are you? Like MI6?"

He snorted. "You watch too many movies. Corps Security is not a government agency."

"So you weren't in the military? You act like a soldier." Or ex-soldier.

"And how does a soldier act?"

I shrugged. "You seem . . . fit." Did I just say that? It reflected an awareness of his person that I did not wish to project. "Like you're used to running five miles before breakfast and eating MREs."

"Definitely too many movies," he repeated with a soft laugh.

"You weren't military, then?"

After a lengthy pause, he admitted. "I was."

"Aha!" I stabbed a finger in the air triumphantly.

"I served in the SAS."

"And what is that?"

"It's a special forces unit of the army."

He was right. I didn't know anything about this kind of thing. The extent of my knowledge was what I gleaned from movies. I'd have to look up the SAS on my phone when he wasn't next to me. "So now you're working private security. I guess that's more . . . stable. Probably less dangerous. Good for a family."

"Do I strike you as a family man?"

"I couldn't say." I shrugged like I wasn't curious. I didn't see a wedding ring, but that didn't mean he didn't have a girlfriend. God, I hoped he was single. I'd feel guilty about last night otherwise. I'd made plenty of mistakes in my past, but I'd never been an adulterer.

"I don't have a family. At least no wife and kids."

Whew. "No? Well, take it from me. You're not missing anything." I winced then. That didn't come out quite right.

"Ah. That's right. The jaded divorcee."

"I'm not jaded." I shook my head. Of course I had heard that allegation before. Men who didn't like what my book stood for. Critics who would never bother to actually read it. The world was full of them.

"Your talk this afternoon. It was interesting."

I fought back a blush. I talked about orgasms in front of people all the time. I could have this discussion with one person. Even if that person happened to be a good-looking guy that had climbed in bed with me last night and brought me right up to the brink. "Apparently not everyone finds it interesting."

"Yes. That gentleman I escorted out from the library took exception."

"A vast number of women appreciate what I have to say."

"'A woman does not need a man for sexual fulfillment'," he quoted.

To hear my words flung back at me in his deep British voice mortified. "Are you mocking me, Mr. Moretti?"

"Not at all."

"It sounds like you are."

"I work for you. It's not my job to sit in judgment. I have no opinions."

"Ha." I crossed my arms. "Said no one ever. Don't try to act like you're some kind of brainless hired muscle. I see the way you scope out every situation for potential threats. Your mind is going a mile a minute, so I know you have opinions."

"Even if I did—"

"You do."

He cut me a glance and my smile widened.

"I'm paid to keep them to myself," he finished.

And that was strangely disappointing. I wanted him to open up—to talk to me. It would be nice to know some of the thoughts behind the gorgeous façade.

I swallowed, tracking my gaze over his thick wrists up his forearms and biceps and shoulders. The jacket he was wearing disguised nothing. I knew what he looked like underneath. At least from the waist up. I could still see him in my mind standing in the gloom at the edge of my bed last night.

I shifted in my leather seat, suddenly uncomfortable. I felt a heavy pulse between my thighs. I crossed and uncrossed and crossed my legs, tugging at the hem of my dress as it rode above my knees with my movements. I should have changed into yoga pants for the drive.

Keep it together, Mathers.

He might not have a wife, but he probably had a girlfriend. When he was done playing protector for the day, he was probably getting in bed with her.

I could easily visualize him tossing his jacket aside and stripping off his shirt. I didn't know if he had a sexy back, but I was guessing he did. Broad at the top with valleys and rises of sinew and muscle tapering to a narrow waist. I envisioned that back and his bare ass, tight and firm, wedging between some anonymous woman's thighs.

I squeezed *my* thighs against the sudden clenching in my core and tried to will the sensation away. I could draw on this fantasy later, when I was alone. That would be better anyway. I knew that for a fact. Sure, he was hot, but that didn't mean he could deliver. He'd come close, but it was doubtful it would have happened. It never did. I knew all about the failure to fulfill.

Men simply didn't know how to get women off. I should know. I'd had three men and none could manage it. Just another reason I had sworn off men. I didn't need them emotionally and I definitely didn't need them for physical gratification. I'd become very proficient at achieving my own releases.

"Do you disagree with me?" I asked, pushing to get to his opinion. "You think women need men?"

"That seems like a loaded question. Nothing I say here is going to be right."

"So you're just going to avoid—"

"People need people," he declared. "We're not meant to be solitary creatures."

Frowning, I sank deeper in my seat. "Well. I've been alone for four years, and I've quite enjoyed it."

Defensiveness lifted off me and swelled in the air around us. We drove along in silence until he said, "My apologies if I've offended. You did ask."

I blinked at the suddenness of his voice beside me and cleared my throat. "Not at all. You can think as you like. I speak my truth the way I see it. You should speak yours."

We drove for several more miles without conversation. Then, he asked, "How did you come to marry three times?"

I inhaled deeply. It was a question put to me several times from different people.

"It boggles the mind, does it not?" I nodded, allowing that. "I often ask myself the same question. How could I be so stupid?"

"You're not stupid. That's obvious to anyone who talks to you for more than thirty seconds."

I absorbed that, letting it make me feel better about myself. Admittedly, it felt good to hear him say such a thing. It felt good knowing he'd thought about me enough to form this assessment.

"I was searching for something," I admitted. "Something outside of myself."

When I left my third ex, I had reached this point of clarity. Unfortunately it took three failed relationships for me to realize I had been going about my life all wrong—that I had been looking outside of myself—in others—for happiness, for a sense of completion. Now I knew what I had done wrong. I wouldn't be that needy person again.

I hadn't sworn off men forever. Just for the rest of my life.

"And what was it you were searching for?"

I shook my head, not really wanting to get into it too deeply with him. And yet I heard myself saying, "I don't think it exists."

"What?" he pressed.

"Happiness. Contentment. A perfect love. Of course, it's a mistake looking outside of one's self for those things."

He shrugged. "Well, you're right about *perfect* not existing, but I don't know. I think happiness and contentment can be had with someone else."

"*With* someone, yes. I don't dispute that. But another person can't solve your dissatisfaction or unhappiness, and that was my mistake."

"Doesn't mean you stop looking though, does it?"

I looked at him closely. "Are *you* looking?"

In my experience, men weren't generally open to admitting they were looking for love. And how hard could it be for this guy to find a woman to love? With that delicious voice and body and face?

I shifted in my seat, suddenly uncomfortable.

"Sure. I'm open to finding someone," he admitted.

I narrowed my gaze on him, assessing for sincerity. He glanced at me and gave me a casual smile and then looked straight ahead again.

Unease shivered down my spine. *Who* was this guy? A unicorn?

I should probably stop talking to him now. The more we talked the more attractive he was becoming, and he was already too attractive.

I turned in the seat, rolling toward the window as much as my seat belt would allow. "I think I'm still jetlagged." I tucked my hand under my cheek.

"Take a nap."

I didn't know how it had come to pass that in so short a time this man had my trust, but he did. He had it. His gentleness after my nightmare combined with his alert, smooth handling of the guy at my signing put me at ease.

I could relax in the seat next to him and give over control. When was the last time I could say that about a man? I winced. I'm not sure any of my exes had ever had that much of my trust. I'd married them full of hope, searching for something more. Something I never found. Something that didn't exist.

It was probably the whole bodyguard thing. Moretti gave off an aura of capability. That was his job. I'm sure it wasn't anything about him specifically. What did I know about him anyway except that he was yummy enough to star as the next James Bond?

I closed my eyes against the darkening landscape, lulled into a sense a security. I suppose that was the point. His reason for being here with me was to keep me safe. That was his job. *Just a job.*

A necessary reminder. It wasn't anything real.

CHAPTER SEVEN

"Hello. You should have a room under V.M. Mathers." I propped my handbag on the reception desk and pulled out my identification for the front desk clerk.

"Of course, Ms. Mathers." Her gaze skipped appraisingly to Moretti beside me before looking back to her computer screen. "Ah, there you are. One king bed."

One king bed? I hesitated. "Uh. Is there an adjoining room for . . . " My hand gestured vaguely to Moretti. I didn't even know what to call him. I should have asked for his first name in the car ride. I couldn't make myself spit out the word 'bodyguard.' It stuck in my throat. And he certainly wasn't my significant other. He wasn't my anything.

He decided to speak up then. "An adjoining room should have been added to the reservation."

The clerk shifted her mouse and clicked a few more times. "Ah. I see in the notes there was a request for an adjoining room *should* one come available."

I shook my head weakly. "*Should?*"

"Yes, I'm sorry we could not accommodate that request. There are several festivals and conferences in town." She gestured around them, encompassing the bustling lobby. "We have no more rooms available."

I could only stare in disbelief, my mind working, wondering what came next. Certainly my publisher did not intend for me to have to share a room with the man they had hired for my protection. That was ridiculous and the height of inappropriateness.

Not to mention way, way too tempting.

I looked to Moretti. "Should we find another hotel?"

Before he could answer, the clerk spoke up. "Oh, I'm afraid it is the same everywhere. The book festival has all the hotels full up. You won't be able to find a room anywhere else in the city." She smiled gently to lessen the bite of this news.

As I stood staring unseeingly at her, grappling with this information, Moretti spoke up again. "Thank you." He extended his arm past me, accepting the key cards. Not that we would need two cards because he would never leave my side, apparently. He sent me a reassuring glance. "I'll sleep on the floor."

A combination of relief and disappointment spiraled through me. I bit my lip, confused at the conflicting emotions.

He gathered up our luggage, motioning with his head that we should proceed to the elevator. The clerk had not been exaggerating. It was a busy weekend, if the crowd was any indication. A horseshoe-shaped bar lined one side of the lobby and people milled around it, drinking and socializing. The buzz of conversation and laughter broke through my daze.

I assumed some of these people were here for the book festival, too. If I was feeling more adventurous, I might go mingle and learn if any of them were authors, too. My small town didn't have any writers in it, unfortunately. Bigger cities had strong writing communities, but it wasn't something I'd had the pleasure of enjoying before.

I sent a furtive glance to the hulking man beside me. How would I explain his presence? I guess I needed to figure out something as he would be lurking about tomorrow, a permanent shadow beside me.

I sighed. It had been a long day. My nap had been less than restful. I was still tired and could happily crawl into bed and sleep for a decade. I just wanted to take a shower and go to sleep, so I would be ready for the festival in the morning.

Of course, there was still the unresolved matter of our sleeping arrangements. It was going to be awkward with him sleeping on the floor. I winced. Maybe I could call down for a cot, because we were definitely not sharing a bed.

That was one of the perks of a divorce—of being alone. I never had to share a bed with anyone again. Any bed I slept in, I could stretch out in luxury. I never had to endure someone farting or snoring next to me or reeking of garlic when he decided to eat an entire roasted bulb of it.

We had to stand in line and wait for the elevator. I swung my bag in front of my body, hugging it as though it could shield me. We waited in silence. I rocked on my heels amid the surrounding revelry.

"After you." Moretti motioned me inside the elevator.

We crowded in with the other guests, waiting in silence and getting off on our floor with another couple who had clearly been drinking. They spoke to each other in French and walked arm in arm in an unsteady line ahead of us. It was hard not to focus on the amorous couple, especially the way the guy slid his hand under his companion's skirt.

My face burned, and I was grateful to reach our room. Moretti used the key card and opened the door for us. I walked in past him and turned to hold it open for him as he carried in our luggage.

I moved inside and the door clicked shut after us. I turned in a small circle, examining our accommodations. "Not very . . . spacious."

"No. It's not." He tossed my suitcase onto the small luggage stand.

I moved to the nightstand and lifted the phone, calling the front desk. Someone answered on the second ring.

"Hi, I was hoping someone could send a roll-away cot to our room."

"Sorry, ma'am. Those have already all been claimed for the night."

Disappointment sank through me. "Oh. Thank you." I hung up and forced my gaze back on him.

"Let me guess. None available."

I nodded.

"Not a problem. I can sleep on the floor."

I know I had that thought earlier, but it just seemed . . . harsh. "That can't be very comfortable."

I hated the thought of that. "I've slept on hard ground plenty of nights. The floor isn't going to hurt me for one night."

The tiny room felt charged with the two of us in it. The bed dominated the room and there really wasn't much space around it.

"Do you need to use the bathroom? I'd like to shower." I moved to unzip my suitcase.

"I'm fine. If you don't mind, I'll just borrow one of your pillows." He brushed against me as he stepped forward to lift one of the pillows off the bed. I sucked in a sharp breath.

He dropped it on the flat carpet near the window. There would be just enough room for him to stretch out between the wall and the side of the bed.

Sighing, I snatched up the pillow and tossed it back on the bed. "You can't sleep on a hotel floor. That's just gross."

I wouldn't sleep a wink with his huge, hard body heating up our shared sheets, but I didn't want to seem like a princess, either. Inviting him to share the bed was just the right thing to do.

He shook his head and stretched a hand for the pillow. "My job is to protect you. Keep you safe. Making you uncomfortable is not part—"

I grabbed his wrist, stalling him. "Safety is just a construct. Nothing is ever safe."

His eyes snapped to my face. "If that were true, I would be in a different line of work." His gaze moved over my face as the air crackled between us. God. Could this room be any smaller?

"You're my bodyguard. We're both adults who can control ourselves. I think I can trust you not to pounce on me. I'll sleep under the covers. You sleep on top."

His gaze dropped from my face to my hand on his arm. I followed his gaze, seeing my fingers not quite wrapped around his wrist. His wrist was too large for that. I snatched my hand away. It was bad enough standing this close to him. I could hardly breathe in such proximity. I didn't need to put hands on him, too.

"I'm going to shower now." I gathered my things from my suitcase.

I deliberately didn't look in his direction as I moved into the bathroom. Closing the door, I flipped on the switch. Blinding fluorescent lighting flooded the small space. I turned on the water and faced my reflection in the mirror as I waited for it to warm up.

I brushed at the small smudges of purple under my eyes. The last few weeks had been one great big push: flying from city to city, event to event. It was a lot. Especially for someone who was accustomed to working from home. I'd quit my job when I signed my contract and knew I had a sizable advance coming. I could always go back to my job as a technical writer if my book-writing career tapered.

I kept my own hours. Slept as late as I wanted. Took naps. Binged Netflix. Walked my dog and worked on the draft of my next writing project at my own leisure. This breakneck pace was an adjustment.

I turned from the mirror and stripped off my clothes. The water was warm enough by now. Steam filled up the bathroom and fogged up the mirror. I stepped beneath the warm spray, ducking my head under the water. I let the liquid warmth wash over me, melting into my muscles and bones. I don't know how long I stood like that, but eventually I lifted my head and forced myself to start washing my body and shampooing my hair.

Turning off the shower, I reached for a towel and wrapped it around my head. Grabbing a second towel, I stepped out and dried off briskly. I'd been in here so long he was probably already asleep. There was that at least. No more awkward confrontations tonight.

I slipped my nightie over my head, wishing I had brought something else to sleep in—something more modest, something that fell a little longer than mid-thigh. Then again, I had never planned on sharing my hotel room with anyone.

I finished my bedtime ritual, brushing my hair and teeth and moisturizing my face. I eased open the bathroom door, mindful of its squeak so that I didn't wake him if he was sleeping already.

I didn't have anything to fear, though. He was awake, reclining on the top of the bed, ankles crossed casually as he read.

My gaze landed on the familiar book in his hands and my chest seized. My book. He had somehow gotten a copy of my book.

Damn it. He was reading *my book* and he was more than halfway through it.

I pointed at the book in his hands as though he were holding a crack pipe. "W-where did you get that?" And how had he already read so much of it? God. He was well past chapter eight. "When did you start it?" We had been practically inseparable. When could have had time to read?

He set the book down and looked at me with a thoughtful gaze. "I got it as soon as I was assigned to protect you."

"Oh?"

"Yeah. It was short notice—"

"Melani mentioned that."

"Yes. I would have been finished otherwise."

"No problem," I said a little breathlessly. "Kind of you to . . . even read it."

He propped himself up on an elbow, looking so very relaxed and at ease in the bed we would share. "So when you said 'a woman does not need a man for sexual fulfillment' what you really meant is that a man never gave *you* sexual fulfillment."

I was well aware of what I had written in that book—that in its pages I had shared that I, a woman of thirty-four, had never experienced an orgasm with any of my past sexual partners.

His dark eyes stared at me, waiting.

I swallowed against the giant lump in my throat and glanced around somewhat wildly. Had this room become even smaller? It felt as though it were only him . . . and me . . . and the bed. I gulped a breath. There was not enough air.

He continued in the face of my silence, "Have I made you uncomfortable? I'm sorry. I did not realize." He motioned to the book in his hand. "You spoke so openly today, and you write so candidly on the matter."

"On the matter of my sex life?" I lifted my chin and reached for the covers, pulling them back on my side of the bed with efficient movements. "Yes. I have nothing to hide. I've bared my soul to the world. What's so shocking is that world cares enough to read my book." I faked nonchalance and shrugged. Inside I still trembled, feeling his dark stare on me . . . feeling that deep voice of his asking me his probing questions.

"Oh, you're a brilliant writer. Very entertaining. Witty."

Heat crept up from my throat to my face, so flattered at the compliment. "Thank you."

"When I heard you speak today, I did not quite grasp your meaning." He gave a small shake of his head. "It's far too incredible. You've been married three times and none of your ex-husbands ever—"

"That's right," I cut him off, bristling. For some reason I didn't want to hear him say it. I admitted it all the time. In my book. At speaking engagements. It's the reason so many men out there were offended. Well, insecure men were offended. It was as though in revealing this truth I was revealing something about them, too.

But I didn't want to hear it from him. It was somehow mortifying to hear the truth I lived fall from his lips.

He shook his head. "You married some absolute tossers."

I blinked and gave a small surprised laugh. "I won't argue that, but they can't be blamed for physiology."

"That's rubbish. A man worth anything can make his woman come."

I gasped at his bold language. And yet I felt those words. I felt them like velvet rubbing all along my skin. And I remembered how close I had been last night when we had been bumping and grinding in bed.

I toyed with the edge of the sheets, still standing beside the bed. Nothing could prompt me to slide in beside him right now. Not while we were talking about things like *coming*.

"It's natural for you to think that way, but women are not often honest about this kind of thing. We're sensitive to our partner's feelings and often pretend we've orgasmed when, in fact, we have not." I smiled down at him.

He scowled. "Spare me your condescension. I can tell if a woman's faking it or not."

I maintained my smile. "I'm sure."

Suddenly he smiled back at me. Only that beautiful smile was slight and pitying. "Poor girl. Have you never had a man bury his face between your thighs until you cry, laugh, and weep all at the same time?"

I couldn't breathe.

"I know when it's real," he added with absolute conviction.

I could only nod.

"I'm sure you give yourself *satisfying orgasms*." He lifted my book with a small wave in the air, and it irked me to hear my own words quoted back at me. "But I can do that too. I can do better than that. Anyone can make themselves come. But there's something different—

stronger, more intense—about not knowing when the next touch will land or what it will be like . . . soft or hard. Fast or slow."

I opened my mouth, but nothing came out. Not a sound. I was aroused. Aching and throbbing with arousal. His words alone had done that.

We stared at each other in the electric silence. My skin felt too tight for my body, vibrating and stretching over muscle and bones that felt suddenly as insubstantial as liquid.

He set the book on the nightstand and rose from the bed. "If you'll excuse me, I'll get ready for bed."

He gathered a few items from his bag and was halfway to the bathroom when he paused to look back at me. In the swirling tension, he suggested, "Perhaps I should sleep on the floor. I'm sure it's the most comfortable scenario—"

"Don't be silly. It can't be comfortable."

"I wasn't speaking of physical comfort."

"Oh." *Ohhh.* He meant it was gonna be super awkward sharing a bed.

Of course that was true. The fact that his words had sent my body into a rage of arousal definitely made things more awkward. At least for me. But I didn't expect him to know that. I could barely admit it in my own head. I was determined to keep it to myself. No way would I reveal it to him.

He would not learn of his effect on me. I'd penned a memoir on the theme of self-reliance and female autonomy and here I was all hot and bothered and . . . *needy.* No. I would not cave to these feelings.

I pulled back the covers and slid beneath them. "Don't worry about it. I'm so tired. I'll be asleep before you even get out of the bathroom." I settled down on my side, hugging the mattress's edge. "This bed is big. I won't even know you're beside me."

"All right." He nodded perfunctorily and disappeared inside the bathroom.

The door clicked after him and the air left me in a whoosh. I rubbed a hand over my face. "God save me," I muttered. Let my words be true. Let me fall asleep so quickly I didn't even have to know he was in the bed with me.

Of course that didn't happen.

I closed my eyes and tried to sleep, but I was keenly sensitive to every sound he made on the other side of that door. The running shower. The squeak of the sink's faucet. The faint scrubbing of bristles on his teeth. The clink of his toothbrush on the basin as he shook it clean.

Then silence.

I imagined him dressing, putting clothes back on that muscly body of his. The body I had felt over me last night and then ogled as he stood beside my bed.

My chest felt suddenly too tight. Had that only been last night? It seemed much longer ago. I fought for an even breath. It felt like I had been together with him much longer than twenty-four hours. I mean . . . I already knew his smell. How his hand loosely rested on the gear stick when he drove. I had the sight of it memorized. The olive-hued skin, the pattern of veins and sparse hair.

The door opened, but I held still, eyes closed, faking sleep. *Faking.* That word conjured up our earlier conversation. Every mortifying bit of it.

I can tell if a woman's faking it or not.

Sure. He was confident. And he seemed a very capable man, but I knew the odds of him delivering an orgasm *every* single time to *every* woman he had ever been with was unlikely, if not impossible. The odds were simply against him.

He was at his suitcase. I held myself tight as a guitar string, listening to the slight rustling with seized breath. A few moments later, his side of the bed sank down with his weight and I managed not to scream even as hysteria bubbled up in my throat.

Oh God Oh God Oh God. I should have taken him up on his offer to take the floor. How could I be in bed with a man? I was a woman who eschewed all men, and with good reason. I now flourished on that platform—on being an independent woman who had come into her own only after she gave up on ever needing or wanting a man again.

He settled down beside me. True to our agreement, he stayed on the top of the bedding, and I felt the pull of the covers as he stretched out beside me.

It's no big deal. You've slept next to plenty of men who never made a move on you. That was, in fact, customary practice.

I grimaced at that truth. The last six months of my marriage to Charlie, we did not touch at all. No sex. No kiss. No fingers brushing as we passed the salt. We were basically roommates, which was fine with him. He was fine with the state of our existence. If I hadn't called it quits, we would probably still be married, still not kissing, touching . . . or fucking. Still just roommates.

My fingers tightened around the edge of the comforter until my knuckles ached. This felt very different from that. Sharing a bed with him would not be a casual thing. For starters, we weren't married. Moretti and I weren't stuck in a sexless rut.

This wasn't a Sunday night where I watched reruns of the *The Big Bang Theory* as my ex snored next to me, drunk from pot roast and a pint of Mint Chocolate Chip. No. This was an entirely different situation from that. Big enough bed or not, I was achingly aware of Moretti beside me.

Sleeping with him would not be sleeping. I mean . . . maybe he could sleep.

I doubted I ever would.

CHAPTER EIGHT

"Are you awake?" I heard myself whisper.

He had been very still for the last couple hours, presumably asleep, but then he spoke, his deep voice quick to reply. As though he had been ready. Waiting.

"Do you want me to move to the floor?"

I ignored his question. It seemed we were well beyond that now. Secure in the darkness, I asked, "What's your name? Your first name?"

It seemed a good thing to know—the name of the man with whom you were sharing a bed.

"Luca."

"Luca," I repeated, testing his name, seeing how it felt on my lips.

"Only a little bit Italian, huh?" he said, and I realized he was teasing.

I laughed nervously. "Yeah."

"You should see Sunday dinner at my parents' house. It's an enormous Italian feast with my family. My parents and grandparents and sister and her family. She's got five kids."

"Wow," I murmured, envisioning the bustling houseful that smelled of fragrant marinara sauce. The good kind you only smelled in a restaurant.

"Have you ever had *zabaglione*?"

I shook my head and then realized he might not be able to see the motion. "No."

"It's a fluffy custard. My mother infuses it with a little cognac."

"It sounds delicious." Suddenly I felt a stab of longing to taste what he was describing for myself. To live it. An Italian feast surrounded by Luca and all his family. That was a little much, of course. I definitely wasn't looking for *that*. No. I was after something else.

"Did you mean what you said . . . Luca?"

Pause. There was just my heartbeat. The whoosh of my pulse in my ears. And all of my thoughts from the last couple hours spinning through me like a pinwheel.

"I always say what I mean."

"About satisfying a woman every time. Is it true?"

"I haven't any ego when it comes to that."

I laced my fingers together across my middle, absorbing that. I licked my dry lips, moistening them. I'd decided I believed him—that he was not one to boast. Somehow I knew that.

Alone in the dark, I'd also decided that I didn't have to be the expert on self-fulfillment. No one had to know what I did behind closed doors.

I drew in a deep breath. "You said you don't have a family. What about a girlfriend?" That was important to know. It mattered before I continued.

"Do you think I'd be in this bed talking about orgasms with you if I had a girlfriend waiting for me somewhere?"

I shrugged one shoulder even as I realized he could not see the motion in the lightless room. "You're working. It's your job."

He grunted at that and I didn't know how to interpret the sound. "The way I've been talking to you and interacting with you . . . that's not my job." He sighed in the dark and in that exhalation of breath he sounded almost angry with himself.

His words served as a confirmation. They made this all seem so much more real. Not a thing I was imagining. Not a thing existing in my head alone.

Something was happening between us, and he knew it, too.

I sucked in a sharp breath and it shuddered out from my lips. "Prove it," I whispered.

Silence.

Maybe I'd spoken too quietly. That meant I could take it back. I could pretend I'd said nothing. Pretend I had not just invited him to give me an orgasm.

But then his voice sliced through the night, filling the darkness between us. "What did you say?"

"Prove it." I suppose I could backpedal from that, but did I really want to? I'd said the words for a reason. His conviction in his sexual prowess and ability to satisfy intrigued me. It was nothing more than that. Well . . . and he made me flush hot all over. There was that.

"For the sake of clarity, what does 'proving it' mean to you?"

"You're the grand orgasm giver. You said you can make a woman come before you even got off." I swallowed, staring blindly into darkness. "Well, prove it. Give me one."

"An orgasm? You want me to make you come? Only you? Not me?" he clarified.

I winced. When he said it like that it seemed horribly one-sided. What was in this for him? "I'm sorry. I don't imagine there is much appeal in that for you." I released a nervous little laugh that died abruptly when the bed squeaked. He turned on his side, looming over me.

"Don't be daft." His hand found mine where it clutched the edge of the comforter. "I love a woman's orgasm on my lips." He seized the edge of the comforter and peeled it off my body.

Cool air caressed me.

"Oh my," I breathed as his big body came up over me then, his knees between my thighs, bumping them apart, forcing my nightie to ride up my thighs and my hips.

He stilled. "Let's be clear what you want from me, Ms. Mathers—"

"Vee—"

Hearing him address me so formally felt ridiculous.

"Let's be clear on what you want, Vee. Say it one more time."

Say it again? I didn't think speech was possible. My heart was lodged somewhere in my throat. I'd have to settle for action. Action was always more effective anyway.

I reached up until my fingers landed on his chest. He'd worn a shirt to bed tonight. It was probably to protect my sensibilities. The soft cotton was warm from his body and my fingertips brushed against it, back and forth.

My hand drifted upward, trailing over his shoulder and then sliding down his arm until I reached where his hand was splayed on the mattress beside me.

I took it. Wrapped my shaking fingers around his thick wrist and tugged until he lifted his hand up from the bed, letting me guide him.

And guide him I did. Directly to my panties. Just so there would be no confusion in what I was asking. In what I wanted.

It was bold of me, but I hadn't been touched by another human, not intimately, in almost four years. And there was the darkness. Courage always found its way through the dark.

I turned his hand so that his fingers slid down the front arrow of my underwear, over my silk of my undies, right over my crotch. Covered up, blocked, shielded by the thin barrier of fabric, I moaned softly at the stroke of his fingers. Even if I was doing it. Even if I was controlling him. Every nerve in my body vibrated and sang its own aria.

"If you want me to do this, then let me," his said in a voice rough as gravel. "Let me do this to you."

I unfurled my fingers from his wrist. My arms fell limply at my sides in surrender.

His fingers remained there between my thighs.

I opened wider, inviting him to do that magical thing he professed to do. Inviting him to take me apart and unravel me. I shifted, wiggled, wondering how long until he started moving—

Welp. And there he went.

His fingers dove downward. Then back up against the seam of me. Then down again, exerting more and more pressure with each passing swipe.

OH MY GOD. This was what he was talking about. I was gasping under him. All kinds of undignified sounds escaped me. I couldn't even compose myself and I supposed that was the point of coming apart. There was no dignity in it.

Suddenly he hooked his fingers around the edge of my underwear and yanked them to the side.

No barrier now. There was a rush of air and then his fingers were directly on me, rubbing against my wetness. I cried out at his first touch on my throbbing flesh, sliding against my folds.

"Oh, you're soaking," he growled, two fingers brushing over my clit. "Is this all for me?" His fingers pushed on, a single one dipping into my opening.

I bit my lip to stop from crying out and nodded jerkily. I swallowed back a sob, wrecked and splayed open before him and not caring. "Y-yes. It's for you."

His thumb moved up, brushing my swollen clit and I shuddered, my hands clenching at my sides, gripping fistfuls of comforter.

He pushed with his thumb, bearing down on my clit as his finger pressed just a fraction deeper inside me, curling up and stroking some unseen velvety sensitized patch of nerves.

It was enough. Enough to make me moan, shake, break.

Enough to push me right over the brink into orgasm.

He had not been bluffing or exaggerating. He was the giver of orgasms. As promised.

Panting, my chest rising and falling rapidly, I came back down to earth only to find his fingers still at work, skimming over me, brushing the entrance to my sex, drifting to softly circle my overly sensitive clit and give it a roll.

Then his hands vanished from between my legs.

I whimpered in disappointment, lifting my head from the bed. "What are you—"

He scooted down my body, disappearing between my legs. My head spun, dizzy with desire and bewilderment. Those hands returned then, closed around the sides of my panties at my hips, and yanked the scrap of fabric down my legs in one clean move. Freed, my legs dropped limply on the bed, where they were not left alone for long. He lifted one and draped it over his shoulder with a plop.

With a growl of satisfaction his mouth closed over me. *Ohhh.* He was doing *that* to me.

He devoured me. Licking with his hot tongue, nibbling with his teeth, turning to press open-mouthed kisses over the sensitive skin of my inner thighs before returning back to my sex.

Now I got it. Now I understood.

Cunnilingus had never been high on the list for any of my exes. It wasn't something I thought I even liked. I certainly never missed it. But that's the thing. You can't miss what you don't know.

And now I not only knew it, but I knew how it could be done . . . how I could be *undone*.

His mouth and grazing teeth become more insistent, more aggressive. I tossed and writhed against him. "Too much," I panted.

"That's it," he growled against me, his tongue swiping and flaying my tender flesh. "When you feel like you can't take it anymore, that's when you're right there."

I screeched, one hand flying to grip his hair while his head pumped and worked between my thighs. I lost all restraint and rocked against that mouth of his, riding his face, driving and seeking my own pleasure like it was the only thing that existed. He worked me furiously, tasting me, sucking me, licking long and deep, making me come in a blinding rush (again) like he had promised he could.

I shuddered, shaking against his mouth, my entire body ravaged.

I flung my arm over my forehead and tried to steady my breathing. I took several deep, gulping breaths. He turned his face and pressed a lingering kiss to the inside of my thigh and that made me shiver.

I released a nervous laugh and glanced at the bedside clock. "It's late."

"I wasn't sleeping anyway." He lifted up from between my legs.

Because of me?

"So much for my theories," I murmured because I had to say *something*. I had challenged him to prove his orgasm-giving abilities, after all.

"Happy to disprove."

I frowned at that. He was happy to disprove *me*.

I wasn't wrong about *everything*. Maybe the odd man like him could provide an orgasm (or two), but that didn't mean I should keep one around. That didn't change anything. I should only rely on myself for happiness and contentment. Expect nothing from anyone. Be an island. That's the safe thing. The smart thing. I still believed in that, even if I did let a guy into my bed.

That didn't mean I was ready to let a guy into my life.

CHAPTER NINE

THE FESTIVAL WAS A BLUR.

Even if I wasn't still reeling from last night, and the fact that Moretti —er, Luca—had smashed all my theories with not one but *two* orgasms, it would have been an overwhelming experience. As it stood, I was reeling . . . and slightly itchy in my own skin. As though the shell of my body no longer quite fit me—as though I was a different person now.

Incredibly, I still throbbed between my legs. At first, I reasoned I was tender from last night's activities. It had been well over four years since a man had touched me, after all. Soreness wasn't an unlikely possibility.

Except the throbbing intensified when I thought about the things he did to me *or* if I looked up and caught sight of him *or* if he stood close enough for me to smell him *or* if I heard him speak. Gah. I thought I could get off from his voice alone.

It was beyond inconvenient. I was in trouble.

Last night had only whetted my taste for more. I felt like such a fraud. How could I even talk about my book at this event with him looking on and listening to my words? I could almost hear his laughter.

It was mortifying.

Staff members escorted me from one panel to another on the grounds and in the buildings of the local university that served as the venue.

Panels ran concurrently throughout the day, and festival attendees had their pick of whom they wanted to hear. Not that any single panel wasn't well-attended. There were over a thousand in attendance. It was a book lover's dream.

I sat on multiple panels with other featured authors. Moretti trailed behind me to each talk, keeping his distance, but lingering nearby while I spoke alongside others on daises that overlooked crowds.

After the previous night, my skin felt extra sensitive. Simply sitting in my chair and trying to concentrate on the questions being put to me was a challenge. I shifted in my seat, my jeans suddenly too tight, the friction of the denim against me too much to bear. I tugged my blazer closer at the front and that was a mistake, too. The fabric chafed my blouse and that chafed my breasts. Breasts he had not even touched and that seemed a travesty now. I heartily wished he had lavished some of his attention there. When I imagined that skilled mouth and tongue of his on my nipples, it made me squirm.

I had a brief break in the green room where lunch was provided to all authors and approved guests. Luca was never far from me through any of it. Even if my gaze didn't seek out his figure like a heat-guided missile, he was hard to ignore. In the green room he stood in a corner, as unobtrusive as a man like him could be. Which wasn't very. He was too big. Too hot. He commanded a room without having to do anything.

He was approached several times by staff and authors alike. I didn't know what he said to put them off, but they always left him alone to continue his silent vigil. At one point a staff member forced a plate of food on him. He accepted, and I was glad to see him eat something.

After lunch, I continued on with more panels and signings. The day ended with a closing ceremony in a giant amphitheater and all the authors assembled on the stage for final remarks and a keynote speech. Luca stood in the wings, not far, never far, waiting for the event to end, his gaze a palpable touch. There was an after party, and I should have wanted to attend. I had thought I would. It was the sociable thing to do, but I did not feel inclined to mingle with a bunch of strangers as Luca stood by silently watching. Not engaging. Not a participant. I knew it was his job. I shouldn't worry about his comfort. I shouldn't care. Watching and *not* engaging was what he was paid to do.

But I did care.

"Do you want to return to the hotel to freshen up before the party?" he asked as I approached him.

I shook my head. "Not really."

He frowned and angled his head thoughtfully. "Oh, did you want to go directly to the—"

"I just want a long hot shower and room service."

He stared at me for a long moment. "You don't want to go to the party?"

I shook my head. "No. It's been a long day. Room service and watching TV sounds wonderful to me."

"If that's what you want," he said slowly, and I didn't care for that.

It made him sound in service to me and subject to my whims, which he was. But after last night . . . his role here with me had become a bit confusing. It was a little less clear now, and I guess that was my fault. The moment I opened my mouth and invited him to prove his orgasm-giving prowess I had thrown everything into chaos.

"I would like it, yes." I turned off the stage and he fell in beside me as we headed out of the amphitheater into the evening. We located the car and I settled back in for the drive to the hotel. It had been a long day, and I was looking forward to staying in for the evening.

Watching his hands on the steering wheel made me think of those hands on me. I wanted to feel those hands on me again. Especially on the places he had not yet touched.

I wanted to get naked with him, and, more importantly, I wanted him naked with me.

It was enough to give me heart palpitations. I needed to compose myself. This wasn't a fling. Last night had simply been an enjoyable experiment. He'd been down for it, but in no way had he indicated he wanted anything more. And he worked for me . . . sort of. Was that weird? I didn't want to make him feel like I was taking advantage of him in this situation.

The hotel lobby was bustling when we arrived. We rode up the crowded elevator to our room, neither one of us speaking. I needed that. Awkward or not, I needed silence to help me compose myself.

We arrived in the room and I kicked off my shoes, dropping my handbag in the chair. "I'm going to take a shower." Escaping under a hot spray of water sounded perfect. "You want to order us dinner?" I asked as I fumbled inside my luggage, gathering some clothes. I avoided my nightie, settling on a T-shirt and shorts.

He moved to the nightstand and picked up the menu. "What would you like?"

"You choose. I love all food."

He nodded and opened up the tri-fold menu.

I ducked into the bathroom. Turning the shower to hot, I quickly stripped off my clothes and then dove beneath the spray. After washing and shampooing, I flattened my palms against the tile and let the water beat down on my shoulders for a long time as I mulled over going back out there, to the place where I had finally achieved orgasm with another person. The room should be designated a historical landmark.

Shutting off the shower, I stepped out and swiped the mirror clean of fog, the glass squeaking under my fingers. For a long moment I stared at my reflection. I looked like I did when I drank a few too many—brown eyes glassy and bright, cheeks flushed like I'd run a couple miles.

I could go back out there, eat dinner, and watch TV and keep things one hundred percent above board. Strictly professional. At least as professional as things could be between two people sharing one bed.

Or I could go back out there and get what I wanted. Which was more than room service. It was more of Luca Moretti.

V.M Mathers, author of *Self Love,* was a woman who went after what she wanted. Sure, I could administer my own orgasms. Or I could achieve them by hooking up with a hot guy in a mutually beneficial and consensual way. Either one of those scenarios would be true to the spirit of my book—and to me.

Nodding confidently, I reached for my clothes and then stopped. I should have gone with the nightie. Putting on a T-shirt and shorts did not spell sexy.

Pulling my hand back I faced myself in the mirror again and readjusted the towel around me, re-knotting it less than securely above my breasts. If it happened to slip and fall, then oh well. It just might help move things along. Definitely not the end of the world.

I stepped out into the hotel room, ready, and in full-on seduction mode.

My gaze scanned the room. Food had been delivered and sat on a tray at the bottom of the bed. Luca was nowhere in sight.

I moved toward the tray and lifted the lid to find a single plate of food. A meal for one. Not two. I lowered the lid. A quick glance around the room revealed no second tray. He had not eaten. And he had definitely left. He had left the room.

My phone rang from inside my bag and I dug it out of my handbag. I answered the unknown number. "Hello?"

"Ms. Mathers. I had to step away. I'll be back. Promise me you won't leave the room." *Ms. Mathers?* That was some bit of nonsense. After where his hands and mouth had been the previous day, I thought we were beyond formalities. I had thought a lot of things, but I guess I was wrong about all of them.

"I won't." I glanced to the tray. "Thanks for ordering me something to eat."

"Of course."

I flexed my fingers around the phone. "Aren't you hungry?"

"I'll get something. Now don't leave the room and don't answer the door."

I nodded as though he could see me. "Okay. I won't."

The phone went dead, and I slowly lowered it back down. I stared at it for a moment in my hand, battling disappointment. I envisioned him somewhere else—in a restaurant or a bar getting something to eat. He probably needed a break from me. That was reasonable. He'd been with me practically twenty-four seven since we met.

Going through the motions, I put my phone on the charger and turned on the TV, finding a show. It appeared to be a comedy, so I decided to leave it. Comedy was a good thing right now when I was feeling especially sorry for myself.

Sorry because my plan to seduce my bodyguard met a dead end. I wouldn't be enjoying his lips on my lips or anywhere else.

I settled on the bed with my food, glad that he hadn't ordered me anything like a salad. I savored the first bite of my fish and chips and focused on the antics playing out on the TV screen.

I finished my food and dressed in the T-shirt and shorts I had originally planned to wear before I had sexy goals. I slid into bed, wondering what was keeping him out even as I told myself it didn't matter. Message received. Last night was a one-time thing.

I dozed off with the TV on, its soft blue glow pervading the room as sounds of laughter from the studio audience lulled me to sleep.

I didn't know how long I slept, but it was disconcertingly dark and silent when I suddenly woke. Propping up on an elbow, I searched the lightless room, orienting myself. It was momentarily bewildering. For a moment I searched for the familiarity of my own bedroom, for the sounds and smells of home, but then I recalled that I wasn't in my home. I was on book tour. I was in Edinburgh. I'd fallen asleep watching TV.

Stretching out my arm, I stroked the space beside me. *Empty.* He wasn't here. He wasn't back yet. Then who turned the TV off?

I reached for my phone and tapped on it so that I had enough light to scan the room and locate him sleeping in the chair. I quickly killed the light and settled back in the bed as quietly as possible, intent on not waking him.

I inhaled and exhaled slowly. He'd returned and opted to sleep in a chair rather than with me again. *He was sleeping in a chair. Rather than with me.*

It was a definite reality check. Last night had been fun, but he wasn't here to be *my* fun. He was here to do a job. That was it.

CHAPTER TEN

THE DRIVE back to London was even quieter than the drive to Edinburgh. We returned to the previous hotel and this time there was no mix up and no over-crowded hotel. We again had adjoining rooms. Not the same room on the fifth floor but an identical room on the seventh floor.

I watched as Luca carried my luggage into one bedroom . . . and then he took his bag into the other bedroom. He would not have to suffer spending the night in a chair again. He'd be in his own room and his own bed. All for the best. For obvious reasons.

He was my bodyguard. There was no relationship beyond that. I'd be on a plane in two days. A swift little pang resulted from that thought, which was entirely inappropriate. I wasn't in junior high, nursing a crush on someone after knowing him for only two days. I was not a raging ball of hormones letting my vagina lead me. Really. I wasn't.

He returned from his room and conducted his familiar inspection. Watching him close the drapes was like déjà vu from the first night. I smiled slightly.

Satisfied, he stopped in front of me. He studied me with an inscrutable gaze. "Your schedule is open until tomorrow night."

"The gala. Yes." I nodded.

"Was there anything you wanted to see tomorrow before the gala?"

I perked up. "As in sightseeing? That wouldn't be too awful for you?"

"I can bear it," he said rather gruffly. "What's on your list?"

Everything.

Smiling widely, the sleeping arrangements bothered me less now. *Bothered?* Yeah. I guess there was no denying it. I was bothered that there was once again appropriate and proper distance between us. That was some irony—and kind of messed up. When I first learned we had to share a bedroom I had been horrified. Now it bothered me that we were *not* sharing a bed? I gave my head a swift shake.

"I pretty much want to see everything," I admitted with a little laugh.

"Ah. We might not get to everything, but we could get an early start in the morning and try to get in as much as we can before the gala tomorrow night." He broke our stare, looking away, down at the floor, at the wall—anywhere but me. A deep breath lifted his chest as though he was collecting himself. As though he needed more air around me, and I understood that. I never felt like I could catch my breath around him.

I nodded again, just once. "That sounds wonderful. Thank you."

I didn't move. Didn't act or, as usual, breathe.

He lifted his gaze back to me and there was such simmering heat there that I felt ensnared, caught, suspended . . . in a state of strange limbo as I looked from his eyes to his mouth and then back to his eyes again. Looking at his wide mouth, at those beautifully carved lips, I couldn't stop thinking that I should know them. I should have kissed him.

I hovered as though this were a turning point. A pivot in which something would happen. Or nothing at all—and I guessed that in this case nothing was something.

I motioned to the small sitting area with its couch and TV. "Did you want to watch a movie? Order a pizza?"

He took a step forward and then stopped, glancing to the couch and then back to his bedroom, and I knew then. His hands flexed at his sides, opening and closing several times before at last falling open.

Nothing was going to happen. We would each go to our separate beds tonight. I would not know his lips on mine. There would be no kissing. There would be nothing.

Nothing.

I felt the disappointment keenly and a sigh welled up, easing out from me. I needed to stop throwing myself at him like something would happen. He didn't want me.

"You know, on second thought," I said, giving us both a way out from this awkward situation. "It's going to be a long day tomorrow. I'm still pretty full from lunch."

"You sure?" His gaze searched my face.

"Yes." It had been hours since we'd eaten lunch, but food didn't seem as important as closing myself up in the privacy of my room. "Good night. I'll see you in the morning."

"Good night, Ms. Mathers."

I was Ms. Mathers again. If I had any doubt that he was determined to put us back in our roles of *specialist* and *principal* it was gone.

"How DID you come to be such a Sherlock Holmes fan?" Luca asked as he handed me my phone after taking another picture of me in front of the Sherlock Holmes Museum. I had Luca snap pictures of me as we visited the sights throughout the morning. It was all terribly touristy of me, but I couldn't help myself.

"Would you like me to take a picture of you both?" a lady asked, motioning to my phone.

"I . . . uh—" I looked uncertainly to Luca.

"Thank you. Yes." He handed the woman my phone.

Luca took me by the elbow and positioned us in front of the black wrought iron fence surrounding the quaint façade of the museum. It took everything in me not to stare at him standing so closely beside me. His broad hand settled against the small of my back and I sucked in a breath at the immediate zing of electricity radiating from that point of contact. I forced my gaze ahead, smiling at the woman snapping our picture.

"Brilliant," she announced. "You're a lovely couple."

My face burned as Luca stepped forward, thanking her and reclaiming my phone.

I nodded my thanks and took my phone back from Luca. I glanced down at the photo and felt a strange flutter in my chest at the sight of us, standing so close. Even Luca was smiling, as handsome as any movie star.

I swiped the screen and realized she had taken more than one photo. She'd caught one of me staring at Luca and I looked utterly mesmerized. There it was. Evidence of my enchantment. I should delete it and yet I couldn't bring myself to do it. I couldn't bring myself to erase any image of the two of us.

Closing my phone, I slipped it into my pocket, determined to keep it and study it more later. At least I would have these photos. Proof that this had happened, that I was not as jaded as I had thought myself to be. That maybe I was open to the idea of romance and love in my life, after all.

"Are they all right?" he inquired.

I smiled and nodded a little too eagerly. "Great."

I didn't need him to see them. One glance of me looking at him so longingly and he would know of my infatuation. I'd keep that picture for my eyes alone.

We fell in step together on the sidewalk. "You were telling me how you came to be such a Sherlock Holmes fan," he reminded.

"Oh. Right. Well, I love all things Sherlock Holmes . . . those books got me through some days."

"Really?"

"It launched me into all things mystery. Agatha Christie, Truman Capote. My small town librarian kept me well supplied. Thankfully the library was in walking distance. Books were my friends . . . and they kept me sane. What about you?"

"What do you mean?"

"As a kid . . . what was your thing?"

"Oh." He blinked. "Sports mostly. I ran track. Played whatever was in season."

"Of course," I said teasingly.

"I had a lot of mates on my street. We were our own football team."

"Football as in . . . soccer?"

He sent me a reproving look. "Of course."

I nodded with a smile and burrowed a little deeper into my sweater.

"Cold?" he asked, gripping the edge of his jacket as though prepared to remove it for me.

"I'm fine," I assured him. "I love this weather. Back home it's still ninety-five degrees right now. You wouldn't know it's fall at all. I've always wanted to live someplace with cool weather. Somewhere with an actual winter."

"Then why don't you?"

"Uh." I blinked. "I don't know. I've always lived in Arkansas."

"Well, do you have to?"

"No. I don't. I can live anywhere . . . write from anywhere, I guess."

I really could. I'd considered it before. The idea had been there, niggling at the back of my mind since my divorce. It just meant gathering my courage and leaving. Picking someplace else to live and settling down there.

We continued down the sidewalk. After a few moments, he asked. "So you read all things mystery and yet you don't write mystery?"

I shrugged with a little laugh. "I always thought about writing a mystery. Never seemed to find the time." I definitely never had encouragement from any of my exes. They didn't understand any endeavor that took attention away from them, let alone one where I didn't get a paycheck up front.

"You wrote a memoir though . . . when you did find the time."

"Yeah. Funny, right? I guess I had something else I wanted to say." Something I *needed* to say.

"And what's next for you? Anything else you want to say?"

"Hm." I angled my head thoughtfully. "That's what everyone keeps asking me." My editors. My agent. Not Mom, though. She kept begging me to say nothing more. To keep my opinions to myself.

We fell silent for a few moments, walking side by side. "That's a lot of pressure," he volunteered as we stopped at a crosswalk, waiting for the pedestrian light to change.

"It can be."

"Don't let it.

"I beg your pardon?

"Don't let it be a pressure."

I considered him sharply. A chill wind tousled his dark hair.

It was always easier for someone else to tell you that. *Don't stress. Don't worry. Don't feel pressured.* Easier said than done.

"What am I supposed to do then? Never write anything again?"

"Yeah. Well. Do you have to?" He lifted a hand out of his pocket and waved it vaguely. "It seems like you've done very well for yourself. Do you need to write another book if you don't want to?"

The light turned and we started across the street. My sneaker caught on the uneven surface of the street, and I stumbled. His hand reached out to grasp my elbow.

"No one has ever suggested that to me before." No one ever told me I could just . . . *stop*. "Well. Except for my mother. But her reasons and motivation are entirely different."

He was coming from some place entirely altruistic. He was being thoughtful and thinking about me . . . about what I might need and want.

"Something to consider. Cut yourself a break. Don't do anything unless you feel an overwhelming urge and desire to do it."

"Is that how you live?" I blurted. "You only do what you want?"

He stopped and faced me. "If it doesn't hurt anyone. Yes. I do what I want."

The air crackled between us. His gaze dropped to my mouth, and I felt certain in that moment that he *wanted* to kiss me. That he was going to kiss me. Finally. His brown eyes seemed to darken, his pupils indiscernible from the irises of his eyes.

People passed us on the sidewalk. I was aware of them in my periphery, but only vaguely. I was centered on him with searing focus. My entire body hummed with awareness. I leaned forward, angling toward him like he was a magnet I could not resist.

"Are you hungry?" he blurted, taking one step back from me, severing the invisible string that had been pulling us closer.

I released a shuddering breath. Okay. Not happening. I guess he didn't want me that much.

I slipped my phone from my pocket and glanced at the time. "Goodness. It's almost two." I took stock of my stomach then. This whole day had been such a distraction. I'd forgotten all about food. I was having a good time. I was having a good time with *him*. "Yeah. I'm starving."

He nodded slowly. "I know a place. Not far from here."

"Great. Let's go then."

We walked the seven blocks to the restaurant. When I reached it, I stopped hard and stared up at the gold scrolling letters stretching above the door and mullioned windows. "Moretti's?"

He pulled open the door for me. "Yeah. It's my family's restaurant."

Delighted, I eagerly stepped inside. Luca followed behind me. It was mere seconds before the restaurant staff identified him. Happy exclamations filled the air amid the delicious smells of marinara, basil, and sizzling meats.

I stood to the side as the hostess and wait staff embraced him.

A tall, silver-haired man exited from the kitchen, crossing the restaurant to fold my big intimidating bodyguard into his arms. He was undoubtedly Luca's father. The resemblance between them was uncanny. It was like glimpsing thirty years into Luca's future. It would be a kind future for him indeed.

"Vee, this is my father, Lorenzo." Luca gestured to his dad and then went on to introduce the lovely hostess. "My sister, Bianca." His father and sister swept me into warm hugs that robbed me of breath.

He introduced the other members of the staff—all names I doubted I could remember.

My attention was trained on his father and sister. I was utterly fascinated . . . and enchanted. The Moretti family was remarkably good looking, and I felt a little gawky standing in the shadow of them. I wished I'd styled my hair instead of sweeping it up into a ponytail for the day.

Conversation whirled around us and I gathered it had been some weeks since Luca had visited the restaurant and they were all taking him to task for the neglect.

"I've been busy with work," he defended, palms face out as Bianca reprimanded him.

"Not too busy, eh?" Lorenzo elbowed his son and sent me a wink.

"Mama is going to be so sad she missed you . . . that she missed you *both*." Bianca looked me over meaningfully.

Heat scored my face. Oh dear. They had the wrong idea about us. I looked at Luca, ready for him to correct his father's and sister's misapprehension.

He did not.

With a hand at the small of my back, he guided me to a booth.

I was reeling. He'd brought me here. To his family's restaurant. Warmth swelled in my chest.

"Have you had lunch?" Bianca asked us, her dark eyes flitting back and forth between us as we settled into the booth.

"No, we have not and we're hungry," Luca declared.

"Famished," I seconded.

Lorenzo clapped his hands. "I will bring you our specials. Beef short rib Bolognese, artichoke ravioli—"

"And mussels in white wine?" Luca asked with a tinge of hope in his voice.

"Of course." Bianca sent me a look. "It's his favorite."

"And garlic bread for the table? And some fresh burrata?"

I gawked. "That's a lot of food." I hoped I could still fit in my dress this evening.

Bianca smiled. "Welcome to Moretti's."

Lorenzo hurried back into the kitchen to start on our order. Bianca lingered and chatted with us, catching up Luca on the latest activities with her husband and kids. They sounded like a handful, but her face flushed pink with obvious love for them.

I listened, charmed at seeing Luca this way, as a real person—a son, a brother, an uncle . . . this glimpse into a real family. It was something I never had.

Lorenzo stuck his head out from the kitchen. "Luca! Come help me load this delivery into the freezer."

Luca looked at me. "I'll be right back."

I watched him trot back into the kitchen, my stupid heart tripping as I tracked him.

"How long have you two been seeing each other?"

My gaze jerked back to Bianca. "I beg your pardon?"

"My brother? You?"

"Oh." Heat swept up my neck to my face. "It's not like that. I'm actually . . . a client."

"A client?"

"Yes. I'm an author. My publisher hired Corps Security while I'm here in town."

"Oh." She frowned. "Well. So this is . . . work? Luca is on the job?"

"Yes," I confessed, wondering why it felt so difficult to admit that.

"Well, I'm not getting that vibe at all."

"I beg your pardon?"

"My brother doesn't bring clients here." She nodded with conviction.

"Oh?"

"I've never met a client of his before. He only ever brings serious girlfriends around us . . . and it's been two years since he had one of those."

I opened and closed my mouth several times, unsure what to say to that. I shrugged awkwardly. "Maybe he just wanted a good meal—"

"No. He's a very thoughtful and deliberate person. He's all about caution." She peered at me contemplatively. "Has he told you about Matti?"

"Matti?" I shook my head. "No."

"Hm," she murmured, her dark eyes probing on me. There was no doubt she was her brother's sister.

"Who is Matti?"

The front door dinged with the arrival of more customers, and Bianca left me to attend to them just as Luca emerged from the kitchen toting plates.

He lowered a plate of steaming garlic bread and a plate of burrata drizzled with olive oil and balsamic vinegar onto the table between us with great flourish.

"Beautiful," I murmured in appreciation.

"You'll love this. It's so fresh." He set small plates in front of each of us and then prepared my plate for me, giving me a hefty spoonful of burrata and several pieces of crusty golden bread.

I couldn't recall any time my exes had ever served me or prepared food of any kind for me. My throat constricted a little as he took such care, making certain I received some of the basil sprig to go along with the burrata.

"Thank you," I murmured, the words thick in my throat.

"Of course." He watched my face carefully at my first bite of burrata-lathered bread. "Oh. My. God." I pressed fingers to my lips in an attempt to stifle my artless moan. "That is amazing."

His eyes fixed on my mouth, his expression losing its levity, becoming a stark and hungry thing. Suddenly I couldn't even taste the food in my mouth. I could only feel his stare, palpable as a touch on my face.

"How is it?" Bianca asked abruptly, appearing beside our table.

I swallowed my bite and nodded doggedly. "It's delicious."

"Just wait until the rest of your food gets here." She patted both our shoulders and then moved away.

We resumed eating, Luca regaling me with tales of growing up in this restaurant. "There's no pot I can't clean," he bragged. "I can scrub and scour to glinting perfection."

"Is that how you got those biceps?"

He looked down at an arm, flexing his impressive bicep. "What these?" He looked up and winked at me. "Flattered you noticed."

I laughed nervously. "Your body is hard to ignore."

Had I just said that? God. I was incorrigible. I didn't know I still knew how to flirt.

He lifted his glass, drinking slowly as he eyed me over the rim. He rubbed some bread in the cheese and oil on his plate and chewed, still looking at me. I felt naked under that stare. In this moment it was easy to remember how his mouth had felt on my sex, so hot and consuming. He ate me out with same intensity and hungry appreciation he gave to the food before him.

I cleared my throat. "Um. Who is Matti?"

He stilled and it occurred to me that in hoping to fill the uncomfortable tension, I'd just plunged us into a completely unknown topic.

His gaze skipped across the restaurant to Bianca. "Let me guess. My sister?"

I nodded.

His lips twisted. "That didn't take long."

"I'm sorry." I shook my head. "I should not have—"

"Matti is Matteo. My younger brother. He died when I was twelve."

"Oh." My stomach sank. *Way to go, Vee. Bring up his dead brother over dinner.* "I'm so sorry."

"We were swimming at the neighborhood pool. One moment he was next to me . . . " His voice faded. He stabbed at the cheese fiercely on his plate. "I should have noticed. No one noticed until it was too late and he was at the bottom of the pool."

"Oh. God." I couldn't imagine it. "That's . . . horrible."

It must have been so difficult for his family. I glanced to where his sister stood chatting with customers. I could hear Italian folk music wafting from the kitchen where his father cooked. They seemed like such happy people . . . and maybe that was because of what they'd lost. Because they understood the value of life better than most. They knew it was to be enjoyed, savored—and not wasted.

Luca shrugged again, except the gesture was anything but casual. I could read that in the tense lines of his face, in the rigid set of his broad shoulders. "I should have been aware. I should have . . . " His voice faded and that's when I understood.

I knew why Luca was a bodyguard. He lived to protect. To help others. To save lives. To make up for what he thought was a failing in his past. It was a compulsion etched deep in his soul, since the age of twelve.

He was staring down at his food, attacking it as though it were the unhappy memories of his past. There would be no telling him *not* to blame himself. These feelings were his, as real as the nose on my face. I would not insult him by telling him they weren't valid.

I stretched my arm across the table, closing my hand around his.

He looked up sharply. Our eyes held. Understanding passed between us.

I didn't say anything. There was no need. We were beyond words.

His hand turned over and he laced his fingers with mine. Our palms pressed flush together, pulses merging and fusing, and in that moment I felt more connected to this man than any other soul before. Not a single person back home. Not my family. Not my exes, even in our happiest of times.

I felt a communion with him—a man I'd known only for a few days. Was I delusional? Or was this truest thing I'd ever experienced?

CHAPTER ELEVEN

I SHOULD HAVE WORN proper shoes.

As in flats. Once the car stopped and we stepped out it didn't take very many steps for me to realize my heels on hard ground = not smart.

To make matters worse, they were new. I thought the strappy gold heels gorgeous and would be very Bond girl—perfect for an autumn gala. Especially with my dress.

I'd taken the advice of the sales clerk and avoided my instinctive need to wear any one of the black dresses I already owned. The woman at the store called the color I had on "sangria" and the word danced through my head every time I caught a glimpse of the satin fabric swishing at my ankles. My dress was fitted through the hips and then slightly flared the rest of the way down to the floor. It felt like another step toward my personal growth. I was wearing a form fitting satin dress. A definite first. I would never have worn this while married to any of my exes. I was too self-conscious of what I believed were my physical short-comings. Now I was happy with myself and would wear whatever dress I wanted to wear.

Luca guided me by the elbow but walked at a much slower pace than that of earlier today. Clearly he was sensitive to the fact that I wasn't wearing tennis shoes anymore.

We'd done practically everything on my list. Except Buckingham.

When I mentioned it following our lunch, he still insisted it was too crowded . . . and he *still* seemed to be laboring under the delusion that I was a person of importance who might be in peril. I didn't dispute it. He'd been kind enough to play tour guide and I'd gotten to see Baker Street and the Sherlock Holmes Museum, after all. My inner book nerd was very happy.

And there had been the highlight of my day. Lunch at Moretti's.

I snuck a glance at Luca's handsome face and felt a painful clench in the center of my chest. I was besotted, and it was really too bad because he clearly had his boundaries. He would not cross the line with me again. As much as he had allowed me glimpses of himself today, as fun and intimate as our time together had been, our relationship was professional. Friendly . . . but professional. That was all I would ever have with him.

People streamed across the plaza. Luca had a word with someone even bigger than he was, if that was possible, and we were ushered past a rope barrier and onto a long red carpet leading up the steps to the museum.

It was like something out of a movie. Cameras clicked as I moved up the red carpet. Someone called my name and I looked in that general direction only to have my picture snapped.

I leaned into Luca. "How do they know who I am? Or that I would even be here?"

He gave me a slightly indulgent look. "The guest list is always released early for these sort of things."

I nodded, but it still struck me as strange that anyone would consider me a celebrity.

Luca released a small huff of breath that was part laugh, part sigh. "You still don't understand that you're a celebrity, do you?"

"I don't feel like I am," I admitted. While my book had been a bestseller for a while now, I still shopped at the local Piggly Wiggly back home with no fanfare whatsoever. No one ever cared to get my picture as I was picking out a nectarine in Four Corners, Arkansas.

Luca shook his head as though I was somehow dense.

I bristled.

"Over here! V. M. Mathers!" I turned at the call, noticing a woman

wildly waving my book and a pen. She hopped in place when she saw
that she had my attention. "Please sign my book! Please!"

I hesitated and then started in her direction.

Luca tightened his grip on my arm. "It's best to keep moving."

"But she—"

"She could have attended your signing." Fair point. But she was here
and looked so very eager and full of longing and it really wouldn't be any
trouble.

"Vee," he said in warning voice, clearing sensing my reluctance to
comply with him. "We need to get inside."

Still, I hesitated, glancing back at the woman shouting my name.

His voice hardened. "Vee, no." I ignored him and inched toward her.

Something whizzed over my shoulder, narrowly missing my head.

Then there was a screech.

I followed the sound to a woman not two feet away from me on the
red carpet. She wore a glittering gown of gold . . . that was presently
covered with some sort of substance. The mess dripped down the front
of her bodice.

"What the . . . " I frowned, peering closer. *Egg.* She'd been struck
with egg.

The stench of it hit my nose. I choked a little.

Rotten egg.

The poor woman held her arms wide at her sides, her face red and
sputtering. I covered my nose with one hand and took a step in her direction. "Are you—"

Luca's fingers circled my bicep and gave me a hard yank, pulling me
from her—just as another object whipped past my head.

There was a sudden shift in the air as pandemonium broke out all
around me.

"Down!" Luca shouted roughly beside me.

"Oof!" Suddenly I was pushed to the ground. His big body covered
mine, smothering me, as a volley of eggs splattered the red carpet all
around us.

I tried to lift my head. "What's happening—"

"Stay down!"

The shower of eggs came to a stop. There was a slight easing of

Luca's weight off me as he lifted his head to inspect the area around us. I knew he wouldn't approve, but I lifted my head and looked around too.

The woman who had been originally struck by egg was full on wailing now. She'd been caught in the crossfire. More slime and bits of shell trickled down her hair and onto her shoulders. Her beautiful gown was ruined.

There was shouting from the other side of the ropes, where the woman waving my book had stood.

A small man was on the ground, pinned beneath a very thick looking knee and thigh, presumably a member of museum security. It didn't seem to discourage him though. He struggled and shouted obscenities as his stare locked dead on me. *Me*. I gulped a shaky breath. I had been his target? He'd been after me.

"Stay here," Luca ground out near my ear and then he was gone, bounding toward the man security was lifting up from the ground.

I sat up, watching as Luca reached the man. He hauled back and struck my would-be attacker with startling ferocity. I heard the crack of his knuckles on the man's face from where I crouched, trembling on the red carpet.

Security quickly stepped in, preventing Luca from another go at the man. Words were exchanged, but I couldn't hear over the loud din and snap and pop of cameras.

Luca returned to me, a feral light in his eyes. I'd never seen him like this. He seemed like an animal just released from his cage.

Grabbing my hand, he hauled me to my feet. This time there was no consideration given to my shoes as he dragged me at a sprint up the steps and into the museum, leaving the melee behind.

We dove inside, dodging people who were flooding outside to see what all the commotion was about. He scarcely slowed his pace once we were in the building. I barely had a moment to process the great domed glass ceiling.

There were so many colors. A kaleidoscope of women in beautiful gowns. Servers weaving through people and high cocktails tables with trays of drink and food.

A familiar face suddenly crossed my line of vision. The photographer who took my photo at the start of this wild ride, and whose work was displayed all over the museum tonight, walked right past. Lilah Rose's chin was tucked, her eyes down, her stylishly tousled dark hair almost masking her face, but it was impossible to miss her in a sleek lady tux that revealed an impressive amount of cleavage.

"Uh . . . Lilah?" I murmured.

She didn't hear me, and Luca didn't let up. We kept walking. His hand clasped tightly around mine as though he thought I might try to make a break for it. We edged the dance floor, and one dancer in particular caught my eye. I did a double take.

"Um. Is that Ian Hale?" He was my favorite actor. And there he was. In the flesh. Sitting all broody at a table beside the dance floor.

Luca didn't bother answering me. He was in a definite zone.

As though there was still a threat nipping at our heels, Luca pulled us deeper inside the grand building. We left the din of conversation behind. He veered left, taking us through the doors into the museum galleries. I saw a flash of a STAFF ONLY sign, but it did not deter him. He pushed ahead until the music from the live band was a faint hum.

"Luca? Where are we going?"

He turned down another hall. We were halfway down its length when he tried a doorknob. The door swung open and he spun me inside ahead of him, finally releasing my hand.

It was a storage room of some kind. Hard to tell what it was storing because sheets and tarps covered so many of the items in the room.

I turned to face him as he closed the door.

He stopped in front of me, his hands closing on my shoulders. He scanned my face and down my body, his dark eyes bright with worry and something else. "Are you okay?"

I nodded jerkily. "Yes. I'm fine." I released a shaky laugh. "That was intense, but I'm okay."

He wrenched his hands away from me as though he suddenly could not bear the feel of me.

I watched him prowl the cramped space, a ball of uneasiness growing in the pit of my belly as he very nearly violently dragged his hands through his hair.

"Luca?"

"Do you understand now?" he growled.

I shook my head. "What do you mean?"

"That you actually need protection." He stopped and glared at me.

"Are you *mad* at *me*?" I demanded, my own temper rising.

"You can't keep your head in the sand when you go to these events. There are some messed up people out there and you can't just skip up to them."

I pointed to the door. "That wasn't my fault out there, and that woman who wanted her book signed wasn't trying to hurt me either."

Bright fire snapped in his eyes. He was furious. "You've got to stop being so clueless and live more cautiously."

"I'm not going to live in fear—"

"How about you just show some common sense?"

I sucked in a sharp breath, galled at his incredible *rudeness*. "Is this how you talk to all your *principals*?"

His mouth closed, the lines on either side of his lips tight. His glare did not ease up on me. If anything, it only burned hotter.

I glared right back at him, lifting my chin a notch.

"No," he finally answered. "I don't speak to all my principals this way, and that's the problem."

"And I guess that's my fault?"

He took another hard step forward, closing the distance between us. I fought the urge to back up and held my ground. "It is. It is your fucking fault. From the moment we met, I've been trying to treat you like any other person I was assigned."

His words flayed me.

He kept coming and I couldn't help myself. He was too relentless. He was like a tsunami coming for me. I backed up until I hit the door. There was nowhere to go now unless I wanted to fling open the door and run. That was too dramatic even in this situation where the pheromones were flying and my blood was pumping and I couldn't stop staring at his mouth.

I wasn't running. We were doing this. Right here. Right now.

His hands came up, landing on either side of my head, flattening against the door. He angled his head and studied me like I was his next meal. I felt my ovaries clench and then combust.

My breath froze, trapped in my lungs, and I flattened my palms against the door behind me, too . . . my fingers digging into the surface, my neatly trimmed nails bending against the pressure as though they could carve out an escape. *Except I didn't really want to escape him.*

There was a party full of celebrities and people with cameras not far outside this room, but I didn't even care. His face was directly above mine. Even in my heels, he was still a few inches taller and I had to tilt my neck to look up at him.

"I can't do it anymore," he announced, the words a warm puff of air on my lips.

"Can't do what?" I countered.

"Treat you like any other principal."

"Oh," I breathed. "W-why not?"

"You have no idea? Really? Do you know how bloody hard it's been to keep my hands off you? Sharing a hotel room with you night after night? Even before that night in Edinburgh when you let me taste you . . . but then afterwards?" He shook his head slowly side to side and leaned in, his nose brushing my hair. "Being with you today was just amazing. And then tonight you're in this dress . . ." I didn't even know he found the dress attractive. He didn't bat an eye when I emerged from the room in it. "Pretending," he continued hoarsely, "that I don't want to do this."

His mouth slammed down on mine, hard and insistent, giving me the kiss I had craved and wanted all my life.

I moaned and he swept in, his tongue claiming, tasting, sliding against my own in sinuous strokes as he leaned full-length into me, pushing me against the door, the bulge of his cock prodding my belly undeniable. His hands came up to hold my face and that just fanned the flames hotter.

I lifted my hands up from the door and wrapped my arms around his broad shoulders. His palms rasped against my cheeks, his fingers spearing through my hair, messing the smooth and elegant arrangement of vintage waves I'd wrought.

I didn't care. The careful side part and elegant waves could be wrecked and that would be an accurate reflection of what was happening inside me.

I held on and kissed him back, hungry and desperate.

He lifted his head and I had to stop myself from chasing after his lips. At least he didn't step away. At least he stayed as he was, his big body pushing mine into the door, his hands framing my face. His gaze moved almost feverishly over my features, his dark eyes absorbing me, studying me in a way that spoke volumes. In those liquid-dark eyes, I knew what he wanted. I read the question there.

I answered him. Not with words though. I unwrapped one arm from around his shoulders and slid it down between us, palming his erection.

I felt my eyes widen and lock on his. I didn't need to hold it directly in my hand to know. He was big.

Curious, and not a little lust mad, I fumbled between us to see it. To see *him*. He didn't help me. I did it all. I freed him and took him out and looked down between us. "Oh, my."

"You ready for it?" he asked roughly, and there was an undercurrent of something vulnerable in his voice. As though he'd faced aversion before. Perhaps rejection. I knew all about vulnerability. I'd vowed never to feel it again. Four years ago I'd made that promise and here I was—as vulnerable as a person could be. Sex did that. No one could hide anything in the throes of it.

He felt like silk on steel in my hand. I ran my thumb over the head of him, reveling in his gasp. I'd never been with a man this endowed.

His voice came out strangled. "Vee?"

I answered him by pumping my hand several times up and down his length.

He moved then. His hands slid down my sides, running over my body, over the satin of my gown. I now heartily wished I had not gone with such a fitted gown. Something with a flared poofy skirt would have been ideal in this moment.

He dropped down and seized the hem of my gown. It took several violent yanks to pull my dress to my hips, and then he squatted again, yanking my panties down to my ankles. I neatly stepped one leg out of them and let the other gold-heeled foot kick them off.

I was really doing this.

I'd shared a hotel room with this guy for several nights and we were finally doing it. Against a door. In a storage closet at a party at the British Museum. I didn't regret it, though. Better late than never. I was leaving tomorrow. *I was leaving tomorrow.* A lump of emotion rose up in my throat and my hunger for him twisted deeper, harder, darker inside me. My sex throbbed almost painfully. I had to have him. Inside me. Quickly.

Rising, he reached inside his jacket, giving me a glimpse of his sidearm. It should have turned me off—reminded me of who he was. Who I was. But it didn't matter. Four plus years was a long time to go without intimacy. A lifetime was even longer to go without the kind of excitement I was feeling right now.

He dug in his wallet and then there was a crinkle and tear of a condom wrapper. He worked fast, sheathing himself and then lifting one of my thighs, positioning it high against his hip. Grabbing my other thigh, he hoisted me up in one move, locking my legs around him.

I gave a small gasp of surprise that turned into a yelp as he entered me in a deep thrust that I felt in my teeth.

"Oh, wow." I inhaled and exhaled deeply, clutching my arms around his shoulders, my fingers digging into him, the tips bloodless white.

He held himself motionless, not moving, not thrusting. He was as still as stone, the only sensation his big throbbing cock inside me. He pulsed and my inner muscles clenched around him.

He groaned, but still didn't move.

I was wedged between the door and his body. His hands slid down, cupping my bottom, holding me up for him. He dropped his forehead against mine, his own panting breath mingling with mine. "Okay?"

"Yes."

"Ah, bloody hell . . . been a while, has it?" His lips twisted in semblance of a smile.

"Yeah." I strangled on a laugh. "Um, yeah, but you might be more, um, than I'm used to . . . give me a minute."

"I'll give you forever," he said right before he kissed me deep—long and hard and thorough. Every stroke of his tongue ratcheted up my desire. I sank deeper on him, inner muscles greedily flexing around him. I whimpered into his mouth. Pinned between the door and his body, it was impossible to pump myself against him, but the impulse was there, and I wiggled.

He got the idea. I was ready, and he bounced me once in his hands, readjusting his grip on my ass.

Oh. I cried out in exultation as he started to move. Long and deep. Never easy. Never soft. Hard, slick thrusts that I felt to my core.

I doubted that gentle existed in him. This, I realized, was what it was to fuck. I'd had sex before. But I'd never been fucked.

He increased his pace, setting a tempo that coalesced each thrust with a bang against the door. I bit my lip, trying to keep silent, dimly aware we were in a public venue, but it was impossible. I couldn't. Every nerve ending was alive and vibrating and singing out in pleasure.

My lip popped free of my teeth, and I cried out. At every plunge, every push, every drive into the door, a cry spilled out. I rode him, sliding up and down against the door with the force of his thrusts, clutching him close, basking in the sounds of his groans in my ear—that he needed me, wanted me in this moment, as much as I wanted him.

Just when I thought I couldn't feel any better, something broke loose inside me. I collapsed, sinking down on him as I released a cry, long and keening. The sound gradually faded and I went limp, my body quivering between the door and him. I drifted back down as tremors rolled through me.

He kept on going. His hands flexed and massaged my ass cheeks as he thrust, anchoring me, marking me in a way that felt indelible. I didn't think there would be a day when I didn't feel the brand of his hands on me—when I didn't close my eyes and remember the sliding friction of him inside me.

Suddenly he stilled, and a hoarse, muffled shout escaped his lips. I felt his release, even through the barrier of a condom. He pulsed and twitched, buried inside me. I watched his face in awe, his expression like nothing I had ever seen in any lover. It was only something I felt. Bliss. Pleasure. Fulfillment. All of this. Now. With him.

He dropped his head into the crook of my neck. Gradually sounds returned. The pants of our breaths. The distant music from the party. Footsteps outside the door. Voices.

He lifted his head and his dark eyes pinned me as effectively as his body had me pinioned to the door. "So. Want to get out of here?"

CHAPTER TWELVE

THE DASH from the museum was a blur. The car ride less so. We sat in the backseat, trying not to be too indiscreet since we weren't alone in the car. Luca sat close, his big hand inching inside the side slit of my dress to caress my thigh, as though he could not *not* touch me.

I held his hand, fingers laced with his—the one that wasn't climbing up the inside of my thigh. Our palms pressed flush, pulse to pulse. Kissing palms.

The driver acted as though we were invisible, but he must have felt the tension on the air, the tightly checked self-restraint.

We made it out of the car and up the elevator without taking off our clothes, but he was peeling off his jacket by the time he crossed the threshold to our hotel room, and we were both fully naked by the time we hit the bed. A condom wrapper ripped and I was grateful he was prepared and took care of that before it even crossed my mind.

I trembled at the sensation of his naked body wrapped around mine. The scratch of hair on his legs rubbed against my skin. The heavy weight of his cock pressed against the inside of my thigh. And there was his mouth consuming me everywhere. First my lips, and then he traveled down my throat. The line of my collarbone. My chest. The undersides of my breasts. My stomach. Yes, even there . . . where I'd always been so self-conscious. He kissed and loved the rounded curve of it, and I moaned, arching under him.

He crawled up me, wedged himself between my thighs and slid home. He lifted one of my legs and flung it over his shoulder, opening me wider for him. He thrust easy and deep, the delicious friction intensifying with each stroke.

We continued on like that. Me under him. Until he rolled nimbly, taking me with him and I was on top then.

I didn't think it could be better than before, but it was.

On top was new. I never got on top. I'd never been comfortable enough, confident enough, but I went with him to the brink, flying over my previous limits.

Straddling him, I settled my weight, sinking down, taking him deep inside. I rocked and controlled the angle of him inside me and that was new and incredible and made me wonder why I'd never done this before . . . but I knew why. I didn't have to wonder. I'd never done it like this before because I'd never been with him before.

Sex was a vulnerable enough act, but sex in a position like this required real trust. For some reason, I trusted him. From the very start, he had evoked feelings of trust. I felt safe with him. Safer than I'd ever felt with any man. Maybe it was his profession, but I suspected it was Luca—the man he was. I didn't trust him because he was a bodyguard. I trusted him because he was the type of man who excelled at being a bodyguard.

He was someone who made people feel safe, and I was no exception.

He was rock solid, a man to depend on. A man who said what he meant, didn't play games, and never backed down. A man like none I'd known.

I rode him, rocking on his cock, arching my back and letting every sound I felt escape with no fear, no concern for our neighbors.

He lifted up on his elbows and devoured my breasts, his tongue and teeth attacking my nipples vigorously. "So sweet," he rasped as I ran fingers through his hair, tugging on the strands and moving him, guiding him where I wanted his mouth to be.

"Harder," I gasped, and he responded, his mouth biting at my nipples. I cried out at the sweet pain of it, feeling a rush of moisture between my legs, slicking the way for him.

His hands latched onto my waist, bringing me down faster, harder on his cock.

He came with a groan. I came much more shrilly. The edges of my vision blurred as I was launched into another orgasm. My hands dropped to his chest, bracing myself as it rolled through me. "Too . . . much," I panted.

He lifted himself up, his hand cupping the back of my head, tugging me closer as his lips closed on my earlobe, softly nipping the sensitive flesh before he whispered, "Never enough."

Never enough.

His words continued to whisper through me even after we'd cleaned up and settled back down in the bed. Even later, after he'd ordered us room service and we binged on steaks, truffle mac and cheese and chocolate cake.

Never enough. Never enough. Never enough.

It would have to be enough because it wasn't as though this could go on. I was leaving tomorrow, and he was staying here.

I lived in another country. We would not be seeing each other again.

He had to know that. It was probably why he was so insatiable. The reason we had sex two more times. He was getting the most he could out of one night together.

My flight wasn't until tomorrow afternoon, but I didn't look forward to the morning. All things appeared in the morning—truths you could avoid at night. The light of day revealed everything.

I didn't look forward to a lingering farewell as he escorted me from the hotel to the airport. Would he turn once again into the *specialist?* That would . . . hurt.

I didn't want to see him like that again. I didn't want him to be that way with me. Not anymore.

We fell asleep, but I didn't know if I would call it restful. Several times I woke, searching for something, discovering that I had drifted to the edge of the bed, away from his heat radiating length. I would scoot back to his gorgeous body and place a hand somewhere on him, just to touch him, to maintain contact, to have that comfort. I could sleep again then.

The next time I woke he was gone. A familiar sinking sensation seized me, and I bolted upright, hugging the sheet to my chest. My gaze shot around the room. Dawn peeked at the edges of my curtains. I slowly eased from the bed and walked from my room into the small sitting area, my feet padding silently on the carpet. That's when I heard water running.

That's when I realized he was taking a shower.

That's when a steady calm came over me and I knew.

I needed to seize this chance and leave. Avoid the awkward good-bye and the uneasy farewell where we were compelled to say things we didn't mean.

Dropping my sheet, I turned and fled into my room, wondering if I could pack and be out of here in less than five minutes.

It took me seven minutes, but brushing my teeth felt very necessary and was worth the extra two.

I pulled my hair into a messy ponytail and tossed everything in my luggage and was out the door to the sound of the shower still running. Lucky for me he enjoyed long showers.

Except as I stumbled across the lobby to ask the doorman to hail me a cab, I didn't feel lucky. I felt . . . sad. Like I was leaving a part of me behind. A part of myself I had just found. Even though I knew that was irrational and fanciful and the kind of stuff a hopeless dreamer would believe, I definitely felt *un*lucky.

I arrived well before my flight departure time, so I didn't have an assigned gate yet, but I still got rid of my bag and went through security. Less harried, I found a bathroom and tried to tidy my decidedly untidy appearance. I even applied minimal makeup, hoping that would make me feel more collected. Following that, I found a coffee shop. An injection of caffeine would make me feel more *me*. I never skipped my morning coffee.

I sat at a corner table with a view of the airport. People walked past, hurrying to either catch a plane or get back home. I was eager for neither. My hands wrapped around my coffee cup, holding tightly as though that might stop them from shaking. I sipped the hot brew for a few minutes, but the caffeine did nothing to steady my nerves.

A waitress came by and I ordered an iced scone, hoping the decadent fare would make me feel better. It failed to offer the usual comfort, however, and sat like a rock in my stomach. I didn't even feel up to browsing the airport bookstores for copies of my book. That always cheered me up. It was one thing to see your book in print and a completely separate thrill to see it in an airport bookstore.

I couldn't help thinking about Luca and wondering at his reaction when he discovered I'd left. Would he be very annoyed or relieved? I'd saved us from an uncomfortable situation, after all. Certainly, he would realize that even if he was initially annoyed that I subverted his protection services again. He'd get over it and so would I.

Eventually, we would both look back on this with fond recollection —like a wonderful vacation with a wonderful friend. No regrets.

The coffee shop had a small TV. I settled into my seat and tried to distract myself by watching it. It didn't work. Every movement, every shift in my seat only served to remind me of my night with Luca. The telltale signs were there, fresh and sharp as a blade against my skin.

My body was sore. My sex still throbbed. My breasts felt heavy, nipples raw and chafing against the inside of my bra. The tiny hairs on my skin quivered as though I'd been shocked with electricity. The flow of blood in my veins felt thicker, hotter. I was aware of myself in a way I never had been before. Each part, each piece of me, felt like its own entity. Its own living being separate from the rest of me.

It would all fade. I knew that. Wilt to memory.

I frowned as I sipped my coffee, sad at the sudden idea that as fresh as last night was now, I'd forget his scent, his taste, the pulse and fullness of him inside me.

My gate was finally posted, and after a little while I gathered my handbag and headed that way. It was a big airport. I wanted to give myself plenty of time. I strolled at any easy pace, letting myself be distracted by the sights, drifting into shops that looked mildly interesting.

I eventually located my gate and took a seat, waiting for boarding to begin, letting the minutes tick by as I tried to get excited. I was going to Paris. That should be the only thing on my mind. I should be brimming with excitement. I was a short plane ride to Paris. My French publicist would collect me at the airport and from there, my French adventure would begin. I had five days in Paris. It should have been the only thing that mattered right then.

Boarding began and they called my row. I fell in line and was soon settling into my seat. Buckled in, I did a quick browse through my phone, sending a quick update to my mom, letting her know where I was headed.

A body dropped down beside me.

My phone slipped from my fingers, tumbling to the small gap of floor at my feet. We bent at the same time to retrieve my phone and our heads collided.

"Ow." I came up, rubbing my skull, then my breath lodged in my throat.

It couldn't be.

But it was.

"What are you doing here?" I blurted, embarrassment and hope and desire tangling and knotted messily in my chest.

Luca deftly claimed my phone and handed it to me. "Going to Paris."

"P-Paris?" I gawked at Luca's face. Light from the window behind me cast his good looks into stark focus. "With me?"

"Of course with you."

He was serious. He was on this plane. I blinked several times, processing that he was beside me and what it could mean.

I moistened my lips. "Did Melani extend your contract to—"

"This has nothing to do with your publisher. I'm here on my own." He took a breath, his gaze steadily fixed on my face. "I'm here for you."

I'm here for you.

My heart hammered like a drum in my chest. "You're here for . . . me?" He'd grabbed his passport, bought a ticket and was on this plane with me. He'd done all that for me.

A smile kicked up one corner of his beautiful mouth. "Are you just going to repeat everything I say?"

"I—I . . ." I could not speak, apparently. I was too stunned at the sight of him. Too stunned to have him right here beside me, crowding me in the tight area of our two-seat row. I swallowed thickly and managed to spit out some words. "Is this something you do?" Was it a casual thing for him to hook up with women and then chase after them because his itch wasn't fully satisfied yet?

"Vee. I'm not an impulsive person." He dragged a hand through his hair, sending locks flying haphazardly in every direction, making him appear younger, more genuine. There was nothing fake about him. "My whole life I've been this organized individual. Someone who stays in the lines. Who follows rules. But with you, I've broken them."

He turned to fully face me in the narrow space—the space that suddenly seemed all the tighter with his big body occupying it. "With you I would break every rule." He seized my hand then, his gaze intent on my face. "Are you ready to say goodbye? Do you never want to be with me again?" Pause. He shook his head as though that would be something terrible indeed, but he would accept it if that's what I wanted. He was a man who kept people safe. He would never do anything that went against my wishes. He took another breath. "*Or do you want to see where this thing goes?*"

Not only could I not speak. I couldn't breathe. Could only think: *yes yes yes yes.*

I want to see where this thing goes.

I didn't *need* him, I realized. That was my mistake before. The old me always felt like I needed one of my exes. I didn't need Luca. But I *wanted* him. And that was okay. It was okay to have someone. It was not weakness. I was fine without him, but I could be better with him.

He continued, "If you want me to leave, just say so. I can still get off this plane. I'll go."

"No," I whispered. "Don't go."

It was hard to believe, but there was something between us—a definite thing. I felt it. He felt it. And I was not ready to let go of it. Not yet.

Maybe even more unbelievable . . . maybe not ever.

He closed the few inches between us and kissed me. His hand slid along my face, fingers and palms rasping my cheek as our mouths fused, tasting and taking and branding. I'd been kissed a lot of times, but this felt different. It felt a lot like forever.

He came up after a long moment to the tune of the flight attendants announcing the closing of the airplane's doors. I smiled at him.

He smiled down at me. "You know the convenient thing about being a writer?"

"What's that?"

"You can do it from anywhere . . . live anywhere."

My smile deepened and I asked lightly, "Is that a fact?"

"Yes. Someone told me that once."

"Well," I said, nodding in agreement, my chest swelling, elation rising up inside me. "That *is* very convenient."

ALSO BY SOPHIE JORDAN

The Debutante Files

A Good Debutante's Guide to Ruin

An Heiress for All Seasons (novella)

All The Ways To Ruin A Rogue

The Forgotten Princess

Wicked In Your Arms

Lessons From A Scandalous Bride

The Earl In My Bed (Novella)

How To Lose A Bride In One Night

The Penwich School for Virtuous Girls

Sins Of A Wicked Duke

In Scandal They Wed

Wicked Nights With A Lover

The Derrings

Once Upon A Wedding Night

Too Wicked To Tame

One Night With You

Surrender To Me

How The Dukes Stole Christmas (Anthology)

YOUNG ADULT

Standalone Novels

The Me I Meant To Be

Kissing Lessons

Reign of Shadows

Reign of Shadows

Rise of Fire

Uninvited

Uninvited

Unleashed

Firelight

Firelight

Vanish

Hidden

Breathless (Novella)

ABOUT THE AUTHOR

Sophie Jordan grew up in the Texas hill country where she wove fantasies of dragons, warriors, and princesses. A former high school English teacher, she's a *New York Times, USA Today* and international bestselling author. She now lives in Houston with her family. When she's not writing, she spends her time overloading on caffeine (lattes and Diet cherry Coke preferred), talking plotlines with anyone who will listen (including her kids), and cramming her DVR with true-crime and reality-TV shows.

Visit her at sophiejordan.net, or sign up for her newsletter at bit.ly/SophieNews.

NOT A BAD BOY

LOUISA EDWARDS

CHAPTER ONE

I YAWNED and reached down to unsnap Pilot's leash, my fingers slipping against the clasp of his leather collar. The next thing I knew, I was lurching forward as Pilot jerked from my grasp to race across the sun-dappled expanse of Primrose Hill, barking his head off like the maniac he was.

Since I was Mallory Pritchard, and I've never had any kind of luck that wasn't bad, I lost my balance completely. I went down. And all I could think, as my ass hit the damp grass, was *of course.*

Of freaking course, because when I winced and turned my head, not only could I see my ridiculous Irish wolfhound/Airedale terrier/Who-The-Hell-Knows mix capering around a magnificently uninterested pit bull, I also caught a glimpse of the other dog's owner.

And holy shit. My heart, which was still pounding from my abrupt collision with the earth, suddenly ramped up to cardiac event levels of beating.

The man currently scanning the grassy hill above Regent's Park for the dummy who couldn't control her dog was Ian Hale.

Ian Hale, last year's Sexiest Man Alive. Ian Hale, star of the biggest action movie franchise in the world. Ian Hale, the man my sister had joked was the reason I moved to London.

"Admit it," I remembered Samantha saying, her voice determinedly light and playful. "You're a writer, you could live anywhere. You picked London hoping to run into Ian Hale."

I'd confined my response to a sigh, because there were about a million things wrong with that statement but it would take a lot of energy to argue them all. And back then I didn't have the energy to do much more than get up in the morning to let Pilot out to pee in the postage stamp backyard of our parents' Brooklyn townhouse.

But I didn't want to make Samantha worry about me, at least not more than she already was, so I said, "Actually, I can't work from anywhere in the world, because I'm researching the history of cookbook writing, and the British Museum holds the best collection of the first commercially available cookbooks by women, so that's where I'm going."

"Right," Samantha agreed. "Potential Ian Hale sightings are just a bonus."

At the time, I'd only sighed again and gone back to packing. I mean, I'd lived in New York City my entire adult life. Celebrity sightings weren't exactly anything new to me. I once saw Kevin Bacon trying on scarves at a Gap on the Upper West Side. He was short. "Come on. Ian Hale is probably a troll in person."

"I bet Ian Hale is as good-looking as he seems on-screen."

"No one could be as good-looking as Ian Hale seems on-screen." I grabbed the book off my bedside table and chucked it into my carry-on. It was the nonfiction title currently burning up the bestseller lists, *Self Love*, and it was all about how women didn't need men for anything. Perfect reading material for my new life in London. "He's probably an asshole in person. And short. I bet he's a short asshole. They always are."

"You don't believe that." Samantha gave me the knowingly scornful look of an older sister who used to trick me into putting peas up my nose as a toddler. "You're a romantic."

"It doesn't matter," I insisted. "Because I'm not going to run into him. And even if I did, I don't gawk at celebrities. I ignore them, like a good New Yorker."

But right here and right now, lying on my back on the grass with the wind knocked out of me and an actual, honest to God movie star leading my scruffy mutt over with one big hand on Pilot's collar, Ian Hale was impossible to ignore.

He loomed up, the huge, dark outline of his shoulders blocking the sun, and I shivered. Breath returned to my lungs in a whoosh, and I gasped in air like a landed trout struggling on the ground. I couldn't make out his expression against the glare. His face was all shadows and angles, and I had a fleeting moment to wonder if I'd been mistaken—it wasn't Ian Hale, after all. That was ridiculous. I must have hit my head.

And then he spoke. His voice curled through my chest like smoke, and I knew I wasn't mistaken. I'd heard that voice before—shouting in anger, broken and brooding, barking commands and whispering tenderness in a darkened movie theater to a captivated audience.

It was Ian Hale. And as he stared down at me on the top of Primrose Hill, in the watery morning sunlight with all of London laid out at our feet, he said, "Is this your dog?"

Pilot stuck his head down and panted happily into my face, his black whiskers tickling over my forehead and cheeks. I had to squeeze my eyes shut to avoid being blinded by drool. This wasn't exactly how my Ian Hale fantasies usually began. "I'm so sorry. He's a menace."

Instead of agreeing with me, Ian Hale paused. His knuckles whitened where he gripped Pilot's collar, and I was pretty sure I could hear a frown in his voice when he said, "He's not. He's a good boy. Just a little high spirits, innit."

The accent. Oh my God, delicious. Less posh than what he did as Zeus in the *Mount Olympus* movies, with a rough undertone that sent a shudder down my spine. My spine, which was still pressed against the dewy wet grass. I flopped around awkwardly and somehow made it up to a kneeling position. I was sure my face was a lovely shade of red; I could feel wispy curls escaping my bun and sticking to my cheeks.

I probably shouldn't have quit Pilates just because it was something Tony and I used to do together.

Well. I also quit because I hated it, and I'd rather spend an hour on the couch cuddling my dog and working my way through a bag of white cheddar popcorn than grunting on a table and activating my nonexistent core. But the Tony thing didn't help.

As soon as I was on his level, Pilot plunged his scruffy face into the side of my neck, and the prickle of his whiskers instantly erased all my annoyance with him. "High spirits is a very kind way of describing it. I really am sorry if he upset your dog."

"Roxanne can take care of herself."

I peered over Pilot's ears at the massive, sleek head of Ian Hale's silvery blue pit bull—probably a Staffordshire terrier. The dog's jaws looked strong enough to bite through concrete. I wrapped an arm around Pilot's neck, belatedly concerned for his foolish life.

"I bet she can," I said, a little nervously.

"She wouldn't hurt anyone except to defend herself." He let go of Pilot's collar and stepped back, the move putting the bulk of his body between his pit bull and me. *Oh man.* My heart clenched when I realized he was actually shielding his dog from me.

I scrambled to my feet, the opposite of graceful, and I wasn't surprised when he didn't reach out a hand to help me up. "Oh, Mr. Hale . . ."

It was clear, the exact moment when he knew I'd recognized him. He looked to the side, the sun finally falling across his rugged, golden-tanned cheekbones and bringing out bronze and copper glints in his hair, which was cropped shorter than the way it looked in the Mount Olympus movies. It was almost buzzed at the sides and back, and allowed to wave a little longer on top. The more modern style gave his handsome face a dangerous edge that struck a deep chord of awareness in my belly.

God, he was beautiful.

A muscle clenched in his hard jaw. Until the moment it vanished, I hadn't appreciated the warmth and vitality of the man I'd been speaking to. He turned to stone right before my eyes.

I was the absolute worst. Here this international movie star was, on his day off, trying to walk his dog in peace. And then he gets besieged by a wild American lady and her mutt. Pilot leaned into my leg as if he could feel me drooping. I wanted to apologize again, this time for knowing who he was, but that seemed nuts. Everyone knew who he was. It was a fact of his life, and I could tell he accepted it, but he didn't like it. Not one bit. I ducked my head, expecting him to just walk away, but he didn't.

Into the excruciatingly awkward silence, I said, "You know, the most decorated dog of World War I was a pit bull named Sergeant Stubby. And not because he was an attack dog or something. His job was comforting wounded soldiers."

He looked down at the solid, well-muscled dog sitting calmly at his side. "Makes sense."

I wondered how much time Roxanne spent comforting Ian Hale. Probably not much, I would have assumed, between all the glamorous parties and awards shows and film sets. But something in the set of the man's insanely broad shoulders said he was thinking of a time when he'd needed the unconditional love of a furry companion.

"The outside of a dog is good for the insides of a man," I blurted, then flushed. "I mean, Winston Churchill said it about horses, but I think it applies to dogs too."

"Nice bits of trivia you have at your fingertips," he offered.

There was a definite crack in the stonework. I grinned. "I'm full of trivia. My sister would say I'm a very trivial person."

Slanting a glance at me from under his ridiculously long lashes, Ian Hale gave me a look I'd swear I never saw on his famous face before. It was the smallest smile, just enough to kick up one corner of his beautifully shaped mouth, but it was completely and entirely genuine. And it was all for me.

It faded between one heartbeat and the next, leaving me wondering if I'd imagined it.

"I don't believe it," he said quietly, and for an instant I didn't know what he was talking about.

When I picked up the thread of the conversation, I laughed, embarrassed. "Well, no. It's kind of true. In the sense that I get easily distracted by little tangents, offshoots of whatever I'm supposed to be looking up—I'm a writer."

"A writer. And an American." He was looking at me now, looking right into my eyes, and it was intense. Like staring into the sun. "And a dog lover."

"If you can call this big baby a dog." I bent at the waist to give Pilot a good snuffle between his perked ears, and when I stood up again, Ian Hale gave me that tiny, unfamiliar, dazzling smile again.

"You love him," he said. "That's good."

"I was only supposed to be fostering him until we could find him a forever home. His first owners left him tied up in their backyard and freaking moved house. Can you believe someone would do that? But in the end, I couldn't let him go. I've never been very good at forever, but we're giving it our best shot."

I bit my lip, aware that I was babbling. But Ian Hale didn't look bored or annoyed. In fact, his whole face had softened until he almost looked approachable, like someone I could go up to and introduce myself . . . if he hadn't been the sexiest man I'd ever seen in my life.

"Roxanne is a rescue too. Abused as a pup."

"Humans are the worst," I offered, my heart swelling.

The entire situation was starting to feel like a dream. I kept expecting to wake up, or at the very least for Ian Hale—movie star Ian Hale!—to take his dog and walk off down the hill and out of my ordinary life for good.

He was nothing like I'd ever imagined him, to the extent that I'd thought of him as a real person at all. And didn't that make me feel like a jerk? Because Ian Hale was very, very real.

It was a crisp, bright morning; a rare fall day in London without rain. I was wearing my "research uniform" of yoga pants and a chunky cable-knit sweater that swung down to my thick thighs. I surreptitiously tugged at the hem to make sure it covered my ample ass.

Ian Hale was wearing a thin white T-shirt. His bare arms, dusted with dark hair and corded with the thick muscle of a man who played a literal Greek god for a living, showed no evidence of feeling the cold breeze.

He emanated a version of the leashed vitality that I'd admired from my seat in a darkened movie theater, chocolate-covered raisins in one hand and Coke in the other. But the difference between Ian Hale as Zeus ruling the world and Ian Hale walking his dog in a baseball cap tugged low over his shockingly blue eyes . . . I couldn't even explain it.

I mean, I would've expected an actor to have charisma. That wasn't some huge surprise. But his intensity, the way he studied my face as if he didn't want to miss a single tiny shift in expression. I never could've predicted that.

And the way it made me feel to be the focus of that close attention?

Also surprising, because I'd always been content to sit in the back of the class and keep my head down. It was easy to hide when you were the fat girl. People's eyes tended to skim right over me, as if my curves made me invisible.

Standing here on this windy hilltop, with Ian Hale's gaze on me, I was having a hard time remembering what it felt like to be unseen.

Pilot whined, his wiry body wriggling with the need to run. With every fiber of my being, I did not want to cut this surreal, once-in-a-life-time encounter short, but . . .

"I should let this guy do his thing," I said reluctantly, glancing at my watch. "The British Museum study room I reserved opens in an hour."

"Are you doing research for a book?"

The strangeness of being asked about my work by an attractive man heated my cheeks with something that was half embarrassment, half pleasure.

"Actually, yeah. That's why I'm in London. I'm here to study the museum's collection of early cookbooks."

"You like to cook, then?" he asked, and I had to laugh, even as I felt my cheeks heat with the familiar embarrassment of admitting that, yes, I was a human person who enjoyed food. As if that wasn't completely normal and universal. Maybe skinny women didn't worry about it? I wouldn't know.

"I guess that's an easy leap to make." I tucked a curl behind my ear self-consciously. "But no, actually, I write nonfiction. Intimate histories of ordinary things."

"So you're not writing a cookbook." He produced a tennis ball from the back pocket of his jeans and showed it to the dogs. Roxanne coiled with graceful strength and sprang after it when her master let it fly. Pilot followed, barking delightedly. "A book . . . about cookbooks?"

"You can learn a lot about a culture by reading its guides to food and cookery. From the evolution of people's understanding of nutrition and wellness to the social implications of who the cookbook writers assume will be doing the cooking—the first major works of cookery writing were by professional chefs, mostly men, and aimed at other professional chefs. I'm interested in the moment when it shifted, in the eighteenth century. When cookbooks started appearing that were by women, for women who were maintaining their own households. Did you know the first cookbook ever published in the American colonies was by a woman? An Englishwoman, in fact. And oh my God, I'm rambling."

I took a breath. *Yikes, Mallory, way to go all nerdy professor on the guy.* "I'm so sorry to go on and on."

"No, it's interesting," he said as Roxanne returned, triumphant, and dropped the ball at his feet while Pilot wagged his tail as proudly as if he were the one who'd caught it. Ian Hale picked up the ball and threw it again. "You're very passionate."

"Huh. That's not what my ex thought." I froze. "I . . . did not mean to say that."

Ian Hale's brows lowered threateningly over his icy blue eyes. "Your ex sounds like a right wanker."

"He really kind of was."

"Is he part of the reason you came to London, then?"

I shrugged, but my heart was racing. We were in the middle of a public park, but somehow this felt like the most intimate conversation I'd had with a man in my whole life. Having already spilled half my guts onto the grass between us, I decided to go full out. I was never going to see this incredible man again, anyway. And the way he was looking at me, as if every word I said mattered to him—it was intoxicating.

"We had a bad breakup, yeah. But it was mostly my fault. No, really. Tony was the first guy I'd been with after a long, shall we say, dry spell. And early on, he seemed great—he paid so much attention to me, he wanted to do everything together, working out and shopping and cooking. And then I realized that all those activities were about changing me. Slimming me down and dressing me up to match some image in his head of what his perfect woman should be, until I barely recognized myself in the mirror. And I decided I'd rather be me, and be alone, than be with someone who didn't even like the real me."

Yup, intoxicating was the right word. I couldn't believe I'd gushed all of that out like a drunk to a sympathetic bartender.

Only Ian Hale didn't look sympathetic. He looked *pissed.*

I flinched back from the anger on his face, and his expression immediately twisted into something anguished before he looked away. His shoulders hunched and he jammed his hands into his pockets as if he was trying to make himself smaller.

Confused, I reached out to him right as Pilot rammed himself into the backs of my knees, nearly buckling them. Grateful for the distraction, I bent down to wrestle the slobbery tennis ball out of his mouth. When I looked up again, Ian Hale was halfway down the hill, striding away with his pit bull trotting obediently at his side.

What the hell just happened?

CHAPTER TWO

"IT'S NOT OVER!" Samantha's face got larger on the screen, like she'd dragged her laptop closer to make her point.

"I dumped a load of drama about my ex-boyfriend onto a complete and total stranger who just happens to be the sexiest man alive." I flopped backward onto my bed, holding my phone up over my head and giving my sister big, tragic eyes.

It was late in London. After a long, very distracted day of taking notes and a bit of dinnertime mooning over a bottle of wine, my tiny image in the corner of the phone screen looked even more disheveled than usual. My sister, even after having arrived home after a long commute from her high-powered corporate job at eight p.m. New York time, looked as fresh as if she'd just brushed bronzer onto her creamy cheeks.

"He talked to you," she insisted. "For like, whole minutes. When he didn't have to. He's into you."

A delicious, full-body shudder made me wriggle a little on the sheets at the very idea. "He's not into me. That's . . . beyond ludicrous, Sam. It's impossible. You didn't see him."

"Oh, I've seen him. I've seen *all* of him." She waggled her straight, full brows, referencing the near full frontal he'd done in *Immortal Wars*.

"Yeah, but he was different in real life. I can't explain it."

"I told you!" she crowed, triumphant. "Hotter in person. Admit it."

I gave in, like I always did. "Yeah, he definitely is."

But that wasn't what I meant. It was more about the way he'd talked, rough and quiet and with as few words as possible. Or the darkness that filtered through the bright blue of his eyes, like the unexplored depths of the ocean. I didn't know how to articulate it to my sister and, totally bizarrely, it almost would have felt like a betrayal to try.

Like a betrayal of Ian Hale, a man I'd met for all of ten minutes, and would never see again except on the cover of a tabloid or on the silver screen. I was losing my damn mind.

I didn't know what Samantha saw in my face, but she got gentle all of a sudden. In that don't-spook-the-horses tone she'd used so much in the wake of Tony, she said, "You think he couldn't be attracted to you because Tony the Tool made you feel unlovable, but it's so not true, Mal. You deserve to be loved."

Always nice to hear, right? And I knew my sister meant it with her whole, huge heart. So how could I ruin the moment by pointing out the elephant in the room?

Okay, that was harsh. I was a healthy woman with lots of curves. It had taken some work, but I didn't hate the way I looked. However, I wasn't enough of a dreamer to delude myself that the rest of the world felt the same. I'd been hearing comments pretty much my entire life about how I'd be so sexy if I only lost twenty pounds, or how I had pretty hair or pretty eyes, because no one who was on the plus side of the scale could ever just be *pretty*, right?

My sister, on the other hand, looked exactly like me, but with all the fat shaved off and the curves trimmed down. She'd been popular, she'd never gone longer than a couple of weeks between boyfriends, and she could look at a magazine or a TV show and see people wearing clothes that would fit her body and look good.

Basically, Samantha didn't get it, and I didn't think she ever would. But she loved me with the fierce loyalty of an older sister who had never once allowed me to be bullied in our neighborhood.

So I didn't say, "Get real, Sam. You think a man who has super-models and A-list actresses hanging all over him is going to look twice at a chubby nerd?"

Instead I said, "I know I deserve to be loved. That's why I ditched Tony, if you recall. But it doesn't matter right now, because not only does Ian Hale not love me, he's gone. He didn't give me his number or ask for mine. I don't know where he lives. And even if I did, what am I supposed to do, stand under his window and yell up to him asking for ten more minutes to lecture him about how the first recipe for ketchup had anchovies in it?"

She flipped a wave of dark hair out of her face. Her eyes, a clear brown just like mine, sparkled with mischief. "You don't need to stalk him at his house. You know where he walks his dog."

So that's how I ended up at Primrose Hill bright and early the very next morning, slightly regretting that bottle of wine but showered and made up and wearing a cute dress. I'd even given Pilot a bath that morning, when I woke up in a panicked sweat at five a.m., nervous about what Samantha had convinced me to do.

Which was to doll up and hunt down a movie star.

I'll just be here, I told myself silently. *I won't bother him, if he seems like he doesn't want to talk. I'll let him approach me. I'll play it cool.*

Play it cool. For the first time in my entire life. No problem.

Pilot nudged my hand with his cold, wet nose. He couldn't figure out why I was clutching that stupid tennis ball instead of throwing it for him to chase. My bare legs goose-pimpled in the morning fog and a light rain started misting down.

I stared around the park. There were a lot fewer people this morning, probably because the weather had turned from yesterday's surprise sunshine back to the regularly scheduled London mist and chill. There was a white couple walking a Labrador retriever, and an older Asian lady on a bench with a sensible mackintosh and a very silly poodle. There was no tall, broad-shouldered movie star anywhere in sight.

"This was a dumb idea," I told Pilot, who looked at me as if to say, "I agree, lady. Now throw that ball."

I'd brought the ball to give back to Ian Hale if I saw him, but who was I kidding? He wasn't going to show up. Yesterday was a fluke, a bizarre and random chance encounter that would never be repeated—most likely because if Ian Hale had any sense, he'd find another park so he could avoid any possibility of running into Pilot and me.

So I sighed and threw the ball, wrapping my cold arms around my torso and staring across the park at the view of central London.

I was pathetic. I couldn't believe I'd let Samantha and Chardonnay talk me into traipsing around London in this stupid getup, pathetically hoping to run into a movie star.

"What are you wearing?"

The gravelly voice made me jump and sent my pulse into overdrive. It was him! I took a deep breath and turned to face Ian Hale, dropping my arms self-consciously to my sides. He was wearing a baseball cap again, tugged low, and a black waxed canvas jacket with a leather collar.

Which made sense, because it was like sixty degrees out, and rainy, and yet here I was in a navy blue cotton dress with tiny white polka dots. It had seemed pretty and feminine when I took it out of my closet, long enough to swirl gracefully below my knees and cover my thick thighs, but darted so that it skimmed my curves instead of hanging like a sack. I originally bought it because it had elbow-length sleeves, and I automatically loved any dress that covered my upper arms, but this one had the added bonus of a sweetheart neckline that made my generous boobs look fantastic.

Or at least that's how I'd felt when I first put it on in my rented flat at oh-my-God-o'clock this morning.

Right now? The misty rain and morning dew had wet the hem enough so that it clung to my pale legs. When I looked down, my boobs still looked fantastic, but my nipples had pebbled up from the cold and were standing proud against the thin cotton of the dress. I felt exposed, suddenly wearing a more revealing, body-hugging outfit than I would normally choose.

I immediately crossed my arms over my chest. It seemed like a real possibility that the rain hitting the heat of my cheeks might create enough steam to completely obscure my face. I could only pray for it to happen.

But since I was Mallory Pritchard, Bad Luck Queen, my face remained completely visible. I imagined the way my makeup was likely running and smearing in the damp and wanted to cry. I tried to smile instead.

"What am I wearing? It's a dress," was my sparkling response.

His mouth twitched. There was even more dark gold stubble lining his hard jaw this morning, and it gave him a rough-and-ready look that made me vividly aware of my inner thighs rubbing together under my skirt.

"Yeah," he said, unsmiling. "You look . . . cold."

Not exactly the impression I'd been hoping to create, but accurate. I glanced down to check that my crossed arms were still shielding my unruly nipples from view. The wind kicked up, and I shivered uncontrollably.

The next thing I knew, warm, stiff folds of fabric were being draped around my shoulders. The collar smelled like leather, smoke, and somehow, impossibly, like the clean salt air of the ocean.

It was Ian Hale's jacket. And it enfolded me as if I were the petite, waifish little thing I used to wish to be, warming me all the way down to my bones. The sleeves hung past my wrists and I immediately curled my fingers into them to wrap the jacket more closely around me.

"You don't have to do that," I protested, because I was never very good at accepting gifts.

He shrugged, massive shoulders straining at the textured cotton of his long-sleeved black Henley. "Cold doesn't bother me."

Of course not, I thought semi-hysterically. No one that hot could ever feel cold.

Before I could collect my thoughts, Pilot raced up the hill, barking madly around the ball clamped in his jaws. The muffled barks didn't seem to unsettle Roxanne, who deigned to sniff curiously at Pilot's ears when he skidded to a stop in front of us. He'd been gone a while, I realized, and he must have found a pretty wonderful mud puddle to play in because my mutt was now filthy. Even better, panting enthusiastically, Pilot dropped the sodden, lightly mauled tennis ball directly on the toe of Ian Hale's battered desert boot. The tan suede darkened under the wet seeping from the mangled ball.

I squeezed my eyes shut. "We brought you your ball back?"

Dear Lord. Why hadn't I figured out what I was going to say if this ridiculous plan worked and I actually saw him again? Mortified, I crouched to grab the ball and try to brush the mud off Ian Hale's probably expensive boot. His foot flexed under my touch, the movement discernible through the sturdy, pliable suede.

He made a low sound above me, a sharp exhalation that was almost a groan. Startled, I turned my face up to find him staring down at me with a heated focus that shot through all my limbs and turned them to jelly.

I hadn't meant to do anything provocative by crouching down. But kneeling there, with his scent and lingering body heat wrapped around me and my face mere inches from the heavy fly of his jeans, I felt an unmistakable filament of sexual awareness spark to life between us.

The look on his handsome, rugged face was . . . hungry. Starved, in fact, and I gasped at the answering lash of ferocious desire that coiled in my lower belly.

"I always seem to end up on my knees in front of you," I said, and the voice didn't even sound like mine. Throaty, sure and unhurried, and I watched the words hit him with an almost palpable shock.

One of his big, raw-knuckled hands reached out, so slowly. I couldn't look away from his eyes, burning in his still face like the hottest part of a flame. My breath caught when his fingers were an inch from my face, and he paused.

I swallowed a whimper, a plea, but he heard it anyway because he let his fingertips ghost over the chilled, sensitized skin of my forehead. My eyes drifted shut and I felt him carefully, almost tenderly, brush back the wet strands of my hair. His hand lingered, broad palm caressing over the crown of my head to cup the back, and I felt myself go hot and liquid between the legs.

My thighs slid apart involuntarily, away from the sweet ache beginning to throb in my pussy, and I let the weight of my head rest in his hand. He bit off a broken noise and my eyes flew open.

Just when I was sure he was going to grab me by the arms and haul me to my feet for a kiss, Ian Hale stepped back.

Strong throat working as he swallowed, voice hoarse, he said, "Get up."

Disbelieving, I knelt there in the rain for a full heartbeat before scrambling to my feet. My flats slipped a bit in the wet grass, adding to the graceless, ungainly sway of my poor, confused body.

Humiliatingly, my first instinct was to apologize. "Sorry! I didn't mean to—"

I broke off, having zero idea how to finish that sentence. What, exactly, was I supposed to be sorry about? It felt like I'd crossed some line, but what? And how was I going to keep from doing it again when I had no clue where that line was?

Realizing that I'd somehow backed into a belief that there was going to be a chance to do *anything* again with Ian Hale, I winced and waited for him to make an excuse and leave. But he didn't.

He never seemed to do what I expected.

Instead of walking away, he took a deep breath and said, "You never said why you're all dressed up today."

Ian Hale—at what point was I allowed to stop thinking of him by his full name? Was it after he'd cupped the back of my head while I knelt at his feet like a supplicant?—*Ian* seemed determined to ignore whatever it was that had almost happened between us. As though he wanted to keep this interaction going as much as I did.

But what was I supposed to say? *I dressed up to attract your attention and I guess it sort of worked!*

That seemed too awkward even for me, so I hedged. "I'm going back to the British Museum today to try again to convince the Britain, Europe and Prehistory curator to let me into the archives. Well, I say try again, but so far I haven't even been able to get a meeting with her. So I thought maybe today I'd try something different. Like maybe it would be better to look a little less as if I rolled out of bed and went straight to work in my pajamas. I don't know. It's probably silly."

He huffed. "Nothing wrong with the way you usually look."

I licked my lips. How did he know what I usually looked like? Had he . . . noticed me before yesterday? "Thanks. I probably would've been better off in yoga pants and a sweater. I certainly would have been warmer."

"Warm enough now?"

I smiled a little and ducked my nose down far enough to catch a whiff of that crazy-addictive salty sunshine leather smell. "I am. Now."

"We should walk these monsters, eh?" Ian gestured down the hill, and Roxanne came to attention. "Sounds like you have places to be."

Now I regretted coming up with a reason that had anything to do with work. How could this be interesting to him? "Oh, well. You know. The museum opens at ten but I'm not sure the curator will be in that early."

We started ambling across Primrose Hill, the low, steel gray clouds veiling the London skyline in the distance, but the city was all around us. Even in the center of this royal park, I could hear the growl and bustle of traffic.

"You think the museum will have what you need."

It wasn't exactly a question, but I answered it anyway, caught up again in the strange, surreal pleasure of having Ian ask about my work. "Sure. They have first editions of the cookbooks I'm most interested in, and probably more that I'm not aware of. A few manuscripts, even! I know I could get my hands on copies of later editions, or even study the originals online, but there's nothing like being face to face with the actual article."

"Sounds like you made the right choice, coming to London."

That was interesting. I thought about it. In reality, I hadn't ever really stopped to consider if I'd made a good adult decision when I packed up, lock, stock and barrel, and moved my ass across the Atlantic.

"I don't know. I think so? It was kind of a snap decision."

"After Tony."

His dark tone made me laugh. "You sound like my sister. She always calls him Tony the Tool."

"I like your sister."

"Me too." I slanted a look at him. "So. You live here?"

He slanted a look back at me. "Yeah. Mostly."

Despite his distracting good looks and sex appeal, Ian was shockingly easy to talk to. But I suddenly remembered that celebrity interviews all mentioned how famously private he was, and how the location of his home was a closely guarded secret, so I let it go. "I'm from New York. Brooklyn."

"I've never been to Brooklyn," Ian said, jamming his hands into his pockets. "The studio usually puts me up at a hotel in Greenwich Village."

It was jarring to hear him reference his movie star life. A reminder of how different we were. "Sure. That's a nice part of town."

He shrugged. "Nice enough. Lonely."

For some reason, my heart picked up the pace. "Most New York hotels are dog friendly. Next time, you should take Roxanne with you."

That got a hint of a smile out of him. "I've thought about it. But it's a bloody long flight."

"I guess you'd have to deal with the other passengers and their exaggerated fears about pit bulls too. That would be annoying. But you've got some trivia to throw at them now, if that would help!"

"Nah, I don't fly commercial anymore. Not after the last time."

Oh, right. Of course Ian Hale crossed the globe in a private jet. What was I thinking? I actually remembered seeing something about that incident in the tabloid headlines at the grocery counter. "The last time. Didn't some out-of-control fan cause such a big disturbance that they actually rerouted your plane and landed in, like, Newfoundland?"

"Ah, that was a mad situation. She wasn't a fan, exactly—just a woman who was off her meds, and thought because I was on the plane it meant that there were terrorists too, and I was there to save them or something. I talked to her for a long time, but I couldn't calm her down." He palmed the back of his head, an unhappy twist to his mouth. "Not much for talking, me. I probably would've done better if there really had been someone to fight."

That hint of vulnerability, hastily papered over with self-directed irony, was the kind of thing I'd never be able to describe to my sister or anyone else—because they'd never believe it. Ian Hale, whose punishing workout routine went viral after the last Mount Olympus movie, vulnerable?

But he was, and it made me want to press one of his big hands between both of mine and kiss his long, blunt-tipped fingers. Then I'd drag his hand down the side of my neck and over my breastbone and then—

I snapped out of it when Ian let out a piercing whistle. Roxanne, who'd been investigating the gnarled roots of an ancient tree, came trotting back to his side, followed closely by Pilot.

"My dog is turning into a little bit of an obsessed stalker," I said with a laugh that I hoped covered up my internal wince. Was that what I was too? An obsessed stalker?

Ian knelt, careless of the mud, to ruffle Roxanne's ears and let her lick his face. There was no earthly reason why that should be so sexy to me, but I had to squeeze my thighs together and swallow a moan.

"He's made friends, hasn't he?" Ian turned his face from side to side so Roxanne could get a good taste of every square, stubbled inch. "Good on him. It's not easy to make friends, is it."

"Don't look at me." I laughed. "My best friend is my sister."

The corner of his mouth kicked up as he glanced at me, Roxanne going to town on the underside of his chin. "My best friend is a dog."

Pilot leaned his entire body weight into my legs, the doggie version of a hug, and my heart clenched. "Solid choice. I had to leave my sister back in New York, but at least I got to bring this guy with me. Can you bring Roxanne on set with you, when you're shooting in the UK?"

I knew it sounded like the kind of question a magazine writer might ask in an interview, but I couldn't help it. I was so curious about what his life was like.

"Sometimes," Ian said, getting to his feet and swiping a casual hand over his damp cheeks and chin. "If it seems like there will be room for her to run. If I'm going to be penned up on a soundstage for days at a time, I leave her with a mate of mine who has a Westie."

A memory stirred in the back of my brain, some adorable video or series of pictures my sister sent me a link to while trying to cheer me up after I moved back home. "Wait. Are you talking about Alec Ramsey?"

It made sense. Alec Ramsey was the classically trained, critically acclaimed actor who'd been brought in to class up the Mount Olympus movies. He played Hades, older brother and nemesis of Ian's character, and a firm fan favorite. The two spent more time on-screen together, and had arguably better chemistry, than either did with any of the various scantily clad love interests who damselled their way through the series getting rescued and ravished by turns.

"Yeah, that's him."

The surrealism of the situation washed over me once more. "Right, sure. Alec Ramsey is your dogsitter."

"Alec's all right," Ian said, as if I'd been making a comment about

Alec's fitness to care for an animal—although now that I thought about it, the things that showed up in the scandal rags about him didn't necessarily inspire a ton of confidence. "But his shooting schedule tends to be pretty similar to mine. When he's busy, Roxy and Alec's pup both go to Damian Moore's. He's the clever one. Got a lovely wife and a little daughter to keep the dogs well occupied."

The wistfulness in Ian's voice distracted me from my starstruck dazzlement that the dog whose butt my dog was currently sniffing was regularly given kibble by either an Oscar winner or a stage actor who had literally played every one of Shakespeare's most challenging roles, to packed houses and standing ovations. And these were Ian's friends.

My friends were either related to me by blood, or had all faded quietly away during my messy breakup.

Attempting to play it cool, I said, "Sounds like Damian has a nice setup."

"I called him the clever one, but maybe he's the lucky one. His little Cora is a firecracker. She keeps us all in fits when we're over for dinner."

"You like kids," I realized. "Do you ever think about having some of your own?"

Oh my God. That was the opposite of cool! It was a super intimate question to ask anyone, let alone a famously private near stranger!

But before I could walk it back, an odd look crossed his face. "Huh. No one's ever asked me that before. I suppose they all assume I like the bachelor life too much to ever give it up."

"There's nothing wrong with being single," I recovered enough to say firmly. I couldn't believe we were having this conversation, or that any of this was happening, really. But I was in it now. "There's nothing wrong with deciding not to have kids with your partner, either. But if you want it, why wouldn't you go for it?"

Jamming his hands in his pockets, Ian angled his body slightly away from me so it was hard to read his expression. "Maybe," he said vaguely. "Someday. But for the moment, I've got to stay accessible. Relevant. I have to keep the fantasy intact for my fans."

"That's . . . honestly, that's kind of messed up." Something about the way he was talking, almost robotically, like he was repeating lines he'd been told to say, bothered me. My inner mouthy New Yorker came out.

"You give your fans your wonderful performances in movies they love! You don't owe them your personal life."

"That's a kind thing to say." He looked right at me, something like a smile pulling at his lips. "You're kind."

I squirmed, cheeks burning. "Another word for it might be 'nosy.' Look, I obviously have no business telling you about *your* business, especially as someone who truly loves her job and would sacrifice a lot for it. But I don't really see why you need to sacrifice your chance at a family to keep being a movie star."

He paused, his gaze finding mine and searching it. For what, I didn't know. "It hasn't been much of a sacrifice so far, to be honest."

I knew what he meant, even if I found it hard to believe. "Don't worry. The right person will come along. Or at least, that's what I've been given to understand by my mother, sister, friends, and many forms of popular entertainment."

He acknowledged that with a slight smile. "I'm not fussed about waiting. For perfection."

My mouth went dry for some reason. "Is that all? You might be waiting a long time."

"Then I'll wait." He blinked those fantastically blue eyes, a small, secret smile tugging at his lips. "But I don't think it will be too much longer."

Heart pounding, I pondered what he could mean by that. It almost felt like he was talking about . . . meeting me? But that couldn't be right. He'd never even laid eyes on me before yesterday. Right?

Before I could figure out how to ask him to clarify, he turned back to me abruptly and said, "I've an idea. We actually shot a few scenes at the British Museum, a couple of films back. I think I still have a contact I can call. Shall we see if they remember me and want to do me a favor by letting my good friend look at the archives?"

I stopped dead on the walking trail. My cheeks went cold and my fingertips tingled as all the blood seemed to rush away from my head. "Are you serious? Oh my God, Ian. But I couldn't ask you to . . ."

"You're not asking, I'm offering."

Temptation wrapped her sticky fingers around my neck and tugged me forward. "If you're sure it wouldn't be too much trouble . . ."

"Will it make you happy?"

"Unbelievably happy," I admitted, already dreaming of getting my hands on the precious manuscripts and preserved letters and menus from Tudor feasts . . . all of it. "Ecstatic, even."

Satisfaction glittered in his crystalline eyes. "Then it's no trouble at all."

Now that I'd given in, I wanted to be at the museum already. Charging down Primrose Hill, it took me a moment to realize that I'd left both my dog and my incredibly unlikely benefactor behind.

Looking back up the hill, I caught a glimpse of an expression I couldn't name on Ian's face. No, that wasn't true. I could name it—I just could barely believe it.

Ian Hale was looking at me, and he looked . . . predatory.

Everything low in my body tightened in a rush. Flooded with heat, my center pulsed a rapid beat in time with the drumming of my heart. I watched him walk toward me, the loose roll of his obscenely trim hips and waist and the sway of his wide, muscular shoulders. He didn't walk, he prowled. His face was still and intent, set in lines of fierce concentration, and his stare never left my face. Ian Hale was hunting.

And I was the only thing in his sights.

As unbelievable as it seemed, maybe my sister was right. Maybe he was into me. I could hardly let myself even think the words without shying away from them, but the look in his eyes . . .

He came to a stop in front of me and I shuddered all over with the uncertainty of it. Part of me wanted to run, to deny that I'd ever even imagined a moment like this. But another, smaller part of me wanted to be brave. To see what might happen if I ignored the voices of the past in my head, telling me I wasn't pretty enough or sexy enough or thin enough to be wanted.

Ian Hale wouldn't look at a woman the way he was looking at me unless she was sexy enough to set him on fire.

Taking heart from the heat in his eyes and the way he leaned in toward me, like we were magnetized together, I lifted my chin and closed my eyes. I could almost taste his kiss.

This was it. It was really happening. I breathed in his scent of brine and smoky leather. I felt a drop of rain hit my forehead and trail gently down my temple. And I waited.

"You should go home," he grated in my ear. "Get dry, change clothes. I'll meet you at the museum in an hour."

My eyes flew open, but all I saw was a repeat of yesterday's view—Ian Hale's magnificently muscled back, striding away from me.

Not. Again.

CHAPTER THREE

It was four in the morning in New York. I couldn't do that to my sister. Besides, she'd only give me more terrible advice about how I should absolutely, one hundred percent believe someone like Ian Hale could ever be romantically interested in someone like me.

But as I numbly washed my hair and soaped up my shivering body, I promised myself I was done. Done with that silly daydream, done with believing in fantasies.

I was done. As long as I ignored the fact that in only a couple of brief encounters, Ian Hale had turned from a fantasy to a flesh and blood man who looked at me as if he'd never seen anything he wanted more.

But not enough to stick around and do anything about it, apparently. So eff him. I was here in London to write a book. A challenging book I'd been planning for a long time, and Ian Hale was going to help me do it. That was all this was. And once I'd graciously accepted his help at the museum today, I would thank him with a note in the acknowledgments and we would never see each other again.

And if that thought was like acid in the back of my throat, well, that was probably just heartburn from all the heavy English food. Which I happened to love. I mean, sausages wrapped in puff pastry and dunked in grainy mustard? How could anyone argue with that?

I zipped up my pencil skirt and got the blouse tucked in and all my various curves strapped down into uncomfortable professionalism. Then I had to spend at least a few minutes pretending I knew what the hell to do with my eyeliner and blush.

I didn't, but I felt that the effort should count for something.

My hair, my one point of vanity, was going to be a frizzy mess in this humidity no matter what I did, so I wound it into my usual topknot and used a few extra bobby pins to try and secure it.

When I was done, I stared at myself in the mirror for the space of a single heartbeat before walking out of my bedroom. Neat and clean. I wasn't shooting for more than that at this point.

I took a moment to mourn my previous carefree days researching books at the New York Public Library, where no one looked at me and it didn't matter if my pants had a zipper or not.

But this was an opportunity, I reminded myself. I was here, in London, to be inspired and broaden my horizons . . . and apparently to fulfill my secret fantasy of meeting Ian Hale.

Charged with anticipation and determination, I gave Pilot a last kiss and locked the door behind me. This time, I hadn't forgotten an umbrella. So, of course, the rain cleared up as soon as I stepped onto the sidewalk. I gritted my teeth and folded the umbrella under my arm. That was great, I could walk. My hips would probably thank me for getting a little exercise.

Maybe if my hips were more slender, if my whole body were shaped more like those waifishly thin, toga-clad starlets in the Mount Olympus movies, maybe then . . .

Pressing my lips together, I stomped down the sidewalk with my laptop bag over one shoulder and a canvas tote holding his air-dried jacket over the other. It was only a block or two before my feet, shoved into sensible pumps, started to protest the unfamiliar activity.

Thankfully, I didn't have far to walk. I'd specifically chosen to lease a flat in the Saint Pancras neighborhood, within walking distance of both the British Library and the British Museum. I had my driver's license, but as a lifelong New Yorker who used the subway to get around, I wasn't all that confident in my ability to drive on the right side of the road . . . much less drive on the wrong side. The London Tube and I had made friends, but I was still glad to be so close to my two major sources of research.

Today, I wished I'd chosen a flat just a little bit farther away. As I rounded the corner of Russell Square, I saw the tall, unmistakably godlike figure of Ian Hale waiting for me at the museum steps, and I knew I wasn't ready to see him again yet.

But since I might never be ready, I supposed I might as well suck it up and at least get the intro to the museum curator. Then I'd send Ian on his merry way, with my heartfelt thanks, and that would be that.

Pasting on a determined smile, I marched up the museum steps. It was cosmically, epically unfair that all it took was a quick shower for Ian Hale to look like the movie star he was. He'd ditched the morning's ripped jeans and Henley for darker jeans and a white collared shirt with the sleeves rolled up to bare his corded forearms. His perfect dark blond hair and perfect stubble were still perfect.

Whereas I, when I looked down, saw a distinct gap between the top buttons of my shirt where the fabric strained over my inconveniently ample boobs. *Very professional.*

Fighting down a blush, I thrust the canvas bag at him. "Here, I brought you back your jacket."

He seemed reluctant to take it. Maybe because the canvas bag I'd randomly grabbed sported hot pink script that spelled out *Bitch, please.* Whoops!

"You can keep it a while longer, if you need it," he said gruffly.

"I have coats of my own."

His shoulders stiffened a little at my abrupt tone. Reminding myself that he was here to do me a gigantic favor, I made an effort to get back on some sort of normal, friendly, but appropriately distant footing.

"Thank you, really. It was very kind of you to lend it to me. But I promise I can take care of myself, even if I seem like a walking disaster."

I smiled to let him in on the joke, but he didn't seem to appreciate my self-deprecating humor. He frowned down at the bag in his hand while I tried to come up with something else to say.

"So! Anyway. I'm here, all clean and pressed and looking as presentable as I can. I hope I won't embarrass you."

He flicked me a searing glance then squeezed his eyes shut. When he huffed out a breath that almost sounded like a laugh, my insides froze.

Oh, God. Was he already embarrassed? Did I really look that bad? My free hand flew to the gap in my blouse, which now in my mind's eye seemed like it was probably wide enough to show the lacy cups of my full-coverage bra. My hips felt as wide as the rear end of a bus all of a sudden, pressing against the tight black wool of the pencil skirt. I probably looked like I'd been melted and poured into this whole outfit, and I was in danger of bursting out of it at any moment.

"We don't have to do this," I said desperately, still tugging at my shirt placket. "Really, you can go home and leave me to it, I'll be fine on my own. I always am. I prefer it, these days."

Stop talking, I moaned silently, waiting in an agony of humiliation to hear Ian's reply.

His frown had deepened, scoring interesting grooves in his cheeks that forecast the rugged beauty we could look forward to as he aged.

"I'm coming in with you. I already called Dr. Georgiana Chesterton, the director."

My breath stuttered. "The head of the entire museum. Oh my God, Ian."

"She's expecting us . . ." He glanced down at the leather-banded watch on his wrist. "Now. We should go in."

But I was a frumpy, embarrassing mess! Surely there was time for me to . . . what? Get a shirt that fit correctly? I wanted to cry. I couldn't make my feet move for a full five seconds.

Ian had already started toward the main entrance, and when he realized I wasn't behind him, he turned. His expression was all determination and purpose, like a general who had decided his troops were going to take that hill, by God, and damn the consequences.

When he saw me rooted to the spot, a spasm of something like frustration crossed his handsome face. "I thought you needed this for your book. Was I wrong?"

The mention of my book anchored me. My book was going to tell the story of women finding independence and renown through cooking. It would explore the ways women historically related to food and its uses, and it mattered to me. It mattered more than my outfit or what my hair was doing or how Ian Hale was probably counting the seconds until his reckless promise of help was fulfilled and he could ditch me.

"Yes." I took a deep breath, clapping a hand over my stretched boob area as I did so. "I really do need to see the parts of the collection that aren't on display. It would help me a lot."

"Let's have at it, then."

It was a slightly grim pair that trudged into the soaring Great Court of the British Museum. I'd seen it before, of course, but that space never failed to take my breath away. The diamond-shaped panes of glass that made up the enormous arched dome of the ceiling let in whatever gray light could filter through the rain clouds above. Two grand staircases curved around the outside of the Reading Room, where I'd whiled away many an hour doing research and getting lost in the ocean of information contained in this venerable old institution.

"Did you know there are more than three thousand glass panels up there?" I said, pointing at the ceiling. "And each one is unique because the Great Court isn't symmetrical. The Reading Room isn't in the exact center."

"I did not know that." Ian stopped with me to stare upward. "It's a bloody big ceiling, all right."

An amused voice from behind us said, "It certainly is. It takes us more than two weeks to clean the entire thing."

The speaker was an incredibly poised, regal-looking Black woman not much older than me—or possibly just a woman with a better moisturizing regimen. Her dark brown skin was certainly flawless, stretched tight over cheekbones sharp enough to make a mortal woman weep with envy. Her black hair was coiled in a chic knot at the nape of her long neck. Tall and trim, she held out a clearly manicured yet unpolished hand to Ian. "Mr. Hale, how lovely to see you again."

The change that came over Ian was fascinating. It was hard to describe—as though he put on a mask and then lit it up. His face relaxed out of the frown I'd grown used to, and into the easy, charming smile that had graced red carpets over the last few years. He took the woman's hand, utterly at ease, loose-limbed and relaxed . . . and yet, there was something so performative about it. Having seen the other Ian, I suddenly didn't buy this version at all.

"Dr. Chesterton," he said smoothly, bowing over her hand in a move that only a movie star could make look cool instead of dorky. "Thank you for meeting with us."

I tried not to thrill at his use of the word "us." It didn't mean anything.

"Yes, thank you! So much. Hi, I'm Mallory Pritchard," I said, sticking out my hand. "It's an honor to meet you, Dr. Chesterton."

She waved that away with an efficient gesture. "Not at all. And please, call me Georgiana. I'm happy to be on a first-name basis with anyone who is passionate about our collection."

Gracious and gorgeous and she had a PhD. *Gah.*

Maybe this was why Ian had been so eager to help me by getting in touch with Dr. Hottie here. I resolutely did not think of them going off together arm in arm to have cocktails or something, after they left me in a dark, dank corner of the museum basement. If I did let myself picture it, though, I'm sure they would have looked good together. They matched. They were the same kind of person. The ridiculously accomplished and attractive kind.

Extraordinary belonged with extraordinary.

But fine. I was fine. I was fine before I randomly ran into a movie star at the dog park, and I would be fine after he sauntered off into the sunset with Dr. Hottie. I didn't need him. I was happy on my own. Well, happy-ish.

Though I might need to find a new place to walk my dog.

In the meantime, I pulled out my biggest, friendliest smile and said, "Well, I don't want to keep you two! Dr. Chesterton, feel free to pass me off to an assistant or an intern. I'm sure they can get me set up in one of the departmental study rooms."

"Oh, no need," she assured me, leading the way across the Great Court to a nearly invisible door set into the wall behind the curved Reading Room wall. "There's a private reading room already earmarked for your use today, and for however long you have need of it. Right this way!"

Gritting my teeth, I resigned myself to a painfully long, polite good-bye. Ian was a silent shadow at our heels, probably counting the seconds until he could be alone with the museum director.

"That's very generous," I said as we trooped down a flight of stairs to a deeper level of the museum than was open to the public. We passed several administrative offices before entering a hallway that smelled reassuringly of old, leather-bound books and dusty papers. One of my favorite smells in the world.

"Here we are." Georgiana pushed open a door on the left to reveal a small, square jewel-box of a room. A sturdy wooden table took up most of the space, and it was topped with a reading lamp and several stacks of heavy books and archival folios that made my fingers itch to touch them.

All the information—the names and places and stories and recipes—contained in those volumes filled my mind in a heady rush. My fingers itched to reach out and touch the dry, brittle pages. The thrill of anticipation almost let me ignore the significant look I caught Ian throwing Dr. Hottie out of the corner of my eye.

"This is amazing," I gushed, bubbling over with nerdy delight. "Thank you so, so much, Dr. Chestert—Georgiana. I can't tell you how much I appreciate it."

"Oh, don't thank me." Georgiana laughed, a husky chuckle that was simultaneously so sexy and so genuine that I couldn't hate her. "Thank Ian here. He's the one who got the ball rolling."

I swallowed hard and turned dutifully to face him. "Thank you, Ian."

He shook his head helplessly, as if he didn't want my thanks, but his gaze searched mine like he was looking for proof that I was really happy with the room.

Caught in the strange, suspended moment, I barely noticed when Georgiana slipped past us to pause in the open doorway. "I'll just leave you to it then, shall I? There's a buzzer on the desk that rings straight through to the curator's desk. Do ring if you need anything or have any questions. And I'll be in my office if you'd like to stop by before you leave, but don't if it's a bore."

And with that, she whisked herself out of the private room, leaving me alone with Ian Hale.

CHAPTER FOUR

"Aren't you going with her?" I blurted out like a fool.

He looked startled for a second, then the lines of his handsome face hardened to stubbornness. "No. I want to stay. I promise I won't get in your way."

"But . . ." My head was spinning. I felt like Pilot's favorite rag doll toy, being vigorously whipped back and forth while clamped in his jaws. All of a sudden, I'd had enough. "Look. What the hell is going on here?"

Ian went into lockdown, his face watchful. "I don't know what you mean."

I stalked around the table to dump my laptop bag on the other side. I needed some space and this room was tiny. "Oh come on! No one is this nice to a total stranger! Certainly not someone like you when the total stranger is someone like me."

"What does that mean?"

"You are Ian Hale, international movie star. And I'm the girl who asked her high school crush to dance at prom and got laughed out of the room. You and I don't match! I mean, just look at us!" I gestured between his perfect, sculpted body in its effortlessly cool clothes that probably cost more than I was paying to rent my London flat, and my soft, too-curvy-for-fashion body in its too-tight outfit. God, I'd put in so much effort to look nice, and I was still a disaster. While Ian had clearly rolled out of bed looking exactly that devastatingly sexy.

Don't think about Ian in bed.

I gulped and tried to hang on to my righteous indignation, but it was getting swamped by the weariness that always accompanied an attack of self-doubt. I knew I needed to ease up on myself. Most of the time, I felt good about the way I looked, but there were always those situations that set off a spiral. That was okay. The longer I lived in my body, the better I got at remembering how to love it.

But no amount of self love was going to change the fact that I was just a regular person. Ian was a star, and mere mortals like myself were not meant to touch the stars. The best we could hope for was to admire them from afar.

I gazed at Ian, who was gazing right back with a look on his face that I couldn't interpret.

"Believe me, I'm looking at you," he ground out, voice rougher than gravel.

It skated over my skin like a touch, and I shivered. Crossing my arms over my chest to hide the way my nipples had perked up as if he'd rubbed his callused thumbs over them, I frowned. "Quit. Doing. That."

"You told me to look at you," he pointed out, frustration leaking into his tone.

"Not that. I mean. Stop acting like you think I'm . . . I don't know, hot or something."

I laughed to show I knew how ridiculous it sounded, but Ian didn't laugh. Instead, he took a prowling step toward me.

"It's not an act."

My mouth dried up so fast, I nearly choked when I tried to swallow. But right on the heels of that burst of glee—Ian Hale thought I was hot! —came a cleansing shot of anger.

"Bullshit," I told him. It was on, now. I'd gone this far, and there was no going back and smoothing it over. So I might as well put it all out there. "At least half the time, you seem like you can barely stand to be near me. You've walked off and left me hanging twice now! Whatever you think about my supposed hotness, you obviously aren't planning to do anything about it. Which leads me to believe you're not really that interested at all."

"Not interested."

Ian blinked, and suddenly the air in the small, cramped room felt supercharged with electric tension. Every hair on my body stood on end.

"You think I'm not interested," Ian repeated, gripping the back of the chair on his side of the table. His big body tensed, the cords of muscle standing out on his bared forearms. I wouldn't have been surprised if the straight-backed wooden chair had snapped like kindling under his clenched fists.

"I know you're not interested," I heard myself say. "If you were interested, you would have kissed me already."

I caught my breath at the boldness he brought out in me. I was baiting the tiger.

Ian's knuckles whitened on the back of the chair. His stare never left my face. "I can't kiss you."

The disappointment was crushing, even if I'd already told myself it wasn't going to happen. "Why not?"

That chair creaked under Ian's grip, but he didn't move. His eyes pinned me in place, like one of the rare butterfly specimens skewered to a display upstairs.

Ian leaned forward, filling my vision. His voice was almost a snarl as he answered, "Because if I start touching you now, I'm never going to stop."

Holy shit.

Everything low in my belly went tight and hot in a dizzying rush. Desire knotted between my thighs, sharp and aching with the emptiness of Ian still being *across the goddamned table from me.*

"So don't stop," I said recklessly, one hand lifting to tug at the open collar of my shirt, which suddenly felt like it was strangling me.

We locked eyes. For a moment, I really thought he was going to do it —upend the table, swipe all the priceless folios and manuscripts onto the floor, and lay me out on top of them like a feast. But when his gaze flicked to the lockless door standing slightly ajar to the hallway, where someone walked by at that exact moment, I knew it wasn't going to happen.

For the sake of the folios and manuscripts, I was relieved. For myself? Not so much.

None of the intensity had drained from Ian's expression. If anything, he was staring at me even more intently. There was a look on his face, something like protectiveness, and it warmed a different part of me than the parts that were still simmering with lust.

But instead of saying something rational and mature and true like, "This isn't the time or place, when anyone could walk in on us and take a cell phone photo that would sell to the tabloids for hundreds of thousands," he put one hand down on the table and lowered his voice to say, "When I touch you for the first time, neither of us will stop for hours. Days, Mallory."

Shock and delight zapped me like a lightning strike.

"Once I get you into my bed, you won't be leaving it until I've tasted every inch of your delicious body," he growled. "Until I've licked your gorgeous breasts and hips, the backs of your knees, your smooth belly, every one of your toes."

His voice caressed each part of my body as he mentioned it, awakening sensation and yearning. My breasts tightened and swelled, nipples aching. My hips wanted to thrust. My knees tingled. My belly quivered.

"You'll wear nothing but me for days on end, nothing to hide you from me, no barriers between us."

I couldn't breathe, couldn't think. My knees went shaky and loose, and I caught myself against the edge of the table. The corner pressed hard into the juncture of my thighs, teasing me through the sensible wool of my skirt. Little explosions of light flickered in my brain and I realized at some point I'd squeezed my eyes shut.

The air was still and thick in the tiny room. All I could hear was the thundering of my heartbeat in my ears. My nipples were tight, aching knots and my legs trembled with the need to push forward and press myself more firmly against the table for some kind of release from the tension.

But the only release came in the form of Ian's soft rumble of a voice.

"When I finally touch you, I'll dip my fingers into your sweetness, one by one, and lick you off them like honey. God, I can't wait to taste you. I'm starved for you."

I gasped, my eyes flying open. He was leaning on the table now, both hands flat against the wood grain. As I watched, they flexed slowly, the scarred knuckles teasing me with flickering fantasies of how they'd feel brushing my soft, inner folds and widening the tight, wet core of me.

"Your body was made for pleasure," he rasped. "And mine was made to give it to you."

My thighs spasmed, internal muscles contracting, and a shuddering breath left my body as I stared into Ian Hale's hot, ravenous eyes and came, completely untouched.

Aftershocks staggered me and I fell against the table. "Oh my God," I panted. "What . . . how . . . ?"

He groaned, fisting his hands and grinding his knuckles into the table hard enough to make his shoulder muscles flex. His beautiful face was set in lines of torment for a long, choked moment while a lethargy I'd never experienced swept over my shivering body.

Those electric blue eyes pierced my bewildered languor. He straightened and ran a shaking hand down his stubbled face. "Fuck me if you aren't the sexiest thing I've ever seen."

The words killed whatever embarrassment might have tried to rise up to overshadow this moment. The way he was looking at me, the way he let me see his honest lust and stark need, didn't allow me to get self-conscious.

And believe me, I wanted to. The part of my brain that was hyper-aware that I'd just soaked my panties in front of the world's biggest movie star, while he talked me to the orgasm of the century—that part of my brain was urging me to run away and hide. Even if it meant leaving before I got the chance to look at that first edition of *The Compleat Housewife*. My heart clenched a little at the thought.

But the biggest part of my brain was more concerned with the fact that Ian was across the table from me, his huge body rock-hard with sexual frustration, and yet he *still* hadn't laid a finger on me. While my body finally began to wind down to a gentle simmer, muscles loosening and relaxing as the wave of pleasure receded, Ian clenched his jaw hard enough to make a muscle jump under his stubble.

So he wouldn't ravish me in a private reading room at the British

Museum. Maybe there was someplace else we could go? "My apartment is like five minutes away," I blurted.

Oh good, there was the awkward, right on cue.

My cheeks went hot as confusion lit his blue eyes, but in the next moment I saw him get it. And I could still hardly believe it, but serious temptation flared in Ian's gaze before he could tamp it down.

"And I'd like to see it sometime," he rasped. "But right now, you have rare books to read."

Warmth kindled in my chest—a different kind of warmth than the fire he'd ignited earlier, but this small candle was no less powerful in its own right. Ian wasn't just the sexiest man who'd ever wanted to get me into bed. He also seemed to care, genuinely, about what I wanted outside the bedroom. It was a completely unique experience in my life so far.

Still, wasn't I supposed to strike while the iron was hot? And looking Ian up and down, from the strain in his jaw to the enticing bulge in his jeans, I could tell that the iron was indeed very, very hot at the moment.

"The books can wait," I offered, licking my lips in the dry air of the room.

"So can I." He said the words like a promise, his gaze turning inward for a moment I didn't quite understand. And in the next heartbeat, he'd relaxed his shoulders and pulled up a version of that small, private smile. "It may take a long, cold shower, but I'll live. And you have work to do."

My gaze slid to the stack of folios and manuscripts sitting on the table, full of secrets and stories and long-gone history. The tips of my fingers twitched in the direction of the top book.

"Well," I said reluctantly. "You did go to an awful lot of trouble to set this up. I'd hate to have wasted your time."

"It was one phone call." He dismissed his own efforts with a shrug, but his stare went sharp on my face. I fiddled with the collar of my shirt, suddenly aware that all the heaving my bosom had recently done had opened the gap between the buttons even wider.

"I'm not winding you up here," he said suddenly. "You know that, don't you?"

My laugh was muffled by the fall of my hair, which finally gave up on its topknot situation and tumbled down to shield my face. "I guess? I mean, yes. You made your point about being into me, and I believe it. It's just hard to keep believing it, if that makes any sense."

He made a frustrated sound. "Mallory."

Gah. My name in that voice, with that accent. And that tone, which did even more than the sex talk to make me believe this was real. It was all fond exasperation, like he kind of wanted to shake some sense into me, but he never would because he liked me too much.

He actually liked me, I realized. Perhaps belatedly, given the orgasm and the favor with the museum director and the way he looked at me. But in fairness to me, nothing even remotely similar to this had ever happened in my life.

"Okay," I said, tossing back my hair. "This is a bonkers situation, but I accept that it's happening. So what's next?"

Approval warmed his ice-chip eyes to ocean blue. "Cold shower for me while you gin up on the right way to roast an ox, and that. And tonight I'll take you out. Anywhere you want to go."

My pulse leapt. "Anywhere?"

A strange, resigned look flickered over his face, there then gone in an instant. When he smiled, it was the big, charming one he'd used on Dr. Chesterton. "Anywhere you like. Top restaurant, posh club. Whatever."

I made a face before I could stop myself. "No thanks. That's not really my scene. I mean, unless that's what you want to do tonight."

I stuttered to a stop, already dreading the prospect of digging through my closet for something to wear to a trendy club, but Ian was shaking his head and smiling his real smile again.

"Nah," he said easily, hands sliding into his jeans pockets. "Not my scene either, as it happens."

"You sure spend a lot of time in places like that, for someone who doesn't like them."

"Part of the job, innit?" He shrugged, resigned again. "Being seen out and about at the right places. Getting papped with the right people. Price I pay for doing the work. Not that high a price, all things being equal."

He was right, of course. He got paid gazillions of dollars to make blockbuster movies, which was probably an easier job than digging ditches for a living. Having to show up at fashion shows and wild parties with a model or two on his arm wasn't exactly a hard life. But that didn't mean he had to love it.

"Could be worse," I agreed. "But I'm not that interested in going somewhere that feels like work to you."

"So where to, then?"

"Take me someplace you've never taken anyone else," I said impulsively. "Someplace you go to have fun."

I loved the way the corners of his eyes crinkled when he smiled. He shook his head slightly. "You don't make it easy, do you?"

Feeling bold, I flirted back. "Do you want easy?"

Sauntering around the edge of the table, Ian headed for the door. He had to pass me to leave, and he came close enough for me to feel the heat from his body and smell his clean, masculine scent.

He leaned in, his lips mere millimeters from my ear and his warm breath sending shivers down my spine.

"Mallory, luv," he whispered, like a confession. "When it comes to you, I want it all."

CHAPTER FIVE

THE PROBLEM with going on a mystery date with a movie star was that I'd left myself with literally no idea of how to dress. I was pretty sure I didn't need club clothes—not that I owned a mesh miniskirt and thigh-high velvet boots, like the starlet who'd accompanied Ian to the opening of L'Etoile. The photos had been all over the newsstands just a month ago, and the memory made my sensible slacks and cardigans look entirely too sad staring back at me from the depths of my closet.

I hadn't gone to the trouble of wrestling my boobs into this low-cut, lacy bra just to swathe them in a thick layer of wool.

I contemplated my underwear-clad body for a moment, palms skimming the curves of my hips. It was the same body I'd had pretty much since puberty, but somehow it looked a little different to me today.

There was still that definite softness to my rounded belly, the too-large breasts that were impossible to hide or downplay. Maybe I didn't need to downplay them though. And maybe being soft where Ian was so hard and chiseled—maybe that would feel good, to both of us. I shivered in the cool air of my flat, and from the bed, Pilot made a whuffling whine in his sleep.

"Easy for you to say," I told him. "You always wear the same outfit, no matter where you're going."

Deciding to take my cue from Pilot, the most confident, outgoing creature I knew, I grabbed a pair of jeans that made my ass look like a bitable peach. Jeans were always good. Ian had been wearing jeans every time I'd seen him. You could dress them up with heels and dangly earrings, or dress them way down with sneakers and a ball cap. For tonight, I'd thread the needle with flats and an emerald green V-neck sweater that clung just enough. The plunging neckline was one I didn't dare often, and it took advantage of my most daring bra, exposing the upper swells of my breasts in a way that felt casually sexy. I was *nailing* this.

Unless Ian's happy place was, like, the opera or something. *Oh, God.*

I wavered for a moment, but the text alert chimed on my phone. Good, it was probably Sam—I could take a quick mirror selfie and get her to sign off on the outfit!

But when I snatched up my phone, the text was from Ian. My heart plummeted—was he canceling on me?—but no, the text said: *Meet me at the Vauxhall tube station.*

My gaze flew to the clock on the wall. It would take half an hour on the tube. I would just barely make it. Relieved not to have any more time to dither about my clothes, I snatched up my crossbody bag and peacoat, and with a last kiss to Pilot's scruffy head, I hurried out the door.

I had thirty minutes on the London Underground to wonder what was at Vauxhall. There were the famous Vauxhall Pleasure Gardens, not that there was anything left of them from their glory days. It was just an inner-city park now, but a very pretty one right on the south bank of the Thames. I'd studied the map of London quite a bit when I first arrived, trying to orient myself, but I hadn't memorized the locations of many restaurants or theaters or whatever Ian might have in mind.

As the train swayed through the dark tunnels and the sleepy-eyed Londoners around me read their books and listened to music on their headphones, I decided to stop trying to guess. Instead, I'd just enjoy the pleasant flutter of anticipation and the sizzle of excitement at the prospect of seeing Ian again.

That sizzle flared into a bright flame in my belly when I jogged up the Underground station stairs and found Ian waiting for me at the top.

He was leaning against an empty red telephone booth, both hands in the front pockets of his jeans and a gray wool ball cap pulled low to shade his handsome face. He stared down at the phone in his hand and didn't look up. To the stream of commuters flooding up the stairs behind me, he must have looked like a regular guy hanging out. No one gave him a second glance.

I wondered how it was possible they didn't recognize him. I felt like I'd know those shoulders, that loose-limbed slouch, the tilt of his head and the hard angle of his jaw, no matter what he was doing or wearing. If nothing else, from the way my entire body instantly zeroed in on him and pulled me forward, as if he'd cast a line and reeled me in.

"Hi," I said, hoping he'd attribute my breathlessness to the fact that I'd just run up a flight of stairs. Not that it said much about my cardio fitness, but it was maybe slightly less embarrassing than betraying the fact that the mere sight of him squeezed my lungs in a tight fist.

He peered up at me from under the brim of his cap, a half-smile tugging at one corner of his perfect lips.

My gaze dropped to those lips in probably the most obvious way possible, but I couldn't help it. I wanted him to kiss me so badly my own lips tingled.

He didn't, but I thought maybe he wanted to. "Come on," was all he said, lifting his chin a fraction to indicate the direction he wanted to go.

We walked toward the river, and I could feel him relaxing beside me as the crowd of commuters thinned out around us.

"So where are we going?" I asked, my curiosity getting the best of me.

"Right now, we're walking along the river." His slight smirk made me grin, even as the non-answer drove me crazy.

"Fine," I huffed, "be all mysterious. I'll find out eventually, you know."

"What if it's only a walk I've got planned?"

Actually, that sounded pretty nice. Not very private, and my impatient body shrieked at the idea of not getting his big, capable hands all over it in the next five seconds, but I could control myself. At least, I'd always been able to control myself before. I'd enjoyed sex in the past. But no man I'd been with had ever made me feel like this.

"Then I'm glad I wore flats instead of heels," I replied gamely. "And that it's such a beautiful evening."

It was too, I finally noticed as the world around us began to filter back into my consciousness. The first few minutes after seeing Ian again were all-consuming for me—a bomb could've gone off five feet away and I probably wouldn't have noticed. But now that I'd acclimated myself to his sexiness again, at least somewhat, I could see that the darkening sky was clear. The streetlamps glowed softly, casting their warm light across the choppy waters of the Thames to our right. Low buildings lined the street, the spaces between them forming spacious plazas dotted with benches.

He shrugged, the movement a little stiff. "Nah, no fear. I only thought . . . where we're going, it's not much. You might not think it's . . . anyway, I thought, a walk. Can't go wrong, can you? Even if the view's not much just here."

"I guess there are more romantic walks in London," I said without thinking, then felt my cheeks catch fire. What was I doing, bringing up romance? This was a sex thing, whatever this thing was between us. It would be insane to expect more than that.

But luckily, he was too much of a gentleman to call me on it, although his shoulders hunched a little in his shearling-lined denim jacket. "Don't be fooled by the movies and gossip rags," he muttered. "I'm not much cop at romance."

"I don't need romance," I rushed to assure him. "I'm fine without it! Can't miss what you never had, right?"

He didn't join in my forced little laugh, and I bit my lip. We trudged on in increasingly awkward silence, past the US Embassy and the New Covent Garden Market, as buildings gave way to the cranes and smoke-stacks of the old Battersea Power Station.

"Here we are, then."

I blinked at his abrupt announcement. Our date was in a decommissioned coal-fired power station? But no, he was leading me toward a nondescript building of beige bricks a little way down the road. I peered at the far side of the building where a modern-looking construction with a rounded glass wall squatted incongruously. I could barely make out the letters of the sign that ran vertically down the wall.

"The Battersea Dogs and Cats Home? You brought me to an animal shelter?"

Ian palmed the back of his neck. "So. Yeah. Sorry."

"Sorry?" I stared at him, my heart battering at my rib cage. "What on earth do you have to be sorry about? This is fantastic! This is where you found Roxy, isn't it?"

A slow, warm smile kindled behind his blue eyes. "It is, yeah."

I couldn't contain my excitement, bouncing on my toes like a kid at Christmas. "Can we go in? I've heard about this place—it's one of the oldest animal shelters in the UK, right?"

"Founded in eighteen sixty," he confirmed, leading me through a high gate and into a pretty little courtyard that seemed to unite the old brick building with the newer construction of glass and chrome. There was a gift shop in the center of the courtyard that looked like a small house painted white with cheerful blue trim and window boxes of flowers.

Utterly charmed, I turned a slow circle and took it all in while Ian chatted to the security guard on duty at the gate. They seemed to have a lot to catch up on.

"Friend of yours?" I asked as Ian rejoined me.

He poked his tongue into his cheek and said, "I may come here quite often. When I'm in town."

"Do you volunteer?" I didn't know if my heart could take this.

"Nah," he shrugged. "Can't commit the time it takes to be a real volunteer. There's weeks of training and the like. Those people are very dedicated. Maybe someday."

He sounded so wistful, it made me sad. What was the point of being an international movie star if it meant you didn't get to do the things you loved? But all I said was, "So what do you do when you come here?"

We had been strolling along the courtyard to a set of glass doors in the new building. Ian pushed the doors open and said, "This."

It was paradise for dog lovers. Spacious enclosures lined the walls, each one inhabited by a bed, bowl, a variety of chew toys . . . and a dog. There were small, scruffy terriers and big, rangy hounds and a placid, yawning Great Dane in the corner. Some of them ignored the new humans in their midst, clearly used to visitors, but a lot of them noticed Ian right away and came wagging up to their enclosure doors.

The dog runs opened onto a play space that looked like an obstacle course, nylon tunnels snaking between ramps set with treads to make them easy for paws to climb. There were trampolines and knotted rope with frayed ends and about a million tennis balls.

"I come here whenever I can," Ian said, shoving his hands into his jeans pockets. "They're not bothered. They let me pet the dogs and play with them. Sometimes I help out when they need an extra pair of hands."

But he wasn't a real volunteer. *Right.*

I watched him glance around the room, his shoulders relaxed and his body language totally open. Ian had taken me at my word. He was happy here, I realized. This was where he came to get away from it all, maybe when he was depressed or stressed, and this place and these animals made him feel better. It was his happy place. And he was sharing it with me.

My heart warmed till it was like a little sun in my chest. It was probably glowing out of my eyes. "Ian," I said helplessly. I didn't even know what I was going to tell him, but a glimpse of movement at the corner of my eye stopped me.

A man I hadn't noticed before stood up from his crouch by one of the dog enclosures at the other end of the hall. He was older, balding and soft in the middle, with very kind eyes that twinkled as he came toward us. "Ian! Back again, are we?"

"Can't get enough, mate." Ian smiled easily and clasped the man's hand, and I was struck by how comfortable he was here. This guy clearly recognized him, but as a person, not a movie star.

"And you've brought a friend, I see." The man shifted his twinkly gaze in my direction and I couldn't help but smile back. "Lester Quinn. Lovely to meet you! I didn't know Ian had any friends of the two-legged variety."

Ian shook his head at the gentle ribbing, but I could tell he was pleased. "Aw, mate. Don't go telling all my secrets. Give me a chance to impress her before she figures out what a sad bastard I am."

"I'm impressed already," I declared, turning in a slow circle. "I mean, look at this place! It's incredible."

"I like her," Lester told Ian.

"So do I."

Ian looked right at me, and I felt myself flush with pleasure. For the first time, I felt my heart open to the possibility that this incredible man actually wanted to be with me. And not for some brief sex thing—because this was not a sexy date.

I mean, it was. Because everything Ian Hale did was sexy, sort of by definition. But it was also more than that. It was an incredibly private man showing me a place he loved, where he was perfectly himself. He'd opened a door to the real man, the real Ian Hale, and invited me in.

And as Lester let us into the playscape and Ian was rushed by a Scottie, a Jack Russell and three Labradors, I let my expectations start to rearrange themselves in my head. Within seconds, though, I had no more time for thinking about anything beyond the wiggle of warm canine bodies winding around my legs and tripping me up, and the joyful growl of Ian's laughter when a poodle mix bowled him over.

We played with the dogs for an hour or so, by the end of which Ian's whole face had been fully tongue bathed several times over—and not by me. I'd never seen anyone give themselves up to doggie kisses the way Ian did. I was utterly delighted by his transparent joy at being slobbered on.

"Sorry to interrupt." Lester appeared at the edge of the playscape. "Ian, can I commandeer the use of your strong back for a bit?"

"Course you can," Ian said at once, climbing to his feet with a last ruffle to the ears of the mutt he'd been communing with.

"Bruno needs a bit of a wash, I'm afraid." Lester tilted his head apologetically, but Ian only laughed.

"Doesn't he always. You can stay here if you like," he told me. "This is going to get messy."

"I don't mind messy," I said confidently, kneeling up and giving Scarlett, a silky-haired spaniel, a gentle push off my lap. She nudged me with her cold, wet nose and I couldn't resist bending down to bury my face in her soft fur for just a moment. She was so sweet, I wished I could take her home.

When I finally managed to stand up, both men were looking at me with identical expressions of approval.

"She'll do," Lester said decisively.

"Was there a test I had to pass before being allowed to wash one of the dogs?" I asked, brushing absently at the fur clinging to my pants. "I'm glad I passed!"

"Well, it's quite the job," Lester allowed, sharing an amused glance with Ian. He led us down the hall to a smaller room with a grooming station and a large tub with a drain and a removable showerhead. "I'll be back with Bruno in just a moment."

Alone for the first time since we arrived at the shelter, I found myself unaccountably shy. Tucking my flyaway curls behind my ears, I attempted a smile and was surprised when it wobbled a little. "This place is wonderful, Ian. Thanks for bringing me here."

He propped his lean hips on the grooming table and crossed his arms over his massive chest, something like satisfaction in his blue eyes. "I knew you'd like it. Well, I didn't *know*. But I hoped."

"It's perfect," I told him. "Best date ever."

His gaze sharpened and heated, a dagger held over an open flame, and the desire that had been banked between us ignited. But all he said was, "You may change your mind about that after you see Bruno."

The door opened before I could reply, and in walked Lester with a hundred and fifty solid pounds of bounding, energetic, absolutely *filthy* Newfoundland puppy.

"Wow," I said, eyes going wide to take in the impressively mud-splattered expanse of dog. "That is a lot of dirty dog."

"It's not too late to back out," Ian said as he stepped forward to take Bruno's lead.

My tongue stuck to the roof of my mouth as he bent down and casually gathered the huge, squirming dog into his arms and lifted him into the waiting tub. The muscles in Ian's back flexed under his thin cotton shirt, and my breath left my lungs in a whoosh.

"No, no," I murmured in a daze. "I'm good here."

"I'll just leave you to it, shall I?" Lester made his escape swiftly. I barely registered the click of the door closing behind him.

Bruno barked happily, wiggling in the tub. His tail banged the metal sides like a drum as he wagged his heart out. Every movement whipped muddy water in an arc across Ian's front, dampening his shirt and dripping down his arms.

"Here now," Ian protested, laughing. "Watch it, pup."

Undeterred, Bruno started trying to get his front paws onto Ian's shoulders. He probably wanted to give him a big, slobbery kiss. I could relate.

"How can I help?" I asked.

"Fetch the soap from the cabinet, if you don't mind?"

I rushed to look for it, coming up with an oatmeal-based dog shampoo in a blue bottle with a triumphant "Ha!"

"Yeah, that's the one," Ian confirmed as he gently wrestled Bruno under the spray of the retractable showerhead. "Bring it here, but stay well back if you don't want to get soaked."

He wasn't kidding. That T-shirt of his was transparent now, the shadows of his abs and the dark points of his nipples showing right through the fabric. I gulped, my eyes riveted to the incredible sight as I absently handed over the shampoo. There was nothing that could've dragged my attention away from a wet, grinning Ian Hale . . .

Except getting splashed full in the face by a Newfoundland puppy shaking his head.

I sputtered, laughing, and Ian cried, "Aw, shite! Bruno!"

"It's fine, I'm fine," I gasped, raking my hair out of my face. "At least it's not cold water."

"And the mud is mostly down the drain." Ian hooked an arm around Bruno's neck and regarded me penitently. "Sorry, Mallory. Truly."

"Honestly, I should've known better. If I was a good planner, I would've packed a change of clothes, since I always seem to get wet when I'm with you."

I registered the double meaning of the words when I saw Ian's eyes widen slightly in shock, then narrow with wicked heat. The corner of his lush mouth quirked up in a smirk. "I'll admit, I definitely intended to get you wet tonight—but not like this."

A full-body shiver racked me, and it wasn't because I was feeling chilled.

"Well. Wow." I swallowed, searching for words. "That's quite a mouth you've got on you, Ian Hale."

One brow arched and a dimple popped into existence in his cheek. "It's a mouth I'd like to get on you, Mallory Pritchard."

And that was it, I was done for. I sputtered a laugh as Ian grinned, wide and happy and so, so fucking handsome it almost hurt to look at him. But it was a pain I wanted to feel. It grounded me in this moment, in this whole surreal day.

Bruno bounded in place, the laughter spinning him up and making him bark excitedly and splatter water all around. Ian held out a hand for the soap and I opened the bottle and squeezed some into his palm.

"Thank you, nurse," he said, waggling his brows and working the shampoo into a frothy lather in Bruno's long, matted fur.

"I always wondered if actors liked role-play in real-life sexy situations," I confessed, "or if it would be like asking an accountant to bring his calculator to bed. Too much like work."

Ian shook his head in bemusement. "I love the mad things that come out of your head."

"Ha! Well, I'm a writer; there's a lot of weird stuff going on in here." I tapped the side of my head, which Bruno seemed to take as an invitation to lick. "Ack!"

"I can't believe how many animals have gotten their tongues on you before I had the chance," Ian grumbled.

Ignoring the flush that warmed the tips of my ears, I reached into the tub to grab the dangling showerhead and started rinsing Bruno off. "I've got to get my kicks somewhere, since you keep refusing to touch me."

Tension crackled between us as we both remembered exactly how I'd already gotten my kicks once today, without Ian laying a hand on me. I was surprised the water in the tub didn't convert instantly to steam, what with the sudden blast of heat. I got caught in Ian's intense stare, a long, breathless moment where I felt every inch of his hard body next to mine, so close and yet so far.

Distracted, Ian lost his grip on Bruno's wet fur when the pup gave a particularly muscular wiggle. Bruno scrambled up and out of the tub so fast, he bowled Ian over onto his ass with a shout of surprise. I grabbed for the dog, but he gave a jubilant bark and evaded me easily, his heavy tail whacking me in the thigh as he skittered across the tiled floor.

"I've got him," I gasped, lunging after him, but the tiles were wet now, and slippery, and my flats provided zero traction to keep me from going down.

Arms pinwheeling like a goddamn cartoon character, my feet slid out from under me and I landed on something unyielding and hot that let out a startled "Oof."

I was laid out on top of Ian, fully horizontal, our fronts pressed together from chest to knees. As if it was answering some ancient instinct, my body immediately softened and molded to his.

Leaning up with my hands pressed on either side of his head, I stared down into his hard, set expression.

"I didn't get him," I said huskily.

Ian's jaw was clenched and his eyes were hot blue, like the summer sky at noon. For the space of several heartbeats, neither of us moved.

Then I felt his big hands come up to clasp my hips, his wide palms burning through the fabric of my jeans. I made a sound I'd never heard myself make before, a sort of bitten-off whimper in the back of my throat, and his fingers flexed on my ass.

I shifted slightly, mindlessly, my legs falling open enough to cradle his hips. And there it was, the solid, unmistakable evidence of exactly how much Ian wanted me.

We both groaned as my softness settled against his hardness, notching together so perfectly and yet so teasingly, tantalizingly not even close to enough.

Desire wiped my mind clean of every thought beyond getting more —more of Ian, more of his touch, more, more, more.

Moving hesitantly, I pressed my hips down and made him shudder under me. Power flooded me in a giddy rush, along with the sweet spike of pleasure from the grind of our bodies. His fingers were iron bars on my ass, the imprint of each digit searing me.

He threw his head back and gritted out, "What are you doing, Mallory? I'm trying to be good."

"You don't have to be a good boy for me," I whispered, aching, and Ian sat up in a single powerful move, as if he didn't have a curvy brunette straddling him. Except I *was* straddling him, and now my legs were parted wide around his lean hips, my empty, throbbing center pressed tight to the shape of his cock under his jeans.

I crossed my ankles behind his back, wound my arms around his neck and held on for dear life as the sensation of being so close to Ian stole the breath from my lungs.

His hands stroked up my back, one tangling in my hair while the other found the tender nape of my neck and squeezed gently.

I gasped and Ian licked into my mouth with a tortured moan.

CHAPTER SIX

His kiss was like nothing I'd ever imagined. Hot and hungry, almost rough but in a way that made me feel so wanted, so desired, so *necessary*. As if he'd rather kiss me than breathe.

Breathing was overrated anyway, I decided muzzily, and kissed him back.

Our tongues tangled, stroking and sliding and thrusting the way our bodies wanted to slide and thrust. It was a tease, but a delicious one—and it satisfied something deep in my heart where I'd struggled to believe, despite everything, that Ian Hale really wanted me.

Well, all that was over now. My doubts burned up and blew away like wisps of paper, like feathers, like tufts of dog fur . . .

My eyes flew up and I surfaced from the kiss with a sputter of shock. That wasn't Ian's hair tickling my forehead.

It was Bruno, standing over us, dripping and panting and obviously very curious about what game the two funny humans were playing now.

I became abruptly aware of the fact that we were sitting on cold, wet tiles and were both wearing damp clothes. There was no way for my superheated body to actually feel chilled, but there were some clamminess issues.

And now there was dog drool. A lot of it. "Gross!"

Ian dropped his forehead to my shoulder with a thud, his big body shaking with suppressed laughter. "That's not the reaction I was hoping for."

"Not you!" I protested, wiping my face on my sleeve. This sweater was basically trashed already anyway. "You are not gross. You're . . . the other thing."

"The other thing?" He tucked his tongue into his cheek, his vivid blue eyes laughing up at me. "Eloquent. Have you thought about becoming a writer?"

I swatted his shoulder, momentarily distracted by the iron-hard muscle beneath my hand. He really was incredibly constructed, this man I was straddling in an animal shelter grooming room. "It's your fault," I told him. "You burned up a lot of brain cells with that kiss. I'm a little insulted that you're still so coherent, actually."

Ian narrowed his eyes. "No, you're not," he said slowly, his hips moving in a small, sensual twist that made me gasp.

"I'm not what?" I really needed to get a handle on this conversation, but it was hard to focus when we were still pressed so closely together.

"Not insulted. You look like the cat who got the cream, licking your whiskers and all."

"Oh, God." I ducked my head, but he reached up to smooth my hair back, not letting me hide.

"No, it's a good look on you," he insisted. "I like to see you smug and confident. Like to know I made you feel that way."

I felt the blush bloom over my cheeks, but I managed to look Ian in the eye. "You told me how you wanted me, and I wanted to believe you, so badly. But a kiss is worth a thousand words. And a kiss like that? Worth maybe a million. Conservative estimate."

He grinned up at me, looking carefree and happy and completely irresistible. Drawn to him like a magnet, I bent my head to get back to the kissing—and Bruno shoved his snout between us with a whuff.

"Okay, mate." Ian surrendered with a shake of his head. "You're right. We're here for you, aren't we?"

"To be fair, he's the one who interrupted bath time in the first place." Reluctantly, I disentangled my legs from Ian's and stood up. My knees wobbled a little, which was an interesting sensation that, up till now, I hadn't believed really happened outside of books.

The Newfie puppy butted his big head into my hip, leaving another wet spot. With a grunt, Ian stood up and unselfconsciously adjusted himself inside his jeans. As if that wasn't enough to make my mouth water, I was then treated to a second viewing of Ian's back muscles tensing and working as he picked up Bruno and heaved him into the tub.

"This really is the best date ever," I sighed, and went to find the shampoo we'd dropped when Bruno made his big escape.

We managed to finish the giant puppy's bath without further incident. When Lester came back to check on us, he was diplomatic enough not to say a word about our damp clothes and mussed hair. We took the towels he offered us and spent a little more time hanging out with the pups in the playroom, drying out, before venturing back into the London night.

Ian tugged the ball cap out of his back pocket and jammed it on his head, pulling it down over his brow and flipping up the collar of his jacket. His shoulders hunched, just a little, and I was amazed to realize that while nothing could completely mask his size, Ian had perfected a posture that made him almost invisible. He was still big, broad and tall and lean-hipped, but without the swagger he wore as Zeus in the Mount Olympus movies, Ian Hale could've almost been a regular guy.

Certainly the people we passed on the sidewalk didn't seem to notice him. I wondered how strange that must be, to be so famous that you had to come up with a way to hide in plain sight, just to go about your life. And Ian Hale was *good* at it.

"I'm impressed," I told him as we walked back toward the tube station. It was the same walk we'd done earlier, in reverse, but so much better. This time, when I shivered a little he put his arm around my shoulders.

"Are you cold?" Ian pressed his lips to my forehead, a tender move that reminded me oddly of the way my mother would check my sister and me for a fever. There was nothing maternal about Ian Hale, but there was a protectiveness I found deeply stirring.

I turned my head into his shoulder, the waxed canvas rough under my cheek. "I'm okay."

"And impressed," he said, reminding me of what I'd been saying.

And incidentally proving that he'd been listening, which was almost the sexiest thing he'd done so far.

Almost.

"With what?" he followed up.

I poked him in the side. "With you! I mean, I guess this is kind of an obvious thing to say, but I see the subtle way you hide in plain sight on the street here and just . . . you're a really good actor."

I expected him to wave it away or shrug it off. He must've heard stuff like that before. What I didn't expect was the way his jaw tightened, a shadow darkening his eyes for a brief second before the practiced smile came out. The fake one he gave late-night talk show hosts and bubbly red carpet presenters.

"Ah, luv, you're too kind."

"I meant it," I said slowly, brow furrowing. "You're good at going unnoticed when you want to, on the street, and you're good as Zeus too. You have to know you are—you're the main reason those movies do so well!"

"Sure, as long as I get my kit off in the first twenty minutes." He laughed, but I didn't like the way it sounded.

The arm over my shoulder felt hard, tensed against something I couldn't quite understand. "I mean, that helps," I joked, trying to lighten the mood, but as soon as I said it, I knew it was exactly the wrong thing.

Because his arm immediately relaxed all the way off my shoulder. I cast him a swift, sideways glance, but his expression was easy and open. Bland.

Fake.

"Wait," I said, "that really bothers you, doesn't it?"

"Why would it? I spend hours, daily, working to maintain this body. Literally half my life is lived in the gym. I see my trainer more than I see my closest friends."

His tone was matter-of-fact, not bragging in any way. If anything, he sounded bored by it. Feeling my way, I said, "That sounds hard."

Ian shrugged those massive shoulders, hunched against the gathering London fog. "It's the job."

I frowned. "I mean, it's part of it, sure."

"It's all of it. My contribution, at any rate."

A blast of cold wind blew in off the Thames, chilling me to the bone. Ignoring the goose bumps, I shook my head. "Ian, no. It really isn't. You do a lot more in those movies than strip down and flex. You know that, right?"

"Look, I'm not complaining. I know how lucky I am. Playing Zeus changed my life. Before *Immortal Wars*, I was nothing. I had nothing. And without it . . ."

I'd be nothing.

He didn't say it, but I heard it in the heavy pulse of silence between us.

I frowned. "But . . . you've done other movies."

"Sure. Other movies with plenty of running, jumping, fighting, and excuses to get naked. In the last ten years, I've done exactly one photo spread for a magazine where the photographer didn't ask me to take my shirt off. But that was with Lilah Rose. She's high-class all the way."

I remembered those shots, I thought. Moody and arty, they'd hinted at hidden depths below the surface charm that was Ian Hale's stock in trade. "What kind of movie would you want to do, if you had your pick? I mean, the Mount Olympus movies can't keep you tied up for the rest of your life."

He grimaced. "You're right about that. My career very definitely has an expiration date on it, which is why I need to work as much as I can, doing what I'm good at, while anyone still cares to watch me do it. Other projects can wait."

Leaving aside the fact that men in Hollywood generally had many more opportunities for long, varied careers than women did, to say nothing of actors of color, of any gender, what concerned me in this conversation was the sense I had once again that Ian was repeating words he'd been told by someone else—someone who clearly didn't want him to think about branching out, away from the big-budget action adventures that had made him famous.

"Who told you that?" I demanded.

He glanced at me, surprise lifting his brows. "My agent."

"No offense, but your agent sounds like a jerk."

That startled a laugh out of Ian. "Well, he's not as big an arsehole as, say, Jeffrey Greenwood," he said, casually referencing a media mogul as if he were a mutual acquaintance, "but yeah, Philip can be blunt. Doesn't mean he's wrong. And it's not been much of an issue, anyhow. Nobody's beating down the door with offers to play Hamlet, looking like this."

A thousand thoughts tumbled through my brain. It had literally never occurred to me, in my life as the fat girl, the funny friend, the sassy sidekick, that the hero of the story could hate his body too.

Or maybe "hate" was too strong—I didn't hate my body, at least not all the time. On my good days, I could see how healthy and strong it was, and appreciate the way it sheltered me and got me from place to place.

But on worse days, it felt like my body was the first and only thing anyone who looked at me saw. No one cared to look deeper. My size and shape defined me. Confined me.

Erased me.

I had to admit, part of me wanted to snap back at him, "Oh, boo hoo, you're the absolute pinnacle of everything society calls beautiful and healthy? That must be awful for you."

But he wasn't saying it was awful. He'd called himself lucky, and I was pretty sure he believed it. At least as much as he believed that the size of his muscles and the attractiveness of his body were the sum total of his value in the world. I felt sick when I realized I'd unconsciously reduced him to nothing more than his hotness in my mind before I met him—and probably even after, for a bit.

That sucked. Because I knew exactly how shitty it felt to be seen as a body first, and a person second. Or not at all.

So I said what I wished someone would have said to twelve-year-old me. "You're more than your body. Don't let your body put limits on what you want to do."

That body, all six-foot-plus of toned, hard-won muscles and coiled tension, came to a full stop. Caught off guard, I was still moving forward when he snagged my hand and pulled me around to face him. Ian stared down at me, his fingers wrapped tightly around mine and his eyes burning with something I couldn't name.

Awareness arced between us like heat lightning, crackling and shocking and sparking. The rest of the world fell away until we were the only two people in the universe. Ian gave my fingers a tug, and we crashed together in a kiss that swept my legs out from under me and stole my breath. His hands came up to cradle the sides of my head, holding me still for his hungry, devouring mouth—but he didn't need to worry about me going anywhere.

All I wanted was to get closer to him.

My arms wound around his waist, under his jacket, the whipcord lines of him tempting my fingers to dig into his back and try to pull him into me. He was deliciously warm. His tongue stroked mine roughly, and his stubble rasped my cheeks, and the tension in my core spiraled tighter and tighter and tighter until—

"Is that Ian Hale?"

He jolted at the sound of his name, and the flash that followed it. In the next instant, Ian had grabbed my hand again and pivoted toward the road. Dazed, I followed blindly as passersby slowed and turned, staring and pointing their phones at us. Some of them started to come closer and Ian picked up the pace until we were practically running and diving headfirst for a sleek, understated black car I hadn't even noticed idling at the curb.

Ian deposited me carefully on the back seat and folded himself in behind me, slamming the door shut with a sharp, "Drive. Now."

At his command, the car pulled smoothly away from the gathering crowd of excited faces and phones poised to record. My heartbeat pounded in my ears, the purr of the car's powerful engine loud in the sudden silence. I couldn't catch my breath.

"What the hell just happened?" I asked stupidly.

"Are you all right?" Ian ran his gaze over me, as if searching for hidden injuries.

"I'm fine. They were just fans, right?" My brain was coming back online.

He sprawled back in his leather seat, a sardonic twist to his lips. "Sure, just fans. And every one of them with a camera phone and a Twitter account."

I looked around the luxurious interior of the car, from the ridiculously spacious, buttery soft seats to the polished burled wood console between them, to the discreet privacy screen separating the front seat from the back. "This is not a cab."

"No, luv."

"This is your car." I tipped my chin toward the invisible front seat. "That's your driver."

"Yeah."

His hooded gaze regarded me from across the two bottles of fancy imported fizzy water nestled into the console cup holders. He was still, like a predator tracking a threat, and he wasn't wrong. Because I was starting to get a picture of what was going on here, and I wasn't sure I liked it.

"So you had your personal chauffeur following us that whole time, in case . . . what? Your Clark Kent disguise failed and people recognized you?"

Ian shrugged, but his eyes were careful. "Partly."

I swallowed against a sudden surge of nausea, but forced myself to keep going. "Which would be bad because of cameras. And word getting out. About you kissing some fat nobody on the street."

The privacy partition whirred shut just as Ian lunged across the console separating us and hauled me into his lap. I squawked, horrifically aware of the heavy, awkward sprawl of my legs. I had to be crushing him, but he gave no indication that I weighed more than a single rose petal.

"That's not what this is about," he said fiercely, directly into my no-doubt shocked face. "That will never, ever be what this is about. I don't want to hide you away. The exact opposite, in fact."

My poor heart was on a roller coaster ride that seemed to be turning corkscrews in midair. Curling my arms around his neck, I allowed myself to settle my weight in his lap and trust that he could take it. "Okay. So why rush us out of there like your hair was on fire?"

"I was protecting you."

"From what? Someone taking my picture? And what, selling it to a tabloid?" I laughed, but it was dawning on me that he was entirely serious. That this was a thing that could happen to me. What even was my life?

With one big hand, Ian tenderly brushed my hair out of my face, the dark curls clinging to his fingers and making his lips tick up at the corners. "The British tabloid press—it's not the same as what you have in

America. It's worse in every possible way. And once they get a whiff of you, they will hound you to the ends of the earth."

It sounded awful, but I couldn't believe anyone would care that much about me. I mean, it wasn't like a high-profile public romance between two movie stars. In practical terms, I *was* a nobody. And maybe that was a good thing.

"I'm not afraid of them," I said, daring to reach up and kiss the serious line of his lips. "If . . . if we're really doing this, if we're really a thing—people are going to find out sooner or later, and I'm sure there will be some interest in who I am and how I caught the eye of the great Ian Hale. But it won't last! I'm boring."

"You're the farthest thing—"

I cut him off with another kiss, indulgent and sweet as sticky toffee pudding. "I don't mean it like that. I only mean . . . I'm not going to sell tons of copies of the *Daily Mail* or whatever. They'll lose interest. It will be fine."

He shook his head, eyes as dark as the sky over the Thames outside, but I kissed him again.

"I'm not afraid of them," I insisted, feeling as brave as I ever had in my life. "As long as you're not ashamed to be seen with me."

"Mallory." My name was a low groan, and between us I felt the thick, unmistakable length of his hard cock. It reassured me like nothing else could have. "Any man would be proud to have you on his arm."

Clearly untrue, but equally clearly, Ian believed every word. I was utterly charmed. "And I can prove it," he continued, staring into my eyes. "There's this gala I have to attend in a couple weeks. I'd like it very much if you'd be my date."

My pulse rate shot through the panoramic moonroof of the car. In a couple weeks. He wanted to make plans for a few weeks from now?

Lost for words, I stared at him for long enough that worry drew his brows together. "I mean, if you'd like to come along with me. No worries if you don't."

I wanted to grin—I wanted to squeal and do a happy dance and immediately call my sister for wardrobe advice. Instead, I cocked my head thoughtfully and said, "Hmm. I don't know. Where is it?"

The flush that briefly stained his cheeks was utterly entrancing to me. "Ah, about that. You know how I pulled a string or two to get access to the British Museum's private collection? Turns out there was a bit of quid pro quo and I promised to show up to their black-tie fundraiser. Apparently it will boost ticket sales if people think they might run into me over the prawn cocktail. It's mad, I know. And it'll probably be a right bore. You should give it a miss."

Shimmying over his lap to face him more fully, I sucked in a gasp as the pressure of his erection rubbed the seam of my jeans in exactly the right spot. I bit my lip and his hands clenched on my hips.

"Are you kidding?" I breathed, scruffing my fingertips through the buzzed short hair at the back of his head. "Of course I'll come with you. I live for prawn cocktail."

"Anything you want," he promised hoarsely. He spread his legs and sank down against the back of the seat until I rose over him like Venus coming out of the waves. And the way he looked up at me, as if I truly was some kind of goddess of sex—it made me giddy. Reckless. And so fucking hungry for him, I couldn't wait another minute to have him.

"What I want," I said, leaning down to whisper into his ear, "is for you to tell me there's no way for that driver to see or hear what we're doing back here."

He swallowed visibly, the strong column of his throat moving, but I didn't let up.

"And then I want to unzip these." With determined boldness, I palmed the worn fly of his jeans.

Ian's head tipped back, the muscles in his forearms standing out ropey and corded as he stared blindly at the roof of the car. My blood sang with heady power.

"And then," I whispered, desire making me relentless and daring, "I want to swallow your cock."

CHAPTER SEVEN

IAN GROWLED and surged up to fasten his mouth to the pulse point in my neck, tangling a hand in my curls and tugging hard enough to sting. Somehow, it only made the fire in my belly burn hotter.

My cheeks were also burning. I couldn't quite believe I'd said it. There was just something so dirty and fantastic about being in the back seat of this fancy car, like we were two teenagers making out on the way to prom. Except unlike my actual prom, tonight had every chance of turning out to be the best night of my life.

I pulled against Ian's hand slightly, just to feel the sting again. His hot mouth opened on the side of my neck, teeth scraping at nerves that were already jangling with sensation. When he groaned again, I felt the rumble of it deep in his chest and it made me shudder. I wanted to hear it again. I wanted to hear it a lot.

The car slowed in traffic, and I took a moment to be grateful for the hazy darkness of the tinted glass in the windows. Because what I was about to do was definitely not street legal.

My heart nervously fluttering, I sent a questing hand down, down, down between our bodies. He sucked in a breath when my knuckles brushed his taut, muscled stomach. His gaze went slumberous and brooding when I lifted away from him enough to wedge my hand against the thick, demanding cock filling out his jeans.

But I was the one whose mouth fell open as my fingers measured his length. Sweet fancy Moses, he was huge. My hand stalled, shock reverberating through me, and my wide eyes flew up to meet his slightly rueful stare.

"Sorry," he said, shifting his hips. "I know it's not everyone's cup of tea."

I wanted to laugh and ask if he was kidding, but it seemed that, incredibly, he was not. And one-sided laughter in these moments never felt good. But I couldn't vouch for what my face was doing when I gently answered, "I'll learn to cope somehow."

There was a strangely satisfied quirk to his mouth. "You're taking the piss."

"No, no," I told him earnestly, walking my fingers up (and up, and up) and down (and down, and down) the rock-hard shape of him. "It might take some training, special warm-up exercises, but I'm committed to this process."

His eyes narrowed to glittering slits. "If it's training you want, we can start with something smaller."

"Like a wine bottle?"

"Like my fingers."

My brain fuzzed out with static when his big hand cupped my jaw, his callused thumb scraping gently across my lower lip. The weight of it made me hyperaware of how plush and open and wet my mouth was, practically watering at the thought of getting to taste him, and I flushed even hotter.

Locking eyes with Ian, I slowly opened my mouth and captured his thumb between my teeth. He sucked in an audible breath when I bit down delicately and his hips gave a quick, pulsing thrust that seemed involuntary.

I closed my lips around his finger and started to suck, tongue lapping at the salt-smoke taste, teeth scraping the sensitive pad. It was so suggestive, such a blatantly sexy thing to do, I had to close my eyes to keep from dying of embarrassment.

But that was a mistake, because with my eyes closed all I could do was feel. And taste. And hear—God. The quiet rasp of his breath, the shift of his hips against the butter-soft leather of the car seat, the muted roar of the powerful engine vibrating through both of us.

Ian slid his thumb out of my mouth and before I could protest he'd replaced it with two of his fingers. They filled my mouth deliciously, stretching my lips just a bit wider and making me squirm to imagine him filling me with something else. Something thicker, hotter, longer . . .

All of a sudden, I couldn't wait another second. I drew off his fingers, savoring the slow slide against my tongue, and opened my eyes. Ian's gaze burned into mine. His hair was mussed, and his cheeks were ruddy under his perfect tan. I leaned down to steal a quick kiss and got lost in it for a long, heart-pounding moment.

But I was a woman on a mission. Thanking God and the good folks at Mercedes-Benz for the generous space between the front seat and the back seat in this car, I slid down to kneel between Ian's spread thighs.

When I looked up, nerves sparking in my belly, the heat of Ian's gaze melted them instantly. He looked like he wanted to eat me alive. And God, but I wanted him to.

First things first, however.

I slid my hands up his thighs, the black denim soft beneath my palms, and savored the taut thickness of his thigh muscles straining the fabric. He was just so big, all over, and it made me shiver with delight. And a tiny bit of apprehension, if I was totally honest.

Best to grab the bull by the horn, I thought a little hysterically, and dove for his zipper.

Ian sucked in a harsh breath as I wrestled with his tight jeans. "Here, let me . . ." he grunted.

With a supple flex of his lean hips, he shifted and pulled his boxer briefs down too, groaning with relief when his cock and balls sprang free. I wanted to groan along with him, but my mouth was watering so much I was honestly afraid I might drool.

He was just so . . . big. And perfectly shaped, thick enough that my jaw ached pleasurably at the sight. He was so hard, his foreskin had rolled back to reveal the flushed, tender head. I stared, enraptured.

Apparently mistaking my awestruck gaping for discomfort, Ian immediately said, "You don't have to, luv. I know it's a lot."

"It is," I said, not taking my eyes off it. "But I've never wanted anything more. Um, I've also never been this close to an uncircumcised penis in the flesh, though, so I might not be any good at this."

"Sweet Mallory. It's you. Your mouth, my skin." His tone was strained, rough with desire, and it enflamed me. "Do anything you like to me. I promise I'll like it too."

It was exactly the permission I needed. Reaching out with bold fingers, I wrapped my hand around the meaty base of his erection and angled it toward my mouth. I licked a stripe up the underside, enjoying the texture of his skin and the salt-and-iron taste and the intensification of his natural musk. Down here, with my face in his lap, I felt surrounded by him. He overwhelmed all my senses. I wanted to live here forever.

I opened my lips and slipped them over the head, letting it bump the roof of my mouth. I bobbed my head and pulled with my fingers, and let my mouth water all it wanted so everything got wet and slippery in the best possible way. Starting up a slow, luxurious rhythm, I lost myself in the scent and taste of Ian Hale.

Above me, Ian bit off a curse. I lifted my heavy lids to gaze up at him, not letting go of my treat. His chest heaved with his breath and his huge hands were clenched by his sides, as if it was taking all his strength not to grab my head or thrust his hips. What a gentleman. It made my heart flutter a little, even as I wondered if I dared to ask for what I really wanted.

Ian hadn't taken his eyes off my face. It was like he was afraid I'd disappear if he even blinked. Passion had blown his pupils wide and black, almost swallowing up the unearthly blue. His hips pulsed once, nudging the head of his cock against the soft back of my throat, and I swallowed reflexively.

He groaned, low and deep, and the sound made me clench around the aching emptiness between my thighs.

When I pulled off his dick to gasp in a breath, his head snapped up, concern crinkling the corners of his eyes. "Are you okay?"

Beyond words, I could only nod vigorously and dive back onto him. But this time I managed to snag one of his big, hard hands and bring it to the side of my head. Maybe that would be enough of a hint?

It was. Ian threaded careful fingers through my hair, and used them to tilt my face up to where he could see my eyes. He raised his brows. When all I did was moan pleadingly and kitten lick the tip of his cock, he cursed and gently, implacably guided me farther down his erection. The pressure of his hand, the slight tug at my hair, the smooth, heated hardness of him in my mouth—it all combined into an intoxicating swirl of sensation and tension that had to find an outlet.

Surrendering to Ian's touch, I let the moment engulf me. The nagging voice in the back of my head, the shrill fear of being not enough or sometimes way too much, even the breathless anticipation of what might come next was all subsumed in the wave of pure physical pleasure.

Sucking him got me so hot I had to touch myself. And luckily, any inhibitions I'd ever had seemed to have been left on the sidewalk when we dived into the back of this car. So I snuck my hand down to investigate the soaked seam of my jeans, shivering a little at the brush of my own fingers on the throbbing, denim-covered flesh.

"Oh bloody hell," Ian grated out. "Are you touching yourself while you suck me?"

I froze, humiliation scorching up the back of my neck like a blowtorch. "I'm sorry," I blurted, pulling back.

Ian blinked once, then scowled. "What the fuck are you sorry for?" he growled. "That was the hottest fucking thing I've ever seen in my life."

"Oh." I wiped my sweaty palms on my thighs. Trust me to shatter the sexiest moment I'd ever personally lived through. "Um, okay? My last boyfriend got annoyed when I was, um . . . distracted during blowjobs. But I can just get back to it, if you want?"

"I want. God, do I want. So many things, and most of them involve you on your knees exactly like that." He ran both hands over his short-cropped hair in a gesture of frustration. "But I admit one or two involve finding and beating the shite out of the wanker who made you think his pleasure mattered more than yours."

I blinked. "That . . . might be the sexiest thing anyone has ever said to me."

And, truly inspired, I got my mouth around the hot, hard length of him and sucked furiously. I was in a frenzy; all I wanted was to taste him, to have the salt and musk of this man in the back of my throat and know down to my bones that I had made him feel good. That I had made him lose control.

Ian didn't disappoint me. Eyes flashing, he hunched forward with a groan I could feel. Cupping my head gently in his giant hands, he whispered, "I can't hold back." When all I did was suck harder and drop my hand between my legs to frantically open my jeans and rub at my aching pussy, he grated out, "God, yes, do it. Make yourself come, gorgeous." And then he shot.

Hard jets of come pulsed from him, filling my mouth before I managed to swallow it down. I'd never loved swallowing before, but there was something about the raw intensity of Ian's release that sent me right over the edge with him. Shuddering, thighs clamping shut, I rode out the tremors of our shared orgasm.

On my knees in the back of a limo, with my hand down my pants and Ian's massive dick still half hard in my mouth, I had the hazy thought that I'd never felt more treasured in my life.

By the time the car glided to a smooth, noiseless stop a few minutes —or hours, who knew?—later, I was sitting sideways on Ian's lap with my head leaning on his shoulder. I'd never been with a man who could make me feel like fine porcelain, delicate—but not weak.

There was nothing weak about the pressure of his long fingers curled possessively around my hip.

The door opened as if on its own, and I immediately wondered if the smell of sex wafted out.

The chauffeur certainly didn't betray it by the flicker of an eyelash, if so. A solidly built white guy only about ten years older than Ian, I thought, although it might have just been a more weathered, rough-hewn face. He looked more like a bodyguard than anything else, and I experienced another of those strange moments of vertigo contemplating Ian's life.

I'd just had car sex with someone who could conceivably and legitimately need a bodyguard.

And the dizzying strangeness wasn't over, because holy shit. A glance past the impassive driver to the street told me it was residential. One of those posh, extremely luxurious and lovely rows of quiet houses curved gently away from us. The car was parked in front of a creamy three-story building with clean lines and high, arched windows. A riotous garden nearly burst over the low brick wall in front of the bright blue door.

"Is this . . . your house?" I asked Ian, dazed.

I hadn't exactly been thinking clearly, but if I had, I would've expected to be brought to a hotel. Or even my own flat. Ian Hale was notorious for guarding his privacy—it was known he lived in London, but nothing else, not even his neighborhood. And yet, here I was, staring around at a pretty Camden Town street.

I'd been right. He lived within walking distance of Primrose Hill, where we met. In the daytime, it must be visible from where we stood.

"Sorry," he said, grimacing slightly. "I shouldn't have assumed. Would you like to come up for a bit?"

The sweetness of this man sent a rush of confidence through my blood that was almost intoxicating. "Oh, honey," I said softly, leaning up on my tiptoes to murmur the words into his ear, "a bit? We're definitely going to need all night."

His eyes fired with possessive need. "What about Pilot?"

I bit my lip and fought off a blush. "Um, you're not the only one who made a few tiny assumptions here and there. I asked my upstairs neighbor to dogsit for the night. Pilot is fine."

"Perfect," Ian rumbled. He gently ushered me out of the car with a hand low on the small of my back. The sound of water shushed and murmured under the distant noise of traffic from Prince Albert Road a block away. The bustle and bright lights of London felt far away, though I knew we were still tucked right into the heart of the city.

"Thanks, Bobby," Ian said to the driver, exchanging a quick, familiar handshake with the man. "This is Mallory Pritchard. Mallory, Robert Martin, one of the best men behind the wheel that you will ever meet."

"Retired stunt driver," Bobby confirmed, tipping two fingers against his nonexistent chauffeur hat.

"What an interesting job," I replied, my mind suddenly whirring with questions, but I reined it in. "Thank you for the rescue back there."

"Yeah, Bobby is the real hero here, I think we can all agree," Ian said, clapping him on the shoulder. "I'm in for the night, mate. Tell Felicia I said thank you for the cottage pie."

"She would've sent along enough to share," the driver said, a smirk tugging at his hard mouth, "had she known you were having company."

For some reason, I blushed at this gentle teasing, but Ian wouldn't let me play it off casually. Interlacing our fingers together, he locked eyes with me and said, "I didn't know myself, until she said yes."

"Miss, I feel I must warn you," Bobby said gravely as I stared back into Ian's mesmerizing gaze. "He's not usually this slick."

"Oi, don't be telling all my secrets," Ian protested, towing me up the walk behind him while I snickered.

"It's okay, I already figured that one out on my own," I told him, waving goodbye at Bobby's delighted face before Ian whisked me inside and shut the blue door behind us.

Ian pivoted and pressed me up against the door, his big, hard body a wall of heat and strength at my front. "Cheeky," he grunted, his nose brushing my temple.

The sound of doggy toenails clattering on hardwood preceded Roxanne into the foyer. The big, muscular dog pranced up to us as if her paws were on springs, tongue lolling and eyes bright with happiness at seeing her human. I was treated to a minute examination with her sensitive nose, inspecting me for any messages from Pilot or hidden treats. Ian and I both simultaneously knelt to say hello, and as our hands smoothed over Roxanne's stout, well-groomed body, my heart swelled with delight. It was just so . . . domestic.

I shivered, my skin instantly feeling oversensitized and too small for my body. Ian looked over with a crinkle between his brows.

"Are you cold? I'm crap at playing host, sorry. Come here, come inside. I'll get you a cuppa."

Before I could protest that I was fine, Ian was pulling me down a narrow hallway, with Roxanne trailing behind. I got a fleeting glimpse of what looked like a cozy library with an armchair and a fireplace through one doorway, and a spacious dining room to the right, before we reached a small, warm kitchen.

The walls were a faded buttery yellow. Copper pots and pans hung from a rack over a wooden butcher-block island. The window over the sink looked out into the back garden, which appeared to be strung with lights hung from the enclosing brick walls. A scarred round table shoved into the corner made a haphazard but inviting nook where Ian clearly spent a lot of his time. The papers and books scattered over its surface gave it a lived-in feel that made me instantly comfortable.

Ian pulled out the lone chair and urged me into it before turning to put the kettle on. He opened a low cupboard that had Roxanne dancing with excitement, and tipped a healthy portion of kibble into the waiting bowl set beneath the butcher block. I propped my elbow on the table and leaned my head into my hand to watch him.

His motions were the graceful, automatic movements of a man who had lived alone and taken care of himself for a long time.

"This is nothing like what I expected," I said thoughtlessly, then cringed a little. "I mean, it's so homey and nice!"

"What were you picturing?" His curious grin flashed as he hitched his narrow hips up to sit on the counter, long legs dangling. "Some sterile bachelor penthouse in Mayfair? A sprawling Georgian terrace in Richmond?"

"Something like that," I admitted. "Not that this isn't fancy! It's really nice! But it's so . . . well, look at you."

"What about me?"

"You're sitting on your kitchen counter," I pointed out, "because there's only one chair at this table."

He studied me silently for a moment. "I'm around people all day, most days. Either at the gym with my trainers, or on set. This place . . . it's my refuge. I only need the one chair because I never bring anyone here."

The hairs on my arms lifted as a sweet thrill coursed through me. "You brought me here."

Ian's gaze sharpened on my face, frustration cutting deep lines in his forehead. "Mallory. Sweet. I've been trying to tell you . . . you're not just anyone."

My heart thundered in my ears as I slowly, deliberately rose and crossed the kitchen until I stood between Ian's spread knees. Peering up into the shadowed planes of his fallen-angel features, I said, "If you don't take me to bed right this minute, I'm leaving."

Ian cupped my upturned face in his big, warm palms, brushing the pads of his thumbs over the fragile skin beneath my eyes and sending shivers all the way through me.

"Baby, don't leave me," he whispered. "Please don't go."

And then he kissed me, and I knew this time there was no turning back.

CHAPTER EIGHT

WE BARELY MADE it up the stairs, pausing to kiss hungrily every few steps and clinging to the balustrade and each other for balance. My weak knees wanted me to just lie down on the landing and do it then and there, but after all this buildup, we needed to do this right.

Besides, it was kind of bright out here on the staircase. And I might be ready to believe that Ian Hale was truly, deeply, and epically attracted to me, but that didn't mean I was ready to give up the chance at flattering lighting when I got naked for the first time.

These thoughts were barely a buzz at the back of my brain though. Most of my consciousness was taken up with the living, breathing reality of the man in my arms, and the way he made me feel.

At the moment? The way he made me feel was hot. Ready.

Desperate.

It would have been frightening, if he hadn't been right there with me, just as needful and hungry.

"Your mouth," he groaned against my lips before angling his head the other way and kissing me again. The wainscoting on the wall dug into my lower back as he pressed against me, full length. I clutched at his shoulders and drowned in the salt-smoke taste of him.

We dragged each other up the last remaining stairs, and Ian apparently didn't want to let go of me even long enough to use a door handle because he kicked open the first door we came to and tugged me inside. In the next heartbeat, we were sprawled sideways across a huge bed.

His eyes gleamed in the darkness as he rose over me and, involuntarily, I arched against the thick, tufted comforter. My greedy hands went to the hem of his T-shirt, pawing at it ineffectually until he crossed his arms and pulled it over his head. It took all my self-control to hold in a moan at the sight of his broad, muscled chest and perfectly sculpted abs. He was ridiculous. I'd always assumed the camera somehow added fifty pounds of muscle, because obviously this could never exist in real life.

And yet here we were.

"You've seen it all before, I know." He ducked his head a little. "On-screen and that. Hope the flesh and blood version doesn't disappoint."

My heart clenched on a swell of tenderness. I leaned up to get my hands around his shoulders and pull him down. He resisted, ever so slightly, the stiffness of his muscles telling me more than words ever could that he knew, intimately, what it felt like to be a stranger in his own skin. I persisted, enfolding him in my arms and holding him tighter and tighter until his big body relaxed into me and he dropped his forehead to rest against mine.

"I could never be disappointed in you," I whispered. "The reality of Ian Hale, the person you are—that's so much better than any silver screen fantasy or action hero character you play. If you're worried that I think I'm in bed with one of the gods of Mount Olympus, don't be. I know who you are. I see you."

His hands spasmed and he groaned deep in his chest, a growl that reverberated through my whole body. "You're the one who is a fantasy. I can't believe you're real."

Heart pounding and breath shortening, I squirmed to get my hands down to the hem of my sweater and yank it off before I lost my nerve. "Believe it, Ian. This is really happening."

"God," he muttered, staring down at my lacy bra which was barely containing my heaving breasts. "You're so fucking lush. You're perfect, Mallory."

And when he skimmed one callused palm reverently down the midline of my body, mapping a line from the base of my throat through the valley of my cleavage and over the quivering softness of my belly, I felt perfect.

This man could have anyone in the world in his bed. And he wanted me.

I spread my legs in an instinctive gesture of invitation, letting our hips slot together more closely and making both of us gasp at the hard press of his denim-clad bulge into the welcoming heat between my thighs. From there, it was a race to see which of us could get our clothes off the fastest, fumbling clumsily and laughing helplessly into each other's mouths as we traded kisses back and forth. I'd never been so eager to get naked in my life. The relief, once we were skin to skin at long last, was immense. Except instead of a release, the tension in my core coiled harder and harder.

We surged together that first time, desire making us impatient and rough. Hot, sucking kisses with a hint of teeth, sweaty and frantic and good.

Hands grasping and stroking and shaping to muscles and curves.

Skin slipping and sliding and sticking.

Ian was a man of his word. Every single thing he'd said to me at the British Museum private reading room, he did to me in his bed that night. And when I was boneless with pleasure and breathless from coming on his fingers and tongue, he gently laid me back on his pillows and settled between my trembling thighs. The sound of the foil condom wrapper ripping open made me clench in anticipation.

His chest heaved as he fought for control, while I did my best to unravel it by reaching down to grasp his hips and pull him into me. The wide head of his cock nudged at my slick lips and made me ache with a sharp emptiness only Ian could fill. I caught my breath at the stretch as he slowly wedged himself into the tight clasp of my pussy. He paused with just the first inch or two inside, gasping for breath and watching me in the darkness. He was as hungry for my reactions as he was for my body.

Heat and pressure and a restless need for friction, for sensation, for *more*.

I threw my head back and crossed my ankles behind his ass, urging him on. The hot, deep press of his cock undid me and remade me, all at once. Ian filled every corner of my being, touching places that had never been touched and making space for himself.

And when that first slow, inexorable push bottomed out, we both shuddered. My walls fluttered around the steely length of him, clenching rhythmically in sweet pulses that brought tears to the corners of my eyes.

"Are you okay?" he rasped. "Is it too much?"

I smiled even as I felt a tear escape my lashes and run down my temple. "I've never felt better in my life."

He breathed out a harsh, shuddering breath, muscles locked in fraught tension above me and around me. I could tell he was still trying to hold back, and I wasn't having it.

Scoring my short nails up the small of his back, I nestled my breasts against his chest and crooned, "Move, Ian. Feel that? You won't break me. We're a perfect fit."

"Perfect," he echoed, deep and rumbly, and that big, thick body started to move. Pleasure seized me and wrung me tight as his hips worked that huge cock in and out of my drenched core. Every deep, plunging thrust electrified me. My eyes wanted to squeeze shut in tormented bliss, but I forced them open to see his gorgeous face set in rigid lines of ecstatic fury.

I'd never felt so full, so taken—or so powerful. I lost all control and all inhibitions. We clung to each other in the midst of the storm of sensation crashing over and through us, and when the wave crested, I broke. For a full minute, I was blind and helpless as Ian fucked me through the aftershocks and drew the rapture out excruciatingly. Ian cried out, grinding his throbbing cock in me to the hilt and setting off another small explosion that wrung me finally and completely dry.

I hung there in the soft, enfolding darkness of his room, anchored to reality only by the bruising width of his cock searing me open. He was still hard, even after coming.

My limp arms fell wide as my aching thighs unclenched and allowed my legs to drop to the bed. Ian shifted inside me, a tiny movement that made me purr exhaustedly before he carefully reached down to deal with the condom as he withdrew.

I stared, unseeing, up at the dim ceiling while Ian flopped down beside me. Searching in the darkness, my hand found his and grabbed on. We lay there in silence, waiting for our heart rates to slow and our overheated bodies to cool. I was so sated, I hardly recognized myself—and yet I'd never felt more completely present in my own skin than I did at that moment, in bed, with Ian a lithe line of muscle along my side.

There were things I wanted to say, wild and tender words I might regret once my brain came back online, but it didn't matter. My body had been through a thing. Sleep reached up and pulled me under without warning.

———

I woke to sunshine streaming in through the huge arched window, filtering through the gauzy green drapes to bathe the bed in hazy morning light, and Ian sitting propped against the headboard with a packet of spiral-bound papers and a stub of a pencil tucked behind one ear.

As I watched, he got a little frown of concentration between his dark-gold brows at whatever he was reading and grabbed the pencil to make a note. Maybe that was a weird thing to get fluttery over, but what could I say? I was a nerd, and he had never looked more delectable.

"If this is a dream," I said lazily, "don't wake me up. I want to enjoy it a little longer."

A slow smile spread over his face as he slanted me a glance. "Go back to sleep, if you like. I'm surprised you're awake, actually, after the way you passed out last night."

I laughed and half buried my face in the pillow. "Well. Someone wore me out."

"How do you feel now?"

Taking stock of my well-used body, I stretched like a cat and all but purred, "I feel like a million bucks. How about you?"

"I feel," he said slowly, tossing aside the papers and turning on his side so we were lying face to face, "as if the day I first saw you on Primrose Hill was the luckiest day of my life. And I've always been a lucky bastard."

My heart swelled even as my ears and cheeks got hot with embarrassed pleasure. "That's funny, that day I fell down in the mud in front of you, I thought I must be the unluckiest woman alive."

"Oh, that wasn't the first day I saw you."

He said it absently while reaching out to brush the curls back from my face, but his hand froze in midair when I sat up straight, suddenly alert. "What do you mean? When did you see me before that?"

"Ah, bollocks," Ian said, covering his face with that big hand. "Bobby was right. I'm not slick at all."

Delighted, I pulled the sheets to cover my naked breasts. I didn't want any distractions from this conversation. "Ian. Tell me."

He flopped onto his back and glared up at the ceiling. "Mallory. I live three blocks from Primrose Hill. Do you honestly think this week is the first time I ever walked my dog there?"

"But I've been taking Pilot there every morning pretty much since I arrived in London a month ago," I protested.

"I know," he said simply, and all the breath left my lungs in a whoosh.

All I could do was stare at him in open-mouthed surprise, but he didn't notice. He was lost in thought, his gaze still on the ceiling above us.

"One day I looked up and there you were. You were wearing red, and your hair was knotted up on top of your head but with little spirals of curls poking out, and you were laughing at something your dog was doing. A game with a stick. He'd get it in his mouth and somehow throw it . . ."

"Reverse fetch," I said, nearly strangling on my embarrassment. "Oh, God."

"Right. He'd throw, and you'd run after it and bring it back, laughing the whole time. For an hour, you played with your dog, and laughed in the sun, as if there was nothing more important to you than making him feel as happy as you were. And I wanted to go up and talk to you, so badly, but . . ."

I swallowed hard, my pulse thundering. "Why didn't you?"

Ian shook his head, a mocking twist to his handsome mouth. "Before you, do you know how long it's been since I arranged a date for myself, with a woman I actually wanted to spend time with? Years."

"But all those models and starlets," I said, feeling stupid and slow.

"They were nice enough, most of them." He shrugged slightly. "Usually they're other clients of my agent, women who need a little PR boost. And they get it, because anyone who goes out with me gets papped."

A little chill ran down my spine at the detached, deadened quality of his voice. "Is that all it ever was? I mean, you didn't actually like any of them?"

"I didn't know any of them," he said quietly, turning his head to spear me with a look. "And they didn't know me. And that's how I preferred it. Until you. I came back to the park every day at the same time when I'd first seen you, and I watched you play with Pilot and talk to him, and I realize that makes me sound like a creepy, sad bastard, but you were so full of life. Alone, always alone like me, and sometimes you seemed sad, and I wanted to know why, but most of the time . . . you smiled. And every day I saw that smile was a good day."

My mind whirled. I couldn't look away from him. I wanted to shake him by the shoulders and ask why he hadn't ever approached me. But how could I, when the only time in my life I'd ever been the one to do the asking, the experience had pushed me so deeply into my shell that I had yet to fully find my way out again?

"I would have said yes," I told him, my throat tight. "I would have said yes to you, to anything you asked me, every one of those days."

Something fierce and aching lit his blue eyes, and when he reached for me, I showed him that "yes" with every inch of myself. He pulled me over him and I braced my hands against the headboard while he buried his face between my legs and devoured me with a hunger that sent me spinning. And when I couldn't stand it for another second, I tore myself away and grabbed a condom from the bedside table. In two seconds, he had himself covered and I knelt over his hips and took him in.

The angle was different, the press of him deeper and more totally claiming, for all that I was the one on top and supposedly in control. His long-fingered hands were tight on my ass, urging me on, and I churned my hips wildly, almost bruising my clit against the hard jut of his pelvis where we were sealed together.

The combination of thick fullness inside, the press of him against my throbbing inner walls, and the scorching friction on my clit was too much. I came, keening, exploding, and he shot up to reverse our positions. His last few powerful thrusts shoved me up the bed and I hung on for dear life while the pounding, shivery, powerful orgasm went on and on and on.

Afterward, when we were finally dragging ourselves out of bed to go in search of caffeinated morning beverages, I winced and said, "Ouch!"

Instantly contrite, Ian reached for me. "Mallory! Was that too much?"

"Your pencil poked me," I complained.

Ian paused. "I've never had it called that before."

"What?" I looked up, confused, then laughed at the expression on his face. Holding up the pencil he'd been using to make notes, I said, "Not that one, this one. I'm afraid we might've gotten . . . effluvia on your papers too. Sorry."

"Effluvia. Good word. You should be a writer."

"Thanks." I found the spiral-bound pages and tried to smooth where they were crumpled. "What is this, anyway? It looks like . . . a script?"

Ian's tension was a sudden, obvious presence in the room, even though he never stopped smiling and his posture remained loose and open. "Nah, it's nothing. Just a bit of light reading."

It was definitely not nothing. "It doesn't look like a Mount Olympus movie," I observed, flipping through the pages and skimming the names of the characters.

"Indie film," he confirmed, turning away to pull on his discarded jeans, as if he didn't care whether I looked at the script or not. Even though the line of his shoulders said he did care, very much. "I get sent scripts all the time. Doesn't mean anything."

I debated putting it down and ignoring it. If he'd asked me to, I certainly would have. But there was something about his elaborately casual reaction that broadcast the importance of this script. And as much as he'd admitted wanting to get to know me after seeing me in the dog park, the feeling was entirely mutual. I desperately wanted to know Ian, the real man behind the star, and my intuition told me that this script was a piece of the puzzle.

"What's it about?"

Voice muffled by the T-shirt he pulled on over his head, he said, "It's a history of a famous mural in East London that commemorates the Cable Street Battle. Bunch of anti-fascist protestors clashed violently with police in nineteen thirty-six. It was a shitshow. We love to act in this country like you Yanks are the only ones with a race problem, but those Black Shirts in England before World War II were plugged into all sorts of hysteria and hatred for immigrants."

He shook his head, jaw tight.

"We've got our own problems. And they haven't gone away—the script goes back and forth between the actual battle and the fight this group of activist artists had to put up to get the mural completed in the early eighties. It's been vandalized multiple times over the years. With the way this country is going? I'd say this movie feels pretty fucking timely."

"That sounds like a story that needs to be told," I said honestly. Internally, I was reeling a bit. I didn't think I'd ever heard gruff, stoic Ian Hale say that many words at a time about anything.

He shrugged. "Maybe, but not by me. I don't do indies."

"You were making notes on the script," I pointed out. "Are you interested in doing this one?"

"No time." He bent down to pluck my underwear from the floor and twirled the scrap of lace around one finger. "Get your kit on, I'm starved all of a sudden."

"What do you mean, no time? I'm sure any director would be willing to work around your schedule for the chance to have you in his movie."

"Her," he said absently. "Director's a woman. And my schedule with the Mount Olympus movies—it's too tight. I need to stay available for the studio. Can't get distracted."

There it was again, that tone to his voice that made it sound like he was speaking someone else's words. I pressed my lips together and caught my panties when he tossed them to me. I didn't trust myself to start this conversation without coffee and on a very empty stomach, so I prioritized getting dressed and trying to corral my curls into something approaching manageable.

Once we'd sorted out our respective caffeine delivery systems, I settled into the kitchen table chair with one bare foot propped up on the seat and watched Ian crack half a dozen eggs into a pan of sizzling butter. Roxanne lounged at my feet, queen of the under-table domain, and alert to the imminent possibility of dropped crumbs. A tray full of chipolata sausages sputtered and spat in the oven. The toaster popped up four slices of golden bread, and Ian flipped them onto a plate with one hand while he seasoned the eggs with the other. My stomach grumbled happily.

Part of me wanted to soak up this unexpectedly domestic scene and enjoy my well-earned breakfast in peace. But at heart, I was a writer. I liked to dig into things and find out more. And no subject had ever interested me more than Ian Hale.

"When you say you can't get distracted from the Mount Olympus movies," I began, "is that something you believe or something your agent told you?"

The spatula clattered briefly against the pan. "Bugger. Roxanne has nothing on you, and she's a fucking bulldog."

"Knowing how much you adore Roxanne, I'm going to take that as a compliment." I gave him a sharp-edged smile that softened when he cast me an unhappy glance over his shoulder. "Ian. You said you preferred for your women not to know you—until I came along. Well, I'm here now and I'm telling you straight out. I want to know you. We don't have to start with work stuff, but we have to start somewhere. And right now, your work is a thing I already know is stressing you out."

Ian was silent for a beat, focused on sliding the cooked eggs out of the pan and onto the plate with the stack of toast. I waited, as patiently as I could, while he buttered the toast and went to the fridge for three different jars of jam. The sausages came out of the oven blistered and glistening, and joined the eggs and toast on the plate. I was starting to feel a little faint.

He brought the mounded platter of food over to the small table, along with a couple of forks. "This looks amazing," I told him. "Thank you."

"Eat," he said tersely, before striding out of the room.

No use trying to batter down the impenetrable wall around Ian Hale's secrets without proper sustenance, I reasoned, grabbing a sausage and biting into it with a snap. Salty, sticky with grease, utterly delicious. Call me a weirdo but God, I loved English food.

I was trying to choose between strawberry jam, gooseberry preserves and orange marmalade when Ian came back in, carrying a squat, squashy-looking armchair. He plunked it down across the table from me and said, "Try the marmalade. It's got whiskey in."

Sold. I slathered a piece of toast and took an enormous bite while Ian forked a couple of eggs onto his slice of bread and doused the whole thing in brown sauce before devouring it in four bites. For the next ten minutes, there was no conversation beyond groans of approval and requests to pass the brown sauce back and forth.

I was just finishing my second piece of toast, savoring the golden sunshine sharpness of the gooseberry jam, when Ian said, "You're right, you know. Phillip is the one who told me not to get distracted. He's working on a deal for three more Olympus movies, and he doesn't want any conflicts."

Suddenly alert, I put down my toast and dusted the crumbs off my fingers. Apparently taking that as a signal that the buffet was closed, Roxanne came to her feet and clicked out of the kitchen to find a patch of sunlight to nap in.

"Your agent doesn't want you to branch out," I mused. "Because he works on commission and the Olympus movies make the biggest bank?"

Ian shrugged and speared the last chipolata with his fork. "He's owed."

The hairs on the back of my neck bristled. "Owed. Ian. I have an agent too—a literary agent, but still. My agent is my partner, my colleague, but absolutely not my boss. I supply the books, she makes the connections with publishers and negotiates the deals. It's a two-way street. I don't *owe* her anything."

Ian closed his eyes for a heartbeat, a breath, during which I could almost sense him weighing out how much information to share. How deeply to let me in. I bit my lip and refused to push, but I did reach across the table to fold my fingers around the rigid tendons of his wrist, simply to let him know I was there and listening.

When he blinked open his eyes, they were dark with memories and secrets. "That's true for you, but it's not true for me, Mallory. I owe Phillip everything. This house, my career. My life."

I sucked in a breath to argue, but he turned his wrist under my hand and pulled back enough to tangle our fingers together.

"I don't mean that figuratively," he said, as if the words were being ripped out of him, simultaneously urgent and reluctant.

The intensity of his gaze rooted me to my chair. I sensed that I was very, very close to hearing something Ian had never spoken about to another living soul.

"I mean," he said hoarsely, "in a very real sense, Phillip Mowbray saved my life. And a lot of shit can be said about Ian Hale, and has, but it'll never be said that I'm a man who doesn't pay his debts."

CHAPTER NINE

"IAN," I said, my chest aching. Our fingers were white-knuckled in their grip together. We were poised at the edge of a rooftop with only one another to cling to for support.

Ian blew out a shaky breath, voice catching on the frayed end of it. "I told you I've always been lucky. Which is true, as far as it goes. I shouldn't have survived my childhood. Loads of my mates from back then didn't. The estate where I grew up—it was bad. Dangerous. Violence, thefts, gangs."

He paused and I tried to swallow around the constriction in my throat. I knew what he meant when he said "estate"—and it wasn't a lovely country house with acreage around it. He meant a tenement, a slum. Poverty-stricken people crammed together, living on top of each other in a situation that became a kind of pressure cooker for violent crime. "I hate that you grew up afraid. I hate that you ever felt unsafe."

His hand spasmed around mine, but he looked me dead in the eye and said, "No, sweet. I wasn't afraid. I was one of the bad ones. People were afraid of me, because I was bigger and stronger than most of the other lads. Most of the grown men too. My mates and I—we weren't the only ones that made that place a hell. We weren't even the worst, maybe. But make no mistake, Mallory. I was a devil, not an angel."

From the way he stared me down, I was certain he expected me to pull away, to condemn him somehow. But I couldn't. "Ian, I don't know what you did to survive when you were younger. I'm sure you made mistakes, and maybe they were terrible ones with terrible consequences. But that's not who you are now."

"No?" The corners of his mouth tilted up, but I'd never seen anything look less like a smile. "You think because I shed the skin of my past like a snake and slithered out of that life, I'm not still poisoned by it?"

"Then make amends," I said fiercely. "Work for change. I don't know, do that movie about the anti-fascists and tell the story of how art can honor the fallen and challenge the present and remind us of what matters."

He came to his feet in a rush of restless power and ran both hands through his hair. "That's what I'm trying to tell you. I can't. If Phillip Mowbray hadn't caught me trying to nick his car one night, or if he'd handed me over to the Met instead of giving me an audition, I'd be dead right now. The path I was on, the people I ran with, the shit they had us doing out on the streets . . . I would not have survived. Or worse, I would have. And it would've been worse, Mallory, because in order to survive I'd've had to become a true monster."

"But you didn't," I argued. "And you can't know what would have happened."

"My father is in prison, hopefully for life. My mother left when I was nine. My older brother lost a knife fight. My best mate started sampling what he was dealing and overdosed." Ian recited his litany of personal tragedy grimly, pacing back and forth across the kitchen like a prowling tiger. "It doesn't take a crystal ball to predict what my future would have been without Phillip Mowbray."

"It wasn't all him! Your talent and your drive and your passion and your hard work—that's what got you here."

"Don't forget my face and my body. Those were my real ticket out, because that's what Phillip Mowbray saw that stopped him from calling the police on a vicious little thug like he would've done if he'd had any sense. But he didn't." Ian sank to sit on his heels beside me, one hand gripping the arm of the chair tightly. "And because of that one bit of luck, I'm this version of myself. I got to keep whatever scrap of a soul I came out of that life with. That's worth a lot to me, Mallory."

I couldn't argue with that, no matter how much I wanted to. "It's a beautiful soul," I told him quietly. "Thank you for telling me all that."

"You had to know. I should've told you last night. You've the right to know what you're getting in bed with."

I could barely breathe. All my fears and doubts and insecurities suddenly felt so tiny, insignificant, in the face of Ian's torment.

"I know who you are," I told him, low and fierce. "You're not a silver screen idol to me anymore. You're a flesh and blood human being who has made mistakes and learned from them, who has a past and secrets and pain—but also a future that can be whatever we want it to be. You're a man I could love, Ian Hale."

He closed his eyes briefly, his big body tilting toward me as if pulled on the tide. In the next instant, his arms had wound round my hips and his face was pressed against my belly.

I made a sound in my throat that hurt. My arms came up to wrap around his head and clutch him to me.

"I need you," Ian rasped, his hold almost bruisingly hard.

"You've got me," I whispered back.

I let him pull me down to the kitchen floor to cover me with his body, and I showed him with mine, in every way I could, that I meant it. And in the back of my head, I tried not to be terrified of how true it was.

This man had me. I was his, body and heart and mind and soul. For as long as he wanted me.

The truly frightening thought that flickered behind my closed eyelids, as he protected us both and then sank into me to the hilt with a harsh groan, was that it no longer mattered if Ian kept wanting me. If this all went south, I wouldn't be able to turn this feeling off and reclaim myself by running away to another continent the way I had with Tony.

If Ian was ever done with me, I would be wrecked. And it was already too late to do anything about it.

THE NEXT FEW days passed in a haze of sex. We barely left Ian's beautiful house. Bobby the chauffeur left with the key to my flat and returned with a wriggling, ecstatic Pilot and a suitcase full of my stuff.

Even still, Ian was true to his word and I mostly wore him, or his clothes, for days on end. Pilot and Roxanne played and ate and slept together as naturally as if they'd been littermates. I hadn't put on pants that zipped in days, and I'd memorized the phone number of Feng Shang Princess, the Chinese takeaway spot a block away.

By silent agreement, we tabled further difficult conversations about the past—and about the future too. There was something intoxicating about living entirely in the present, moment to moment, and discovering exactly how much I could enjoy another person's company.

Of course, we talked. We shared little stories, intimate details of past relationships, the names of our first pets. I told him all about my family, which he soaked up like a flower growing in parched earth. He especially loved hearing about my exploits with Samantha, and claimed he couldn't wait to meet her.

In fact, Sam was the only person I'd spoken to other than Ian in days. Well, not counting thanking Bobby for the run to my flat, and my daily calls to order the seafood fried rice in XO sauce that I was now addicted to.

"We're both between projects," I reminded Sam on our video call, leaning my head against the back of the low-slung lounge chair and enjoying the brisk chill of the late fall afternoon. I turned my head far enough to get a hit of Ian's salt-smoke scent off the rolled collar of his cable-knit fisherman's sweater, which engulfed me like a comforter. "Ian's expecting to be called in for reshoots on the last Olympus movie any day now, but nothing yet so the only time we spend apart is when he meets his trainers at the gym. That's where he is right now."

"Are you writing?"

I squirmed in my seat a little and avoided looking at the screen of my phone. "I'm still in the planning stages."

"Which means you haven't even opened your laptop."

That stung, especially since I already felt hideously guilty that I hadn't been back to take advantage of my amazing British Museum access since that first day. "I don't have a contract for this book. It's not as if I'm under deadline!"

Sam snorted, her pretty features twisting with wry, older sister amusement. "Right. Why work if there's no deadline?"

"I've always said I'm like Calvin from the comic strip. It's not that I work best under pressure, it's that I work *only* under pressure."

That usually got at least a grin out of Samantha, but this time she just glanced away. I sat up straighter in the chair, my feet bracing firmly against the ground. "Sam, what's wrong?"

She huffed out a breath. "Nothing. Just. I don't want you to get too wrapped up in all this, Mal. Ian sounds great but . . ."

"But what?" I demanded, feeling the blood rush to my cheeks. "Don't get too attached, because someone like Ian Hale obviously can't be serious about someone like me?"

"That's not what I meant," Sam insisted. "At all. But Mal, it's been a week! And you've basically moved in with him! Don't you think that seems a little intense?"

I subsided with a sigh. "Intense is a good word for it. But that doesn't mean it's a mistake. I care about him, Sam. I think . . . God, it sounds impossible when I even think about saying the words, but I think this could be something real. Something good. Something that lasts."

On the tiny screen, I saw my sister's eyes fill with tears, which she quickly dashed away with the heel of her palm. A determined smile didn't quite erase the persistent lines of tension around her eyes. "That's that, then. Go for it. Don't worry about anything else."

I frowned. "Wait. What else should I be worried about?"

Sam froze for long enough that I half wondered if we'd lost our connection. "Nothing. That's what I'm saying. Enjoy the new-romance glow! You know, stay holed up a while longer. Forget what I was saying about work. The world will still be there waiting when you and Ian are solid and ready to face it."

Something about her brisk, cheery advice chilled my soul. "Samantha. What is going on."

She scrunched up her face. "Okay. Okay, maybe you need to know."

Worst-case scenarios—Mom was sick, Dad was sick, she was sick, oh God—raced through my head. "Tell me right this minute!"

"The tabloids figured out who you are. There are photos from that night you went out to the dog place last week—pretty hot ones too, good work, sis—and they've gotten a lot of play. Like, a *lot* a lot."

My stomach roiled unpleasantly, but I took a deep breath. "That's fine. I expected that. They'll drop it soon enough when everyone realizes how boring I am."

Sam hesitated. "I'm not sure about that. It wasn't so bad at first, just a couple of guys out front, but the last few days . . . "

I gripped the phone so tightly my fingers ached. "What do you mean?"

"They didn't only find you, Mal." Samantha sighed and raked back her wavy hair with a pale hand. She looked tired, I noted, shaky and a little drawn, the way she got when she didn't sleep well and her anxieties flared up. "They found us too. Since there haven't been new pics of you or Ian in a week, they're out for whatever they can get. I guess the family of Ian's new flame is better than nothing? I've got quite a collection of photographers staking out my block now. They're camped out at the brownstone too. The last time Mom tried to leave the house, one of them tried to harass her into giving up some clue about where you were."

Without even meaning to, I leapt to my feet. "Samantha! Holy crap, why didn't any of you tell me?"

"Because Mom's fine," Samantha said firmly. "Nothing happened. She went back inside and they're getting groceries and stuff delivered."

"What about you?" I demanded, voice shaking.

"I can get groceries delivered too."

"That's not what I meant."

She sighed. "I know. I'm fine too. This is . . . bizarre, and a little scary, but we can weather this, Mallory, if you're really sure he's the one."

"I'm not sure of anything right now." I hugged myself tight and wavered on my feet. What should I do about this? What *could* I do?

By the time Ian got back, freshly showered and wearing what I called his don't-notice-me costume of dark jeans, black waxed canvas jacket and ball cap, I had worked myself into a frenzy. I had also gotten dressed in my own clothes, which felt strangely tight and restricting, and put on makeup.

The minute Ian walked in the door, I barreled into his arms. When they instantly encircled me, I breathed out a shaky sigh of relief at the sensation of things slotting into place. The rightness that permeated the very air I breathed when we were together. This *was* real.

But did that give me the right to mess with my parents' lives? To send my sister into an anxiety spiral?

"Mallory, luv. What's happened?"

Ian's deep voice, so concerned and caring, made my throat burn with the onset of tears. "I want to go out. Right now. Let's go out and sit down somewhere in a café and have a cup of coffee. In public."

He stiffened against me, muscles locking down in rejection. "Not a good idea."

I pulled away from him. I needed to get a good look at his face. "Why not?"

To his credit, he didn't try to distract me or soft-pedal it. "Some photos got into the gossip rags, of us kissing, and there's been a bit of a thing about it. Mystery woman, Ian's loved up, blah blah blah."

"Thank you for telling me now," I said quietly, folding my arms around myself. "But I wish you had filled me in when it first started happening. I don't need people protecting me from the choices I make."

Ian's jawline was as hard as granite. "Protecting you is not negotiable. And if we go out right now, I can't guarantee there won't be more photos. More attention."

I lifted my chin defiantly, even though it felt like I'd suddenly swallowed a pound of gravel. "Good. Let them take my picture. Maybe then they'll leave my family alone."

He raised his brows and I answered his unspoken question, filling him in on my conversation with Samantha. When my trembling voice faded to silence, he clenched his fists at his sides. "I'm sorry, Mallory."

"It's not your fault." I grabbed one of his tense fists and lifted it to my face for a fierce kiss. "Ian, look at me, it's not your fault."

"But it's because of me," he argued.

"It's because of both of us," I said firmly, feeling the truth of it down to my bones. "We are in this together now, and if I'm going to make this choice that affects so many people I love, I need to know what I'm choosing. I can't hide in your house forever, and I can't use my family as some kind of shield. I won't do that to them. I need to face the press for myself, and start getting used to dealing with it. If this is going to be my life . . . our life."

I blushed as I said it, but I stood tall and kept my head up. And I wasn't surprised when Ian's eyes flashed with heat and he curled his other hand behind the nape of my neck to haul me close. "I want that. I want you."

Against his lips, I said, "Then take me out and let's show the world we're together, and we're not afraid."

A muscle clenched in Ian's cheek as he turned his face away for a moment. I could tell he didn't want to do this, that he'd rather be doing anything else, but he said, "Let's go."

It wasn't until much later that I was able to read the emotion that flashed across his handsome face as he turned to open the door. Something like sadness mixed with resignation and dread, but something more as well. I puzzled over it as I shrugged into my coat and wound a light scarf around my neck, but then he gave me a smile and took my hand, and I forgot about it.

Only afterward, when I looked back on that moment, did I understand.

Ian *was* afraid.

CHAPTER TEN

HEARING about the hordes of paparazzi outside my sister's apartment in Clinton Hill and my parents' brownstone, I half expected to have to shield my eyes from the flash of cameras the instant I set foot outside Ian's house.

But of course there was no one there. The location of Ian's London home was a secret I was beginning to appreciate. It must have taken quite a bit of maneuvering to keep gossip journalists from digging it up or following him home.

We held hands and walked down the street, as if we were any other couple out for a stroll. But I knew my palm was clammy with nerves, and my chest felt tight. Although maybe that was just the effect of wearing a bra with an underwire for the first time in seven days.

As we turned onto Regent's Park Road, traffic rushed past us in a steady stream of cars, black cabs, and red double-decker buses. There was more foot traffic too, Londoners bustling home from work and tourists wandering over from the park to take pictures of the canal that ran behind Ian's street. No one seemed to pay us any attention, and my shoulders started to drop from their defensive position up by my ears.

"Maybe it's all blown over," I suggested, hope flickering to life beneath my breastbone.

He didn't reply, just led me down a wooded path that followed the canal. It took us past a gorgeous old stone church and out to the noise and commotion of Prince Albert Road.

"Where are we going?" I asked as our sidewalk turned into a pedestrian footbridge over the thoroughfare. It looked as if we were headed in the direction of Primrose Hill, but that couldn't be right since we'd left the dogs at home, lounging in the back garden. Come to think of it, Primrose Hill would be a terrible place to find paparazzi since Ian apparently went there all the time and they hadn't mobbed the place yet. "How do paparazzi find celebrities?"

He shrugged, a sneer pulling at his mouth. "They're vultures. They mostly hang about outside the hot clubs and restaurants, or they pay staff to tip them off. If they know where you live, they'll camp outside and hound you down the road."

Chilled, I jammed my hands into my pockets as Ian draped one muscled arm over my shoulders like a weighted security blanket. "Now I understand why you work so hard to keep your address a secret."

"That's for the fans too." Ian tilted his head. "Most of them are lovely, don't get me wrong. They just want an autograph or a photo with me to show their friends, and most of the time, that's fine. Part of the gig. But a few years ago, when I lived in Islington, I had a woman show up at my flat and refuse to leave. It was a right mess. I got more careful after that."

"Yikes," I said, snugging in close to him as we started down the stairs on the other side of the footbridge. "That sounds scary."

"Fame will do your head in if you let it," Ian said, all matter-of-fact. "People who see you in movies and interviews start to think they know you, or they're entitled to something from you. Boundaries become important."

I wanted to apologize for asking him to push the edges of his boundaries, but instead I pressed my lips together. We were going to have to figure out new boundaries together for this to work. "So are we going to one of those restaurants where the celebrity photographers hang out?"

Ian shook his head, and pointed to a sign at the corner ahead where our path merged with something called the Broad Walk. My memory pinged with something I'd read while eagerly researching the area of London I'd found a flat in. The Broad Walk ran north to south through the entirety of Regent's Park, linking the English gardens in the lower part of the park to . . .

"The London Zoo!"

A smile lit Ian's eyes without doing more than twitch at his lips. "Yeah. You been?"

"No," I breathed, excitement speeding my pulse. "I keep meaning to take a weekend and go, but I was so caught up in research. And, you know. Moping at home with my dog, feeling dejected."

I laughed a little, hardly able to remember that person now. What had she been so upset about? Offloading Tony the Tool, who made her feel like crap? Good riddance.

"It's great," Ian said. "But I always get recognized, so I don't go often."

The Olympus movies had been a big hit with kids as well as adults, I remembered. Then I frowned as a thought occurred to me. "But there won't be paparazzi."

Ian looked grim. "Hopefully not."

I sighed. "Ian, come on. I'm trying to work out how I feel about this."

That stubborn, hard-jawed look was back. "So we start with fans. Dip a toe. It's all part of it, Mallory—no reason you have to jump in and immediately start swimming with the sharks."

The urge to argue rose up hard enough to nearly choke me, but I throttled it back and tried to look at things from his perspective. He was already doing something that went against the grain, deliberately exposing himself to being spotted and besieged by fans. More than that, he was exposing me to it. And I knew that was hard for him.

"Okay," I said, giving him a tremulous smile. "We'll start in the shallow end."

He smiled back, that slow, small, sunrise-on-the-horizon smile that made everything inside me melt because it felt like it was for me alone.

We crossed over Regent's Canal where it widened and turned to follow the northern edge of the park. Other walkers swirled around us, many of them tourists and families leaving the zoo, carrying plastic bags of souvenirs and looking tired and happy. So far no one had paid much attention to us, everyone more interested in getting home or back to their hotels than taking note of strangers walking near them.

Before long, a low building with a stucco roof and slim white columns spread in front of us. It was late enough in the day and close enough to closing time that we were the only people at the entrance to buy tickets. The bored teenager who sold them never looked away from his phone as he mechanically took Ian's money and passed back the tickets. I started to understand how Ian was able to pass through the world unobserved so much of the time. People were largely much too involved in their own lives to notice the celebrity in their midst.

"Oh," the ticket agent said, finally glancing up. "Park's about to close, you've only an hour or so."

"Got it, thanks," I smiled back, and in the instant before I turned around, I saw the kid's eyes widen and dart to the man at my side. I held my breath—but nothing happened. We kept walking, and the kid kept quiet, and it was fine.

It did ratchet up my tension, however. Wandering down the path hand in hand, I found myself scanning the faces of the other zoogoers, nervously anticipating the moment one of them would look over and recognize Ian Hale, star of Hollywood's biggest blockbuster series in history.

True to form, nerves transmuted to words spilling out of my mouth. "Did you know that during World War I, the zoo let the army train their seals to detect submarines? But by the time they were trained and ready to be deployed in the Channel and the North Sea, someone had invented the hydrophone and the seals were obsolete, so they got to come home to the zoo."

"Fascinating," Ian said gravely, although I could see a muscle tick in his cheek as he tried to suppress a grin.

In retaliation, I was just about to launch into a lecture about how the first zoo in London had actually started as a collection of gifts made to the monarch of live animals from around the globe, and was housed in the Tower of London for six hundred years before this Regent's Park zoo opened. But before I could get to the really interesting details about how several of the animals protested their cramped enclosures by mauling zookeepers and visitors, I heard someone cough politely behind us.

I cast a swift, sideways glance at Ian, who had donned his public mask of blandly charming smile and easy, unthreatening grace, before looking around to find a deeply tanned middle-aged woman with her hand on the shoulder of a skinny boy.

The boy looked up at Ian and squeaked, nearly vibrating with excitement. "Mum, it's him! It's really him!"

"I see that, Oliver." The mother grimaced a faint smile and waggled her phone diffidently. "We're so sorry to trouble you, Mr. Hale. But would you mind posing for a picture with my son? *In the Time of the Sun* is his favorite movie."

As I watched, Ian's fake public smile turned more genuine when he crouched to address the boy face-to-face. "That was a fun one to make. Thanks for watching, Oliver."

He turned to smile up into the woman's phone camera while Oliver grinned so hard it looked like his cheeks might crack. "Thank you," the boy said, before running back to the rope encircling the lion enclosure with his mother. She gave Ian a nod, and me a curious look, before following her son.

I breathed out. "Well, that wasn't too bad!"

Getting to his feet, I could see that Ian still hadn't lost the stilted, out-in-public expression. "Not so fast, sweet. Here they come."

He was right. The phone pic with Oliver was only the beginning. It seemed to have opened the floodgates, giving other bystanders and fans and curious zoogoers the permission to throng around us in a big, jostling group. Within seconds, we'd been surrounded. People shoved bits of paper and pencils at me, begging me to get Ian's attention. He kept that damn smile in place and signed as many as he could, using his height and long reach to great effect, while always keeping me sheltered securely against his side.

It was overwhelming, a din of voices and laughter and excitement, but I didn't sense anything truly frightening from this bunch of fans. No one got out of hand. They were thrilled to see their idol out and about, enjoying the zoo the same way they were, and once they'd gotten their autograph or photo with Ian and had been acknowledged by him in some way, they mostly drifted off to exclaim with one another about the incident or call their friends to share the story.

I didn't think anyone was paying too much attention to me until a young Black woman with a nose piercing asked for my autograph too. "You're his girlfriend, right? You must be famous too."

"Oh, I'm not," I hurried to assure her, pushing away the pen she offered me. "Really, I'm no one."

"That's not what it looks like," she said skeptically, brandishing the pen again.

Feeling extremely foolish, I took the pen and scrawled my name on the corner of her zoo map. She thanked me and faded away, to be replaced by a few more people who wanted a picture or an autograph, and it was fine. Weird, but fine.

At last, we seemed to have spoken with everyone who was still at the zoo and cared about movies. People gave us space, throwing us the occasional smile and watching us either overtly or out of the corners of their eyes as we stepped closer to the lion enclosure and stood side by side in pensive silence.

Ian was holding himself so still, he could've been carved from the golden sandstone that formed the lion's den in the elaborate habitat before us.

I took a deep breath. "We survived."

His shoulders relaxed almost imperceptibly. "You were brilliant."

That made me laugh and run a self-conscious hand over my curls. "I was awkward, but that's okay. I'll get better at it."

Between us, his hand reached for mine and tangled our fingers together. "So. Not a deal breaker, then."

Relief bloomed in my chest as I realized. "No. No, it really isn't."

I turned to him with a huge smile, and was a little startled to see the set expression creasing his brow. Catching my eyes, he immediately smiled back and squeezed my hand, but I could tell he was worried.

Well, nothing but time would cure that, I reasoned silently. This thing between us was still fragile, as brittle and delicate as a finely preserved piece of ancient parchment. We weren't sure of each other yet. How could we be, after a week?

"We're going to be fine," I told him. "I can handle this."

"Don't make any promises yet." His gaze turned distant. "You haven't seen the worst of it."

Still riding the high of surviving my first fan encounter, I easily shrugged off his doom and gloom attitude. "Quit worrying! Come on, I want to see the penguins before they close. And I want a cotton candy. I mean candy floss. Whatever you call it, the pink spun sugar on a stick. Let's go!"

I pulled Ian along in my wake, and he seemed to perk up as we made a quick loop around the Penguin Pond before heading back toward the front of the zoo. By the time we got back, the zoo had cleared out quite a bit. Even so, Ian reached into his back jeans pocket and pulled out his folded-up ball cap, and put it on. I didn't object. We'd done enough for one day.

"Hey," I said. "So when one or two of the people who took pictures with you today post them online, do you think it could take some of the pressure off my family? Make the photographers calm down and leave them alone?"

Ian gave a reluctant shake of his head. "Not likely. Blood in the water brings more and more sharks to circle around."

A chill raced through me. "God. Okay. Well, what would do it?"

He moved his shoulders restlessly, the big muscles bunching. "Mostly, stay boring and don't get caught acting like a wally anywhere in public. Then there are actors who court the paparazzi. Make friends, give them enough to keep them happy in exchange for being left alone most of the time."

I made a face and pushed out through the metal turnstile at the zoo exit. "That sounds like a devil's bargain, but if it keeps my family from having to deal with—"

A man jumped out of the lengthening shadows thrown by the pillars holding up the entrance hall. "Ian! Ian! Over here!"

Ian shot forward like a racehorse hearing the starting pistol. Grabbing my hand, he hauled me up and got me moving before I could do more than squeak.

"Head down," he instructed as we moved at a fast clip toward the Broad Walk. "Don't look at them, no matter what they say. They need a shot of your face, and once they know they can get you to react they'll never leave you alone."

"They?" I gasped out, suddenly aware of the patter of sneakers on pavement behind us. It definitely sounded like more than one guy, and as we walked swiftly toward the turnoff to cross the canal, I saw another man come lunging up the stairs with his camera already pointed in my direction.

Ian immediately veered away, leading us over the footbridge as our pack of hyenas followed closely, cajoling us to stop, to turn around, to give them a smile. The wind rushed in my ears and the breath sawed in and out of my lungs in a painful rasp. I couldn't see where we were going. I held on to Ian's hand and followed where he pulled me, focusing numbly on my low-heeled boots clicking rapidly along the sidewalk.

"Come on, luv, give us something," came a voice almost directly behind me. Harsh and grating, the man brayed, "Don't let Ian keep you all to himself, that sly dog. A rack like that belongs in the spotlight."

I cringed, instinctively bringing my free hand up to my chest, but I managed not to turn around. Ian, on the other hand—I felt his steps slow ominously, and a shot of real fear detonated in my heart. This time, I was the one pulling him forward.

"Let's just get out of here," I begged, and he listened. We kept moving, faster and faster until we were almost running past St. Mark's. The church and the trees and the people who stopped to stare and point were nothing but a blur in my tearing eyes.

Then that same voice came again, shredding through the chaos like a hacksaw. "Hey, Plumpy. Plumpy! Plumpy Pritchard, look at me."

Horror flushed through me, wrenching a sob out of the depths of my chest. The meanness of it, the casual cruelty, nearly knocked me off my feet for a second. I swayed and nearly fell over, and then I realized it was because Ian had let go of my hand.

I whirled to see him strike out with the speed of a hunting panther at the sneering man at the head of the gaggle of camera-wielding white guys. Ian gripped the man by the lapels of his cheap sport coat and lifted him clear off the ground, shaking him with a spine-rattling snap.

"Ian, stop," I cried, reaching for him, but he was gone, so far beyond my reach in every possible way. Rage had overwritten his beautifully chiseled features with a hardness I'd never seen before, and as the photographer took it in, his sleazy sneer dissolved into something closer to panic.

"Listen, chief, I didn't mean it," he babbled. "I didn't even come up with it. They're all calling her that, all the tabs, it's not my fault. I'm just doing me job."

It's a shitty job, I wanted to tell him, but there was no time because rather than bother replying, Ian set the man back on his feet. Almost gently.

And just as the photographer inhaled a sigh of relief, Ian hauled off and punched him in the face. Blood spurted from the man's nose in a geyser as he doubled over, shrieking. The other paps reacted, some running away but most staying to pop their flashes in Ian's face and get the best shot they could of this horrible, nightmare moment.

The moment when Ian Hale completely lost it.

Because of me.

The thought broke the nauseating paralysis that had gripped me since hearing the nickname I'd been given by the British tabloid press. I leaped forward and snagged the back of Ian's jacket, pulling hard enough to get him swinging around toward me, anger still simmering in his eyes. When he saw my face, no doubt white with the sick feeling of shock churning in my belly, the anger faded away.

I enfolded his hand, the one he'd used to hit that photographer, in both of mine. The big knuckles were already swelling, but he didn't flinch when I brushed over the raw, tender places.

"Ian. Take me away from here. Please."

He nodded once, never looking away from my eyes, and we turned and walked off into the deepening darkness of oncoming night.

This time, no one followed us.

CHAPTER ELEVEN

WHEN WE FINALLY GOT BACK TO Ian's house it was fully dark. I walked straight down the hall, through the kitchen and out into the back garden to sink to my knees and bury my face in Pilot's shaggy, warm fur.

He greeted me the way he always did, wagging his tail so hard it wiggled the entire back half of his body, but he held still and let me hug him the instant he sensed my distress. Roxanne whuffed softly, and I knew Ian had stepped outside. My breath shuddered out of me in a damp rush, but I forced myself to my feet.

"Come to the bathroom. Let me take a look at your hand."

Ian flinched a bit at the deadened tone of my voice, but I couldn't let any emotions through. I had a stranglehold on the fuckers right now, but if I eased up for even an instant, it was going to be a feelingspalooza over here.

He silently preceded me to the bathroom, pausing only to pour out two bowls of kibble for the dogs, who were immediately distracted from our silly human problems. That gave us the chance to get out the first aid kit and examine Ian's hand without two curious pups underfoot.

Moment to moment, task by task. That's what I could handle.

I set out the antiseptic wash and the cotton balls, then reached for Ian's hand. He'd already taken off his jacket so I didn't have to turn back the cuff. That was good.

As always, I shivered a bit at the first brush of skin on skin, but the reaction was heavily dampened this time by the strange dichotomy of being close enough to touch—and feeling further apart than ever before.

A yawning chasm had opened up between us, and I didn't know how to bridge it.

I didn't try. I focused on the red, abraded patches on his knuckles. Wetting the first cotton ball, I dabbed at the spots. My hands were steady. I was vaguely proud of that.

"It's not always that bad," Ian said suddenly, the words rough and rushed, and I immediately dropped the cotton ball. So much for being cool under pressure.

Crouching down to pick it up, I tossed it in the garbage and stood to wet another puff. I kept my gaze lowered, zeroed in on my job, and pressed the new puff to Ian's wounds.

His other hand covered mine, stilling my fingers.

"Can't you even look at me," he said hoarsely.

My eyes shot up to meet his despairing stare. "Ian," was all I could get out before my throat closed.

"I thought we'd be okay at the zoo." His words ran together, tumbled over one another in his hurry to explain. "Fans don't usually call the paparazzi to tip them off. I mean it happens, but not often. Usually it's an employee or something."

My mind flashed up an image of the ticket-taking teen who'd seemed to recognize us in the instant before we entered the zoo, and I closed my eyes briefly in regret. I should have said something to Ian about it at the time, but it was too late now. The damage had been done.

All I cared about now was what happened next.

"I don't know what to say to make this better," Ian murmured, voice fraying at the edges, and the jagged pain in his eyes made mine well with tears.

I bent over our intertwined hands, head and throat and heart aching to see tears splash down on his bruised, scraped knuckles. "You bled for me."

"He made you cry. I'd do it again, and worse," he growled, and I shot to my feet.

"No!" I pressed my cold, clammy hands to my damp cheeks and

tried to think rationally, but my internal monologue was basically a keysmash of anger, fear, dread . . . and something sharp and hungry lurking under it all. "God, Ian. That's the last thing I want, for you to be hurt because of me."

There it was—that's what was layered under everything else I was feeling. Guilt. The moment when I realized Ian was going to throw a punch and either get hurt or hurt someone else on my behalf—it was the kind of thing that sounded sexy on paper, but the reality? Made me feel sick to my stomach.

How could I have let that happen? Maybe if I had been braver, stronger, if I hadn't let that awful nickname get to me . . .

Ian was shaking his head as if he knew what I was thinking. "It won't be that bad next time. We'll do what we talked about before, make arrangements with them, make friends—"

I snorted, folding my arms across my body to hold back the creeping chill. "Oh sure, after you just declared war on them. I bet they'll be real happy to play nice."

His expression turned bleak as midwinter before he managed to get it under control. "What are you saying?"

"I don't know!" Feeling abruptly hemmed in by the cramped confines of the bathroom, I paced out into the hall. "I just . . . I don't understand how you can be so matter-of-fact about all this."

"It's part of the deal," he said, coming to stand in the doorway. He leaned against the doorjamb, filling the frame with his massive shoulders. "It's my life."

"How can you want a life like this?" I cried, then instantly wished I could take it back when I felt the way he pulled away from me. Not physically; he was still there, in the hall, watching me with those intense blue eyes that seemed to be cataloging every feature like he'd have to draw them from memory later. But at the same time, I sensed his sudden reserve.

"I *don't* want this life," he gritted. "But I can't leave it. Do you know how lucky I am to have gotten out, starting where I started? I'm living out my second chance here, Mallory, and I owe it to the blokes I knew back on the estate to make the most of it. Most of them didn't even get a chance to live past their teens."

"I get that. I really do. And it would be one thing if you were at least doing the kind of acting you want to do. Then maybe it would be worth it! But for movies you seem to hate, playing a character you don't like, trading on your looks when there's so much more to you than that." I choked on the last part, my whole chest feeling crushed under an enormous weight. "It's not healthy. It's eating away at you, bit by bit, and I can see it even if you can't. I saw it the moment I met you. You're not happy."

He shook his head, as if he barely understood the concept, and a piece of my heart shattered like glass.

Pressing a hand to my breastbone to contain the pain, I doggedly went on. This fight had morphed into something bigger than a single unpleasant run-in with tabloid photographers. I didn't know where it was going, but I had to see it through.

"I understand making sacrifices for your work, or for the people you love—people who would do the same for you in return." I strode back down the hall to him, to reach up and press my hands against his cheeks as if I could press my meaning straight into his brain. "But Ian, these Mount Olympus movies and your agent who doesn't seem to care that you're miserable . . . you don't owe them your sanity."

He was a marble statue under my palms, cold and still, but his eyes burned into mine. "Yeah. I do."

I fell back a step as though he'd shoved me. Cold spread through me, numbing my fingertips and stealing my breath. "I don't know if I can do this."

Every muscle in his body tightened at once, as if he was absorbing a blow. Then he breathed out a long exhalation and said, "I know. I shouldn't have brought you here. I thought I could keep you safe, but I was being stupid. I wanted you too much."

Dimly, I understood that all of this was going to hurt, so much, when I looked back on it later. Every word was a killing blow. But for now, I was lucky. The numbness had taken hold and spread to my chest. "That's not what I mean. I could deal with the fame stuff, the paparazzi, being laughed at and called names by strangers. It sucks, but it's survivable. What I can't stand is having a front-row seat while you slowly kill yourself doing work you hate until you believe you're not capable of anything more."

We stared at each other across the canyon of his back hallway. Neither of us made a move. My bones felt heavy, like they'd been filled with ice. A wave of despair broke over my head. I couldn't believe what I was about to say, but it was the only thing I could say.

"I need to leave."

I saw him flinch, taking the hit, and in a cruel trick of memory, all I could think of suddenly was the one time I'd threatened to leave before. More of a tease than a threat, and then his serious reply: *Baby, don't leave me. Please don't go.*

A sob caught in my throat, and tears washed out my vision so I stumbled on my way to the stairs. If he said it again, I wouldn't be able to leave, and I had to. I needed time, and space, and sleep, and a chance to breathe without wanting to throw myself into his arms and promise to be whatever he needed for as long as he needed me.

When he caught my wrist in a gentle hold, I struggled and cried harder. He let go at once, but I couldn't escape his ragged words as easily.

"Mallory. *You* make me happy."

The ice around my heart cracked and pierced me through. I looked down, half surprised not to see blood dripping onto the polished hardwood floor.

"I can't be the only one responsible for your happiness," I choked out. "It's too much. You need to fight for it too."

Changing course, I turned away from the stairs and grabbed Pilot's leash from the front hallway table. I could get my stuff later. "Pilot, here boy!"

He came racing from the kitchen on thundering paws and skidded to a stop next to me, all bright-eyed anticipation of walkies.

"At least let me call Bobby," Ian said hoarsely. In my peripheral vision, I could see that he was holding himself in the doorway, every muscle straining against some invisible barrier.

I had to get out of here, before his resolve crumbled. Or mine did. "It's not far. We'll walk."

"No. It's not safe."

Turning back to the hallway table, I snatched up the gray wool ball cap Ian had tossed there when we came in, and plunked it on my head. "There, I'm wearing your disguise. No one will recognize me. And I pity anyone who tries to bother me while Pilot is keeping watch."

Ian nodded once, slow and jerky. I couldn't believe he was letting me walk away. I couldn't believe I was going.

From start to finish, this whole relationship had been unbelievable, I thought hysterically. And the thought that it *was* finished shoved me toward the door.

"Take care of yourself," I managed to say, my hand on the doorknob. Just as I stepped out onto the front stoop, his voice came to me from the dark depths of the hallway. Every word ground out like broken glass.

"I told you once I was waiting for perfection. Even if it couldn't last . . . thank you for giving me a glimpse of it."

My fingers clenched, my steps faltered. I almost dropped to my knees. His final words propped me up long enough to make my escape.

"Goodbye, Mallory Pritchard."

THE FIRST FEW days were the worst. Almost instantly, I was aware I'd made a huge mistake. I was paralyzed with regret, obsessively remembering the way Ian had sounded when he said goodbye.

I'd thrown away a chance at real happiness. It was over. And it was all my fault.

For a week, I did nothing but mope around my flat and miss Ian so much I could barely breathe through it. Oh, I also managed to cry. A lot. And I went down about a million internet rabbit holes looking for pictures of Ian and me together.

There weren't that many; what I saw a lot of was speculation about our relationship and commentary about my size. A lot of it negative and hurtful, which I tried to ignore. But I was surprised to discover that there were a lot of people out there who were rooting for us, fiercely. I read a few posts that made me cry—again, not difficult—from women who wrote about how much it meant to them to see someone who looked like them locked in a passionate embrace with a man who clearly fancied the pants off her.

They'd even come up with a nickname to counter what I'd been dubbed by the tabloid press, and when I first read it, I felt it spread like a soothing balm over the raw place that afternoon outside the zoo had left in my psyche. Instead of "Plumpy Pritchard," they were calling me "Magnificent Mallory." And even though I'd never felt less magnificent in my life, I appreciated the support with every fiber of my grief-wrung being.

Of course, the internet was never entirely healing. There were plenty of people who hated me on sight, or judged Ian for his strange choice of girlfriend, or speculated that it was already over since no one had seen us together in days. That last one hurt the most, since it was, after all, correct.

Finally sick of the emotional roller coaster, I bailed out of the celebrity gossip sites and banned myself from looking at click-bait headlines. The only exception I made was for any news that looked like it might be about Ian getting in trouble for punching that smarmy photographer, but I never saw any. His agent must have smoothed it over. At least he was good for something.

I swallowed against the tang of bitterness at the back of my throat, and forced my attention back to the book in front of me.

Today was different. Today, I'd reserved a spot in one of the public study rooms at the British Museum and I was attempting to get back to work. It was going . . . not great, but that was at least partly because the reference librarian hadn't had all the materials I'd requested in my application when I arrived. I had to explain that I'd been given special dispensation by Dr. Chesterton to view the books, which brought up all kinds of memories that made me blush and stammer.

The librarian had given me what she did have and told me the rest would be brought over when they were pulled from the stacks. So I'd settled at my spot and propped the first book up against the large easel that stretched the length of the narrow table.

The reading light illuminated the pages as I turned them, but I wish I could say I noted their contents with fascination. Distracted and depressed, I lectured myself silently about taking up a coveted study room seat and not making the most of it, and vowed to focus.

I had finally managed to get involved in comparing the recipes for fertility tonics in *The Compleat Housewife* and *The Experienced English Housekeeper* when someone appeared at my elbow. The blue carpet had muffled the sound of footsteps walking toward me, and I was startled to see Dr. Chesterton herself standing beside me.

She was as stunning as ever, a flowy, ivory silk shell showing off her beautifully toned brown arms and making me wish I'd put in a little more effort than black stretchy ponté pants and a gray cowl-neck sweater.

Reminding myself that what I looked like literally could not matter less in this moment, I summoned up a smile that barely wobbled at all. *Go me.* "Hello, Dr. Chesterton. How are you?"

"Georgiana," she reminded me gently as she laid several heavy tomes on the table beside my laptop. "Here are the rest of your research materials."

"Wow, thank you." A flush heated the back of my neck. "You must have better things to do than hand-deliver books to writers."

She turned her slim wrist up to check her delicate gold watch. "As a matter of fact, I've a board meeting in about five minutes, but I wanted to drop by and take the opportunity to make certain you know your invitation to the Common Harvest Gala is still very much on the table."

"Oh!" Nonplussed, I tapped a nervous finger on the stack of books. "That's, ah, very kind of you."

"Not at all." She smiled, a flash of brilliantly white teeth. "I should have mentioned when last we met, I very much enjoy your books. *The Secret Life of Cotton* is a particular favorite; extremely interesting and entertaining. I'm honored that you're using our library here, and I would be pleased to see you at the gala. But of course, you are not obligated to attend."

There was a delicate pause while I tried to figure out how to gracefully say that I'd rather eat a bag of raw dicks than go to a fancy fundraiser where I might come face to face with the man I sobbed my heart out over every night.

She shrugged and turned to leave. Over her shoulder, she tossed off,

"Ian told me you wouldn't be joining us, but men don't always know what to do for the best, do they?" Then she was gone, trailing a cloud of expensive perfume in her wake.

Well, shit. I sighed to myself and began gathering up the books I'd borrowed. There was zero chance of getting anything productive done after that. I dropped them at the reference desk and let them know I hoped to check them out again soon. Then I headed out into the drizzly mist of another rainy London afternoon.

Rummaging in my bag for my phone to check the time, I frowned when I saw that I had five missed calls from my sister. I'd had my phone off, as per the study room rules, and I quickly thumbed in Sam's number, heart thudding heavily against my ribs.

"Is everyone okay?" I demanded the instant my sister picked up.

"What? Yes, oh my God, check your email. I sent you a link to a *Variety* article."

Confused, I said, "Okaaaaay . . ."

"Go read it," Sam instructed, "then call me back."

Samantha was the only person I'd told the whole story to, including how painful I'd found it to read all the gossip about my relationship with Ian. She knew I was trying to wean myself off Ian Hale headlines. So if she thought I needed to see this . . . what could it be?

The rain started pelting down harder, making me curse and scattering the groups of students and tourists who habitually used the front steps of the museum as a meetup spot. Pulse racing, I found a tea shop across Great Russell Street and ducked inside to shake the water from my hair.

There was a tiny table tucked into the front corner by the window, and I ordered a cup of Darjeeling and a cheese and pickle sandwich before snagging it. Finally settled, I hurriedly opened my email and clicked through to the link Sam had sent.

It was short, not even a real article—just a few paragraphs announcing the news that *Immortal Wars* actor Ian Hale had stepped into a key role in the independent film *The Battle of Cable Street*, and had also signed on as an executive producer.

I sat in that tea shop and cried. At least this time, there was joy mixed in with the pain.

Still sniffling, I called Samantha. "He did it," I cried into the phone. "He really did it. I can't believe it."

"I have to admit, I'm impressed," my older sister said. "As a gesture, it's better than a dozen roses."

My mouth went dry. "You think he's sending me some kind of message?"

She snorted as though the answer was obvious, but I was already shaking my head and trying to squash the tiny tendril of hope. I had to remember the finality in Ian's voice when he'd said goodbye. It was over. "No, no. If it had anything to do with me, why haven't I heard from him?"

"Maybe he's tired of being the only one putting himself out there."

I rocked back in my seat, all the wind knocked out of me. "What the hell is that supposed to mean?"

"Mallory." I could vividly picture Samantha pulling her own hair out in exasperation based on the tone of her voice. "You are my baby sister, and I love you, but do you know why you dated Tony the Tool?"

My mouth dropped open, but nothing came out.

"Because he asked you," Sam said, with emphasis. "And on some level, you didn't think you could do any better."

"I didn't know he was a tool when he asked me out!"

"So defensive," Sam tutted. "Maybe because you know I'm right. You stayed with him for over a year, Mal."

"Look, I know I was stupid for not kicking Tony to the curb sooner."

"Hey. You're not stupid," Samantha said firmly. "But you haven't really put yourself out there since you asked that asshole to dance at prom."

I sat bolt upright. "So I'm not stupid, I'm a coward?"

A white-mustached, bespectacled gentleman a few tables over cleared his throat and rustled his newspaper in my general direction. Taking the very British hint, I lowered my voice and turned my body slightly toward the rain-spattered window.

"That's not fair, Sam. I write books and publish them! Every single time, I know I'm opening myself up to criticism and bad reviews and readers who just don't like them. It's hard and scary every time, but I do it."

"Yes, you are brave in your professional life," Sam agreed. "But what about your personal life?"

Slumping, I barely noticed when the waitress set down my tea and sandwich. The moment when eighteen-year-old Mallory screwed up all her courage and approached Michael Trombley for a dance, and he and his friends guffawed with laughter, blazed through me in an instant, leaving its familiar sickly smear of shame and sadness. "Look, we weren't all born with perfect hair and faces and bodies and the confidence to match. Some of us actually know what rejection feels like, so we avoid it!"

"There it is." She didn't sound satisfied, only resigned. "The real reason you didn't pick up your phone and call Ian the minute you saw that movie deal. You're so scared of rejection, you won't make a single move to fight for what you want."

I can't be the only one responsible for your happiness. It's too much. You need to fight for it too.

My mouth went dry. I took a sip of tea and the porcelain clattered against my teeth. Was Samantha right? All the way along, through every step with Ian, I had felt like I was taking a huge risk. Like I was putting myself out there, as Sam suggested. But was I? Looking back, Ian was the one who initiated every encounter. He did the asking out, he invited me back to his flat.

He made it clear, over and over, that he wanted me. That he wanted to be with me, in every way.

And what did I do? I lapped up all that intoxicating attention and swore I believed he meant it . . . then I told him he wasn't fighting hard enough, and I left him.

"Take it from me," Samantha said softly. "Nobody's appearance is some kind of vaccine against insecurity."

"You're right," I breathed, the enormity of my mistake crushing my chest. "I'm the worst."

"You're not the worst." Samantha was as staunch in her defense as she had been brutal in her wake-up call. "You're human. Humans make mistakes. They're only unforgivable if you don't do anything to make it right."

How could I expect Ian to forgive me, when I could barely imagine forgiving myself? For the first time in a week I let myself look back on the night I'd left and remember not my own pain, but his. The expression on his face when I told him I had to go . . .

My heart jumped into my throat like it was trying to make a quick getaway. The temptation to get down and roll around in the guilt and regret was strong. But my eyes strayed to the clock over the fireplace on the wall opposite my table.

I didn't have time. I had somewhere I needed to be.

"Sam, I need your help."

"Anything," was her instant reply. "Does this mean you're going after your man?"

I threw money down on the table and snatched up my laptop case, determination firing every cell of my being. "If Ian can be brave, I can too."

CHAPTER TWELVE

Two hours later, back at the British Museum, being brave felt harder than it had seemed alone in my flat. I glanced at the banner by the door, elegant russet and gold lettering that proclaimed this the First Annual Common Harvest Gala. The whole evening appeared to be in support of an education initiative around sustainable farming, which was a great cause. Certainly worth the money I'd spent on this dress at the last minute.

Whoever had sponsored the fundraiser—the Pella Group, according to the banner—obviously had plenty of money, I mused as I gazed with awe at the transformation of the huge, circular Great Court.

It was a fancy event planner's fever dream of the world's swankiest fall festival. The glass-domed ceiling glittered under the fading sunset sky, limned in shades of red and orange from carefully placed lights. The Great Court was filled with gold-draped tables and a dance floor with a raised dais at one end for the live band. At intervals around the perimeter of the space, gorgeously moody black-and-white photographs of farms and farmers were perfectly lit for the perusal of the admiring guests. Autumnal garlands festooned the walls, and everywhere I looked there were centerpieces bursting with ripe pomegranates, golden tufts of wheat, ruffled dahlias and spiky tassels of Amaranthus.

The lady guests appeared to all have received some sort of memo about the color theme of the evening, because their gowns were an array of rich browns, crimsons, yellows, and metallics, with the occasional tasteful black thrown in.

I, however, had not gotten the memo.

Swallowing hard, I touched a hand to the smooth, silky fabric of my brilliant purple gown. The one that was more daring than anything I'd ever worn in my life before—something I wouldn't have dreamed of even trying on before I met Ian.

I'd specifically chosen it for this event, anticipating a phalanx of photographers out front. I'd pictured myself boldly marching past them, my magnificence on full, confident display, and maybe throwing a smile and an upraised middle finger over my shoulder as I swept inside.

Now I reached down deep inside for that fuck-off energy I'd had when I looked in the mirror before I left the house. I could use some of that energy to get through this evening, even if it wouldn't help with photographers. By the time I'd arrived, I'd missed whatever red carpet situation there had been.

I also appeared to have missed the speeches, since the dancing was in full swing.

That's good, I told myself. *That's what you're here for.*

The internal pep talk didn't do much to calm my nerves. I stopped touching my dress, suddenly sure I was leaving stains from my clammy palms on the delicate silk. Oh God, sweat stains. My armpits suddenly felt unbearably humid. The Reading Room, usually chilly enough to require a cardigan, felt more like a sauna tonight with all the wealthy, beautiful people circulating and chatting and drinking and laughing.

The room swirled in my vision slightly, the colored lights dancing behind my eyelids even when I closed my eyes to get my bearings for a second. The music seemed to swell and fade in a wave, along with the tinkle of ice in glasses and the scrape of forks on plates, and the low, constant buzz of champagne-lubricated conversation.

I desperately wished for a glass of liquid courage right at that moment. But I definitely didn't need anything that would make it even harder for me to balance in the ridiculously high heels I needed to go with a dress I hadn't had time to hem.

The song ended, smoky jazz saxophone trailing off into a smattering of applause from the couples dancing. As they began to drift off the dance floor, my view of the other side of the room cleared . . . and there he was.

Ian. Devastating in a perfectly tailored three-piece suit, complete with a gold watch chain glinting at the pocket of his waistcoat. One of the only men not in a tux, he would've stood out no matter what—if not for his fallen-angel good looks and the impossible breadth of his shoulders then for the impenetrable aura of aloneness that surrounded him like a barrier.

Ian sat at a table with nine other people, his chair kicked out slightly so his long body was angled away from the rest of them as they laughed and talked and toasted one another. Ian's strong thighs were parted, feet solidly planted, as he leaned back in his chair with a glass dangling from the fingers of one hand. His posture could have looked lazy or careless, but instead he gave the impression of brooding alone in the dark with his thoughts and a glass of whiskey.

As I watched, the woman to his right tried to engage him in conversation. He turned his head to indicate he was listening, and he seemed to respond politely enough, but when he immediately faced forward again and took a sip of his drink, she gave up with a bit of a huff. Ian might as well have been encased in ice for how much anything around him seemed to touch him.

He hadn't even bothered to haul out his movie star smile and practiced charm for this evening. He'd shown up, as promised, and that was it. Because he was loyal, and he lived up to his word. Even when he was miserable.

Determination and agonized fear swelled in me, propelling me forward. Eyes trained on Ian's face, I cut across the dance floor. Every step reminded me of that stupid senior dance, and my stupid crush on that stupid boy.

This was different, I reminded myself. Ian was a grown man, and I was a grown woman, and no matter what, he wasn't going to laugh in my face. Probably.

But that didn't mean he wouldn't reject me, I knew. He might. He might not be kind about it—he might lash out, and I had to acknowledge that his feelings were at least partially justified. I was ready to take whatever he dished out. Because whatever happened next, at least I would know I had tried. I hadn't waited and let life happen to me like I was a secondary character instead of the heroine of my own story.

The fat friend, not the girl who got the guy.

Well, fuck that. I was Mallory Pritchard, published author and beloved sister and loving dog owner and the woman who could make Ian Hale happy. This was my goddamned story, and no one was going to write the ending for me.

I marched right up to Ian's table and stopped directly in front of him. All conversation at the table, and at some of the ones nearest us, ceased as guests nudged one another and stared. I didn't care. I waited while Ian's hooded gaze traveled from the tips of my silvery pumps, up the slinky lines of my unapologetically body-hugging sheath dress, to the proud swell of my breasts over the low, straight neckline.

When he finally looked up at my face, the smoldering heat in his heart-of-the-flame blue eyes nearly singed my eyebrows off.

I didn't wait for him to speak. I held out my hand, and my voice didn't waver or break when I said, "Care to dance with me?"

There was a quiet gasp from the woman who'd been trying to talk to Ian a minute ago, but it barely scratched the surface of my focus on Ian. He was studying me like there was going to be a test later, and he was determined to ace it. I kept my hand out, waiting, and when he reached to grasp it, a full-body shiver raced through me.

At the first brush of our fingers, that connection I thought I'd shattered snapped back into place between us.

"I'd be honored," he rasped, that low, smoky voice that went straight to my core.

He stood in a lithe, powerful rush that made me want to scale him like a mountain. Instead I grinned in elation as I walked backward, towing him onto the dance floor. The band had slowed way down, a tune I couldn't name but that beat in my blood like the first stirrings of desire.

My plan had been to sweep him off his feet, but when he whirled me in close and held me to his body with a strong arm across my back, I was the one who nearly swooned. Pulling myself together, I let Ian move us slowly, sensually around the dance floor while I remembered what I'd come there to say.

"Congratulations on the new movie deal," I said. Our faces were so close, I could see the flecks of silvery gray in his irises as his eyes widened.

"Saw that, did you," he rumbled.

"I hope your agent wasn't too upset." I one hundred percent did not care if that jackwagon was upset, but I knew it would have been hard on Ian.

Brows lifted to show he had his doubts about my complete sincerity, Ian said, "Turned out all right in the end. I told Phillip to go ahead with the Mount Olympus deal too. I'll make time for both."

He said it with a touch of defiance, as if he expected me to berate him for not quitting the blockbuster franchise that had made him a household name.

"That sounds like a good compromise," I told him, squeezing his hand reassuringly.

"You were right. I'm glad I went for it." Ian spun me out into an exuberant twirl then pulled me back in, laughing and flushed and exhilarated. "I missed you," he murmured into my ear, and I turned my face into his neck to drown myself in the woodsmoke and sea salt scent of his skin.

"I could barely breathe without you," I whispered, my lips buzzing with sensation where they brushed the hint of stubble under his jaw.

I could feel the press of each individual fingertip as Ian firmed his grip on my back. "If there weren't at least fifty people watching us right now, I'd give you mouth-to-mouth."

"Let them watch," I said dizzily, light-headed with relief and happiness and anticipation. "I don't care."

"I care," Ian growled. "You're mine. I'm not in the mood to share."

Somewhere behind us, at the other end of the massive Reading Room, indistinct voices shouted. The music faltered, and Ian used his height to squint over the crowd.

"What's going on?" I asked.

He frowned. "Looks like some sort of fight. I can't see what's happening, but someone is causing quite the scene."

As I glanced around us at the partygoers who had been staring our way a few moments ago, I realized Ian was right. Everyone was looking toward the commotion at the back of the room, some even migrating in that direction to get a better look, and I realized we'd never have a better chance to slip away unobserved.

"Come on," I muttered, slipping out of my heels and carrying them in one hand as we made our way quickly off the dance floor and out the side door that led to the stairwell.

"Where are we going?" Ian asked, highly entertained, if the look on his handsome face was anything to go by.

"Somewhere private enough to do this," I countered, pulling him to a stop while I was still on the landing. He'd already gone down one stair, and that put his lips at the exact perfect height for kissing.

Spearing my hands into his dark blond hair, I ravaged his mouth with a hunger I couldn't conceal. I didn't even bother to try—I wanted him to know.

Which reminded me, there were things I still needed to say. Breaking the kiss with a gasp, I tried to gather my wits.

"Wait, Ian. Before we go any further, there's something I have to say."

He pulled back far enough to search my expression. Whatever he saw in my face made him lower his brow intently as he waited.

I swallowed my nerves and prepared to break a lifelong habit of self-protection.

"You said I was right when I told you to go for it," I began, biting my lip. "And I'm so, so glad it worked out and I think you'll be amazing in that movie and the producing thing is very cool, and if anything I said helped make that happen—I'm ecstatic about it. Truly. But Ian, I was wrong to leave you the way I did."

He opened his mouth, a protective frown pinching his forehead, and it was so gallant but I couldn't take the easy way out this time or it would become a pattern I'd never shift.

"Please let me finish. I have to apologize. For implying that you didn't fight for what you want, when you've been the one fighting for this, for us, since the very beginning. All I've done is let you pull me along while you did all the heavy lifting, and if I had to guess . . . it's made you think, maybe, I'm not as into this as you are."

For the first time since I appeared in front of him tonight, Ian deliberately looked away from me. A muscle ticked in his temple, but his voice was mild. "It's not a problem."

Dying inside, I insisted, "It *is*—"

But before I could explain, he rounded on me, eyes blazing. With one swift step, he'd backed me up to the wall and caged me there with his hands braced on either side of my head. "No. It's not. I'd rather have a piece of you than nothing at all."

"But that's what I'm trying to tell you," I cried, my heart thumping so hard it hurt. "You have all of me, Ian. I love you."

Disbelief gave way to triumphant joy in his eyes in the split second before he kissed me. Moaning, I threw my arms around his taut, muscled waist and kissed him back.

He was mine. A man I could trust with every part of myself—my fears, my doubts, my flaws, my joys, my hopes. And as for me? I made a silent vow, then and there, to be a woman Ian could trust. A woman who would love him, and not leave him when things got tough. A woman who would see, and cherish, every part of him, his past . . . and his future.

Needing to get it all out in the open between us, I confessed, "I don't know if I can promise the perfection you were looking for. But I can promise to be brave. I can promise to be with you. And I promise that as long as we're together, we can take on the whole world and make our lives whatever we want them to be."

"Mallory. Sweet." Ian tilted up my chin with one gentle finger. "If you're with me, it will be perfect. You're all I need. I love you."

My entire body lit up with fireworks. Savoring every shiver that ran through both of us, reveling in Ian's hardness pressed against my softness, I smiled up at him. "I know. You showed me in a hundred ways before either of us said the words."

Ian smiled back. "I'll never stop showing you."

I knew it was true. Ian Hale was a man of his word.

Which he proved, right then and there, in that stairwell at the British Museum, with a huge party carrying on above us and the quiet archives of books stacked up below us, and he was right.

It was perfect.

ALSO BY LOUISA EDWARDS

ABOUT THE AUTHOR

Louisa Edwards is the award-winning author of the Recipe for Love contemporary romance series. Under the name Lily Everett, she also writes the Sanctuary Island books. She stole her first romance novel from her grandmother at age eleven and never looked back. Louisa lives in Austin, Texas with her husband, their toddler, and an ancient terrier.

Visit her at www.louisaedwards.com.

SONGBIRD

TESSA GRATTON

CHAPTER ONE

OF THE VILLAGES Daniel Kelly had personally invaded, Caerafon was certainly the most picturesque.

Settled just north of Snowdonia National Park, the Welsh village boasted a rail stop, a small mining museum, a forest excursion site, and two rivers that crashed together just outside the village green where the ruins of an 800-year-old fort gathered moss and tourist tracks. Daniel had studied the specs: 587 residents, but capable of housing more than twice that many at the highest point of tourist season, thanks to several inns, guesthouses, and two campgrounds in the forest-encircling town. It was spitting distance to at least five castles, not to mention Snowdonia itself, a train museum, old burial mounds, and a handful of standing stones in a cow field.

He stared down the verdant hillside into the village. Colorful cars zipped between gray- and blue-stone row houses and shops, and the forest bent inward around it like an embrace. Afon Glas, one of the rivers, churned alongside the highway, slipping around boulders and beneath centuries-old bridges, out of sight south of town.

Daniel had parked his rental on the pullout to take in the view and start establishing a contextual map to go with maps he'd studied: basic Google map, the accordion road map he'd bought for six pounds at a gas station in Shrewsbury before crossing into Wales itself, and the Ordnance Survey of Northern Snowdonia that was so detailed and useful he could've planned an invasion campaign with nothing else.

The area was idyllic, he supposed, leaning a hip on the buttercup yellow hood of the car, and he had to admit the air smelled clean. Fresh, even, and just a bit damp. He drew a deep breath and exhaled to a slow ten-count. There was a pleasant breeze and the afternoon sun tinted the light emerald and dewy. He'd struggle to last a day.

There was no doubt in Daniel's mind that he would succeed in the mission he'd been assigned by his great uncle, vice president of Pella Group: close the deal with Ms. Elspeth Gwenlan to sell her bar to the corporation.

But the secondary mission was to take a break in a beautiful Welsh forest, the opposite of arid Afghanistan plains in almost every way, over the third anniversary of the worst day of his life.

Great Uncle Edward meant well. Daniel's parents meant well. Well enough to ship him across the ocean to work for the UK branch of Pella. Where nobody knew him or his history.

He dug the engraved black lighter out of the pocket of his slacks. Flicked it open, flicked it closed, and folded himself back into the car to drive into town.

Daniel rolled down the windows so he could keep breathing in that clean, damp air as he roared into Caerafon proper. It was a few weeks past the summer season, but still bustling with residents and tourists—mostly in the form of hikers. The national parks and forest excursions remained open for business. He left his car in the narrow car park next to the Blue Garden Guesthouse where he was booked for the next ten days, deciding to walk to Elspeth Gwenlan's pub.

He left his bag in the trunk, grabbing only his cell, wallet, sunglasses, and Alvin's lighter.

Taking the long way around the village green, Daniel walked along a gray cobbled sidewalk, enjoying the casual feel of the place. Nobody was rushing, there were folks on little stone patios outside of a cafe, school children in uniform crushed in a small mob under a bus stop labeled in English and Welsh, and a line of young men in hiking books and neon windbreakers, with hats and well-stocked backpacks. One of the men laughed suddenly, high-pitched and loud, and Daniel reached into his pocket for the lighter.

But he stopped himself, dashed across the street, and cut through the village green. The grass was thick and too wet in some places, marked for a soccer field. Daniel cycled through his breathing exercise and focused on the pub at the far end.

The Fort was the only stand-alone pub in Caerafon and did decent business, according to Pella researchers, but could do better with a fuller menu and more infrastructure—which Pella was glad to provide if the Gwenlans would sign it over.

Thanks to the intel he'd received from the initial information gathering and whatever official approach Pella had made to the Gwenlans, Daniel had been doing research on Welsh sustainability practices, local providers, and food health, and was developing what he considered an excellent pitch for Elspeth Gwenlan based on her known interests. His strategy was two-pronged: convince her the pub could make a positive, lasting impact on the community if it fostered local sellers and community giving, and outline the potential revenue streams from which she and her family could personally benefit. He couldn't imagine anyone not responding well to more money and a better community, especially not a woman spearheading a borough-wide farm-to-table group. And he'd gotten good at gently arguing pro-Pella itself, with a charming smile, intentional gestures, and several facts about how even a corporation like Pella could shift their in-house culture toward making the world a better place.

It wasn't *all* bullshit.

The façade of The Fort looked just like every other building in Caerafon: gray stone with white trim around the door and windows, deep gables, and dark slate roofing tiles. A large wooden sign swung over the entrance, painted with a peeling white stone tower like the castle of a chess set. Beneath it were laurel branches and curlicue lettering declaring *The Fort* in gold.

Charming and quaint, but ready for an upgrade.

Daniel pushed inside, noting the thump of a wooden green man mask that hung from the inside handle and acted as a dull door chime. There was a narrow, dark entryway and a second door propped open, and beyond it the warm oak and whitewash of a classic-looking pub. Low ceiling with exposed, worn black beams, a bar notched and stained, with short saddle stools tucked up, four beers on tap, and a back wall of mostly whiskey. Two more exits: an archway into the kitchen that had an external door, too, according to the blueprints, and a narrow closed door leading to a staircase up to a second floor that used to be a flat but was unused now, and ought to be transitioned into additional seating, or maybe a private party space. Beneath his feet the old floorboards warped unevenly, but not dangerously.

Behind the bar was a young man with honey-brown skin and slicked black hair skimming his ears, wearing a Nirvana T-shirt. Definitely not Elspeth Gwenlan. Daniel nodded at him, and wandered to the center of the floor, taking the place in.

"Order up here," the young man said in what Daniel was fairly sure was an accent from south of London, not Snowdonia. Daniel nodded again, continuing to scan his surroundings. Two of the deep booths were occupied, one with a family of four, another with a quiet couple on their phones. And an older man hunched over a pint at a tall table, his work boots muddy and hooked around the stool rung.

Pictures of the local landscape filled the walls haphazardly, some obviously old—black and white, or grainy sepia—others glossy and new. Ruins and majestic castle towers dominated the imagery, as well as the sweeping, bare mountains, and lush river valleys. Some photographer a few decades ago had gone through a train-tracks phase. Near the south corner a cubby was cut into the wall and filled with ratty paperback books. The southwest wall was windows, but the small-paned, poured glass kind that let in light but not much in the way of a view.

The low music that Daniel had identified as vaguely classical swelled into vocals and he realized it was opera. A duet in Italian. Very interesting choice for a tourist pub. But not really his problem. He only needed a signature.

Just as he frowned, a voice called, "Sorry I'm late, Asra!"

Daniel turned as Elspeth Gwenlan breezed into the pub, hair wild and a merry grimace playing across her expression. He barely had a moment to appreciate the lightweight sundress fluttering around her curves before she dropped a ragged reusable grocery bag onto the bar, then smoothly leveraged herself up, swinging her long, bare white legs over the bar, thumping boots down hard on the other side. The young man—Asra—steadied her as she landed. "S'all right, sis," he said.

Something about it made her laugh, and her bright eyes widened with easy humor. She touched Asra's Nirvana T-shirt with a purple-manicured hand, shoving him back, and reached for an apron on a hook next to the top-shelf whiskey. "Any news?" she asked, turning finally to glance around at the pub and whatever customers she might have.

Her gaze fell on Daniel, who hadn't taken a breath since she'd appeared, and as he stared at the spikes and curls of her autumn-brown hair, the vivid hazel of her eyes, her pink-flushed cheeks, and the earnest brightening of her smile, he changed his entire strategy.

CHAPTER TWO

ELSPETH READ, a long time ago, that wolves had been hunted to extinction in Wales by the turn of the sixteenth century, but she was pretty certain at least one was back. And he was coming right for her.

Her heart already thrummed from her race across the green to reach The Fort—then back to the market again because she'd left her bag on the checkout counter when Mrs. Morgan distracted her with a half-dozen questions about the buy-local initiative meeting next week. Elspeth had been on her way again when Agatha at the Blue Garden flapped her hand from the guesthouse patio and asked if Elspeth had seen a dapper American who left his car in the guesthouse's car park but hadn't stopped in. Elspeth had grimaced and in her best singsong voice promised to keep her eyes out.

Tying on her apron as Asra told her something about one of the taps acting up, Elspeth certainly made good on that promise. She couldn't take her eyes *off* the man stalking slowly around the perimeter of her place, closer and closer to the bar.

He was the kind of tall that seemed even taller by the tapering angle of shoulders to hips and long legs in charcoal gray slacks. It was a three-piece suit so well fitting she assumed it was very expensive, either one of many or a splurge to look good on vacation.

Asra bumped his shoulder into Elspeth's and took off with a chin nod. He'd be back this evening with Mary for the busy shift. Elspeth grabbed herself a seltzer from the minifridge under the bar and when she stood, the wolf was right there.

Elspeth tilted her face and offered a winning smile—her usual for new customers.

He didn't smile back at first, as his serious eyes slid down her face to her mouth. Those eyes were dark brown like bitter chocolate, and when he looked back up at hers, *then* he smiled.

All teeth, all trouble, and Elspeth felt a fluttering laugh trying to excavate itself from her stomach.

It had been too long since she'd felt anything like that.

"Hi," he said, gaze stuck on her as he slowly slid onto one of the stools and leaned his elbows against the bar. And Elspeth decided the fancy suit was one of many: nobody with only a single pricey suit would so casually touch his elbows to an unknown bar. Agatha had said he was *dapper,* after all.

Elspeth grinned. "What's your pleasure?"

"Hmm," he seemed to purr, finally looking away from her to skim the shelves behind. Elspeth caught her breath at his eyelashes, at their soft curl, and was thinking about how they'd tickle against her throat. Then she thought about his mouth under her ear.

Shocked at the path of her thoughts, Elspeth blinked rapidly. She wasn't one to immediately fantasize about tourists. Or anybody, really. Anybody flesh and blood shifting on the barstool like his cock was too big, pursing full lips and intently considering her whiskey.

Her pulse had already been high. She was flushed from her run in ankle boots not meant for running and a dress too fine for the cold wind. Her body was primed for a wild ride with somebody. And Jesus Christ, what a somebody.

She studied the square of his jaw and long lines of his sun-tanned throat, disappearing under the crisp collar and wide knot of a silver-lavender tie that tucked neatly into the waistcoat. His black hair was slicked back in thick waves, shorter in the back, and she thought she saw the shine of scars licking behind his right ear. *She* wanted to lick behind his—

"Jameson?" he suggested, after a long enough pause it occurred to her he'd been allowing her to stare.

"You can get that in America," she teased breathlessly, trying to salvage some pride.

"What do you recommend then?" the American smiled again, just a sly curve of lips this time.

"Hmm," Elspeth murmured, copying his purr as she turned and tilted her face up to consider her stock, too. Looking away brought only a little relief, because now she felt his gaze down her spine, drawing heat with it, lower and lower. What was her next move? Did she try to impress him, or tease him again, or give him her own favorite? Was he noticing that her bra was too tight, band cutting into her back fat, or horrified by her tangled hair, and worried the Welsh never bathed?

Elspeth briefly closed her eyes, remembered his smile—hooked up like a secret—and made her decision: humor.

She hopped onto her little step stool and grabbed the Black Barrel Jameson—the kind they aged in charred barrels—and plunked it down in front of him with a grin.

"Jameson," he said, voice deepening with amusement.

Elspeth slid her hand down the bottle in a brief caress. "Well, it's always a solid choice, but this fancy bottle I can upcharge to my heart's content."

A laugh burst out of him, deep and raw as if despite his wolfish grin laughing wasn't something his body was accustomed to, either. He nodded once, still chuckling, and Elspeth felt a thrill of satisfaction that danced down to the soles of her feet.

She poured him a double without asking how he liked it, then returned the bottle to its high shelf. When she looked back, he'd taken his tumbler and wandered away from the bar, giving her a fine view of his ass and the perfect way the dark gray waistcoat hugged his waist and framed his shoulders.

Oh, Elspeth was done for.

And then she noticed he'd left his jacket there on the bar for her. Like a promise.

Biting her lip a little, she lifted the jacket up and took it to one of the old boat cleats hammered to the wall for hanging hats. She settled the jacket into place and smoothed it with her knuckles.

For the next hour, Elspeth watched him nurse that double of Jameson while he perched at a high table against the back wall, flipping through the stack of old paperbacks in the built-in cubby. They were a mix of thrillers, romance, high fantasy, and a few literary classics Elspeth didn't absolutely hate. All of them reread until the pages were soft as butter and the corners of the covers worn away, the spines cracked in ten places. Many had been her dad's, a few she'd picked up in her teens, and three donated by regulars. She let people borrow them sometimes, if they promised to bring them back, or offered replacements equally loved.

The tourist family paid and departed, and Mr. Cutter, and the later afternoon crowd, filled in—mostly more tourists and a few locals—and Elspeth was constantly pouring drinks and washing dishes in the back, dipping chips in and out of the hot oil until Mrs. Morgan and her sons came with the evening pies—three sweet and two meat—the only real food on Elspeth's menu. It was exactly the right amount of busy to keep her in motion but not quite enough that she needed help.

A perfect afternoon, especially with the American giving her something pretty to look at. This was the sort of day when she couldn't imagine selling The Fort, no matter the money, no matter how it could free her up to do—well, anything. Go back to finish her degree, or travel, or push full-time on the buy-local groups.

No, on a day like today The Fort was hers, a shell of armor against the world, warm and sweet and smoky inside, and she controlled what happened within—who was welcome, what she served, with whom she flirted. Just as before it had been her father's, and his mother's, and his mother's father's, back to 1857. Elspeth could never be the Gwenlan to end the tradition. She'd been born in the bathtub upstairs, for Chrissakes. For better or worse, she couldn't leave it, and memories of her dad, behind.

Smiling sadly to herself, thinking of rubbing down this chipped bar for the rest of her life, she pushed at stains with her old rag like they were anxieties she could save for later. When she glanced again at the American curled over his Jameson and the paperbacks, she realized she didn't know his name. She'd lusted after him harder than she could remember in her life, and hadn't even introduced herself. Three novels piled next to his tumbler, and as she watched, he took the one in his large hand, flipped to the end, and started reading the last chapter!

As if sensing her horror, he glanced up. Whatever her face was doing surprised him, and he lifted his eyebrows. Elspeth shook her head, too overcome.

Sauntering over with two of the books and his near-finished whiskey, he said, "You don't think I'll like this one?" holding up the Nora Roberts he'd so blithely desecrated.

"No, I think you *will*," Elspeth tried to pull back into flirtatious instead of flabbergasted. "But you read the ending!"

"I had to make sure it wouldn't make me sad," he said with a one-shoulder shrug, entirely unapologetic.

Before she could react, he held up the Kate Elliott with the beautifully illustrated knight in golden armor. "This one clearly doesn't end well."

"That," Elspeth said, reaching for it, "is the first book in an epic seven-book series, so of course it doesn't end well—it doesn't end at all."

He handed over the fantasy novel. Elspeth cradled it against her breast, and slowly realized what he'd said. "You don't like sad books?" she murmured, barely audible over the three hikers who'd just come in, trailing mud and yelling pleasantly as they tried to choose a table.

The American's expression fell into something a little bit hard and a little bit vulnerable, and all Elspeth could do was stare at the bend of his lovely mouth and feel rather tenderly.

Probably, he was sussing her out the way she'd teased him with the Jameson.

She said, "None of the books over there are sad. Bad things happen, but villains don't win for long."

"I'm safe with you—with your books," he corrected himself quietly.

That was definitely a slip on purpose, and Elspeth narrowed her eyes. "Yes," she said. "But stick with the romances and mysteries if you want a tight turnaround on happy endings."

"Okay, beautiful," he said, slow and deliberate.

"I'm Elspeth," she corrected smoothly, despite the heat climbing down her vertebrae.

"Daniel. But my friends call me Kel."

"And what should I call you?"

"Depends on what you'd like to be," Daniel replied matter-of-factly, then knocked back the rest of the whiskey.

She rather felt like she'd downed a shot of the water of life herself, and carefully breathed through her nose.

Daniel slid his tumbler gently toward her and Elspeth asked, "Another?"

"How about a ginger ale? And a piece of that pie?" He glanced at the man down the bar making enthusiastic progress on a slice of steak pie.

Elspeth wrinkled her nose at the flavor combination, but nodded, pointing for him to have a seat.

He obeyed, positioning himself at the inner end of the bar where he could face the whole pub. While she grabbed a can of Seagram's from the minifridge, he unbuttoned his cuffs and began rolling his shirtsleeves up.

Elspeth cracked open the pop-top and set down his drink, eyes trailing up the suntanned lines of his forearms. As his hands moved, the muscles shifted, and she focused on the bone of his wrist, then the trio of thin scars down the back of his left hand, shining and pale pink, then his knuckles and the wide spread of his fingers, and before she could help it she imagined them on her waist, sliding down her hips to press into her thighs. It was all she could do not to roll her hips with anticipation.

"Thanks," Daniel said, taking the ginger ale.

Elspeth snapped her eyes up to his and nodded. She spun away to fetch a slice of steak pie, a hearty one, too; *he'll need his energy later if I get my way*, she thought, putting a little bounce in her step. Then she laughed at herself, knowing she'd never go through with it. She was behaving monstrously.

After serving him, she was distracted with an order for six black velvets and by the time she returned he'd eaten enough of the pie that she knew he liked it. Elspeth leaned her elbows on the bar and licked her bottom lip. "How's it?"

"I don't understand why meat pies like this never caught on in America." Daniel lifted another forkful and ate it.

"Goes better with a lager," Elspeth said.

"Probably, but I needed an alcohol break."

"I don't believe you're a lightweight for a cold second."

"Not usually, but I hadn't eaten since this biscuit and cream for breakfast in London."

"Morgan's pie will fix you right up then."

"Morgan?"

"From the market on the other side of the green. Just past the Blue Garden Guesthouse," Elspeth added cheekily.

Daniel had the decency to look chagrined. "I left my car there, without saying hello."

"Agatha has likely told half the town to be on the lookout for her missing American."

"I really wanted a drink," he said. He brought a hand up to rub gently behind his ear and she saw the tip of a tattoo peeking down from his rolled shirtsleeves, there at the delicate inside of his elbow. Impossible to know what it pictured.

Funny, she thought, *how he hasn't even loosened his tie or unbuttoned the form-fitting waistcoat, but only rolled up those sleeves. Like a deliberate attempt to convince himself that he is relaxing, without really doing so.*

"You're smiling at something, I sure wouldn't mind knowing what," he said, and Elspeth remembered he wasn't part of her fantasy quite yet.

"Well," she said, going all in, "you're rather good-looking."

With perfect timing, Mary Lannish arrived for her shift. Mary was nineteen and everything about her, from her personality to her ponytail, was pert and sweet. She tied on an apron and slipped into the kitchen to take over frying chips and fire up the oven to roast some brussels sprouts she'd fancy up with spices and oil into something serviceable.

Daniel remained at the bar and picked up the romance novel, reading from the beginning, like any sane person would do. Elspeth made him a Jameson and ginger, with ginger beer much spicier than the Seagram's he'd been drinking. Then she settled into the evening, breathing deep of the laughter and sour spilled beer, the rhythm of building a good pour, hurrying to fill a new basket of chips, taking orders and closing out tabs. Asra showed up, too, and Elspeth could relax or take off for home anytime.

But she didn't want to go home.

Daniel had set the book down and was chatting with a few locals, at ease and leaning on the bar like he belonged. He watched everything carefully, eyes always going to the door when somebody new arrived, and he kept his back to the wall like he was holding court. But she appreciated the way Daniel studied The Fort: the patrons, the smoke-stained whitewash of the ceiling, the clomp of boots, and calls for another round. He studied it like it mattered, not just out of curiosity. He caught her eye when a couple of tourist ladies sidled up to him to flirt, then threw up their hands when his accent revealed him to be just as American as they were. He bought them all shots of her fancy Jameson. They each left their own big tips. Impressive—in Elspeth's experience, American white ladies were shit tippers.

Elspeth leaned across the bar and said to Daniel, "I should hire you to flirt with my customers."

"I'm really just trying to impress you." He leaned closer, too.

Oh, how Elspeth wanted to hop over the bar and dig her hands in his hair, scratch little pink lines down the sides of his neck, and grab the knot of his tie. She'd stare into his eyes, demanding, until he lifted his chin for her, and then with gentle, sure little tugs, loosen the tie, pull it away to get to the ivory buttons at his collar. Flick one open, then the second, and maybe a third, who knew?

Elspeth released a long, slow sigh, pursing her lips in an almost-whistle.

Daniel looked at her mouth, and his hand curled hard around the cut-glass tumbler. "I really had better go get settled before Agatha of the Blue Garden Guesthouse gives away my room."

"She might show up with her dog, drag you out by your ankles."

"Can't have anyone witnessing such indignity."

Just as she opened her mouth to offer to walk him over, John Surley called her name, waving her over to a small group of tourists with empty baskets of chips. She smiled bright with regret at Daniel. "Asra can close you out."

He smiled. "I'll be in town a couple weeks," he said as if she'd asked.

Elspeth felt her whole body straighten and when she swung out from behind the bar—the proper way—she did it with a bit of a silly shimmy. Then grimaced at herself, but laughed and headed for John Surley.

When she glanced back over her shoulder like an eager ingenue, he was watching, and held up the romance novel, one beautiful eyebrow arced in a question.

She nodded, and he pressed it flat to his chest, hand splayed over the gilded cover to hold it against his heart.

The next time Elspeth looked, he was gone.

CHAPTER THREE

BEFORE THE SUN rose Friday morning, Elspeth was in her running clothes and heading into the chilly dawn with a tray of scones for Agatha. She dropped off nine every other day, from her mother's fresh batches. Then she went for a jog up the mountain past the old chapel ruins to the Neolithic burial chamber, on a rough route she'd perfected over the past three years.

Her bare knees and arms were freezing, thanks to the spandex shorts and exercise top she wore, but she'd be glad in half an hour, working up a sweat along the winding road. Elspeth walked as fast as she could across the dark sidewalk without disrupting the cloth-covered scones. She was sleepy but brightening in the brisk breeze that pebbled her skin. It was a short walk from the cottage she shared with her mum to the guesthouse, too near to bother driving unless it poured rain.

The sky overhead was dark blue, stars twinkling everywhere but in the east, where just over the canopy of trees and shadow of the mountain, dawn pressed silver fingers. Nobody else was out so early, though the first bus would arrive soon, and the lights were on in the Morgans' back room. A tiny part of Elspeth wished she'd catch a glimpse of the American, who her mum had told her was called Daniel Kelly, which she'd heard in turn from Mrs. Morgan with a little sniff at the Irish. Elspeth had laughed and given her mum the whole rundown of the evening, only censoring the exact intensity of her lust. Mum had been encouraging, though wary of Daniel's sheer Americanness—America was too far away for a relationship. Since Elspeth's mum had started quietly seeing Asra's dad, who was a Londoner, Mum had appointed herself quite the expert on how distant a long-distance relationship had any right to be.

Elspeth had extricated herself with a defiant insistence that *relationship* wasn't the correct term to describe her interest in Daniel Kelly, fleeing before her mum's scandalized cry. She'd been up half the night obsessed with the idea of licking the tip of that tattoo peeking out of his rolled shirtsleeves, without even knowing what it was a tattoo of! It could be the base of a sleek anchor or a camo-painted rifle or the slender foot of one of those pin-up girls they used to paint on the side of planes with offensive gravity-defying tits, and she wouldn't care. Elspeth was betting it was military of some kind, but for all she knew it was a tattoo of a heart with his mum's name and she'd still die to put her mouth on it.

She sure couldn't explain *that* to her own mum. Especially when either of them having any romantic interest at all, much less discussing men together, was too new, too delicate, to ruin with serious engagement.

But the memory made her laugh again, and she admitted to herself that she was fairly sure she'd take anything from Mr. My Friends Call Me Kel. Good thing he'd be tucked away in the dark guesthouse this early.

But a thrill of fear stopped her cold at the flicker of firelight on the guesthouse patio. The firelight appeared, disappeared, appeared again. Like a bobbing corpse candle.

Elspeth blew out an aggravated breath; it was only a man, not a premonition of death.

Though . . . she forced herself to keep walking at a casual pace.

Daniel. It was Daniel Kelly.

He slouched on the delicate wrought-iron garden chair set against the façade of the guesthouse, one elbow propped on the equally florid wrought-iron tea table. His long legs stretched before him, crossed at the ankles, and his black hair flopped over his forehead, shadowing his eyes even when the lighter in his hand flicked on again, casting a fiendish glow against his stomach.

Elspeth swallowed the bubbling thrill, stepped past the last of the decorative birch trees lining the sidewalk along this stretch of the main road, and came into his view.

The lighter flicked on, and remained on as Daniel lifted his chin and stared at her.

Oh, he looked like an elf prince or the devil himself.

"Elspeth," he said, and she felt his voice touch her, slipping along the cold bare skin of her arms and legs, upwards and inwards, gathering in a tight, hot bow right in her belly.

She walked to the patio, stepped up the slight rise, and looked down at him. "You're awake early," she said lightly, trying for blithe.

"Jet lag," he said, snapping the lighter closed again. He didn't move at all to straighten his shoulders or move his long legs. But his eyes, impossibly dark in the pre-dawn gray, looked slowly at Elspeth's entire being, and she clenched her fingers around the tray too hard.

"Isn't it the middle of the night in the States?" she challenged, to put herself on firmer ground.

He smiled dark and slow. "Okay, beautiful. Jet lag and insomnia."

"Maybe if you didn't smoke, you'd sleep better."

Daniel caressed the lighter with his thumb, the air around him thick with sorrow, then tucked it into the pocket of his slacks. Same ones from yesterday. But he wore a thick sweater over the slacks, and his shoes were polished black military boots, one cuff half tucked in, the other slumped over his laces. "It isn't mine," he said abruptly.

Then he drew up his legs, planting his boots solidly on the patio. He leaned forward, gaze down. "It was my friend Alvin's. He died three years ago this Tuesday."

"I'm sorry," Elspeth whispered, gutted by the years. Her dad had been dead the same amount of time.

"I sleep worse this time of year, since." He lifted his eyes, and in the dim pre-dawn they looked to have a swirl of grief, until he spread his lovely mouth in a smile. "But I was glad to have your book, keeping me company."

Elspeth returned his gentle smile. "Oh, good. I hope you liked it."

"Got me rather hot and bothered, too," Daniel added.

"Oh," Elspeth said again, the tray of scones cutting into her stomach, she pressed it so hard.

He stood. "What's this?" he asked, moving close enough only the tray kept them apart. She had to look up just a little bit. Rising silver-gray light softened the cut of his jaw and she found a cool glint in those bitter-chocolate eyes. Last night, she'd put him around thirty years old, but in this moment, he was ageless and perfect as that elf prince she'd imagined.

"Scones from my mum," she murmured. "For your breakfast."

"Can I help you with them?"

Elspeth nodded wordlessly, and Daniel took the tray, but he didn't back off. Her tongue was dry, and she didn't want the eerie, timeless moment to end.

A breeze blew and Elspeth shivered noticeably.

Daniel frowned. "You're cold. Do you . . . want a jacket?"

She smiled at the helpless-sounding offer. "I just need to get going on my run. Want to come?"

Surprise at her own invitation kept her lips parted after the last word. She never had company for her runs—for three years they'd been her time to expunge whatever anger and grief plagued her most, so she could put it aside and help her mum or run The Fort. It had been more than a year since she'd broken down in sobs halfway up the mountain, but she still needed the routine to herself.

Daniel's eyes shifted down to her mouth, then back to her widened eyes. He started to decline.

"No, I mean it," Elspeth insisted. She nodded firmly. She did mean it, she wanted him to say yes, wanted him to go with her. "Go with me. Exercise helps with insomnia, too!" she added the last as a cheerful challenge. She'd wager he couldn't back down from a challenge.

"Okay, I'll take these in and put on the right shoes," he said, turning with the tray of scones.

Elspeth followed into the warm guesthouse, feeling like the world was tipping under her feet.

CHAPTER FOUR

DANIEL DID NOT KNOW why he'd told her about the lighter. Or Alvin.

No, he did know, and since his therapist liked to say he couldn't work through his trauma if he couldn't be honest with himself about what he felt when, Daniel forced himself to admit he'd told her because he'd wanted to. He felt like if Elspeth Gwenlan gave him half a chance, he'd never stop talking. He'd tell her whatever she'd listen to, just so she'd stay close, stay looking at him in that hungry, sultry way.

He didn't remember the last time he'd craved confession.

As long as he didn't confess he worked for Pella. It was too late for that now, after not coming out with it last night.

He dashed upstairs and pulled on Army sweats, a T-shirt and his trainers. It couldn't have been more than a few minutes before he jogged back down to find Elspeth hugging her bare arms while she talked to Agatha Priddy, her back to him.

The spandex shorts she wore were so tight he could see the imprint of the line of her panties pressing the flesh of her ass, and he wanted to bury his face in it. Kneel down, peel off the spandex, grab her thighs, and lift her up so she had to brace forward on the counter, and find out what Elspeth tasted like.

God, he was hard just thinking it, and hadn't even touched her yet.

Agatha said, "Daniel, take one of my water bottles, this one refuses."

Cold panic flashed through him.

He'd forgotten the older woman was even in the kitchen, and she was standing right there. He'd not been aware of everything in the room —he had to stay aware. If he didn't keep track of every inch of space around him—

But it was only a damned guesthouse. This was Wales. Nothing was going to explode.

Fuck this anniversary.

"It isn't that far, Agatha," Elspeth said, turning to flash him a grin. Her reddish-brown flyaway hair was in two short pigtails, and when her gilded eyes met his, Daniel felt his chest loosen. He was fine. Everything was fine.

With a half-smile, he said to Agatha, "I'll have to defer to my guide on this one, Mrs. Priddy."

"Off we go, then," Elspeth sang, actually pushing on his chest to back him away.

Before he could do much more than register her hands on him, brushing against his nipple through the T-shirt, they were out the door and into the cold dawn, and Elspeth jogged past him.

"Come on!" she said, and took off.

Daniel took a deep breath of the cold air and followed. Behind her, he had an excellent view of her long legs, that delicious ass, waist pinched in by her spandex, and the soft dips of her back where her sports bra bound her tight. He wanted his hands all over her. It was so good to simply *want*.

He was going to fuck this up. *Honestly*, he reminded himself, *I already have.*

That relaxed him a little bit more. If he'd already ruined his chances by not telling her who he was, he didn't have anything to lose.

Elspeth led him northwest out of town, and thanks to his memorization of the Ordnance Survey, he knew the road she turned onto would wind up the small mountain. The pavement crumbled into hard, furrowed mud, twisting between trees. Under the canopy it was dark, and he saw the little flashes of reflectors on her trainers.

The road was steep, and it wasn't long before he had to concentrate on the exercise instead of the way her body bounced. Elspeth kept her pace, never flagging, though she did glance back at him sometimes and smile. She seemed so pleased he was there, exactly the same distance behind her; it pleased him in turn. Time stretched, and the glow of dawn slowly soaked the forest. Birds tweeted, the breeze rustled the full, still-green leaves, and their footsteps crunched in perfect rhythm.

When they burst out of the forest and onto a gorse-covered hillside, the sun flared on Elspeth's hair, casting it gold and Daniel pushed harder to catch up with her. "Where are we headed?" he asked, voice rough from hard work and disuse.

"There's some ruins another quarter mile up," she said, sounding like she'd been doing nothing more strenuous than a nature walk.

"Sure," he said, and couldn't help adding, "You're not even winded."

Elspeth laughed. "I usually sing full-out while I make that run, so this was a break."

"Sing!" That hadn't been what he'd expected.

She slowed down to a quick walk and her smile broke off as she looked away from him. "It keeps my lungs at their best potential, and is better than . . ."

In her trailing quiet, Daniel thought he understood what she'd been about to say. Better than crying. There was a longing in how she stared out over the valley.

Resisting the urge to touch her cheek, he followed her gaze. The valley was lush and dark green in most places, with a few gray slate roofs peeking out along the edges of town, and he could just see the open space where the village green had to be. The sky, though, was pink and orange and brilliant blue, with silver-edged clouds rippling near the horizon. Epic and open. Daniel took another deep breath, filling his own lungs, and thought about that: keeping her lungs in shape. A few things fell into place. "Opera," he said.

Startled, Elspeth looked at him. "How . . . I . . ." her mouth gaped adorably.

Daniel moved closer to her, so their arms brushed. "I thought it was an odd choice for a tourist pub to be playing Italian opera."

"Oh, of course," she said, and *now* she sounded breathless, which Daniel liked.

He leaned nearer, holding her gaze for a longer moment. Her

creamy cheeks had gone pink, and she suddenly took his hand, glancing down at it. Her fingers were cold and dry, and Daniel curled his around hers, ecstatic at the contact. It was barely anything, but he felt it down to his bones.

She said, "I left school when my dad got sick, but I was studying opera, of all things. Nobody studies opera anymore."

Keeping hold of her hand, Daniel tugged her on again.

They walked in silence for a moment, until she nodded at his sweatpants and said, "Were you in the Army? Are you . . . still?"

It was stamped along his thigh. ARMY in bold proclamation. Daniel nodded. "For six years, but no, not anymore. Not since . . ."

"Three years ago." Next she'd ask what happened. "Why did you join?" she asked instead.

Relieved, he quickly replied, "To piss off my folks."

Elspeth laughed brightly. She squeezed his hand.

"It's true," Daniel smiled nostalgically, thinking of his stupid, defiant twenty-one-year-old self. "My family business is business, two generations before me, the self-made kind that has this sense we paid our dues a hundred years ago, so now the world owes us success. I hated it, and other than studying opera probably, the military horrified them most."

Her laugh this time was louder, but trailed off, and she said softly, "My dad didn't understand opera, but it didn't matter. He bought me this soundtrack to a movie—*Children of Men*, I saw it too young, I think, but I barely remember what happened, because I was so taken by the singing. It was opera, but eerie and disorienting. I asked to see the movie again and again and finally he realized what I truly wanted, and bought me the soundtrack. I repaid him by trying to sing it myself, while doing chores. I screeched like a cat, but I loved it. He told me I could work for singing lessons, and, well . . ."

"Sing something for me," Daniel said. "If I'm what's keeping you from your morning song, don't let that stop you."

Elspeth slid him a wry look, and when he kept his expression as open as possible, she pursed her lips.

He was going to kiss her. It was the only thing he wanted more than to hear her sing.

She let go of his hand and ran.

Daniel chased after. He caught up around a bend, and Elspeth flashed her teeth at him, pushed harder, and he had to work to pull ahead. They both were laughing, gasping for breath, when suddenly Elspeth darted off the road, vaulted a crumbling stone wall, and landed hard in an overgrown, scraggly field. "Watch out for shit!" she called merrily as he scrambled after, grimacing as his trainers landed in damp grass. But he didn't let it stop him.

Elspeth had slowed, picking over the uneven ground.

The smell of sheep lifted off the earth, though Daniel couldn't see any. The hill bent up and away, and at the crest there were two big standing stones tipped against each other.

Elspeth pointed and he nodded, and they trudged up the field.

When they reached the stones, Elspeth immediately flattened her hand against one. She smiled almost tenderly, and he had the urge to disrupt the moment. Daniel put his hand on her back, just like she touched the rock.

He felt her surprise, but she didn't pull away. It was as if for that moment they were both part of the ruins, connected by touch and purpose and mystery.

Then Elspeth slowly turned, letting his fingers trail along her shoulder, over it, and onto her collar.

Pushing gently, Daniel backed her up until she was fully against the standing stone. Her chin tipped up, almost defiant, as she stood there, chest hardly rising though she breathed hard. He stared down, loving the play of sunlight on her hair, the way it plastered against the gritty gray rock, and her flushed cheeks. The skin beneath his splayed fingers was so pale he could see its flush, too. His eyes drifted lower over the shell-pink exercise top to tightly bound breasts. That sports bra, the tight pants, they looked good, but they'd be a bitch to get into. Especially on this inhospitable hillside. Would she even let him try? He slid his thumb along the edge of her shirt. At her soft inhale, he looked at her eyes again. She stared intently at him. Waiting. She was nearly as tall as him, so he didn't have to lean down, just bend toward her.

Then Elspeth lifted her hands, grabbing his shoulders.

The breeze was cold, pinching his sweat and reminding him just how warm he was, his body thrumming with race adrenaline. Her fingers dug into his T-shirt, then she slid them to his neck, nails scraping the nape, and Daniel kissed her.

Her mouth was hot and sweet, and she opened up immediately, lifting herself onto her toes like she was eating him for breakfast. Daniel groaned low in his chest and pressed full against her, moving his hand from her collar down over a breast and her ribs, and he took her thick hips in both hands, grateful for the spandex. She arched against him, her mouth demanding his attention again with slow, eager kisses.

He tugged her bottom lip with his teeth, then kissed her jaw, nuzzling to her ear and whispered, "Sing for me."

Elspeth grasped at his hair, where it was too short, and her nails scraped lightly again and again.

"Sing something," he repeated, then bit her earlobe.

Her gentle cry was almost like a song.

Working along her neck, he kissed and sucked, holding her hips firmly against him. He groaned again at the pressure on his cock, how warm she was, with only thin material between them.

"Oh," she whispered.

Daniel caught her mouth again, sweeping his lips against hers, dipping inside. Her arms wrapped around his neck now, all her weight against him or the standing stone.

He kissed lightly at the corner of her mouth and insisted, "Sing."

Her smile curved against his own. "I'm busy," she murmured, pulling herself up, sliding one thigh up his.

Grabbing that thigh, he moved his other hand to her ass and picked her up properly, pressing his hard cock right at her center.

Elspeth gasped a perfect, singsong note, rolling her hips to rub against him.

"There you go," he managed, catching her eye. "A song just for me."

With a moan that vibrated through her and into him, she hid her face in his neck, tightening her thighs around his hips. She was laughing softly.

Daniel rocked against her again, and she moved with him, her whole body working. All he had to do was support her, hands on that ass; he could feel the muscles through the flesh, soft and hard and soft as she flexed into him, and his breath fluttered. Elspeth put her lips to his ear and deliberately sang a soft, "ah," shifting herself on him, giving him exactly what he'd asked for, and goddamn did he want inside her.

"Elspeth," he said, and her head fell back, revealing her throat. He put his lips to the hollow and dragged up, biting just enough she moaned again and rocked faster against him. He could feel himself tightening, feel the close, closer, hot sinking feeling before he came and he couldn't *believe* it. "Elspeth," he said again, surprise lightening the tone.

She nodded, and didn't stop nodding, and swiveled her hips. "Yes," she said, and her hands were lost in his hair, scrambling over his ears, cupping his face, and she tugged until he met her eyes. Elspeth's were wide, bright with the rising sun, and she moved still, her lips apart, gasping little notes of passion, the best song he'd ever heard, faster and faster, eyes locked to his until he was terrified of what she might see. Just before he could no longer bear it, her eyes fell shut and her brow wrinkled and she stopped moving, holding still with her pussy pressed perfectly hot on him. A shiver ripped through her, and she sighed.

Daniel kissed her mouth, and moved himself, rubbing in longer strokes. She wiggled, but held on, and it was easy for him to coax her into meeting his long strokes with her own, her body looser now, and her movements languorous, teasing almost. "Daniel," she said, and it sounded like a promise. God, he wanted inside her. He wanted—he was so close to her skin, barely separated, and he imagined it, the hot opening very ready for him, slick and pink and eager.

"I'll sing you a better song," she murmured, squeezing her thighs. "Come on, darling, I promise. If you come for me."

Her voice was deeper, the words so sexy and commanding, and it rattled something loose in him. He wanted to give her what she wanted, do exactly as she ordered, to feel her clenching around him. "I want—I want to be inside you."

"Me too," she answered, kissing his jaw. "It would be so good," she said. "So good. Come for me like this, and later—later it'll be my mouth on you."

"Elspeth," he said, almost begging, and she licked at his mouth, offering her tongue to him, then she pulled his bottom lip into hers and sucked.

The orgasm hit and he groaned, nearly dropping her as his body jerked again and again. But he held on, and she held on, arms wrapped about his head, riding it with him. He put one hand against the standing stone, shuddering, pressing her between the rock and him, as if they could both melt into it.

His knees needed to bend, so he carefully set her down, going with her, and with an arm around her waist he sat on the cold earth, back to the stone. Elspeth tucked against him, and let out a great sigh. Her hand fluttered at his chest, then down his stomach, pressing to the muscles. She wrapped it around his waist so they held each other.

As the cold seeped into his back and ass, Daniel became too aware of the sticky cum in his briefs and wrinkled his nose. "I haven't done this since I was a fucking teenager," he said, huffing a laugh.

"I didn't think I *could* do this," she said, face against his chest so her words were muffled. "I didn't even—we didn't even . . ." Elspeth giggled. She tipped her head up, and he kissed her forehead.

"Next time, I'll bring a condom on our run."

Her eyes got huge. "Oh, my God, if I buy condoms without going fifty miles out of town, everyone will know why."

Daniel snorted.

Elspeth burrowed closer. "It's cold now," she whispered.

"We could race back." He didn't want to get up.

"I think I'm too—um. Wet. To run."

"Christ," he knocked his head back against the stone to sabotage the renewed lust at the thought of her wet and hot, and what he could do with his fingers.

As if reading his mind, she slid her hand slowly down his stomach to his hipbone. Hesitated, and when he fell still, she dipped her fingers under the band of his sweats.

Daniel clenched his jaw, but couldn't quite stop the twitch at how cold her skin was.

Elspeth laughed and pulled her hand up to her own stomach.

With a sorry groan, he began to sit up.

"Wait." Elspeth leaned away and faced him. Her hair fell out of her pigtails in such a mess, and her mouth was raw pink. She stared earnestly at him, licked her lips, then said in a rush, "I promised you a song."

Warmth blossomed inside his chest, and he felt an honest smile soften his own mouth. "Yeah, you did," he said. He lifted his eyebrows expectantly.

She moved onto her knees, leaning back on her ankles, posture straight and her hands flat on her thighs. Her fingertips were pink in the cold, and Daniel nearly told her to keep the song for later. But he was too damn selfish.

Elspeth took a long, preparatory breath and sang.

At first, her voice trembled, and she kept her eyes closed. Daniel stared at her lips and hints of her tongue, taking her all in as her voice grew stronger, lifting on waves of melody.

It was Italian, and distantly familiar, like he'd heard it in a movie maybe, since he'd never purposefully listened to opera in his life.

She was gorgeous, and her voice was filled with passion. It rang out in the cold morning, and Daniel felt . . . new. Sweaty, sticky, cold, nowhere near satisfied, but wanting more because this was perfect.

Elspeth opened her eyes, and at the sight of him staring her words faltered and she smiled with a little embarrassment. The shape of her mouth changed the tone of the song, and she schooled herself again, lifting her face slightly for the swell of music.

The final note swept up, and she held it out, softening so that it drifted in the air, finally fading as she blinked quickly. Looking down, she took another shuddering breath before glancing at him with obvious vulnerability and flushed pride.

"Beautiful," he said, and brushed his thumb along her bottom lip. "What was it?"

"Mozart."

"I've heard of him," Daniel said.

It worked to make her laugh, chasing away the vulnerable sheen in her big hazel eyes. "I haven't sung for an audience in . . . quite some time."

"Thank you," he said seriously.

She got to her feet. "We should go."

Standing, he nodded and offered his hand. It felt like more—like offering her more than he could know.

Elspeth slid her fingers along his palm until they wove with his.

CHAPTER FIVE

ELSPETH'S HEART hadn't stopped pounding for hours.

It was mid-afternoon and the Friday rush had begun, but she barely felt it, having been high on sex, singing, anticipation, and emotional clarity since leaving Daniel at the guesthouse this morning. And not just emotional clarity, but *shared* emotional clarity. Elspeth was certain he understood why she sang only on her morning constitutional, and she understood the rippling confusion and grief an anniversary could compel.

Plus, thanks to his T-shirt, she'd gotten a good look at the tattoo curving up from his inner elbow along the strong line of his bicep: it was a wicked-looking knife. The military kind with a serrated spine. Elspeth had never particularly noticed blades other than to avoid slicing herself open chopping veggies, but she still wanted to suck on his. In fact, she was developing a quick obsession.

She'd put on a pop music internet station when she opened up The Fort, and still danced around as she poured and served and wiped up spills, grinning, flirting with the regulars and even accidentally with Asra when he arrived. He instantly dragged her into the kitchen and demanded to know if she'd fucked the American. "No," Elspeth had said, then laughed. "Not yet. Not quite." And she'd twisted her lips into a thoughtful frown, wondering what exactly counted. Maybe she had? "Maybe?"

As she worked through the exact series of events at the burial site, her skin grew warm again, and her breath shallow, and Asra pushed away from her. "Nasty," he laughed. "If my dad marries your mum, we definitely have to stop having conversations like this."

"You brought it up," she reminded him.

"My mistake, sis."

"Don't tell anybody!" she hissed.

Asra eyed her with the intense skepticism of a twenty-year old. "Your whole . . . aura . . . is telling enough."

He vanished out to the bar, calling a greeting to someone, and Elspeth closed her eyes, knocking her head back against the wall. She drew a few long, deep breaths to calm down.

It took three rounds of frying chips before Elspeth was certain she could smile like a sane person and allowed herself to reemerge.

Of course, he was there.

Her heart started back up again, and she felt her cheeks flush. Daniel had tucked himself into the farthest booth, with his back to the wall beside the cubby of books. He already had a pint of lager, and wore another three-piece suit, sans tie, jacket hooked on a cleat beside the booth. This suit was black and crisp, with a dark pink shirt. Elspeth tried to smile plainly at him, but the corners of her mouth curled too slowly, too wide, and when he dipped his chin in acknowledgment—not with a smile, but hard eye contact—she felt the heat snap straight to her pussy. She spun away, tingling all over, and ducked behind the bar to hide.

The rhythm of her life took over.

Elspeth lost track of time in her business, teasing Asra as they danced around each other behind the bar, taking the day's pies from the Morgan sons—five extra for Friday night—answering the phone once or twice, glad when Rhys arrived to wash dishes. Because Asra had started Daniel off, it was Asra who took him another beer and reported back that the American was charming Mr. Griffiths and Evan Hughes, who'd served in the Welsh Guard until retirement. Evan sometimes gave informal tours of the old fort ruins down at the river and was in the middle of lecturing Daniel on the entire marshal history of the region. Asra promised Elspeth her American seemed into it.

It made her happy to think of him interested in local history, which made her think about the standing stones, which made her think about his mouth and tongue, and the feel of his hips between her thighs as he pinned her to the stone. The feel of his cock right there against her, the friction on her clit, and his aching whisper when he said he wanted to be inside her. God, the things she'd said in response! She'd never been so bold before, though at the time she'd only felt eager.

Elspeth had to stop and clench all her muscles, pressing her legs together behind the bar. She laughed a little at herself, and was relieved when Cathy Lewis and Thomasina Bevin popped in, sidling up to the bar.

Contemporaries of her mum, Cath and Thom were a pair of old white lesbians still pretending they were roommates, with separate bedrooms in their pristine cottage halfway up the mountain where they offered rooms and quick breakfast during the peak season. Cath, her silver hair swept up in an elegant chignon out of step with her track pants and bulky hoodie, ordered a Pimm's, and Thom, who liked lipstick and sweater dresses, asked Elspeth to make her something purple.

While she played with creme de violet, Elspeth listened to the pair tell her about the married French couple who'd just checked out, the wife who never got off her phone, using an app to lead her husband around and get odd little tidbits about trees and street corners and ruins and all manner of random facts. At first they'd been dismissive of the technology, but then the woman told them the year their own cottage had been built! Can you even believe it, Elspeth?

No, she barely could. Elspeth had widened her eyes appreciatively as she set down a coup glass for Thom to try, with gin, violet, lemon, and splash of a weird herbal simple Mary had concocted.

"How long until you have to decide about that offer for this good old place?" Cath asked.

Elspeth's spine stiffened. "Ah, end of next week. Or as soon as I like," she managed through a dry throat. She hated that it was *her* choice. Mum thought she was being kind, putting Elspeth's future in her own hands, only it wasn't only her future. Caerafon itself had a huge stake in it. Over the decades a few hotels and shops had accepted corporate sponsorship, but nobody was outright owned by outside business. Much less a multi-national drug corporation trying to shine up their reputation with a ready-made sustainability façade.

Bitterness drained into her stomach. She wished her dad were here.

"Your mum showed us the proposal, and it looks a delight—and all that money!" Cath said.

"It's only what The Fort is worth," Elspeth insisted.

Thom raised her coup glass. "That it is."

"Once they own it, they don't have to stick to the proposal. They could level the building and put something" —Elspeth flapped her hands in the air— "I don't know—modern!"

"And you could go back to school, or travel, and your mum could marry that Pakistani man from London without a worry for you. It would be good for her to go on an adventure," Thom finished mildly.

"I know." Elspeth nodded. She did know. "And his name is Kam."

"You'd still have roots here, sweetheart, and nobody will forget your dad," Cath said, expression drooping into sympathy.

"I know," Elspeth repeated. She fought against the fluttering threat of tears, pressing a smile on. "I have to go clear a table."

They let her flee, and Elspeth made a beeline, shining eyes and all, for Daniel's table.

"Hi," she said, plopping down on the edge of the booth bench. She let her smile spread to old Evan Hughes—Mr. Griffiths had moved to a tall table with some other locals. Evan patted her hand and lifted his nearly empty pint glass.

"Hi, El. Good chatting with you, young man," he said, his accent thicker, as usual when he performed for foreigners. It lightened Elspeth's heart a bit, and she said, "I didn't mean to chase you off, Evan."

"No bother!" he declared. "You're much prettier company for the lad."

With that, he hobbled with his glass to Mr. Griffith's side.

Elspeth turned to Daniel, expecting a flirting comment about Evan being right about the prettiness of his new company, but instead Daniel leaned in so his arm brushed hers, and dipped his chin.

"You're sad," he murmured, then his gaze flashed past her. "What did those old birds do to make you sad?"

Opening her mouth to put him off, she stopped. He smelled like some earthy hair product and she really wanted to press her face to his and stay there. With somebody who didn't care if she sold, somebody who didn't have any stake in Caerafon, only in getting into her pants. That's what she needed. So she grabbed his lager and took a drink.

Then Elspeth said, "They think I should sell The Fort."

Daniel hesitated, and then he frowned. "Thinking about selling it makes you sad?"

She drew a hard breath, and pushed it out, nodding. Her fingers played along his pint glass. She should get him a new one. "Yes. But . . . so does thinking about not selling. I'm a mess."

He smiled softly and reached for the lager, wrapping his hand around hers. Her entire body reacted, longing for more, as he shifted to face her, and murmured in her ear, "You don't seem a mess to me."

Elspeth shivered and did not lean in, or she'd melt into his lap in front of the whole pub. She glanced at him from the corner of her eyes. "What you think I seem like isn't to be trusted."

A soft intake of breath alerted her to his surprise, and Daniel's hand fell away from hers. He started to speak, but she interrupted.

"I mean," she said, only as loud as necessary to be heard in the lively room, "that when you're here, what I'm feeling changes. Like that physics thing we learned in school—just observing particles maybe changes their behavior?" Elspeth wrinkled her nose. "Or maybe it was atoms specifically. But that—that's you, looking at me, changing how all my atoms behave."

"Exciting your elements," he said, slowly, like each word was dragged up his throat. "Christ, Elspeth."

Her face was fully turned to him, now, and her knee pressed on his. She parted her lips. She had to breathe through her mouth, to taste the flavor of his presence. "Uh-huh," she murmured.

"So you behave differently around me."

"I most certainly have never behaved like I did this morning ever before. Next to a Neolithic burial site, no less."

"Do you go for a run every morning?" Daniel asked with a very distinct insinuation.

"No," she whispered, eyes lowering to his mouth.

"Then when do I get to kiss you again?"

Elspeth watched his lips form the words more than she heard them, feeling them brush against her neck, down between her breasts, trailing imaginary kisses along the inside of her thighs. "Tuesday," she said too loudly.

Daniel fell still, vibrating sudden tension as if her word had been lightning and they awaited the thunder.

Her gaze flew to his, and it was his turn to seem sad. Devastated, more like. Because of the anniversary. She nodded; she'd remembered. "It's my day off," she said lightly. "And I hear you like local military history, so I thought I could take you to see a few castles."

His jaw clenched briefly. He barely moved to say, "Okay. Tuesday." The date sounded like a death sentence. Then with a marshaling of will she could trace in the muscles relaxing around his dark chocolate eyes, he gave her that wolfish smile from the moment they'd met. "No kissing allowed on the weekend?" he teased.

Finishing his beer before answering to give herself a moment to compose, she said, "The weekend is the busiest here, most of the year. Day-trippers, hikers, you name it. I'll be busy constantly."

"And Monday?"

"Inventory and weekly deliveries. And cleaning. The Fort isn't open, but I'm here dawn to dusk."

"Alone?"

"Sometimes—usually. My dad liked to be alone for it, to fill the place up with just him, he'd say." Elspeth twisted and pointed at one of the photos at the end of the long cluster of them, next to the bar. "That's him, with me and my grandad. Then above it, Dad, Grandmum, and Great-Grandad. His father opened The Fort, but we don't have a picture of him."

She felt his fingers light at the nape of her neck, there and gone, a comforting, teasing touch before he said, "That's why it makes you sad to think of selling. When you're alone here, you're alone with him."

Nodding, she turned back to him. He understood her so easily. It

was soothing, like she wasn't bizarre for thinking it if he could understand. "Yes. It's my family, and it's good here, you know? I like it: the
people and this place. It's a good life," she added firmly.

Daniel tilted his head in acknowledgement, and his eyes riveted her
in place; his whole physicality drew her, the broad angle of shoulders
and the tight black waistcoat narrowing his waist, crisp slacks and lush
pink shirt. It should've been pretty, but instead they were dangerous—he
was dangerous. Her sad, hungry wolf.

Elspeth thought she should change the subject, sneak out back with
him and tear his waistcoat off, maybe, see if she could snap the buttons,
when Daniel very softly said, "But it's not the life you want."

Her breath caught painfully in her throat, and she got up from the
booth so quickly she nearly stumbled. He knew her. How was it possible
he knew her so well? She wanted him to tell her more about herself, dive
deeper into her depths, but it was impossible. Something she wanted so
badly couldn't be real.

"Elspeth," he said, reaching for her.

"I'm fine—I'm fine." Elspeth turned on her best customer service
smile and plucked his glass off the table. "You need a refill." She spun,
and felt his eyes on her the whole time. Even when she was behind the
bar again, choosing a new pint glass, setting it under the spout, he
watched her, and she flicked her eyes up to his once, saw his regard, felt
her insides melting, and like a coward sent the lager over with Asra.

CHAPTER SIX

ELSPETH CHANGED the streaming music to her usual classical music station, welcoming the familiar as she poured and flirted and cut a fresh batch of lemons and limes, and changed the tap on the always popular Guinness, glad Monday would see new kegs—and that Asra was coming by to help clean the lines.

She avoided looking at Daniel, ate a sandwich her mum brought by, chipped a fingernail, and resigned herself to not having time to reapply polish until Wednesday. She could at least scour it all off first thing in the morning.

Daniel only had that second beer, then Asra closed him out. Asra bumped into Elspeth and nodded his chin at the departing American. Daniel was slipping his jacket on as he stalked away, and at the last moment turned to look directly at her. She caught her breath and he smiled apologetically at her, like he'd done something wrong.

Elspeth stood frozen to the spot as he exited past three new customers. Asra and Rhys buzzed around her filling orders, and Elspeth suddenly caught Rhys's shoulder. "I'm taking my break, I'll be back in fifteen."

Without waiting for acknowledgement, Elspeth darted around the back of the bar, wove through the middling crowd, and burst outside.

It was dusk, and chilly, the sky striped purple with clouds, and cars with their headlamps on zipped past, heading out of town mostly, but all the lights remained on along the line of shops bracketing the village green. She hugged her arms around herself, glad for the thin cardigan she wore over a plain green T-shirt, plainer jeans, and flat ankle boots.

There he was—Daniel striding across the street, and up onto the cobbled sidewalk. Elspeth dashed after him, unsure about calling his name.

She dodged a cyclist in a reflective helmet and jogged faster, just about to reach for him when he stopped and turned smoothly—a predator aware of his surroundings. His guarded expression opened up at the sight of her, and Elspeth put her mouth in a determined line, grabbed his hand, and dragged him down a narrow alley between the post office and the old bookstore.

Daniel said nothing, going with her easily down the unlit path, and she pulled him around to the back where the forest crept all the way up to the gravel delivery road. Ancient trees towered in straight columns, surrounded by lush undergrowth and younger trees, everything mysterious deep brown and evening gray-purple, the twilight coaxing her to this boldness. Wind hissed like distant applause in the high branches. "Here," she murmured, leading him in, disregarding his fine slacks and polished shoes. The earth was softened with fallen leaves and mud, and she spun, put her hands on his face, and kissed him.

Her ears roared with a rush of embarrassment in the second it took him to respond, but then he wrapped his arms around her and pushed her mouth open with his. She leaned in and Daniel's tongue swept into her with a demanding heat. Elspeth dug her hands into his hair, grasping his head.

He tasted like beer, and she laughed breathlessly, tugging his bottom lip with her teeth. She arched her back to press the length of her body against his as Daniel dragged his hands down her spine, down and down to her hips, where he hooked his fingers under her cardigan and T-shirt. His fingers were cold, and she gasped. He spread his hands against the small of her back, pulling her hips against him and she felt his hard desire against her belly through the rough denim of her jeans.

"Oh," she said, tilting away to look down. Daniel kissed her cheek, her temple, down her jaw, but Elspeth did not offer him better access;

she was too interested in his cock under those crisp black slacks. Even in the shadowed evening she could see the shape it made, and she slid her hand down the lapel of his jacket, over his tightly buttoned waistcoat, to his belt and started undoing it.

"Elspeth," he said raggedly.

She hummed distractedly, pulling the slick leather free of the buckle. With a little tug she unhooked it, and Daniel groaned, moving his hands to her shoulders, gripping them.

The tip of his cock waited right there, pressing at the button, through the thin material of his knickers. She couldn't help but skim her fingers against it, shuddering as he shuddered. Carefully, Elspeth unbuttoned the slacks and lowered the zipper.

Daniel backed up, hands on her shoulders guiding her with him, until he pressed against one of the trees. Elspeth kissed him softly, licking at his lips until he opened them, and she leaned in, her hands on his chest. His erection pressed to her belly, thick and so very warm. Just like his mouth. His hands moved into her hair, cupping her head, and Elspeth wanted to smile, it felt so good, but she was too busy to smile. She stroked her belly against his cock and Daniel moaned into her mouth.

Lowering her hands again, she slipped one under the waistband of his knickers. His hips jumped at the touch of her fingers around his crown, and Elspeth's breath hitched. She rubbed her thumb along the slit as her nipples hardened, then she dove right in, grasping him. Her hand encircled him, and she lightly squeezed. Daniel was panting, his arms up, hands fisted together in his own hair, his face a dream of desire, lips parted, eyes closed.

She loved it, and slid her hand along him again, exploring the shape, the smoothness and slight curve. Rougher hairs brushed the back of her knuckles, and she wanted them on her cheek, she wanted her mouth around him, to taste the tiny beads of precum at his tip. She wanted floodlights to see everything, and time to enjoy it fully.

Gripping his hip with her other hand, Elspeth leaned in, brushing her nipples against him, suddenly remembering they were both fully clothed, him in his dangerous black suit, pressed and fine, except for his cock in her hand, and his exposed throat as his head fell back against the tree. Every lean inch of him pulled taught just for her.

She stroked slowly up his cock, then down again, touching the base and Daniel hissed her name again helplessly.

Distantly aware of cars and shops just outside the line of trees, the village closing down, Elspeth moved a little bit faster, and Daniel suddenly grasped her face and kissed her, then he took her wrist and squeezed, making her let go. She did with a tiny whimper of loss, replacing that hand with the other. Daniel tried to smile and brought her hand up to his mouth. He licked her forefinger, then her middle finger, and brought both into his mouth, sucking firmly.

It was Elspeth's turn to moan. The suction pulled from her fingertips, along her hot veins, straight to her core, and she ached. Her pussy was enflamed; she could feel it throbbing with her pulse, so good it almost hurt.

Daniel licked her fingers again, and her ring and pinky fingers, then bit her thumb teasingly. He caught her gaze, licked again, kissed her fingertips with little flicks of his tongue, then kissed the heart of her palm. She shivered, and he licked her there, dragging his tongue where his kiss had been. And then Daniel put her hand right back on his cock.

Oh.

Elspeth smiled, panting now, and slicked her damp hand against him. Daniel's hand followed hers, and he touched her finger to his slit, smearing the precum there, and together their hands drifted down his cock. He squeezed her fingers around him, and she smiled wide enough that her teeth shone, learning what he liked and loving the tremble of his body against hers. When his other hand found her breast, he pinched her nipple and she gasped at the pleasure. He didn't let go, caressing and pinching through her shirt and bra, and his forehead fell forward to knock gently against hers. Their breath chased back and forth as his hips moved, pushing his cock in their hands.

"Elspeth," he said through clenched teeth.

"Daniel," she answered, holding on to him with her other hand, wanting to shove it down her own pants and relieve the fiery, building pressure there. But she thought she'd fall over if she let go of him, and just the slick, hard feel of him in her hand, covered in turn by his hand, was so desperately perfect she couldn't risk it.

His breath drew in, and he stopped, and managed to say, "I'm—"

Elspeth gasped and hopped away, eyes wide, watching as he stroked himself once more, twice, and then he came with his whole body.

That's when she did it: she unbuttoned her jeans and slid her hand into her pussy, shocked at the heat and wetness, and she pressed on herself, cupping herself with her hand. Elspeth rolled her hips, legs shaking, as Daniel's orgasm splattered up his perfect black waistcoat and he staggered back against the tree again. He was so open, so raw. Elspeth put her other hand to her mouth, covering her tiny sighs of admiration and lust, and rubbed her clit, pushing her fingers lower to skim against her hole, and up, down and up, imagining his hand back over hers, sharing this. She stared at him, and when he opened his eyes, *saw* her, her orgasm hit.

Elspeth bit her own knuckles, pushing firmly on herself as she stood there riding the waves, desperate not to fall over. It added an edge to the orgasm, and her cheeks were hot because she'd just done that in front of him, in the forest a few meters from the bookstore and across the street from The Fort itself. Out in the open. Again. Only worse.

Better, she thought.

Shivering, Elspeth stroked herself lightly as she withdrew her hand, knees weak, and almost rubbed her hand on her jeans before remembering she had to go back to The Fort, *right now*.

"Elspeth," Daniel said just as raggedly as before. "Come here."

He leaned heavily against the tree, pants undone, hair mussed, and all the rest of him perfect but for the streak of cum on his waist.

All the visions this morning of elfin princes and the devil lounging under that flickering fire returned, here in the dark forest, awakening this uncontrollable lust.

She went to him.

Daniel took her hand—the one covered in her own wetness—and brought it to his mouth.

At her gasp, he grinned, and slid her first two fingers past his lips, sucking only very gently. He licked her hand all over again, this time not preparing her for anything, but finishing her off.

Elspeth couldn't breathe, caught in the perfect, filthy, beautiful moment.

Then Daniel put her hand against his heart, pressing it to the waist-coat, and covered it with the lapel of his jacket.

"I have to go back," she whispered.

"I know." He left her hand against his muscled chest and refastened her jeans, eyes locked on hers the whole time.

The little tugs on her pants made her hot again. And when he let go, she pulled her hands against her own chest, backing away. "Good night," she said.

He didn't move, still undone, a line of skin shining at his waistband, and shadowy hair disappearing into his knickers. Watching her.

This time she wasn't fleeing when she walked quickly away, but maybe heading towards something instead.

CHAPTER SEVEN

DANIEL KNEW he was going to hell. And his mom would be the one to throw him headfirst into the pit.

He'd called her on Saturday so she wouldn't call him instead, and the entire time he listened to the recent shenanigans of his nieces and answered her questions about Wales and what he was eating, he'd thought about Elspeth. Because for the first time in a long time he wanted to tell his mom about a girl.

But if he told his mom, he'd be lying to her, too.

And despite having served three tours in the hot mess of the Middle East, Daniel Kelly suspected this could be the worst thing he'd ever done.

At first it had felt good to keep the secret, to know it was too late for them before they'd even begun. If he'd already ruined their chances, he could just be himself, could just go where Elspeth took him, where his body and needs took him. Eventually she'd find out, understand he'd betrayed her before he ever opened his mouth, and they'd be done.

Seeing the end so clearly had made taking the steps to get there feel simpler, more relaxed, more *right*. Like her books, where knowing the ending wouldn't let you down allowed you to enjoy the journey.

But what if he didn't want that end? What if he liked her too much?

Christ, he liked her. Not only the way her body moved—spontaneous and light-footed; not only her mouth—with a hundred different smiles; not only her melodic voice and fleshy hips, or her wide-ranging style—he'd seen her in a summer dress, a cardigan set, a tank top, a sequined T-shirt; not only her tangled hair and certainly not only how wet she got for him. He liked how she thought about her family and struggled with protecting its legacy. He liked that she knew local from tourist at a glance and how she built a Guinness.

He liked how when she decided to take what she wanted from him she'd dragged him barely into the forest and just done it.

Daniel had yet to notice a thing about Elspeth he didn't like.

Which is why he was standing outside The Fort on Monday, late morning, knowing it was closed, but also knowing she was in there, and alone.

They hadn't been alone since Friday night in the forest. Because he'd been avoiding her.

After speaking with his mom Saturday morning, he'd gotten to know Caerafon properly, wandering the village with packs of tourists. He tried to feel the ground beneath his feet, take deep breaths, really ground himself in the day to day like he was supposed to. He ran into Evan Hughes out at the ruins of the old black stone fortress that once had guarded this beautiful valley where the two rivers came together. When Evan took him back to the ruin's namesake for a pint, Daniel could hardly say no, but he managed to do nothing more than get caught staring at her bent neck as she concentrated on twisting a perfect orange peel and setting it alight in some fancy whiskey drink. The round of applause from her tourist customers brought her face up, flushed and grinning, and she saw him. Her lips had fallen open just slightly, and Daniel felt himself getting hard.

He'd asked Evan if all the photos on the wall were about Caerafon history, which set the old man talking for over an hour, and Daniel made his escape.

After another sleepless night, on Sunday he researched the most strenuous hikes on Snowdon Mountain and ended up walking a narrow gravel path that snaked along the steep, rocky slopes past lakes, cutting up in switchbacks toward an incredible ridge with views that knocked his breath away.

It had been the hardest he'd pushed his body since the Army had pushed it for him.

The land was desolate: treeless mountainsides covered in rough green moss and scraggly short bushes and grass. Sharp boulders that looked like they'd been shattered off even higher peaks were strewn about. It was cool and damp, gray light filtering through low clouds that misted as he returned to his car, but he was grateful the rain reminded him this was no desert mountain. The lighter pressed heavily in his pocket, and when the wind gusted, Daniel kept catching himself searching the sky for a helicopter he knew was never coming.

He ate that night at the Royal Vic Hotel, guiltily drinking a pint poured by some other bartender. One without a single smile, much less a hundred.

In his room at the guesthouse he'd watched some murder show set in a town a lot like Caerafon, but somewhere in Yorkshire, on his iPad, then tried to read, but it wasn't one of the used-up paperbacks from Elspeth's shelf. He couldn't pretend to sleep yet, he couldn't just lie there only to avoid thinking about fire and Alvin's laugh by imagining her hands and the rough bark of the tree on his ass, how luminous her eyes had been in the dark while she got herself off just looking at him.

Of course he'd gone hard again remembering, and pulled himself off in the luridly floral guest room. Twice.

Lust-induced insomnia was better than his usual.

At dawn he slumped on the floor, back to the bed and the lights off, having managed to doze. He merely held onto the lighter, not flicking it on or off. That was an improvement, he told himself. Holding it without the nervous tick. If he could just remember Alvin in peace, remember the rest of his team without the panic . . .

As Daniel breathed in long ten-count patterns, wishing he was better at meditation without his therapist guiding him, he heard the quiet of the house break.

A gentle knock on the front door, the creak of Agatha's steps down the front hall below him. The murmur of voices.

Scones. It had to be Elspeth at the door. Delivering her mother's predawn scones, in those tight running clothes. Christ, the way the sports bra pressed her breasts together, squeezing her back to highlight the strength in her shoulders, pinching around her ribs . . . He wanted to dig his hands under and unhook it. Set her free and knead his fingers where the bra had probably reddened her skin.

If he went down, she'd let him join her. Exercise would do him good. And a taste of her, more direct than licking her off her fingers.

But Daniel had closed his eyes and let his head fall back. He'd go tell her the truth. Later, after he showered and dressed, after he wrangled himself into looking better than the exhausted, gouge-eye depressive motherfucker he no doubt resembled at the moment.

The lighter was in his hand, the metal warm from being held. Daniel looked at it, settled in his palm with a little black shine.

The door downstairs had closed again, and he'd imagined he could hear her jogging away. He wondered if she'd sing on the way up the mountain.

When he finally went down to breakfast, the other guests had already been and departed for the day, so Daniel had gotten quite a lot of information out of Agatha regarding Elspeth's family in general, and Elspeth in particular. Apparently, Elspeth had been disappointed not to see him, despite the dawn hour. Daniel had admitted that he'd spent more time with Elspeth last week, and that was all it took for Agatha to decide to help him in his cause, and she spilled. Some of it he knew already, from Pella's file, but the neighborly finesse meant more than distant facts.

Elspeth was twenty-five years old, a Capricorn, and had left the Royal Welsh College of Music and Drama one semester short of her degree in music performance because her dad was too sick to run The Fort and her mom was a wreck. She'd taken over during the last stages of Malcom Gwenlan's cancer, and after he died, she didn't leave because there was nobody else, the poor dear. Once several of the town ladies took a road trip to Cardiff to hear her perform, and Agatha went on a tangent about how beautiful it had been, and what a tragedy Elspeth had never returned to her music. But wasn't she making a fine show of the pub, and wouldn't her father be proud?

Daniel made all the right noises, mostly just eating three of the scones and a slab of fried ham, and all the tea Agatha put in front of him. Then Agatha brought up the offer to buy The Fort by some fancy company out of London and America—Pella, had he heard of it? He was American after all—and Elspeth was keeping her plans to herself, not even telling her mother what she wanted most to do. Her mother was dating a Londoner, and Agatha was proud of Alys for getting back out into the world, and she hoped Elspeth could do the same thing. Here Agatha smiled prettily at Daniel, green eyes nearly vanishing behind a fall of wrinkles, and he understood that was to be his role: romancing Elspeth.

He wanted to.

So at quarter past eleven a.m., Daniel arrived at The Fort in his best navy blue suit with the silver-mint checkered vest, freshly shaved and carrying a plastic bag with two egg salad sandwiches. He didn't think it was the kind of lunch that lent itself toward the mouth-to-mouth contact he longed for, but Agatha swore it was Elspeth's favorite, so egg salad is what he brought.

From inside he heard the sound of opera. He knocked, but she probably couldn't hear over the rising vocals and cello. After knocking again, he tried the knob—open.

Daniel pushed through the door, sure to let the green man make its usual announcing thump. He didn't want to startle her. Stools were up on the bar, chairs and other stools piled on the tables and booths. He began to call her name, but she was there in the middle of the pub, on her hands and knees in cut-off sweats, scooting backwards toward him.

He started to sweat.

Elspeth was mopping with a wide rag, singing as she stroked the long wooden panels, shoulders strong and ass in the air. It was the floor of a pub. Foul for sure, but all Daniel wanted was to drop everything and grab her. Pin her face to the floor and with his other hand pull off those tattered gray sweats. In his imagination, she wasn't wearing anything under them. And she was wet.

Choking slightly on the overwhelming desire, Daniel closed his eyes and sucked in air through his teeth. "Elspeth," he said, but it hardly made a dent in the opera.

"Elspeth," he nearly yelled.

She yelped, spinning hard to land on that fine ass, and brought the rag up in front of her like a shield.

They stared for a moment: Daniel tight and hot in his body, clenching the grocery bag like a lifeline; Elspeth's eyes huge and her mouth open, cheeks rising pink. Her hair was falling out of a high ponytail and her arms held out still, warding him off with the rag.

Then Elspeth started laughing. Her entire face transformed and she dropped her hands, shaking all over with mirth.

Daniel let out a relieved sigh and felt a smile creep over his own mouth. "I'm sorry," he said loudly. "I knocked, but . . . "

"But the music!" she yelled back, waving him off when he offered her a hand to her feet. She darted to the bar for her phone and turned the volume low enough they could talk.

Swallowing, and trying not to walk weird because of his hard-on, Daniel joined her at the bar. He leaned against it and pinched a wisp of auburn hair that curled beside her cheek. "I brought you lunch."

Her eyes flicked down, and she tilted her head closer to his hand. Daniel cupped her face, and her skin was hot in his palm. Then he kissed her.

Like a lying bastard.

Elspeth darted her tongue playfully against his lips, then pressed her entire body against him. She didn't touch her hands to him at all, only using her mouth and body. Just as Daniel raised his other hand to her hip, she danced away. "Good, I'm starving," she said. "Ginger ale?"

Breathless, Daniel nodded. He dragged a stool one-handed off the bar, and thunked it down, then one more. He sank onto one, needing the support, and with careful focus unloaded the sandwiches, napkins, and bags of vinegar potato chips. The crisp sound of pop-tops alerted him to her standing directly across the bar from him, and she set them down.

Daniel removed his jacket, folded it over the rungs of another stool atop the bar, and unbuttoned the cuff of his shirt. As he rolled the sleeve, he realized Elspeth had gone perfectly still. Worried, he looked, and caught her staring with her bottom lip in her teeth. Staring at his forearm.

He unbuttoned the other cuff and held his arm toward her.

Her startled eyes flew to his.

Daniel gazed at her, giving her whatever permission she liked.

Taking a deep breath, she held his upturned hand, sliding her fingers to his wrist. Carefully she took the cuff and folded it over, then again. Her fingers skimmed his, the chipped purple nails delicate on his inner wrist. It was too light, too careful, like the promise of kisses or blazing eye contact across a crowded room. Daniel felt his pulse pop under her hand.

Elspeth leaned nearer and nearer, bent at the waist across the bar as she worked.

Each fold felt like it ricocheted into his chest cavity, and each flick of her knuckles against his forearm made him more desperate to grab her. Standing there, unmoving but for his quickened breathing, was the most erotic thing he'd ever experienced. She pushed the sleeve over his elbow, caressed the soft flesh on the inside, and Daniel gave in to a shiver.

Her eyes rose, and she smiled. "I've wanted to lick your tattoo since the moment I saw it—just that tip of it, peeking out."

Throat dry, Daniel nodded. She could color the tattoo in with green and purple stripes if she wanted to. He hoped his voice sounded deep and sexy rather than helpless when he said, "Maybe after lunch."

Casually, Elspeth shrugged and let his arm go, moving away.

Daniel had never felt less casual in his life.

He couldn't lose this. Lose her. If he told her about Pella, he would.

For the first time in years he wanted something. Didn't he owe it to himself to follow the road?

He drank a third of the ginger ale in one go, then she was beside him, arms raised as she retied her ponytail. It put her chest on display; she was wearing a sports bra again under her worn T-shirt. Her nipples were hard.

Daniel cast about for a topic of conversation as he distracted himself unwrapping his sandwich. "Do you have, ah, merchandise?"

"Merchandise?" She reached for her sandwich.

"Like, T-shirts with The Fort logo?"

"We don't even really have a logo," she said with a wry smile.

He didn't suggest she have one designed. This was dangerous territory already; he was an idiot.

"Pella will make one, if I sell, I'm sure." Elspeth opened her sandwich. "Egg! How did you know?"

"Agatha," he said quickly, grasping the change of subject. He lifted his sandwich in a toast. "She told me a lot."

Elspeth winced cutely. "Oh?"

"About your singing. She told me about the time she and some of her friends drove to Cardiff to hear you. I wanted to brag that I got a private performance."

Her giggle was a good reward. She took a bite, and so Daniel did the same. It needed hot sauce. Or to be a hamburger.

Elspeth's smile faded, but not with upset; it just slowly tilted down into a gentle, old sorrow. "She told you why I'm not a famous singer already? About my dad?"

"Yeah."

"He wouldn't have liked you," she said.

Daniel's brow shot up. "I'm very likable."

"Not if he noticed how you look at his daughter."

Thank God for the egg in his mouth tamping down his lust, because she'd lowered her lashes as she said it. Daniel swallowed, washed it down with ginger ale, and pushed his sandwich away. It wasn't worth it. He leaned toward her. "And how do I look at his daughter?"

"Like you want to eat her for lunch."

Nodding slowly, Daniel said, "As soon as she finishes her own meal, maybe I will."

CHAPTER EIGHT

ELSPETH HAD BECOME A SEX MONSTER, after merely the slight encouragement of two erotic encounters on the same day. Days ago. But here she was, flirting at the expense of her deceased father, because she couldn't contain herself.

Here she was, sweaty and eating egg salad, just thinking about how to get his hands between her legs. She didn't even recognize herself.

All weekend she'd been distracted with anticipation of him appearing in The Fort, and it was a physical ache sometimes. Not just in her pussy, but spiking in her brain, too, and at first she'd been irritated that a day without him could make her so addlepated, but as Sunday went on and she still hadn't seen him, she realized it was *hope*.

When she imagined seeing him again, it made her smile.

Elspeth hadn't ever been a sad person, and she knew the difference between sadness and grief. But she'd gotten used to being just a little bit sad all the time, in addition to the clarifying moments of intense loss, intimate regret, light nostalgia that plagued her grief. And anger, too. It was better this year than the one before, and certainly the year before that, but Elspeth realized she'd taught herself to expect to be sad.

That hope, that longing to see Daniel again was the first time she remembered expecting *not* to be.

Daniel made her want to remember what happiness felt like.

And also to have constant sex for at least a week.

Elspeth said, "I hardly saw you this weekend. Which was fine!" She smiled encouragingly. "I . . . What were you . . . up to?"

He leaned his elbow on the bar, clearly finished with his barely eaten lunch. "I learned everything Evan Hughes knows about the ruins over the river on Saturday, and on Sunday I hiked Snowdon Mountain."

"Oh? How was it?"

Daniel paused, and Elspeth started to flush at the inane question, but his posture relaxed slightly, and when he spoke it was gentle. A little . . . sad. "I probably shouldn't do it alone again."

He wasn't flirting, though with a different tone, he might've been.

She skimmed her hand against his knuckles in sympathy, though she did not truly understand. She wasn't sure she needed to. In her experience, nobody who hadn't lost a parent they loved quite understood even if they perfectly empathized, and if his anxiety had to do with war, it likely didn't matter what he said. She couldn't understand. "Well, you won't be alone tomorrow, and the castles sometimes require a lot of walking."

"Sounds good."

They each smiled tightly. Daniel watched her as she finished her sandwich to the rousing aria of Isolde's Liebestod from Wagner's *Tristan und Isolde*, gradually realizing what a bad omen it was, despite the violent beauty of the singing. She reached over and tapped her phone to pass it. Skipped the next from *Madama Butterfly,* and it landed on "Song of the Angel" from the *Children of Men* score. The song that had made her a singer.

"Listen," she said, sliding the volume up.

Elspeth closed her eyes. She knew so much about the song, the composer John Tavener, the mezzo-soprano Sarah Connolly, and she knew how this song affected her. She wasn't sure she could bear to see Daniel dismiss it, yet she had to let it play.

First Connolly's voice began low and wide, moving up through alleluias, and gradually the violins pierced her voice. The two wove in and out of each other, sewing a gorgeous, chilling duet. There had been a time in her life when Elspeth's only ambition was to have this control, this ability to take her voice and ruin someone with only an alleluia.

The song was just over four minutes, and Elspeth did not move, nor did she hear Daniel so much as shift on his stool.

When the music trailed away, Elspeth gasped herself out of her trance and paused her phone. It was kind to give Daniel a moment to craft his reaction; he couldn't possibly have missed how much the song meant to her.

Elspeth looked at him, schooling her expression as best she could.

His eyes were on her, dark and sad, but something in his brow or the lay of his lips gave her hope. He said, "That was beautiful. And . . . disturbing."

Though it was not a word she'd have used, she appreciated that it was clearly a genuine reaction. She nodded to encourage him.

"It was so wistful," he said. "I don't think she gets what she's reaching for."

"She's praying, so probably not," Elspeth whispered.

Daniel stood. "Put it on again. On repeat."

Elspeth caught her breath and stared at him. He moved so his hip touched her bent knee. Then he took her phone gently and his quick fingers did the work for her.

Then he smiled his slow wolf smile. "Are you done with your lunch? I'm ready for mine."

"Oh," Elspeth said, or rather moaned softly.

Daniel abruptly strode away. She squeaked disappointment, but he only turned the bolt on the front door, dropped the old-fashioned slide lock down into the hole in the floor.

Elspeth pressed her hands flat to her belly.

Alleluia, she thought.

She didn't know what to do as he returned. She still didn't have any condoms or she'd have invited him upstairs. A droopy, wide, old sofa slouched up there still. And a shag rug. She pressed her lips shut around a bubble of laughter.

Returning, instead of touching her, Daniel cleared up the remnants of their lunch, pushing it all aside. Then he took his lovely suit jacket and spread it on the bar like a picnic blanket.

Elspeth's eyes widened.

Daniel glanced at her, smirked a little, and slid one finger inside the waistband of her cut-off sweats. He tugged and she stumbled against him, lips parted eagerly.

Dragging that one finger along her hip, he put the forefinger of his other hand down the other side. Elspeth leaned up to kiss him, and he met her with his mouth open, breathing her in, keeping the kiss as tentative and promising as the song rising around them.

Their tongues touched lightly, and he glanced his nose to hers, a sweet gesture belying the dig of his fingers on her bare hips. He walked those fingers down and grabbed her bottom, pulling her against his very hard cock. Elspeth hummed happily, in tone with the song as it quieted and started over.

Daniel carefully, purposefully, pushed her sweats down her hips, leaving her in only her cotton knickers.

She kissed him again, letting him trace the lines of cotton gently pressing her hips. He slid his palm along the curve of her lower belly, two fingers and thumb dipping under the knickers to brush the top of the fluff of her hair. "Yes," she whispered against the corner of his mouth, tasting along his jaw.

He fell to his knees, leaving her bereft of a mouth to kiss or a neck to nuzzle, and with him he took her knickers.

With a gasp, Elspeth looked down at Daniel, crouched so his face was flush with her pussy, her shorts and knickers around her ankles. He leaned in and brushed his lips to the top of her mound, breathing in slowly enough to tickle. She put her hands in his hair, digging into the layers, and watched him.

It is obscene, she thought lazily, *standing half naked in my own pub*. In her family's pub. But his nose traced a line along her belly to the indent where it met her hip, and she thought maybe it was romantic instead. Daniel helped her hop out of her knickers. Then he stood up, his body skimming along hers.

"Hold on," he murmured against her cheek, and she grasped his shoulders as he hefted her off her feet and set her down on his spread jacket there on the edge of the bar.

He'd pushed between her knees before she realized what was happening, opening her up to display.

"Oh my God," she breathed, embarrassed, her thighs squeezing his hips. Cool air directly on her most intimate parts was shocking. And his attention! Her nipples ached as they tightened, as her whole body flushed with need. She took a deep breath, her ribs pushed at the tight binding of her sports bra, and even as she wanted to cover herself up, she wanted to bust out of the bra and arch her back and just be naked and free.

"No?" Daniel asked her, catching her eyes. His hands were on her thighs.

She stared into his bitter-chocolate irises and said, "Yes, please."

His wolfish smile appeared, with all its teeth.

Elspeth moaned, her head falling back, and the ripple of motion rolled her hips forward; she'd have tumbled off the edge of the bar if not for his grip.

Then his breath touched her inner thigh, and his lips grazed the sensitive join of leg to torso, and she felt like heat was just pouring out of her. She melted toward him.

Fingers spread her apart, and she shuddered, knees closing around his shoulders, and he kissed her right on her clit—a tease only—before licking softly, following with little circles.

Elspeth gasped. She thought of health codes suddenly, and that Asra had a key! She panted, mind spinning, and leaned back on her elbows, body taught with holding herself up and the intense joy zipping up her spine from his kisses. Then Daniel's mouth pressed down, and his tongue entered her, and there were no more thoughts in her head.

The song started over again, and Elspeth opened her mouth, breathily crying out and the music and his lips and tongue mingled together in a hot ache that rang in her ears, echoed in her chest, and burned to her core.

Daniel slid one hand under her thigh, holding her tight against him as she struggled to contain her need to move, to beg him to put something inside her, to relieve the desperate ache: he sucked at her, swirled his tongue in long strokes, and she panted, "Daniel, Daniel, please."

She was so ready she barely felt the slide of his fingers entering her, until he moved them, pushing inside, still kissing her and sucking at her clit, and she pushed back, trying to fuck his hand and face, gone in the need, entirely gone, but the crescendo of her song—her favorite song— pierced her low moan, and when she came it was to a thrill of violin.

Daniel did not let her fall back across the bar, but kissed up her belly and wrapped his arms around her waist, holding her as she shuddered and sighed. Elspeth wrapped her legs around him, and as her heels knocked into him she realized she was still wearing her trainers.

CHAPTER NINE

GIVEN the nature of their relationship thus far, Elspeth was glad to discover on Tuesday that she could enjoy hours in Daniel's presence without either of them having an orgasm.

They began their castle adventure that morning at Beaumaris, in an adorable seaside town on Anglesey with sweeping green marshes and a view of stark, low mountains across the strait. The castle was one of Edward I's, like most of the castles in Elspeth's part of Wales, built in the late thirteenth century. That was most of what she knew about it, but she still babbled random facts she suddenly remembered about Welsh princes and certain revolts as they strolled hand in hand along the curtain wall.

Daniel only took his eyes off the gray-white stones and crumbling crenellations to glance at her or ask a question she didn't have an answer to without looking it up on her phone.

Sometimes, his thumb stroked hers and she lost track of her thoughts. As they ducked into a hollowed-out tower, necks craning to stare up at the hooded remains of ancient hearths and notches where floor beams used to insert, he stepped behind her and put both hands on her shoulders, leaning close, and she felt him breathe in the scent of her hair and the valley behind her ear.

"This is good," he said, his tone almost like he was reminding himself. Elspeth reached up to touch one of his hands but said nothing. If today was the anniversary of his friend's death, she knew better than to try to mold it in any particular way. She hated it when others imposed their assumptions about grief onto her; she wouldn't do that.

As they left Beaumaris Castle, Daniel purchased the thin yellow Cadw Guidebook, and as she drove them back to the mainland on the way to Caernarfon, he flipped through, reading tidbits of the history and filling in gaps in her knowledge. They ate power bars he'd packed alongside bottled water, umbrellas, a jacket, maps, and his wallet in a small hiking knapsack. She pointed out the village of Llanfairpwllgwyngyllgogerychwyrndrobwllllantysiliogogogoch and laughed as he tried to pronounce the full name—the longest place-name in Europe—several times, even pulling up videos of various attempts by news anchors.

Everything was natural between them, easy and domestic, and Elspeth relaxed moment to moment. She'd been nervous after yesterday, after coming all over her bar. Daniel had offered to stay through the afternoon to help with her chores, but she'd told him they wouldn't get anything done, eyeing the rather excessive bulge in his pants.

He'd had to agree with her, watching as she reluctantly pulled her sweats back on, and she held his gaze, licking her lips as she offered to get him off, too. Daniel had kissed her forehead and promised to take care of himself before she lost any more time away from work.

With a boldness that took her own breath away, Elspeth had asked to watch.

And he'd let her.

In the tiny, dark-paneled bathroom, she'd leaned against the door and stared, hot and excited enough it would've been easy to bring herself again, too. Instead, she'd forced her anticipation into a panting need, a pain, while he stroked and fingered himself, lashes lowered except for when he occasionally snapped his gaze to hers and seemed to glare with passion.

Elspeth had realized in that drawn-out, deliciously dirty moment that she liked needing something so badly, something that would *definitely* make her happy. It was a perfect ache, wanting something new—a future apart from the expectations of grief or the past, different from selling or not selling. Another option, not either/or, but more.

Her heart blew out and open while he gave her the gift she'd asked for, coming messy and with gritted teeth, in his fancy suit and his big dick reddened and spent.

As he'd shivered and breathed himself calmer, reaching for paper towels, Elspeth had fled.

She'd dived back into cleaning the bar, gave up mopping, and had the stools and tables nearly set to rights again when he emerged, perfectly coiffed, from polished shoes to slick black hair. She said, "I'll pick you up at half-eight tomorrow morning."

"I'll pack snacks," he had answered with a friendly smile, and as he walked past, he took his jacket, which Elspeth had folded carefully.

They'd not seen each other again until she pulled into the Blue Garden Guesthouse car park at eight-thirty sharp, and he walked out in jeans and a dark green sweater, knapsack arms clipped across his chest in a way that accentuated the breadth of his shoulders.

It had been the most glorious day, sun-bright and green, warm despite the cool wind gusting off the ocean. After Beaumaris, they wove along the coast to Caernarfon, another Edward I castle with layers of squared-off towers, this one in a larger town, its walls surrounded by ocean, city, and a long car park. This castle had been more rebuilt, and they could explore different levels, climbing up into the ramparts to gaze out over the gray roofs of the city while wind snapped royal flags above their heads. They weren't alone at all, and Daniel had bought his Cadw book at the start this time so he could read things as they went, exploring slowly. Elspeth was more than content to go where he willed, reading placards and discussing what it must have smelled like eight hundred years ago.

Especially because he continued to hold her hand.

Once he'd frozen in a tower room clustered with a dozen other tourists, his body suddenly rigid, but before Elspeth could tug him into the next room or ask if he was all right, he blew out a long breath and let go of whatever had happened. With a sad, self-deprecating smile he'd said, "Sorry."

"For what?" she'd replied, and they'd stepped together into a long inner hall, filled with exhibits of weaponry and uniforms and flags. It was the Royal Welch Fusiliers Museum, housed there at Caernarfon.

Daniel took his time, and Elspeth followed, wondering if being surrounded by the trappings of war made this day better or worse for him. Wondering when he'd tell her what had happened to him—or if he ever would, and whether she could stomach not knowing.

She was thinking long-term, she realized. After five days, she was wondering if it would be months or years before she knew him completely.

"I've read some of his poetry," Daniel said, before a display of a lovely silver cross medal with a white and purple ribbon.

Elspeth leaned closer. It was a Military Cross, awarded to Second Lieutenant Siegfried Loraine Sassoon in 1916. "Oh," she murmured.

"He was not a fan of war."

"Is anybody?"

Daniel slid her a look that was less sad and more knowing. "Yeah."

Elspeth put her hand in his again, curling their fingers together. "I didn't know you like poetry."

"My therapist gave it to me—Sassoon had PTSD, too, and wrote poetry and memoirs. I read some."

He said it all so lightly, especially the *too*, that Elspeth could've ignored the implications. All she did was nod.

"He lost several very good friends and his brother," Daniel said.

Did you? She wanted desperately to ask.

"Too bad I'm shit at writing poetry."

"You're good at *other* things," Elspeth murmured.

Daniel's eyes lit up, and the surprise in his smile put a real jump to her pulse. "I sure am," he said slowly.

They'd left the museum and wandered the rest of the grounds, until it was time to find lunch.

As they ate, in a low-ceilinged café with sandwiches and Elspeth's favorite lager, she told him about coming here as a little girl with a school trip, and Daniel told her about his family.

Mom and Dad living in Chicago, both working in the family business—which started as a corner pharmacy in the early 1900s and grew, thanks to hard work and his grandmother's money. She'd been a rich Protestant who'd nearly been disowned for marrying a Catholic, but when the profits began to accrue, she was forgiven. Elspeth said she didn't realize things like that happened in America.

"Rich people everywhere are like that," he'd said.

"I wouldn't know," she teased, and Daniel had cocked his lips and said, "Maybe you will someday."

Certainly—certainly—he meant when she accepted that offer for The Fort, or if she managed to be a world-class singer. But she wanted him to mean because she'd be *his*.

Elspeth was smitten.

He also had a sister and brother-in-law and two nieces, and he related the shenanigans his mum had reported when he called her Saturday morning.

He voluntarily called his mother. Elspeth grinned.

"I like that one," Daniel had said.

"What one?"

"That smile."

Her joy drifted away into flirtatious amusement. "My smile."

"You have so many different ones." His voice was low burning embers, his eyes insistent. "For different customers, different emotions, even a sad smile. And one for me, when you're about to command me to . . . do what you want. And that one from just now. The wide-open grin."

Elspeth felt her face falling away from every possible smile, she was so touched. She stood up, hands on the table, and leaned over to kiss him.

Daniel returned it, fitting their lips together, just barely parted, and when she pulled back, Elspeth said, "We have another stop to make."

CHAPTER TEN

ELSPETH DRAGGED him down the road to a corner store.

"Wait here," she said, voice higher than usual, but Daniel nodded, sliding his hands into his pockets, and she darted inside.

This town was rushing with cars and people, on a bright Tuesday afternoon. The castle wall rose over rows of converted shops and quaint cafes, and Daniel looked up at the flag snapping high against the blue, blue sky. They'd stood beside it only a couple of hours ago.

He took a breath and let his finger skim along Alvin's lighter at the bottom of his jeans pocket. He hadn't pulled it out all day, even when that woman's laugh had so sharply triggered a memory, and not in the car this morning as Elspeth drove him mostly in companionable silence. They'd swept along narrow roads through forest and hill to the island of Anglesey, and he'd enjoyed looking at her profile as she drove with her chin slightly raised, like she was ready to literally fight traffic. Not that there was much of it.

He'd enjoyed everything today.

For a while he even forgot it was the anniversary, and forgot he was lying to her, too.

Nothing had ever made him as eager and constantly turned on as Elspeth Gwenlan, and he felt like a kid waiting to open presents on Christmas morning every time she looked at him. Would she tell him she wanted to watch him masturbate again? Christ, he hoped so. Would she talk about some damn opera and wiggle at the way it made her feel? Or grow thoughtful as her mind whirled, each twist and turn splattered across her face? Or would she give him that smile again? The one that said, *you make me happy. You make me happy, and I didn't know I could be happy again.*

Daniel leaned against the external wall of the corner store, and hung his head to look down at his feet so nobody could see that he was smiling, too. The gesture pulled the scars on his back, the ones trailing up his neck from burns and skin grafts. The sensation always made him a little nauseated, but this time he wondered if maybe Elspeth wouldn't mind them.

He wondered if maybe he could give her everything she wanted, and then leave before she knew he was a liar. Make this good enough she never regretted it, even if she hated him after.

She'd been inside for a long time.

At least seven or eight minutes. What could she possibly need in there?

He checked his phone, ignoring the work emails like he'd been ignoring everything from Pella for days. He had a few news items and notifications he deleted, since he was supposed to be on a recovery vacation. Far, far away from stress. He didn't delete the email from Alvin's brother, who always emailed this time of year. Daniel always responded about a month late. It was the best he could do.

His shoulder muscles were stiffening with tension. Last year he'd been so wound up he punched a manager in the face for he didn't even *remember* what. Except he'd been so fucking frustrated. The year before that he'd spent today drunk.

Daniel needed Elspeth back. Before he got too fidgety. Before he lost it and snapped or—or cried.

A traitor thought whispered, *what if she doesn't mind your tears, you coward.*

Pushing off the wall, he spun to escape himself, charging for the door.

It swished open and there was Elspeth, cheeks bright pink, eyes wide as she nearly ran into him.

She had a single plastic bag crushed to her chest, and tried to smile.

"Elspeth," he said, gripping her arms, frowning too hard because he wanted to know why she was too upset to smile.

With a broad grimace, she shook her head.

Not upset. Embarrassed. Acutely embarrassed.

Biting her bottom lip until it turned white, she opened the bag. "I just stood there for so long, staring. Reading the boxes! There weren't even that many to choose from, but I didn't know . . . "

Daniel's whole body felt like it was glowing, pushing out and out and out until he'd float away like a hot air balloon. The bag had several different kinds of condoms. His breath hissed through his teeth. She wanted him. She wanted him enough to— "You got plenty," he managed to strangle out, sure he was holding her too tightly.

"I didn't know what was best! What . . ." her voice dropped. "You just seem . . . large. But just because you're bigger than Alfie and Sam— the only other—well. It doesn't mean . . . I . . . So I don't know how to tell what is . . . Does it matter? And so I stared and stared, and I *Googled it*, Daniel. I Googled it while I was standing there! And then someone . . ." Her eyes dropped shut as if she couldn't bear it. "Someone asked if I needed help. It was mortifying."

Daniel had never been so charmed in his life. He let go of her shoulders and cupped her face. "Okay, beautiful," he murmured, then kissed her forehead. She smelled indefinably good. His own smile grew, even though she couldn't see it. As Elspeth melted into him, arms (and sack of condoms) going around his waist, he whispered, "I'm sorry my penis is so big."

Her body went rigid and she gasped.

There in the bright afternoon street, he held her, eyes closed and face pressed to her hair, and Elspeth slowly started to shake with laughter.

CHAPTER ELEVEN

It was five p.m. Tuesday, and they climbed the loose rubble path up the hill to the last castle of their day: Dolwyddelan, only twenty minutes south of Caerafon. Elspeth wanted to show him a true Welsh castle, built by a Welsh prince, and she had a meeting at six. Maybe they'd take another castle day, and see Harlech, or go up to Conwy.

Dolwyddelan was the ruins of an old square keep built on a knoll overlooking a valley. They walked a long path up steps and rough-cut terrain, but through idyllic forest and past a stream. They climbed over the crumbling curtain wall and stood in the grass looking up at the old keep.

They were alone. The sun lowered in the west, and Daniel walked ahead, jogging up the old stone stairs to the dark arched doorway into the keep.

Elspeth hugged herself. She'd been here several times throughout her life and liked letting him explore on his own. He'd return to her.

Green hills lifted all around the site, and clouds rolled, and everything was glorious. She hummed the ridiculous "Papagena-Papageno" from *The Magic Flute*. A silly lover's song, that sounded the way her heart felt.

"Elspeth!" Daniel called, peering out from the high entrance. He waved her to him.

She went, joining him inside the empty old room, with its pale wooden floor and bare stone walls.

Daniel caught her from behind, wrapping his arms around her. "I don't know why you didn't come with me."

"I was enjoying the outside. Singing."

"Oh? It will echo nicely in here."

Leaning her head back, she caught his eye. "I'll sing for you later. After my meeting."

"I know," he nuzzled her neck. "Ten p.m., at The Fort."

"Come prepared to stay the night."

He hummed darkly against her skin, and she closed her eyes, holding his hands as they held her. The musty stone and dust smell didn't even bother her; it was cool and soothing inside the old keep. Especially with his strong chest behind her, arms around her, and hot lips exploring the lines and hollows of her neck and jaw.

Elspeth controlled herself carefully, fully aware if she sank into this, they'd end up doing something unforgivable in this governmentally protected historic site.

Daniel seemed to sense her peace, and kissed her jaw, her cheek, and then leaned his temple to her head. He breathed so slowly and carefully.

"I like this. I like how it feels," he said.

"How does it feel?" Her heart thrummed along with her body, wanting something intangible, but etched in delicate lines with hope.

"Constant," he said, then repeated it, more firmly. "Constant. I constantly think about you, constantly want you. Constantly like you. I'm not used to that."

Elspeth managed to nod, and her fingers tightened against his hands, too tight, really. But her knees were weak. Her center ached again, gentler than yesterday, but the slightest encouragement would revive her desperation.

Daniel pressed against her, and then suddenly let go. "If I have to wait until ten o'clock tonight, I better not get started."

"I'm sorry." She turned. "I wish I could cancel."

"It's good for me. I can be alone for a few hours. Your sustainability stuff matters."

Elspeth snorted. "My sustainability *stuff*. Yes. All right." She let out a shaky breath. "But at two minutes past ten, you be ready, Daniel Kelly."

He laughed, warm and eager, and with a jaunty bow—which she could hardly take with a straight face—charged off to finish exploring the ruins.

CHAPTER TWELVE

DANIEL SHOWED up at The Fort at nine-thirteen. Asra was tending bar, and warned him they closed at nine-thirty on Tuesday nights.

"I'm meeting Elspeth after her meeting," he said, sure of himself, and it worked. He enjoyed a whiskey until the last customer was shooed out, then offered to help Asra tidy up while they waited for Elspeth. The music playing had been quiet old jigs, and Asra changed it to a current alternative station, pushing the volume to a better level for cleaning.

Daniel dried dishes and packaged up the few perishable bar ingredients for the overnight fridge while Asra swept through the rest of his checklist. Just as they were finishing, the door in the wall opened, and Elspeth appeared.

"How long have you been here?" Asra's eyes went wide.

"I used the back stair," she answered, but her eyes were all on Daniel.

His pulse had jumped at her sudden arrival, and his neck crawled knowing she'd been right upstairs, moving around, this whole time. But the tension shifted to lust as he looked at her, in a soft red sweater and tight jeans, her hair frazzled and loose as he'd never seen it, tumbling around her shoulders.

"Hi," she said to him. Her lips were pink, shining ever so slightly in the yellow pub lights.

"Hi," he answered, aware it was more a vibration than a word. His awareness sank lower and lower down his spine. He wanted to stride over, grab her up, and ravish her mouth. Walk her back to the wall, and—

Asra smirked and asked how the meeting had gone.

Elspeth blinked; so did Daniel.

"Great," Elspeth said. "Great, yes. And Mrs. Templeton laid out her distribution plan, and we nailed down how much capital it will take, oh! And a specialist contractor is coming up from Aberystwyth to look at where we can put solar panels so I have to get all the official paperwork about where we're allowed to 'ruin the quaint beauty of the rooflines.'"

"I thought you were focusing on farm-to-table and local growing?" Asra said.

"Yes, but when people get excited about something, I have to encourage it."

Daniel stepped closer to Elspeth and turned a dark look on Asra. "This seems like a riveting conversation—for tomorrow."

Asra laughed. "Sure thing, man. See you tomorrow, sis."

Once he was gone, Elspeth just stared at him.

"Can I come up?" he asked.

With a sweet, nervous nod, she turned and put her bright purple flat to the first stair. She held out her hand and without hesitation, Daniel went to her and took it.

The narrow stairs closed around him too tightly, too darkly, but he held her hand and followed, trusting her to pull him up into light again.

Candlelight greeted them, from three wide white candles set on a short circular coffee table, flickering merrily over a nest of blankets and corduroy pillows pulled off the sagging sofa shoved in the corner. She had a small electric camp light, too, and wine and green plastic stemless glasses.

Elspeth let go of him and rubbed her palms on her thighs. "It's so ridiculous. But I still live with my mother, and you're at Agatha's, so . . ."

Stepping across the uneven floor, he took her head in his hands and kissed her, showing her exactly how good everything was. Her hands gripped his jeans, then slid around to duck in his rear pockets and pull him against her.

They kissed, pressed fully together, and Daniel loved the eager lick of her tongue asking for more. He opened his mouth; she followed. He dug his fingers into her wild hair, smiling against her mouth, and Elspeth nibbled his bottom lip, biting gently, tugging a little. He captured her mouth again, tasting her tongue, scraping light against her teeth. The heat seemed to pass between them, and her fingers pressed through his jeans into his ass. She rubbed her body against his and hummed in pleasure.

Disengaging, Daniel stripped off his sweater, tossing it aside. Beneath was only a T-shirt. Elspeth did the same, revealing nothing under hers but a plain black bra edged in lace.

She started to say something, but Daniel took her ribs and bent her to him, leaning to rub his cheek against the swell of one heavy breast, then run his tongue where the bra cut slightly against her flesh. He dragged his hands up, flicking his thumb over her nipple, and again, and he felt it pebble.

He sighed with intense satisfaction, and put his mouth to her other breast, and found that already-hard nipple with the flat of his tongue. The thin cotton separating him from her dampened, and he teased with his teeth.

Elspeth grabbed his head, arching her back.

Daniel kissed up her sternum to her throat, and she directed his mouth to hers again, kissing him deeply. He reached around and unhooked her bra. Her little gasp lit him up, and he was so hard, trapped in his goddamn jeans.

Shrugging out of her bra, Elspeth unhooked her own jeans, and started wiggling her hips to get them off. "Just, hurry up," she panted.

He laughed, but it was breathless too, and followed her example, ripping down his jeans and briefs simultaneously—a little too enthusiastically, and it rubbed his cock a little raw, but Christ, he wanted her. His T-shirt followed, and then they were both naked.

Daniel braced himself, feeling the phantom heat of the scar curling over his shoulder like the fire that put it there, waving, waiting to derail them.

But she didn't even seem to see it.

"Oh," Elspeth whispered, reaching for his cock. She wrapped both hands around it, pressing a thumb against the crown, and as his eyes involuntarily fluttered shut, he saw the tip of her tongue breach her lips, like just the sight of him this way starved her.

She stroked him gently, palms soft and dry, and her fingers danced down to his base, one hand cupping his balls, sliding around to feel the hidden juncture with his ass. He widened his stance for her as she explored, standing there as still as he could, but wrenched open his eyes to watch her bright cheeks, her eager eyes. Naked, she was like a goddess, confident as she touched him, grinning to herself even, distinctly possessive.

"Oh, I like this," she said, glancing up at his eyes.

In answer he brought his hands to her breasts. He copied her exploring motions, gently hefting, pinching, and he leaned his hips toward her, skimming the tip of his cock against her belly.

Abruptly, Elspeth jerked away. She took two long steps around the nest of blankets and dug into her plastic sack, coming up with a handful of condoms. She raised her eyebrows. Daniel pointed to the gold one.

She ripped open his selection as she returned to him, and carefully positioned it. Her lips were parted, her body giving off heat, and he gently held her shoulders, watching.

Her hands were *trembling*.

Daniel's hips jerked a little, desperate, as she rolled the condom on.

"Elspeth?" he murmured. It was the best he could do.

"I need you so badly," she said, voice a little scratchy.

Daniel immediately touched her pussy, sliding a finger past the dark curling hair, between her folds where she was so hot and slick. Elspeth moaned, and he pushed deeper, holding her in the palm of his hand, and fingered her opening. If possible, his cock got even harder.

She nudged her hips forward, deepening his touch, but then shook her head. "Just—" Elspeth fluttered her hands toward the nest of blankets. "Get down there."

Laughing, he obeyed. He spread on his back, cock bobbing a little, and he gave himself a single stroke, to check the condom, before raising his arms, folding his hands beneath his head. His entire body stretched on display for her, and he felt so strong.

Elspeth said, "I love it when you do that. Touch yourself," she added.

He moved to do it again for her, but she stepped around him, feet on either side of his hips. The light caught her round hip, the underside of her large, perfect breasts, and up her throat, gilding her. Daniel barely breathed—too much and he could come just like this. Just with her looking, wanting as badly as he wanted.

Gracefully, Elspeth knelt, hands on his chest, sinking down just below his cock, and all that heat focused against his balls. Daniel hissed in pleasure as she moved against him, sliding her wet center up along him. She moaned, and put both her own hands against herself, rubbing down. Her thighs shuddered against his hips, then she took his cock and put it where she wanted it: right at her hole. Elspeth's mouth fell open. Daniel did his best not to move.

She slowly, achingly slowly, took him in, making little gasping notes.

Daniel made fists in his own hair, pulling tight enough to hurt.

He only tilted his hips to help, and Elspeth let out the deepest groan as she fit fully against him, hot and perfectly tight. The need to move spread up his body like wildfire, and he gritted his teeth, because he knew—he *knew*—what it was like to be burning, but this didn't scream on his skin so violently it surpassed pain, this was good, better than good. This heat put him back together from the inside instead of tearing him apart.

Her hands flattened on his chest, two brands, and she stared down at him, bright eyes round. "It hurts," she whispered, but wonderingly, and then she moved, just a little, keeping him inside her as she squeezed and moved around him, shifting her hips, gasping and then smiling a slow, burning smile.

He flexed his stomach, performing a quick sit-up, and she laughed as he caught her around her hips, pulling her down on his cock again. He kissed her, then she began thrusting down again and again, and he held her hips. It wouldn't be long. He seethed through his teeth, her lips found his forehead and pressed there. She put her arms around his neck and held on, and her moans deepened, her body clenched around him, and Daniel wanted to touch her center while she rode him, while she thrust herself so passionately onto him.

But she shook her head when he moved his hands, until he grabbed her ass again, and she said *yes yes*. Daniel dug his fingers in, pulling her closer, as he ached to throw her down and take over, move harder, faster. But Elspeth grabbed his neck and held his eyes, hers wide and wild. He wasn't sure he'd ever looked straight into a woman while she fucked him and it was so good his orgasm tightened sharply.

"I'm going to come," he said raggedly.

"Me too," she hissed, and threw back her head, pulling his face to her throat. Daniel dragged his tongue against her neck, bit her, and when she cried out, he let it all go, coming eagerly and unrestrained.

Elspeth sang pretty gasping cries, still moving, rolling her hips with the pulsing of his orgasm like she could feel it, too, and then in a drawn-out cry she pushed low and lower, shuddering around him. Her mouth was beautiful and wide, and sweat glistened down her sternum where Daniel buried his mouth, breathing her in.

"Daniel," she whispered tenderly.

He never wanted to move again. His pulse thrummed. His bones seemed lighter.

But Elspeth slid off of him, melting rather, and curled on the blankets. Sweat glistened on her ribs and temple. She smiled smugly, even with her eyes closed.

Daniel leaned onto his shoulder and caressed the line of her cheek, loving it. Loving her.

He felt completely relaxed for the first time since . . . well the last time Elspeth had had her way with him. He wanted to keep her.

"Is there a bathroom up here?" he asked softly.

Her nod was lazy, and she pointed with a limp hand.

With care, Daniel stood and made his way into the tiny closet with its old toilet and a sink the size of a cereal bowl. Through a narrow door was a tiled room with a stand-alone tub. He cleaned himself off, startling suddenly at the squeal of the faucet.

When he walked back into the main room, she was staring at him through the wavering light, still naked, and she hadn't pulled any blankets over herself.

He grabbed the bottle of wine, already open with the cork stuck half back in. He poured two glasses and brought them to her. "Here, beautiful."

Stretching like a cat, she pushed up to sit on her hip and accepted. Her eyes held his over the rim. "I want to clean up, too, but I'm pretty sure I'm just going to get messy again," she said plainly.

Possibly it was his imagination, but her accent seemed to roll more gently. Like a purr.

"I hope so," he said.

"I did buy a whole stone of condoms."

Daniel barked a laugh, and drank some of the dry, cheap wine. She smiled pertly and did the same.

And they kept staring at each other, not speaking, but silently teasing. She lifted one eyebrow; he showed her his teeth. She pursed his lips in pretend fear, exaggerated like a silent-film star. He leaned in and kissed her. One hand skimmed along the curve of her breast and she pressed closer.

Daniel leaned away to set his wine down safely, and she said, "Daniel?"

The hesitation in her voice told him what she was looking at before he turned back to see her eyes, indeed, trailing along his shoulder where a moment before he'd offered a glimpse of his scar. Expecting her to finally ask what had happened, he braced himself. He'd decided to try to answer. "Elspeth," he said simply.

She got to her knees, putting her glass right on the sloping wooden floor, and moved behind him. Her hand reached out and she touched the tip of the scar, high on his right trapezius. "Can you feel this?"

It wasn't the question he'd anticipated, and his shoulders tensed anyway. He felt the pressure of her touch, moving along the ripple and shine of the scar, which widened down his shoulder blade and back like a tongue of fire. "I . . . feel the sensation, but it isn't the same. It's like when you push on a limb that's fallen asleep. Some pressure, and I know where you are. It's strange, and used to be disorienting," he confessed, far more than he'd even said to his doctor.

"What about this," she murmured, moving her face closer. She kissed his rippled flesh and he brought up his knees to lean his arms against, balancing his whole body.

"Does it upset you? I'm sorry."

"No, it's all right," he said, uncertain he meant it.

"Good." Elspeth moved fully behind him, skimming her hands on his shoulders, then down his back, tracing the edges of the scar with her mouth and tongue, like she was going to lick the scar off him, leaving him fresh and new. Her hands kneaded his ribs, moved around him to find his belly and climb up to his nipples. She flicked them and pressed against his back. When her breasts touched him, he flinched at the pleasure, striking directly to his cock.

"Daniel?" she asked, putting soothing kisses along his neck up to his ear.

"I like it," he said.

"Good," she repeated, and reached for his cock again with both hands.

CHAPTER THIRTEEN

THE HOURS of the night expanded along with Elspeth's heart. They fucked and drank the whole bottle of wine she'd grabbed at the end of the meeting in Morgan's back room, cuddled, whispered little things like favorite movies and first times, and fucked some more. Elspeth was sore, and she liked it, though probably would skip her morning run.

Her entire body tingled and tickled—overly sensitive and raw, inside and out. Finally, she had to wrap up in a blanket and press fully against his side, head on his arm. It was the deepest part of the night, when all the world was quiet. The moon had set, too, and all the candles guttered out. Daniel put his mouth to her temple and in the absolute darkness told her he'd been in a helicopter crash, in Afghanistan, and his friend Alvin had died in the fireball that burned off half Daniel's back. Alvin died protecting him, because Daniel had been already injured—hit with a ricochet bullet and that's why the med-evac in the first place. He didn't embellish, but only said the words soft and fast. Elspeth had stroked her palm over his heart and said, "You made it through another anniversary."

"It's like leaving them behind." His voice shook. "I hate it."

Elspeth nodded. She whispered, "I know."

She wanted to say more, to sleepily confess she knew she had to stop letting imagined obligations make her future for her, but it was too dark, too quiet, too much like letting go. And Daniel tightened his hold on her.

When sunlight crept through the threadbare old drapes on the narrow windows, Elspeth opened her eyes to find Daniel watching her sleepily.

"Did you sleep at all?" she murmured.

"A little."

"If you want to brush your teeth, I brought fresh things, and then we can . . . do it again before I go downstairs to make coffee." Elspeth blushed.

Daniel's slow smile curled her toes.

He started to sit, but she caught his hand, suddenly desperate to know. "Daniel, how long are you staying with me?"

Elspeth let go, covering her mouth. She'd not meant to add those last two words.

Turning toward her, Daniel brushed hair out of her face, combing it gently back. His own hair stuck up wildly, a mess of product and sleep, but still devastating. *Mine is probably matted*, she thought, trying to think of anything but his answer.

He swallowed, and said, "I have to be back in London on Saturday afternoon."

Three and a half days. Taking a deep breath, Elspeth nodded. "Okay. I have to decide if I'm selling by then. The Fort," she clarified, then grimaced. As if he'd forgotten. "If I do, I'm supposed to be in London on Friday for a meeting."

"I can . . . drive you," he offered.

Stomach gone a little sour, Elspeth put on a brave smile. "That sounds delightful—but only if you don't mind driving Mum, too." Then she pushed up fast and beat him into the tiny bathroom.

CHAPTER FOURTEEN

ELSPETH WAS DETERMINED NOT to ruin her delicious affair with Daniel Kelly by hyper-focusing on whether or not it was ending in London. She knew she should just ask him, but didn't want to hear an answer she didn't like. Besides, she had her own choices to make.

So she'd enjoy what time they had, be wild, take what made her happy.

That afternoon when he walked into The Fort, Elspeth met him halfway across the floor and kissed him in front of all her customers.

He responded immediately, lifting her slightly, spinning in time to the swell of the pretty piano haunting the speakers, and dipped her deeply.

She gasped and laughed, and when they whipped up to their feet, The Fort erupted in applause.

Elspeth shooed Howell Jenkins off the stool at the far end of the bar and enthroned Daniel there, as it was his favorite seat in the place—close to her, with his back to the wall. She put on a streaming channel with West End hits and when a love song started, she did her best to wink at him as she sang along.

It turned into an impromptu musical, with regulars and even some game tourists joining in, filling The Fort with off-pitch harmonies and carousing versions of songs from *Phantom* and *West Side Story*, and memorably, *The Lion King*.

Daniel laughed and tapped his hands on the bar, but didn't sing. He caught her once, as she spun between tall tables singing "A Lovely Night" from Rodgers and Hammerstein's *Cinderella*. His hands gripped her ribs and he kissed her, more than a sweet public snog, and she melted against his chest.

The story spread fast enough Elspeth's *mum* appeared in The Fort, which she'd avoided whenever possible since her husband died. Mum made a beeline for the American, and by the time she departed they were fast friends. Daniel even charmed her out of the story behind Elspeth's name, and crowed with delight to discover she was named after a princess in an old fantasy novel. There wasn't a single drop of sadness in his eyes.

For dinner he took her forty minutes away to Tyddyn Llan restaurant and inn for a real date, and she drank a cocktail made by a stranger with fancy botanical gin, wearing high heels and a strappy dress it was really too cold for. And Daniel looked at her once or twice like he was thinking of staying longer than the end of the week. The look burned her, so hot she struggled not to squirm in her dainty chair, and all she did was reach for his hand and bring it to her mouth to kiss the pad of his finger.

They made love languidly back home on the first floor of The Fort, and when Elspeth was filled up with him, she blinked away tears before he could see—she was so happy, and ready for more.

To recover, Elspeth blindfolded him with his tie and stood over him with shaking knees, telling him what she wanted him to do to himself while she watched.

After, Daniel hugged her, rubbing his hand along her arm, and she brought up her knee, wrapping her leg around him.

"You're so tense, beautiful," he said.

"What happens after London?" she asked casually, trying to sound like she didn't care very much.

For several long breaths he didn't answer, his chest lifting up and down slowly. She flattened her hand on his sternum, over his diaphragm, and considered teaching him to breathe like a singer.

She blinked, her lashes brushing his clavicle. He kissed her hair.

Then he said, "I don't know."

It was a quiet confession, filled with layers of meaning she thought she could read: he wanted more than he thought he could give.

Elspeth rolled on top of him. The lights were out, and only pale moonlight slid through the windows. In the dark his handsome jaw begged to be kissed. His lips parted with secrets. And he stared up at her openly, not hiding the admiration in his gaze, or the sorrow, or the hunger. He touched her hips, her breasts, her cheeks, and drew her face down to his.

"I want you, Elspeth," he whispered against her lips.

She laughed; she couldn't help it. Hearing him say so made her want to keep laughing, to squeal, even. To sing a silly song. Like something from Disney.

"Elspeth," he said, a little chiding that she'd laughed at him, but his lips drew out into a smile, too. In the dark, he was the devil again, dangerous but oh-so good.

"I want you, too," she said merrily.

Sitting, he caught her as she fell back, and she wrapped around him again. She was so naked and sticky, she should have felt awkward, but didn't.

"No matter what, I'll still want you after London," he whispered against her lips.

"Me too," she said.

"Promise," he said, but didn't give her a chance to reply, otherwise occupying her lips and tongue and voice.

CHAPTER FIFTEEN

THURSDAY MORNING, Elspeth jogged alongside Daniel, up the winding road to the burial mound. Overcast skies fought a battle with the sun to drag out the dawn, so they ran through dim gray, and the chilly wind was damp. She'd given in to autumn and put on yoga pants and a thin fleece, and sadly acknowledged to herself when her heart lit up at the sight of Daniel in his sweats hanging off those lanky hips, that it was too damned cold for any funny business. Too bad, because she felt so good in her body. She felt light, strong, ready.

She felt like tomorrow wasn't the end for them.

They had today, then tomorrow they headed to London for her meeting with Pella—if she was going to sell. Which she thought she would. She was almost certain. And it wouldn't be an end for The Fort, either.

Nothing had to end that she didn't want to end.

No matter what, Daniel had said. No matter if he was in America or London or Caerafon. No matter distance or The Fort, no matter if she went back to school or stayed here to create some kind of real job involved in sustainability. There were so many possibilities.

She could do anything. Elspeth stopped, a-flutter to the point of near panic.

"Daniel."

He ran a few more steps before slowly turning, jogging backwards, his brows raised playfully. "What's wrong? Surely not tired! Something cutting into your sleep?"

Elspeth smiled. "You know it is, Yank."

Tilting his head charmingly, he jogged in place.

Her pulse raced; she felt it in her ears and palms, and fluttering in her chest. "What should I do? Should I stay? Run The Fort? Or sell it? Tell me."

Daniel stopped moving, staring at her with a frown.

"You've never said what you think I should do," she pressed.

"I can't tell you what to do with The Fort."

"But you're not a villager, you haven't been attached to The Fort your whole life. You're not even Welsh!" She threw up her hands. "You're objective. Lend me that objectivity."

For a second, he still did not move. Then his entire demeanor snapped harder. In a wave of predatory grace, he stalked to her and took her face in his hands. "I am not objective. Not when it comes to you, Elspeth Gwenlan." His voice was rough—too rough. "Not at all. Not remotely."

Shaken at the sudden emotion on display, she only whispered, "Oh."

"Oh," he said, and kissed her so deeply he seemed to find places inside her she'd never noticed before.

The kiss was hot, his mouth was hot, but damp air clung to them, and she shivered. She wanted to tell him she loved him, she didn't want this to be over—and why should it be? She could do anything she liked.

Elspeth broke away, staring at him breathlessly.

She knew. She knew what to do. Sell. Her dad would have wanted her to. Because—because he'd given her music, he'd sent her to school. He'd never once said anything to make her think he expected her to come home for The Fort. The pub was never meant to be a weight around her neck. Not when he'd been alive, and he'd never do that to her just because he died.

Daniel stroked her cheeks, staring into her eyes, his brow forming lines of worry. "Elspeth?" he murmured.

She couldn't close her mouth, but only gape breathlessly at her simple, obvious revelation.

"Elspeth," he repeated. "What happened?"

"I'm well, I'm . . . well." Leaning against him, she took the comfort of his embrace, and whispered, "I'm selling. That's it, that's the choice."

His body seemed to shudder as he held her, and he nodded. "Good. I . . . if that is what you want."

"It is."

"Good." This time it was a firm word, and Daniel said, "I want to take you to London. Today. Put you up somewhere nice. Have the whole weekend to celebrate."

Elspeth felt like she might lift off the ground, float up the mountain. She nodded, joy and the rightness of the choice buoying her. A laugh found its way out of her mouth. She grasped his face, pecked his lips with hers, and pushed away. Spinning, she flung up her arms to wave as she ran back down the road, toward town. "I'll start making arrangements," she cried. "I'll need a few hours, but lunchtime? I'll see you then!"

She laughed again at his stunned expression, but turned away, breathless and ecstatic.

When she burst into her mum's cottage fifteen minutes later, she was flushed and too thrilled to do anything but call, "Mum! Where are you!" as she dashed into the kitchen.

Her mum was there, with Agatha, despite the breakfast hour.

Both women looked glum, stunned, and were huddled around Mum's laptop.

A snake of premonition slithered into Elspeth's stomach.

"Mum?" she whispered, crashing.

With a pretty frown, and such grave concern in her bright green eyes, her mum said, "Did you know Daniel's family is on the board of Pella?"

CHAPTER SIXTEEN

NERVES HAD NEVER PLAGUED Daniel as badly as they were as he waited for Elspeth to come outside. He was going to drive her to London, put her in a fancy room, and then tell her everything.

It wasn't even that much to tell, really. He'd been careful not to influence her thinking, he'd been himself. So much himself he realized he'd been acting like a stranger for years.

He loved her.

He'd known her a week, and he loved her.

It hurt his chest to think about.

Leaning on the door of his bright yellow rental, Daniel pulled out Alvin's lighter, rubbing it with his thumb.

Elspeth would arrive, he'd get her and her things into the car, then for the entire drive ask her about her future. Help her spin out whatever dreams she wanted for the next week, month, year, decade. And after they arrived at her hotel, he'd have a bottle of wine sent up, and he'd sit her down and tell her why he'd really come to Caerafon, and why he'd changed his plans, why he'd kept it from her.

It would be *fine*. She'd be angry, definitely, hurt maybe. But she'd forgive him. She had to. Maybe it was a good thing, even, because they'd found each other, and it hadn't changed her decision.

"Right?" he muttered to the lighter. Then he shoved it back in the pocket of his slacks.

Come on, Elspeth, he thought, looking down the short bricked path to the cottage front door. Mere hours had passed since she'd run joyfully down the mountain away from him, leaving him bereft and half hard.

Nothing seemed to be happening in the cottage. The frilled curtains on the small square windows to either side of the front door were still; he heard no muffled music or anything but the bustle of the village up the road.

He wanted to see her bedroom. It had been hers all her life, but for those few years at university, and Daniel wanted to see the inevitable fine art prints and framed posters from the London Coliseum. He wanted to know what she kept in her underwear drawer and the brand of toothpaste she used.

Just as he pushed off the car, the front door opened.

Daniel's relieved smile froze at the sight of her.

Elspeth remained in her yoga pants, and a baggy sweater fell off one shoulder. She had on wooly socks, no shoes, and her hair was loose and kinked from braids. But none of that would have mattered except for how pale she was. *Drawn,* was the word.

"Elspeth?" he said, striding for her. Something was wrong. Something had happened.

"Stop." Her voice cut harshly, and she thrust out a hand, fingers splayed.

He stopped.

"Go to London without me." She closed her eyes, but the words couldn't possible have hurt her as badly as they did him. "I knew you were a wolf the moment I saw you. I knew."

The breath blew out of him. He said, "Elspeth."

"Mum will drive me tomorrow. I don't want to see you there, at the meeting. I can't watch you . . . gloat." With that, she finally looked at his eyes.

Her anger hit him like a swift concussion wave. Faltering back, Daniel involuntarily lifted his hands for his helmet and—he stopped. She knew. It didn't matter how she'd found out. Daniel stared at her, not knowing what the fuck he could possibly do to defend himself.

"I'm sorry," he said hoarsely.

"No, you're not. You got everything you wanted, plus some—some . . ." the rest of her sentence shuddered out as a terrible sigh. "I can't look at you much longer," she whispered. "Don't make me."

"Elspet . . ."

"No, *Mr. Kelly*. Get out of my village. Go back and tell them I'll be in tomorrow to sign over the fucking pub. You win."

"This isn't what I wanted," he tried again.

"I don't care." Elspeth spun and marched back to her house, and there in the door was both Mrs. Gwenlan and a disgusted-looking Agatha.

Daniel met the sharp old eyes of his hostess, but she shook her head, wrinkled lips pressed so firmly they were near invisible.

The two women parted to let Elspeth past them.

Then they closed the door.

Daniel turned and put both hands on the roof of his rental, leaning in, and let his head hang. He felt gutted. Ruined.

This time, he had no insurgents or missiles to blame for his ruin. No orders or brave idiot friends. Not even alcohol. Just himself.

His jaw clenched, he bent his arms like he'd do a pushup against the car, mind burning, scars pulling, all of him a sudden cold typhoon of grief and guilt and anger.

He took deep breaths, slow and steady—at least he could get his heart rate under better control. No panic now. No outburst. *Just breathe,* he told himself.

It worked, marginally. The ringing in his ears faded a bit, and when he opened his eyes the light wasn't so bright it hurt.

Daniel jerked open the car door, slid inside, and did exactly what Elspeth had commanded.

CHAPTER SEVENTEEN

THE HOTEL ROOM WAS SILENT.

Pristine white walls and gilded moulding, with heavy curtains striped gold and mint-green pulled back over floor-to-ceiling windows overlooking the Thames itself and half of London. The massive bed was more than enough for Elspeth and her mother, but Mum would be staying, she hoped, with Kam tonight, after the party they'd agreed to attend. As special guests of Pella Group.

God, Elspeth had liked to say no, but Mr. Harcourt from Pella insisted, eager to keep proving how ready they were to be good, and Mum had thought it would be fun. Good for Elspeth to dress up, drink champagne at the British Museum, and remember what society could feel like. So they'd gone from the meeting where Elspeth and her mum signed their names at least twenty-seven times, to a luxury department store for clothes and shoes, lunch with Kam, and now here Elspeth perched on the overlarge bed in a hotel room the likes of which she might never experience again.

Alone.

In silence.

Her phone sat face down on the quilt. She had so much music loaded, and a speaker leaned unobtrusively beside a potted orchid. With

Bluetooth. She could fill the opulent room with opera, or haunting instrumental, or even just a comforting old ballad. Anything.

But Elspeth chose silence, because even her favorite song in the world was broken now. She couldn't guess how long before she'd be able to even think of listening to it again, much less singing.

The things she'd let herself do this past week forced her eyes closed. She'd gone on dates and climbed castles. She'd desecrated the burial grounds more than once. She'd let him eat her out on the bar of her family business! She'd let herself be wildly in love. She'd been bold. Demanding. Hungry. The words she'd said, the things she'd asked for, had been so good. Deeply good.

Elspeth felt her face crumple but refused tears a place.

It was done.

At least she knew now, she told herself, what it was possible to feel, how filled up she could be, how happy. She'd learned too much about grief the past three years not to get to learn bliss, too.

That's what she told herself.

A knock came at the outer door, through the bright sitting room. Elspeth had ordered ridiculous pink wine from the room service menu. It was all on Pella.

Standing, she smoothed the skirt over her thighs and went barefoot on the thick carpet to answer. Soon—after at least one massive glass of wine—she'd strip off the rest of her only business suit, and put on the new, glittering jumpsuit and high heels. They'd go for appetizers at this posh tapas place Kam liked, then walk two blocks to the museum.

Elspeth opened the door, tip in hand, and caught her breath to see Daniel Kelly standing there in his navy blue suit without the jacket, waistcoat accentuating his torso and shoulder, the shirtsleeves rolled *perfectly*. His hair flopped in his eye, not quite as perfect, which made it better, of bloody course. It was unfair for him to be so sexy. How dare she like it? How dare he make her want him still?

"I told you," she said, in her best prima donna tone, "I do not wish to see you gloat, or to see you at all."

She started to close the door, but he stepped in. "Please, Elspeth, please," he said. "I just want to say something, and if you hate it, I'll never bother you again."

He sounded desperate.

Good. Elspeth turned her back to him. She walked across the fine sitting room and knelt before the elegant chest of drawers hiding the minibar. She didn't have to wait for room service. "How did you even find me?" she demanded.

Daniel stood, one hand in his pocket, looking for all the world right at home in this fancy place. He winced.

"Oh," Elspeth said. "Right. Your company made the arrangements."

His bitter-chocolate eyes drilled into her. "I love you."

Elspeth sat back on her heels and stared up at him, trying to be unmoved, trying to hear anything else over the roar in her ears. She said nothing. Her mouth wanted to fall open in horror, but she didn't allow it. Her heart wanted to tear out of her chest, but she didn't allow that either. She wanted him to say it again. But she wouldn't give him the satisfaction.

"I should have told you yesterday," he continued in her silence. "Or when I realized it, at Dolwyddelan Castle."

She scoffed in defense, frustrated at how well he'd pronounced it. She could not think about standing with his arms around her in the hollowed-out keep. She'd remember her tender feelings, her fucking *happiness.*

Quietly, dangerously, she said, "*That* is not what you should have told me."

Daniel dropped into a crouch. His hands opened, pleading. "If I'd said I worked for Pella, it would have changed everything."

"Not as much as it does *now.*"

His anxious press of lips was so beautiful, Elspeth wanted to touch his jaw, where he needed a shave, and she knew how good that rough skin felt, so she imagined telling him to undo his pants and—

Closing her eyes, she said, "It's too late."

"It can't be. There must be something I can do, Elspeth, because I love you."

"Those words aren't a weapon!" she cried. She stood and went to the window, pressing her hand to the cold glass. Heat spread like a ghost around her fingers. Blurring out London and the clouds.

"I don't have any weapons," he said, standing, but staying back. "Not when it comes to you. I want you, and I know I should have told you. I should have done a lot of things. But after that first day, I didn't want to risk what we had. I'd lose you, and I've never wanted to keep someone this badly."

Leaning in, Elspeth put her forehead to the glass. She believed him. Her chest ached, her heart ached, because she believed him. She turned around, pressing her whole body against the window. Showing him how far away she needed to be. "But you don't respect me," she said. "If you did, you'd have told me who you work for."

Daniel shook his head. "You're wrong. I didn't tell you that because I'm a selfish bastard, not because I don't know you're amazing. You gave up so much for your family, you not only ran your business, but expanded—and dragged the whole village in. You have everyone's respect, Elspeth, not only mine. Everyone's. That's why they love you, and want you to be happy. And why I do."

"*You* cannot make me happy," she said, translating the line from a tragic opera. A hard aria of refusal. Elspeth swallowed. "There's no such thing as *no matter what*. It's over."

Another knock sounded at the door.

"That's my wine. Let them in, would you, and then go."

"Elspeth . . ."

"You used to pretend to *like* doing what I told you to do, so—so do it now." Elspeth went into the bedroom and sat on the chair beside the gilded vanity. She was shaking.

The knock came again. She listened. He moved too quietly, but there was his dark voice at the door, thanking the attendant, tipping him, and then . . . the door closed.

She breathed too hard, waiting, listening carefully. She prayed he was gone, but hoped, like a fool, that he'd stayed.

After a moment, Elspeth went into the sitting room. The wine service waited, elegant, silver, and so very lonely.

CHAPTER EIGHTEEN

THERE WAS no part of Daniel ready to play the charming American businessman for three hours at the British Museum, chatting about corporate nonsense and keeping to the *yes, Pella is expanding into world-improvement* party line. Usually he got through these things by flirting with literally everyone, from hot arm-candy to retired board members and everyone in between. There was even a movie star here tonight. After all, nobody hated being flirted with by a man who looked as good in a tux as Daniel Kelly, regardless of marital status or position on the sexuality spectrum.

Trouble was, tonight he didn't want to flirt, and had no backup strategy.

Everything running in the background turned back to Elspeth Elspeth Elspeth. How to win her back, when to try to see her again, how long did she need, where would she go, was there an Ordnance Survey somewhere he could study to build a road back to her?

Daniel was a goddamn wreck.

Harcourt and Godfrey had unpleasantly double-teamed him until he agreed to give a damned speech—*just the basic thank you folderol,* Godfrey said with a hand wave, and Harcourt frowned as he added, *but make it sexy* in the stuffiest possible way.

Valiantly refusing whiskey until after he talked, Daniel mingled with a single flute of champagne for the meet-and-greet portion of the evening. He'd never been to the British Museum before, and had to admit the massive party space and clean white walls were like the inner keep of a brilliant modern castle. The gala curved around the tower of the Reading Room, elegant tall tables decorated with pomegranates and ruffled flowers, and the lighting was warm orange and reddish, projecting oak leaves against the tower in falling motion that was mesmerizing if he stared too long while the brittle old woman in sequins with whom he was currently discussing something about tariffs went off on a tangent.

For a while Harcourt hustled him around, made him talk about the US side of Pella, and how smoothly the transitions had gone when Pella incorporated Kelly Pharma six years ago. Daniel wanted to remind everyone he'd been in fucking Anbar at the time, so it was all hearsay to him anyway.

He thought he saw Elspeth at least eight times.

It was the red-orange lights, surely, casting auburn shadows on every upswept bun or messy fall of curls.

He'd give anything for it to actually be her. She'd like the Lilah Rose photographs on display, most of which had the same kind of intimacy as the ones hanging on the wall at The Fort. Maybe she'd come—he knew Harcourt had invited her, but couldn't bring himself to ask the old man what she'd said. If she'd refused, it would only be because she hated him, and just the thought soured the champagne in his stomach.

When he was finally introduced to the stage by a dangerous-looking archeologist with broad shoulders, Daniel set his empty flute down and put on a minimal-watt smile. "Thanks for the intro," he said, leaning into the mic. The only pure light in the room glared hotly on him. He looked out, ready to cast a net of charm so it wouldn't matter what he actually said.

The entire place stared at him, gleaming eyes and rainbows of evening gowns, gray-black-blue suits and tuxes stock-still, with the servers silently moving among it all. Daniel's heart rate increased for no good reason. He got started.

"Pella started in 1863, not nearly old enough to have a place in this museum," he said. "But my family's company, Kelly Pharmacy, is even younger—though by American standards, we're ancient. Nearly a whole century since my great-grandfather founded it." He gave a quick few lines about the history of his family, and how the merger with Pella came about—the official version, having only to do with progress. Then he said, "So it really depends on who you're talking to whether something is old or new, exciting or dull. That's why perspective alone can make an endeavor worthwhile, and motivation drives progress. For a while, Kelly Pharma and Pella were motivated by science, agricultural politics, and, let's not forget, making money." He grinned, and was rewarded by scattered laughter. "But part of our integration has been coming to understand that the world itself has problems that only people with motivation, perspective, and resources can fix—or we're all doomed. Pella Group is dedicated to making sure we aren't doomed. And we're thrilled to have opportunities like this to create space for intellectual debate and scientific investigation into new ways to push worldwide agriculture with a real eye toward sustainability."

Applause interrupted him, and he paused.

That's when he saw her.

It was really her this time, not a phantom with red-glinting hair.

She'd come.

Elspeth stood beside one of the tall tables in a dark blue jumpsuit with a plunging neckline that hugged her glorious breasts and pinched in at her waist, falling in velvety lines over her round hips. Her bare shoulders were strong and pale, her neck was encircled by layers of sparkling chains he wanted to rip off to see her throat, to put his tongue there in worship.

Curls tumbled around her face, pinned up somehow, and worst of all, she was looking right at him with her big eyes. Not happy, not angry, not anything of passion. She looked devastated.

Daniel missed his cue as the applause faded, staring like he'd never seen beauty in his life, and every piece of him insisted he leap off the dais and go to her, take her away and make her have him. If he had to devour her inch by inch to do it.

He wasn't breathing right.

From two feet away, he heard Harcourt hiss his name.

Swallowing, Daniel gave the crowd his smile again, though his ears rang.

She was here.

"I . . ." he started, and it hung there, and shit, soon they'd all think he was drunk or an idiot.

He was one of those things.

Daniel's smile tilted, he felt the protection of it, his old cocked smile, and he said, "Only yesterday, Pella closed a deal to put down a new kind of local roots, on a much smaller than usual scale. But as you know, sometimes the best endeavors must start off with a seed. There's a village called Caerafon, about five hours' drive from here, in northern Wales. They're doing incredible work to open up old traditions and make way for innovation in small business. Farm-to-table initiatives, the kind only neighbors can arrange, people in a community who know what they need, who know what their land needs. So they're working with clean energy like those mountains deserve, and being as rebellious as I've recently learned the Welsh could always be when it comes to invaders. Invaders like me."

Below him, Elspeth started to back away.

"I met a woman," he said, looking right at her. "A woman not only trying to do everything for her family, her village, her land, but succeeding. And she taught me something about sustainability. It's a word we throw around a lot, but this woman, Elspeth Gwenlan, helped me see that you have to understand who you are in order to know how you fit into your community, or how you can make a better world. You have to face who you are before you can give best. And you have to understand who others are and what makes them special. Because real sustainability isn't going to be about any of the things we—Pella—already bring to the table. Perspective, motivation, and resources. It's going to be about figuring out what part we all can play in the future, the part that fits us best, and then fitting ourselves into the wider world, making it our mission to keep those connections—our relationships—with each other and the land—the planet—strong."

It was a mess, not what he'd intended to say at all.

Daniel shook his head. The speech didn't matter. Only Elspeth mattered. "This woman, I didn't tell her I had a stake in whether or not she sold her pub, her life, to Pella and let us come in to transform her village, our reputation. Change her life. I didn't tell her because the moment I saw her, I knew nothing about what *I* was mattered. She was gonna make her own future, and that was . . . spectacular. Who I thought I was, what I thought I wanted, that was irrelevant. She was *constant*. Real. You showed me who I can be, Elspeth." He laughed. It wasn't a fake laugh, built for charm, but the kind of soft, real laugh he couldn't hold back, the resulting chemical reaction to a truth he'd just realized. "You showed me who I *want* to be. That's like the refrain to a song, and you probably know it. I don't. If I did, I'd sing it right now, in front of all these people." He stepped back and spread his arms.

Elspeth shook her head. *Don't.*

"I won't, beautiful." Daniel glanced at Harcourt, who was blotchy red in the face. "Anyway, thanks for coming, enjoy the champagne—we have a lot to celebrate tonight."

With that, he strode down the shallow steps and away from the dais.

By the time he reached the table where she'd been, Elspeth was gone.

CHAPTER NINETEEN

ELSPETH GRABBED another flute of champagne from a tray of them perfectly balanced on the hand of a harried young server. She drank a third of it in one go, and nearly burped outrageously. She'd forgotten it was *champagne*.

Blinking her eyes at the discomfort, she kept moving—more like mincing—in her high heels. The soles were too slick for this expansive marble floor and dreamy red-shadow light. Daniel's voice had heated her body, turning her nipples and spine traitors. But that one word, *constant,* the thing he'd said to her at the castle, that's the word that took a detour along the way from her ears to her pussy, and encircled her heart.

Maybe her heart was a traitor, too.

Elspeth should've run straight out the entryway and hailed a taxi. Mum would understand, even if she and Kam had been having a good time. Mum knew what Daniel had done. She'd know that speech was just words, they didn't change anything. Couldn't.

Somebody else was giving a speech now, and she closed her eyes with relief at the nasal voice. She leaned against the dark information desk, sipping her champagne.

There she remained, until the speeches ended and a floor was cleared for dancing. The crowd shifted, and an old crooner came over the speakers. Elspeth knew she should move, or he'd find her.

Heading toward the Mesopotamian floor, she set her flute down. She'd be fine if she could only hide, or find somebody else, somebody hotter, to dance with.

The song changed.

She recognized "Voi che sapete" from *The Marriage of Figaro*.

It was not dancing music.

But it was the Mozart she'd sung for him that first day at the burial chamber.

Elspeth froze. Her eyes closed and she recalled so vividly the cold air on her flushed cheeks, her pulsing, post-orgasmic core, her rising hope, and Daniel's dark eyes.

Just thinking of it filled her with longing—and made her wet.

She listened to the entire song there at the edges of the crowd, knowing when she turned he'd be there. Knowing it. And while she stood still, not turning, she felt something she hadn't felt in years: stage fright.

Not the sweaty, nightmare kind, but the good, necessary thrill of fear at what-ifs and possibilities. The tension just before the curtain rose, just before she found out if she could do it this time, if she'd startle or cough or go sharp. It was the best feeling, one she and others at school had chased. Without it, performances fell flat or drifted into rote submission. A commanding performance required friction inside.

Oh God, she had it now. Friction aplenty.

Elspeth swallowed, and turned.

Daniel smiled with extreme solicitude. Then he bowed very slightly, and in his perfect tux, he was irresistible.

She drifted to him, took his hand, and he swept her onto the dance floor.

The music was back to crooning. Smooth jazz, with piano and steel brushes. George Michael. "Kissing a Fool."

Elspeth felt a wave of relief at identifying the song, as if knowing its name put her on even ground. Despite the subject matter. Then Daniel pulled her into his arms.

Her body pressed his, and the loose trousers of her jumpsuit flared around her ankles. She let her fingers slip along his hairline, and he leaned in. It was all right. She'd be all right.

There—Mum was dancing with Kam, and they'd shifted nearer. Mum gave her big-eyes, but Elspeth shook her head. In the slipping reddish lights, she saw her mum's smile curl with a little hope.

Elspeth closed her eyes. Her feelings were a mess, but her body knew what it wanted.

"I didn't know you'd be here," Daniel murmured, voice rumbling from his chest to hers. Indecently. She loved it. "But I'm glad you are."

"Your speech was a lot of bullshit," she whispered.

"Not all of it. Not the important parts."

"Sustainability is important."

"Not like you are."

Elspeth sighed into him. She put her cheek to his jaw, letting the whole length of her brush against him, and she felt it: he was hard.

He wove their fingers together, and as they moved—she shouldn't be surprised he was a good dancer—he pushed against her, backed away, spun her, pulled her back in, and slid his hand around her waist, finally pressing her firmly against him. It was delicious.

Elspeth rolled her hips a little, and in the dim red shadows of the dance floor, dragged her hand from his shoulder, down his chest, past the form-fitting cummerbund, and pressed it between them. She grabbed his cock and let go.

"Christ," he whispered.

She was ruining her knickers. Her very nice knickers, and the under-armor pressing her into the shape she'd needed for this jumpsuit. The lace cupping her breasts could hardly even be called a bra, and she wanted him to see it, wanted to see him see it.

Why shouldn't she take what she wanted? He certainly had.

"Come with me," she said, leaning in to lick his jawline.

Then she let go and walked away.

Elspeth was trembling.

If she did this, it would mean something: she couldn't give herself this and then let him go.

She stopped.

Daniel's hands landed gently on her shoulders, and he held her without pressing close. "Forgive me," he murmured.

When she moved on again he slid one hand down her arm and offered it to her. She let their fingers play together, walking close, too close together, and she ducked around a corner. Their footsteps echoed. They passed three people with champagne flutes looking at the Rosetta Stone, continued on, and Elspeth ducked left past sandstone griffons, into a long empty hall with nothing but ancient reliefs on the wall, meters and meters of them. She pulled Daniel on, her pulse picking up speed, a counterpoint to the tattoo of her heels on the stone floor. She turned again, onto tiles in a sea-foam green room with more reliefs and only very dim lighting.

"Here." Elspeth stopped, squeezing his hand. She turned and kissed him, arms sliding around his waist.

Daniel sighed into her, hands finding her ass. He pulled her tight.

She nudged past his lips, tasting the full flavor of heat and champagne on his tongue. Her body tingled, burned, with need and racing nerves. Her breath thinned and she nipped at his mouth, dragged her hands up his chest to his hair and held his head, fingernails digging. Daniel groaned and Elspeth arched her back, her breasts to his chest. Her heels put her center right over his, and she rubbed against his cock, her belly tight. Oh, this was dangerous, thrilling. She shivered and pushed harshly back from him.

Daniel gasped softly, reaching for her, but she put one hand out, stopping him.

His mouth looked crushed, he breathed past slightly parted lips, and when she met his gaze there was such longing in those dark eyes. Longing, lust, and . . . surrender.

As she stared, Daniel sank to his knees. He tilted his head, watching her the whole time, until his face angled up toward her, his wide hands splayed on his thighs. So put together, perfect in his tux but for a slight rumple where she'd dislodged the bowtie and the press of his cock ruining the crease of slacks.

Elspeth swallowed a moan. Her knees trembled and she managed to whisper, "Take it out for me."

"Elspeth," he answered hoarsely, a hand going automatically to his zipper.

She glanced out into the long hallway of reliefs. "I can see all the way to the exit. I'll see if anyone . . ." Elspeth looked back at him. "I want to see you. I want . . ." She licked her lips.

He nodded. Light from the hallway highlighted half his face, his shoulder and ruffled black hair; the other side was shadowed, fading into the other room. Daniel knelt in the threshold, where hall became room, stone became tile.

Elspeth felt her heart crashing in her chest. She could still hear the distant music from the gala.

Daniel flicked open his pants, slowly unzipped, and his fingers disappeared into the silky-looking waistband of his knickers. Elspeth held her breath as he touched himself, drawing his cock free for her.

She bit her lip, hard, and crossed her arms, holding her own elbows to keep herself together.

Air hissed through Daniel's teeth as he gave himself a stroke, then another, tentative and gentle, it seemed to her. He toyed with his tip, eyelashes fluttering but he held her gaze even as his cheeks reddened, as his teeth gleamed in the half-light.

Elspeth leaned back against the wide wall of the doorway, the only part of the wall free of ancient art. She kept her attention on him, holding herself, aware of the empty hall, aware of being alone but oh-so-close to other people, to dancers, to the gala, to her mum. Sweat broke out along her spine; she wanted to fall forward and suck him off herself, taste his cock on her tongue, swallow him up. She whispered, "I want to swallow you up, Daniel Kelly."

His hips lurched, and he worked faster. "I wish I had some of your heat on me, slicking me."

"There's so much for you," she said, panting a little. Her pussy ached, all her desire dripping to her core to gather in a hard knot. She didn't give in, didn't press a hand there over her jumpsuit, just watched him, aching and longing. It felt so good.

"Elspeth," he said breathlessly, both hands around himself, one deeper than the other, hidden in his pants, the other working the shaft and crown almost frantically.

"Daniel," she answered, letting her suffering through in a soft moan.

"What do you—want—me to do?"

"Come, darling, right now," she whispered, leaning eagerly forward, ass propped on the wall so she didn't collapse.

His jaw clenched and his eyes widened before squeezing closed and he hissed again, his entire body wracked with orgasm. He caught some of the cum, but it smeared along his waistcoat, along the inner jacket, and Daniel sagged back opposite her, sinking onto his heels, his back and head leaning on the wall. His shoulders heaved and shuddered, the lashes of his closed eyes flickered; he took a deep breath and his lips relaxed. He looked relaxed. Peaceful. Both hands covering himself but for just the slightest hint of the crown of his cock.

Elspeth shook with desire, and power, and love. She stared down at him and felt so alive. Like she'd just performed the greatest show of her life, the kind that echoed forever, forwards and backwards, changing who she'd been every day before, and who she'd become every day in the future.

"I love you, too," she said.

Daniel sucked in a breath, his entire person suddenly alert. He stood, awkwardly wiping his hands in his pockets, and putting himself away. He reached for her but stopped.

Elspeth nodded. She meant it. "Let's get you to the washroom."

He stepped into her path, using his body, not his hands, not touching her. "Will you . . . take off your necklace?"

Lifting her eyebrows, she did, fumbling slightly as the heavy ropes of glass slid down her collar and she caught it.

Daniel moved closer, and Elspeth caught her breath again, aching everywhere. She was so hot and wet she couldn't believe herself, and her eyes drifted closed as he pressed nearer, bending his head to touch his lips to her neck.

Elspeth sighed long and hard, so very pleased at the soft heat of his mouth, and his tongue as he pressed it to her throat, kissing along the ring where the necklace had been. "I love you," he said against her skin.

Together they looked for the washrooms. Elspeth walked as quickly as she could; each step was friction on her thighs, tightening and loosening her desire. She leaned against him, and he kissed her temple.

They had to move through the gala again, but didn't stop, didn't sway or accept another drink. When Daniel paused at the entrance to the men's room, he leaned in and said quietly in her ear, "Come in with me. You haven't gotten off."

Elspeth shivered with pleasure. "I like it," she said.

His laugh was low, his breath hot.

"I do." She turned her face and kissed his jaw. She licked his bottom lip. "It feels unfinished. Full of potential."

For a moment Daniel said nothing, then he ducked his head and caught her gaze. "You don't want to be finished."

"Not with you," she confessed.

His mouth found hers and he swallowed her words, lips pulling into too much of a smile for the kiss to be good—instead it was perfect. She felt his teeth and remembered his broad wolf grin.

Elspeth rubbed her cheek along his, and said, "Go clean up. I want to dance again."

"And again and again?"

"As long as we like."

"I'd like to have forever," Daniel said softly.

She leaned back and touched his lips as they curved into that smile. "Keep saying that, and I think you might just get it. Now go—come back fast."

Daniel broadened his wolfish smile and obeyed.

ALSO BY TESSA GRATTON

NIGHT SHINE

STRANGE GRACE

Novels of Innis Lear:
THE QUEENS OF INNIS LEAR
LADY HOTSPUR

The Blood Journals:
BLOOD MAGIC
THE BLOOD KEEPER

The Gods of New Asgard:
Book One: THE LOST SUN
Book Two: THE STRANGE MAID
Book Three: THE APPLE THRONE
Novellas:
GOLD RUNNER
LADY BERSERK
GLORY'S TEETH
collected as THE WEIGHT OF STARS

ABOUT THE AUTHOR

Tessa Gratton is the author of adult and young adult fantasy novels including *The Queens of Innis Lear* and *Lady Hotspur* from Tor Books, and the YA original fairy tales *Strange Grace* and *Night Shine* from McElderry Books. Tessa's critically acclaimed novels and short stories have been translated into twenty-two languages. Though she has lived all over the world, she currently resides at the edge of the Kansas prairie with her wife. *Naughty Brits* is her inaugural foray into writing romance, and she is thrilled to be here.

Visit her at tessagratton.com.

You can sign up for Tessa's newsletter here: https://tinyletter.com/TessaGratton

SUPPLICANT

SIERRA SIMONE

HE'S LATE.

(James Church Cason is never late.)

He's stuck in traffic. He's lost. Something happened.

(Nothing keeps Church from what he wants. Ever.)

He loves me. He wouldn't do this to me.

(But do I *know* that? Beyond a shadow of a doubt? Do I really know him well enough to say?)

He's not coming.

And on that point, I'm forced to finally face the truth.

He's not coming.

"Would you like to try him again?" the woman next to me asks kindly, nodding down at the phone in my hand. She's a stranger—someone employed by the church to facilitate wedding ceremonies—and her warmth and concern are blistering. I'm blistered with it. My face is hot, my eyes are seared with unshed tears, my voice is burnt and dry when I speak.

"No, thank you," I rasp. "I think—I think it won't do much good. I'm so sorry, but do you have any water?"

I hate the tenderness in her eyes when she nods, because it brings me that much closer to breaking, and I can't break. I won't. Not yet and not here. I look over at my little brother, twelve and fidgeting in his tuxedo, his blue eyes wide with worry. I offer him a wobbly smile.

"It's going to be okay," I say, reaching out to squeeze his hand. "At least no boring ceremony to sit through, hey?"

He looks like he's about to cry, and that also brings me closer to the brink, so I look away. Through the cracked door that separates the narthex from the nave.

There's only a smattering of people inside—fifteen, maybe, in a church that could seat five hundred. They're all here for me—fellow volunteers at the museum and friends from college. No family other than Jax, because our mother died a few years back and our father is a piece of shit who'd rather get stoned than do anything else.

No one is here for Church. No one. There's no sight of his parents, his brother, the niece who was supposed to be the flower girl, the sister who was supposed to do a reading. No friends. No other sharply dressed professors or sun-drenched archaeologist types.

Stupid, Charley. You've been stupid.

The vicar clears his throat and begins making his way down the aisle to me, to the great interest of the worried guests, and when he slips in through the door, he takes my hand.

"My dear," he starts, and he doesn't have to finish. He's been waiting up by the altar for almost an hour. I know what he's going to say.

"Yes," I say. "I should—I need to go."

"Of course," he says, just as kindly as the event planner had. "I'll tell the guests. Something vague, naturally."

Well, he could hardly be specific, could he? Since even *I* don't know why my wedding is missing its groom.

"Thank you," I say. My eyes are burning something fierce, and I know I only have minutes before I disintegrate. "Is there a side door I can—"

The event planner returns with a cup of water and an expression of supreme discomfort. "Ms. Tenpenny," she starts, using the water as an excuse not to meet my gaze, "there is a driver out front—your fiancé's driver."

There's a collective wince as we all think the same thing. Is someone still your fiancé after they leave you at the altar?

"Er, Mr. Cason's driver, I mean," she hurriedly revises. "He says Mr. Cason sent him to give you a ride to your home."

Church sent his driver.

On our wedding day.

To take me back to my place.

"Oh, did he?" I say. Softly.

A blunt, iron ball of anger sinks through all the hurt, through all the embarrassment and vulnerability, sinks right into the pit of my stomach. My anger will anchor me to the earth, it will keep me from floating away, and so I hold on to it with eager hands. Because Church doesn't get to have this. He doesn't get to have helping me, he doesn't get to have a *gesture*, no matter how pitifully small it is. He doesn't get to feel good about a single damn part of today, he doesn't get the satisfaction of looking back on the day he left a bride alone to be humiliated and heart-broken and think *but at least I took care of her.*

No.

He doesn't get that. Especially when it's coupled with waving his family's obscene wealth in my face at the same time.

I take a drink of the water the planner brought and then hand it back to her. I take Jax's hand in mine and meet the vicar's concerned stare. "So is there a side door?"

It turns out that I used the last of my pride on turning down the driver. I gathered my things into a holdall and left the church without bothering to change, which meant shoving my fluffy white skirt and petticoats through the narrow turnstiles at the Tube station, and having my little brother hold the train of my gown on the escalator so it wouldn't catch at the bottom. And then we rode the Tube home in silence, me trying not to cry and Jax practically vibrating with confused adolescent worry.

He was going to walk me down the aisle.

Now he's helping me jam my wedding dress in and out of Tube-car doors and turnstiles.

Of course he's worried.

What comes next? I have no idea. All my plans for the last few months started and ended with Church, with the dark-haired god in suits so crisp they made the rest of the world seem soft. Compared to those sapphire eyes and that hungry mouth, nothing else seemed to matter: not my terrible, barely there dad, not my little brother growing increasingly lost and uninterested in school, not the bills piling up on our kitchen table. With Church, I'd been able to pretend that everything would be okay, because how *wouldn't* it be okay in the arms of a man like him?

Jesus. What a fool I've been.

Not for the first time, I wish I had friends. Real friends, not just a handful of people who know my name and vaguely wish me well.

I'd ask them if I'd been oblivious. Naïve .

After all, in what world did Charley Tenpenny—a destitute college student with an American accent—have to offer a man like him? Other than hours and hours of dark, delicious sex?

I blow out a long breath as Jax and I climb the stairs to our dank, tiny flat.

I won't think of the sex. I won't think of the way Church's fingers felt wrapped around my hips or curling inside me. I won't think of how wild those blue eyes would look when they lit on me, as if the mere sight of me turned him into an animal. *My angry god,* I'd whisper in his ear, leaning in close so he could feel my lips brush against his skin. *My temple. My Church.* And then I'd be seized and dragged to the nearest appropriate place for fucking. Sometimes even not that appropriate, because he could never wait.

You are my church, he'd growl in response as he pinned me against the first convenient surface and took me. His voice would be smoky and carnal. *You are all I see. All I pray.*

Unholy obsession. Hard sex. When he proposed, it felt like a fairy tale.

How could I have been so stupid? Men like him don't marry the girls they fuck in corners.

But then why did he buy me a ring? A dress? Why did he call me Charlotte Cason, as if I were already his wife?

The flat's door is hanging open when we reach it, and I'm jerked out of my thoughts so fast I nearly lose my breath. Dust swirls in the weak light coming in through the kitchen window, and from here I can detect the stale beer-and-cigarettes smell that suffuses our home. Our life. Our nasty, tattered life.

How did I ever think I could be Mrs. Cason?

"Charley?" Jax asks uncertainly.

Jax. You have to focus for your brother.

"Wait here, buddy," I tell him, handing him my phone. "Call 999 if I'm not back out in just a minute, okay?"

He nods, scared, and it's for his sake, all for him, that I muster up a wobbly smile and then push through the opened door, my wedding dress brushing against the old, stained carpet as I do.

"Dad?" I call out, expecting to see him asleep on the sofa or perhaps stumbling out of the back bedroom, stoned and bleary.

There's only silence.

I check the kitchen and the bathroom, then mine and Jax's room, and then his room. There's no one here. "It's okay, kiddo," I call out, and then turn back to look at Dad's room again, noticing for the first time what's missing.

His clothes. His phone charger.

The keys to the only car we have.

Dread claws its way up to my spine—dread just as terrible and carnivorous as standing in a church waiting for a groom who will never come—and I go back into my room and lift up my mattress.

My meager savings—scraped together from working at a café near my school and stuffed into a worn envelope—are gone. I don't need to look at my banking app to know that my account—shared with my dad—is cleaned out too. The shared account was the very reason I'd needed to stuff money under the bed, in case there came a month when we needed extra to cover rent or food because Dad had spent everything else on booze or bets or worse. It happened regularly enough that I never could build up a healthy reserve, but still, I'd managed to put enough under the mattress to supplement my tuition fees for next semester.

And now there won't be enough. Not for school, and maybe not for rent either, and oh God. I haven't just lost Church today, I think maybe . . .

Maybe I've lost everything.

Not just a future with him, but a future at all.

What am I going to do?

Focus. Focus for Jax.

"Is Dad gone?" Jax asks, his voice too solemn for such a sweet boy. "He . . . left?"

It's too much. I nod, my chin quavering and my throat aching, and then I sink onto my bed. The white skirts of my wedding dress rustle and fluff around me.

"Do you want a hug?" Jax asks, looking like he needs it more than me.

Openly crying now, I open my arms and draw my little brother into the world's longest, teariest hug, no longer able to stop the sobs from tearing through my body.

Tomorrow.

Tomorrow, I will be brave. Tomorrow, I will focus.

I'll unenroll from UCL, I'll quit volunteering at the British Museum because a resume for a career that needs a graduate degree to get started is now the least of my worries.

I'll get a job, or two or three. I'll find us a cheaper flat and buy us good food and make sure Jax is on time to school every day. I'll be the sister and guardian Jax deserves.

And I will never, ever forgive Church Cason.

But all of that is tomorrow, and right now it's today, and so I weep. I clutch my brother close and I let every single moment of agony rip through my chest and out of my throat. I give in to every horrible, self-hating thought I have, I curse myself for being stupid and poor and plain, and I curse Church for being perfect and cruel and wealthy enough to send a driver when he couldn't be bothered to show up himself. I cry until I'm lightheaded and swollen-eyed and exhausted. I cry a thousand tears for every second I stood alone waiting for Church and for every pound note my asshole father stole from me and for every class I won't get to take.

Tomorrow, I'll be furious. Tomorrow, I'll become the icy warrior I'll need to survive.

But today, when I cry, I cry for a broken heart.

And for a man with dark, dark blue eyes and a voice like smoke and sin.

CHAPTER ONE

FOUR YEARS LATER

"Stop chatting and go faster on the champagne," Martin snaps as he shoves by. "They're drinking it faster than you're serving it."

"It's a gala for celebrities and society twats, what do you expect?" Twyla mutters, rolling her eyes at me and obviously not caring if he sees. She's a server with Hart Catering like me, but she's only doing it as a nights-and-weekends gig when she's not in class, and really, it's only to prove some kind of point to her parents, who are always begging to send her money. She only needs this job in an abstract sense, and so she tends to get mouthy with Martin The Boss.

Not me. As much as I'd love to give Martin a piece of my mind, I need Hart Catering because it dovetails perfectly with my days working at a supermarket—and I require both to keep paying bills.

Ergo, I keep my eyes down and my mouth shut.

Two more years. Two more years and Jax will be off to university and maybe something will change. Maybe I can go back to school. I'll be twenty-six then, it won't be *too* weird, right? The other students won't look at me like I'm pathetic? Or a pensioner? Like I've missed my chance and now I'm doomed to work at Tesco forever?

Here's the thing.

I never let myself dwell on Church and what he did to me. I never let myself admit—even in the privacy of my own mind—that I might still be in love with him. That I'm still nursing my broken heart because the broken heart is all I have left.

But sometimes—when I'm exhausted from working two full-time jobs plus parenting a hormonal teenager, when Martin is being a real dick, when the bills are piled so high I think they'll bury me—I let myself dwell on what life would have been like if Church had shown up on our wedding day. If he'd married me and then whisked me and Jax off to his Chelsea townhouse, so I'd be free from paying rent and could keep paying tuition.

If I'd graduated with the degree I wanted and was working for the museum where I'm currently passing out canapés instead.

If my days were filled with kisses like good gin—clean and cool and biting.

If my nights were filled with gasping, uncivilized fucks.

Stop. It.

That's the danger of dwelling on the future I wanted—it turns into pining for the man who took so much of it away. I make myself remember the gutting, lonely moments alone in the narthex, the slow heat of the tears when I realized he wasn't coming. When I realized that I'd been made a fool of—and worse.

When I realized I loved someone more than he loved me.

There's no word for stupidity that profound.

I pop open a bottle and start pouring, and Martin fusses off somewhere else in the back room, probably to scold someone else for being slow. Twyla snags one of the flutes I've just filled and knocks it back in one go.

"Come on," she coaxes as she sees my small smile. "Have one. Fuck knows this is the best shit we'll get to taste in a while."

I want to. I really, really want to. I want to have a glass of champagne and disappear into some of my favorite exhibits and forget—just for twenty minutes—that my life is a sleepless grind of work and debt and putting on a brave face for Jax, who needs to have as normal an upbringing as I can manage.

I stare at the bubbling flute for a moment, and then I sigh. "With my terrible luck, Martin will smell it on me."

"Ah yes," Twyla says, grabbing another flute as I open up a new bottle. "This mysterious bad luck of yours. Are you ever going to tell me about it?"

What would I even say?

It's nothing, really. Just got left at the altar by a scowling god—a god who still rules over the university department I had to leave because I was too broke. Oh, yes, he was my professor too, how thoughtful of you to ask.

It would make a great party story. If only I had time for parties.

Blocking Twyla's reach for a third flute, I slide the now-full tray onto my hand. "It's a tale for when we have something a lot stronger than champagne," I say with a forced grin, and then I push out the door and follow the faint strains of music to the Great Court and the event itself.

***

THE GALA IS in full swing now, the autumn sky just beginning to fade over the glass canopy that covers the court. The conversation and music together make for a dull, boozy roar in the echoing space.

I fix my *of course I'm happy to carry a heavy tray around* smile on my face and begin circulating through the room, unloading flutes at a rate that would horrify Martin all over again. With each step, the second-hand shoes I'm wearing pinch my toes and send pain rolling up the balls of my feet and into my heels, but still I keep the smile plastered on. Martin won't care if my feet hurt, but if there's one whiff of bad attitude among the staff, he'll unleash hell, and I can't afford hell. Not for another two years, at any rate.

I play one of my favorite games while I circulate to keep myself from focusing on my feet, where I pretend I'm David Attenborough observing the habits of rich people. Silently, I narrate all the elaborate mating and dominance rituals unfolding around me; I describe the elaborate plumage of the subjects, their bizarre status symbols and hierarchical negotiations.

It's a game I've been playing since I went through a fervent Attenborough stage after my first anthropology course at UCL, and sometimes Church and I would even play it togeth—

Nope. No Church. Just Attenborough. The one man who could never let me down.

I'm gestured over by a pale woman in a ball gown, her eyes glued to someone younger, prettier, and possibly more interesting than her, given the way the younger woman seems to be holding court in the semi-circle of people in which they are standing. The older woman's eyes never leave her rival as she efficiently plucks a glass of champagne from my tray, and the younger woman, who clearly is paying more attention than she lets on, reaches over and does the same, so that they're matching each other flute for flute like antagonistic cowboys matching each other shot for shot in an old Western film.

Here is the cold-blooded society maven forced to defend her committee territory from a young upstart. The upstart will have a name like Summer or Vervain, and the maven will make sure to say it as often as possible to highlight how ridiculous her very existence is. Both will use the champagne as a way to buy time for the next cutting remark.

I leave the maven and Summer/Vervain to move along the curve of the Reading Room wall, which is practically glowing against the darkening sky outside. I approach a group of men and women who are all dressed crisply and conservatively and arguing vehemently about the impact of the Asian markets on pharmaceutical investments.

Bankers. A totally different tribe than the maven and her rival.

I hand out flutes as I narrate—the voice in my head sounding like Attenborough's, old and wise and fond. *Jostling for status, these young and hungry creatures must always be looking for prey, even at a gala—*

My narration is interrupted by the slow fade of the music and a tide of polite applause. And then a voice I never thought I'd hear again rolls through the court, amplified by a microphone.

"Good evening," Professor Church Cason says.

Those few syllables—smoky and burned around the edges—spark fires everywhere inside me. Fires of panic and shock and sizzling lust.

I freeze next to the bankers, who take my stillness and the oncoming speech as an invitation to relieve me of the rest of my champagne.

Church continues, his voice coming from someplace I can't see, his words effortless and casual, like he's not slicing me open with every single one of them. "On behalf of the Institute of Archaeology at UCL, the Friends of the British Museum, and the Pella Group, thank you for coming here tonight to support Common Harvest. It's our hope that programs teaching students about the history of food sustainability and food culture will help shape contemporary attitudes to food and agriculture, as well as increase awareness and support of sustainable farming around the globe. We're all here because we're invested in the future of Common Harvest, this museum, and our young people. And because we like free drinks," he adds dryly. Everyone laughs, as if they didn't donate an obscene amount of money to be here. Those *free* drinks are probably worth hundreds of pounds a pop.

Tray picked clean by the banker-hyenas, I start sidling away, the Attenborough narration in my head completely silent, my own thoughts completely silent, everything gone except for Church's voice and the thud of my heart. He continues to speak as I angle away from the Reading Room to head back to where the caterers have staged. He gives some kind of introduction to tonight's big donor, and I think I'm going to make it without actually having to see him. I'll escape without having to see him in a tuxedo—not unlike what he should have been wearing that day four years ago.

But I don't make it.

There's more applause, and my new vantage means that I'm able to see the raised stage near the entrance to the Ancient Egypt exhibit. I'm able to see Church—so much of Church. So much of that thick, dark hair I used to pull on, so much of those powerful shoulders testing the seams of his tuxedo. He's turned away from me, he's shaking hands with another man who could rival Church in tuxedo-seam-testing, now he's stepping down right into the arms of—*oh*.

Oh.

A woman—tall and blond and in her thirties like him—hugs him briefly before giving him a soft kiss on the lips, a kiss which Church permits but doesn't return. She pulls back from him and gives him a happy smile, already talking, and he gives her an unreadable expression as he leads her away from the stage where the handsome donor begins his speech about his corporation and why they care about food sustainability and research. Tax write-offs, one would assume, but he can hardly admit that to a party of schmoozy do-gooders.

I don't know what line he ends up feeding the crowd, because I'm not actually listening to a word he's saying. My attention is solely on Church and his blonde.

I want to hate this woman currently lacing arms with my ex-fiancé. In fact, the hate is right there at my fingertips, burning against the cool tray and begging to be unleashed.

Hate for her. Hate for him.

Hate for this terrible, itchy white shirt that marks me as staff and not as a guest, not as someone who matters.

But even as I force myself to take a step to the side—and then another, and another, until I finally have to tear my eyes away and watch where I'm going—the Attenborough in my mind can't help but be fair to his date. As pretty and well-turned out as she is, she's clearly not a society maven or a Vervain or a banker. Like Church, her skin is the kind of half-tan that comes from a fair person spending days and weeks outside. And though she seems comfortable in her dress and heels, she's without lipstick or painted nails. She's approached even more than Church is as they step away from the stage, and her friendly demeanor and immediate engagement with everyone who comes up to her is disarming.

No, she's not a Vervain. If I had to guess, she's another archaeologist or professor. Like I should have been.

It's not her fault. None of this is her fault. I'm just jealous that she's on the receiving end of kisses and amusement. That she gets to hear that low voice in her ear when she comes.

I decide I can still hate Church though. That seems fair.

I have to go.

I can't go.

But I don't know how I'm going to make it through the rest of tonight with Church here breathing the same air as me. Leaving isn't an option —I'm not Twyla, who's only a tourist in the Land of Unpaid Bills—I actually live there and I can't risk losing a job as steady as the one I have at Hart.

But I also can't face him. I can't be close to him, I can't talk to him, I can't pretend to be okay while he plucks a champagne flute off my tray.

If he sees me and he ignores me, I'll die. If he tries to talk to me, I'll die.

If he looks at me, and in those dark blue eyes I see any combination of regret or pity or indifference—I'll die.

How the hell am I going to survive the rest of tonight?

I can't help it; I turn back around.

It's not like this is the last time I'll ever see him; if I listen to my pride or my bank account or my self-discipline, I'll be back out here with a fresh tray in just a minute anyway—although I'll definitely be avoiding him and his pretty date if I can help it.

No, this isn't about pride or holding my ground or proving something to myself. This isn't about strength. It's about one moment—just *one*, haven't I earned that much?—of weakness.

Church is turned in my direction now, listening to someone who's chattering away at his date as said date chatters back and rubs an absentminded hand up and down his arm. He's wearing the expression he wore the day we met here at this very museum—an expression like he's waiting to be intellectually and morally disappointed by the person he's listening to. His sharp-edged mouth is in a neutral line that might pull into an irritated frown at any moment, and his jaw works ever so subtly to the side, as if it's trying his patience simply to exchange the usual social mundanities. The lights have begun transitioning to muted reds and oranges as the cocktail tables are discreetly moved to the sides to allow for dancing, and even in autumnal event lighting, he is arresting.

Arresting. Not perfect. Not beautiful. The unforgiving mouth and stern features preclude beauty; the scar slashing across his cheek from a dig accident in Jordan makes him look cruel and ruthless, which he is.

I should know.

I've often wondered if there's something wrong with me, some kind of masochistic sequence in my DNA that's somehow managed to defy evolution and common sense and lead me right into the arms of a man who could eat my heart raw . . . and did.

Even now, after he cracked my soul open, poured petrol inside, and lit me on fire, I want him. Every cruel and terrible part of him. His brilliance and his disdain and his carnality hiding underneath it all. His rough voice and midnight eyes and the way his need for me always seemed to stun him, like he hadn't planned on me but once he'd had me, there would be no getting enough, no possible satiation. I was his to consume and his hunger was infinite, like a god's.

What would Attenborough say about that, I wonder? Are there animals in the wild who willingly snuggle up to the bigger animals who want to eat them? Are there bunnies that can't help but hop after snarling foxes? Big-eyed deer that nuzzle against the throats of wolves?

No, of course not. There's only museum-loving girls who fall obliviously and deliriously in love with their brutally depraved professors.

I hate him, of course, I'll hate him forever for lying to me, for humiliating me, for shredding my heart in an unfamiliar narthex with only an event planner and my baby brother for comfort—but I could never hate him for that depravity. Or his indifference, or his arrogance. They were the things that made me fall in love with him, senseless bunny that I was, and even now as I'm watching him barely rein in his impatience with gala small talk, I can't help but fall in love with him again, just a little bit. Just with that crisp tuxedo and with the way the reddish gala lighting makes his restless gaze a deep violet hue. Just with that mouth that used to mark sin and possession all over me in between murmured lectures about ancient religion.

It's in this single moment of weakness, this one moment I've given myself in *four years* to remember how beautiful and daunting he is, that his eyes meet mine and he sees me.

He sees me.

His face goes from bored to stunned to avid to angry in the space of a heartbeat—in the space of *my* heartbeat, as my heart surges once in my chest and then begins frantically beating out a tattoo of fury and retreat. A message even my dumb bunny brain can understand.

Go.

Flee.

Before you kill him.

Church says something to his date and their conversant, and then begins pushing his way through the crowd toward me, determination carving his proud features into something equal parts sexy as hell and terrifying as fuck.

I see the moment his eyes rake over me completely, when he takes in the catering uniform and the empty tray in my hand. More shock ripples through him, followed by more determination, his mouth sharpening into a blade as he cuts toward me through the crowd.

Go, you stupid bunny, the Attenborough in my mind chides me, and I finally listen, unfreezing and darting towards the hallway, looking over my shoulder just once to see Church moving faster, walking with long, powerful strides.

"Charlotte," I see him say. Growl. I know it's a growl even though I can't hear him over the music and the hobnobbing. His dark eyebrows are pulled together and his hands are flexing at his sides, like he's itching to grab me and hoist me over his shoulder like he used to do before the wedding. I used to joke that studying primitive history had made him primitive indeed, and he'd simply smile back and dare, *but tell me you don't like it, little supplicant,* and I never could tell him that, because I did, I did like it. I liked everything we ever did together until the day I had to ride the Tube home in my wedding dress, and then I liked nothing ever again.

The truth is that I'm a mean, tired, furious bunny—a little supplicant turned apostate and unbeliever—and I'm not hiding because I'm scared. I'm running from him because if he catches me, I will kill him.

I will scratch out his eyes while reciting passages from the Egyptian Book of the Dead, I will hum Latin hymns while I bite his heart out. I don't care what kind of god he is, he is a dead god to me, and I will build a temple to bitterness out of his bones. He will be my burnt offering and I will send that smoke all the way to heaven. I will char the world with the pride he stole from me.

Stay away, Church.

Don't you dare.

I duck down the hallway, but I know Church and I know he'll follow me right back to the kitchens if he has to, and so I set my tray against the wall, accept the annoying possibility that Martin might upbraid me later, and then scurry through a narrow door that spits me back out into the Great Court. And then I jog into the exhibits, pushing past the scattered gala-goers in Egypt and Greece until I get to the empty stairs, and I can climb up to the deserted upper galleries to wait him out. There's no one up here, and my footsteps echo loudly on the wood floors as I move from Ancient Levant to Ancient Mesopotamia.

I think I lost him.

Thank God; it would be extra awkward to explain to Martin why I abandoned my champagne-slinging duties and also murdered a guest. Hart would lose its catering contract with the museum for sure, and I'd probably be fired. You know, after the trial for homicide.

I stop in front of a case displaying a cuneiform tablet, and I allow myself to breathe all the breaths I couldn't earlier. I stare blankly at my pale reflection in the glass, not bothering to absorb either the smudges under my eyes, or the tight, scraped-back ponytail I have to wear for the event, or even the clay tablet itself. I just breathe and will my heart to stop hammering against the walls of my chest.

I don't have to kill Church. I don't have to see him.

I don't have to remember all over again why I fell in love with him.

Slowly, too slowly for comfort, my pulse begins to slow and the adrenaline begins to dissolve in my blood. Exhaustion takes its place, and tears sting pointlessly at the backs of my eyes. When will it end? When will I be free? I suddenly wish I *had* left London four years ago like I made him think; I wish I'd fought harder to get Jax and me back to America so I'd never have to see or think or *feel* about Church Cason ever again.

Hot tears start rolling down my face, and I hate them, I hate the wet slide of them, I hate how I'm weak and angry and empty and it's from the mere sight of him. The mere presence of him.

Dammit.

I swipe at the tears and suck in a shuddering breath—and that's when I hear his low, furious voice.

"Hiding from me, little supplicant?"

CHAPTER TWO

CHARLEY

FIVE YEARS AGO, I'd been a baby museum volunteer, tasked to shadow one of the docents giving a private tour of the Mesopotamian and Levantine galleries. Except said docent suddenly took ill—the kind of violent, stomach-cramping ill that can't be endured anywhere except on a toilet —and I was stuck giving the tour with no training and barely any detailed familiarity with the objects on display.

The added joy? The tour group was a cluster of visiting *history professors*. You know, the exact group of people who would notice I had no idea what the hell I was talking about.

But I made the most of it. We'd had a section on Mesopotamia in my Neolithic Revolution course the previous semester, and so I faked it pretty well, adding in a few jokes and dimple-buttoned smiles to make the most of my sunny Americanness. By the middle of the tour, everyone seemed charmed, except for a lone, scowling professor in the back. Church.

I found out later that he'd drawn the short straw in his department and was tasked with babysitting the out-of-town colleagues while they were in the Big Smoke for a conference. For a reserved man like Church, not only was spending the day with a group of strangers nigh on unbearable, but subjecting him to a tour of a British Museum gallery was akin to subjecting Vermeer to a primary school art class. Church had dug things out of the ground that now resided in the museum; they'd consulted him when reworking their Religion and Belief narrative. There was nothing a second-year undergrad could tell him about the galleries that he didn't already know so well he could put the actual curators to shame.

It was near the end, when I was pleasantly bluffing my way through a description of a Babylonian tablet depicting a naked, winged goddess, when Church finally asked a question.

"Why?" he asked in his low voice.

I paused my bullshitting, my brain stuttering at the interruption. "Pardon?"

"Why," Church asked, putting a hand into the pocket of suit trousers too expensive for a professor to be wearing, "did the Babylonians do this? What was the instinct that drove them to mold Ishtar onto this tablet? Why do you think they needed to depict her—or any deity for that matter?"

It was an unfair question to ask any volunteer docent, no matter how seasoned, and the other professors seemed to know it, shifting uncomfortably and starting to make noises like they were going to answer on my behalf.

Except I found myself answering before I could think better of it. "I think that's a reductive question. Sir," I added, so I wouldn't seem too rude. But really. It was a stupid question, on top of a *mean* question, and it was clearly designed to embarrass me. It didn't matter how well this scowling jerk wore a suit or how narrow his waist seemed under all that sleek, tailored wool. Or how devastatingly sexy that scar looked running down his chiseled cheek.

Nope. Not having it. Not even from the embodiment of every dirty professor fantasy I'd ever had.

Church's lips had parted the tiniest bit at my challenge, and then he'd drawn his lower lip between his teeth for the barest instant at the word *sir*. Like hearing me say that word was enough to make him hungry and ever so slightly unsure at the same time.

I managed to drag my stare from his mouth to his eyes as I decided to say more. I wasn't a total dumbass about this shit, and also fuck him. "What comes first, deity or depiction? Depiction forces us to manifest the god into reality. Trying to diagnose the *why* of depiction misses the better question of *how*—how did these gods actually become gods? How did the Mesopotamians leapfrog from faceless pillars at Göbekli Tepe to the fully realized form of Ishtar here on this tablet?"

The other professors murmured in approval, but Church seemed to notice them not at all. He stepped forward, blue eyes alight and mouth twitching at the corner. Not quite like a smile, but like—well, like he was enjoying himself a little. I got the feeling he was surprised by this, that he was planning on being both disappointed and vindicated in his own superiority by my answer, and the fact that I hadn't just rolled over and given him an easy victory was . . . pleasing.

But his intense stare and cruel mouth made it very clear that he would have a victory from me of some sort. And boy if that didn't make my lower belly flutter just the tiniest bit, if it didn't make the Attenborough in my mind notice how primed I was to receive his mating display of intellectual feathers.

"So, Charlotte," he said, reading my name off the tag pinned to my blouse.

"Charley," I corrected with my dimples out, partly to goad him (he didn't seem like the type to indulge in nicknames, not for himself and not for other people) and also partly because I wanted him to know. I wanted to hear him grate it out against my neck while he fucked me. I blushed a little at this realization, which he noticed.

The corner of his mouth twisted even more; the fox had just seen how little self-preservation this bunny actually had when it came to asshole professors.

Hell, the bunny was only just now realizing it about herself too.

"Charley," he said, letting his rough voice linger over the syllables as he watched me lick at the corner of my mouth.

"Yes?" I whispered.

"That was a very pert little answer you gave me. But you answered a question with another question, and I don't allow that."

"We're not in your classroom," I said, a bit fuzzily. His stern "see me after class, you bad girl" voice was really making it hard to think clearly.

Or remember the actual tour group now ping-ponging their attention between Church and me as we talked.

"I'm not finished yet, Charlotte."

His refusal to use my nickname let me know that I was at the end of his indulgence. *Mmm, I wonder what happens at the end of his indulgence. Spankings?*

He said, "I want you to answer your own question."

My own question. Uh, what was that again?

Oh right. The *how.*

From the rapt gazes of the tour group, I knew I'd get no help from that quarter, and from an intuition that—aside from recent revelations about the state of my panties in the presence of scarred, argumentative men—never failed me, I knew I was in choppy waters now. I didn't know enough, hadn't thought enough about this to discept ancient iconography with him.

But when I looked at him again, I could see something almost *fascinated* in his expression, and I didn't want that fascination to go away. Not because I pussed out on a hard question.

"I think cultural advances drive religious advances," I hedge.

"Most people would say it's the other way around," he countered before I could finish. "Göbekli Tepe predates the agricultural revolution, suggesting that religious practices were already transitioning before the prevailing way of life changed."

I shook my head. "I think living religions respond to the time they're in, and so it's impossible to say that the complex at Göbekli Tepe meant the same thing to the people who built it as it did to the people who worshipped in it generations later. And I think the invention of cuneiform writing meant, for the first time, gods could be described in detail and these descriptions could survive and take on mimetic life. I think the invention of papyrus and paper meant these descriptions could reach people farther away than ever before. The increasing efficiency of weapons, war, and administration meant that religion was no longer localized but nationalized. Imperialized. All of these things forced deities and philosophies to evolve in complexity and depth in a way they never would have if our technology never moved beyond carving ivory or stone."

Church stared at me for a long minute after that, and then he nodded. The effect of his nod was like having him cup a hand between my legs.

"That's a good answer," he said. "You're still wrong. But it's a good answer nevertheless."

I couldn't help it, I laughed. And when I laughed, everyone else laughed too—except for Church, who was looking at my mouth like he wanted to bite it.

Everyone chimed in then, talking about whether or not it was even fair to compare a pre-pottery temple complex with the pinnacle of Babylonian cultic expression, and then I managed to move the tour on and finish it out without any more pointed questions from Professor Midnight Eyes.

And then after I walked them down to the Great Court and not-so-subtly pointed out the places where they could spend money on scones and scarves and soap shaped like mummies, Church stayed by my side as the rest dispersed to go buy mummy soaps.

"Am I correct," he said, studying my face, "in assuming you've never given that tour before?"

My cheeks burned again, but he took my hand, enveloped it in his large, strong ones. Calluses in contrast to his cool, suited demeanor stroked rough against my skin.

"You did brilliantly," he said quietly. "No other tour guide would have been able to answer me like that, not even one who's been doing this for years. You should be proud."

"Thanks?" I said hesitantly, going all fuzzy again from the touch of his skin on mine.

"Are you in school?" he asked with sudden urgency.

"University," I said. "I—um. Second year."

Relief flooded his expression, followed by something else I didn't understand. "I should go," he murmured, and to my eternal disappointment, he dropped my hand. "Goodbye, Charlotte."

***

.   .   .

Except it wasn't goodbye.

The next day I was shadowing yet another docent through a private tour of Ancient Greece when I became aware of a lean, suited predator stalking my steps. As the tour moved into the next room, Church cupped a hand around my elbow and led me back into the deserted Nereid Monument room.

"Come back for more clay tablet debate?" I teased, a bit breathlessly because oh my God, he was so unbearably sexy and severe. And tall. And nice-smelling—something that reminded me of incense—woody and smoky and rich. Like he really was a church, like he was a temple. A shrine to classical masculinity.

"No," he said. "I came back for you."

CHAPTER THREE

CHARLEY

"I'M NOT HIDING FROM YOU," I tell Church all these years later, as I spin to face him. "I'm hiding *for* you. So I don't murder you."

I expect Church to have some kind of riposte for this because he always had a riposte for everything, but instead he goes completely still, looking like someone just kicked him in the chest. Too late I remember the tears on my face, my missing piercing, the weight I've lost. The eternal bags under my eyes. I don't look like the happy, freckly coed he was going to marry once upon a time; I look like someone who works two jobs and has a full-time internship at How to Parent a Damn Teenager, Inc.

"Christ," he whispers, his eyes tracing me all over. The cheap shoes, the borrowed uniform, the blond hair scraped into a short, stubby ponytail. The fingernails ragged from tearing open boxes at the supermarket. "Little one."

Which is when I see he looks nearly as bad off as me.

His face—always rather forbidding—has grown leaner. Harsher. His body too, which used to be gracefully clad in muscle, now seems hardened and ruthless under his tuxedo, as if he's spent the last four years trying to push-up his demons away. A permanent line has carved itself between his brows, his mouth looks like it's never known a smile, and his eyes are the bleak blue of the coldest, deepest oceans.

He looks . . . empty. Grim and hollow and past all hope.

God, what happened to him?

And why does seeing him like this hurt as much as seeing him, period?

"No," I say, to him and to my traitorous heart, taking a step to the side. Towards Ancient Levant and the staircase. Towards not-murder, and also towards not feeling all these terrible *non*-murdery feelings. Feelings like I missed him, like I want to trace the pale scar on his cheek. "Don't *little one* me. You lost that right four years ago."

He takes a step to match mine but goes no farther. He's not close enough to touch me, but he's close enough for me to see the pulse in his neck, the tic of his jaw as he works it slowly to the side.

"You said you were going back to America to live with your mother's family," he accuses softly. "I looked for you everywhere."

"Well, I lied," I say, taking another step back. The overhead gallery lights mean his long eyelashes cast shadows over his eyes, which must be why they look so haunted right now. Why he looks like he's in pain.

"Why did you lie?"

Oh fuck him. "Why did you leave me in a church, asshole?"

He takes a step closer. "I don't want to talk about it right now."

"What does it matter? It's not like I'm going to show up in your classroom and beg you to finish what you started, it's not like it can make a single bit of difference. It's *over—*"

His eyes flash at that, and suddenly he's close, too close, close enough that if he wanted, he could slide those strong, archaeologist's hands around my hips and yank me against him. Yank me up so I could wrap my legs around his waist.

Just the thought of it has heat flushing all over me, tightness twisting between my thighs.

Scared of my body's reaction to him, I stumble back and away. He lets me, but he doesn't stop prowling closer and closer, stalking me until I'm literally backed against a wall.

He stops, just out of reach, and stares at me like I'm a virgin chained to his altar.

"It's not over," he says with so much raw determination that I almost believe him.

"It is," I say, for myself as much as for him. "It is, and you're the one who ended it."

He sucks in a breath at that, closing his eyes for a single moment, before opening them again. "Why are you working here?" he asks. "You should be in a doctoral program. You should be in the field or the lab or in your own classroom. Not as a—" he makes a vague gesture at my uniform, like even the act of articulating the word *server* is beneath him.

"You gave up the right to know what I'm doing with my life at the same time you gave up the right to call me yours." I fold my arms over my chest and try to muster my best glare while my face is still wet with tears.

Tears that seem to horrify and fascinate him all at the same time. *My depraved Church, my angry god—*

No. Not my Church.

"Let me kiss you," he says abruptly.

I stare at him like he's a lunatic, and he has to be, because there's no way in hell . . .

He steps forward, close enough that our shoes bump, and I can smell him. I can smell the incense scent of him and I can count each individual eyelash fanning above his lapis-colored eyes. "No," I say, a little distractedly. "You could have had a kiss at the altar, and then every day after that. You have any idea how often I would have kissed you if I'd been your wife? You called me a supplicant before, but I would have been a zealot for you. I would have kissed your throat every morning and your feet every night, and you would have been anointed hourly by my mouth. *You* gave that up, Church, not me."

His voice is honest and bare when he answers, "Not a day goes by when I don't think about what I could have had, Charlotte. You think I didn't want your zeal? Your mouth on my throat and feet? You think I still don't want it?"

I should push back. I should say I don't care what he wanted or what he wants. But fuck if being wanted by him isn't as intoxicating as it ever was, and the admission of his desire has hot knots of excitement tying themselves in my stomach.

He nudges closer, one shiny dress shoe pressing between my feet, and his mouth now inches from mine. "Simply one kiss," he murmurs, his stare hot on my mouth. "Surely I owe you that? At the very least?"

"You owe me everything," I whisper.

His eyes darken. "I know," he says.

Needing to see something other than him so I can just *think*, I turn so that I'm facing the wall, which is stupid, because what's my plan here? To stare at the wall until he goes away? To hope that if I can't see his sculpted mouth or haunted eyes I might regain my will to murder him? Or at the very least go back downstairs to Twyla and my champagne duties?

The other reason this is a stupid plan presents itself immediately; a large hand plants itself on the wall by my head, and I feel the ghost of a warm finger trace the curve of my shoulder.

As if Church needs my mouth or even my full attention to work his god-magic on me. Fully clothed and staring at a blank wall, I'm still trembling on the edge of senselessness and all from a single brush of his finger.

"I first found you here," he says, his finger following the seam of my shirt to its collar. "In this very room. My greatest treasure, and like all great treasures, I nearly missed seeing you, buried as you were in the crush of the ordinary and the mundane." The pad of his finger—warm and rough—whispers across my nape, and a shiver skips all the way down my spine. "I nearly walked away, and if I had, some other lover would have found you and your mind, not me."

His fingers move around the edges of my hairline, and then suddenly my ponytail holder is tugged free and my hair is loose and sifting down around my shoulders. He runs his fingers through it, he massages at my scalp and rubs away the tenderness from where it's been pulling all night.

My eyes flutter closed at the pleasure, but I still manage to say, "You ended up missing me anyway. At the church, remember?"

He ignores this, still rubbing and stroking along my scalp until my toes are curling. Or they would curl if my damn shoes weren't so tight. "The night after we met, I swore to myself that I wouldn't come back. You were too young, and I'd been a churl to you. And on top of it all, I wanted to tie you to the bed and make you talk about religious iconography while I buried myself in your cunt—and never, ever have I wanted something as powerfully as I wanted that. As I wanted you."

His fingers follow the curve of my jaw until they get to my chin and then my head is tilted back to rest against his shoulder. With one hand still against the wall and his other now toying idly with the top button of my shirt, I'm enveloped in his embrace. His chest is warm against my back, even through his tuxedo, and against my skirted bottom—

I shiver again, unable to resist the urge to press against him. Just a little. Just to confirm that his erection is as thick and hard as it ever was, a beautiful, massive thing that proved Church's divinity, because no mortal could have a cock like that. It wouldn't be fair to the other men of the world.

His breath catches as I press against him, but he doesn't move otherwise, he doesn't hoist me over his shoulder to find the nearest spot to fuck me in, he doesn't shove me to my knees to fix the problem I made— all things he would have done four years ago.

He does none of this, and that's when I know I'm in real trouble. He's going to exploit that horrible, all-consuming *thing* that's always been between us. That thing when a supplicant finally finds the temple in which to prostrate herself, when a wolf finally finds a bunny that will hop after him and seek shelter between his paws. He's making me feel it all over again.

His fingers drop to my hip, now to my thigh, now to my knee.

"You have a date here tonight," I say, pointlessly.

"And?"

Typical Church answer. Asshole.

"I—I was going to murder you," I say as his fingers hook under the hem of my skirt and trace maddening circles up my bare thigh. It's a place where I haven't been touched in years, and my body is having all kinds of wet, shivery feelings about him touching it now.

I should stop this. Yes, I should definitely stop this.

I'm going to stop it so hard.

In, like, a minute.

"You can still murder me," Church says soothingly, his fingers now stroking along the line of my panties. My head is lolling against his shoulder and my hips are pushing against his touch, trying to get his fingers to more interesting places. "I'll let you murder me all you want. But let me make you feel better first, hmm? Just rub it all better."

He emphasizes his point by sliding a single finger under the cotton and running it over the curl-covered swell he finds there.

I gasp, and in the space of that gasp, he's rucked my skirt up to my waist and slid his whole hand down the front of my panties. He cups me hard, like he used to do every chance he got before, and my body remembers. My body remembers what my mind tries so hard to forget—that this is a man I used to trust so completely, with every cell in my body, and there was a time he rewarded that trust with a breathless worship of his own. A fierce adoration and pride.

Pride.

It was always pride with us. Pride that irritated him into aggressing a poor tour guide, pride that made me fire back. Pride that kept both of us from backing down from danger when I walked into his classroom a week after the tour and realized the mysterious man I'd been fucking for the last six nights was my new professor.

"I shouldn't teach you."

"I promise to behave."

"Liar. Luckily for you, I don't trust anyone else with your education."

So we'd done it—we'd played the promising student/flinty professor game during his lectures, and then the moment we were alone, footsteps of my classmates still echoing down the hall, I'd be yanked onto his lap and bitten and licked. In between bites, he told me everything I got wrong in my last assignment. At his flat, we'd punctuate arguments about Mircea Eliade's approach to comparative religion with hard squeezes and strokes and orgasms, and I'd tell him he was wrong about human symbolic thinking in the Lower Paleolithic while he wrapped me in rope and then fucked me however he saw fit. He graded my papers while balancing his laptop on my back as I lay limp and well-used in his bed. And whenever I said something insightful in class, whenever I won an argument, whenever I hit on something clever in my papers, I was rewarded just as ferociously as when I was corrected.

No, not rewarded. *Reverenced.*

Revered and venerated and cherished.

You're going to be cleverer than me soon, he'd murmur against my skin. *You'll outshine everyone. The other professors, me, the whole world.*

It was possibly the highest praise Church could give, since he arrogantly—but also correctly—assumed he was the smartest person in every room he strode into, and so his praise and petting over my intellectual successes never felt patronizing or supercilious. Superior, yes—asking James Church Cason to be anything else would be like asking a lion to be a mouse—but superior in a way that made me into a lion too.

For all that I later resented feeling like an idiot animal of prey, until he'd left me at the altar, he made me feel brilliant and immortal. Yes, he fucked me like an altar sacrifice, refused to accept any work or thought or argument from me that wasn't the absolute best—but there was no disharmony in that, not for us. He could be reduced to cinders by my potential and then still fuck me like I was his temple prostitute, and we moved from one dynamic to the other like hopping between trenches at a dig. And like a dig, it would look like chaos to the uninitiated—simultaneously dirty and yet regulated, both inchoate and bizarrely intricate—but to us it was home.

Until our wedding day.

Remembering that now, my cheeks heat and my eyes fly open. "Fuck you," I say, right as his middle finger grazes over my clit, and then my curse turns into a low whimper.

"A fine plan," he murmurs in my ear. "Because you were always mine to fuck, sweet Charlotte, from the moment I laid eyes on you."

His finger is perfect, it's the kiss of heaven, it's big and blunt and firm, and it's right where I need it, right where it feels *so good.* Good enough to push my murdery urges to the edge of my mind, just for a moment, just for right now.

"I'm not yours," I manage. And I mostly mean it, but I can still feel his smirk curving against the shell of my ear, because he knows *mostly mean it* is a world away from *absolutely and definitely mean it,* and he won't let me forget it.

For some reason.

"Why?" I ask on a gasp—he's just slid his fingers down to toy with my vagina, to probe possessively at where he used to own me—and then

I inhale again as he pushes his finger inside and sends sparks skittering everywhere across my skin.

Four years. It's been four years without being touched by this man, and it's like taking a full breath of air after a deep, dark dive. Oxygen and life flood me, my body sends *yes please yes please* chemicals swimming through my blood, and the bright, heady wash of it all makes me dizzy. I slump back against him even more as he slides out enough to tease my clit again. "Why are you doing this?"

"Because I need to," he grates out. "Because you belong to me."

His finger penetrates me again, then a second finger. They slide and curl and stroke, and my body sings at being filled by him, filled by his will and his arrogance and his hunger. The hunger that even now has him growling low in my ear as his indelible erection makes its needs known against the soft curve of my bottom.

I try valiantly for a dig, for something that would give me some control, but not enough to control to leave. I don't want to leave. I don't want to stop. I want to ride his hand and then murder him for being the most selfish man on the planet. "Doesn't your date belong to you?"

"No," he says shortly, not elaborating and his fingers not pausing in their rhythm.

"But—"

"But she's not here with me between her legs, now is she?"

"God, you're such a dick," I groan, chasing his touch with my hips so that I'm riding his hand in truth. I reach over my shoulder and behind me to fist my hand in his tuxedo jacket, the other I brace against his hard thigh for balance as I rock against his touch.

"And you're the wettest thing I've ever felt," he says. "Helpless girl, fucking my hand. Do you miss it? Me?"

"No."

"Sweet Charlotte, you can lie with your words all you want, and I'll still know the truth." His hand molds to the shape of me—his palm grinding against my clit as his fingers press and curl inside—and he buries his face in my neck. Inhales. "Who's touched this since you left me?"

"None of your fucking business," I breathe.

Oh, he doesn't like this, not at all. I can feel his body tense against mine; his hand in my skirt is merciless, determined, it will wring an orgasm from me at all costs now, simply to erase any memory that's not of him. I should hate that, I should stop it. Shove him away and tell him he doesn't get to make me come, and he doesn't get to care about the people who *do* get to make me come.

Or better yet, I could knee him in his giant dick and then go back to my job, the one I have to keep for at least two more years.

But *fuck*, he's good at this. Even angry and jealous—or maybe it's because of the anger and jealousy—his touch is sex itself. Primitive. Greedy. Unapologetic. His palm is pure rolling pressure on my clit, his fingers are long and skilled inside me, and liquid fire is pooling in my lower belly, burning at the apex of my thighs and down my quads. He's going to make me come, and there's no doubt in my mind that he thinks he's winning some crucial point here, that he's conquering, when really I still hate him and his perfect, godlike penis, and I'm one the who's winning. I'll take my orgasm, tell him to fuck off back to hell, and then walk out of here having been pleasured *and* with the upper hand.

Ha.

"Are you thinking about it?" I provoke. "Me fucking other people?"

"Yes," he says sharply. "And I'm thinking about how I'm going to fuck you in very short order, my little supplicant, and the minute I do, you'll forget about anyone else. You'll forget about anyone but me."

Memories flash—his body toiling over mine, his firm buttocks flexing and thrusting as I clutched and scratched for him to go harder and faster; his big, rough hands covering my naked tits as he bounced me on his lap like a doll. His cruel mouth between my legs, insatiable and as merciless as the rest of him, licking and sucking me as his muscled arm bunched and moved just out of view so he could masturbate while he ate me.

There was nothing like Church in the grip of an orgasm. It was like watching potency itself, and it was so erotic to see his jaw flex and his eyes hood and his stomach and thighs jerk with the force of his spend that I'd usually come again just from witnessing it.

Oh God.

I definitely miss sex with him, and I'm definitely going to come right now, and I definitely wish he was going to come too.

No. No pleasure for him. You take yours and get the fuck out.

Oh, I'm going to take mine. Any minute now, any second, so long as he keeps giving me that hand to use . . .

Church, predator that he is, scents his impending victory. "That's right," he says. "I'm going to fuck you again, Charlotte. And again and again and again, until you're too worn out to run away from me again."

"Dream—" *moan* "—on—"

"I already dream of you," he whispers. The hand that's fucking me pushes my ass tighter against his hips, and the bar of his erect cock rocks against my bottom. "Every night. I dream of the way your wet cunt tastes. Of the way it looks. Do you remember the day I came back for you? Do you remember how I ate you that night?"

"Yes," I breathe. "*Yes.*"

"I was lost then. The moment my lips brushed against you, it was over; I was lost and you were mine. But you were mine before that, weren't you? You were mine the moment I saw you. Right here, right in this very room, I saw you. Clever and original and so kissable with that bold mouth. You laughed at me, do you remember that? Maybe that's when I knew."

I'm so close, close enough that my knees are all the way buckled and my head is thrashing on his shoulder. "Knew what?" I manage.

"That you could survive me."

That you could survive me.

But did I survive him? Could I call the last four years *surviving* when everything that made me that electric, ambitious girl four years ago was subsumed in the crush of loneliness and poverty? Were we the perfect example of why gods and mortals don't mix?

"Church . . ." It's half curse, half plea. I'm going to come harder than I have in four years, and I hate him, and I've missed him so much that I'm going to fly apart with it.

"Charlotte." He breathes me in as his touch works me over the edge and coaxes me right into sheer, filthy bliss.

Release sears me—sparkling, squeezing, hot—it starts right behind my clit and rolls everywhere: my belly, my breasts, down my thighs to my curling toes. Church makes a ragged noise into my neck as he feels my pussy clutch at him, and I know he's thinking of how it would feel around his cock. How wet and tight. How good.

The thought of his cock in me, of him spending inside of me, drives my climax higher and harder, until I'm supported completely by the hand still working my cunt and his other arm, which comes away from the wall to band across my ribs and keep me upright as I shake and shudder my way through the feeling.

It feels nothing like coming alone in my narrow bed and nothing like the few drunken orgasms I'd received from a Dutch bartender three years ago before she moved back to Maastricht and I gave up on post-Church dating altogether.

No, this is the dictionary definition of *good*, this is the kind of *good* one uses to describe sixteen-year-old scotch or a virgin dig site with bones and sherds only inches below the surface. This is the kind of good that can change your life, that can lash you to a beautiful god and lead you down the path to ruin . . .

The kind of good that not only blinds you, but binds you.

Except I'm not bound.

Church made sure of that.

What he and I had is dead, and he killed it, and it's nothing but a relic. It could be in its very own glass case in this gallery, that's how broken and inert it is.

He slides his hand free of my sex and raises it to his mouth to lick it clean, nuzzling me between tastes, as if to praise me—and God, I like it, I like it too much, it's dangerous how much his raw animalism stirs me.

I wriggle free of his hold and stumble away, my body still trembling and my cunt wet and pulsing and already aching for him *again*, the stupid thing.

"Charlotte," he warns in a low voice.

I spin around, staggering back enough to put real distance between us. He stands there looking impeccable and barely rumpled at all, as if he went for a stroll through the exhibits and didn't just finger-fuck a server to hell and back. Only his dark, hungry gaze and the fingers he's still licking clean speak to the licentious things he's just done.

"Thanks for the orgasm," I say in a shaky voice. "Now fuck off."

A slight twitch in his jaw. "No."

"I mean it, Church. You ruined us, you ruined me, you ruined everything. Now please let me live my goddamn ruined life in peace."

"And what is that life, Charlotte?" he asks, intensity burning beneath the surface of his voice. "What is this? I don't understand how my little one is here in clothes that don't fit, too pale, too tired, too thin. How could my supplicant, my brilliant one, end up in the shadows like this?"

Rage, white-hot and poisonous, floods my veins.

"You want answers?" I hiss. "You should have been there to ask the questions when it would have mattered."

His jaw twitches again. He knows I'm right.

"So you answer your own question, Professor Cason, because I'm not your fuckable little prodigy anymore."

"That was never how I thought—"

"I'm leaving now," I interrupt. "Going back to my *shadows*."

"Charlotte."

I glare at him as I retuck my shirt into the waist of my skirt. "Don't follow me, don't talk to me. Don't even think about me, or I'll drive my knee so far between your legs you'll have a dent in your heart, got it?"

His eyes narrow, ever so slightly—a god assessing a rebellious mortal—and then he nods, his eyes menacingly pretty.

"Good night, little supplicant," he says softly, in a voice I know means he thinks it isn't over.

But it is. It is over.

There's no unsinning those sins of his.

CHAPTER FOUR

CHURCH

THERE'S a Ray Bradbury story about God. Well, there're several, actually, but one in particular captivated me as a child. It's called "The Man."

In the story, a rocket ship full of explorers lands on a planet, and upon landing, they learn that God has just been there. The planet's inhabitants—joyous with their newfound revelations—invite the explorers to stay, to hear what The Man has told them. All of the explorers agree, save for the captain. Bitter and blustering on about proof, he decides to chase after The Man, to follow him to the next planet and the next and the next, until he catches Him. Until he can pin Him down and look at Him with his own two eyes.

The captain is clearly the villain of the story; a man incapable of humility and incapable of faith. He believes that if God can be chased, then God can be caught. And if God can be caught, then God can fix the unhappiness inside him. And the story says that's bad for all the usual Bradbury reasons of humanity and love being more important than ambition and greed and so forth . . . but as a child, I couldn't help but empathize with the captain. Couldn't help but think I'd be climbing back into my rocket ship too, if I knew how to chase God through space.

So I grew up and taught myself how to chase God another way. Through time instead.

I became convinced that if I simply unearthed the right temple complex or cradled the right figurine in my hands, I'd finally behold the face of God. Not in an idol-worshipping sense, but in a sacred sense, a discarnate one—my mind able to brush against God's mind, if only for a second, if only for a brief moment as I dusted ochre-stained dirt from a piece of bone or stood on a wind-whipped ridge overlooking a ritual landscape.

Unlike the captain in the story, however, I was perfectly content merely to chase. To chase was also to understand in its own way, and therefore the chasing became the singular goal of my life. To dig, to study, to write. To teach, because teaching was how one was able to dig and study. My career was more than a *profession*—it was a vocation as cherished and holy to me as a priest's. It was the one thing that mattered, the only thing I held dear.

The only thing, that is, until I was manipulated into taking a group of visiting colleagues on a tour and I first laid eyes on Charlotte Tenpenny.

She was winsomely brash and happy and faking her way through that tour with adorable aplomb. She had wild, curling hair and a spray of freckles across her pale nose and rosy cheeks.

She had eyes the color of a rainy day. A nose ring and a dimple.

And most damning of all for me, a freckle on her lower lip.

I couldn't stop staring at it. Of all the depraved shit I've done, all the men and women I've fucked and wrecked, somehow that freckled lip was the single most obscene thing I'd ever seen. *She* was the single most obscene thing I'd ever seen, and nobody else around me realized it. They were fooled by her friendly accent and her cheap business-casual clothes, by her confidence and sunniness.

She played the role of cheery intern well, but I could see the truth all over her.

She needed biting. She needed licking. She needed me.

And after she snapped back at me, held her ground against my admittedly unmannerly questions? Revealed that singular mind to me? Then I knew something much worse.

I needed her.

I tried to fight it—I did, and I'll swear it to God Himself once I find Him—but I only lasted a day. And then I was back for her and that freckled fucking lip.

***

YES, it's as bad as you think. I did what you think I did, and I didn't do it for some hidden, noble goal. If you're looking for a reason to absolve me, you won't find it. I can't be absolved. I'm selfish, I'm vain, I chose that selfishness and vanity over Charlotte—and yet.

And yet.

The day my director presented the options to me—marry this bold, brilliant student of mine and lose everything, or break it off and keep the destiny I'd been promised—was the day my life ended. I didn't know it at the time, I didn't perceive the knife sliding cleanly between my ribs, but there it was, a blade so long and so sharp that it severed everything inside my chest, it bled me dry until I was a shell, a husk.

You could survive me. That's what I told her last night at the gala.

A pointless observation, really, because what mattered in the end was that I couldn't survive *her*. I didn't survive her. I've spent the last four years in the opposite of survival, in the land of the dead, chanting her name to myself through the fog and incense of this netherworld I created for myself.

If you marry a student—one who was your *student*, the director had said, *it's over. You may scrape by with your job, but any hope of moving up, of getting funding—gone. You know how vicious academia can be. And her? Do you think she'll ever command any respect or find a job of her own if she marries* the *Professor Cason? You'll kill her future in this field before it ever starts.*

He was right. If I married her, it was over, for both of us. But what I should have known was that it was over from the minute I saw her. From the first moment I beheld that freckled lip.

She'll never forgive me. And she shouldn't.

So then why did I take the trouble of interrogating her prick of a boss to find where she works during the day? Why am I here? Inside this dingy superstore listening to children cry and trolleys rattle through the aisles?

You know why.

Because last night, with my fingers inside her body and her body inside my arms, I felt alive for the first time in four years, for the first time since I let my slutty little supplicant face the worst on her own in that church.

And more importantly, she came back to life too, fucking my hand like a beautiful whore, murmuring husky threats as her body squirmed against my touch. There was no trace of the weary server then, no sign of that tearful, tired girl. She was once again my obscene little genius, my own pillar of flame.

If I had any heart in me left, it would have broken again seeing what the last four years had ground out of her, but those same years have turned me into a vessel of ashes, and so I felt only the usual bleakness, although it's worse today. Emptier and grimmer than usual.

I suppose it could be remorse?

It's not an emotion I'd particularly ascribed to my personality—I may be fascinated by religion and God, but I'm not a kind man or a warm one. I don't even know if I'm a moral one. My only compunctions about fucking Charlotte after I learned she was my student were intellectual, were concerned with the quality of education I'd be able to give someone I also needed to see tied to my bed on a regular basis. But seeing her unhappy and worn down last night . . .

That knife is moving between my ribs again as I methodically walk the aisles looking for her. I thought I'd saved both our futures by abandoning her, but last night demonstrated that I definitely hadn't saved hers. Somehow she'd gone from horizons of unbounded academic ambition to—well, whatever the hell this is. Shelving cheap food and carrying trays around and making me want to crawl to her feet the way she used to crawl to mine.

Except her crawling was bedroom play. There would be nothing playful about my crawling. Nothing sweet about a dead man begging for one last glimpse of life.

Is this remorse, then? Does it even matter?

I find her at the end of a long aisle, stocking a display of discounted biscuits, wearing a blue shirt and black pants that should look completely boring but instead draw attention to the swell of her hips and the small, pert curves of her tits. She doesn't see me yet; she's straightening up to stretch her back and bat at the stubborn curls wafting into her raincloud eyes, and that knife-that-could-be-remorse severs something crucial inside of me, something that had grown back since I saw her last night.

I bleed out internally all over again, I die again, I die miserably like I deserve.

What would she have looked like in her wedding dress?

What kind of rain would I have seen in those eyes as she walked down the aisle to me?

And then she sighs and looks longingly down the aisle towards the front of the store, as if hoping to see that time has raced by and her day is almost done, and I see the freckle on her lip. A teasing flaw right in the middle of that plush pink mouth, and hot, dark urges whisper through me.

I have to bite her again. I have to taste her cunt.

Just as I acknowledge these things, she sees me. Her eyes widen fractionally—surprise and longing and anger all swirling through those gray depths—and then she narrows her eyes in a such a way that makes her look like an avenging goddess. She could be Ishtar or Lillit. She could be Nemesis or Morrigan or Kali.

Fuck, she's beautiful.

It's not that I've forgotten over the past four years—on the contrary, I torture myself to visions of her perfection daily and nightly—but confronted with it in the flesh . . .

Well, it unmade me last night. It's unmaking me now.

Spots of pink glow under her freckles as she takes a step toward me. "What are you doing here?" she demands, keeping her voice down. She casts a quick look around to make sure we're alone, which we are—mostly. Shoppers mill around us, but they're too preoccupied with squirming children or their phones to pay us any mind.

I try to think of a good answer to her question. I used to be good at answers, I used to be better at answers than almost anything else.

I'm all out of answers now; all I have are formless, urgent questions. *Find something, Church. Find something to say.*

"Last night wasn't enough."

It's the wrong thing to say, and if I thought Charlotte looked furious before, it's nothing compared to now. Her cheeks are red and her chest is rising and falling fast under her shirt. "Not *enough?*" she repeats in a low, dangerous voice. "You don't get to even *think* about having more with me. Exactly who the hell do you think you are?"

The answer comes faster than any answer has in four years. "Nobody. I'm nothing and nobody, but I don't even care about the nothingness when I can see your face. I'll be nobody forever, Charlotte, if it means I can touch you again."

Her lips part and purse and part again, like she doesn't know what to say to this, and I don't blame her. What is there to say? She shouldn't let me touch her, she shouldn't let me near her. We both know what I've done. But losing her has carved me up and scraped me clean, and I'm beyond doing the right thing now, I'm beyond everything but total honesty and raw need.

Anger settles back over her face. "Do you remember what you said to me when I returned the ring?"

The invisible knife between my ribs jabs at me. "Yes."

"You said you couldn't marry me, but you wouldn't tell me why."

Because I knew it was a shitty reason even then, I want to tell her. *I couldn't bear seeing your face when I told you that I'd chosen our careers over our worship.* But I don't tell her this. Maybe I'm still a coward.

"And then you said," Charlotte continues, and there's a thickness in her voice that betrays the tears she's pushing back, "that we could still fuck. Do you know what that was like to hear? That you'd condescend to screw me, but not to marry me? For some reason you wouldn't bother to explain?"

Knife, knife, knife. Right into the heart.

"I couldn't fathom giving you up," I admit. I'm not proud of how hoarse and desperate my voice sounds, but pride was the first thing to die after I realized what I'd done to myself and to her. I drowned it in gin and hours-long runs; I strangled it nightly as I fucked my fist to memories of her. "The idea of being without you was beyond contemplation."

"But you wouldn't marry me? *After you asked me to marry you?* God, do you even hear how fucked up that sounds?"

"Yes," I say, almost angrily. "I'm well aware."

Her eyes blaze like molten silver. "And now here you are, four years later, wanting . . . what, exactly? To berate me for not surviving you? To tie me to your bed when you still won't tie me to your life?"

"Charlotte—"

"*This* is why I told you I was going back to America," she says, spinning half away from me and yanking on her ponytail in frustration. "Because if you'd found a way to say that shit to me again, if you'd shown up with this whole 'we can still be lovers' line, I would have torn out your tongue and thrown it in the river."

"Charlotte."

"And I'm better than that. I was better than being left embarrassed and hurt in a church. And I'm better than being your hookup girl now."

"*Charlotte.*"

She finally turns and looks at me, tears shimmering over her glare. My heart kicks and bleeds and aches, and my cock gives a lazy, yawning stir and starts lengthening down the leg of my trousers. Her tears always did get me hard, but to be fair, they were usually tears from a good spanking or a deep, mascara-smearing blowjob. Tears that we agreed to.

But we didn't agree to these tears, and I caused them anyway—and I'm hurting for her and hard for her and so fucking ashamed and also so fucking obsessed and there's nothing that can break this miserable, muddy tide between us, nothing that can ease her tears and my hunger for her at the same time. Nothing that can make me deserve her and nothing that can make me stop wanting to deserve her.

I take her hand and pull, and she's off-kilter enough that she lets me, she lets me drag her back to the hallway that leads to the break room and staff toilet, and it isn't until I've pulled her into an empty manager's office that the murder threats start coming.

"I'm going to kill you," she says. "Let go of my hand so I can kill you."

I kick the door shut and let go of her hand—so I can plant my own hands against the wall on either side of her head. "Twenty minutes," I say. "I need twenty minutes."

She glares at me. "Twenty minutes before I kill you?"

Four years ago, I would have spun her around and seared her bottom pink with my palm for a comment like that. But I'm immediately and painfully distracted by the track of a lingering tear on her face as it rolls down her cheek to the corner of her mouth.

And then onto that goddamned freckled lip.

With a growl, I'm on her, I'm against her, I'm biting and sucking on that lip—my entire world the taste of her tears and her mouth—and she doesn't murder me even in the slightest. The minute I kiss her, her hands weave through my hair and tighten, not trying to pull me away, but keeping me close. Her hips begin rocking mindlessly against mine and she pants into my mouth whenever we separate long enough to suck in a breath.

"*Shit*," she hisses, and I know she's furious with herself. But even in her fury, she can't stop grinding her needy cunt against my clothed erection. It swells to full hardness to meet her. "*Fuck.*"

"Twenty minutes," I demand in between bites. "Give me twenty minutes with you."

"And just what do you think you'll accomplish in twenty minutes?" she gasps out, hands sliding beneath my coat and sweater to tug at the buttons of the Oxford shirt I wear underneath it all. She's always been a glutton for my body. Matched only by my terminal gluttony for hers.

"Orgasms," I promise, moving to her neck and sucking the skin there until she groans. "One for every year we've been apart."

Her hands are under my shirt now, running up and down my abdomen with greedy caresses. The caresses are awkward because our lower halves are still grinding and mashing together, but she keeps rubbing her sex against me anyway, arching her back to get a better angle against my cock.

"You," she pants, "don't get"—*pant pant*—"to just come here"—*pant*—"and fuck me with your giant penis."

I move my mouth to her ear and feel how she shudders with the tiniest licks, the smallest of nips. "Who said anything about that? I'm going to lick those orgasms out of you. I'm going to kiss them right out of your little pussy. I'm going to fuck you with my mouth, and you're going to be so soft and swollen and hungry for more after that you're going to give me what I really want."

I pull back so I can look into her eyes—silver and glistening even in the cloudy light coming in through the office window—and so I see how they war between wary and aroused. "And what do you really want?" she asks. Her hands are roaming down to my arse now, like she can't help herself even when she's supposed to be negotiating—or murdering me, according to her.

"To be your temple again."

I think the noise she makes was meant to be a scoff, but it comes out like a choked sob. "You'll never get that back from me."

I know that. I know that like I know the feel of my own palm around my cock. But it's gutting to hear her say it aloud, and I press my face back into her neck so she doesn't see how she's hurt me.

Her hands move back up to my chest, then my shoulders, then my hair, and I think *this is it,* this is the moment she's going to push me away, and I won't get to taste her, I won't get to pour every hour of my emptiness and misery into the kinds of intimate kisses that I would rip my soul out to give her. I breathe in the sweet, soap-smelling warmth of her neck, I tell myself to enjoy this last moment of her body against mine, her hands in my hair, and I brace myself for the rejection I've earned. The rejection I deserve.

It doesn't come.

Instead, she pushes my head down—down, down, down, until I'm kneeling at her feet. "Four orgasms," she says as she pushes me down her body. "Four and I might consider not tearing your throat out with my teeth. And you only have fifteen minutes."

I peer up at her like she's a goddess who's just spared my life, and I don't miss the tremble in her chin as she looks back down at me. Nor do I miss the flush on her neck or the hard nipples pressing against her shirt. She hates me and wants me all at the same time, and I can't blame her, because I hate myself and want her all at the same time too. Want her so much that atonement and morality are nothing right now, they are non-concepts, they can't exist when heaven itself is a mere few inches away from my lips.

No, I have to taste her. I have to lick her and bite her and scent her and mark her and remember. Remember this holy ritual we used to act out faithfully every chance we got—sometimes in bed, sometimes with her cuffed and spread for me, sometimes in my office at the university—this sacred act where I drank of her like communion wine. Where I breathed her in like the divine air of Delphi. She called me her angry god, and I was, I was her jealous, fierce, imperfect god, but we'd both known the truth. We both knew who actually worshipped whom.

She was my wind-whipped ridge over the temple complex, she was my precious artifact. When I held her close, I held God close, when I was with her, God was with me. Experiencing her is experiencing everything I've spent my life chasing after, just like the captain in the story.

My little supplicant, I think wildly, pressing my mouth to the apex of her thighs and kissing her fabric-covered cunt. *My little one. How I need you.*

I don't give her a chance to rethink this; I can't. I reach for the button of her pants and unfasten them, tugging them around her hips and bottom to her knees and then I bury my face against her white cotton knickers. I inhale her, shoving my nose into her body and making her gasp with the coarse animality of it. The minute her scent kicks into my nostrils, my cock responds with a jerking leap in the leg of my trousers, wanting out to play.

"I smell you," I murmur, angling so that I can bite gently at the cotton-covered folds. "I know you've been needing this. I know you've been thinking of me and how good it felt to fuck my hand last night."

She shudders, her fingers tightening in my hair.

"You've always liked it a little wrong, Charlotte. A little bad. And you need it so often, my sweetheart. I've never met anyone who needs release as much as you."

She shivers again, whimpering as I give her mound a final kiss over the cotton and then begin tugging her knickers down to reveal her gold-covered cunt. My own sweet chalice, my own reliquary. Gilded and gorgeous and protecting the real gift inside.

I kiss her as reverently as a priest kisses his stole, soft kisses along her silky curls until I get to her clit, which is plump and swollen, and sweet as any berry, a little fruit waiting to be plucked. I kiss it too, relishing her small jump as I do, and then I tease at it with the tip of my tongue, finally, *finally* tasting her. The unique, intimate taste that's sweet and earthy and so goddamn addictive that I've been starving for it since before our ill-fated wedding day four years ago. And the moment it hits my tongue, I need more, I need so much more and I use my thumbs to spread her apart so I can lick deeper, farther, I need it to be the only thing I taste for the rest of my life.

She gives a cry and slumps back against the wall.

"Everything," I breathe into her, barely able to stop myself from tasting her long enough to speak, "this is everything. *Fuck.*"

And after that, I can't speak. Me, the teacher. Me, the writer. And all my words are gone, totally subsumed. Burned away in the face of my need to drink her down, to mark every hidden corner of her with my kiss, and have her break apart against my lips. I keep her spread with one hand and then use the other to push her pants and knickers down to her ankles, enough to free one leg, which I sling over my shoulder. God, yes, *this*—this right here, with her thigh warming my ear and her hips angled just right against my face—I have to live the rest of my life like this. My face buried in her and my nose bumping her clit as I fuck her with my tongue, as I stab into her and swirl and lick, and then move up to suckle at her while her pleasure slicks all over my face.

"Church, you—I wanted this—so much—" Her words are barely there, just mindless pleasure words wrung from the circumstances, but I steal them for my jealous, bleeding heart anyway, I tuck them against the wounds there like bandages.

"You're so soft," I growl into her, before shoving my whole face back in again like a fucking animal. "You're so soft and you're about to get even softer, aren't you? About to make this place all swollen and slick for me?"

"I—" She can't finish. But she doesn't need to—a long, lingering suck on her clit sends her over the edge and she starts riding my mouth like she paid for it. I groan into her as she comes, as spots dance before my eyes, as my cock strains against the fabric of my trousers and tries to get closer to the person who really owns it.

"That's one," I say, pulling back the slightest bit to breathe in the Charlotte-scented air. Then I start in again, this time slowly teasing her sheath with my finger, playing with her inner folds and pressing gently against the edges of her until she's trying to drop herself onto my finger, until she's making mumbling, fussy noises as she chases my touch with her hips. Finally I indulge her whining and press all the way inside, pulling my mouth away so that I can look up at her as she writhes on my hand.

"You wish it was my cock, don't you?" I say in a low voice. "You wish you were impaled on me, feeling every throb of me. Every inch of me."

"Too many inches," she complains, but the hitch of excitement in her voice betrays how little of a complaint it actually is. "You're abnormal down there."

"Built for you," I say. The honesty and longing in my voice must tug at her, because she blinks down at me with those raincloud eyes. "Every part of my body was built for you."

"You don't believe that," she says, but she sounds a little uncertain. "You don't believe in those kinds of things."

"I do now," I whisper, leaning back in to kiss around my finger as it works inside her. "I do after the last four years without you."

"As if you've been pining. Please." She tries to scoff, but it's at the same time I add a second finger, and so it comes out as a moan instead.

I'm not wounded by this, but only because there's nothing left to wound. I close my eyes and rest my forehead against her stomach. "I can't sleep," I confess, my lips brushing against her intimate skin as I talk, as if I'm confiding into her body. "I can barely work; I can barely even tolerate *thinking* about work because it reminds me of you. I had to stop drinking because I drank too much with you gone. And I hate every person I see that isn't you."

"Except for the people you fuck."

It's a fair comment—before her, fucking was as necessary to me as eating, as digging—and my particular tastes usually entailed transactional liaisons with a myriad of partners. When one wanted to be worshipped in bed, one had to be careful only to find lovers who wanted to worship. Or more plainly put, I only inflicted myself on the willing. Those people whose tastes matched mine. But then I met Charlotte, and Charlotte became my taste, she become the only taste worth having.

"I haven't fucked anyone in four years, Charlotte. Since the day I met you, you've been it for me. Even in your absence, you've been it."

I say this into her skin, breathing the truth into her secret places as I continue to fuck her with my fingers, but she still hears me. She uses her fingers in my hair to pull my head back so she can search my face.

"What about your date at the gala?"

"A colleague."

"She kissed you."

I lift up a shoulder as I stare up at her. "Katie would like there to be more between us, but there's not. I don't push her away in public so I can spare her the embarrassment, but I've made it very clear that's all she can expect from me."

"I don't believe you," she says, but I know she does, I know the truth of it is etched into every part of my face.

"It doesn't matter," I say, looking up at her. "Whether you believe it or not, it's true. I was, am, and will always be your temple. Body and mind."

I don't give her a chance to argue about this; instead, I prove my words true by kissing her and then teasing her with my tongue as I work my fingers inside her. I prove my words by drawing another culmination from her adorable, half-uniform-clad body.

I prove to her that our bodies know things our minds don't.

She arches her back as she comes, her ponytail swishing against the wall as she thrashes through it, and before she's even finished contracting on my fingers, I start up again, sucking on her juicy little bud until I can practically feel it throb on my tongue. Throbbing in time to the urgent ache in my cock, which is beyond hard at this point. Tasting her, smelling her, having her slickness all over my fingers . . . watching that flush crawl up her neck as she comes . . .

I have to close my eyes as her third orgasm peaks, because otherwise I'll orgasm too. I might do it anyway, even with my eyes closed—the slightest contact from my trousers against my swollen tip has me rocking my hips—because it's just too much to be tasting her and fingering her all at once. Too much to hear her low cries and gasps.

"One more," I say. "Give me one more."

She's still clamping down on my fingers from the last one, and she tries to push my head away from her. "No," she moans. "I can't. I can't take it."

"You will," I growl. I draw a finger through her pouty seam, and then use the gathered slickness there to press against the pleated rim behind her pussy. "You'll give me my last orgasm, little one. You're through running from me."

The moment my finger breaches her tight rear entrance, she lets out a ragged sob. "Church," she chokes out. "Church. *Fuuuuck.*"

She's filled in both channels now, stretched around my knuckles as I kiss her everywhere, as I use my tongue on her plump button and on the sensitive petals gloving my fingers. "Keep saying my name," I order her, chancing a look up to see her staring down at me in flushed, rumpled awe. Awe that shoots through my veins like a drug, a pure dose of heady worship going right to my heart and then back out to every square inch of me, sizzling through my bloodstream until my very skin is on fire with it.

"Church," she breathes. "*Church.*"

Which I can't handle. I can't handle her chanting my name like a prayer, not with that open, unshuttered expression on her face, not with her eyes like silver rain. Not with her body hot and wet and swollen with pleasure.

I make an animal noise against her skin as I use my free hand to tear open my trousers and pull my cock free. I shouldn't come, I don't deserve to come, I don't deserve to feel anything other than grateful that she's letting me do this, but as I said earlier, I'm not sure how moral I actually am. Like everything else in me, my morality begins and ends with Charlotte, and when I feel her tremble like a leaf caught in the wind when she realizes I'm beating off, that's all the absolution I need. She always did like it more if I drained myself during oral sex, and she enjoyed watching me handle my needs so much that I'd reward her with it sometimes. A dirty show just for her peeping little heart.

My hips punch forward into my clumsy, left-handed touch as I use my other hand to wring my last climax out of Charlotte.

"Church," she says again. "Oh fuck, Church, please fuck me. Please please please—"

Her broken words are changing into broken cries, and I relish the sound of them, relish the sound of her begging and craving even after three orgasms. I relish it so much that my starved body releases with a shudder and sends long, hot ropes of cum between her legs, marking the wall, her ankle, part of her pants.

It's the first decent climax I've had in four years, and it wrecks me from head to toe. It ends all thought, all movement, all feeling except the dizzying, floating relief of coming home again.

I didn't even realize I'd stopped eating her until my pulses slowed, and now she's grabbing at my hand to fuck her again, her eyes wide and wild at the sight of my cock and also at my seed everywhere and also at my rough, lewd hand between her legs.

"God, I wish I could fuck you," she says in a pant. "Really fuck you. Hours and hours, riding your giant cock until I can't stop coming—" Her own words send her over, and the fourth orgasm detonates through her. The contractions around my fingers are hard and fast and merciless, and she bends forward at the waist, curling over me as she grips my hair hard and gasps through the sharp, biting pleasure of it.

She cries my name a final time—*Church*—as her body wrings itself free of all the adoration she's soaked up from my touch. Everything is wet and sex-smelling and the pain in my scalp is nothing compared to the jagged joy I feel at seeing and feeling her like this—utterly carnal and completely euphoric. In a state of Church-induced rapture. And then her knees give out, and even though I can catch her before she falls, we end up rolling to the floor in a tangle of legs and arms and expensive wool and cheap uniform polyester.

She blinks down at me with something like bemusement, like she's just awoken from some kind of spell and can't remember how we got here. And I can see it—I can see the very moment self-loathing darkens her eyes and pulls at the nibble-worthy corners of her mouth. She's angry with herself for succumbing to me again. It makes *me* feel angry to witness—angry with myself and her and with everything—and I wish I could just *atone* once and for all, no matter the price. All my money, my property, a finger, a kidney—anything, I would pay any cost, because nothing is as costly as being without her.

Curls the color of white gold have worked their way free from her ponytail and now fly free around her face. They beg to be pulled and I ache to pull them.

I reach up, wind a curl around my finger, and tug.

Her lips part, putting my favorite freckle on delicious display, and then her eyes flutter and widen as the familiar cocktail of pain-induced neuropeptides and hormones lace her blood. Adrenaline, endorphins, dopamine, oxytocin—our altar wine.

I tug again for the sheer pleasure of it, for the drop in my own blood pressure, my own dopamine and oxytocin hits, for the deeper and beyond-chemical joy of seeing her release her clenched grip on her thoughts and hurts and sink completely into the here and now with me. Fuck, I love her. I love her when she wants to murder me, I love her when she resists me, I love her when she surrenders to me. If I were a cleric and not an academic—one of the faithful instead of whatever the skeptical but obsessed fuck I am—this is how I would feel about God too. Full of so much love and adoration that I'd do anything right now to show her, any scourging or fasting she asked.

"You asshole," she whispers, and then fists her hands in my sweater and rolls to the side, so that she's on her back and yanking me over top of her so that I'm braced on my forearms and caging her with muscle and will.

"You missed this," I tell her. I don't need to ask. One doesn't pull a Dominant ex-lover on top of them if one doesn't miss it.

"You asshole," she repeats, but her eyes are shining with tears. She tries to look away, but there's nowhere to turn her head that isn't into my arms, so it's more a nuzzle than an escape.

Tenderness—the thing I've only ever felt with her—surges up inside me. "You know this is what I meant when I said I wanted to be your temple," I say, fingers finding her hair and stroking the silk there. "The temple to keep you and shelter you and protect you. The temple you could come to for safety and hope and rest. I wanted *this*," and I tighten my arms and legs around her to make my point. That if there was a way I could carry her through the world tucked up inside of myself, I would do it.

"You just want me to worship you again," she sniffs.

That's undeniably true, even if it's not the only thing that's true. "Well. Yes."

"I knew it."

"That doesn't make me a liar, little supplicant. Temples are for the worshippers, not for the worshipped. Is it so hard to believe that I want to give you this more than I want to enjoy you taking it?"

"You left me," she says into my arm, not looking at me. "You were supposed to promise to be my temple forever and you left me."

This is also undeniably true. "I did."

"Why?" she asks brokenly, finally turning her eyes up to me. They are every cloud I've ever seen, every drop of rain, every lonely puddle in the road. "*Why?*"

It's those eyes that finally break me, that gut me. No longer a knife in the heart but through the soul. And I deserve it, because it's as bad as she believes it to be. It might be worse.

"For work," I answer after all these years, and I want to close my eyes right now, a cowardly move but one that's almost irresistibly tempting right now. Because how pathetic it sounds, how stupid and how utterly mundane. She's waited four years to hear that her fiancé and god was more concerned with keeping the right office in the right building than pledging his love to her.

"For work," she repeats, looking confused. "Church, we fucked for a year before the wedding. I wasn't even your student that semester. If you were really worried about work, then why propose? Why go through the whole song and dance of helping me find a venue? Paying for my dress?"

"You would have been my student again," I point out, even though it doesn't matter now. But with our department the way it was and with Charlotte as clever and driven as she was—and with me as possessive as I was—it would have been inevitable. In the classroom or on a dig—she would have been mine again. And I would have made sure it was so, because I never did trust anyone else with the jewel that is my Charlotte's mind. "But that you *had* been, that you were still enrolled at the university, that was damning enough. And I didn't realize it until the director told me."

Her brows pull together. "The director?"

"He came to my flat the morning of the wedding. You may

remember that he was dating my sister at the time—and it was my sister who took the liberty of calling my guests and telling them the wedding was off before I knew anything about it."

Her eyes close for a moment. "So that's why none of your guests were there."

"Yes. And he persuaded me that it would be the end of my career in every meaningful sense if I married a student—not to mention it would have ended your career too, before it had ever started."

The furrow between her brow hasn't gone away, and I kiss it because I can't help myself. "I don't see how my career would have been affected."

"Can you not? How many people would've assumed that you'd fucked your way to prominence instead of earning it on your own merit? We'd know differently, but that hardly matters when the doubt would've pervaded every space you worked in. I couldn't lose my work, Charlotte, but just as much, I refused to lose yours. I couldn't bear the thought of stamping out your future just so I could stamp my name on your legal existence." But my hold on her tightens as I consider that none of it mattered anyway. She still lost her future.

"Then why didn't you answer my calls? Why didn't you *show up* to tell me this? Why didn't you face the aborted ceremony with me? Why didn't you find me that night? Why didn't you find me the next day?"

This. I'm ashamed of this almost more than the decision not to show up to my own wedding. I owed her everything, and I especially owed her the truth. "It took me two or three hours to persuade the director not to make our engagement known, even after I decided not to go the wedding. We've never gotten along, him and me, and he was torn between finally having some kind of political leverage over me or being tainted by association, since he was fucking my sister. By the time I'd convinced him not to poison my career and yours, the wedding was long over—it was why I'd sent the car, you understand. Not to be high-handed or dismissive, although I admit I'm often that, but because I was determined to save the future before I fixed the present, and I wouldn't leave him until I had his word he wouldn't tarnish our names."

She searches my face. "I don't forgive you."

"You shouldn't."

"You did it as much as for yourself as you did it for me."

"I did." I bend my head down so I can smell her neck, her hair, nuzzle my cheek against hers. "I'm sorry, Charlotte. It was selfish and hollow and arrogant of me. I thought if I gave up my chase for God, I'd be giving up myself. But of course, I lost myself the minute I gave you up, and it didn't matter. I damned myself that day, and for nothing."

I can feel her breathing underneath me—the fast, panting swell of her ribcage against mine, the thrum of her pulse against my nose as I run it along the column of her neck.

"And that night, I—" I spare telling her the whole truth, the truth of what I became and what I did to my own house as the horror of what I'd done unfolded inside me. I'm still finding shards of glass four years later. "I wasn't fit to come to you. And when I was more composed, I felt you were owed an explanation beyond a phone call. So I came to your flat to find you the next day."

"I went to the library to use the public computers to look for a job," she says. "I wasn't home."

"I waited for a while, but I was—I'm afraid I still wasn't in the right frame of mind." I'd been like a wounded animal that day, snarling and snapping at everything, and I'd dimly recognized in my hurt and anger that I was likely to shred something between us that couldn't be stitched back together. So like an animal in truth, I'd followed my instincts to the water. I watched night blacken the Thames into a slick of oil, reflecting as much light as it swallowed, and I imagined that cold oil as my shame, coating everything inside of me until it was ready to be lit on fire. Charred to oblivion because everything already felt charred without Charlotte in my arms. Worse than charred.

A world without my little one was a world too dead to burn.

"And I came to find you the next day," she recalls, and I think of a memory colder than that night by the Thames.

"Yes, you did."

At the time, I'd been still too raw, still too arrogant to consider that it was truly the end. She'd walked into my office and set the engagement ring on my desk, and a desperation like I've never known clawed hold of me.

"You can put that ring anywhere you'd like, but you're still mine."

"I believed that until two days ago, Church. I don't think I believe anything right now, especially since you won't tell me why."

Panic. Terror. Shame.

If I told her why, she'd leave. She'd leave and she'd never come back.

Fear boiled in my veins as I tried to convince her and deflect from the terrible truth at the same time.

"We don't need a wedding, Charlotte, nor a marriage nor a mortgage together to prove what we have."

"We don't have anything. Not anymore."

I'd kissed her then, getting to my feet and hauling her into my arms, feeling her shiver and cling to me just as she always did. Feeling her mouth open to mine and accept me. "I acknowledge I've fucked up, little one, but you can't lie to yourself about what we have or don't have. I still need you in my bed and you still need to be there. The rest we can figure out in time."

"I won't go to another church alone," she said against my lips.

The mere mention of what she suffered at my hands made my bones ache and my body throb. "Maybe churches aren't for us. But my bed is. But this is."

I pulled her back to my mouth and she let me. She let me take a deep, lingering kiss.

Because it was her kiss goodbye.

"I came by for more than giving back the ring," she said, breaking our kiss. "I'm leaving."

I tightened my arms around her. "We'll leave together. Go to my flat. We can work things out there."

"Not leaving your office," she clarified. "Leaving London. Leaving the UK. I'm going back home."

"Home?" I asked, agitated. "Explain yourself, Charlotte, because your home is with me."

She pushed away from me. "There's nothing to explain. I'm going to America and I'm never going to see you again."

I think even then I still hadn't truly believed her, not really. But within a week her flat was empty and she was unenrolled from UCL. She was gone. And the only comfort I had was that somewhere across the ocean, she was fulfilling the promise of that brilliant mind. A promise that was at least undimmed by a connection with me. If nothing else, I spared her that.

"So now you know," I tell her. "I didn't want to tell you, then or last night, because it was so incredibly foolish of me. Selfish, and unforgivably so. But you deserved the truth as much as you deserved my shame, and I didn't give it to you. I'm so sorry, little one. I owed it to you, just as I owe you so much else."

All at once, all the fight seems to leave her. She closes her eyes, her body going still beneath mine. "Now I know," she murmurs, as if to herself. "Now I know."

I drop my forehead to her cheek, and for a moment, we just breathe. Joined together in this wound I gave her.

I know it can't last. We're cold and sticky and tangled, and I haven't forgotten that she needs to get back to work, but the very idea of separating from her *again* has me miserable. I curl my fingers in her cheap work shirt and root through her curls to bury my nose in her scent. She smells clean and floral, like she's just removed a crown of flowers from her hair, and I can't get enough of it.

"I have to go," she says.

"You didn't even murder me. Would you still like to?"

She sighs, and it's not a happy sigh or an amused sigh—or any kind of good sigh. It's the sigh of someone so hurt and so tired that each breath feels like work.

"No, Church," she says wearily. "I don't want to murder you."

I raise up so I can look down at her. A tiny flame of hope curls in my chest. "You don't?"

"That doesn't mean I forgive you," she says pointedly. "And I would like very much never to see you again after this."

I stare down into her perfect face—pert and freckled and stubborn. Can I give her my absence? Now that I know she's here in London? That she's been suffering?

Was I ever capable of it?

Am I a moral man?

Can I be for her?

"Is that what you want from me? Is that the *only* thing you want from me?"

Fuck, this feels worse than bleeding out, than burning, than emptiness and ashes. This is bleeding *in*, this is growing something brand new, just for her. And it hurts. It hurts worse than anything, because before I had no choice, but now I'm agreeing. I'm agreeing to lose her once again.

She hesitates, then the stubbornness reasserts itself in the pull of her mouth and the jut of her chin. "Yes."

"Then you have my word."

She narrows her eyes up at me. "Nothing's ever this easy with you."

Jesus Christ. *Easy?* She thinks this is going to be *easy?* I push up to my feet, wrapping my hands around her elbows and setting her on her own feet in the process. "There's nothing easy about this, Charlotte," I tell her in a sharp voice. "If I had my way, you'd be over my fucking shoulder right now, and I'd be hauling you to my bed where you belong. I'd have you trussed up and so thoroughly fucked that the only thing you would want to do next is nestle into my arms and sleep. I'd be with you when you woke up—then and every day after—and you would go back to the things that made you smile, and you'd stop all this nonsense." I nod at her uniform shirt.

Her face, which had been rapt during my little speech, now grows mulish.

"It's my nonsense, Church. And you're *not* going to have it your way. Even gods have to acknowledge free will," she says, yanking out of my touch.

"Am I still your god then?"

"I don't belong to you anymore, dickhead. There's your answer."

The laugh that leaves my lips is broken and dry. "That may be true, but don't you see it doesn't matter? I belong to you, sweet genius. You've made me your own, and your body feels it even now. Or are those nipples still hard for someone else?"

Spots of color rouge up her cheeks as she starts setting herself to rights. It's hard to say if she's angry with my observation or flushing in response to my heavy cock, which is semi-erect even as I zip my trousers closed. Her eyes follow the movement with unmistakable hunger, but her voice shakes with emotion when she says, "This can't happen again. This *won't* happen again."

I take a long moment to answer, smoothing my clothes and then tucking her curls back behind her ears. She wants to bat me away, I can see, but the minute my fingertips touch her face, her eyes close and her lips part. Drugged like an initiate into esoteric mysteries. Power flowing from me into her, and then back into me again.

"I am your temple no matter what. Your god, your own. When you need me, I'll be there."

A slow shiver moves through her, a dimpling in her chin like she might cry—something I feel like seven thousand arrows—and then she tugs herself away.

"Goodbye, Church."

"Wait."

I have no right to this, I know, and I know more than anything she wants me gone. And I'll go and stay gone, even though I know exactly what ash-dusted tomb I'm consigning myself to—but before I do, I have to know.

"How did this happen, Charlotte?" I ask. "Did you need help finding a job after you graduated?" The thought is actually painful, that she needed help I could have so easily given, and she didn't ask it of me. "Do you still need help? I know you don't want to see me, but I can still—"

She jerks her head to the side, silencing me. "I don't need help," she says tightly. "I'm *fine*."

"You're not." It's shitty and over-familiar of me, maybe. But it's one thing to have work you choose and another thing entirely to have your choices taken away. And everything about her vibrates with the pain of having her choices stripped from her.

She glares again, but she doesn't contradict me.

"I won't apologize for having the audacity to be right, little one."

Her gaze flares to a molten silver and I think for a moment that she's going to shove right past me without answering, that she's going to leave without dignifying my intrusion with a response—but all at once, the anger goes out of her and her shoulders slump. Her eyes drop to the floor and she takes in a long breath that seems to do nothing to make her feel better.

If I thought she looked tired before—hurt, fatigued, alone—then I see it clearly now. The toll her life has taken on her. It's like dying all over again to see it, but of course that's nothing compared to hearing what she says next.

"I didn't need help finding a job after I graduated because I *didn't* graduate. I couldn't—I couldn't even finish the semester. I came back from what was supposed to be our wedding to discover that my father—" she grits out the word with a lifetime of bitterness behind it "—had stolen everything we had and left. Just . . . left. Me and my brother and our flat and everything."

Rage—clean and pure—whitens my vision until I force myself to take a breath. "He abandoned you?"

Simply left his children? One, a college student who was still finding her equilibrium after he'd uprooted the family from America to come back to his own country, and the other, a literal child who had years left of school?

Charlotte cuts a look at me. "Sound familiar? Seems to be a theme with the men in my life."

I wish I could say that shame erases the rage, that I'm humble enough to accept that I can't stand in judgement of others given my own past—but alas. I still want to fling her father into the river.

"I haven't talked to him since then, and I have no idea where he is. I managed to get legal custody of Jax and tried to keep things normal for him, but . . ." She looks down again. "I couldn't afford to stay in school and pay for the rent and food and everything else. I have to work two jobs as it is, just to scrape by, and to have to manage tuition on top of that? And even without tuition, whatever's left of my time belongs to Jax. Helping him with school, making sure he's ready for his exams, taking him to art studio and his flute lessons and keeping an eye on his group of friends . . ."

She puffs out a breath. "Maybe my father thought because I was marrying someone, we didn't need him around anymore. Or maybe I'm giving him too much credit by imagining he thought about us at all. But the upshot is that I was completely and utterly alone. I had nothing, and I had no one, and yeah, it fucking sucks that I couldn't finish school and follow the path I wanted. But you know what? I'm fucking *here*. My brother is here. We're sheltered and fed and safe, and that's because of me. That's because of what I gave up and what I worked for, and I refuse to let you make me feel like shit about it, okay? I'm better than that. My efforts are better than that."

She is. They are.

And I am nothing. Nothing in the shape of a man.

"Goodbye, Church," she says again, and this time I don't stop her.

This time I let her go.

CHAPTER FIVE

CHARLEY

UNDEFENDED AND ALONE, now the girl must make a nest of pillows and blankets to protect herself. Tomorrow, the harsh London wilderness will be waiting. But tonight the girl must retreat and recoup. And cry.

I know things have to be bad if I'm Attenboroughing myself. Dazed and dizzy from three solid hours of sobbing, I manage to fake my way through dinner and homework with Jax, and then I collapse into a fitful sleep. Tomorrow is a double shift at Tesco, and the day after will be Tesco plus a catering gig, and I don't *have time* for Church to be in my thoughts like this. For his words to be swimming through my veins and crawling inside of my heart.

Since the day I met you, you've been it for me.

Do I believe that? Does it matter even if I do?

I am your temple no matter what.

When you need me, I'll be there.

Liar. He's a liar. He wasn't there when I needed him, he wasn't there when he said he would be.

Except you never gave him a chance to be after the day of the wedding, a voice reminds me. *You made sure he thought you were gone— you made sure he couldn't be there for you at all.*

Well, I refuse to feel bad about that. He did the worst thing, and when someone does the worst thing, they don't get second chances. Especially when that worst thing was to save their career.

And yours, the voice says. Which makes me scowl. My career was lost anyway, and besides, I'm not interested in forgiving him for choosing *anything* over me. Not when there were seventeen thousand other ways he could have handled things. Number one of which was to have told the director to fuck off and then shown up to our goddamn wedding.

But you know what it means to him. His job is the literal manifestation of his desire to find God. Can you really blame him for that?

I want to. And I think I do, but in order to keep the blame bigger than the sympathy, I have to forget what an amazing teacher he was. How carefully he mentored all of his students and the pains he took to help each one of them improve. I have to forget about how he lit up on a dig site, becoming smiley and boyish and excited; I have to forget the awe in his voice and the humility in his face when he cupped fragments of forgotten worlds in his hands.

But I will forget it. I will if it's the last thing I ever do. I'm not going to forgive him, and I'm not going to keep thinking about his cruel mouth and glittering eyes and smoky voice. I'm *definitely* not going to remember the jolt of pure rightness I felt when he told me that he belonged to me, that he wanted to be my temple again. I won't remember the gouging agony in his expression as I told him exactly how hard the last four years have been, and I won't remember his stern words when he refused to let me hide my pain from him.

I won't apologize for having the audacity to be right, little one.

Nope. Not interested. Still a mean little bunny. Still smarter than falling in love with a broken, miserable god. I will forget the last two nights ever happened and go back to the safer—if lifeless—way things were before, and that's just how it's going to be.

***

· · ·

EXCEPT THE NEXT MORNING, I wake up with a tender pussy and my heart in my throat. I wake up with Church's words still whispering in my mind.

Am I cursed? Is this what a curse is?

It feels very Greek to me, very much like I'm the victim of some capricious divine whim. Doomed to long for someone who fucked me over.

Hungry for the touch of someone who thinks me worthless.

Okay, maybe that's not . . . *entirely* fair.

Church was never the kind of man to be interested in something inferior; he didn't waste his time with anything cheap or dull. He thought me brilliant and adept and *his*. And I know all that because he told me so. And the only time Church ever lied was the day he failed to show up for our wedding, and even then, he didn't lie with his words, only his actions. In fact, for all his cruelty, all his arrogance, and all his ice, Church was always unfailingly, painfully honest.

Maybe he's being honest now?

I'm so sorry, little one.

I am your temple no matter what.

It doesn't matter, I tell myself. It doesn't matter how sorry he is, it doesn't matter how right and alive I felt with him yesterday, it doesn't matter how he sees me exactly as I need to be seen.

Because I'll never forgive him for not seeing me when it mattered.

I get dressed with a huffy forcefulness, as if that will prove to some invisible audience that I'm really done thinking about Church and not at all noticing how my well-pleasured body twinges with every movement. I see my brother off to school, and then I stop by the landlord's flat on the ground floor to drop off this month's rent before I go in to work.

Roksana, my landlord, narrows her eyes when she opens the door to me. "You can't take it back," she says with a sniff. "I've already started spending it. Repairs, if you must know."

"Uh," I say, glancing behind me to make sure there isn't some other tenant she's talking to. Seeing no one, I decide to pretend the last ten seconds didn't just happen. "I brought this month's rent for you. I'm sorry I didn't get it to you on Friday, but I got home from work so late, and I didn't want to wake you—"

She doesn't take the envelope from me. Instead she sniffs again. "You can't take it back."

"Take what back?"

"If you want to add it to what you've already paid this morning, you can, but you can't take it back and then pay me for only this month instead. Like I told you, I've already spent a lot of it."

"Roksana, I think there must be some kind of mistake. I haven't paid you yet."

She narrows her eyes even more and sucks her teeth. "First thing this morning, I was on the phone with a man who seemed to know you. I assumed it was a boyfriend at first, but he was quite cold with me, I'll have you know, and very impatient. I thought then maybe he was a solicitor of yours, or a banker. He wired the next twelve months' rent right into my account."

Quite cold. Very impatient.

And could drop a year's rent into someone's account at the drop of a hat.

A white, angry static crackles in my vision and my hearing and I can feel it singe the inside of my veins. "He didn't happen to give his name, did he?"

Roksana shrugs. "Church something. Churchwell? Churchhill?"

James Church Cason. My hand fists around the envelope and Roksana glances down at it, shrewd assessment in her gaze. "You could give me that for safekeeping," she says. "In case this Church man changes his mind."

"I think I better hang on to it," I manage, anger coursing through me so hot and bright that I can't even remember why I didn't murder him the last two times I saw him. "If you'll excuse me, I need to make a phone call."

***

THE WALK to work is windy, with that kind of autumnal spatter that can't decide if it wants to rain or what, and it matches my shitty mood perfectly when Church answers my call. A shitty mood that's exacerbated by the fact that I still have his phone number memorized after four years. *What is wrong with me?!*

"What the hell do you think you're doing?" I demand, before he can say a single word. "This is way out of line, even for you."

"Hello, Charlotte," Church says softly.

"Don't *hello, Charlotte* me. You had no right to pay for my rent. *None.*"

"It's a gift," he says. His voice is still soft, but threaded through the words is an unmistakable edge. The one that kept me coming back to Church's bed over and over again—the cold imperiousness that thaws only for me. "It's freely given. I don't expect anything in return, little one." Even with the strange combination of softness and arrogance, honesty still rings through his words. He's telling the truth—or thinks he is.

I still say, "Oh, really?" because that's just who I am.

"Yes, really. I wanted to ease something for you that was in my power to ease, Charlotte. I wanted to make something—anything—better for you and Jax."

I flush with more than anger, although I'm not sure what for. Embarrassment that he so easily peeled back the lid on my shitty, cash-strapped life? Or something much, much more dangerous?

Am I . . . *touched?* That he notices me and thinks of me? Am I turned on by the fact that he still wants to care for me? Am I grateful that he picked the single biggest source of my misery to ameliorate?

Ugh.

Maybe.

Stupid bunny.

My footsteps become more like stomps as my irritation with myself spills over to him again. "You still should have asked, you interfering prick."

The silence following my insult scratches at me, if I'm honest. I've always been colorful with my language around him—prick, bastard, asshole, *arse*hole if I was in the mood to make fun of him—and I've never stepped back from provoking him. But my little rebellions and challenges were always met with scrumptious wrath; more often than not, I was hauled over his lap and spanked until I was begging to be fucked. Sometimes he would wait to punish me for my brattiness, letting the anticipation worm its way under my skin until I was near crazed with it, and then finally tying me to his bed and tracing rebuke all over my body with his tongue and teeth.

And yes, okay, sometimes I provoked him *because* I wanted some spanking and bondage. Sometimes a girl needs to savor the sweet displeasure of her god, what can I say?

But right now, he's saying nothing. He's not purring sexy threats into my ear, he's not dryly musing aloud about whether his bratty supplicant needs to be bitten or ridden or both. He's quiet and I find that I hate it.

"Aren't you going to say something?" I demand.

Church sighs. "What is there to say? That the only thing that kept me on this side of sane for the last four years was the mistaken hope that you were in the States building a life for yourself? That knowing you've been suffering, that you've been alone, that every day has not only been a struggle but a slow starvation of the things that used to feed you—that the knowledge is fucking damning? And I can barely swim through the hours knowing it?"

The pain in his voice saws right through me, and I stop walking.

"I don't care if I'm the villain. I don't mind being the bastard. If I can do anything to ease your suffering, if you sleep better for just one hour of just one night, then it is worth you hating me more than you did before."

The insides of my eyelids burn a little at that, and I duck my head so no passersby will notice how fiercely my chin is wobbling. The words *I don't think I hate you* are on the tip of my tongue and they sting more than the unshed tears.

"You can't atone for what you did," I say in a whisper instead.

"I'm not trying to, Charlotte, not anymore. I know I can't buy your forgiveness. Now all that's left for me is to live with myself and what I've done."

It's his raw but honest admission that pushes the first sob out of me.

"Little one," he says, sounding as broken as I feel. "Are you crying? Are you that furious with me?"

"Yes. No." Another wet, gasping sob. "I don't know, Church. I don't know. Some moments I think I hate you, and then other moments, like right now, I wish you were here."

"That's the pain talking," he says gently. "You don't really."

The tears are flowing fast and freely now, mingling with the cool drops of rain. "You have no right to say what part of me is talking and what isn't," I say, knowing it sounds like nonsense and not caring.

"Of course," he murmurs.

"And you have no right to decide what will ease any of my sufferings," I mumble.

He hums in agreement, a soothing noise that immediately makes me feel safe and small and loved.

I'm reminded of all the times I showed up in his office, shaky and exhausted from a night guarding Jax from my father's drunkenness, a sleepless night sitting against the inside of our bedroom door, terrified that my dad would beat it down at any moment. Me, I looked too much like his dead wife to scream at, but Jax? Jax was the perfect target. And Jax only had me to protect him. Which meant once or twice a month, I'd see Jax safely to school and then stagger to the one place I felt safe.

With Church.

He'd take one look at me and then somehow I'd end up in his lap, cradled against his chest as I cried myself to sleep right there in his office, and then I'd wake up on the settee he kept for students to sit on during meetings.

After the second time it happened, he took out one of the bookshelves in his office and bought a long sofa to replace the settee, so that then I'd wake up several hours later on plush cushions with a pillow under my head and a soft blanket pulled over me. Groggy but protected. Cared for. And he listened when I begged him not to get involved, although he did inform me that the next time my father did anything more than look at my brother, he'd be stepping in.

For a kinky, autocratic monster, he was always careful with the boundaries I needed him to be careful with. He only invaded the parts of my heart marked for invasion.

I miss him. I don't hate him and I can't forgive him and I miss him.

"Church?"

"Yes, Charlotte?"

"Will I still be your little supplicant even now? Now that I've told you to stay away? And now that you can't ever make up for what you did?"

His voice is pure Church when he answers—like the still, small voice Elijah heard outside the cave: quiet and boundless all at once. "Always. You have the right to ask me to stay away, but there is one thing you can never ask of me, and that is for me to stop loving you. It would be easier to ask me to stop breathing."

I feel like I can't breathe myself. I certainly can't speak. I can't even cry properly; the tears are just leaking out now without any effort from me.

He makes another one of those noises that makes me feel like I'm tucked against him, listening to the steady, reassuring beat of his heart while he sifts through my hair. "I love you too much not to give you what you need. I won't approach you, I won't call, and you are certainly entitled to give back the money if you need."

The rain comes down harder now, hard enough that it makes it difficult to hear his final words. But I do hear them. I hear them and begin weeping in earnest.

"Be well, little one," he says, love and arrogance winding through his words in that way I adore so much. "You, Charlotte Tenpenny, smartest and bravest person I know, will always be my heart and my faith."

And then he hangs up.

CHAPTER SIX

CHARLEY

I MAKE IT A WEEK.

Barely.

The morning of the seventh day, I'm caught in a slurry of UCL students, tourists, and commuters pushing impatiently out of Euston Station as I make my way to the archaeology building to find Church. Gordon Square is spitting wet leaves in shades of red and gold onto the street, and I try not to think about how many peaceful hours I spent in that damp and rustling stretch of trees and grass while I was a student here. I try not to remember what it was like to stare at the window I knew belonged to Church's office, a smile on my lips to match the secret tucked away in my chest.

I mumble apologies as I push past the students and make my way into the building, ducking through hallways filled with chatter about soil micromorphology and ceramic petrography. I pass by labs and lecture rooms; I catch the familiar scents of coffee and climate-controlled air. Longing for this place fills me up like heavy water as I climb the stairs.

I was happy here.

I could have been happier still.

No sense in rehashing all that now. I'll be back. If not here, then somewhere else, and I'll kick ass there instead. I'll make up for all the lost time and then some.

Bolstered by the thought, I reach Church's floor, taking deep breaths in an effort to steady my thumping heart. What will he say when he sees me? Will he be angry? Will he be frustrated? After all, it was me who demanded space, and now here I am waltzing right into his.

He's a smart man, I remind myself. He'll understand that just for today, I need to reopen communication, and anyway, if *he'd* asked for space, then of course I would respect that. But he didn't, and a not-so-small part of me flutters at the thought that he didn't ask for it because he wants me to change my mind. Because he wants to be open and available in case I do.

Which I am.

Because I have to give the rent back.

I wish it was because of pride. I wish I could say it's because I've taken care of Jax and myself *just fine* for four years, and I don't need to ruin my streak with some man's guilt-money. I wish I could say that making any part of my life easier on his account irrevocably taints my honor and it just can't be borne.

But none of that's true. I've been poor my whole life and desperately so for the last four years; if everything else about me and Church were different, I'd take his money just like I took all those orgasms from him a week ago and walk away without looking back.

No, it's a bigger sin than pride that compels me today.

I can admit it now, after this last awful week. I love him. Stupid bunny that I am, I love him and crave him and want to forgive him. And maybe . . . maybe I already have forgiven him? There's a difference between forgiveness and trust, right?

I can forgive him without trusting him, I can let go of my pain without giving him the power to hurt me again.

The problem is that I want more than just to forgive, bloodlessly and from a distance.

I want to curl up in his lap and sob into his strong chest. I want to be angry with him, I want to hate him, and I want him to be strong enough to take it, to hold me while I cry over the hurts he gave me.

And then I want every dirty, sacred moment I missed with him over the last four years. Every moment I'm owed.

But how can I want that without betraying the girl he hurt? I demand of myself. *How can I want to be his again without betraying myself?*

I can't.

But I also can't have his gift haunting me. It's like the ghost of his smoky, spicy scent; it's like the still-warm imprint of him in my bed. So long as the money is there, Church is there. And every moment free from worry is now laden with memories of him—the midnight eyes, the harsh mouth. The *words*.

I am your temple no matter what.

There is one thing you can never ask of me, and that is for me to stop loving you.

Fuck, I have to give that money back. I have to be free of this.

Church's office is tucked away on an upper floor, on the side overlooking Gordon Square, and it's impossible not to have a Pavlovian response as I approach it, even after all this time. My heart thuds wildly, my belly feels hot and tight, everywhere my skin begs for touch, for teeth. Sometimes I'd be summoned here, sometimes I'd surprise him, but more often than not, I was hauled here by the elbow and then covered with his trembling body the minute the door clicked shut.

That infinite god-hunger of his. How I delighted in being his sacrifice over and over and over again . . .

Fitting that it ended at a literal altar.

Maybe it doesn't have to end, a traitorous hope murmurs. *Maybe he'll spread you out on his desk and . . .*

I ache with the thought—a deep, shuddering ache that only Church can soothe. I should leave. I shouldn't knock on his door like this, wet and ready for him to ease his heavy cock inside me, but I am knocking, I am opening the door, knowing full well if he so much as looks at me, I'll fall to his feet and beg for just one more minute of supplication. One more act of worship.

But when I open the door, it doesn't reveal my flawed deity, but an utterly empty room. There're no books on the shelves, there's no antique desk with a drawer for the little depravities we couldn't help but indulge on campus. There's no sofa for a scared, exhausted girl to crash on after keeping watch over her brother, and there's no basket next to it for a soft blanket to cover her with.

There's nothing and no one.

Church is gone.

But when? How? *Why?*

This should be the one constant—the one thing that holds the universe together.

Church teaches. Church teaches so Church can chase God through muddy fields and underneath crumbling tells. This is his life, his only passion. His calling.

And he's fucking brilliant at it.

"Looking for someone?" a voice asks from behind me.

I'm frozen in the doorway, almost unwilling to turn around and leave this moment of shock behind because I know what comes after it will be worse. But I do turn around, and when I do, I see the director. Officious and reedy and pinch-lipped.

It's the same director who told Church he couldn't go through with our wedding.

I have no idea if he recognizes me or not, and in this moment, I couldn't give a rat's ass. "Where is he?" I demand. "Where are his things?"

"He left," the director says. His words hold just the faintest whiff of smugness, but there is a tightness to his face that suggests he's unhappy too. Which makes sense. Whatever his personal feelings towards Church, he just lost the brightest star in his institute, not to mention the best teacher. Church's students went on to do great things—good-for-alumni-brochure things—and most importantly, people left his classes changed for the better. Smarter and more perceptive and more imaginative than they were before.

He's an amazing teacher.

And he's not here.

"He *left*?" I repeat, as if the director must be mistaken. "He wouldn't leave. This is—this is everything to him. It's everything he ever wanted."

The director shrugs gracelessly. "Apparently not."

"But . . ." I turn and look back into the office. Outside the windows, Gordon Square is wet and bright with autumn colors. Behind me are the faint noises of doors closing, people murmuring, someone rolling a cart down the hall. This was his world. His entire world was this place.

"He left," the director repeats, "in the middle of term and with no notice. I told him he'd never find a position again quitting like this, but he said he didn't care." The director scoffs. "Probably with as much money as he's got, he doesn't have to care."

I'd really like to tell this guy to eat a bag of dicks, because this job was the *only* thing Church cared about—even more than he cared about me. He was frequently impatient with the bureaucracy, with the labyrinthine politics, with how difficult it was to secure permission and funding to do the things he *really* loved, but never, ever in the time we were together did he raise the possibility of quitting. *Never.* So what could have changed?

Me?

No. Surely not. Church isn't stupid; I told him he couldn't atone. And he's not a liar—he told me he wasn't trying to.

So then why would he do this idiotic, self-destructive, selfish, cowardly thing? How could he do this to the students who needed him? How could he do this to *himself*? How could he rob himself of his future and his passion and the only part of him that resembled a soul?

I turn back to the director, and whatever is in my face has him taking a step back.

"Listen, madam," he says, "there's no need to be angry with *me*, it was entirely his decision—"

"Where is he now?" I snap, not interested in playing nice.

"I presume at home? He cleaned out the office yesterday—"

I'm already pushing past him to get to the stairs, and within a few minutes, I'm hopping down the stairs to Russell Square Station and catching a Piccadilly line train. I'm not sure what my plan is—I'm not sure I really had a plan in the first place, even before I knew he'd quit teaching—but I'm certain some yelling is going to be involved. Maybe some light murder is back on the table.

I mean, really. What the hell? After leaving me at the literal altar for this job, he's not going to keep it? After making me the burnt offering for his career, he's just going to walk away?

Screw. That.

He is going to get that job back and he is going to fulfill his promise as a professor and as an archaeologist. It makes no sense for him to waste his mind and his gifts like this. It makes about as much sense as me dropping out of school, except in my case, I literally had no other choice. Yet he's awash in choices, he's buried up to his neck in them.

So why *this* choice?

Yes, murder is back on the table now. And this time it's not for hurting me, it's for hurting himself.

When I get to his Belgravia townhouse—a graceful rise of white Georgian architecture set against the frowning sky—the door is hanging open as a young man lugs photography equipment inside. A crisp-looking woman in perfectly hemmed wide-leg trousers is talking to someone else on the front steps.

"We should wait for a sunny day for the rooftop photos," the person says back to her. They seem to be looking through the weather app on their phone, oblivious to the woman's eye roll.

"In October?" she asks impatiently. "I think we'll be waiting a while. And he wants the listing up tomorrow. We're doing it today."

The person on their phone sighs but accepts her decision. "I suppose if he's listing it under market value anyway . . ."

The woman nods, like this is all something the person should have already put together.

Jesus Christ. He's selling his house.

The woman—his estate agent, I presume—finally catches me hovering on the sidewalk, assessing in an instant that I am not a potential buyer for a multimillion-pound home and narrowing her eyes at me. "Can I help you?"

I'm too shocked and angry to put on the dimple-and-freckles act for her. "Yes. I'm looking for James Cason."

If the agent is surprised a girl in a sweater dress and scuffed boots knows the owner of the house, she doesn't show it. "He's not here. We're preparing the house for market, as you can see, and he told us he'd spend the day at his second home to give us space to work. And no—" she adds, seeing me open my mouth "—I don't know when he'll be back. Perhaps you could try calling him."

"Perhaps I could," I say, already walking away. I don't need to call him, because I already know where he is. He doesn't have a second home in the city, but he does have one place here that he loves above all others.

"Thank you," I tell the agent over my shoulder, and then I retrace my steps all the way back to the Tube and back to Russell Square Station.

CHAPTER SEVEN

CHURCH

THERE WAS a practice among the ancient Celts.

They would make swords inlaid with gold and precious stones. They would polish stone axe heads for thousands of hours until the stones gleamed like glass. They would make intricate necklaces and bracelets and rings. Anything could work really, so long as it was very difficult to make and too precious to lose.

And then they would break these things.

Swords were curled into circles, axes cracked in half. Jewelry was bent and scored and cut. The objects weren't just marred, they weren't just broken—they were *ruined*. They were killed until there was no question of them ever being useful again.

Then these beautiful, dead gifts were given to the waters, to the lakes and rivers and bogs where the gods lived. An offering. A sacrifice.

Sometimes, if I close my eyes and I still my breathing, I can imagine the flashing and glinting of the bent swords as they drop through the water to the depths below. I can see the last glimmer of the necklaces as they slip into the shadows.

The final gasp of things that were made only to be broken, things made only to be given up to dark and never seen again.

I wonder if this is Charlotte and me—except if it is, then who is the slayer and who is the offering?

Who did the making and who did the breaking?

***

THE MUSEUM IS QUIET TODAY, which suits me just fine. I drift through the European rooms and then the British rooms, looking at all the torcs and shields that long-dead priests gave to the waters, and I miss Charlotte. I stare at the Sutton Hoo exhibit and glance at the various belts and knives and cauldrons liberated from hoards and burials, and I miss Charlotte. I sit down on a bench and stare at my pointless hands, my empty hands—hands that should be cradling and petting and spanking—and I miss Charlotte.

We're both the offerings, I think tiredly. I broke her, then she broke me.

No. She'd already broken me. From that very first day. From that very first moment right here in the museum. I saw her and then I was bent for her. Cracked and killed. All for Charlotte Tenpenny.

Everything else was just flashes and glimmers in the dark.

I'm not sure how much of the morning I pass in this fashion, haunting the exhibits and missing Charlotte as only a broken thing can, but when I wander over to the Mesopotamia room, I find it empty. The neighboring room is closed for a new case installation, and the exhibit two rooms down is roped off for something that involves a camera crew, and the cumulative effect is that it seems to deter traffic away from Mesopotamia.

I don't mind. I rather like being alone with my agony. It feels fitting.

I'm staring at the relief of Ishtar that started it all when I hear the footsteps. The quick, angry slap of boots on the wood flooring, and before I have a chance to look up, she's excoriating me with her words.

"Just what the *fuck* do you think you're doing?" she hisses, stomping towards me. Her hair is down, making a halo of soft, curling gold around her face, and all her stomping has sent an appealing pink blooming under her freckles. And that lip—God, that lip. Even now, even broken, my body responds to that sinfully freckled mouth like she's already promised it back to me.

She's still striding towards me and berating me all the while, and all I can think about is how beautiful she is. How perfect. The hem of her sweater dress doesn't quite reach the over-the-knee socks she's wearing under her boots, and slivers of pale, freckled thighs tease me with every step. Her dress hugs her body, as if in worship, clinging to her breasts and hips, hanging down to cover her hands to keep them warm. I wish very suddenly that I could keep her hands warm, but I know if I reach out to wrap them in my own, she'll leave, and I don't want her to leave.

I want her to stay here in this dim museum twilight and keep abusing me in that sweet, angry voice of hers. If she wanted to scream at me forever, I would let her happily. With all the relief I could ever feel.

I'm still staring at her with a smile on my face when she reaches me and takes a big breath. She narrows her eyes. "Are you even listening to me?"

I shake my head, daring to reach out and tuck a wild curl behind her ear. "But keep talking, please. I deserve all of it."

She huffs, very adorably, and crosses her arms over her chest. "Your reverse psychology won't work on me."

I just want to gather her in my arms and prop her on my lap and murmur every beautiful thing about her into her ear. I want to spend days memorizing the freckles on her shoulder. I want to spend the rest of my life with my nose buried in the curve of her neck. "Please," I say. My voice is soft, but earnest enough that it makes her hesitate. "Keep going. I want to hear you."

She glares at me a little like she still thinks it's some kind of trick, but then she relents, too furious with me to bottle it inside any longer. "Fine, *professor*," she seethes, sticking a finger against my chest. Warmth blooms from where she's touching me to everywhere else in my body, sending something hotter than heat all the way to the whorls of my fingers and the soles of my feet. Happiness, I think. Joy.

Love.

I want to press my body to hers, my broken heart to her broken heart and just let the jagged edges stab and shred us all over again.

She's still going. "You're going to hear me, because what kind of self-destructive moron leaves the only job they've ever wanted, and I know you're not a liar, and I know you said you weren't trying to atone, so then what could possibly have motivated such a fucked-up decision—and how could you do that to your students and to *yourself*, you're going to be so miserable, and do you want to be miserable? Because I don't see any other way—"

I surrender to the need to touch her, and I take the hand currently against my chest and cradle it in my own. I bring it to my lips and simply touch them there. Her skin against mine. It's heaven.

Her rant is brought to halt by this, and I can feel her pulse speed in her wrist at my touch. I can hear the hitch in her breath as I kiss her knuckle and then her palm and then her fingertip.

"You look like shit," she grumbles, unable to keep scolding me but also unable to completely let it go.

"I know." I say the words against her skin. "I know."

"Church," she whispers. "Why?"

That's been this whole week between us—the *whys*—although I know for her it's been much longer. Four years of *why*, and I'll never be able to make that up to her. I need her to know that as much as I need to savor these last few seconds between us. She'll leave and I'll let her, and then I'll let myself sink into the dark. Find some cottage somewhere and live out the rest of my days as the shattered man I am.

"It wasn't to prove something to you," I tell her, looking up to her face. Her eyes shine with angry tears, and my heart rips a little. "I swear, Charlotte, I swear on everything I've ever cared about. This wasn't a grand gesture. I wasn't trying to—"

I can't finish the words. Because while I'm not trying to win her back, while I know I can never make up for what I've done, my instinct is still to pin her by the wrists to the nearest wall and kiss her breathless. My instinct is still to take her home, cage her with my body, and tell her *mine, mine, mine* until we both believe it again.

So it's very hard to say *I wasn't trying to get you back*, not because it's not true—it is—but because I'll always want her back. Always, until I die, and then even in the realms past death. She is my own soul.

"I wasn't trying to earn your forgiveness or your pity," I say instead, straightening up. I don't let go of her hand, however, and she doesn't make me. "I need you to know that."

"I do know that, *asshole*," she fumes, tears spilling over. "I know that, and that makes it worse, because it means your only other motive was hurting yourself, and I hate it. I hate that you've cut yourself off from the thing you've dedicated your life to."

My thumb can't stop rubbing at the skin of her wrist. If I could stop time, I'd stop it right here—my thumb brushing against her very pulse, her face teary and gorgeous and lit by the carefully muted bulbs of the exhibit cases.

"Why are you looking at me like that?" she sniffles, trying to duck her face away from me. It's habit—and probably a bad one—when I don't let her. I catch her face with my other hand and make it so our eyes meet.

"Looking at you like how?" I murmur. Even though I already know.

"You know how," she mumbles, because she knows that I know. It's why I knew she'd survive me when I first saw her—because she's always seen straight through my games. And then chosen to play along anyway. "All puppy-dog-eyed. And . . ."

She reaches up and touches the edge of my mouth. I think I might expire in agony. I love her so fucking much.

"You're smiling," she says on an exhale, her voice and fingertips trembling. "This is a *smile*."

"I have been known to smile, little one. Especially around you."

She shakes her head, her eyes tracing the curve of my lips. "No. Not this kind of smile. Not like you're happy when you have every reason *not* to be happy."

I can feel my lips tilt even more against her touch, and I want to nip at her fingers so badly, I want to take one into my mouth and flick my tongue against the tiny whorls and ridges of the tip until she's whimpering for me to tongue her clit. I know any moment this will stop and she will walk away and I will never see her again, but maybe she wouldn't mind one last little bite. One final kiss to last me the rest of my pointless, lonely life.

"You—I told you to stay away from me," she goes on. "I told you I wouldn't forgive you. And then you left your work, which is the only thing you've ever loved. You shouldn't be smiling."

"I'm smiling because I'm looking at you, darling girl."

"But—"

It's my turn to shake my head. "There're no buts, Charlotte. No qualifiers. You are the very expression of the sacred. You are my holiness. Seeing you is like being transfigured, heartbeat by heartbeat, breath by breath, into light itself." A tear slides down her cheek at my words, and I frown at it. "I know there's no act I can lay at your feet to redeem my selfishness, and I almost don't want there to be, because I don't deserve even the comfort that it could be possible. But how could I keep living with the wages of my sins after knowing how much they'd cost you? These last four years, I've been sustaining myself on the lie that you were better off without me. But you weren't. And I can't serve any longer the idol I chose over you. You say my work is the only thing I ever loved, but it was *you*, Charlotte. How could I still pretend to chase God when I'd already let the divine slip through my fingers?"

Another big tear slips down her cheek, and I'm going to hell, but it'll be worth it for this one stolen taste. I lean in and kiss that tear away, letting the salt bloom on my tongue, and she shivers against me.

"Don't cry," I murmur. "It'll be okay."

I start to pull back, and then she grabs the front of my sweater and twists her fingers in, holding me close. She's still trembling. "It won't be okay," she whispers. "It can't be okay now. Not when I need—"

She stops herself abruptly, and worry twists my guts. She needs something? Is there more financial worry? Is her father back and causing trouble? "Tell me and I'll make it happen. Do you need money? Help? For me to leave right now?"

Her eyes meet mine in a scorch of silver. "I need *you*," she chokes out, and it stuns us both. It stuns me so much that I'm totally unprepared for her to yank me down to her mouth and kiss me like it's the only thing that can keep her alive.

CHAPTER EIGHT

CHARLEY

FOR A FEW GENTLE but breathless moments, Church's mouth is pliant against mine. In fact, all of him is pliant—soft and surprised and yielding. I pull him closer to me, and he lets me, and I part his lips with my own to taste him, and he lets me. I slide my hands up so that I can wrap my arms around his neck and I kiss all of my need into him, all of my anger and hurt and loneliness and longing. The horrible tangle of *wanting* to hate him, but knowing I'll always, always love him.

And he lets me, he lets me, he lets me.

If I hadn't seen the truth in his shattered gaze, if I hadn't heard the honesty in his tired, smoky voice, then I would feel it in his body now: he didn't expect this. He didn't expect anything from me.

He meant everything he said.

His hands are slow and shaking as they touch my back, his body is totally frozen against mine. Through our clothes, I feel the pound of his heart, and when I break our kiss and open my eyes, I find his already open, watching me with something beyond awe, something purer than awe, because it's stripped of all hope. It's pure humility, pure adoration.

It's worship.

I used to be the cleverest girl in class, but I'm all out of answers right now. Because he's looking at me like that, his eyes are a deep ocean blue like that, and he's still *smiling* like that.

And what possible answer can I have? To him? To the strange and terrible and undeniable fact that I forgive him? Everyone I know would tell me it's stupid, everyone I know would tell me that he doesn't deserve it, that I deserve better, and logically, it all adds up: he hurt me, therefore fuck him.

But maybe . . . maybe logic isn't all of love. Maybe it isn't even half, maybe not even a quarter. Because I do love him, damn my eyes, and what I wouldn't give for some new kind of logic, a logic that could account for *fuck him* and also *let's fuck him.* A formula that could compute *I love him* and *I can't trust him* and *I don't know how to trust him again* but also *I'd like to try.*

There's no logic like that, there are no answers. Which means I'm only going to listen to the questions right now. Namely, one question.

What is the one thing I know I want with all my heart in this very moment?

That . . . that I do know the answer to, and I pull him back to me for a second kiss.

It's like a match is struck.

Church's pliancy burns clean away and blazes into something else. Something firm and fierce and possessive. *He's* the one to chase my mouth now, he's the one fisting and yanking at my sweater, and he's the one kissing with his whole body: his hands shoving at the hem of my dress, a hard thigh pushing between mine, an arm now banding behind my back so that I can feel his hardness everywhere. His erection, his stomach, his chest. Everywhere he is granite—if granite can be ferocious and greedy and hot.

"Little supplicant," he breathes against my mouth. In just those two words, I hear *him*, my Church, my angry god. And I also hear this new Church, this man so broken with love for me that he won't even pray for atonement because he knows he doesn't deserve it. I hear both versions of him, and I think I love both. I love him both godlike and mortal, I love him in his cold, marble perfection and I love him shattered.

"Please," I kiss-mumble, trying to climb him, wishing I could climb *inside* him, wishing there was something closer than close. And I don't even know what I'm saying *please* to, just that I need to say it, and I need him to hear it. I need him to know that I meant *I need you* in every possible way.

I'm not a small woman, but Church takes me easily in his arms, biting at my jaw and neck as he carries me to the corner of the room. Each bite sends sparks shivering across my skin; each bite reminds me of what I've always needed, which is this. Which is him.

I scan the room as he bites my throat and his hands flex under my thighs. He sets me down and pins me against the side of an exhibit case with his chest and hips, while his hands keep roaming up and down the bare skin of my thighs under my dress.

I twist my head to check that the exhibit room is still empty—we're partially hidden from view, but it wouldn't take someone very long to figure out there's a girl getting felt up in the corner. My turning deprives him of my throat and he growls my name.

"Just making sure no one sees," I say—my words choked off by a large hand palming my breast and the resulting surge of heat between my legs. As if he knows—he always knows—Church presses his hips in and uses the giant rod of his erection to rub against me.

"Don't I always make sure you're safe?" he asks, fucking me slowly through our clothes. He pushes up my dress so that it's only his trousers and my knickers between us and I groan. "Have I ever let a stranger see what's mine?"

"N-no." My teeth are chattering, and I can't stop shaking. Each grind of his cock against me has my eyes fluttering. "You never let anyone see."

It's the truth. Church had always been as careful as he was insatiable, and as many times as I'd been fucked, fingered, or eaten in public, I'd never been seen. I was never sure if it was because he was possessive or thoughtful or some heady mix of both, but the result was the same: Church took care of me as he took what he wanted from me, and every needy, breathless fuck that we stole in public was as safe as it was urgent.

He rakes his teeth over my throat as I realize he's angled our bodies so that even the security cameras can't see us. "Do you trust me?"

God, he wants an answer that I don't have. "I trust you with this," I finally say, and he nods, as if he already knew the answer. But when my eyes catch his, I see a turbulent midnight there. He thinks this is our goodbye fuck, this is some final gift he doesn't deserve but can't keep himself from taking.

I don't want it to be our goodbye fuck. I don't want that at all. But before I can tell him this, his big hands are in my panties, finding my wet place and penetrating me without warning.

I gasp and arch against him, the small bite of pain heavenly against the pleasure, like salt on chocolate. But that's nothing compared to what happens to him. As my body clasps his fingers, he gives a fierce growl against my neck, like an animal that's just scented his mate, and suddenly he's yanking my panties down and tearing at his belt.

"Need inside," he grunts.

"God, yes, fucking *yes*, do it, do it—"

He frees his cock and I nearly expire at the sight of it. It's thick and straight and a yummy dusky color, and it wedges its way through his opened trousers like a weapon. Like a scepter. Ready to ruin me and rule me.

I can't wait. Like literally can't wait. I'm arching and mewing against him like a fussy kitten.

He reaches for his pocket and his head snaps up. "I don't have a condom."

For a moment, I'm speechless—Church *always* had condoms because I always needed fucking, and usually more than once—but then I let out a giggle that echoes around the exhibit.

His broken-soft smile returns, although his eyes are still wild animal eyes. "What, Miss Tenpenny?"

"Just—" I cradle his jaw with my hand. "If I hadn't believed you weren't planning on being forgiven before, I believe it now. Because if you thought there was any chance of this happening, I know you would have had like twenty condoms in your wallet."

He shakes his head, then presses his lips to my palm. "What have I told you about hyperbole? It's beneath your intellect. Naturally, I would've only put ten condoms in there."

I laugh again and he bites my palm.

"I have an IUD now," I tell him, my laughter edging back into fervent need. "And I'm clean. Church, if you mean it, if you meant what you said about not being with anyone since me—"

"I meant it. You want me inside you now? Bare?"

His words are hungry, and that hunger stirs me past enduring. I've never had him like this, raw and intimate. Just Church. Primal, naked Church.

"Please," I beg, pushing my hips forward. My panties are down far enough that I kick them to one side and I use a hand to hold up my dress so he can see the place I need filled. I don't want there to be any mistaking what's his to take. What's his to ease himself with.

Church gives a low groan and his erection surges, growing even thicker, the skin pulling taut and shiny. "I need to fuck you," he says, somehow both coldly and hoarsely in that contradictory way of his.

"Please take it, God, just *please*," I whine, reaching for him, but he stops my hands by grabbing my wrists and pinning them above my head with one hand as he gives the room a quick search.

Then he takes himself in a big hand and notches himself right at my pussy. I wrap a leg around his waist to open myself up to him, and the action spreads my flesh open so that now the searing heat of his crown is pushed right against where I'm wettest.

A hollow groan escapes his throat, and his head drops down between his shoulders, as if even this small contact is too much to bear. For a moment, we just breathe and shiver like this, with his head ducked and his cock spreading me open and his hips poised to thrust.

"Church," I breathe.

"I know," he breathes back. "I'm just—*fuck*, I need it, but I also need a moment to be grateful for this, Charlotte, because I am grateful. So fucking grateful. Just a moment more, just be patient a moment more for me."

Grateful.

His gratitude guts me. I'm slain by it, and I'll be slain every time I think of it for the rest of my life, but even in broken gratitude, Church keeps my hands pinned, and when his head lifts, his expression is my favorite one in the world. The one of a god with a sacrifice to devour.

"Now for the rest," he says arrogantly, but also reverently, and pushes up into me. Just the head, no more than an inch, but already I feel pierced by him, invaded and spread. I'm wet—wetter than I've ever been maybe—but Church's cock is no laughing matter. He gives me another fat inch, and I suck in a breath, writhing on it.

It aches. It feels perfect.

It aches.

It feels perfect.

"Problem?" he murmurs, giving me even more and splitting me in two in the process.

My head hits the case behind me. "I . . . forgot."

The corner of his sharp mouth curves—not his soft smile from earlier, but that familiar cruel one I love so much. "Forgot what, Charlotte? How hard this cock gets for you?"

Another shove, another inch—and another gasp pinched out of me.

"How deep I go? Or how much your sweet body has to work to take me?"

He's only about halfway in, and everything below my navel feels like it's being squeezed in a massive fist. I'm panting, rolling my head along the case wall behind me, and he slides a hand between my thigh and his waist and then pushes me open. He pulls back a few inches and slides back in, my body letting him go deeper this time.

He lets out a very male, very satisfied grunt. "Good girl."

I look down to where we're joined and moan. The hard flesh spearing me is straight from mythology—or maybe pornography. Maybe both. "You're a giant," I manage. "Or some kind of mutant, maybe."

"Sorry," he says, forcing his way deeper and making my eyes flutter in the process.

"You don't sound sorry," I manage.

"I'm not," he says.

"Asshole."

One of his dark eyebrows lifts in amusement. "What should I say, Charlotte? It's terrible to see you flushed and panting as you try to take my cock? I hate feeling you squeezed so tight around me that I can barely move? Sorry my penis is so big?"

"It would be a start," I mumble.

Church looks down then to see what I just saw—the place where his velvet-smooth organ breaches me, and his jaw tics. His grip tightens on my wrists and thigh, as he seems to struggle with some powerful urge.

I know what it is.

"Take it," I say. There's no brattiness in my voice just now, and no legitimate anger. There's no hurt, and no blame. There's only the love for him that five years ago fell on me like a curse, in this very room. The love that was born to be offered and then taken. A love for temples and secret sacrifices in the dark.

His head snaps up and his eyes meet mine and they're pure, liquid midnight. And then I'm impaled on him, lanced all the way up to my heart.

There's pressure and heat and an urgent tightness twisting into something too unformed to be called pleasure. The raw place where pain met bliss was Church's favorite place to keep me, and he didn't need ropes or floggers to do it. Just his long, perfect body. Just his huge hands pinning me still and forcing me open for his erection.

I have to bite my lip to keep myself from coming right then and there.

"Little supplicant," he breathes and then his forehead rests against mine as we pant and tremble together. "You feel—fuck—how will I live without the way you feel? The way you shiver against me when you're getting close? The way you bite at that freckled lip? How?"

I part my lips to say something—I'm not sure what, but something about how I don't want him to live without it either—and he kisses me with a sudden fierceness that steals my breath and my words.

I can taste gratitude all over his kiss, and when I lick it off his tongue, when I search out more from inside his mouth, his grip on me turns punishing. Below our kiss, he starts the fucking, moving in shallow, grinding thrusts that have an orgasm burning bright and hot behind my clit, and I'm going to come already, I'm going to come after only a few seconds with my Church inside me—

I look down again, unable to resist the carnal mechanics of it all, the animal sight of it.

"Do it," Church orders. "Give me what's mine."

I break apart for him, on him, around him. I can't see and I can't hear—I can only feel and thrash and cry his name as my pussy clenches and releases in abrupt, shuddering waves. It's all hot, mindless sensa-tion, and it's flowing everywhere in my body, from my seizing lower belly down to the soles of my feet and the aching beads of my nipples. Everything feels and aches and unravels for my Church, and he knows it, he knows it's all for him, that my pleasure is his, my pain is his, that *I* am his. He may think I'm only his right here in this moment, he may think that he'll never get to own me again after this, but that doesn't erase the totality of his possession. Of his need to brand me inside and out.

As my body wrings itself out with release, Church seems to lose all patience. All control. My wrists are dropped so he can shove my dress up even higher and squeeze my breast; my thigh is pressed against the case so that my cunt is completely open for his needs. His inhales come in rasping snarls and his exhales in short, angry growls.

And his fucking—his fucking is unstoppable. A cruel weapon meant to command me, and my pulsing sex is evidence that he already does. Not that he seems satisfied with a single orgasm from me. No, he won't be satisfied until I'm wrecked, until I can barely stand and his fuck is the only thing keeping me upright.

"Give me more," he whispers in my ear. "Give me everything until it's all mine."

I can't speak, I can't hardly breathe—this was how it used to be between us, this is what I've been secretly keening for: this ravenous hunger he had for me, like he'll die if he doesn't swallow me whole.

And it turns out that in order to live, I need to be eaten alive.

What a lewd picture we make. Anyone walking in could see this cold, dangerous boy with his belt dangling around his hips, his angry cock buried inside a squirming girl with her dress shoved up to her waist and her cheeks flushed from his dirty, filthy attentions.

Anyone could see this for what it is—a liturgy as frantic as it is holy. A sacrifice being taken.

I come again.

Now, it is really only him keeping me pinned against the wall, and as he grinds into me with that massive thing, I slowly melt against him. My hands paw limply at his biceps as my head drops onto his shoulder and lolls there, like a doll's. And he fucks me like a doll, like a plaything.

"You were right," I tell him, the words husky and air-starved from all the orgasms. "You are still my temple."

"And you are my prayer," he growls back. "*Mine.*"

Underneath my fingertips and against my stomach and between his legs, all of him goes impossibly taut, impossibly hard. Even as one part of him surges into me, the rest of him trembles and shakes and shivers, like he's got a fever. Like he's sick with needing to come.

And then he does.

His eyelids lower, his jaw flexes, and every single muscle in his body seems intent on pushing in deeper, on pumping into me harder, and right when he gives a thrust so fierce I feel my foot lift off the floor, he gives a darkly erotic growl, and releases into me with long, heavy pulses.

He keeps me pinned as he fills me, and it's all so wet, so dirty, to feel him like this without a condom, and I love it, I want more of it, I want it all the time.

He stabs into me again and again, using his own spend to make the slides slick and fast as he chases the last clenches of his pleasure and makes sure he leaves every last drop between my legs. But for as carnal and raw as it all is below, his hands are grabbing and grabbing above, like he can't get me close enough. Like I'll never be close enough to his heart.

We're sweating, indecent, and still so very exposed, but I never want to move. I just want to curl into his strong chest forever.

I feel his lips on my hair, and then his nose as he breathes me in.

"Charlotte," he says miserably. "My sweet, brilliant Charlotte."

"Church, I—"

"You don't have to tell me," he says, pressing his lips to my temple and then easing free of my body. "I know."

I huff. "I don't think you do."

He doesn't respond to me with anything other than a nod of resignation. He thinks I'm about to tell him to go to hell, and he would go there meekly if I did. *Meekly.*

My Church, meek and mortal, and all because he thinks he deserves the worst. I mean, he does, but it's also not the point right now.

The point is that I don't want to tell him to go to hell. I don't want him to go away. I don't want him going anywhere except everywhere I'm going.

He kneels to tug my dress down and help me step into my panties. "Will you listen to me?" I ask.

"Of course," he says.

"I love you," I say and then my breath gets all stuttery and short, because suddenly nothing feels as important as getting this right. "I love you and I don't want you to stay away from me. I want you close. I want you next to me, inside me. I want to belong to you again."

He's looking up from where he kneels at my feet, and I see a thousand expressions passing over his face. Shock and then hope and then guarded concern. "We just fucked, Charlotte. I don't think it's the right time for you to make concessions—"

"They're not concessions," I say. I run a fingertip over the scar on his cheek and then trail my fingers down to his jaw so I can keep his face lifted to mine. "They're what I want."

"But I fucked up," he says hoarsely. "You shouldn't want them."

"Maybe," I say, using my other hand to brush the dark hair away from his forehead. "But I do. So."

My words do nothing to ease the turmoil in his expression, and he closes his eyes, as if he can't look at me while he says what he says next because otherwise he won't have the strength to say it. "Charlotte, please. Please don't compromise on this. Don't compromise for me."

I don't spare him the truth. "I'm not," I tell him bluntly. "I don't trust you right now and I can't tell you that tomorrow will be the same as today. I definitely can't promise you that I'll ever put on a wedding dress for you again."

His eyes open at this, full of shame, and I hate that my proud Church is willing to look my blame in the face but not my love.

"I don't have answers to a lot of questions about us," I admit, and I think of the four-years-ago Charlotte, trying not to cry on the Tube while people politely ignored the way her dress spilled over their feet. I won't betray that Charlotte by unequivocally forgiving what was done to her. But I also can't betray the Charlotte I am today—the one who is desperately in love with the possessive, hungry mystery that is James Cason. "But when I ask myself, *what do I want today*, I know the answer to that. I want you. I want to see if I can find all those other answers in your arms. I want that more than anything."

His sapphire eyes search mine. "Are you sure, Charlotte?"

I take a deep breath. It feels good to admit this, it feels so good to set down resentment to reach for something sweeter. "Today, Church. Today, I'm sure."

He gets slowly to his feet, setting his clothes to rights without ever taking his eyes from mine. Once he's completely dressed again, he puts his hand over my heart, like he owns it.

"This is mine again?" he asks in a low, shaking voice. There's fear there, and awe, and hope. Trembling, eager hope.

"Today, Church. And you can ask me again tomorrow."

He leans and catches my mouth with his—a brushing, stirring kiss that promises wicked, greedy things. "Then I better make today count."

And in true Church fashion, he tugs me impatiently out of the exhibit and down the stairs. He tugs me all the way to his house—and once the estate agent is booted from the premises and my brother knows I'll be out late—we finally do what we want most in the world to do.

We worship.

EPILOGUE

CHURCH

"I DON'T WANT to go home," Charlotte says with a sigh. In front of her, the Mediterranean sparkles blue and brilliant, and a warm Tel Aviv breeze toys with her curls, occasionally revealing flashes of her delightfully freckled neck.

"I'll bring you back," I say, coming to join her on the balcony. "You'll need to have more experience out here if you want to curate Levantine collections anyway."

She pouts a little, that freckled lower lip making a plump little curve. "Do we really have to go back to Oxford?"

"We do," I tell her, wrapping her in my arms and pulling her so her back rests against my chest. We look out at the turquoise sea together while I nuzzle against her hair. She smells like sunshine and shampoo—when we got back to Tel Aviv and a real hotel after four weeks digging near a dusty tell, she went straight for the shower and scrubbed her hair for about forty minutes. "But I'll take you to that standing stone you like and fuck you for hours next to it. Will that scratch your prehistory itch?"

"It's not the same," she fusses, but she does push her bottom against my lap. "But you can still fuck me for hours. That part's okay."

"Hmm. How about we start on it now?"

"But we're supposed to go to dinner with—"

I'm already slinging her over my shoulder and taking her back to the bed. I give her backside a swat before throwing her on the bed and then crawling over her. "Legs open, little supplicant. Show me what I want."

I'm barely patient enough to wait for her to obey, wanting to tear her dress off with my teeth and then spear her with my neglected cock. Having Charlotte on a dig with me again was profoundly wonderful—I loved seeing her face as she finally freed some tiny, broken treasure from the earth, and I savored having her thoughts and observations available to me in the field. But it was also a problem, because all of the things that made it fulfilling also made me fucking horny. And turns out it's next to impossible to get a leg over in the middle of the desert, so I've been very, very deprived.

Since that day three years ago in the museum, it feels like everything and nothing has changed. I rented a modest flat in London and stayed close to Charlotte while Jax finished school. Charlotte refused to move in with me—but she did finally accept my gift of rent that first year, which meant she could quit catering and sign up for night classes at UCL. She graduated—with honors—at the same time Jax did. And now she's pursuing her graduate degree at Oxford, where I've also taken a post. Apparently my reputation was good enough to withstand my abrupt departure from UCL, and since we both came to Oxford at the same time, it was easy to prevent any nepotist speculation from the get-go.

Besides, I'm only at Oxford because she's there. Once she wants to leave, I'll follow her to wherever she finds the job of her dreams. She's my passion now, and my calling.

Three years ago, Charlotte said five fateful words to me. *Today, the answer is yes.* And I've spent every day since then asking her, as gently and patiently as a monster like me is able, *what about today?*

Every day, in a blessing I don't understand or deserve, the answer has been the same as it was on the first.

Charlotte pulls up her dress and spreads her thighs and I feel as thunderstruck by the sight as I did the first time I saw it seven years ago. Without bothering to do anything else, I pull my linen pants down to expose my aching erection and then push it against where she's wet. I love this part, when I can just begin to feel the tight grip of her, because it means I'm about to be as close to her as I possibly can. It means that, at least for a while, I'll be able to make her feel as breathless and split open as she makes me.

"I forgot to ask this morning," I say as I jab forward. Her back arches deliciously and I lean down to bite at my favorite freckle. "What about today?"

I expect her to give her usual answer, and so I'm already stroking my cock into her pussy, ready to segue to the part of the fucking where she's too well-pleasured for conversation, when she says, "Today, the answer is forever."

My body gets the message before my mind can process it, and I go still, looking down at her. "What?" I ask blankly.

Her mouth twitches in a small smile that's smug, and a little nervous. She reaches into the pocket of her dress, and I feel her slim fingers brushing against my hip as she searches.

And then she pulls out a ring.

It's a silky, matte gold, finely—but still visibly—beaten, with the small hammer marks making angles and faces all around the band.

"I made it," she says shyly. "There's a local blacksmith who helped. I couldn't find a ring antique enough to be interesting to us, so I thought I'd fashion it myself."

"Charlotte," I say, trying to be careful, but failing, failing. My heart is massive, huge, it's taking up my entire body—except, of course, the part still nestled in Charlotte's snug warmth. That part just continues to throb happily. "What is this?"

"It's an engagement ring," she says. "Will you marry me?"

I can barely think over my giant, bloody heart. "Do you—are you very sure, little one? Because I don't need this. I'll live the rest of my life as the happiest man alive even if we're still taking it day by day."

She shakes her head on the pillow, gray eyes clear but serious. "I don't want that. I needed time to trust you again—and trust myself. I needed space to see my promises to myself and my brother through. I needed to make sure that if I forgave you, I was doing it for the right reasons. But the past three years have given me that. And I want more. I want everything."

"I do owe you everything."

"You do."

"I don't deserve to give it you."

She pulls one lovely shoulder up to her ear in the laying-down version of a shrug. "I'm ready for you to deserve it."

I didn't think my heart could get any bigger, but here it is, bigger than me, big enough to hold her inside it. "Charlott . . ."

She smiles up at me. "What about your answer, my Church? What about today?"

I take in a long breath that's full of her and our sex and the sparkling Tel Aviv evening. If she's ready for me to deserve it, then I shall, and I'll give her everything in return. "Today, the answer is forever," I tell her.

Her smile is so big, it could light up all of Tel Aviv. She reaches for my hand, and soon I have her ring on it. I can barely take my eyes off it, but I do, because nothing is ever as beautiful as my sunny little supplicant.

Tears burn behind my eyes as I scoop my arms underneath her and begin thrusting into my perfect girl, and I murmur everything into her hair as I strum orgasms out of her like music from a harp. I murmur every last word about how gorgeous she is, how clever, how blessed I am, how wrecked she makes me, how I'll never, ever abandon her again. And when I finally come with the sea rushing outside and her ring glinting on my hand, I'm not an angry god or a cold temple.

I am *her* supplicant.

And I will worship at her feet forever.

ALSO BY SIERRA SIMONE

Thornchapel:

A Lesson in Thorns

Feast of Sparks

Harvest of Sighs

Door of Bruises

Misadventures:

Misadventures with a Professor

Misadventures of a Curvy Girl

Misadventures in Blue

The New Camelot Trilogy:

American Queen

American Prince

American King

The Moon (Merlin's Novella)

American Squire (A Thornchapel and New Camelot Crossover)

The Priest Series:

Priest

Midnight Mass: A Priest Novella

Sinner

Co-Written with Laurelin Paige

Porn Star

Hot Cop

ABOUT THE AUTHOR

Sierra Simone is a *USA Today* bestselling former librarian who spent too much time reading romance novels at the information desk. She lives with her husband and family in Kansas City.

Sign up for her newsletter to be notified of releases, books going on sale, events, and other news!

www.thesierrasimone.com
thesierrasimone@gmail.com

CPSIA information can be obtained
at www.ICGtesting.com
Printed in the USA
LVHW041139250920
667084LV00001B/7